TILL
DEATH

I BIND MYSELF TO YOU FROM THIS DAY...

TILL DEATH

MIRANDA LYN

Till Death— 1st Edition
© 2024, Miranda Lyn
All rights reserved

No part of this publication may be reproduced, stored in a retrieval system, stored in a database and/or published in any form or by any means, electronic, mechanical, photocopying, recording or otherwise, without the prior written permission of the publisher. This book is a work of fiction. The names, characters, places, and incidents are products of the writer's imagination. Any resemblance to persons, living or dead, is entirely coincidental.

Cover Designer—Tairelei—www.facebook.com/Tairelei/

Copy Editor—The Ryter's Proof

Maps—Virginia Allyn—www.virginiaallyn.com

Print Part Page Art—https://thewonderwitchemporium.com/

Print Chapter Heading Art—https://lilaraymond.com/lettersbylila-links

CONTENT WARNING: Threats of Violence, Language, Explicit Sexual Content, Gore, Morally Gray MMC (he's probably going to do some red flag shit... you've been warned)

TRIGGER WARNING: Violence, Death, Murder, Imprisonment, Mentions of Drug and Alcohol Use, Kidnapping, Torture, Grief, Parental Death

ENDORSEMENTS FOR TILL DEATH

"Utterly brilliant with everything you need to lose yourself in a world of betrayal, passion, and the unexpected."

-Melissa K. Roehrich, author of the *Lady of Darkness* series

"From the very first chapters, Lyn grabs you and doesn't let you go. It's a story of deceit, of betrayal, of impossible choices, found family, redemption and love. A true enemies to lovers, dark fantasy."

- Olivia Wildenstein, author of *The Kingdom of Crows* series

"Fans of Kerri Maniscalco's Kingdom of the Wicked and Stephanie Garber's Caraval will love this story of the Death Maiden's one chance to defy Death himself, combined with a searing romance that adds an irresistible layer of passion."

-Jessica, @books_and_crafts

"Get lost in this rich and decadent moulin rouge inspired world, filled with death magic and forbidden love. A must-read for those who want to be swept away into a world full of dark devotion, where the hero may just be the villain."

-Sam, @haus.of.fables

"Till Death is the romantasy standalone story readers have been craving. It is not just an epic enemies-to-lovers tale but a unique world that will leave you asking for more."

- Sarah, @rosebudmode

For Jeanne

And to my readers:
You never let someone defeat you. You stand. You step. You rise.
This world will eat you whole if you let it.

ALSO BY MIRANDA LYN

FAE RISING:

BLOOD AND PROMISE

CHAOS AND DESTINY

FATE AND FLAME

TIDES AND RUIN

UNMARKED:

THE UNMARKED WITCH

THE UNBOUND WITCH

THE UNBLESSED WITCH

COMING SOON

NEVERMORE

www.authormirandalyn.com

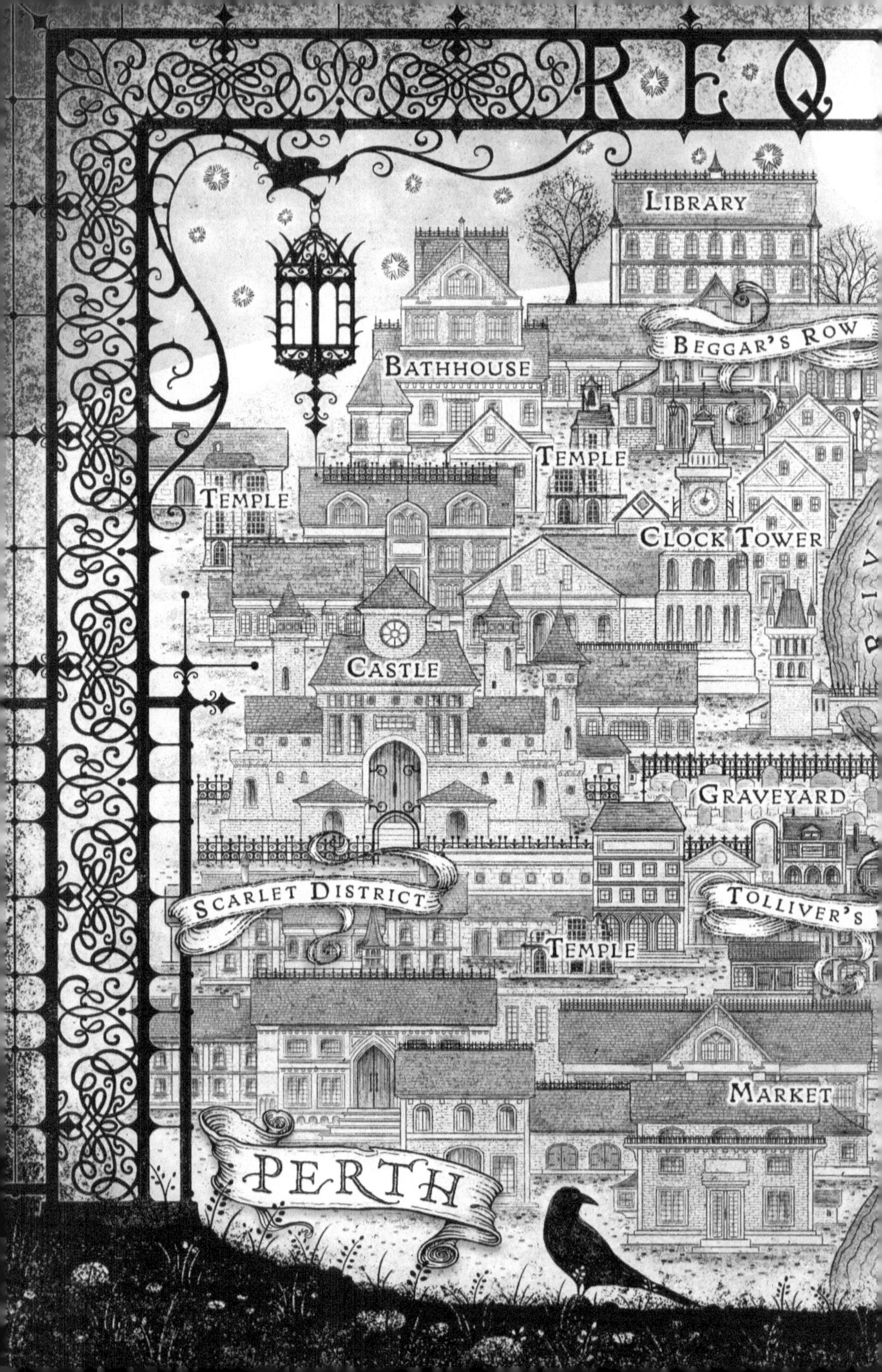

PERTH
LIBRARY
BEGGAR'S ROW
BATHHOUSE
TEMPLE
TEMPLE
CLOCK TOWER
CASTLE
GRAVEYARD
SCARLET DISTRICT
TOLLIVER'S
TEMPLE
MARKET

ALSO BY MIRANDA LYN

FAE RISING:

BLOOD AND PROMISE

CHAOS AND DESTINY

FATE AND FLAME

TIDES AND RUIN

UNMARKED:

THE UNMARKED WITCH

THE UNBOUND WITCH

THE UNBLESSED WITCH

COMING SOON

NEVERMORE

www.authormirandalyn.com

R E Q
LIBRARY
BEGGAR'S ROW
BATHHOUSE
TEMPLE
CLOCK TOWER
TEMPLE
CASTLE
GRAVEYARD
SCARLET DISTRICT
TOLLIVER'S
TEMPLE
MARKET
PERTH

SYNDICATE HOUSE
SINNER'S SQUARE
DANCING GHOST
MISERY'S END
GAMBLER'S QUARTER
TEMPLE
CASTLE
HALLOWED
SILK ROAD
BATHHOUSE
TEMPLE
SILBATH

PART ONE

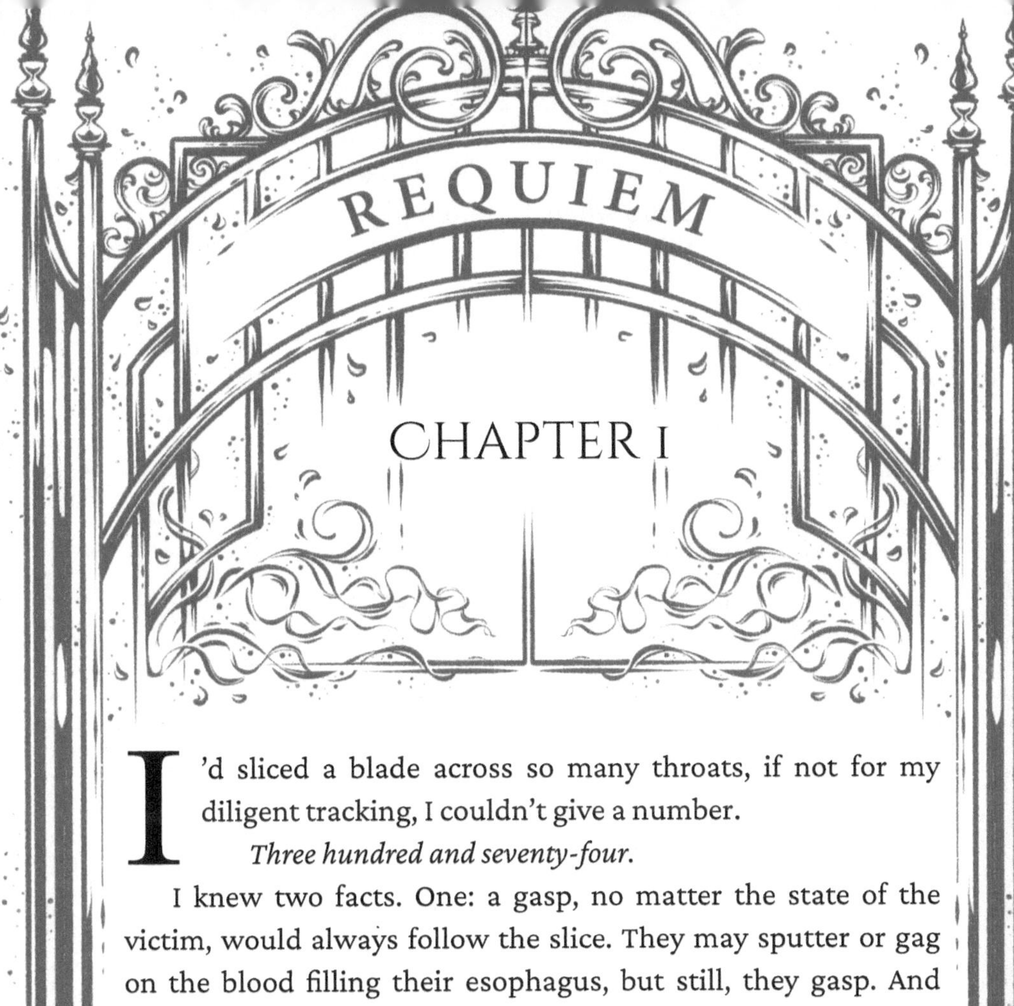

CHAPTER I

I'd sliced a blade across so many throats, if not for my diligent tracking, I couldn't give a number.

Three hundred and seventy-four.

I knew two facts. One: a gasp, no matter the state of the victim, would always follow the slice. They may sputter or gag on the blood filling their esophagus, but still, they gasp. And two: they won't die unless I'm the one holding the blade.

I didn't know a person could smell worse than the sodden alleyway behind Lady Visha's brothel. Something putrid wafting off Death's appointed target had proven me wrong. It was either him or the blonde prostitute hanging off his good arm. Based on his stumble and the perfect cadence of her gloriously high heels, he was a good bet for the lack of hygiene. Her patron must have paid very well, even though he didn't have a pot to piss in. That, or she'd found herself in severe debt to Lady Visha.

I didn't need to lean over the wrought-iron railing circling the rooftop to see where they were going, nor rely on Death's magic to guide me. Thomas Vanhutes had been the object of my obsession for days. Since the night Death delivered his name, I knew where he lived and where he found pleasure. He slept on a stained mattress older than he was, with no linens, and his crumbling apartment boasted a leaky faucet. Not surprising for someone living on Beggar's Row. At least he had shelter, which was more than most in that district. Including the giant black crows that hounded the vagrants. They were always watching. Perth's most notorious plague.

I leaped from the rooftop, avoiding the puddles that inundated the narrow alleyway like an incurable illness, clinging to the shadows along the close brick buildings. Crossing the uneven brick road to stay close to Thomas, I quickly scaled the next building, digging into the dilapidated edifice I'd grown so familiar with. Most dwellers of the twin kingdoms could navigate these roads in pitch black. The water reflected enough of the streetlamp's cool glow to guide the way.

The birds pecking at the gaps between the bricks scattered when Thomas stumbled by. And, though he wobbled, and his company clacked, I was as silent as the deaths I delivered. A weapon. Honed and sheathed for as long as I could resist the magic.

A woman's faint pants echoed through the next alleyway until she grew to a fake climax, satisfying her third patron of the night. The red-haired woman had perfected those moans, and Lady Visha had likely become even more wealthy because of it. As I passed, she held her breath. As if she'd felt me from above, Death's Maiden, like a promise of deliverance from her plight. There was hope in that breath. A wish, though she'd never know I was there, having honed my skills by the age of thirteen. Some miserable souls were just more desperate than others.

I crept away, eyes focused once more. She'd wipe the remnants of that man from between her legs with a dirty rag and move on to the next within the hour. There was no saving her. Though that was not my job. The twin kingdoms were full of dark merchants, crime lords, thieves, and brothels. Every person needed to be rescued from something, even the Perth king's daughter. I'd sooner fall under the thumb of a crime lord than endeavor to save the world.

I stalked Thomas from the apartment rooftops, crouching and watching my victim carry on, his silhouette elongating as he neared his favorite alehouse. Every third night, he stopped at the Badger Hole for one final nightcap, and I preferred to avoid the street rats that swarmed outside.

He hesitated for only a second before letting the prostitute tug on his good arm, probably eager to end her suffering. Like most dwellers of Beggar's Row, she didn't flinch at the rodents outside his home. They were more welcomed in this city than the failing king.

Heel to toe, I paced along the adjacent rooftop, placating the magic with my movements; not to grant Thomas a final tupping before his ultimate demise, but to give the woman time to pay her debt. A mercy for him, perhaps.

The door would squeak if I opened it. Lifting or pressing down on the handle wouldn't stop the squeal, so I opted for the window when Death's magic became too strong to resist. The bars had rusted away long ago, and I fit easily. Aside from the snoring, the space was eerily quiet. The prostitute had never left, but I wasn't expecting to find her naked, and on her back, tied to the kitchen table, a look of boredom on her face.

The leaky faucet dripped into a puddle on the piss-stained floor, and the woman lay spread open with Thomas passed out in the corner. Based on the scene, he'd had far bigger plans than his drunken stupor would allow. As I neared him, the visions began. Death's magic showed me all the ways I could kill this man. Breaking every bone in his body until his tortured screams were no longer audible. Slicing him from nose to navel, letting his innards slink to the floor, leaving him to drown in his own blood.

Hand gripping the knife strapped to my waist, I fought the power that would eventually win long enough to free the whimpering woman. She rolled away with a groan before scrambling until her back hit the wall as realization sank in. My presence in the dead of night meant only one thing.

"Deyanira." The chokehold of shock rippled over her trembling features.

I didn't begrudge her for neglecting to use my title. Folding my arms across my chest, I let the blade of my curved knife show. "Is the debt paid?"

She held an arm up to count the red bands before nodding.

"You can stay and watch, but he'll be here in five minutes."

Dull brown eyes rimmed in smeared mascara widened, followed by the first authentic gasp of the night. She didn't say another word, only grabbed her clothes and hurried out of the apartment, naked, the squeal of the door, the final goodbye.

"I don't blame you," I managed, unable to fight the magic any longer.

A silent slice and the second gasp, the one I'd anticipated, satisfied the power throbbing through my body. *A name given; a body delivered.* That was my true role. That of a harbinger. A lone assassin in a world of none. Death's Maiden.

The gargle was hardly audible over the sound of the shrill ringing in my ears, the eerie retraction of magic leaving traces behind, reminding me I was still human, though every kill carried me one step closer to Death's court.

Three hundred and seventy-five.

Sliding the only chair from the table, I sat, thrumming fingers along the surface, waiting, hating the relief that coalesced with the guilt. Each second was a heartbeat. Each one of Thomas's slowing rasps, a promise. I no longer watched the final rise and fall of a chest cavity. Though the first had conjured tears, by the fiftieth, my heart had turned to stone. The gods had abandoned us to Death's ultimate reign, and this was the world he reaped. And I was his weapon.

Death came without ceremony this time. His shrouded figure was no more than an ominous mystery until he swept his shadowed hood back, revealing the face of a beautiful monster. The most stunning man one may ever see, his immortal, god-like features were every bit the trap. Jet black hair and a perfectly angular face only set the tone for those obsidian eyes.

"My darling," he purred as I bowed low. "You have never been a disappointment, Deyanira."

His voice was the sound a throat coated in warm, golden honey might be, but I knew better than to utter words in his presence, especially when he tucked a finger under my chin, pulling me from the rancid floor while I watched the name burned into my palm wither away to embers and ash.

Death pressed cool lips to my cheek as he did with every meeting. Floating above my victim, he drew Thomas's soul from his body, eyes glistening with mirth before he laughed and dragged him off to his eternal court.

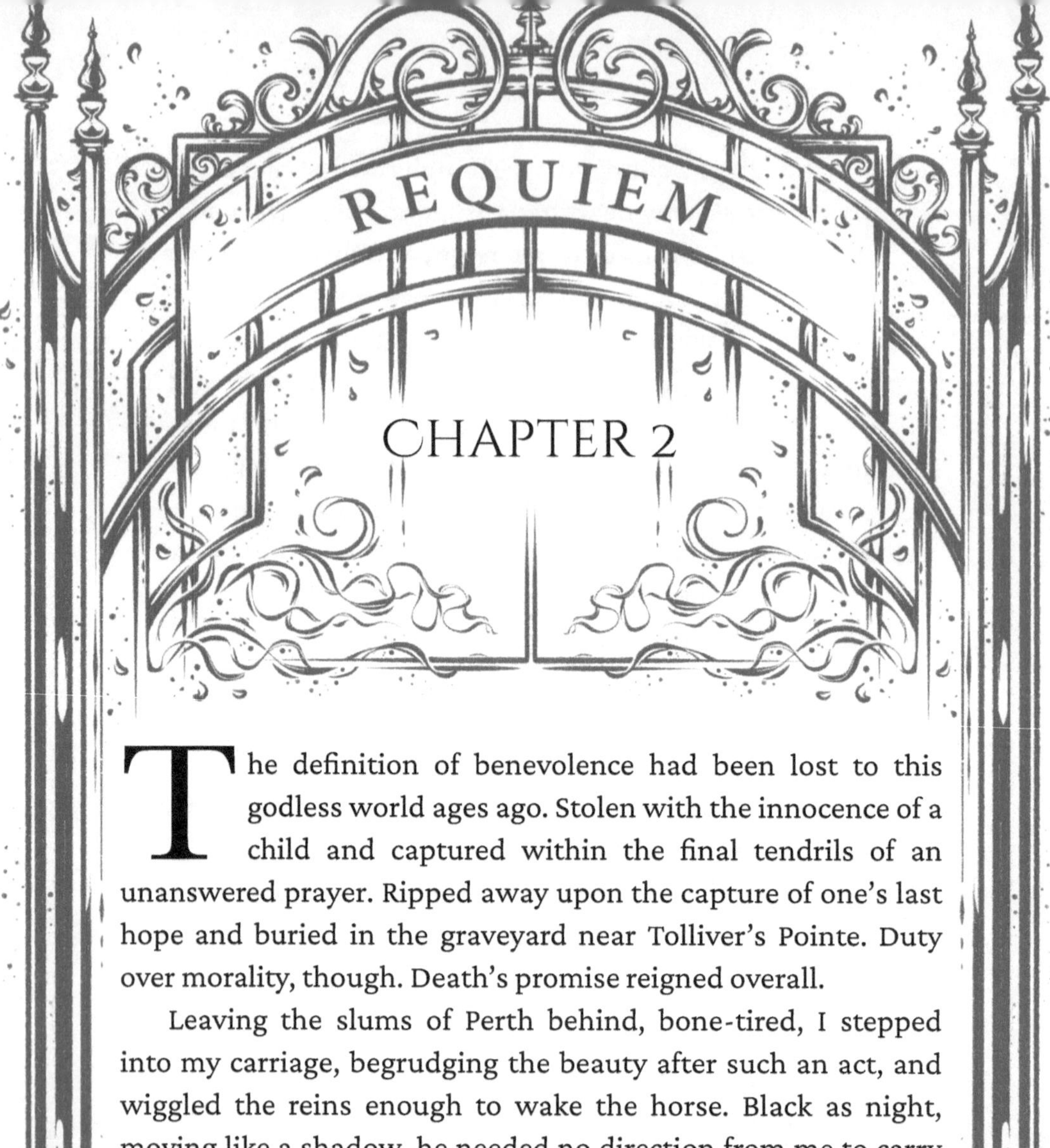

CHAPTER 2

The definition of benevolence had been lost to this godless world ages ago. Stolen with the innocence of a child and captured within the final tendrils of an unanswered prayer. Ripped away upon the capture of one's last hope and buried in the graveyard near Tolliver's Pointe. Duty over morality, though. Death's promise reigned overall.

Leaving the slums of Perth behind, bone-tired, I stepped into my carriage, begrudging the beauty after such an act, and wiggled the reins enough to wake the horse. Black as night, moving like a shadow, he needed no direction from me to carry us through the narrow streets, past the barrage of flickering streetlamps, and on to my father's home, my prison. A constant reminder that, had I not been born with my supreme title as Death's Maiden, *princess* might've led me through a completely different life. A life with a mother.

An hour later, Regulas stood at my bedroom door with perfect posture, perfectly pressed black clothing, and a perfect sneer on his aged face. "He's waiting."

"He is always waiting."

"For his beloved daughter," he said, eager to emphasize each sarcastic syllable of that word.

This particular member of my father's council used to fear me. As most did. But over the years, his fear changed into smugness. And, while I could reach out and snap his unnaturally thick neck, the baser part of me remembered that I was not like the Maidens and Lords that came before me. I was a weapon by fate, not choice. And a princess, all the same.

Planting my feet, I straightened my spine and ran a finger over the ornate design on Chaos's curved handle, finding comfort in the weapon that never left my thigh. "I am a member of this royal house, Regulas." I narrowed my gaze until he flinched. "You will not forget yourself again."

He bowed, clearing his throat, though his words were laced with annoyance. "Forgive me, Your Royal Highness."

"Just because my father has chosen to forgo formalities with you within the walls of his castle, does not mean I have. Should you wish to see the sun again, don't forget your place. I answer to Death first and my king second."

Holding himself bent at the waist while waiting for my dismissal, his balding head flushed, the lights along the ceiling illuminating the bulging veins. I checked for dirt beneath my nails and the corners for cobwebs before finally dismissing him. Setting my hand on the cold metal knob, I contemplated the escape of my bedroom. Such luxury would have to wait, though. My father was not a patient king.

He'd meet me in the throne room and nowhere else, choosing formality in every moment we shared. My father resented Death and the power he stole by selecting me in the womb as Maiden, the first and only royal to hold the title. A king deserves power over his kingdom but covets control over his family.

Two heavily armed guards, both with expressionless faces

and long swords crossing their backs, opened the doors in unison, never bothering to look at me, though I could see the Adam's apple bob in one's throat as I passed. His weapons were for show, good for maiming at best; mine were soul suckers, a guaranteed eternity in Death's court.

The obsidian columns wrapped in iron burst from the floor as if they'd been banished from hell and sent to hold my father's throne room erect. And at the top of fifty towering stairs, he sat on his dais, staring down at the world like he'd summoned them instead.

"Deyanira." His voice echoed off the walls. "Must you always disappoint me?"

Ten years ago, his words might have inspired a reaction, but after so long, I'd become numb to him, confident it was better to hold my tongue than engage. Instead, I silently begged the old gods for reprieve of this torture. Of this life where I'd never know love or kindness or laughter. The closest I would ever have was Ro. And even she was fickle. Still, my eyes flashed to Regulas, who was standing behind him, mumbling something with the same sneer on his face as earlier.

I didn't move, flinch, or breathe as I stood waiting for him to begin. Eventually, he gripped the smooth edges of his throne and descended the steps, one loud booted step at a time. Clasping his hands behind him, he circled me like a vulture, assessing as he always did.

"Report!" he demanded.

I stared straight ahead, unwilling to let my green eyes, the twin to his, fall. "The victim's name was Thomas Vanhutes. He rented a rundown apartment in Beggar's Row, near the Badger Hole. He died in hi—"

"His sleep. Yes. You are a merciful murderer. And the Maestro? Does he continue to hunt you?"

"Of course, he does, but there were no signs of him or his men."

"Don't you find it odd that you miraculously avoid him? You wouldn't be keeping secrets from me, would you?"

I sighed, drawing the same repetitive explanation forward. "It's not a miracle, Father. It's a skill. I'm always aware of my surroundings and danger."

"How lucky for all of us."

Teeth clenched, I didn't miss the indignation in his tone. He knew I could have tortured them all. He assumed Death's magic begged me to slaughter. But my stubborn will allowed me one grace. Choice.

"And the Life Maiden?"

I gulped. "No news."

"We haven't had a Life Maiden in twenty-six years. More people than ever are sick, with no one to heal them. She must be hiding. It's impossible that you haven't heard a single word, Deyanira," Regulas said from behind my father's throne, his puny voice echoing off the brushed gold walls until it crept down my spine. He'd purposely left my title out.

"I'm not the Huntress. Blame someone else. Blame yourself, *councilman*," I snapped at him.

He crept down the steps as formidably as my father had, mirroring the king's stately posture, stopping three steps from the bottom to ensure he could still look down on me. "Our guards are training more aggressively than ever before. There's fighting amongst Requiem along the Hallowed River. If you were to use more... persuasive measures to seek answers, perhaps you would have more."

"I am not a spy."

"You are hardly anything," Regulas answered.

I'd barely registered my own movement until his high-pitched scream ripped through the room. One moment, the snide man was standing, the next, his feet flew from beneath him as Chaos collided with his shoulder.

I climbed the steps as slowly as he had descended, pressing my boot into his arm as I ripped the blade from his body and wiped the fresh blood on his pants. Crouching, I glared. "I have trained my entire life to be able to kill you with less than a thought. Should you wish to reach your one-hundredth year, you will never speak to me again."

"M-my king?" he stammered, not daring to rise.

I stood, turning to finally look my father in the face. The kernel of pride might have shocked me, had I never known his love for violence. His intentional distance had only sharpened the edges of everything I was. To raise a child without a single touch, a single soft word, grows a beast in slumber. A person with no knowledge of love or light. A woman with no compassion. Still, as if it'd been planted in my soul before I was born, I cared. I wanted to experience love and kindness more desperately than he could ever fathom. Maybe the yearning was what kept me human.

Years ago, I'd disguised myself and went to the inner city to seduce a man. After several visits and several easily swayed partners, I'd learned that touch was not enough. Forced passion didn't placate the desire for someone to see beyond the mask.

The king moved to my side. "If one continues to play with fire, they will get burned. Especially if that fire is my daughter. Go clean yourself up, Regulas. You're an embarrassment."

A flicker of satisfaction settled in my gut. Upon the click of the great door in the back of the throne room, my father continued his careful assessment, shaking his head as he surveyed my unpolished boots. I stiffened, falling right back in line.

"What have you heard of Silbath?"

"Nothing new."

Again, he tsked. "I demand you be of use to me. And as I cannot marry you off because your poor husband would likely wet the marital bed every night in fear of you, you must have another use, Deyanira. You refuse to kill on my behalf. So, what good are you?"

His rhetorical question echoed through my memories, pinging off each and every time he'd uttered those vicious words until that kernel disintegrated to ash.

"The old gods damned and abandoned us." He spun on a heel and paced behind me, each step in a synchronized rhythm. "War would be so much easier."

I bit my tongue, letting the coppery taste of blood fill my mouth. There would be no use arguing with my father. He didn't understand the finality of murder the same way I did, and thus, war.

Many generations ago, the two kingdoms of this world had nearly killed each other off. Rampaged by war and famine, had Death not stepped in and taken away our ability to die for one hundred years, there would be no one left. A reprieve for everyone but kings seeking land and people to imprison.

He climbed the steps back to his throne and sat heavily, twisting his silver mustache until it curled at the ends. I waited for my dismissal, knowing he would stretch it out, just as I had done to Regulas. Perhaps I was more like my father than I'd realized. Eventually, he cleared his throat and waved me away without another word.

By the time I made it to my room, the exhaustion of my task, of the magic that had compelled me until my free will was gone, forced every muscle and every bone to grow heavy. Death's magic was so potent, it could not have been meant for mere humans. The second my mind had wandered to the hidden vulnerability of Maidens, I pushed those thoughts away, just as Death had warned me to do the first time I'd ever seen him.

When he promised me an eternity and warned me of an early end.

Because, though magic was rare, and so powerful it should not have existed in humans, I would always be the exception. Along with the Life Maiden, should she ever be found. The brush of sheer curtains caught by a cool breeze trailed over my skin as I stood on the balcony, staring down at a world hunted, one soul at a time.

The moon was hardly a crescent, and difficult to discern, but still, it provided just enough light to guide me back through the massive bedroom and to a full-length mirror leaning against the wall. I ran tired fingers over the gilded filigree along the top, noting where it'd begun to wear down over the years.

"Ro?" I whispered, shifting toward my reflection.

The glass rippled like an awakened pond in response to my voice.

Holding my breath, I stepped through, into a world that I once believed was only for me, though the years had taught me differently. This world was hers. A sanctuary from the evils of mine.

"Back so soon?" The familiar voice wrapped me in comfort as I strode into Ro's home.

"Unfortunately." I navigated her peculiar hall of mirrors and descended the squeaky steps into the cottage, pushing through the vines of various plants growing from the ceiling until I found her, watering can in hand.

"You are a conundrum, Dey."

"Why?"

"Because you wear your burdens so visibly. There are days it hurts to look at you."

"It hurts more to *be* me. But those must be the days you deny me entry."

"No." She winked. "I'm usually entertaining someone far more handsome."

The loose wrap of her navy robes showcased her golden-brown skin while still highlighting her piercing dark honey eyes. Though I'd visited her more times than I could ever count, her beauty always stole my breath. Even as a child, I would come through the mirror and stare at her in silent moments, wondering why she hardly aged and seemed to grow more beautiful. But a child never sees the subtle signs, the tiny wrinkles gathering at the eyes or the small strands of gray hair. In truth, I didn't know Ro's age.

I reached for the waxy leaf of a nearby plant to keep my hands busy. "I'm confident he's the one entertaining you."

"You would not judge me if you knew what you were missing."

I snorted. "I'm not innocent, Ro. I know exactly what I'm missing."

"A single dip of a stick by a mere boy does not teach you what you are missing. You need a man to throw you around a little bit."

"If a man ever tried to throw me around, I'd cut his balls off before he had the chance to empty them."

The edges of her mouth curved into a wry smile. "I've tried that. It's not nearly as fun. They scream a lot."

Gesturing to the door along the back wall, I followed her into the main room of her home, slumping onto a velvet couch as she poured two glasses full of amber liquid and passed me the first. Hers was empty before I could take a sip of mine, though I'd never seen her swallow a drop. The alcohol was a ritual at this point, carrying us through the motions on habit alone.

"We don't have to." She carried her words as if in song. "If the tasks are wearing on you, perhaps it's time to embrace this gift."

I narrowed my eyes, sharing a deadly look that would rattle a weaker person. "We have very different opinions on what a gift is."

"Mm-hmm. Just don't let me catch any rumors about how I maim you for fun."

I took another giant swing of the whiskey. "To be fair, this *was* your idea."

"How was I supposed to know you would keep it going after all these years?" Dainty fingers disappeared within the folds of her navy robes as she took a seat directly across from me, pulling out a small metal box.

My eyes flicked to the ruby embedded into the top. My late mother's. She was my first kill, her soul the path by which I entered this world like a battering ram, and the jewel was my gift to Ro for being here for me when no one else was.

She lifted her chin. "Off with it."

Slamming back the last swallow of the drink, I let the amber liquid burn a familiar path down my throat. I set the glass on the table and stood, removing my shirt to give her easy access to my spine. Sinking onto the colorful rug before her, I clutched my knees to my chest and let myself experience a modicum of vulnerability, remembering the small details I'd learned of Thomas's life, of his friendship with the man who worked the predominantly rotten fruit stand in Silbath's square. Of the neighbor he'd robbed. He wasn't a decent man, but he'd had a life, and if not for me, he would at least have had time for redemption.

Metal scraped metal as Ro opened her precious box, removed the ink and needle, and began to tattoo the three hundred and seventy-fifth flower petal along my back. The vine was sprawling and the dainty flowers unique to her imagination. I'd run out of room one day.

After my mother's untimely murder, Death had given me the mercy of sixteen years to train. But that second kill, when I was still a child, still unsure of why my father's court shied away from me, destroyed something in my soul. Ripped away my ability to feel and think. And when I'd cried, staring at myself in the mirror, wondering what kind of a monster I'd become, Ro saved me. She'd revealed herself, welcoming me into her home, if I were brave enough to step beyond my reflection.

Enamored by her beauty, I followed her into this haven, wondering why she wasn't afraid of me, like the others. She knew who I was, *what* I was, and still, she did not shy away. When I'd told her of my numbness and the fear that consumed me, that one day I'd take so many lives, I would no longer remember them, she offered this service. And the second that needle pierced my flesh, it was like inflating a punctured lung. Allowing me to feel and breathe, if only for a moment. And I'd needed that desperately, time and time again. Until a single flower became a garden. And a scared girl became a woman—lacking, but a woman, nonetheless.

"Ro," I whispered, lost in my memories.

She placed a hand on my shoulder. "I see where your mind wanders when you come to me. I offer you solace because we are kindred spirits. But must we discuss it every time?"

"Knowledge is power, and magic is a burden. Maybe if I understood it, I could fight it more."

"Magic is a gift and yes, oftentimes, a burden. But as there are so few of us with it, there is nothing to understand. You are the result of a promise from Death. He stood upon a broken realm of two cities, destroyed by war and famine, and took away the ease of mortality among our ancestors, promising a Maiden to remind us of the fragility of life. You are a blessing, even if you cannot see beyond the burden." She'd spoken those words with no emotion behind them. Reminding me that this was the history and the religion of our world. A truth everyone knew and accepted.

"I know." I lowered my head onto my knees. "It doesn't make it any easier."

She stood, circling to sit cross-legged on the floor before me, lifting my chin with a finger. "Last week, I visited the bathhouse in Perth. I watched a woman wrestling her child to simply bathe. She slipped and fell, and that single act would have taken her life because she cracked her head on the tile. She had four children with her. I know it doesn't feel like it means something, but your burden saved her life. You must think of those moments, Dey."

"If I could—"

"No. These thoughts will rot your mind. We've been doing this for ten years. Ten years of tattoos and sorrows and loathing yourself. When will it be enough?"

"The day you leave me."

"I am far from one hundred. We have so much time left together."

"And if I am given your name?"

She grabbed my hands, the human connection still stunning me after all these years. "Then we will hold the blade together, you will close your eyes, and we will have our final moments in peace before I am sent to Death's court."

The ringing in my ears and the weight on my heart did not leave me that night. Not as I climbed those steps and walked back through the mirror, or when I closed my eyes, begging for sleep. I think I could stomach the loss of just about anyone else. Even my father. But never Ro.

CHAPTER 3

Thick fingers gripped the sides of my face as Death hovered above me, cunning, dark eyes inches from mine as his hot breath melted down my cheeks. "You are so beautiful, my Deyanira."

Fighting the urge to cringe in my dream, mere weeks after Thomas's murder, I turned my face away, and he vanished, appearing even closer than he was before. He reached for my forearm, his grip like talons as he studied my palm, nearly salivating.

The first time he'd seared my skin with a name, I'd screamed, and a wretched smile unfurled across his beautiful face, stopping my heart. He relished in misery and fear, and it ruined something within me that had hoped he truly was the savior our history had made him out to be. I'd never made a sound again. Never spoken a word.

"What do you dream of when you are not here?" he asked, knowing I wouldn't answer. "Is it the final scream of your victims? Do they wet themselves in your dreams, Deyanira, or do you leave that part out?"

Toying with me, he waited until I looked at him. When I was seventeen, I'd refused, and he'd held me in sleep for three days, his eternal patience everlasting. I broke then, and it remained a challenge for him each time. A game I had no desire to play. So, I succumbed.

I hated how beautiful his smile was when he approved, seconds before burning the name of the next victim into my palm, skin sizzling as the smell of my burning flesh filled my nostrils. White-hot pain raced up my arm. Every part of me wanted to buckle, but I remained steady, unflinching as he stared at me, hunting for my breaking point.

"I will see you in a few days, my beauty. I have a good feeling about this one."

He'd spoken those words to me every single time. As if he hoped this kill would deliver him a worthwhile soul. Each name given was a charge, an invisible line of magic binding them to me for the rest of their short lives, but only I was aware of the string.

Death's court, also accurately known as hell, was permanently lit by two moons in eternal night, a realm unlike mine. To stand before his haunted castle, the silhouette of colossal black spires stretching across the hazy ground was not intimidating. But the hellhounds that sat before the gates that seemed to reach the heavens, ruby eyes stone cold and unmoving, certainly were.

The soul of every person I'd ever killed lived in this realm. Those who reached their one-hundredth year without the touch of a harbinger were said to be saved by the old gods and rested for an eternity in peace or reincarnated to repeat their miserable life cycle. But there was only one of *us* in every generation. One dead, another born. My mother was trapped here simply because she'd seen a Life Maiden after marrying my father, and that simple visit increased her fertility. A mistake I would never have the chance to make if she could not be found. Curing those with debilitating injuries and disease while inspiring fertility, the Life Maiden was always welcomed with gifts and smiles, the stories said. Perhaps I'd never know.

Brazen curiosity burned as stoutly as my palm, though I did not peek at the name, choosing to close my eyes instead until I woke. Death's low chuckle and his cold kiss on my cheek were my fading goodbye as I woke in my bedroom.

Bram Ellis.

The second I read the name, Death's magic pulsed. Pushed. Urged me out of bed as my toxic world spun with recognition. I moved my fingers over the burnt edges of the name, convinced it could not be real. What was Death playing at? I loathed being given the name of someone I recognized. That was rare. But not as rare as this.

I stepped into black full-body leathers, buckling the straps across my thighs, and slipped a mask across my face. With a full head of black hair, I didn't need a hood, but there was comfort in shadows. I used to wear a cape, as well, but it took one strong man to grip the edges and yank before I sliced it off, freeing myself. Never again. I'd need every advantage I could get for this hunt. And every weapon, should things go wrong.

I'd never asked my father for a single piece of lace or string of pearls. Not one frilly dress or stallion. Instead, I'd arranged a secret room to be built on my own. The Death Maidens that came before me killed for Death and themselves, instilling a fear that resided in so many hearts that people rarely told me no. With three walls of weapons, I studied my options pointedly, feeding the magic that begged me to use them all. I'd never go without Chaos, but I'd already strapped her onto my thigh. Throwing knives would definitely be needed. I skipped a whip but snagged an iron-tooth chain. Dainty enough to wear and dangerous enough to sever an arm, she'd saved me on several occasions. With poison, a change of clothes, and perfume for good measure, I couldn't have been more prepared without hauling the entire arsenal.

My position was revered by many. Terrified glances and wide berths greeted me in royal halls and among busy streets. But those that lurked within the damp alleys typically carried vendettas, and though they could not kill me, they could easily incapacitate me for the rest of my life. And I was partial to my arms and legs. If I could not kill for Death, I'd fall to madness, the magic poisoning my mind.

Many hours later, I'd left Perth behind, using rooftops to cross to the border of Silbath. Only the Hallowed River separated the realm of two cities. Our long and sordid history, that of a single kingdom split in two, always flashed across my mind when I passed the opposing guards. But even they would not stop me. I was Death's tool. His promise to our people that should we sink so low again, and reach a boiling point of hatred, he would remove the mortality restriction and let us burn this world to the ground. Though hated, the Death Maiden was still respected on both sides of that pointless border.

The talk was cheap amongst the guards, who stood vigilant as they faced off, weapons drawn. The numbers here had tripled in size over the past couple of months, and though I knew the people would be the ones who would suffer a war, there was nothing anyone could do to make peace. Hatred was bred along kingdom borders and within the minds of aggressive soldiers and sniveling councilmen with far too much time on their hands and no true vision of the people who suffered below their massive boots. The tension had grown so strong you could taste it in the misty air.

Riddled with slums, buildings with iron bars, and rodent infestations, our kingdoms were nearly identical. Silbath was larger, but Perth was slightly richer, and something within those negligible differences held a waning border. The only thing that flourished in this world was misery. And the gods-damned crows.

Traveling the Silk Road, I avoided the hustle of the market, winding myself through damp alleys past the Dancing Ghost, thanking the old gods for yet another overcast sky until my target appeared in the southern distance. Some would say the Silk Road was safe, but anyone with eyes could see the disease-riddled market for what it was: a haven for thieves and the Maestro's lackeys, who fed on the unfortunate.

Magic kept me focused, concentrating on light and movements and sounds and smells as I developed a viable plan of action before I reached Silbath's great stone castle. Confidence would only carry me so far. Bram Ellis held a position of rank, and that fact alone would mean evading guards. My favorite fucking pastime.

It was not a day for murder. As long as I could fight the magic, I would, buying my prey as much time as possible. The weapons were only a safeguard. A failsafe should this go horribly wrong. Today, I only needed to be near enough to appease the pressure. Stalking and learning while my veins throbbed but acquiesced.

I'd killed a mark here three summers ago and knew exactly how to get into the castle. As there would be no foot traffic within the bailey, a fact well-known, I had to watch the king's guard on the parapet while changing into something water-proof. Then I'd wait for the opening to cross the stockade and leap into the putrid moat.

The murky water, green and mossy, was nearly impossible to swim through. Still, I managed, taking careful breaths as needed to keep an eye on the guard patrolling the wall. This castle, once a stronghold for all of Silbath, had become nothing more than a symbol of hierarchy and wealth among riffraff.

The shallow water of the half-empty moat circled the castle, allowing me to enter through a grate and climb into a great stone room that once housed boats, but now only held decayed wood tied to a sunken dock.

I quickly changed, discarding the noxious clothing I'd have to slip back on to leave, scaring the rats away before dotting perfume on my neck. It'd take hours for the smell of that cesspool to leave me if I didn't change, and if I meant to hide within the walls, I had no intention of raising a single warning bell in Silbath's castle today.

Pushing the door open no more than an inch, I listened first and stepped out only when I knew no one was nearby. I made it halfway to the hidden door I'd found last time before I was spotted.

"Death Maiden?" a young girl said with a gasp, blue eyes already watering.

Rounding on her, I drew my blade and pinned her with a glare. "If you treasure your life, you'll leave me and speak of this to no one. One peep out of you, and I'll hunt you for sport. Understand?"

"Is... is it my father?" she managed, trembling hands disappearing into her skirts.

"Would you really want to know if it was?"

Dark lashes cast down toward the floor, but she kept her chin raised. "Yes."

"Then make sure he knows how much you love him, just in case," I said from behind the mask. "And pray to whatever gods you believe in."

Her eyes flashed to my hands, but black gloves blocked her view. I took one step toward her, inciting enough fear to send her darting away with a sob. Perhaps she'd tell, but it changed nothing. By the end of this week, Bram Ellis would be dead, or I would. There was no stopping Death's coercion over fate.

Following a familiar path, I managed to sneak into the hidden passages of the castle, where light was scarce and people more so. The spiders didn't bother me as long as I left them alone. Though an occasional high guard would pass through, I'd mastered vanishing into the shadows by the time I was seven. Back when training was fun and only one death haunted me.

"The king is ready for war, and I say more power to him. Why should we fear Perth?" A court member's shrill voice carried through the thin walls.

My heart stopped my feet for only a moment as my father's fears were confirmed.

"Aren't you afraid?" another answered.

"Why should I fear war when it is my husband that will fight? Perhaps I'll be a widow by year's end," the woman said excitedly.

"If not a thrall, Agria. Imagine being forced into the Scarlet District."

"The men are ready. The people are ready. We're double their numbers, last I checked. It'll be nothing at all to conquer that entire wretched kingdom."

I continued on, letting the voices fade away. My father would have planted me there to spy for hours had he known I could navigate these passages. I'd considered it once, knowing it might be the only thing I could ever do for him. But Silbath's king hated Perth's king, and the people in the middle would suffer the same, regardless. A war between our kingdoms felt imminent, no matter what. And the people would not die. They would be mutilated and left to suffer or forced into servitude until their hundredth year.

Eventually, I made it to the walls skirting the king's council room, and while I expected to find a guard or servant eavesdropping, the area was clear. Crouching, I drew a long rectangle in the dirt on the floor and placed each voice to a seat until I'd narrowed down who might sit within the room. The king's aged words carried through as he spoke of visits to Lady Visha's and the last cunt he'd tasted. The valuable information was looser on the tongues of the court.

"Do make sure our seats are cleaned before we get to the theater," the king was saying. "I don't like attention before the show."

I straightened, listening in order to decipher the plans as their voices quieted. It would be far easier to kill Bram Ellis if he was not behind castle walls. But the second the magic followed my train of thought, I had to fight the urge to storm into the room and claim my victim prematurely. Compulsion riled within me. I could end it now without the hunt. I could take out the guards at the door with throwing knives before they could think of defending the room's occupants. And none of the men at that table were a threat to me.

The click of a door down the passageway was my only warning before a royal guard stepped beyond the threshold. I jumped backward, hoping he hadn't seen me with my ear to the wall, but his hurried footsteps were his own damnation. I lunged before he could make a sound, landing on his back with an arm around his neck. Clad in black armor, I thanked the old gods he hadn't worn a helmet before I smashed Chaos's hilt into his skull.

The brute could take a hit, though, stumbling around for several seconds as I rode on his back. He smashed my spine into a wall, trying to free himself, but one more well-placed bash and that was it.

With adrenaline coursing through my veins, confident I hadn't killed him, I threw my own body below his to quiet the ungraceful fall, twisting my ankle. Shoving him until he rolled, I managed to wiggle free.

It was always the fucking guards in this palace. Last time, I had to tie two in the dungeons. And only the old gods knew how long it'd taken for them to free themselves. Still, if I left this one here like this, he'd squeal as soon as his vision was clear enough to get out of the passage. And then everyone would be locked down and on high alert, and that wasn't a problem I wanted.

Stripping away every piece of armor that made him heavier, I admired his chiseled body for only seconds as I drafted a plan. I gripped his ankles and tugged the king's guard inch by inch down the passage, praying even to Death himself that no one else would come. I'd have to start killing at that point, just to make it out alive.

Lugging a giant guard through the narrow passageways of Silbath's castle was not how I'd envisioned my day going. In fact, I could think of exactly five hundred and seventy-two other things I'd rather be doing. I'd counted with each fucking step I'd hauled the bastard.

He'd be found too quickly near the council chambers. If not by a nosy servant, then by a courtesan seeking the king or another high-ranking scumbag. I'd have to get him into a space that no one would stumble across, and, unfortunately for me, that meant going all the way around the central meeting rooms, far beyond the kitchens, and toward one of the old bedrooms that were no longer used. The king had no children. Most of the rooms of his castle housed more dust than dignitaries.

When he woke up, he'd be in pain for days. If not for the pounding headache, then from getting the shit beat out of him as I dragged him, unceremoniously, over rocks, through rats' nests, and even into a few walls when his body didn't want to turn the way I needed it to. Even still, it wouldn't be enough to keep him silent.

Once we were far enough away, I slipped the vial of poison from a hidden pocket. Double-checking that my mask was secure to avoid the fumes, I pried his drooling mouth open and deposited three drops on his tongue. But as I surveyed his body one final time, I added one more for good measure.

"You won't die," I promised. "But you're going to hate your life for at least a week. You're welcome."

I ran back through to gather his gear and dropped it with him on the way out. He didn't move an inch when the heavy steel landed on his torso. Maybe four drops were overkill.

Two days later, I forwent the mask, opting for something that would blend in a crowd. Still, dresses weren't for me, but I twisted my dark hair out of my face, donned a simple blonde wig, applied red lipstick, and went for a long brown cloak with a deep hood. A perfect disguise I'd used several times, because no one outside of my father's castle ever looked hard enough. Though children were scarcer now, with no Life Maiden around, there were still a few. And if I weren't disguised, their mothers would clench their shoulders, hiding them away as I passed, teaching them without words that a Death Maiden would always be someone to fear.

They were not wrong. But then the people would talk, giving me away. And the magic was already thrumming within me, pushing me to study the name etched into my palm. To visualize Bram Ellis's death and deliver his body.

I rarely went a full day without stalking my victim. Never two. But these special circumstances had required a different kind of reconnaissance. By the time I set out to fulfill my duty as Maiden, I knew the exit plan for my mark to leave Silbath's castle. I knew which carriage he'd be in and who would ride with him, as well as the names of all of his closest companions, their bonded wives, their whores, and even which bathhouse most of them frequented, though most of that knowledge had come from previous trips to the castle.

Bram Ellis preferred an opium den owned by the Maestro blocks away from the Dancing Ghost, and that would be my backup plan, should tonight go to shit. But the theater would be the better option. He'd travel alone afterward, giving me a ten-minute window.

I'd only need one.

Giant black crows rested on glowing streetlamps, watching the dark, misty world from their posts, as the richest and vilest of Requiem gathered outside of Misery's End, the Maestro's dark burlesque show. Years ago, my father refused his request to open his theater in Perth, but the Silbath king feared him more. Though no one used his given name, Drexel Vanhoff was, at his core, a magic-bearing crime lord anyone would have been hard-pressed to go toe to toe with. Many of our kingdom's people donned the Maestro's blue bands around their arms, proof they'd become magically bound to the repugnant man.

I kept to the back of the building a few blocks down, pacing as I waited for the line of carriages to descend upon the infamous theater, adrenaline racing as I felt the danger to my very core. Like clockwork, the Maestro arrived first. The spokes of his carriage imitated the keys of a grand piano, and the black iron doors were molded to replicate curtains. Polished boots splashed in a puddle as he exited, placing his signature top hat upon his head and flexing his fingers in leather gloves. I couldn't see his face from here, but I knew the scar down his cheek would be there. The mark of a man that even I would rather avoid. A man who had hunted me since I was a child.

Five women wearing just enough fabric and feathers to cover their bits accompanied him as he leaned on the cane he didn't need. He waved to the growing crowd, his coat tails shifting along his calves as he followed his personal guard inside.

The king of Silbath was next. And though he did not don the adoration of those gathered, they still managed to bow and silence themselves as he and his entourage entered Misery's End. Death's magic roared in my veins, urging me to follow, to stalk, to kill.

The patrons would enter through the front of the building instead of the back. I contemplated the rooftop access, but the Maestro's security was infamous and brutal. I didn't need extra roadblocks tonight, knowing what was to come, so I hid the weapons they'd take at the door. Each harbinger carried themselves differently. Most commanded attention and were unapologetically ruthless, killing for Death less than they killed for themselves, but I preferred solitude and respite from people.

Stashing my weapons and circling the building to the main entrance, I managed to slip into the line in front of two women fighting over the man between them. I didn't need to go in, and probably shouldn't, but there were few places in Silbath I'd never been, and knowledge was always power. Anytime I'd hunted a patron obsessed with the scandalous show, I waited until after the curtains fell, content to end them in their sleep. Due to the nature of this kill, I'd need to keep eyes on Bram Ellis at all times. Anything could change in an instant, and if I didn't kill him soon, the magic would completely consume me, driving me to madness until I took him out. And when I was pushed that far, carnage followed. I'd learned the hard way that nothing fed Death's magic like murder. Copious amounts of it, if I lost control. So, I'd stay nearby and keep my wits about me. The ramifications of this night would already be severe without mistakes.

A hulking man at the door, with fists the size of sledgehammers, stood beside a beautiful tanned woman with stunning eyes, one green and one blue, who surveyed the crowd as thoroughly as I had, though she was dressed in a sheer gown. A performer watching the door. Interesting. Her gaze landed on me for mere seconds before she moved on, searching for some-thing, or some*one*. When I approached to enter, the man held an arm out to stop me.

"You're new."

I narrowed a glare. "You're observant."

The woman cleared her throat but did not speak.

"It's three coins to enter, four if you're looking for work. Did Lady Visha send you?"

I drew an even breath, pulling coins from a small bag in my pocket. "I'm not a whore."

The woman piped up, assessing me with an unamused sneer. "Spoken like a member of high society. Anyone worth their death knows most of the women ensnared are not whores. They're too poor or too indebted to save themselves."

I handed over the coins without responding and slipped inside the theater. She was right, of course. And that was why I didn't begrudge this world its disgusting nature. We were simply a product of our self-inflicted misery.

The entry room was no more than two grand staircases to the left and right. People pressed into me, shoving me toward the group of guards dressed in all black, siphoning us into a single file line.

"If you have any weapons, now's the time to say," the closest said, gesturing for me to turn around.

I had to tilt my head back to look into his mutilated face. "No weapons," I answered, omitting the tiny throwing knives sewn into the hem of my pants.

Rough hands trailed down my spine, making my skin crawl. I gasped, trying to remember the last time anyone other than Ro had touched me. Years. It'd been years. He slipped one hand up the inside of my thigh, the salacious look on his face turning my stomach as he moved down the other side, enjoying his job far too much.

He gripped my ass, and I stumbled forward before rounding on him. "Touch me again, and I promise you'll be eating the rest of your meals through a fucking straw."

"I doubt that, sweetheart, but it sounds like a good night. Come find me after the show."

"Go fuck yourself."

He sniffed the hand he'd groped me with. "Maybe I will."

"Keep it moving," another guard from down the line shouted, pinning me with a stare as if I'd been the one to hold everyone up.

Shuffling forward, I hustled up one side of the grand staircase and stepped into a different world. A world of elegant obsidian finishes and dim lighting focusing down on a stage draped in black velvet curtains. The outside of the building gave nothing away to indicate such finesse lay within. Its decayed edifice fit right in, mere blocks from an opium den. This was why my father hated and feared the Maestro in equal measure. His wealth and power and his ability to bind people into magical contracts made him the uncrowned third king. He had every opportunity to conceal himself in plain sight, and an unofficial army of prisoners to protect him.

I let my fingers trail up the carved railing, trying desperately to keep the awe from my face. Entering Misery's End was like stepping through one of Ro's mirrors and into a different world and time, though paintings of naked people, lost in the throes of passion, adorned the walls. Somehow that vision in dark alleyways sickened me, but here, they were perfectly placed, as if each tousle of a woman's hair, each strain of masculine muscle told a beautiful, passionate story.

The theater, bathed in a palette of black and gold, seemed to pulse as I entered. Opulent chandeliers suspended above dripped with cascades of shimmering crystals, which cast scattered shards of light that danced playfully across the dimly lit space, hinting at a giant birdcage just to the right of the stage, though I couldn't see much of it beyond the darkness.

"First time?"

I whipped around, surprised to find a polished man standing beside me, running his fingers through thick brown hair. I noticed the weapons before anything else. The kick-engaged blade embedded into his left boot, the stiff wrist indicating a hidden knife in his sleeve, the leather whip on his side, and the obvious emerald-encrusted dagger sitting comfortably in his belt.

The lower half of his face remained hidden beneath a mask, but he was neatly draped in a green tailored suit, the richness of the fabric accentuating his broad chest, coattails cascading gracefully behind him.

"It is," I answered, looking back at the drapery, moving the wig so it covered more of my face.

"Don't let the Maestro see you admiring his handy work. He loves to collect pretty girls. If you have a weakness, he'll hunt you down and exploit it."

I gripped the railing in front of me. "I have no weakness."

The smoky tone of his deep voice coiled around me as he chuckled, cinnamon eyes glinting. "Everyone's got a weakness, sweetheart. Some just don't know what it is until it's too late."

"I'll keep that in mind." Pausing, I spun to face him, shocked to see the way he held eye contact with me. If only he knew I was Death's weapon... Even now, a small tendril of magic wove around my heart, begging me to swipe his blade and plunge it into his heart. "What's with the whip?"

He lifted a shoulder, never looking away. "Makes me look tougher."

"You might want to reevaluate that. Maybe try a hammer or a hellhound or something."

An onslaught of wrinkles formed around his charming eyes, giving away his hidden smile. "I'll keep that in mind during the show."

"You're a performer?"

"I am many things," he said, as if it were a promise to himself. "But tonight, I'll be the final act on a new mission to leave you breathless. Gotta see if I can find a dog before then."

I lifted a brow. "If you're doing something sensual, maybe skip the dog."

He smoothed a hand down his lapel, leaning toward me, that hint of a smile peeking through again. "Guess I'll have to reevaluate the whole performance, then."

"Might be for the best."

A single sharp chord of music, a bow across tightly wound strings, echoed through the hall.

"That's my cue. Happy gawking, first-timer."

I glared. "I wasn't gawking."

He answered without looking back. "Whatever helps you sleep at night."

A swell of pain burned its way through my veins. I'd denied the magic for longer than it would allow. The second the throbbing started, I nearly ran to get eyes on my victim, just to soothe the growing pain. I searched for a seat with a perfect view of my target. The king and his council sat in a special section high above everyone else, though Bram's dark eyes stared at the stage in wonder.

Rather than moving down into the audience, I found another set of stairs, which were strangely unoccupied. The lights went out, and I took the opportunity to slip into a vacant box directly across from my target, with a perfect view of the stage to satiate my curiosity, while still tracking, still letting the magic thrum.

Barely dressed women with feathers for collars and jewels for undergarments traipsed through the section across from me, delivering drinks and flirting with the handsy king. Some bore red rings around their wrists, but most had blue. Each one was a magically binding debt to Lady Visha or the Maestro.

The sharp click of a cane colliding with the stage floor stole my focus. A foreign sense of anticipation swelled within me, matching the crescendo of murmurs and whispers in the growing audience that was pouring in. Time seemed to slow, as if the world held its breath, waiting for the Maestro to seduce them with his spectacle. Each of my muscles relaxed, one by one, the intoxicating thrill of the unknown baiting me. Drawing me in.

"Welcome," the Maestro shouted, his voice carrying around the full theater in perfect pitch, "to a place where seduction and secrets intertwine, where dreams and desires find their stage and consume your senses to leave you trembling in ecstasy. Every movement, every touch will be carefully choreographed to awaken the depths of your darkest appetites." Drexel Vanhoff commanded his silent audience, enthralling them with his smooth tone. He paced back and forth, promising a show unlike any other, and I fell deeper and deeper into the growl of his words. Until his gaze snapped to me. Until I knew, without a doubt, he saw me hidden in the shadows. Until a serpentine smile crept in, distorting the scar and lifting the curl in his red mustache. He seemed to speak only to me, his enchanting voice curling around my ear until the hair on my arms stood. "Tonight, my dear, I'll show you a world where pleasure and need intertwine, where submission and dominance create a symphony of lust."

I could feel every inch of my skin. As if he'd somehow touched me with his words. I couldn't stand it, yet I couldn't look away. I forced thoughts of Bram Ellis into my mind, coaxing the magic forward to overpower whatever hold the Maestro seemed to have over me. The second the desire to kill forced my eyes to Bram, I sucked in a sharp breath and considered leaving the theater immediately.

Before I could talk myself into straying from the plan, the lights went out, thrusting the entire theater into pitch black. A minor piano chord played, the dramatic sound the only one heard as a spotlight sprung to life on the ceiling, pinpointing a single diamond. As the light grew, revealing two strings of jewels hanging from the ceiling, a feminine voice as pure as honey encompassed the room, stealing my breath. The light fell onto the singer, and my heart stopped. She hung from the ceiling on a diamond swing, her body bathed in a shimmer with only enough yellow rhinestones to cover her nipples. With her long legs crossed, I couldn't tell if she was naked from the waist down or not.

The audience gasped, collectively moving to the edges of their seats as the woman sang her song, swinging back and forth in tune with the music now seeping from the orchestra pit directly in front of the stage.

No one breathed when her final note was sung. They simply stared in awe as the stunning woman leaned all the way back in her swing until she was parallel to the floor and screamed just as the light flickered out. Seconds later, the stage was lit, and the woman and her diamond swing were nowhere to be seen.

I scanned the shadows, looking for her, refusing to let my mind be tricked by the Maestro and his show. But as if he'd anticipated that, the drums began to beat, and the stage filled with men, completely naked, covering their fronts with varying shades of feathers. My heart thrummed in my chest with every pound of the drums. Each turn the muscled men took awoke something inside of me, their lithe bodies every bit as alluring as their master had promised.

They moved together, faces fierce and forward as women in matching feathers cascaded onto the stage from either side. The audience erupted into cheers, breaking my trance enough to spy on Bram Ellis. His only movement since last I looked was the slackened jaw. I took a step away, but the second I considered leaving, the music took a sharp turn, and a row of spotlights turned red, pouring down onto a giant birdcage.

The men on stage trailed their fingers over the bodies of the women, stretching their muscles and bending as they danced together in a way I'd never seen before. They moved as one pulse, one beat at a time toward the cage until the women were all inside. The men slipped into the darkness at the back of the stage as all eyes were meant to follow the women. Feathers were removed one by one until the cage held fourteen completely bare women, still dancing with the rhythm of the haunted music pouring over us.

Squeezing my eyes shut, I forced myself to listen and not watch. To focus on reality until I realized the truth behind Drexel Vanhoff's sensual show. Magic. A thick layer crept up the walls and permeated the air, gripping every patron by the throat and holding them in their seat, forcing them to sit, to stay, to drown. And most of the people in this room didn't have enough experience with magic to recognize its talons.

As the night carried on, Death's magic thrummed below my skin, hunting for violence and begging to be unleashed. My fingers trembled as I fought the madness within me. Distracting myself, I studied the footwork of the dancers, pushing away the compulsion to kill.

I'd trained with my father's guard until I could best ten at once, and it usually came down to footwork. A fighter's tell was either in his feet or his eyes. When I stopped, he'd told me it was because I had nothing more to learn, but years later, I'd heard it was because the men grew scared. That's when the Maestro's henchmen slowly started circling. As if he'd heard I'd stopped training and it would somehow make me weaker.

Drexel used to send lavish gifts to the castle when I was a child. My father would make me sit and watch as he burned every single one. A lesson in self-indulgence he'd said, warning me that the Maestro was the most dangerous person in Requiem, and should I ever be captured by him, I'd never be welcomed home, and if I came back, he'd find a way to seal me in a box. As if I was ever truly welcome in the first place. But still, the lectures had wrapped around my heart like steel until the Maestro became a common enemy between me and my father. And as I grew, I'd learned the reason. If captured and bound to the Maestro, my life, my free will, would be lost forever.

His men had closed in a few times, but it became clear early on that, though the Maestro could have forced them to capture me, and they'd be magically bound in a never-ending pursuit, none were relentless enough. He hadn't used his power. Not yet, though I wasn't sure why.

Eventually, sweat beaded, coating my heated skin.

Look at the name, the internal voice of madness demanded.

I could look if I wanted. I should look. Appease the pressure to move. To get my weapons. To hunt. To kill.

To kill.

Time was nearing for Bram Ellis. I rose, eager to leave, denying the magic that tried to keep my eyes glued to the stage. When the cool night air kissed the back of my neck, I sighed in relief. There was something unsettling about Misery's End and the Maestro's curated world of choreographed lust. It was one thing to witness a tupping in a dark alleyway, but it was quite another to see it dished up for entertainment.

The carriages I needed had been perfectly tucked away right where I'd planned for them to be. And though one of Drexel's guards paced before them, it was nothing at all to sneak past after I'd gotten my hidden blades and helped myself inside the carriage trimmed in gold. I waited in the shadows, wishing I'd brought my mask. I found a modicum of comfort in killing as the Death Maiden, and not as Deyanira Sariah Hark.

Death's magic coiled down and down, the anticipation taking over every last ounce of control I could muster. When the door swung open and the drunk man crawled inside, resting his head across from me with bloodshot eyes, the magic burst. I tried like hell to fight it, even though I'd prepared myself. The monster, Death's weapon, would not be deterred. The slice across his throat was clean. The blood spatter was not. He gasped and gurgled as the cart lurched forward. Somewhere far, far away I heard the sound of a haunting cello pouring over the night as I watched and waited for Bram Ellis to die and Death to steal his soul while I sat in a carriage smothered in blood.

"The name. Give me the name so we can be done with this." My father's cold eyes bore into my soul as I clasped my hands, no longer burdened by a name, behind my back. I hadn't wanted to tell him. Of all the names in the world, not this one. Still, I obeyed. "Bram Ellis."

He shot off his throne faster than I'd seen him move in years. "Surely I've misheard you."

I shook my head.

"You killed the fucking king of Silbath, Deyanira?"

CHAPTER 5

I hadn't eaten for two days. My callous father told the cooks to refuse me. I could have gone into Perth and fed myself, but I found more comfort in solitude than I ever had before. No maids entered my room; Regulas hadn't been perched outside of my door. I was alone. And content. Though the hunger pains had started this morning.

War was imminent regardless, but there was nothing I could say to my father now that would make him see that it wasn't my fault. Death's Maiden, true enemy to all.

Standing before the filagree-trimmed mirror, I called Ro once more, but she still didn't answer. Not unlike her, but disheartening. She was the only one in the whole world who made me feel worth my death. The only person that didn't seem to fear me.

My entire life was a compilation of patience. I waited for my father's summons. I waited for the Maestro to order my capture by his henchmen. I waited for Death's visits to my dreams. I waited for the magic to consume me on a repeated cycle, and these days, even after I'd killed a king and turned the world upside down, were no different. I'd never contribute a thing to this plagued realm of two cities. Instead, I'd always take. Lives and love and happiness.

Three knocks on my bedroom door shattered the respite I'd found in my coveted isolation. "Princess Deyanira, your father summons you to the council chambers. You're to leave all weapons behind."

Whoever'd been charged to deliver my father's message hadn't bothered to open the door. And, as the small footsteps hurried down the hallway, it was clear I was not to be escorted. Which was likely better. I'm surprised he hadn't posted a full guard outside my doors, just to keep me in, as it were. I didn't go anywhere without Chaos, and his order wouldn't change that. Especially when he was so angry with me.

I walked the buzzing halls lined with paintings, keeping my chin high, all the same. Listening to the court whisper. The fallout of killing a king was never going to be peaceful silence.

"Ah, the king slayer, war bringer," Regulas said from his seat at the lengthy table when I entered. "I see you didn't bother dressing up for the occasion. Join us, won't you?" A hint of glee sparkled in his typically dull eyes.

I glanced at my black leather pants and collared shirt hidden mostly by an expensive green jacket with golden stitched vines. Not improper, but also not a dress, though it was likely the blade on my thigh that bothered him and not the casual attire.

No one rose. No one bowed. Instead, the other council members kept their eyes down, focusing on the polished marble floor with their mouths shut. Whatever was about to happen could not be good.

I raised an eyebrow. "How's the shoulder, Reg?"

"I'm not sure what you mean," he said through a forced smile.

"The old memory starting to fade? How close are you to your one-hundredth?"

My father cleared his throat. "Deyanira…"

I curtsied. "My king."

The doors behind me creaked open, and a line of servants entered, the scent of freshly broiled pork and roasted vegetables hammering me before I could rise.

"I hope you don't mind, Princess Deyanira," Regulas fucking chirped. "We've worked up quite an appetite."

I blinked slowly, rising. "Why would I mind?"

My blood boiled. Not because of Regulas, but my father's silence as he watched me, waiting to see how I would respond. He would never be a shield for me, and his council knew that. His silence taught me to be stronger. And alone. To never need a person's approval or defense. But it also taught them to allow their resentment to show.

He'd been icy my entire life, staring down the murderer of his beloved, a woman he kept so private all portraits were removed so I could never look upon her face and see my own.

"Thought I heard your stomach growling." Regulas's ugly face twisted when I glared at him.

The rest of the council said nothing, and no one moved. My father's appointed hand was nothing if not predictable, but though I usually kept my composure, which was why he felt at liberty to speak to me this way, today was not the fucking day.

I sauntered forward, circling the table as I closed the distance between us. Fear shone in his eyes as he realized he'd pushed too far.

"Deyanira," my father warned.

But I did not listen. The pull of my dagger and the lethal smile on my face was accompanied by the sound of piss dripping from Regulas's seat.

I leaned over to whisper in his ear. "Once again, you forget yourself." In a quick motion, I spun the knife in my hand, grazing his ear before stabbing the meat in the center of the table. Aside from my father, the room collectively jumped. Sinking my teeth into the pork and letting the juices slide down my chin, I used Regulas's jacket to wipe Chaos clean. "I think you've wet yourself, councilman." My father cleared his throat, forcing my eyes to him. "Did you need something from me, my king? Or have I been summoned to watch you dine?"

He pushed himself away from the table, the scowl enough to make a lesser man cower. "Silbath crowns their new king in three days."

"What does that have to do with me?"

"In one hour, you will join us in the throne room with your mouth shut and your weapons in your room. You will not disobey that order again, do you understand?"

I considered the presence of his council for half a second before responding. "There's nothing you could say to convince me to abandon this blade. You can try to lock me in your dungeons, tie me up, chain me down, whatever you'd like, but I won't be left unarmed. Ever."

"You would disobey your king?" one of the elder councilmen asked. "On the brink of war?"

I made eye contact with my father before continuing. "Shall I answer that honestly, my king?"

"Please," he answered, lifting a goblet full of wine and sinking back into his chair as if this show was merely an inconvenience.

"I could kill any of you in this room with my bare hands before you knew it was happening. I don't need a weapon to be Death's Maiden. But my father knows me well enough to know that's the one order I will not obey. He's asking me only to placate you all. And I'm simply telling you it's not going to happen."

"You've heard my demand of her," the king said, casually biting into a potato. "It was requested that she be unarmed. What she chooses to do beyond that command is her will alone."

"Who requested?" I asked, shifting toward him.

"Sit. Eat."

"You realize Regulas just pissed himself three feet from where you're dining, don't you?"

My heart raced, wondering what the great secret was. He wasn't letting me leave this room, and there was a reason. I'd never been invited to a meal with my father in my life.

"Then stand there and deny yourself. It makes no difference to me."

Out of sheer stubbornness, I locked my hands behind my back and waited, ignoring the food covering the table, the pig-like sounds the council made as they dined, and even the maids who eventually emptied the table.

"Let us visit with our guests," my father said, gesturing toward the door.

The council went first. The second they exited the room, the king gripped my shoulder so hard that if I hadn't been conditioned to his tactics, I might have winced. "Whatever the outcome of this meeting, you will do as you are told. You openly defied me in front of my council, which I allowed. It will not happen again. For once in your life, Deyanira, be useful."

I dipped low, wondering why his brow twisted as if he were worried. "Yes, my king."

We stood outside the doors of the throne room for several minutes. I tried not to fidget or let my mind wander, but there was really only one man who could shake my father. But why would the Maestro be here? Sticking his nose into royal politics wasn't like him. He'd come to court on occasion, just to rile my father for the theatrics. He'd once bound one of my father's court members during a ball, right in the middle of the ball-room. Then made the man circle the room, singing off-key for an hour before my father simply closed down the event and sent everyone home. It was a pissing match more than anything, Drexel Vanhoff reminding the city that he was a servant to no kingdom.

My father adjusted the golden crown on his gray hair and smoothed the front of his royal purple jacket, avoiding the brass buttons before nodding to the guards. When the doors opened and we entered, all eyes fell upon us, watching every step as if they all held their breath. I followed my father through the hall, past each of the obsidian pillars, up every single step of his towering dais, and stood silently beside him without scanning the anxious crowd. If Drexel Vanhoff was there, I would not give him the satisfaction of my curiosity. But when a line of familiar faces stepped forward, the edges of their boots kicking the dais, I realized the true reason for my father's feelings.

"Councilmen," my father said by way of greeting, ignoring the gathered court that came to gawk.

They bowed collectively before the one with a round belly, wearing the official green sash of Silbath decorated in several metal pins, spoke. "We agreed that she would not be armed."

"No," my father answered coolly. "We agreed that she would be asked to leave her weapons behind. My council can attest that she was instructed to do so and disobeyed."

They shared wary glances before a man with long white hair, save the massive bald spot on his shining head, spoke. "Princess Deyanira Hark, Death Maiden and heir to the throne of Perth, you are hereby charged with high treason and the murder of our beloved king, His Royal Highness, Bram Ellis, may he rest in peace."

"May he rest in peace," the gathered repeated, including my father.

"What say you?"

A thousand-pound weight dropped into my stomach as my ears began to ring.

"Speak," my father commanded.

I curtsied to him to buy myself time, dragging in a steady breath. "It is unfortunate that Death delivered the name of your king, but as Maiden, it is my obligation to fulfill the demand of Death, even above my own father's rule. A Maiden cannot be held responsible for the whims of Death. That is the law."

"And why should we believe you were not acting on your father's behalf?" one of the councilmen asked.

"Have you not asked him yourself?"

The man's voice remained dull, as if he read from a script. "We have."

I gripped the hilt of my dagger to keep myself calm and rational. This was merely protocol. They would have their answer and be on their way. "And are you calling him a liar?"

Several of my father's court shifted in their chairs, sharing glances and whispers as the question hung in the air.

"I am calling you a murderer."

"Because I am," I said, mimicking my father's cool tone. "I recognize your voice. You spoke in the halls outside your former king's council chambers and said, 'The king is ready for war, and I say more power to him. Why should we fear Perth?'"

"I certainly did not."

I could feel my father's razor-sharp glare on the back of my neck. I'd withheld that information. "So, you're calling me a liar? In my father's kingdom? As you accuse him and me of conspiring to kill your king. Does that sum it up?"

"In a thousand years, since our kingdom's fate was saved by Death, he's never ordered the life of a king to end. Ironic now, that the first time a royal is chosen as Maiden, and as the unrest between our kingdoms is nearly at a boiling point, our king should be murdered. Is it not?"

"No."

"Elaborate."

I walked forward, taking several steps down the stairs to make sure my voice was heard all the way to the back of the room.

"I don't pretend to know what Death's motive is for a single name that's burned into my palm. It's not my business, and it isn't yours. But aside from one terrible tragedy, I've never taken a life that was not ordered. However, the only people that push for war work within the walls of a castle. The people, councilman, those you speak for, want far simpler things. Like food, shelter, and warmth. Your kingdom is being taken over by a crime lord running a burlesque show with too much power, and it's allowed because you get a cut of the profit. They do not call him the Maestro for nothing. Eventually, he will silence you, and your kingdom will be the one to pay."

"I have every guard in our kingdom standing at your borders, ready to attack. Do you threaten me, Princess?"

I moved until I stood three steps above him. "I am not threatening you. I am speaking for the people of your kingdom because you will not. If you're so concerned for the well-being of this gods-abandoned world, maybe you should find something more worthy to occupy your time."

The man adjusted his collar and shifted around me to look up at my father. "Have you considered our proposal?"

"We have, and we agree to the terms."

"And does the princess agree?"

"She does."

His quick answer sent chills down my spine. They couldn't lock me away. I'd threatened to let him try, but the outcome would be disastrous. Death's magic would consume me.

I straightened, letting the world spin around me as my mouth fell open. What had he done?

"You have five days."

My world faded to dark, curdling screams from my past drowning everything around me. Panic set it. I couldn't drag a single breath into my lungs. I couldn't grip Chaos tight enough to ground me to the steps. I could not hear beyond my own thundering heartbeat.

The room was empty when I finally regained enough composure to turn, facing the man who'd just damned me.

"I cannot be imprisoned," I whispered. "You know what will happen."

He'd been lost in thought, hand resting on his chin as he stared out the stained-glass window, casting the room in a marbled, vibrant glow.

"You will not be imprisoned, Deyanira. You will be married."

CHAPTER 6

"What do you mean, *married*? To whom?"

"To the next king of Silbath, whomever he may be."

I stumbled backward, nearly falling off the final three steps. "You don't even know who you've sworn me off to. That's..." I couldn't finish the sentence. Not without breaking there and then in front of my father. "Why?"

"Are you so blind that you can't see the favor I've given? They would have bound you up, had I not suggested this marriage."

"You... you suggested it?"

"This is the role of princesses, and I will not explain myself to you. I demand that you be of use to me. You will be my eyes inside that castle. You will find your new husband's weakness, no matter how long it takes you, and you will deliver that information to me by whatever means necessary. You will become the temporary queen of a temporary kingdom, and that is all. In the end, your new kingdom will be mine."

"I'm your only heir. Who'll rule here if something happens to you?"

"That's why we seek the Life Maiden so desperately."

Ah. The nail in my coffin. He didn't wish to groom me as queen. He wished for another. Someone else. Anyone other than Death's Maiden.

"Am I dismissed?" I asked, measuring breaths to steady my hands.

"For now."

"PLEASE, RO," I whispered, standing before the mirror, limbs trembling with fear and anger.

The mirror rippled like liquid silver, soothing my heart. My shoulders sank as I stepped through the enchanted portal into her second realm. The air crackled with an electric pulse as I emerged on the other side, finding myself enveloped by a forest draped in twilight hues.

"Where are we?" I asked as I left the free-standing mirror behind, staring at the shafts of muted light piercing through the thick canopy.

"In a sanctuary," she answered, tugging on her emerald scarf until her luscious hair fell loose onto golden brown skin.

The air carried a heavy scent, the earthy aroma of decaying leaves mingling with a hint of melancholy. It felt as though I had entered a world caught in the throes of lingering sadness.

Ro, with her mischievous smile subdued, gasped the moment her eyes landed on me. She rushed forward, placing her cool palm on my cheek as she searched my eyes. "You look like shit, Dey. What's wrong?"

"Have you heard about Bram Ellis?"

She nodded. "I was visiting a *friend* in the Scarlet District when news arrived of the Silbath king. You cannot possibly think you had a choice. This is the cycle and the way of the magic. We've been over this time and time again."

I turned away, squeezing my eyes shut. I could be hard as nails when I had to be, but I was still a person. "It's not that I blame myself more than usual. It's everyone else. Well, the Silbath council, at least. I stand accused of killing on my father's behalf. And now, to appease the assholes, I have to marry the new king. Whomever that may be."

"So... what's the problem?"

My voice shook in disbelief. "The marrying part. The king slayer part. The upheaval of my life part. Take your pick. I'm trapped."

Her eyes narrowed, shifting between mine for several moments before she answered. "You have more poise and restraint than you give yourself credit for. You could refuse and kill the man who makes these demands, yet you care enough, despite everything, to refrain. You have a moral code that none before you had. But the way you are feeling is how you should be feeling. Change can be a cruel master. It pulls us in unexpected directions, leaving us feeling lost and uncertain. But even in the depths of darkness, there's a sliver of hope. Maybe this betrothal is an opportunity for transformation, for rediscovering the light within you. You've been suffering for such a long time."

"I'm not suffering. I hate this life, this godsdamn title, but I am happy." I lifted a leaf from the ground. "In my own way."

"Maybe becoming a wife means you'll have more things to find happiness in. Like discovering your bedroom is for more than sleeping and scheming. Come. We're celebrating." Yanking my hand, she led me back to the portal, pulling me through and into the hall of mirrors in her home.

"Why should we celebrate?"

She tugged me through her atrium and to the room we always ended up in, though the couches had been pushed toward the outer walls, and none of the dainty tables held their usual teacups and trinkets. "Because it's time to leave your father's world behind and become a woman. A queen even. It doesn't matter who you marry. He has to be better than this existence, and you get to start over. Fall in love." She held out the final word in her sing-song way.

"No one is going to love the Death Maiden."

She stopped in the middle of the room, and I nearly collided with her back. She turned, her beautiful face instantly sad. "*I love you, Deyanira. You are my only real friend.*"

I'd never heard those words spoken to me. I'd never felt the strange warmth they coaxed, nor the way my heart clenched. I'd wanted that devotion so desperately, but what had I done to deserve it? "I'm sorry, Ro. Of course."

I couldn't speak the words back, no matter how much I wanted to. They felt foreign on my tongue. A language I understood but did not speak.

"There now. Hold that thought." She turned to rummage through a tall cabinet in the corner I'd never seen. Standing on her tiptoes, she pulled a bottle of blue liquid with an intricate glass topper from the shelf.

I studied the room to fill the silence, noting all the changes since I'd been here weeks ago. She was never content with her furniture, and the small endearment of a salacious woman felt so intimate to know.

"Stop staring at my couches, Dey."

"I just don't understand why you move everything around so much."

She lifted a shoulder with a smile. "Unlike some people, I appreciate change. Drink."

"What is it?" I scowled.

"It's something I've saved for a special occasion. Don't ask questions."

The sweet, syrupy liquid exploded on my tongue before coating my throat. I coughed, handing her back the glass. "That's terrible."

She laughed, the trill bouncing off the walls. "It really is too sweet. Let's have another."

"I haven't eaten in days. If I have another, I might be sick."

She stilled. "Why haven't you eaten?"

"My father forbade the cooks, and I had no fight in me."

She set her glass down, taking mine and doing the same. Leading me to the couch, she tugged until we both sat, still holding her hand. "Deyanira Sariah Hark, Death Maiden, Princess of Perth... you never, ever lose your fight. You never let someone defeat you. You never falter. You stand. You step. You rise. This world will eat you whole if you let it. Even the disease crawling on our streets is thick enough to take you down. We don't show weakness or cower in the dark. Promise me."

I nodded, leaning my forehead to hers. "I promise."

"You will be the only reason our world does not fall to war. You will be the savior of our time. This is the chance you've asked for. This is your gift to your people. You'll eat, and I'll add a flower for the fallen king. And then you will go home and prepare for your life to change for the better. Deal?"

I closed my eyes with a heavy sigh. Maybe she was right. "Deal."

"Ouch." I winced, trying not to glare at the seamstress as she pinned yards of black, lacy fabric to my body for the third day in a row. If I scared her off, I'd have nothing to wear to my wedding. The three silent women surrounding her brought pins and threads and heaps of judgment and fear, adding to the overall ambiance of dread.

A woman who resembled a mouse had come the first day, and she'd flinched anytime I moved a muscle. She didn't speak a word, yet tears fell, and she rushed out before she could finish.

"Again, Princess Deyanira," a shrewd woman, sitting in the corner every day since, managed from behind the group of silent women hustling around my bedroom. With permanently flushed cheeks and fingers that looked like sausages, she took notes and tsked at everything I said or did. She'd been appointed Courtier of Nuptials by my father. "Proper etiquette only."

I set my jaw, staring straight at the mirror ahead of me, ignoring my long, dark braid pinned to my head to stay out of the way.

"The black veil is to be pinned on by a child so only the face of an innocent sees me before my future beloved. I'm to stare only at my feet, walk up the aisle, and stand in silence for the entirety of the ceremony. The new king will join me beneath the veil but will not look at me. We're to seek each other's hands in the dark, to represent finding each other without interference from anyone outside of our unity. His wrist will be placed over mine, and we will speak the solemn vow, igniting the only magic everyone in this kingdom is entitled to."

"The binding." The seamstress's breathy voice shocked me. She slapped her hands over her mouth. "I'm so sorry, Princess. P-please forgive me."

The Courtier cleared her throat, but naturally, I ignored her.

"You don't have to apologize."

"The magic is the best part," she said, sharing a tentative smile.

My cynical response rolled right off my tongue without a thought. "Magic always comes with a price."

The seamstress paused, meeting my eyes for only a moment. "We thank you, truly. For this marriage. Our people... We're grateful. It is no small thing, and the masses know that."

"And the Sacred Pact?" the Courtier interrupted.

No one had ever thanked me before. I spoke numbly, letting the words pass by without acknowledgement. "A kiss on the wedding day will reverse The Binding, and therefore, it is forbidden."

"The worst part," the seamstress added, the girls around her finally cracking their silence to snicker.

"That will be all for today," the Courtier interrupted, standing to huff with every step toward the door. "Tomorrow, your father will visit you first. He will bring the child to fasten the veil. You'll walk down the aisle silently and with proper posture, following the rules we've been over. Do you have any last-minute questions?"

"No."

I'd spoken the word with a tone of finality that shook me to my core. I was doing this. Marrying a stranger at the behest of my father, just like many women before me. I'd become someone else's problem, from my father's perspective, and maybe, somewhere in there, our people would see the sacrifice for what it ultimately was: the loss of one's freedom for the good of the kingdom. Tomorrow, I'd marry a perfect stranger, and I could only hope he would be kinder to me than my current king.

THE SCRAPE of a boot across the rug on my floor yanked me from my final night's sleep in my father's castle. Someone was in my bedroom. Hand gripped firmly around Chaos, I held my eyes closed, listening. Breaths slow and measured.

Closer and closer the intruder crept, their right footstep slightly heavier than their left, though they moved nearly silently. Injured left leg. Noted. Lying on my side, I held my breath for the final step. The second they were within viable reach, I jerked upward, knife extended, stopped only by the solid grip of a man on my forearm.

My eyes took longer to adjust to the silvery hues of moonlight flooding the room from the open balcony than my brain did. I'd broken his grip and smashed an elbow across his face before I could see a single feature.

As he stumbled back, my sleepy vision finally cooperating, I leaped from the bed, landing on him as he fell backward, that left leg catching a knee as he went down. Deep brown eyes stared back at me from behind my dagger sitting gracefully upon this stranger's throat.

"Who the fuck are you, and why are you in my room?"

I could see the wheels of his mind spinning as he took me in, realizing only now who perched above him.

"My name is—" He gulped, the blade scraping the stubble on his neck. "Forgive me, Death Maiden. My name is Icharius Fern, and I'm to be your husband."

CHAPTER 7

Chestnut brown hair fell effortlessly over the stranger's forehead, framing his face, while his sharply defined jawline gave away the clench to his teeth. His penetrating brown eyes, so dark they could have been black, locked on to mine. Though he lay beneath me, his long, muscular physique radiated power, filling the space with a heady presence. The slight tilt of his lips gave away the cocky thoughts in his pretty head.

"Why are you in my room?" I narrowed my eyes until I knew he could feel the wrath behind them.

He cleared his throat. "Surely you've heard my name spoken before this moment."

I leaned in until we were nose to nose. "Of course, I have. But you still haven't told me why you're here."

In truth, I had no idea what my betrothed's name was or what he looked like. My father had intentionally kept all details from me, knowing I could easily hunt down any prey, gather information, and potentially kill him. I could have done it anyway. The alleys of Silbath were just as loud as those of Perth, but my curiosity hadn't piqued. Instead, I'd avoided the topic every chance I got.

"If I could stand, Princess—er, Maiden. How should I refer to you?"

I didn't budge an inch, and his solid body beneath me hadn't protested. "My name is Princess Deyanira Sariah Hark, Death's Maiden, heir to the throne of Perth. Take your fucking pick."

Something mischievous crossed his face like a passing shadow. He smiled. "Deyanira Sariah Hark, Death's Maiden, heir to the throne of Perth, nearly *queen* to the Silbath throne, future *wife* of King Icharius Fern, would you mind moving your right knee just a hair? Otherwise, we may never have children."

"If you do not live to see the sunrise, there will also be no children."

"Ah. Yes, I can see how that would pose a problem."

Despite my better judgment, I shuffled backward, letting him up before crossing my arms over my chest, still gripping Chaos in a tight fist as I waited. Those eyes scanned my silk nightgown, starting at my feet, lingering over the lace on my breasts, and stopping only when he met my unamused glare.

"Get your fill, King?"

"Sorry," he snapped, whipping around.

"Only a fool would turn their back on the Death Maiden, knowing she holds a blade."

"Did you want me to face you? I am a man standing before a stunning creature in her... unmentionables. I cannot be held to proprietary standards."

"You're a scoundrel and nothing more if you can't keep your eyes from my body."

"A test, then," he said, slowly turning. "Should I look anywhere but your face, Princess Deyanira Sariah Hark, Death's

Maiden, heir to the throne of Perth, you may take your dagger and plunge it into my heart with no protest from me."

The way he held my gaze unnerved me.

"Why are you here?"

He ran his fingers through a crown of thick hair, nearly the shade of mine, but those careful eyes didn't falter. "I'm... well, you see... tomorrow isn't about us. It's about them and their will for the kingdoms and whatever else they have planned for our future. Does that make sense?"

"If any of this is a shock to you, Icky, you have a lot to learn about being a royal. Where the hell did they find you?"

Despite the obvious desire to hold back his smile, he grinned, and something deep in my soul flinched when he perked an eyebrow. "Icky?"

"I guarantee that's the least tame option running through my mind. I was going to make fun of the last name, but Icky feels right, considering the present circumstances."

He took a step forward, stealing my breath as his fingers intentionally held my bare arms. Aside from Ro, no one touched me. Ever. I could hardly think beyond the way he continued to hold my gaze fearlessly.

"Marry me, Princess Deyanira Sariah Hark, Death's Maiden, heir to the throne of Perth. Tomorrow for the crowds and the kingdoms, but tonight, for us. They will never know, but we can take the choice away from them. We'll marry on our terms and not theirs."

Every muscle in my face slackened until my jaw hung open.

He slid careful fingers up to my shoulders, never breaking contact. "In twelve hours, you will be mine anyway. You'll wear the dress, and the people will cheer, and we'll leave this castle behind. I'm sure that's not a fate you wished upon yourself, but in this moment, you can choose me without them."

"I don't... Why would..." I shook my head, trying to clear the fog that'd settled over me, starting the moment he'd pinned me with that unwavering stare. "I am Death's Maiden. I am the harbinger, the king slayer, the only true person to fear in this world. Why aren't you cowering? Why would you choose this?"

"Because..." He forced me to turn until we stared into Ru's mirror. "I'm standing before the most beautiful woman I've ever laid eyes on, and somehow, the gods have blessed me again this week. First, I'm told I'm the distant relative of a fallen king, and I'm crowned the next day. But then"—his palm moved to the small of my back, pushing me forward until we stood so close to the mirror, we filled the frame—"they told me I'm to take a wife of their choosing. You could have been anyone. Any age, any beauty. You could have been a nightmare. And yet, it was as if the heavens conspired, and fate itself intervened to grant me this privilege."

His words resonated deep within my being, their sincerity and passion igniting a flame within my heart. I allowed myself to be drawn closer, my eyes still holding his in the reflection of the mirror. The weight of his grip on me, both commanding and tender, sent shivers down my spine, awakening a whirlwind of emotions I had never experienced before.

He leaned over until his voice was no more than a deep whisper in my ear. "The choice of our hearts should never be dictated by the whims of kingdoms or the expectations of others. We shouldn't be forced into the confines of tradition. Let me prove to you, future wife, that I am worthy and willing without the order from my council."

There was a gravity to his words. An ethereal silence. A plea and desperate wish. The room seemed to hold its breath, the moonlight filtering through the sheer curtains casting a soft glow upon our faces as he waited.

I couldn't deny the urge to defy my father for the sake of having a choice. And this man, this conundrum of a person, had put it all on the line and still agreed to marry me, not only without a fight, but he was fighting *for* it. For us. Here and now. Still, my mind told me this was a bad idea.

"Pretty words and a man's conviction rarely end in bliss."

"I'll make you a deal. You can pick any challenge you want, and I will best you. If you lose, you agree to marry me tonight."

"And if *you* lose?"

"Then I will refuse to marry you tomorrow, and you can walk away, free of the obligation."

"I can assure you, neither of us is walking away tomorrow. We will be married no matter what."

"Pick your challenge. Let me prove that I'm worthy of you."

I walked away, shaking my head. "You're persistent. I'll give you that. At least let me dress, and then I'll be happy to kick your ass for a while. We can consider it a warmup for our marriage."

He rubbed his hands together, flashing a knee-buckling smile, that chiseled jawline somehow growing more defined. "I might surprise you."

"I highly doubt it," I called over my shoulder, heading into the bathing room for privacy.

I dressed in my usual black leathers, arming myself with every weapon I kept hidden in the small room as an idea formed in my mind. Nothing would truly make him worthy, but perhaps instilling a little fear would be a good life lesson.

He stood on the balcony with his back to me, staring out over Perth with his hands clasped behind his back. The second I moved toward him, he turned, though his eyes still never left my face.

"If you want to impress me, Icky"—I flipped my blade in my hand for show—"disarm me."

He pushed aside the sheer curtain. "With my charm or wit?"

"With your hands, King. But… if I remove your weapons first, I win."

"Who says I'm wearing any weapons?"

"You've got a knife strapped onto your back, and there's a holster beneath your shirt. I'd wager it holds another blade, but it could be your diary, I suppose. I'd bet my last coin you've got at least one weapon in your right boot. Your left is likely clear since it's injured."

He sauntered back into the room, his eyes finally dropping to survey me before rubbing his face. "Okay. I'm ready. I'll be gentle… mostly."

"I make no such promises," I countered, planting my feet shoulder-width apart.

He dove as expected, and I spun with ease, avoiding his grip but managing to hook a finger into his belt and engage the blade on my wrist.

"I believe you missed," he said, seconds before his pants fell to his ankles.

"Rule number one, Icky. I never miss."

Fighting the urge to look down, I laughed, letting him pull his pants back up with a huff.

"Don't worry, I left enough of your belt to be of use. You'll just have to cinch a little tighter. I'm sure you can manage."

"How considerate."

I didn't bother getting into position this time. He was sloppy, and I was highly trained and always ready. He lunged for me again, snagging my wrist and stealing the little knife I'd used before I ever saw his hand move.

"That's one for me and none for you."

"Good boy," I chided. "Again."

He moved without fear, looking directly into my eyes with solid composure. I'd never felt so bare before another. This time, he didn't charge me. Instead, he feigned left and spun right, and when I caught his arm, shoving him away from my ribs, the look of surprise on his face was a victory I didn't know I needed.

The king didn't hesitate, hitting the ground to sweep his leg below me, knocking me down. Springing into action, he flipped over me, swiping the tiny throwing knives on my rib cage.

Rolling, I crashed into him, throwing a punch to his ribs before stealing, not one, but two of his blades, which were exactly where I'd predicted they were. I grabbed his right foot and cranked it sideways until he twisted enough for me to yank the boot free and dump the third blade.

"At least you were smart enough to come armed, Icky."

"I'm beginning to hate that nickname," he growled, moving into position once more, something far darker passing across his face. "What's the score?"

"Three for me, three for you."

He tsked, opening his fist to reveal the serrated arrowhead I had sewn into the inside liner of my sleeve. Raising my arm, I cursed, studying the fresh slice into my favorite shirt. That clever asshole.

"I hate you more now than I did five seconds ago."

He inched forward. "Which of us are you trying to convince you're not having fun?"

He was right, and that pissed me off, too. My world had been a constant rotation of disappointing people for as long as I could remember. This was foreign. And enjoyable. And for just a second, I let myself wish there could be a sliver of hope and light in my future.

The new king moved closer again, a dare in his eyes as he reached for Chaos.

I hesitated for only a second before bringing a swift fist down on his forearm. "You'll have to pry that one from my cold, dead fingers."

"And this one?" he asked, pointing to the throwing knife still in place at my shoulder.

I twisted my lips into a smirk. "Try, King."

He matched my smile, and something sparked between us. Something I felt so strongly that I could barely hide the tiny gasp.

My back collided with the wall. He'd been stalking, and I'd been inching away without realizing, too consumed by his effortless distractions. He pressed his chest into me, and I shoved him, but his muscled body didn't budge an inch. That cocky smile returned, lighting his eyes. There were probably a hundred things I could have done to escape the arms that caged me in. But this was supposed to be a test.

"You're making me uncomfortable."

He searched my eyes before simply dropping his hands and stepping away. "I'm sorry."

My heart thundered in my chest, betraying all my emotions. He'd passed. And I think I wanted him to. Not because I was thrilled to marry a perfect stranger, but because tomorrow I would stand beside a man that didn't tremble at the thought of marrying me. If I never laid in his bed or shared a meal with him, that was fine. If he didn't come for advice on running his kingdom or share secrets with me, if we didn't walk the gardens hand in hand or spend a night in front of a fire telling stories, I could live with that. As long as he could look me in the eye when we passed in the halls, as long as he wasn't my enemy from the second we became bonded, I could handle it.

"Take the blade," I whispered.

He pulled the weapon at my shoulder in slow motion. Our gazes locked. The clatter to the floor didn't break the spell, nor did his bare knuckles brushing my arm where my shirt had been ripped. "I will replace your shirt. You have my word."

"After I marry you," I said, letting the moon-bathed world around us fade away.

"*If* you'll marry me," he corrected, lowering his voice.

"You haven't fully disarmed me, King," I said with no conviction whatsoever. Because in truth, he'd been flawlessly chipping away at my armor the whole time.

Ro's words echoed in my mind.

It doesn't matter who you marry, you get to start over. Fall in love.

I didn't know love. I'd hardly known kindness. But here, my future stood before me, wishing only for me, despite our titles and circumstances. How could I deny him tonight and marry him tomorrow when he'd so readily offered me something I was secretly desperate for?

"Tell me what is happening in that pretty head of yours, Princess Deyanira Sariah Hark, Death's Maiden, heir to the throne of Perth."

"I don't trust you enough to share my thoughts."

"I am definitely a scoundrel," he said, handing me the little arrowhead. "I wouldn't trust me either."

I bit my bottom lip, holding out one of his knives. "You're also hideous to look at."

"And I chew with my mouth open," he countered.

"I bet you snore."

"I should really see a doctor for that. And the morning breath is atrocious."

"Because you're a mouth breather?"

"Helps with the snoring."

"Makes sense. And what are you doing for that balding patch on the back of your head?"

He threw his palms up. "Whoa, whoa, Princess. It's all fun and games until you cross the line. This hair is and always will be perfect."

"Well, that's the deal-breaker. I can't marry someone with fragile masculinity."

He wanted to move forward so badly, to reenter my space, to overwhelm me. But the foot he'd lifted to take a step with replanted itself, showing his restraint as he clasped his hands behind his back.

Still, he practically growled at me, his eyes darkening. "If you crave masculinity, I'm certain I can deliver."

"That's an awfully bold statement for someone that just had their pants around their ankles."

He softened. "Don't pretend you didn't want to look."

"Don't pretend you didn't want me to... So, let's say I agree to marry you twelve hours early. What's your plan? We just stand here and initiate the binding? Is that what you want?"

"What do you want, Deyanira?"

The way he spoke my name, the way his voice tumbled down my spine, enraptured me. For a second, I felt weak, but the way he looked at me, the way he spoke to me, made me feel more. Stronger. Enough.

"I'll marry you anywhere but in my father's castle. If we're taking our future into our own hands, it should be on our terms. No traditions. Just our solemn vows and the binding. But should I wear the veil?"

He picked his weapons off the floor, stowing them into their rightful places before coming to stand before me and taking my hands. Intentionally touching me once again. "No. Save the veil for tomorrow. I think I'd prefer to watch you make the biggest mistake of your life."

"At least we can agree on one thing."

"Most women tend to find me very agreeable."

"Perfect statement to tell your future wife the day you meet."

He locked his fingers with mine, tugging me toward the window. "Come on, fearsome, king-slaying Death Maiden with thirty-two titles. Let's ruin everyone's plans."

CHAPTER 8

Chasing the king through the narrow alleyways of Perth as he tried and failed to avoid most people was entertaining. He'd go left, change his mind, pull me right, and continue on.

"Do you have a plan, or are we wandering aimlessly until the sun rises and you can change your mind?"

He stopped, pressing into me, and my back collided with a damp brick wall as two drunks passed by, stumbling and cackling with laughter. Caged between his arms, our world felt different from theirs. My heart raced beneath his amber gaze.

He leaned down to whisper, "Sorry for this, but the best plans are the ones that go awry. They won't recognize me, but they will notice you, and if word gets out that the princess was seen with a strange man the night before her nuptials, we'll have more explaining to do than I care for."

"There's an abandoned temple four blocks north, next to the graveyard on Tolliver's Pointe. We can get to the rooftop from the outside, and no one goes there because they don't want to anger the old gods."

His eyes glistened. "They are old gods for a reason. But if we're to be married, I guess a temple is appropriate, as long as we don't go inside. I hate them."

Staring down at me, his mouth so close I could feel his breath, he dropped his arms, lifting a finger to run it down my cheek. Always touching me. And I hated that it didn't make my skin crawl.

"No kissing," I whispered. "It's a tradition we have to keep if we don't want to revoke the binding."

A thumb brushed over my lips. "It is the worst one."

"I don't know," I said, ducking away from him to catch my breath. "You don't have to wear the veil."

"See? There are gods."

To my utter surprise, the king found no issue scaling the building. I had to keep reminding myself that he didn't grow up in a castle. He'd have survival skills most in the cities carried. Perhaps the beautiful exterior mixed with the roughness would do something good for this world.

"It's beautiful from up here." Icharius gripped the intricate iron railing, peering down over the city. "We're far enough away, and it's dark enough out, you almost can't see the rot."

"Almost." I moved to stand beside him, studying a broken city from a vantage point I'd used many times.

The harsh reality of the city's underbelly could not be hidden, even within the darkest moments of the night. Carriages trundled along the streets, their wheels echoing on the cobblestones. Pedestrians, wrapped in threadbare clothing on their frail frames, huddled together, limping through the mist, their footsteps muffled but resolute. Bent over, their bodies seemed burdened by the weight of the world, their gaunt forms betraying the toll of hardship and destitution. Hollow eyes, haunted by sorrow, stared into an unforgiving void.

The gravity of the moment wasn't lost on me. I'd only ever

taken from this world. I was merely a symbol of promised pain. But in this one act, in marrying a king to ensure peace—though I would have to defy my father eventually—I would make the ultimate eternal sacrifice for a struggling people. Somewhere in the depths of my soul, I hoped and even prayed to the gods that had abandoned us, this act would be felt by the people of this world. That they could look at me, and maybe fear me, but hold a sliver of gratitude that I'd married for their sake and not my own.

The silver light of the moon rimmed each of the headstones in the graveyard. Each death, a marker of a Maiden's presence. A silent tally of our murderous history.

I kicked a toe into the crack between weather-worn mosaic tiles laid centuries ago. The funerals I'd watched replayed in my mind. Moss and lichen clung tenaciously in scattered patches over the old building.

"You can nearly see the pulse of the city from up here," he said, unaware that I'd looked away.

I nodded. "Can you imagine what it was like before the wars? Before Death spared us from extinction?"

He turned, taking in my solemn face as I tucked a damp lock of hair behind an ear. "Maybe we should get this over with."

"A true romantic if ever I've seen one." This time, his smile didn't meet his eyes.

"You could always change your mind."

He shook his head, sodden hair falling across his brow. "Not on your life, Princess Deyanira Sariah Hark, Death's Maiden, heir to the throne of Perth, future queen of Silbath."

"Dey," I whispered.

"I'm sorry?"

"You can call me Dey."

He titled his head. "That feels like a win."

"It's not a win, Icky. It's just a concession."

"My friends call me Orin."

I couldn't help the urge to push the rogue hair from his brow. "That's an odd nickname for Icharius."

He leaned in with a smile. "It's better than Icky."

"Depends on who you ask, I guess."

He took a solid breath, his broad chest rising. "Close your eyes."

"I don't trust you, and I'm standing on one of the tallest buildings in Perth. I'll pass."

Closing the distance, he gripped my hands. "You can trust me, Deyanira."

"I trust no one, King. Not even my own father."

"Take out your blade."

"What?"

"Take your knife and press it to my throat. If it brings you peace of mind, then hold me at Death's edge, and let me marry you."

I gripped Chaos's handle, the familiar grooves bringing me solace. But I did not unsheathe her. Instead, I simply let my lashes fall heavily to my cheeks, droplets of water falling silently.

"It's the most beautiful sunny day you've ever seen, and you're standing at the back of your castle's garden. Though your veil shields you from the world, you can smell the flowers. You can hear the soft murmurs of the crowd. The haunted tones of a cello call you forward. Toward me."

A breath shuddered through my lungs as he built the scene in my mind. He plucked my hand free of the dagger and placed his wrist on mine.

"I don't have religious words or earthly vows to promise. The titles are gone. I am simply a man standing before you with a heart that is both eager and hesitant. Though we begin this journey as strangers, I am drawn to you, and I vow to discover the intricacies of your mind with reverence and awe."

I opened my eyes to stare into the sincere face of a perfect stranger who'd stolen me from my bed to make secret promises. With one wrist still laid over mine, he used his other hand to wipe the rain from my cheek.

"With Death's blessing and the gods watching over us, I bind myself to you from this day, till death."

I couldn't help the smile as a burning pulse heated my wrist.

"Your turn," he whispered.

Managing a breath, I began. "As Death weaves his narrative into the fabric of our story, I vow to navigate this marriage with grace and an open heart. I give you my hesitant, yet sincere vow to embark on this journey together, with a promise of devotion and careful discovery. I vow to form a bond that transcends time and reaches into the realm of eternity. With Death's blessing and the gods watching over us, I bind myself to you from this day, till death."

As the final tendrils of magic bound our lives together, I could hardly resist the pull to him until he started laughing, breaking the spell that'd fallen over us.

"What's so funny?" I asked, yanking my hand away from him.

"I think you just used your wedding vows to damn me to Death's court for eternity."

"Intentional." I laughed, despite myself. "If you wake me in the middle of the night again, it's a guarantee."

"Should we shake on it?"

I held out my hand, eyes locked on the fresh golden band of magic circling my wrist.

He tugged his sleeve only high enough to reveal his own marking and gripped my palm, giving one vigorous shake before pulling me forward and into his arms. "Goodnight, Wife. This is where we part. I hope you wake with no regrets."

"And I hope you wake, remembering you've just married Death's Maiden and somehow still show up tomorrow with some color on your face."

"I'll see you on the other end of the aisle." He swiped another soaked hair from my forehead, cursing the rain before walking away.

I watched him leave, his silhouette fading into the mist the second he moved beyond the streetlamps. Lifting my scarf to hide behind the familiarity of a mask, I descended the building moments later, rushing past the tapestry of neglect and poverty, over the gathered puddles, and on to my father's castle.

Tossing and turning through the rest of the night, I rose to watch the sun attempt its rise, replaying every second of my secret wedding. I'd just finished tying a small ribbon around my wrist when my bedroom doors flew open, crashing against the wall as my father stormed inside. It was the first time in my life he'd ever entered my bedroom.

"I want no surprises, Deyanira. Do you understand? If you mess this up, there will be a war by nightfall. Today, you are a demur, subservient daughter and wife."

I watched over my father's adorned shoulder, waiting for Regulas to arrive with his normal bullshit, but he didn't come.

"Yes, father," I said, dipping low, though something within me wanted to rebel, knowing I was now a queen and his equal.

"You're to eat in your rooms, dress in your rooms, and speak to no one. I want nothing to interfere with this marriage ceremony. Your groom is set to arrive within the hour, and if I get the feeling you've left this room to find him, I'll open the dungeons and lock you away, letting the madness rot your mind."

I rose to my full height, glaring as coiled steel surged through my veins. "If you try to trap me, on this day or any other, I will kill you where you stand. I am no longer the daughter of a desperate king. I will be the wife of a worthy king. Your threats hold no value over me any longer. You may lock yourself behind your castle walls and weep over the state of your dwindling kingdom. You may swim in your coffers, clinging to the only reason Silbath has not attacked and imprisoned our people. You may even take whores to your bed at night and act like no one else knows of your dalliances. But you may *not* threaten me again."

The hatred burning through his eyes mirrored my own. He rushed forward. I held myself in place as a fist crashed down upon me, rings splitting my lip, beautiful pain racing across my face.

I lowered my chin, bold enough to breathe hate into my words. "Congratulations, Father. You've finally taught me a lesson."

Fist in the air once more, he growled. "And what lesson might that be?"

"Shiny kings upon their thrones have tongues of serpents but strike like boys."

I dodged his next swing with ease.

He huffed, stomping out of the room without a single look back. I'd never felt so fucking vindicated in all my life. Somehow, the last twelve hours had been the greatest of my existence. There was nothing that could sour this day for me. Though I was already bound to Orin, a king who had more potential than I'd seen from anyone else, I was about to perform an act that would finally show this kingdom that I was willing to make sacrifices for them.

There was nothing to be done to hide my swollen split lip. The blood had stopped with a cool rag, but I'd wear my father's marking the rest of the week, no doubt. Still, the women came silently, eyeing me with trepidation as I stepped into the long, black lace gown that fit me like a glove, showing skin through the intricate weavings of the seamstress's craft.

Before the child came, I stood in front of Ro's mirror one final time, taking in the weight of this day and the symbolism of the gown, letting my eyes fall upon the small hint of the binding hidden beneath the ribbon on my wrist. When the reflection rippled, I knew she was watching. I imagined her prideful face staring back at me. She'd be in the crowd, I was sure. Watching amongst all the other strangers, but this moment was for her and me, even if she wouldn't step into my room with the other women. Her power was her secret alone, and I respected that boundary.

When the courtiers left and the young girl was finally sent in, tears streaking down her cheeks, I knelt, attempting a smile without cracking open the fresh wound. Her giant blue eyes stared back at me as she trembled.

I showed her my palm. "You need not fear me, child. I bear no name today."

She nodded, swiping away a tear before she whispered, "You are still beautiful, Princess, even if you killed my aunt."

Her words struck me right in the gut as she grabbed the edges of the solid black veil and pulled it over my head, concealing my stunned face. My father had selected her for a reason. Poor child. I followed the sounds of the little girl's foot-steps out of my room, in complete darkness. Every step, with only a single weapon, felt foreign to me. Especially as I navi-gated my father's halls, knowing how furious he was with me. Knowing I'd done something so reckless last night when there was such a delicate peace between our fragile cities.

Heart pounding like a wild beast yearning for freedom, I crept along. The familiar scent of polished wood and aged parchment filled the air, challenging my senses to stay aware of my location. My footsteps echoed softly against the cold stone floor as I followed the sound of the young child's anxious breaths through familiar hallways, all the way to the castle's main doors.

The trembling touch of her hand gripped mine tightly, her

fingers cold and clammy. A stark contrast to the warmth that should radiate from the touch of an innocent. Her fear was palpable, a heavy cloak draped over her small frame, seeping into my senses.

As we ventured past the gardens and toward the forgotten temple, the cacophony of distant voices grew louder, mimicking the child's unease. The courtiers' whispers and the servants' hushed tones blended with the rhythmic thud of my anxious heartbeat. The dissonance of somber music reached my ears, a mournful melody that mirrored the child's shaking grip. The haunting notes wove through the air, whispering of uncertainty, grief, and trepidation, which had become the soundtrack of my existence.

Loose stones turned to solid bricks as we approached the grand doors of the castle's temple. The whoosh of air accompanied the squeal of the doors opening, letting the music rain down upon us. The second she could, the little girl broke free and ran.

Swallowing my nerves, my heart steadied, finding solace in the knowledge that this procession was merely a façade. This day, only an illusion of unity existed between our kingdoms. A fragile shield against forces that sought to tear them apart.

The world silenced. I closed my eyes, picturing Orin's brutally beautiful face as I stepped, one foot in front of the other, up the black, carpeted aisle. I pictured my father standing there in purple, regal attire and my husband in green.

The shiny finish of recently polished boots came into view as my father cleared his throat, indicating I'd gone far enough. As one, the gathered audience took a resounding breath, following my father's orders to be seated. Though I'd only known Orin for what seemed like moments, I felt myself shifting toward those boots on the floor, truly feeling like he may be the only soul in the room who wanted me there.

Several moments later, as my father spoke about abandoned gods and Death's promise to save us all, he inched away from me, and my heart sank. Perhaps last night was only a show, and today, when he stepped below this veil, things would be different, yet normal in every way I'd always known.

I couldn't help the lump that formed in my throat, and no matter how many times I tried to swallow it down, it grew sharper, forcing tears to my eyes. This was likely the biggest mistake of my life, and I was in too deep to escape now. He'd tried to warn me last night.

Lost in my own thoughts, I'd hardly registered the choir boys singing their beautiful songs. I didn't hear the lighting of the candles surrounding us. I missed my father's recognition of Icharius Fern's new position as king of Silbath. I only heard my future looming closer and closer as my bonded husband continued to move away from me. Perhaps he would stumble into one of the candles and light himself on fire. I managed a smile as I pictured the face he'd given last night when his pants fell. It likely would have been the same.

"... not only to witness the union of two souls but also to celebrate a bond that holds the promise of peace and prosperity for both our lands. In the absence of divine guidance, Death stands as a constant companion, a reminder of the fleeting nature of our existence..."

As my father praised Death as an ally, my stomach churned with a mixture of disgust and apprehension. I knew his true intentions, the dark machinations that swirled within a wretched king's mind. The marriage that was meant to bring harmony and peace was nothing more than a pawn in his grand scheme for power.

Still, the ceremony continued, until the long pause before the vows were to be spoken and the bond we already made, sealed.

"Join now your future wife below her veil. Join hands and deliver your solemn vows."

Thick fingers gripped the edge of the veil, but before I could finally see his face, the doors in the back of the temple slammed open, and a very familiar voice shouted from the door, "Hate to interrupt the festivities, but it seems your princess is already married. To me."

CHAPTER 10

Reality, the full truth, crashed into me as I stumbled backward.

"That is my wife. We were bound last night." Orin's voice rang through the temple with unhurried conviction.

"Impossible," my father barked.

"Search her wrist," my *husband* yelled from halfway up the aisle. "See our bond for yourself. She wasn't worthy of a king. In fact, she hardly protested at all."

Though pinned, the black veil was ripped from my head, taking a chunk of hair with it as I stared up into the vengeful eyes of the real Icharius Fern, an absolute stranger with a halo of blond hair and cold, dark eyes. He snatched my wrist and tore the lace, showcasing the fresh golden band for all to see.

"Who are you?" I asked Orin through gritted teeth, peering into the face of the only person in the world I'd ever wanted to murder. He'd lied. He'd manipulated me. He'd embarrassed me beyond any shred of dignity.

"Orin Faber, *Wife.*"

My world nearly collapsed. My only chance to give anything to this world had been swept away with the pretty words of a liar. And I'd fallen for it easily. Chasing the idea that someone might actually want me. Choose me. Fury built from the bottom of my toes, inching its way so powerfully through my body, if not for the humiliation, rage would be the only emotion I'd ever feel again as I stared at the cocky grin of a hateful bastard.

"Deyanira! Explain yourself," my father said, his voice so cold and low only a trained ear would note the vulnerable shake in his words.

"He... tricked me."

Orin leveled a glare right back at me. "No offense, Your Grace, but it was hardly a challenge. She was quite eager. A trait I hope she takes as strongly to the marriage bed."

"You bastard," I snarled.

Pandemonium erupted in the temple. The gathered people started yelling their outrage for the jilted king.

Out of the corner of my eye, I caught my father's movement just in time to duck, still locked in Icharius's grasp. Though my father missed, the new king raised a fist the size of a hammer, hauling back. I kicked up my skirt and yanked Chaos free, causing the room to still.

"Let me go, or today will be your last," I demanded of King Icharius.

Though he obeyed, he also balked. "You dare threaten a king? No wonder your father had to beat you into submission this morning."

Rotating the blade so I held the hilt firmly, pointing toward the ground, I drew back and smashed his godsdamned nose in, throwing all my anger with Orin behind the punch.

Standing at the front of the aisle, surrounded by candles and beyond that a riotous crowd, I considered my options. I searched face after face, but Ro was nowhere to be seen. Leaping over the candles, I made it a little over halfway back down the aisle before my father commanded control of his court and those of Silbath.

"Silence!"

The room stilled.

"Deyanira Sariah Hark, you are hereby stripped of your title. You are no longer heir to the throne of Perth, betrothed to the king of Silbath, nor are you welcome in my kingdom. You are banished. And should Death have something to say about that, he can find me in my godsdamned chambers."

I turned slowly, aiming to look my father in the eye one final time when a crack reverberated around the room, splitting the aisle in two as a plume of black shadow crept from the crevice like fingers, the cavity birthing none other than Death himself. My heart stopped beating.

A single sob from the back was the only sound as he rose, floating toward me with a face completely hidden within the depths of his hood.

"My beautiful Deyanira," he purred, reaching for my face as he stroked a thumb over my father's marking. "Who dares strike my Maiden?"

I spoke no words, but my eyes betrayed me as they fell on the King of Perth, who'd been attempting to back away. In a single thought, Death left me standing in the aisle to circle my father in a symphony of screaming shadows. When he pulled away, my father's face had gone ashen. Though his shoulders still rose and fell, the essence of the tyrannical king had faded away.

A man three rows ahead of me gulped, the sound so loud in the silence that Death turned to face him. The woman holding the man's hand fainted. Death's deep and tumultuous laugh reverberated over the temple walls as he came back to my side.

"Will you finally speak to me, my beauty? Will you tell me what has happened here?"

I stared straight ahead, my defiance utterly annoying him, though I knew he would not display that emotion in front of the court. He reached for my hand, examining the golden band before delivering a dark chuckle and leaning forward to whisper, "A wedding gift, then, my Deyanira."

Searing pain ripped through my palm as my flesh burned. The two courts, now unsettled, shuffled toward the outer walls, but Death cast shadows over the door and all the windows, shrouding the temple in darkness, apart from the flickering circle of candles at the front of the aisle.

Despite my own stubborn will, anger, embarrassment, and a torrent of other emotions crashed over me, pushing the tears from my flooded eyes. I raised my palm, blinking away my sorrow to read the name I'd been given.

Demir Altruis Hark.

My father.

Magical compulsion unlike anything I'd ever felt overtook me.

I shook my head, protesting, trying to plant my feet, though they betrayed me. Not in front of all these people. I didn't want to become the monster they imagined.

"Even now, after all of his faults, you would save him?" Death asked, his voice no more than an echo in my mind. "How absolutely intriguing, my beauty."

He'd been an unbearable father, unwavering in harsh lessons and cruel words. But I was born from love. He had the capacity. And in his own way, he'd shaped me into a warrior. A woman who could and would defend herself in a cutthroat world where no one would hold my hand. No one would fight alongside me, and he'd made sure I'd survive it. I was never going to be his heir, but I was still his. He was a product of an environment that would have devoured him had he been any other way. And he was my father.

Gripping the knife, I stalked up the aisle, letting the tears fall freely. "Please don't do this," I begged, the first words I'd spoken to Death in ages.

His eyes glimmered with malice. How could they not see him for the beautiful monster he was? How could they still consider him a savior when their skin turned to ice with fear?

Regulas finally emerged from behind a pillar in the back of the room. It could have been his name. It should have been, for all the hatred and evil he'd injected into the relationship between my father and me. Pulling a sword, he meant to intervene.

"Guards!" he shouted, speaking for my motionless father. "Protect your king."

None moved. None were willing to step into Death's path.

"Please," I whispered, though I knew the crowd nor the gods that had left this world to destroy itself would not hear me. "I am not this."

Standing between my father and me, Regulas held a trembling sword across his body, loyal to the very end. Magic seared across my mind, enveloping me in visions of my own father's death. Slitting his throat was last in line. I saw his head fall to the marble floor. I saw my own hands reach into his severed belly, ripping him to shreds. I watched myself slaughter a man I'd loathed for so long, yet still did not wish to end.

Fighting the magic until pain ripped through my body, I blinked away tears, glancing over my shoulder, beyond Death to stare into Orin's piercing gaze.

"I hate you!" I screamed, shoving Regulas to the side and whipping Chaos across my father's throat.

The eruption of hysteria behind me alluded to Death's dramatic departure. He'd let everyone watch as he coaxed my father's soul from his fallen body while the powerful magic, stronger from his close proximity, no doubt, receded, leaving me in a state of shock, exhaustion, and suffocating numbness.

Somewhere in the commotion, my unfortunate betrothed had ordered my capture. The hurried noise of people scrambling was drowned out by the buzzing in my ears. I willed my legs to move, but they did not obey.

The guards, those dressed in purple and the ones in green, closed in, but I had no fire. Even when I could hear Ro in my mind, screaming for me to fight, to rise. To run. Nothing worked. Not until a solid shoulder collided with my stomach, my feet left the ground, and I was hauled out of the temple like a rag doll.

"So help me gods, if you don't put me down—"

"Yes, I know. Threats and violence and long-drawn-out murders. Be silent. You lost, Maiden."

Orin.

I landed a well-placed punch to his kidney, and he winced with a shout before overcorrecting and falling to the pebbled earth. Guards and courtesans and their bonded spouses poured from the temple behind us.

Orin jumped to his feet, lunging for me with far more grace than he'd had last night and no limp in his left leg. Fucking liar all the way around.

"Keep your hands off me!" I screamed as he snatched me around my hips from behind.

I cracked an elbow into his face, but he didn't budge. The guards were closer now, and I'd never be able to fight them all. He leaned back, lifting me from the ground as he tried to run, but I wouldn't be taken prisoner. I kicked and flailed, fighting like a wild animal, until his grip slipped, and he dropped me.

"I'm not going to pretend I'm sorry about this... *Wife*." The final word dripped from his hateful mouth like poison as he struck me solidly in the back of the head with the hilt of a sword. I hadn't even seen it coming.

"I'VE NEVER KNOWN anyone to sleep ugly."

Deep, resounding echoes of pain ricocheted off the walls of my throbbing mind as the blurry world righted itself. A surge of fury washed over me, amplifying the disorientation caused by the unfamiliar space.

Orin Faber leaned against a dusty dresser across a foreign bedroom, with his arms folded over his chest, glaring at me as if I'd been the one to ruin his life.

"Go fuck yourself," I groaned, untangling my feet from the lacy edges of my tattered wedding gown so I could stand, though the world tipped, and an ache raced down my spine.

"Steady there, King Slayer. I've never been good with poisons."

I grabbed my stomach to keep from hurling as the room spun. Poison... I should have known. "I've been taking heavy doses of poison to build a tolerance since I was fourteen," I slurred. "You'll have to try better than that."

Three of him now stood where one did moments ago. I blinked, willing my vision to right itself.

"Looks like it." He flipped a knife in his hands, the familiar ruby drawing my attention, even while battling poison. My blade. Chaos.

"I'll be taking that back." I stumbled forward, throwing an arm out for balance.

"Come and get it, first-timer."

I'd heard that name before. My head snapped up to look into eyes I hadn't recognized. The masked performer from Misery's End. One of the Maestro's bound men. "You... Gods, of *course*. You work for *him*."

He took a step toward me, lowering his chin. "For someone who throws her ability to kill around like she's planting a fucking farm, you're not very smart."

"Neither are you."

He'd stepped too close. I lunged, fighting the disorientation enough to snatch Chaos from his loose grip, whirl behind him, and point the tip directly into his back, though my stomach rolled in protest.

"Now, tell me who you are and why I'm here."

He lifted his hands into the air and shifted forward, but I moved with him, keeping the dagger pressed firmly against his spine. "More poison next time. Noted."

I scoffed. "This is the last time you're going to see my face until I'm standing over you for the kill."

"You enjoy it, don't you? The kill? Acting as Death's whore?

Throwing threats to make sure everyone hates you. We know. We get it. The victims of this world are warned from birth to stay the hell away from you."

"You know nothing about me."

He turned in a flash, his hand gripping mine as it held the blade. "Do it. Kill another person for your own glory. Do they keep a tally in Death's court? Of all the lives taken? Those with the highest numbers live eternity on some kind of fucking pedestal?"

I paused, anger coiling as I stared into his furious eyes. "Who was it? Who did I take from you?"

He leaned closer, hunching over the blade, not bothered by its proximity to his abdomen, as he growled. "My brother. My father. An old woman who used to live across the street and helped my mother feed us when we had nothing. You are the single enemy of this world."

"I am not your enemy."

He swiped the dagger away and grabbed my throat, slamming me against the wall. "You *are* my enemy."

My eyes fell to his lips. If twenty-four hours hadn't passed, I could break the bond.

He squeezed, knowing exactly where my mind had gone. "You're too late, Maiden. You've been asleep for two days."

The gods truly had abandoned me.

Shoulders heaving inches from my face, I didn't fear him. He couldn't kill me. He had no more weapons to hurt me. His fingers pinned around my throat barely stole my breath.

"Are you eager now, Wife? Now that the whole world knows you're nothing but a desperate, hateful murderer who couldn't be counted on for one honorable task to save this world from war?"

Coiled rage exploded within me as I remembered his words from the temple. The embarrassment. The way I'd begged before everyone and still murdered my father. The single moment Death had touched me so intimately for all to witness. I swallowed against his fingers. "I'm going to give you one chance to back the fuck up, and then this is over. How it ends will be up to you."

His grip tightened until I was sure I would bruise. "Shall I count to ten?"

Swallowing the new wave of nausea, I drew the blade and shoved it forward, barely missing him as he jumped away, venom dripping from his hateful glare.

"You're going to have to be faster than that, Maiden."

"I have a name."

"I know. It's annoying to say."

I lunged. He spun, swiping a dusty floor lamp from the corner and swinging it at me with full force. Taking the heavy base of the lamp right in the gut, I doubled over, confident anger was the only thing keeping me from throwing up.

The impact of the floor lamp sent a shockwave of pain through my body, but it only fueled my determination.

Gasping for air, I straightened myself and narrowed my eyes at Orin. Hatred simmered within me, boiling over in a torrent of words. "Get your shit together. I've seen more strength in a stableboy."

He smirked, his eyes glinting with malicious delight. "Oh, I'm well aware of your exploits. But a high body count doesn't make you invincible, only more undesirable. A nightmare."

I lunged again, this time with a swift and precise strike, though his hurtful words were their own kind of weapon against me. My fist collided with his jaw, sending him stumbling back against the dusty dresser, a discarded vase of wilted flowers shattering on the floor. With a surge of adrenaline, I launched myself at him, unleashing a flurry of punches and kicks, some landing and some blocked, though considering the poison, the playing field was nearly level. Occasionally, I surprised him, but not often enough.

Orin retaliated, his movements fluid and precise. We clashed and circled each other, locked in a dangerous dance of violence. The room became a battleground, with shattered furniture and scattered debris bearing witness to our shared rage.

"Shall we consider this our wedding night, Wife?"

"You fucking talk too much," I spat, wiping blood from the corner of my mouth.

I threw a fist into his face. He kicked my thigh. Each blow landed with bone-crushing force, but neither was willing to yield, stubbornness and anger driving us beyond reason.

He'd taken me. He'd fooled me. He'd stood at the back of that temple and ruined everything. He'd made a choice when I had none at all. There was nothing in me that could care anymore. I'd tried that. I'd relented to my father on the mere chance of having someone give a shit about me. Someone forced to remain on this side of the mirror.

He paused as new fury swelled within me. As every single piece of life as I'd known it fell to the floor with my realization that I had nowhere to go. My father had disowned and stripped me of my title in front of the whole court.

"You giving up already, Nightmare?" Orin held a fist in front of his face like a true fighter, ready to block as he bounced on his toes.

I was done. Done with everyone and everything, but especially that smug grin as I stalked forward, hauled back, and threw all my emotions into one solid punch that sent him flying backward and crumpling to the floor.

"Nightmare, huh? Sweet dreams, asshole."

Setting the edge of my dagger in the hollow of his throat, I let my eyes drink in his brutally handsome face. I should have watched for a breath, the rise and fall of a rib cage, anything that might indicate I hadn't already killed him, but as strange voices called up the stairs beyond the doorway, there was no time. And despite my fury, I couldn't find it in me to press the blade home.

I took a second to glance around the room, taking in the destruction we'd wrought before grabbing the damn lamp and sending it through the floor-length windows across from the bed, letting the glass shards scatter.

Securing Chaos to my thigh, I pressed my back against the wall, my breathing ragged, my heart pounding in my chest. I summoned every bit of anger, hurt, and resilience, allowing them to swirl within me, a storm of emotions that fueled my determination. Out of desperation alone, I launched myself toward the broken window, leaped over the threshold, crossed the balcony, and jumped over the railing.

The world blurred around me as I descended through the open air, gravity pulling me mercilessly towards the ground. There was no safety net, no comforting presence to catch my fall. I braced myself for impact, knowing it would be bone-rattling.

As the ground rushed up to meet me, I tucked into a protective roll, instinctively absorbing the force of the fall. Pain reverberated through my body, threatening to incapacitate me. But I gritted my teeth, refusing to surrender to the breathtaking agony.

I could be weak when I was alone and safe, and, though I didn't know when or where that would be, I limped away from Orin's prison, wondering if I'd just sealed my husband's fate, if that final strike had been his ultimate demise.

CHAPTER 12

Though I was still draped in a tattered black lace wedding gown, injured and seething, I found my way through the thick trees, crossed into Silbath, and sank back into the comfort of the city. The outskirts were a place most didn't bother traveling. Nothing surrounded the cities' borders but desolation, and wounded souls craved company.

I kept all thoughts of self-pity away as I pressed more and more weight on my aching leg until I could walk an even stride. I could not be weak, and I would not be prey. The Maestro's men lurked most heavily in the streets near the Dancing Ghost and his magical theater, Misery's End.

The elusive sun slipped beneath the horizon, an invitation from the world for me to fall back into the darkness I was so used to. Using the downspouts and worn ornamental ledges, I managed to scale a building I was becoming too familiar with. It took longer than I would have liked, and I stumbled once, barely catching myself, but each movement was a necessary evil, an escape.

The rooftops were a balm. A second realm of solitude I'd

played in as a child, the appalling sights within the city raising me. I knew them like a baker knew his recipes, or a dancer, her steps. I could draw a map with my eyes shut, learning first this world above and then the one below. The city's seedy underbelly was no place for a child. It was hardly a place for a woman with a title, but I'd grown there, too. I'd learned what a man might say to a lady to take her to bed. Or what she might say before stealing his wallet. I'd learned which streets were always violent and what Lady Visha looked for in her prostitutes. I'd learned intimately about the depths of jealousy while watching other people have the freedom to live when I was damned with the charge to kill.

But the one person I'd avoided, above all else, was Drexel Vanhoff, the Lord of the Underworld, if his nefarious position held a proper title. Because at the core of who he was, the Maestro was a collector. Using his magic to bind every poor soul he could, building an army, if ever he decided to turn on the royals.

I'd never challenge for my kingdom title. A small part of me, buried beneath the anger and the sadness, was glad to be rid of the burden. To go to war with this strange new king would be one thing, a guaranteed failure ending in misery for all of Perth. But if history had taught me anything, an unknown king didn't rise without the heavy hand of someone else. And the only one with that much power was Drexel. But he was as dangerous as they came, and I'd rather gut myself than sit before him, fight against him, or even exchange words.

Still, I was a Hark. And while Death became my master the second my mother died, branding me the harbinger, I could do something, *anything,* to stop the downfall of this realm. My counterpart had to be out there somewhere, hidden in the underbelly. Someone knew where she was, and now that I had nothing left to lose—no genuine friends, no family, no royal title—perhaps she was the last thing I could give to this diseased world. I might have been born Death's Maiden, but I could die a savior.

Squatting in the heart of Silbath was not a good idea. I needed to get to Perth, but first, perched above Misery's end, I watched. And waited. I wanted to know why Orin had broken into the castle. And why, of all things, had he married me when he hated me from his very core?

Though I might have left him there for Death to reap his soul, I knew he must've been more than a simple performer, more than an attractive guy with a solid right hook.

But no one came. The building might as well have been abandoned for all the attention it received from the passersby. No one stopped. No lights shone. There was no crowd, no carriages. Nothing.

A single parchment pinned to the door grabbed my attention, but from this vantage point, though it lifted into the wind and a few letters were legible, I couldn't read the announcement, nor discern the image.

I paced, shooing away the crows that gathered as I debated my next move. Rain fell, as it always did, soaking the frayed wedding gown. It took exactly four seconds for me to slice off the bottom half, but it was still restricting and could get me into more trouble than it was worth. Dropping the lower half of my dress below, confident a vagrant would find some use of it, I lowered myself to the familiar, dark seclusion of the cobblestone alleyway.

Avoiding the light cast from dim streetlamps, I hustled toward the theater, snatched the paper, and darted for the nearest alcove. The new king's face stared back at me.

Be it proclaimed with great splendor and regal fervor that on this momentous day, the old gods bear witness to the joyous union of His Royal Highness, the illustrious King Icharius Fern, with the esteemed Death Maiden, Princess Deyanira Sariah Hark.
In celebration of this sacred matrimony, the grand spectacle of Misery's End has been rescheduled to grace the kingdom's revelry.

Today's show.

That... prick. Orin had lied. Again. A damn kiss could have broken the bond between us hours ago. He'd proven his point by canceling my marriage and single-handedly ripping my title from me. He'd taken everything and seared the image of me killing my father into so many minds. As the anger stirred, heating my veins, I pushed away from the wall, feeling like I didn't have nearly enough weapons to take on the fucking world. And I certainly wasn't going to do it in a wedding gown.

For a second, I turned, wondering if there was time to go back and kiss a dead man, but perhaps his eternity in the Death Court would be sufficient. The binding to him wouldn't matter, it would only be a golden band around my wrist, a reminder that I was a fool and pretty words had ruined me. And if he was still alive, I hoped the mark burned like hell every time he looked at it.

At this moment, with no home and no money, trapped in godsdamned lace, I had no option but to cross the border to get to the clock tower in Perth. I'd kept troves of weapons in several places throughout the cities. Learning where I could leave valuables the world would never find had been a game when I was a teen. I'd likely lost half my father's wealth playing, but somehow, the value of those items always found their way back. That was the savage cycle of a monarchy. Though the people were poor and haggard, they'd still funnel what little they had back to the overseer. By choice or thievery, it would happen, nonetheless.

The dilapidated temples of the old gods were the safest sanctuary, but there were superstitions and boundaries even I avoided. The stench in the narrow alleys turned my stomach as I delved deeper into their dimly lit recesses. Filth and corrosion clung to every surface. But I stayed in the shadows, navigating the darkest corners despite the repulsive surroundings, fully aware that I'd need boots to jump across the rooftops.

The shredded remains of my dress had nearly stripped away my ability to hide, leaving me exposed in a way that made my skin crawl. I preferred my mask and every weapon I owned. I preferred solitude and the deepest recesses. Especially now, with a scorned king likely hunting me. I avoided eye contact with the destitute souls who huddled in the alleyways, their hollow gazes reflecting the desperation I sought to escape.

I pressed my back to a building as a towering figure hiding beneath a cloak limped by. The second he'd shuffled passed, he paused, as if trying to convince himself he'd just seen Death's harbinger, but when he turned to face me, I'd already rounded the corner, only glancing over my shoulder to catch him scratching his head and continuing on.

Watching the man, I hadn't noticed another until I slammed right into him.

"Watch it," he growled, shoving me to the side.

I ducked, but I wasn't fast enough. Maybe the remnants of poison lingered. He snatched my wrist and yanked, his rancid breath creeping into my nose as he huffed.

"I'd let go if I were you," I warned, snatching Chaos in a swift but effective maneuver, her ruby pressing into my palm.

He released my arm but still loomed too close. I took a step away; he followed as if trying to make out my face through the murky shadows of the alley.

"Whatever you're thinking, it's a really fucking bad idea."

"You have no idea what I'm thinking."

I pressed the blade to the base of his throat. "I've had a shitty day and honestly don't care what it is. You've been warned. Anything beyond this moment is a direct result of what you choose to do with that information."

"Maiden," he gasped, but didn't make a move, as if he were stunned.

"You have three seconds to turn and walk away before this blade finds a new home in your esophagus."

"And if—"

"One."

"You're shorter than—"

"Two."

He stepped backward, still staring, but I took the window of opportunity and spun, hustling away.

"What's everyone so afraid of?" he yelled.

A drunk man was always more ballsy than a sober one and typically far more stupid. I kept moving beyond the cluster of buildings, block after block, past the pubs, the prostitutes, and the few carriages on the streets. Beyond the Silk Road and to the Hallowed River between the cities.

I expected guards. Hordes of them dressed in green on the Silbath side and purple just beyond the river. But no one patrolled the border. Something was wrong. I backed away, wanting desperately to watch the city from above and see what I could learn. But I was an easy target right now. And if the new king had put a bounty on me for drawing a weapon on him, I could be overpowered. I could be locked away. And that was not an option. So, I steeled my veins, checked over my shoulder once, and ran like hell, passing over the long stone bridge and shooting into the gap between two nearby buildings before turning back. Curiosity forced me to watch, unable to tear myself away from the questions lingering along an unmanned border.

If my father died with no heir, wouldn't Perth, the council... find a replacement, just as Silbath had done when Bram Ellis died? The border had never truly been a roadblock for anyone crossing, but there had always been angry guards on both sides.

Mere blocks from the clock tower, I stopped, swinging a hard left, passing by the Badger Hole, and stepping over the rats to enter the nearby apartment of Thomas Vanhutes. Based on the smell alone, his decaying body must've remained for several days before the gravedigger had come to remove it. But I wasn't here for the memories. Thomas had a long mirror in his hall, and, though it was cracked, it would serve a purpose.

"Ro," I whispered, placing my hand on the reflective surface.

Nothing.

Damnit.

"Seriously, Ro. I need you."

I didn't know if she'd let me stay for long, but surely a few days while I worked out a plan couldn't hurt. She'd know every-thing going on between the two kingdoms, as she always did, using her mirrors to spy. But it didn't matter because she didn't answer.

I placed my hand on the mirror once more, a plea more than anything. Still, she didn't budge. And, as my only friend, this was as good as it would ever be for me.

"Fine," I scowled, stomping out of the apartment.

The clock tower seemed to have grown an extra twenty feet overnight. With my lack of boots and no trust in the slippers, I'd gone up as far as I could inside the building before tossing them to the side and stepping out onto the ledge of the window bare-foot. There were times in my life when this was fun, and times like now, when I'd lost a weapon or needed a change of clothes, and it became impossibly far to climb.

Wind had casually brushed my skin while I was on the ground, but this far up, my dark hair lashed across my face, blinding me. Digging my fingers into the crevices between cracks, bare toes curling for as much grip as they could get, I continued, until I missed a stone, and my feet slipped, leaving me dangling at a dangerous height with sore shoulders, raw feet, and hardly any strength left. Sheer stubborn will was the only thing that saved me as I regained my footing, cursed every old god, and crept to the top, slipping into the wide crack behind the rusted clock face with a huff.

With shifting gears for a floor and crow nests for company, it was not a place for sleeping or shelter, but I'd kept a change of clothing and a box of weapons and jewels hidden beyond a panel on the north side of the exposed space. I changed quickly and loaded myself down with everything I now owned in the world. The gems would be pointless to most of society. But I was no longer hunting the vagrants. I was weak. There was only one woman who could and would pay a decent price. And though I'd have to be careful with each word and agreement, Orin Faber had left me with no choice but to pay a visit to Lady Visha.

"Maiden," the dark brown man, over a head taller than me, said, gripping the lapel of his coat as he stepped to the side. I could almost hear his heart thundering when he reached and twisted the iron knob.

As I strode through the entrance of the brothel, the world transformed into a realm of clandestine desires and hidden pleasures. Sconces cast a seductive glow, their dim light revealing just enough to tantalize the senses while shrouding the illicit activities in an air of secrecy.

The musty aroma mingled with the haze of opium smoke, enveloping the hallway in a hushed, intoxicating atmosphere of lust and sex, cheap perfume, and stale cigarettes, weaving a story that spoke of every encounter behind sheer curtains.

Murmured voices floated through, their soft timbre hinting at whispered secrets. I listened carefully, confident the truths I needed could be hidden between these walls, but I couldn't grasp words beyond the opioid haze slowly taking over my mind.

I'd been lost to the seduction of opium dens only once, ten

years ago. When tragedy struck and I had nowhere else to go, when I couldn't deal with the reality of death, I'd fallen into the darkness of that underworld, trading jewels to keep the memories at bay. It was only when Ro refused to see me that I walked away. Still, my heart yearned for the numbness the haze offered, as if a smoky finger beckoned me forward, promising me temporary escape.

A scream of pleasure pierced the veil of my mind, bringing me back, intermingling with a soft, feminine giggle. The tapping of a long cigarette on an ashtray provided a broken rhythm to the symphony of sensuality.

The atmosphere within the brothel mirrored the complex tapestry of its occupants. Patrons, frantic for attention and seeking temporary solace from their hardships, mingled with servers who themselves were desperate to repay their debts to Lady Visha. The women working here wore masks of forced smiles, concealing the sadness that lingered in their eyes. It was a world where desires met with transactional encounters, where emotions were carefully guarded.

Stepping into the main room, beyond the long hall that carried me through a world of varying degrees of promised pleasure, I moved to the red velvet couch but considered what fluids might be lingering and opted to stand as I waited for Lady Visha's invitation. This was her world. And she was happy to let her patrons see the Death Maiden within these walls. Happy to let the world see that her power stretched beyond fear.

A reasonably attractive man, with cropped brown hair nearly hidden beneath a top hat, had no such reservations as he sprawled across another couch, his dark eyes watching the courtesans pass by. When one walked by, wearing nothing but a sheer robe and the highest heels I'd ever seen, he grabbed her wrist, pulling her onto his lap. Sad eyes met mine for only a moment before she tilted her head and laughed. Ink from the man's fingers transferred onto her beautiful golden skin as he rubbed her back.

When she tried to pull away and he refused to let her up, protective anger surged through me, and I made it all of three paces toward the asshole before Cordelia, one of Lady Visha's favorites, cleared her throat from the doorway. I made a mental note to pay the printer a little visit the next time I was around. Though I wasn't sure he'd seen me beyond his lust.

Making eye contact with the woman that'd saved that man's testicles, I wondered if she would have done that, had she not been Lady Visha's favorite. I'd never seen another of the courtesans remain untouched. Though there was only one red band on her arm, a debt easily paid, some would say, she stayed by choice, the hostess to the Goddess of Pleasure, should such a title exist. Visha stacked her debts, each band countable, whereas the Maestro locked a person down with time. That was perhaps the only difference between them. Still, I followed the woman all the same, down the dark halls and into the serpent's office.

"I've always known you to be smart, Prin—forgive me. It's no longer princess, is it?" Lady Visha rested one arm on the plush red velvet chair, and with the other, cracked her long cigarette on the side of her mahogany desk, letting the ashes fall to the richly patterned rug.

The chestnut-haired shadow at her side rushed in, sweeping away the mess. I watched the band on her arm, but it did not fade or falter. How many debts had she agreed to with that single ring?

I didn't respond. She'd asked me to forgive her but, while I didn't think there could possibly be a binding contract in there, the last twenty-four hours had taught me new lessons.

"On edge, Maiden?" Lady Visha leaned forward, adjusting the collar of her feathered red robe as she lowered her dark lashes, her soft golden curls falling onto her shoulders. "One could hardly blame you after jilting the new king."

"Something like that." I took three steps into the room, pulled out the chair opposite of her desk, and sat.

"I assume you've come to ask for help? Taking back your father's throne? I am not a miracle worker, Deyanira. But if you'd be willing to swear yourself to me, I could pull a few strings, loosen a few others." Her gaze narrowed as gracefully as a serpent ready to strike. She nodded to Cordelia, who crossed the room, her long, perfectly groomed legs peeking from beneath her robes as she poured two glasses and delivered them without spilling a drop or lifting her eyes to me.

I took the drink. I knew the drill. If I didn't, Lady Visha would end the meeting. There were certain battles I had to let her win, but the liquid burned all the way down, leaving a boulder in my stomach. I hadn't eaten, and mixed with the opium haze and poison, I could feel myself melting, my shoulders relaxing, my thoughts fogging over with each second that passed. Pressing my nails into the skin on my hands, I forced myself to focus. "I have no interest in my father's kingdom."

She clicked her tongue. The sound echoed in my mind. "Pity. My little Petals tell me Icharius Fern has moved his soldiers into Perth."

"Maybe you could tell me how a person no one has heard of managed to rise to king of the world in a span of days."

She stood from her desk, walking around to perch on the front, leaning forward as she dragged a finger below my chin without an ounce of fear. "What is that information worth to you, beautiful girl?"

I snatched her wrist, yanking her face to mine. "I've told you a hundred times, I'm not going to fall for your tricks. Keep your secrets, Visha. I'm here to make a trade."

Her golden eyes fell to Chaos, sitting at my waist. "What kind of trade? A desperate one, I hope."

"I'm not desperate."

"If you keep those silly morals, you will be."

"Refusing to kill isn't a silly moral; otherwise, you'd be lying on the floor, and I'd already be gone."

She stood, all dramatics and seduction leaving her tone. "Spoken like a magic wielder that doesn't understand what it's really like to taste the power. Tell me what you want, Deyanira."

She'd taken less time to crack than normal. Thank the old gods. Still, my tongue numbed, and the room rippled. "Five hundred coins and I'll let you see what I've brought first. Three hundred and you can buy it for less, sight unseen."

The trill of her laughter coiled around the room as she moved to a bookshelf and withdrew an old leather tome. A game. Bargaining gave her a high as potent as the opium haze swirling through her brothel. But she would never seem eager, nor rushed. Nor out of control of every possible scenario. I forced my eyes to focus, studying the tapestries on the walls, each depicting a lusty scene of two lovers tangled in various poses.

"Cordelia, would you come here, Petal?" The words had barely left her stained red lips before her favorite courtesan was at her side, eyes trained to the carpet, dark lashes grazing her pink cheeks.

"Yes, Lady Visha," she murmured as quietly and gently as I'd ever heard her.

"I need Everen from the peacock room, if you wouldn't mind?"

Cordelia bobbed down in a small curtsey. "Yes, Madame."

When the door clicked shut, Visha set her book down and came to stand before me. "Your father's throne is lost. It's wise to stay away from Icharius Fern. While you may have never heard his name, we in the Scarlet District certainly have. He beats my girls and shows no mercy if he thinks he's being pushed around. There's something very dangerous about him."

"Do you think he's working with the Maestro?"

She tapped the side of her nose and winked without verbally confirming. If Lady Visha was being careful in her own brothel, even in front of her courtesans, something was definitely brewing.

She gripped my arms and examined me more seriously than I'd ever seen her, golden eyes flickering in the lamplight. "The Maestro doesn't care for politics, and everyone knows that."

Watching closely, she waited for me to connect the dots she would not speak aloud, but the drink mixed with that fucking haze had fogged my mind. She'd never spoken to me so frankly, and though I would wager her aim was to create a false sense of security, I still had to fight to trust the tone in her voice. The desperation on her face. She may have had an angle here, but she wasn't lying.

There was a link between the Maestro and the real Icharius Fern, and if it wasn't about the politics, it had to be something else.

"The Life Maiden?" I mouthed without making a sound.

Shaking her head, she turned away just in time for Cordelia and a completely naked, black-haired woman to stride in, fingers clasped around the navy straps of two high heels, bouncing off her thigh as she walked. She didn't recognize me at first. Maybe my stance was too loose, my muscles too relaxed to be dangerous.

Her breath caught in her throat, giving away the exact second she'd figured it out. Stumbling over her bare feet, she nearly fell, trying to run back out of the door. Cordelia was faster, slamming it shut to stop her, as her mistress would have demanded, had she needed to.

"Relax, Petal." Visha moved to stand before Everen, drawing a manicured nail across her collarbone, up her neck, and to her chin before brushing a thumb over her bottom lip. "I will protect you."

The light's glow reflected off the tears welling in her soft blue eyes as she slowly nodded. I withheld my snort at the notion. As if she had any sway over Death's magic.

Lady Visha moved her hand down her courtesan's trembling arm, stopping just below the four red bands marking her a thrall. "Who do you see standing in this room?"

Everen drew her head back in confusion, eyes falling to me, then Cordelia and back to her mistress. "Just the three—"

The brothel owner brought a swift slap down on Everen's hand before repeating the question. Without missing a beat, the woman answered. "I see no one, Madame."

"Good." The seductive and lingering tone to her smoky voice had returned. "Today, you have a choice to win your freedom. Shall we play a game?"

Her eyes doubled in size. "Will I have to leave? If I win?"

"Perhaps," her mistress drawled.

I shuffled my feet, feeling the heat of the alcohol creeping up my neck until I was sure my cheeks flushed, and the room had tilted.

"This is my home, and I'm safe in the Scarlet District."

This time, I couldn't help the huff of laughter. "No one is safe here, especially this close to Beggar's Row. Don't fool yourself, sweetheart."

Lady Visha's golden eyes snapped to mine. She did not approve, and I couldn't afford to piss her off. I apologized, but the words fell too easily from my mouth.

"Will you force me?" Everen asked.

"No, little Petal. Not today." She kissed the courtesan's cheek and turned away. "You see, Maiden, I'm confident you are desperate. You've lost your kingdom, you're bound to a stranger, and you've never had friends. I have to believe you are just like Everen and wouldn't dare bite the final hand that could feed you."

"Perhaps," I said, echoing the tone she'd taken with her worker.

She whipped around, moving in a blur. Her saccharine voice had vanished, revealing the serpent. "Do not mock me, Deyanira. It will serve no purpose. Do you want to make a deal with me or not?"

I almost answered. But saying yes might have bound me into a deal I certainly didn't want to make. "I will make no open-ended deal, Visha. No matter what you slipped into that drink, I know better."

"Perhaps I should drag this out further, give it a few more seconds to take effect."

Biting the inside of my cheek, I stepped toward the door, setting the trap. She was cunning, but so, so easy to manipulate. "Suit yourself. I'll find another buyer for my father's jewels."

"Stop," she barked. "I'll give you the three hundred."

I pulled the less expensive necklace from my boot, keeping it concealed within my fingers until she dropped a bag of coins at my feet. The pendant was worth that, if not a bit more, but had she paid the five hundred, I would have given her the satchel of rubies in my other boot. Lady Visha was a serpent. A magic-wielding thorn in this world, but she kept her girls safe, and by that choice alone, I'd never slight her.

She snatched the jewelry from my hand, examining it for several minutes, everything in the air shifting until it felt like this was her world and we were just living in it.

There were lessons to be learned here, though. A seed to plant among the gossiping prostitutes of Perth's underbelly, as I was dragged into my new reality with absolutely no one and nothing but Chaos at my side. When you dance among demons, you cannot be the weakest creature.

I stepped to the door, and Visha clicked her tongue, spurring Cordelia to move in front of it until her mistress gave me leave. But I was Death's Maiden. The last in a line of killers, cultivating a title to be feared and respected. Maybe I wasn't like those who came before me, but I was like no one else, either.

I pulled my infamous blade from my belt as the world swayed again. The grip along the groves designed for my deadly hands steadied me. I placed the flat edge of the blade to Cordelia's neck and smiled. "Don't let your mistress fool you, Courtesan. Those who feel safe are the easiest to hunt."

"Deyanira," Lady Visha shouted, the delicate thread of desperation riding the edge of her voice. "That is enough."

I glared, the dark walls beyond the brothel owner blurring. "Of the four people standing in this room, I hold the most power. Isn't that why you let me walk in here? Isn't that why you bargain with Death's Maiden? You don't give a shit about the jewels. You certainly don't need the coins you parted with. It's always a game for you. A challenge. Every word you utter serves a single purpose as you try and fail to trap me."

Cordelia's squeal as the edge of the dagger pressed into her neck was enough to hold Lady Visha in place. "I am not weak. I am not desperate. I could end your life right now and take this building as my own, and who would stop me? The new king? His guards? I am not afraid of them. Be grateful for my human-ity, Visha. This conversation could have gone in a completely different direction."

It might have been the adrenaline from shoving steel into my veins, it might have been the lack of food or the alcohol, it might have been Orin's leftover poison or my weakening resolve, but whatever had happened, I didn't register my knees buckling until I was on the floor.

"All bark and no bite," Lady Visha purred, the honey returning to her voice. She moved to crouch before me on the floor. "This world can still break you, but I can keep you safe. Let me help you, Deyanira."

She held a hand forward, those eyes softening as she waited for me to take it. Cordelia murmured something, Everen answered, but the mumbling voices held no diction as if they'd been spoken underwater. I blinked several times, trying to clear my mind. She wiggled her fingers. "You can stay here, with me, forever if you'd like."

Each breath was a drumbeat, each blink, the cymbals crashing. My heart, my lonely, eviscerated heart, knew that I needed her. That I could trust her without question. But something in my brain warned me of the serpent, of the familiar taste of magic seeping down the walls.

The door slammed open behind us, breaking the spell as the last person I'd ever expect to see in Lady Visha's brothel strode in, her face as hard as steel as she grabbed my jacket and helped me to my feet.

Ro.

"There's a special place in Death's court for you, *Visha*," she snapped, shoving me toward the door.

"Yes," the brothel owner called back. "Anyone worth their death knows that. Do save me a seat, kitty cat."

The patrons and courtesans scattered as we stormed down the hall. I tried not to breathe in any more of the toxic haze.

"Unless you're here to get railed, Deyanira, you have to stay away from the Scarlet District."

"What the fuck do you care?" I asked, yanking free of her arm. "You're only around when it's convenient for you."

"Yes, Dey. I have a life and friends, and you aren't the only person I talk to. I don't sit waiting for you to come see me, and I won't feel guilty about that."

"No, you'll just hide and spy on the world from a fucking pedestal."

The last word was a slur, but as she stopped dead in her tracks, dark eyes lowering, I knew I'd struck a chord.

"I am the only one that has stuck by your side for all these years, Deyanira. Be careful how you speak to me."

I faltered. She was right, of course.

Taking a slow breath, letting the fury and adrenaline loose, I dropped my head. "I'm sorry, Ro. It's been a really shitty day."

"I can imagine," she said, the bite still riding the wave of her softening voice. "Go out the back door. I'll take the front and make sure no one is following us."

"Surely there's a mirror—"

"Shh," she snapped, covering my mouth with her hand. "For once in your life, just do as I say, Deyanira."

The instant need to pull a weapon jolted through my arms and to my fingertips. My patience with people was wearing too thin. I said no more as I walked away from her, strolling to the opposite end of the hall, not hearing a peep from those hidden behind the sheer curtains. I shoved the door open, dragging in a deep lungful of fresh air before nearly tripping on the guard that had let me in. He lay knocked out in the alleyway.

Pulling Chaos on instinct alone, I cleared every thought from my mind as I stepped over the man and into the alley, moving away from the simple carriage waiting there. I lifted the mask to hide my face, but it didn't matter. The dancer from Misery's End with two different colored eyes slipped out from behind the carriage wearing a tight corset and long gown. The glare on her face hinted she wasn't bothered by the beast I'd become if she made a move against me. Orin Faber followed. I took three steps back before slamming into a wall of solid muscle. A man who might've been a giant in a past life wrapped arms of steel around me.

I fought like a wild animal until his grip slackened just enough for me to slip free, but I was slow. Orin lunged, and I didn't feel the blade go in, only the warmth as blood seeped from my abdomen.

The massive arms surrounded me again, knocking into the handle of the blade, ripping the hole until I screamed in pain. My inevitable submission as the dark-haired demon, my very alive bonded husband, moved in front of me with a victorious smile.

"Please continue to fight, Little Nightmare. I love a good challenge."

"I say let her bleed for a while," the woman said as they threw me into the carriage, pain racing through my abdomen. "Let her suffer."

"We aren't barbarians, Paesha," Orin said.

"You just stabbed your wife in the Scarlet District, and now you're dragging her ass home for the second time in so many hours. I'd define barbarianism to you if I thought it would matter."

Each breath I took was a rise of strength countered by complete loss. If I thought I could hurl myself out of the carriage and escape, I'd still try. But they'd only hunt me, and three assholes against one injured person with absolutely nowhere to go didn't seem like a safe bet. I hoped my scream of rage was enough to keep Ro at bay.

I checked for weapons first. Chaos was gone, though I'd bet my death, the pouch of coins, and the rubies that remained in my pocket that Orin had taken her. I still had a small throwing knife in my sleeve, but, lying on the rattling bed of the carriage, I couldn't tell if they'd emptied my boots. If I shifted at all to check, I'd give myself away.

"We'll clean it," Orin said, answering a question I hadn't heard.

"I'm confident a little Maiden blood is probably the least of the vile things that have leaked into this carriage," Paesha added.

"I'll take care of it," the giant man answered.

"If you feel so inclined, Jarek," the dancer said. "I won't stop you."

When they'd thrown me into the carriage, I'd clenched my teeth in pain, but I hadn't moved again, pretending to be knocked out by the blow of my head crashing into the opposite door. Curiosity drove me to peek an eye open.

Jarek's voice carried through the space like a growl. "We send it back like this, the Maestro's going to take it out on one of you."

I couldn't see Orin, but I could feel his boot on my spine as we traveled down the road. The low rumble of his words still jarred me. "He's right. We return the carriage how we found it."

If they hadn't stolen Chaos from my side, I would have dragged her sharpened edge down the leather seat on my way out. The cart came to a halt, and I wondered for only a moment who'd driven it before everyone jumped out. Orin was gentler than I'd known him to be as he maneuvered me toward him. I remained limp, eyes almost closed. He was a blur, but there was no mistaking his build or the darkness that seemed to consume him. He ran a finger over my rib where the knife had gone in, then reached for my face, swiping the hair away.

My skin crawled at his gentle touch. It took everything in me to hold still. To lie and wait. But as soon as he lifted me, wound be damned, I snatched Chaos from her stolen sheath at his waist and jumped free of him, hissing as my body protested.

"Don't be foolish, Nightmare. You can't escape."

"You don't…" I stumbled, pulling my fingers from the gash to see the blood was still running. "Don't call me that."

"I'll call you whatever the hell I want to call you, Maiden." He lunged, tossing bulky arms around my waist just to throw me over his shoulder, with no concern for my wound.

I screamed in pain, piercing the night as I hauled the knife back and would have buried it into his ass had Paesha not been there to catch my arm and take the blade from my weakened hands.

"I'll never stop fighting you," I growled.

"I'd be disappointed if you did," Orin answered, his voice far calmer than I would have liked, as I struck him over and over with a fist.

As we neared a door of the odd, towering home, I lost my will to fight and pleaded, hating the way it sounded, but I was desperate. "Please. Please don't lock me in. I can't stay here. I have to go. You don't understand."

He dropped me into the empty room, and my hip cracked on the bare wood floor. "You can't be allowed to roam free, either."

The second I was shut in the room, the walls moved in. Closer and closer they inched. I crawled, banging on the locked door. Pounding on the ground. Screaming as loudly as I could. Adrenaline mixed with fear as I became consumed by space. Every bit of air in the room grew heavier, a chore to drag into my lungs. I struck the wood until my gloves wore down, and after I removed them, beating until my knuckles were bloody and the skin on my palms raw. Until the tears no longer fell, and I had no voice remaining. I could handle a lot. But the single thing that would end me, that would turn me into the monster they feared… the monster *I* feared, was captivity.

I was born to be the most powerful person in the world, and it was crushing me.

When I woke, lying in a pool of my blood, weak and defeated, I stared at a half-filled glass of water and a sandwich set on the floor just inside the room. I wasn't proud, lifting the water to my lips, forcing myself to sip instead of gulp. I reached for the sandwich. The immediate pain from the movement was severe. And defeating.

"Would you like some more water?" a high-pitched feminine voice asked from the hall.

"Yes, please," I rasped, desperate for the door to open.

"Move back against the far wall. If you do, I can help you."

There was no way in hell. If not because it might be my only chance at escape, then because I could hardly lift my head to finish the last swallow of water.

"I can't," I whispered, clearing my throat before trying again. "I can't."

The door inched open, and a woman with short red hair and rosy cheeks popped her head in, the soft smile on her face fading away as she saw me lying on the ground. "That's... that's a lot of blood."

"Sorry."

"Did you just apologize for bleeding?" She knelt down before me, but as soon as she opened her mouth to speak, she was interrupted.

"Godsdammit all, Althea," Orin roared from behind her. "Are you trying to get yourself killed?"

The door swung open, slamming into my feet. I groaned from the jarring pain stabbing through my abdomen. Orin's golden eyes scanned me from head to toe, his fist clenching before he rested a hand on Althea's shoulder. "Go get my mother's medical kit and meet us in the kitchen."

I hissed in protest when he hoisted me from the floor and carried me through the house, the eyes of several strangers falling on us as we passed. He laid me on a sturdy wooden table, fully clothed, and though I could barely open my eyes, I still managed to glare.

Gripping the edge of the table, Orin eyed my stomach. "You remove the shirt, or I do. Your choice."

"Go fuck yourself."

"You have three seconds to decide. One."

My eyes fell shut.

"Two."

"Two and a half," I groaned.

"You and I both know you aren't going to die. I could just leave you to suffer."

Fire surged through me. I didn't need a thing from him, especially insinuated mercy. "Then do it."

"I can do it, Orin, if you want me to," that soft voice said. "It might be better if I—"

"Leave us," he barked, and the door snicked shut.

"Eager to get a peek at your handy work?"

A line formed between his brows. "You've never had to fight you, and it shows. You left me no choice, Nightmare."

"Stop calling me that."

He ignored me, eyes pinned to mine as he grabbed the cowl neck of my hood, pulling it carefully over my head before dropping it onto the floor. He studied the leather buckles and straps across my chest.

"I can do it. Just leave me."

Orin's eyes gleamed with a mixture of amusement and malice as he towered over me, deep brown hair falling into his brow. Ignoring my demand, he started on the intricate harness that once held my weapons and now concealed the stab wound. With each strap he unbuckled, I winced in pain.

"You can't be left alone. You'll be off murdering some poor, innocent soul by night's end."

I turned to my side and tried like hell to haul myself up, but blood began dripping like crimson tears on the scuffed kitchen floor.

"Don't pretend you know anything about me, Orin Faber."

He crossed his arms over his chest, scanning my body until my heart rate quickened. "I'll just sit back and watch you struggle until you pass out."

"Are you mocking me for *bleeding* when it's *your* fault?"

"Had I known you were so fragile, I would have been more careful."

"I think we both know I'm anything but fragile. Now get out."

"Make. Me."

Though it hurt like hell, I rolled to my side, gripping the table and shifting until one leg touched the floor. Only with monumental effort did I get the second leg down.

He smirked, studying me as he took a single step forward, grabbed the final buckle, and said, "Not sorry about this," before ripping it free.

My vision turned white. My legs gave in. The harness dropped to the ground, shredding away what was left of the fresh scab on my abdomen. Somehow, he managed to catch me before I hit the floor.

"I hate you," I mumbled.

Orin's hot breath curled around my ear as he leaned close, the deep timbre of his voice causing the hair on my arms to rise. "I hate you, too."

He laid me back down on the table, pulled up the remnants of my shirt, but left my breasts covered, and then yanked off my boots. His hands burned into me. His touch was like a thousand needless as he worked. I wanted to protest again, to tell him to leave me alone. But I knew the wound needed to be cleaned. I knew few things sounded better than washing away the layer of dried blood on my skin, and I knew, above all else, he wasn't going to fucking listen to me, anyway.

I couldn't figure him out. I hoped eventually I'd stop trying. Every word he'd spoken on that roof felt so sincere. The way he'd looked into my eyes had stripped me bare. But then what did I know of genuine sincerity? He'd merely played the part well. And when we fought, he hadn't held back. He'd taken and given every blow as if it might be his last. I didn't miss the darkness in his eyes when he stabbed me. He'd meant to. I could see how much my pain had brought him happiness.

Yet, now, I lay before him, hardly able to keep my eyes open, weak from blood loss, and he'd insisted on caring for me. He'd carried me out of that prison himself. His prison. I didn't understand.

There was a pause before he removed my leather pants, but when I looked up at him, expecting those fiery eyes to be staring at my undergarments, I was surprised to see him looking at my face. As if he watched the wheels of my mind turning, trying, and failing to figure him out.

"You've got blood in your hair, and I have to rinse the wound before it can be bandaged. Hot or cold water?"

"Why do you care?"

"I don't. But no one in the house slept last night with all the racket, so I'm hoping this wears you out."

I laid my head on the table, too tired to keep it upright. "Maybe you shouldn't lock people up. Then you wouldn't have to bother at all."

He went with the cold water, which matched his icy exterior as he let it drip. I gasped, but he pinned me down without much effort, keeping me from ripping the skin around my abdomen any more. Orin used a cloth and proficiently cleaned, his knuckles grazing my skin, fingertips constantly touching as he worked while I wished to be anywhere else.

"Here," he said, offering a metal flask.

"I'd rather die."

"Suit yourself, but this is going to hurt."

I counted three blinks, staring at a patched ceiling. "I'll survive."

His eyes didn't leave mine as he took the flask and poured its contents into the open wound, the alcohol every bit as excruciating as I imagined, and then some. He held my shoulder down, but my stomach roiled, and I wanted nothing more than to turn over and vomit. Another basin of lukewarm water later, and it took every ounce of strength I had to sit up so he could wrap the bandage while holding eye contact, daring me to show weakness at his touch. But this was a silent war, and I was very good at his game.

"The blade went all the way in," Orin said. "It's going to take days to heal."

"Longer," I rasped. "Your giant friend hit the handle, and I think the blade nicked something."

"We contemplated asking nicely, but it didn't pass the vote. Lie back."

"How fucking generous." I waited a beat before adding, "Prick."

"Not the worst thing I've been called. Pretty sure that's not even the worst thing *you've* called me. Now, lie back."

"Can't. I'll throw up."

He gripped my bare arm, staring down at me. "You'll be fine, *Nightmare*."

I laid slowly, his grasp never faltering as I rested my head on the table. "I prefer Maiden."

"Maiden," he drawled, refusing to look me in the eye. "So eager for a battle, even when you're broken."

The corners of his mouth fought the grin as he moved away, that beautiful, brutal face full of cocky indignation.

The scent of lavender filled the air as he dipped a cloth into a basin of warm water, wringing it out before carefully wiping away the blood that matted my hair. His touch was surprisingly tender, each stroke soothing the ache in my head. He smoothed a finger over my neck, pulling my collar down, no doubt gazing over the tattoo that crept up from my back.

Warm water seeped into my scalp, and he buried his hands into my hair, massaging every inch, applying more soap, and scrubbing. Those fingers got lost, digging every discomfort from my mind.

I looked up to see him staring into my eyes and immediately snapped mine shut. Whatever this was, he was still my enemy. I'm sure he didn't want me staining the floors of his massive house with blood. He didn't want me screaming in despair either. If he locked me in that fucking room again, well, it was just going to be round two. But for now, all thoughts of rebellion and all the ways I should make him suffer went to the wayside as he scrubbed until I fell asleep.

"Hello, my beautiful Deyanira."

Falling into Death's court would never be something I got used to. Setting my jaw, I shifted into the silent but obedient servant I'd learned to be with him. He curled a finger toward me, his magic drawing me closer. I'd killed my father only days ago, and while I thought that might, at the very least, win me some time, Death was never predictable.

His dark eyes held mine. "Tell me you're playing hard to get with your new husband. Do you want his name, my beauty?"

I said nothing, hardly daring to blink as he leaned closer, near enough to whisper in my ear, sliding his hand down my arm to take my wrist and turn my palm. His intentional touch sent shivers down my spine as he dragged a finger over my sensitive skin.

My breath hitched.

He whispered, "I could mark this perfect skin with his name. I could take you to your knees with desperation to kill him, my Deyanira."

The way his voice purred was an illusion compared to the lethal darkness in his eyes. His eager drive to reap and hunt, to pluck another soul from our realm of two cities was insatiable. This was not a man who saved our world. No matter what the historians would have had us believe, he just wasn't. But that was a speculated truth that would never leave my lips.

"Speak. Say his name and it will be done."

I wanted to. The old gods knew I did. But that would be an indirect way of choosing someone else's fate. The single thing Orin had accused me of. There was still a kernel of goodness in me, something deep that kept me sane and proud. I would never take a life. The woman who killed for Death was a separate part of me. A beast and a monster, but she wasn't all of me. So, I held my tongue.

"Come, my darling," he said, stepping away, though he clenched my hand until the bones ground together.

He led me down the dark stone path outside of his infamous gates. Two moons cast a hue of blue across his haunted eternity. The closer we stepped to his towering hellhounds, the more my sleeping heart raced. Their ruby eyes pinned me down, turning my feet immobile until their master chuckled.

"Stand down. She isn't a threat to you." He winked at me. "They will not harm you as long as you draw no weapon and I do not command it."

I wondered if he would lead me beyond the swirling iron gate to the castle and court. I wondered for only a moment if he would keep me here. And worse, I did not loathe the thought.

One day, I would return and never leave, embracing eternity in hell. One day, I would stand before my mother and find the words to apologize. I would see my father again and stand or break before him.

"Touch him," Death commanded, the power in his voice potent.

Though trembling, I did as I was told, burying my fingers into short, coarse hair. When the hound jumped at my contact, a low growl rumbling in his chest, it took every ounce of strength to keep from running.

"She is mine, Aetherius. There is no need to fear her."

And though I knew Death had gotten it wrong, that it was not the hounds' but my own dread filling the air, I remained silent, stroking the animal while Death moved away, giving attention to the other beast before turning to study me, to watch the way my hands moved over his beloved pet. I met his eyes without shame, but I couldn't say it was without fear. There were chords wound tightly within me that Death knew how to strike.

"You are different, my beauty," he said, inviting me to his side with another gesture. "Why do you not crave the death of your enemies?"

A breath in. A breath out.

"One day, I will break you." His promise filled the air as he snatched my hand and burned the name into my palm. His handsome face showed every bit of delight as pain overtook me. "I have a good feeling about this one," he purred, seconds before everything vanished and I opened my eyes.

Though covered with a blanket, I lie on the floor of Orin's prison room once more, Death's magic pulsing through me, begging me to claw my way through the walls to hunt my newest target.

CHAPTER 15

I f ever there was a person in this gods-abandoned world whose name I truly might have given to Death, it would have been Orin Faber. And staring at the burn marks in my flesh, though I'd half-expected Death to plant his name there anyway, I felt no sense of relief when I read the name given.

Arabella Grenwich.

My instincts wanted me to lean into the magic and let it give me a sense of direction, but as I stared at the gleaming door-knob, fear crept up my throat, gripping me in a vise. I'd have to resist the manic urge as long as possible. Because every second until I was out of this room was going to drive me to madness. A madness I'd had experience with. A kind of madness that had once broken me to stealing the lives of twenty-three people in a single night.

I refused to look at the name, refused to think about it, or remember the edges of the seared skin on my hand. Refused to think of the weapons I didn't have or wonder which city she might reside in. Instead, I moved to the center of the hollow room, my abdomen still sore, but better, and I sat with my knees to my chest, rocking back and forth, ignoring the way the walls moved in.

"One," I whispered. "Anika Sariah Hark."

A breath.

"Two. Garrit Faden."

Another breath.

"Three. Marian Achlen."

Face after face, name after name poured through my mind. Starting with my mother and ending now with my father. "A name given; a body delivered. Always the same. Not my fault. Not my choice. Breathe."

Move.

The magic had its own sort of voice in my mind. A physical command over my body, as if it wrapped itself around every muscle. Every tendon. Every bone.

Now.

"Three hundred forty-six, Sibylla Rikket." The names came faster, desperately tumbling from my lips as I rocked, digging my nails into my legs until I broke the skin. "Three hundred forty-seven, Ezra Prophet."

Stand up.

"No," I said aloud, gripping the sides of my head. "No."

"Three hundred for... forty-eight. Esb—"

TOUCH THE DOOR!

I jumped to my feet and ran to the door, needing to be near the handle. Needing to stare at the way the flickering light on the wall shined upon the beautiful curve.

Touch it.

The words were not magic; they were the poison of my own mind. They were me. All of this was. Every choice. Every death. Every drop of blood. Me. *Me.* I wanted this. I craved this. I needed death. The satisfaction. The blade. The blood. The blood.

The blood.

"Stop it." I dug my fingers into my thick hair, pulling until the pain turned to numbness and the pieces came out in clumps. "This isn't you."

"This isn't you."

"This isn't you."

I couldn't fight the drag of my eyes back to the brass knob.

It's cool. Touch it.

"It'll be cold in my hands. Comforting."

Yes.

"No." I backed all the way to the opposite side of the room.

The walls are thin.

"The walls are thin. I could claw my way through. The blood. The death. The kill."

Yes.

"No. No. No."

Heart racing, I ran to the door and gripped the cool knob, letting that single sensation comfort every vibrating nerve.

"There."

Turn it.

"Fight it."

Arabella Grenwich.

I could picture her in my mind. The single, beautiful slice across her throat. I could hear the curdled gasp. See the moment the life left her eyes and her soul vanished.

I turned the knob slowly, my heart fighting every single inch as the knob gave a little more and a little more, until it passed where a door lock would have kept it.

He hadn't locked me in. I was free.

The magic became quiet.

Satiated.

Only the haunting remnants of my past echoed around me

as I crept into the hallway, pushed my back against the wall, and slid to the floor. The madness had nearly consumed me, and I wasn't even trapped. I was a victim of my mind. My fear. And had that door been locked, eventually, I would have broken through it. Or clawed my way through the walls. Because no matter how much I tried to fight this power, the second I lost control, it was over.

"Maiden?" that kind, feminine voice from before said. She poked her head around the corner, a smudge of ash on her face, the sun beaming down the hallway, enveloping her hair in a halo of glorious red as she tucked a hammer into a loop on her belt. "Are you okay?"

"The door was unlocked. I didn't break it."

She moved tentatively until she was across the narrow space from me, sinking down the wall just as I had, our feet nearly touching. "I know."

"Was it a mistake? The door being unlocked, I mean."

Her smile was genuine but careful. "No."

"So, I'm free to leave? Or will I be stabbed and dragged back to this prison again?"

"The Syndicate house is not a prison. It's a home, and I won't stand by and see it become anything else."

I replayed the map of the home I'd seen in my mind, calculating how many steps to the knives in the kitchen, and how many more to the door. I could jump out a window again, though preferably something closer to the ground. A single pulse of power reminded me I would need to leave sooner rather than later. But I had no intention of staying, anyway.

Rising, I dusted my hands on my pants, only then realizing I wasn't in the same clothes I'd been stabbed in. Nor the wedding dress. But still my wardrobe. Something from my closet... in my father's castle.

Confused, I looked back at the woman, and a trill of a laugh escaped before she covered her mouth with her hand. "Don't worry, Maiden. Paesha and I dressed you. Not Orin."

"Who are you?" I asked, drawing back.

Green eyes stared into mine, but no answer came.

"It's fine. You don't have to tell me. It's better if I don't know."

I walked away, leaving the woman on the floor as I made my way to the kitchen. Another woman, older, with dark hair and a nose that matched Orin's, spun the second I entered the room. His mother, maybe. She gasped and backed away, arms gripping the counter.

"I won't hurt you. But it's dangerous to travel completely unarmed." I swiped an abandoned kitchen knife off the table and made to leave.

"Wait," she called after me.

My throat closed. I was already on edge, and whatever she would ask of me, of my dealings with a man who was potentially her son, I wasn't ready to answer. Nor did I trust that she wouldn't find another blade and plunge it into my skull if she was anything like her asshole child.

"Here." She held out a dagger. "I'd prefer to keep the other one. If it's all the same to you."

I studied those dark chocolate eyes for only a second before carefully handing back her blade, handle first. She gave up the dagger, and something about it felt a little too easy. Why would they have captured me last night, only to let me leave today? Each interaction in this house became more and more odd as I made my way to the door, wondering if *he* was the only one who demanded I stay.

"Will you come back, Maiden?" the redhead asked, following me as I snaked my way through the next hall, searching for the front door.

"No."

"If I asked nicely, would you consider it? Please?"

"No," I growled.

"Here, then," she said, tossing my coin bag at me the second I faced her. "My name is Althea Washburn, and if you need a friend, you can find me here, outside in my forge, or in the warehouse behind Misery's End."

She tucked her cropped hair behind an ear. The loose sleeve of her shirt fell just enough to show the blue band around her wrist. I'd never been more confused in my life. The mystery of this so-called Syndicate intrigued me. The temptation to ask her why she was being so nice that it felt like a trick sat waiting on my lips.

But the magic pulsed again, pushing me out the door, and though I half-expected a group of Drexel's armed lackeys waiting to trap me again, standing with cigarettes hanging from scared faces, no one was there. Only a worn path through a long grass field that led into the line of oak trees.

I turned once, looking back at the gables and turrets of the home in waves of distrust and confusion. The charcoal dwelling, a relic really, held its own sort of mystery; a tapestry of varying styles and mismatched levels, which seemed to fit the occupants of the strange house. Dilapidated windows, adorned with ironwork lattices, peered out from the depths like watchful eyes. Also fitting. But what the fuck was the Syndicate for?

SNAKING THROUGH THE DRIED-UP ALLEYWAYS, the sun that rarely shone in the cities revealed every nook and cranny of disrepair. Silbath's bricks crumbled, and walls cracked. There were fewer shadows to hide within and more people to avoid. Hunting during the day felt like more of an intrusion on my victim's life. Still, Lady Visha's women, though fewer, perched on streets and leaned against the walls, wiping sweat from their brows, adjusting melting makeup in silver compacts, and eyeing every person, man or woman, that ambled by.

The rutting was calmer in the day, and less gritty from the rooftops. Moaning danced through the alleyways at night in fervor because alcohol was a cheap escape, and so was an orgasm. Three men poured from the door in an alley, each wearing long coats and leather gloves similar to what I'd expected to see of people lingering outside the Syndicate house. The Maestro's gangsters circled another man thrown from the same doorway. The squelch of leather resonated as they moved like vultures, rubbing their fists into their hands. One pulled a crowbar and lifted it above his head with a snarl. I turned away, feeling like it was too early to see two acts of violence this early in the day.

Arabella Grenwich leaned against a lamppost, oblivious to the starving raven scavenging around her as much as the murderer perched above her. The apron at her waist served as a place for her to wipe the ink from the newspapers she sold. She'd swiped the sweat from her face twice. Each time left a black mark almost as dark as her eyes upon her golden skin.

"The king of Perth has fallen. Slayed by his own daughter moments after he denounced her. Read all about it. Two coin. The Death Maiden is on the run!"

I was pretty sure anyone standing close enough to me could hear my eyes roll. "Old news."

Still, a little old couple crossed the uneven street and traded their coin for the gossip, standing to read the paper, hunched shoulder to shoulder.

"Icharius Fern joins the realms. Two coin. Read all about it. Written in his own words!"

I stared at the woman, Death's magic thrumming within me. This proximity would be enough to hold the power back.

The hunting and closeness always was at first, but something urged me forward. My own mind, potentially. Fear of capture after being subdued twice. If I didn't end her life and wound up imprisoned by the king, the madness would consume me. I no longer had the precious luxury of time. She'd have to die today.

A prick of anticipation struck me. That power coiled around my muscles as I looked for another way but found none. I waited for the old couple to wander down the street before leaping into the alley behind Arabella. At first, she paid me no mind, likely assuming I was just a beggar or otherwise. And I wished I could have been. I wished the daylight didn't have to see the stain on my soul. But wishes were for dreamers, and my dreams conjured nightmares.

I stepped onto the sidewalk, pulling the dagger. Sheer force of will shoved me back into the alley. I pushed my spine against the wall. Sucking in three sharp breaths, I moved again, creeping up behind Arabella, wrapping my hands around her mouth and dragging her backward. She kicked and screamed, and the old gods knew I wanted to cater, to cave to the begging. I wanted to be more than what I was damned to be.

"I'm sorry," I whispered.

She went rigid, only then putting together who'd taken her. I should have pushed the knife home and ran, but she deserved a moment. It was the only thing I could give her, if not the peace of a death in her sleep.

"Please," she managed. "Please, I have to take care of my mother. She's... She's sick."

My stomach roiled. My fingers loosened on the blade. I was a monster. Her monster. Her nightmare.

"Before you die, do you know anything about the Life Maiden?"

"No. I swear it. No one has seen her, please. I'll pay you," she pleaded, turning to face me as my grip loosened. "I don't have much, but I've got a bit. I've been saving to find us a home. You can have it."

I shook my head, fingers instinctively caressing the mask on my face to make sure she couldn't see the tremble in my façade. I was a killer.

"I can—"

The blade across her throat was a clean cut. So clean that for just a moment, it looked as if it hadn't happened at all. Only when her eyes widened, and the scarlet blood poured from the fresh wound, did I look away. She gasped. They always gasped. The only consistent thing in my life, beyond my title as Death Maiden.

It took him longer to come this time, but when Death appeared in broad daylight, I held my chin high, my eyes narrowed, and said nothing as he kissed my cheek and wrenched the harvested soul back to his court. His collection.

Exhausted, I stood in that alley for what must have been hours. The world passed by in a blur, hardly anyone paying any mind to the body of Arabella Grenwich. They'd looted her papers, and someone had tried to steal her shoes before they eyed me standing vigil. But she lay alone. Just like me.

These moments of desolation had defined me for so long. I felt as though my life was just happening around me, and I was nothing more than a pawn for the villain, an enemy for the masses that saw him as a god, and a victim of myself. I'd lost control of everything.

Staring down at the vacant face of the woman I'd murdered, I realized whatever my plight, it could've been so much worse. And I could let myself be a victim, or I could fucking rise. And I wanted nothing to do with the bottomless pit of my own emotions.

Forcing my legs to move beyond the exhaustion that rattled me within the abyss of spent magic, I shoved my arms under

Arabella's fallen body, lifted her from the ground, and walked out. I carried that woman down the middle of the godsdamned street, eyes and whispers and shouts of horror be damned as I moved. They would have sooner seen her rot than do the same, and I was not like them, despite the things they thought they all knew about me.

She grew heavy by the time I got to the empty bridge at Perth. Heavier so by the time I made it to Tolliver's Pointe. But that was my own burden to bear.

"Fredrik?" I called, kicking on the door of a house nearby.

When the man, who had to be nearing his hundredth year, inched the door open, I gave him three seconds to take it all in before the door shut in my face; a chain could be heard sliding out of its locking mechanism, and he joined me on the crumbling step.

He slipped a hat onto his head and let his wrinkled face fall only inches. "Put her in the wagon, Maiden. What's the name? For the stone."

"Arabella Grenwich. She has a mother somewhere that'll be worried."

He nodded, pulling on his gloves. I hated to burden the old man with digging a grave, but as I dropped two coins into his hand, I knew he needed those as much as the next person.

"There's another bag of coins in her apron. Make sure her mother gets them."

He sighed, using immense effort to creep down the step. "Yes, Maiden."

It was rare that I delivered a body to the grave keeper. Rarer so when it happened in broad daylight. But those who watched never followed, anyway.

From Tolliver's Pointe, I could see the turrets and battlements of my father's castle bathing in the last few moments of daylight. I found myself ambling down that familiar road, wondering what I might find, should I walk through the gate. If Regulas would still be there, kissing the ass of whatever nobleman Icharius Fern shoved into my father's bed, or if he'd tucked tail and run off.

The red lights of the Scarlet District flickered to life, casting the world in Lady Visha's favorite hue as I faded into the shadows, grabbed a familiar railing, and scaled a vacant warehouse, purely exhausted from my trek and the expenditure of magic.

Lying flat on the roof, I stared up into the starless sky. I could sleep here, but it was only getting colder. I would be too exposed, and I needed to hunt for the Life Maiden. It was important, but it seemed such a massive task when I didn't even have a bed to crawl into. I had an invitation, though, and that thought lingered in my mind as a familiar voice growled.

"Tell me what you know."

My heart leaped into my throat. Rolling over, I searched the skyline before realizing that Orin was somewhere below me. I crept like a feline to the very edge of the roof, holding my breath as I peeked over, only far enough to see Orin holding a man pinned against a wall. I might not have recognized him behind the mask, but I knew the shape, and gods help me, I think there was even familiarity in the build of his shoulders and the bulk of his legs.

"Tell me where they are," he seethed, shifting just enough for me to see a knife held to his victim's Adam's apple.

The man shook his head, and before I could process what was happening, Orin took his blade, plunged it into his poor victim's chest, and watched him crumble to the ground. I waited a heartbeat and then another. After ripping off his mask, Orin lifted his head to the sky, spreading his arms wide as if daring the clouds to finally break and pour down on him. With his eyes closed, face cast in the red glow of the nearby lights, he might have been beautiful, if he wasn't such a bastard.

A voice at the other end of the street broke whatever power had held Orin in place. He lifted his hood and snuck away, never once looking back at the man he'd injured. I waited. Perhaps I could follow his victim and learn more. Learn whatever knowledge he was looking for or find whomever it was that was missing. But the minutes turned into more than an hour and the man hadn't moved an inch. Not even when the rats came.

He couldn't be dead, but why had he laid there, not bothering to call for help? When I approached him, I half-expected to smell the alcohol he must have reeked of. A drunk passed out on the streets of the Scarlet District could be found on every corner. But when I rolled the man over with my scuffed boot, trying to wake him, vacant eyes stared up at me.

He was dead. Orin Faber had killed a man… and Death never came to collect his soul.

CHAPTER 16

Any time I'd seen Death, he'd always appeared in his full, viciously dark form, rattling my nerves with his proximity as if he could sway my stubborn will to his own. The shadows that peeked from the ground had been different. A collection of sorts, but not what I'd experienced with Death.

Orin was a killer. The single thing he'd claimed to hate me for, yet there was darkness in him. A hypocritical, murderous darkness. I'd seen it in his eyes when we'd fought. I'd heard it in the raspy tone of his deep voice when he'd said he hated me.

Erratic thoughts howled in my mind. Since the moment that man had stepped foot into my bedroom, everything had changed, and nothing made sense. Aside from the violent and sometimes disgusting nature of the general population, everything I'd come to know of life and people had been decimated. Iron truth wrapped around my heart. None could kill, apart from the Death Maiden, and there could be only one. Me.

But I couldn't deny what I'd just seen.

Before I knew where I was going, I hauled my tired body to a rooftop and started moving. Spiraling. Running through everything I knew of life and death. Could Orin somehow be the Life Maiden, and had he twisted that magic? A life lord? On and on I walked, leaping from roof to roof after crossing the Hallowed River. With no destination, only a desire for truth, I found myself standing across from Misery's End, staring into the crowd of lingering people, eager to step inside the Maestro's show, if not for the entertainment, then to bathe in the intoxicating magic seeping down the walls.

I crouched on my perch, watching as the crowd dwindled, feeding into Misery's End. Orin was bound by magic to Drexel. The blue band around his arm had proven that. He'd likely have to be here before the show started if he was indeed a performer, but trusting anything from his mouth would be foolish. Orin was keeping secrets, and I desperately needed to know why. If he couldn't be of Death, because that role was taken, then maybe a pawn for the God of Life. And that's why no one could find the missing Maiden. She wasn't a woman, as she'd always been in the past, but a man. And maybe Drexel had found someone with the power to twist or reverse magic, and he'd used it on Orin. What better skill to give a lackey than murder in an immortal world?

My heart hammered into my throat as all the pieces fell into place. There'd been talk that Drexel had made a deal with Death a long time ago. And though some questioned it, this revelation seemed to prove it. And what a discovery it was.

Curiosity forced me down the building, pushing me to make reckless decisions as I circled Misery's End, looking for a way in. I couldn't walk through the front door. I'd made too many enemies to be impetuous. With no idea whose eyes would be searching for me, nor Orin's influence over the rest of the workers, I had to tread lightly. Especially when the Maestro was still the biggest threat.

I'd known about the window in the back when I'd considered all escape routes while plotting to kill King Ellis. The problem was, I didn't know how well it was guarded. The warehouse behind Misery's End was my next option. I'd seen many performers enter and never exit, leading me to believe there must have been a tunnel between the two buildings running beneath the street. But minutes before a show started, it was likely packed with performers. Including a certain dark-haired, brooding husband of mine.

With two options, the theater's window or crossing the street to the warehouse, I decided to take my chances against the guards and focus on the window. I could get to the top of the building and leap down onto the sill. Then I'd have to decide from there the best route.

I wasn't expecting the voices coming from the rooftop as I held the drainpipe firmly, steadying myself the second I heard shouting.

"You do not make decisions within or outside of these walls. Am I understood? You are mine." Though the voice was missing his usual flair, there was no mistaking the Maestro's tone or his composed fury.

I couldn't hear the response, only the shuffle of several sets of feet. Discovering what was happening was not worth the risk of being seen by a man who collected people as prisoners, as thralls, as bodies forced to do his bidding. I hunkered down, willing my heart to silence until the voices receded and the cool night air was my only companion. Even then, I waited for my muscles to protest and the music to come alive before climbing the rest of the way up and landing as silently as possible, side-stepping the fresh blood pooled on the roof near a door. It would certainly be guarded, though. I'd have to use the window.

I crept to the sidewall of the massive building, hiding behind the twisted iron railing. I peeked between the spindles to be sure no one was watching before swinging myself over the top, barely missing the sharpened finial across my ribs. Gripping tight, I held on, praying until my boot tips met the ridge of the window without shattering the glass.

But I wasn't lucky. The ledge was too narrow, and, had the music not been at a crescendo, the sound of the break would have been heard for blocks. As it was, I had no choice but to swing myself into the theater and prepare for damage control. I landed lightly, crouching to cushion the fall with my hood as far forward as possible. The room was so dark, I couldn't make out a thing, but it smelled of clean leather and maybe a hint of blood. I pressed my back to the wall and quickly felt my way down it, kicking a bookcase before reaching the doorknob. Holding my breath, I pressed an ear to the wood, but there was nothing to be heard beyond the heart-pounding music.

Falling to my stomach, I watched through the crack below the door, seeing two sets of boots standing across the narrow hallway. And a third with feet facing me. I had half a second to roll away before the door swung inward. Using the lack of light to my advantage, with nowhere to go, I jumped to my toes and hid behind the open door.

Somewhere in the room, a light turned on, and I held my breath behind the mask, hoping it was anyone but the Maestro. Seconds turned into minutes, minutes into an eternity as the music flowed and stopped on a dramatic note, followed by an uproarious applause. The Maestro's theater voice seeped into his office as he promised the crowd the end of tonight's show would be something they'd never forget. Likely, a repeated promise from the skilled showman with a golden tongue.

The second round of applause muted as the room's visitor walked back out, shutting the door. They'd left the light on, though, illuminating the office in a deep, warm glow. Tapestries covered the walls in tightly woven masterpieces of our world's history before the old gods abandoned us. I glanced over most, having seen similar works before, but an aged map caught my attention.

I studied the intricate details woven into the fabric. Among the familiar streets of our two cities, though they were much larger in these former times, each temple was marked with precision, and the names of the gods and goddesses whispered to me from the ancient threads. In a lower corner of Silbath set the grand temple of Verus, God of Illusions, its golden rays wavering, stretching toward the heavens. Nearby, Serene, the Goddess of Loss and Lust's temple, stood with its silver adornments glistening in the moonlight.

Further across the map, several blocks away from what I knew to be the Scarlet District, the temple of Eiria, Goddess of Life, Truth, and Reflection, was depicted—a place where prayers were offered for health and fertility. I moved my fingers over the tightly woven threads, wondering if I could find any clues about the Life Maiden in that temple. I pressed on to find another nestled in a secluded grove, hidden from prying eyes: The temple of Irri, God of Broken Things.

There wasn't a person alive who could tell you which fallen temple belonged to which god or goddess. Perhaps aside from the Maestro, who kept his map displayed like artwork. There were so many temple ruins in the city that most had been forgotten. A space we'd seen but never explored until our minds told us to forget they were there, as the old gods had done to Requiem.

After scanning the otherwise vacant office, I moved back to the door, peeking below to examine the hallway, or what I could see of it in my very limited view. Empty. As if those from before were not guards for the Maestro, but instead, keeping watch for whoever had snuck in. I cursed myself for not paying more attention as I slipped out. A woman's pure and powerful voice became the ambiance as I crept down the hall, turned into a dark passage deeper into the theater, and found myself sandwiched between two thick, black pieces of fabric.

The heat of the spotlights, the smell of the dusty curtains, the creak of the wood floor...

Shit. Shit. Shit.

I'd accidentally stumbled backstage. Moving as the reticent killer of this world, careful not to touch either curtain, I inched down and around until I came to the side stage. If I stepped into the light, those working would see me. If I stayed here and the curtains were pulled for any reason, I'd be seen by everyone else.

I quickly ripped the mask from my face, shoved my hood back, and hopped into a small gathering of women, all dressed in high heels and corsets with feathers in their hair and deep red lipstick, watching whatever was happening on stage more intently than they were their own surroundings. Using that to my advantage, I swiped a hand fan and feather boa from a cart nearby, and walked with a purpose, as if I had all the right in the world to be there.

The power that seeped through the Maestro's theater was palpable. I could feel it in every step I took away from the stage, drawing me back as if I were somehow linked. Could he have two forms of magic? He was most notoriously known for his contractual binding, the blue bands around the wrists of those indebted to him, but could he have a second power? Magic was so rare. Why would that be?

There were, of course, the Life and Death Maidens, and Lady Visha and her binding, which was also odd. Why would there be two with that power? And then Ro with her mirrors, and certain people had been rumored to have other forms. Strength and speed and skills in cooking and building. One woman claimed to speak to the birds, but she'd lost her mind and had been locked away long ago, the second she started claiming Death was not the savior we'd made him out to be. Those were dangerous words when this world was his domain. Though now, I wondered just how wrong she really was.

No one paid much attention to me as I hustled through. A familiar voice caught my ear, but I didn't look at Althea. If she knew I was here, she might tell Orin, and I wasn't ready for him just yet. I needed more answers.

"Are you lost, Little Dove?" An old man's soft voice halted me.

Keeping my face down, I shook my head and tried to shuffle away.

He called again. "You're headed straight toward the boss. Come this way."

The most impeccably dressed old man I'd ever seen in my life clasped his hands together, eyes beseeching. Though his hair was hidden beneath the firm brim of a violet top hat, his bushy white eyebrows gave away the color. He held a respectful hand over the heart of his finely pressed green suit, the trim detailing done in a beautiful golden hue.

"Not to worry, Little Dove, I'll get you the best seat in the house." He lowered his voice. "Come now. Before you're caught somewhere you ought not to be."

I opened my mouth to say something rude, but the pink in his cheeks and genuine smile halted me. I could trust no one. Least of all, a man who likely had a blue band on his arm, but he hadn't sounded an alarm or called for backup yet, and that was enough for me. I wasn't afraid to face the Maestro if it came to it. But I was cautious.

"Thank you," I answered, my voice unsteady as he gestured down a small hall to the right.

He tugged on a long golden chain, revealing a finely etched pocket watch he clicked open. "You'll want to hurry. The lights will turn off for fifteen seconds at the conclusion of this song.

Take the third seat in the fourth row and don't sit down until everyone else around you does."

I hustled, following his directions exactly until I reached the door at the end of the hall.

The old man threw his hand out. "Wait for the song to end."

"Why would you help me?" I asked.

He pulled the hat from his head and placed it over his heart. "Because my younger sister was your predecessor, Maiden. Your burdens are heavy."

The lights fell with my jaw.

"Go," he barked from the dark. "Fifteen seconds."

There could have been a team of guards waiting for me on the other side of that door. There could have been a magical menace, or even a scorned king, but instead, it was simply the audience, bathed in shadow, breaths held for whatever dramatic event the Maestro might have been concocting. I slipped into the exact seat I was directed, standing with the crowd until purple lights flooded the black stage, and everyone roared in applause as two women stood, back-to-back, with chests heaving and swords raised high.

I sat when the crowd did, expecting my view to be obstructed this close to the stage, but this particular spot sat at just the right height and angle to have a clear, glorious view. The orchestra crept to life, starting their melody as a single note, then growing until my heart was racing in tune with the show, timed with each dangerous step of the women sword fighting on the stage in the most beautifully choreographed dance. They traced their fingers up each other's bodies, having undressed until they were nearly bare. They'd wiggled and laughed and put on an alluring, erotic show. And I loved it. I'd felt my fingers twitching, wishing I could meet them. Touch them.

It took me three more songs, including one with the woman falling from the ceiling again before I noticed the little girl in the birdcage, watching as a patron and not a part of it, licking a sucker, her legs swaying back and forth from the swing dangling in the middle of her tiny prison.

Her wild brown hair was a calling card. A halo of perfect curls that might have swallowed her whole one day. She was dressed in a fine gown, emphasizing her light blue eyes against olive skin, even from this distance. She would have fit right into my father's court. I studied the audience more than the performers now, but no one seemed to notice the child. The woman next to me glanced over to see what I was watching. It was as if her eyes had passed right over her.

The theater fell into darkness again. If not for the ominous boots crossing the stage, then the sharp clack of the cane gave away the Maestro seconds before a single crimson spotlight poured over him. His eyes scanned the audience as he plastered a sinister smile across his face, twisting his red mustache at the tip with a pristine, white-gloved hand.

"Ladies and gentlemen, esteemed patrons of Misery's End, gather around. For tonight, we are about to embark on a journey like no other. Let me regale you with a tale of old gods and legends, a story of how they once graced our world, only to turn away, leaving us to fend for ourselves when we were ravished by war and dying.

"But fear not, for when the gods abandoned us to bloodshed, Death himself appeared with a grand proposition. He bestowed upon us a gift, a boon of immortality for a hundred years, ensuring that we may revel in the splendors of life without the fear of its inevitable end. Death is our savior, our mighty god. But, my dear audience, even he is indebted to me." A deep chuckle left his throat as he let the gasps fill the space, relishing in every second of his theatrics. "Did I promise you a spectacle unlike anything you've ever witnessed? Did I promise you violence?"

The crowd began to cheer, and as those vicious eyes swept toward me, I clapped, though I kept my face cast as far down as possible, heart thundering as he spoke of Death's debt, confirming my theory of Orin's twisted power, or so it seemed.

"Is my audience not interested?" He pretended to pout, turning away. The crowd tripled in volume, stomping and clapping and screaming for the Maestro. Just as he'd wanted. A master manipulator.

"Oh, there you are." He tossed his head back and laughed so loud, so guttural, it must have shaken the rafters. "You seek disorder tonight, and I shall deliver. Behold, a show that will set your hearts ablaze and stir your souls to dance in the dangerous embrace of fear. We shall summon forth the very essence of the Death Court, and from the depths, a hellhound, a creature of myth and terror, a manifestation of our deepest desires and darkest fears, shall appear. They say you should never look him in the eyes. But can you resist?"

My heart did not beat. My breaths did not come. He could not really mean that Death's hound would appear. The beast of nightmares would devour this entire theater. I gripped the edges of my seat, dread turning my skin ice cold as the Maestro's gaze finally landed upon me, and absolute delight filled his dark eyes. As if he spoke to me alone, as if he walked down that platform, stood before me, and shoved his hand into my chest, just to be sure I knew he had seen me.

"Orin Faber, bonded husband to Death's precious Maiden, please join me on stage."

CHAPTER 17

ased on the way Orin's shirt clung to his side, it was clear he'd been the one attacked on the rooftop, and Drexel and his henchmen hadn't bothered to stop the bleeding. I watched from my seat as my prick of a husband stood ramrod straight, staring at the back of the theater as if the red spotlight held him in place. But the bruises were there upon his face, and the wound in his thigh still dripped blood. And though he was dressed for the show, black coat with tails and a fresh peony stuck into his chest pocket, he looked like complete shit.

My gaze found the hands that had washed my hair so tenderly, the mouth that whispered his hatred, the eyes that burned into mine. Orin Faber was a conundrum. A murderer and liar. He'd ruined the trajectory of my entire life. Perhaps he deserved to stand before Death's hound. Especially if he was hiding the power of Life and letting this world go to waste. But he didn't feel like my counterpart. He wasn't the balance. Just the thorn.

The Maestro gestured to his side, and the kind old man who'd led me to my seat struggled onto the stage, carrying a cello that was taller than he was and likely heavier. He glanced at the little girl in the cage and managed a very subtle shake of his head, but she'd turned away, her sucker loose in her fingers as dread filled her tiny face. She opened the door to her cage, sneaking out, and somehow, no one had noticed. She might as well have been a wraith.

"Please," the Maestro said to Orin. "Play for your audience."

The beautiful man did not balk or flinch or even scowl. Orin simply swept his coattails to the side and sat before the instrument, taking the bow from the old man, who then scurried off the stage.

The world faded away as that first haunted chord pierced the silent theater. The magic of Misery's End pulsed, enrapturing the crowd as Orin leaned into his cello, closed his eyes, and graced the world with his exquisite, tormented melody. His hands moved as if he wasn't dripping blood, his face, that stunning fucking face, changed, feeling each and every note, coating the theater in his song. He was a performer. But at this moment, he was also a god. Transcending time. Taking every one of us to a place no one deserved. With a song. A lament.

Tears filled my eyes, and I could not wipe them away. I couldn't move. Only feel the burn of our bond pulsing in my wrist, telling my heart, no matter the history between us, that man was mine. If only for these few precious moments before reality returned. He was a disaster. But so was I.

The woman in the chair next to me gripped my hand. I jerked, the spell Orin had spun, breaking. Only then did I see the fiery ruby eyes. Only then did I remember Drexel's promise.

My heart dropped into my throat as the violation of the theater's magic had once again controlled me. I hated it. All of it, but I could not look away as a giant black hellhound moved from the shadows, each paw, each massive claw, digging into the stage as he padded forward, straight for Orin.

I believed the man to be so lost in his song that he had no idea of the danger he was in, but a scream from off-stage ripped him back to reality just in time for him to roll from his seat and watch as Death's hound pulverized his precious cello.

He wasn't as lucky the second time. The claws of the hound collided with his stomach, ripping into his skin so thoroughly the tear was not a sound anyone here would forget. And, just as I expected the audience to protest in horror, a great round of applause and cheering rattled me.

But that sound, that horrifying sound was muted by the deep, jarring growl of the beast. Two men and five women, one of them Althea Washburn, appeared on the stage, holding groupings of golden bars. It wasn't until they moved in, their faces horrified, Althea's stained with tears, that I realized what they meant to do. Coming together as one, they trapped Orin in a pop-up prison, stealing any chance of escaping from Death's hound.

"No." The word left my lips in a whisper, though I didn't mean to make a sound.

The woman beside me finally turned to look. All color left her face as she realized who sat beside her. She was more scared of me than the beast meant to butcher beyond repair.

Orin's back collided with the cage, and the audience began to boo him, desperate for a show. He ducked and rolled, dodging the snap of venomous jaws, but the audience only grew louder. Heart pounding, I looked over my shoulder at the exit. If I stood and walked out, who would notice? Who would peel their attention from the mutilation of a man?

Looking back at Orin, who stood only to the beast's shoulder, blood dripped. His bruised face stared at the hound, feigning right, moving left, just as another swipe came for him. When the beast's paw hit the stage, Death's shadows billowed out in a cloud, smothering Orin.

His scream was the last straw, my complete breaking point as I rose from my chair, audience be damned, and stormed to the back of the theater, throwing the doors open, no matter how much that toxic magic tried to pull me back in, and descended the stairs.

I almost made it to the front, my peaceful escape, before I was stopped by the woman with one green and one blue eye. Apart from her beauty, it was her most recognizable feature. Paesha, they'd called her. "Going somewhere, Maiden?"

"Get the fuck out of my way before I drop you where you stand."

I hadn't seen the little girl until she stepped out from behind the woman, clutching her hand.

"She doesn't mean it, does she, Paesha?"

The woman's deadly smile was a contradiction to the lace corset and the row of feathers that showed off every inch of her long, golden legs. "I think she does."

"She absolutely does." I scowled, drawing my knife and holding it to the woman's throat before she had time to blink. "I will not repeat myself."

She stepped backward, pushing the blade away with a finger. "I don't think Orin's mother will appreciate the fact that her knife was just pressed to my throat."

"You say that as if I should care."

She made a weak attempt to take the knife. The little girl gasped, and in three steps, I had Paesha's back slammed against the wall.

"Rule number one, asshole. Never try to take a knife from Death's Maiden."

She seethed, eerie eyes narrowing. "The Maestro has summoned you, King Slayer."

"The Maestro can kiss my perky ass." I left her standing as I walked out of the theater.

A gift.

CHAPTER 18

The Syndicate house looked far less daunting when I returned of my own accord. The patchwork rooms on the exterior seemed to fit better in the moonlight. The lean silhouette of Orin's mother could be seen from the tree line. She sipped a drink, staring off at nothing.

I walked toward the home without hiding myself, keeping my hood down and the mask in a cowl around my neck. Maybe I wasn't truly welcome here, but I had questions. A million of them, and if tonight was any indication, though they were bound to the Maestro, they were not his family. They probably didn't even like him.

"You came back," his mother said. Not a question. "Have you eaten?"

I shook my head, playing the part of an innocent woman in need.

"There's dinner on the table. Help yourself."

She stepped to the side, and I hesitated, staring at a home that'd been my prison twice.

"If you eat and leave before they come home, I won't tell

them you were here."

"Why would you do that?"

Smoothing a finger over the rim of her chipped teacup, she said, "We feed who we can and care for those that need it. This home will never know a stranger. But maybe you should ask yourself why you came back instead."

I considered her question as I walked past her, directly to the kitchen, and picked up two slices of bread on the table to make a sandwich. I knew why I'd come back. Orin had killed a man and shouldn't have been able to. The old man... had helped me, and I didn't know why. I wasn't sure if he lived here, but the child was a link to Paesha, and she was here with Orin. Althea had called this a Syndicate house. And I'd do whatever it took to unwrap the mystery circling my dear, sweet husband. Because that asshole had stabbed me. And apparently, I could have died.

I could have died.

Sighing, I let my shoulders drop. He hadn't patched me up or washed my hair because there was something good in him. He'd done it because if I died, when his friends knew he was the one who'd stabbed me, they would also know he was a killer. I couldn't believe I hadn't put it together before the Maestro's show. He might've been the Lord of Life in hiding, but he was still a prick.

"There's tea," Orin's mother said. "I'll pour you a cup."

I plastered a smile on my face to hide the sneer. "That's so kind. Thank you."

The front door squeaked open, and a man I'd seen once before, the giant Black man with a long tan jacket, weapons on his side, and dirt coating his hair, poked his head into the kitchen. "Orin?"

She answered with a shake of her head, and he gave a curt nod before stepping back out. He hadn't even knocked.

"Do you see that band on your wrist? You are my child now,

like it or not."

"I wasn't aware I needed a new parent." The second the words were out of my mouth, I bit the inside of my cheek, cursing my snarky tongue. I could only push so hard before the welcome wore off, and I needed to be here. Though I was beginning to think they'd take any riffraff off the street to support whatever their cause was.

She set her cup down, gathering her hair in her hands to tie it back. "Where are your parents now? Where is your family? Where are your friends, Deyanira?"

My cheeks flushed, anger surging to life. I stepped toward the door.

"I don't say those things to hurt you. You've already been invited to stay here, and it seems you have no one."

I wanted to scream at her. To remind her that she didn't know a single thing about me beyond her own misconceptions. But I could play my part, be the demure daughter of a fallen king and not Death's Maiden.

"Thank you for the welcome."

She walked toward me, curtsying as low and refined as anyone I'd ever seen, though she wore no gown. "My name is Elowen Faber, and I give you my name as a peace offering, child. Do with it what you will."

With her eyes cast down, something about the curtsy felt like an abomination. I had no right to that, and she and I both knew it.

"The knowledge of the name makes no difference to Death's selection. Prepare your heart all the same, Elowen Faber. Your son won't enter this house the same way he left."

I walked out to the sound of her falling the rest of the way to the floor.

The sandwich in my stomach churned as I sank into the darkness on the side of the house opposite the moon, seeking the comfort of my lonely shadows. Hours passed. Elowen returned to her stoop, her breathing normal, but I could see the subtle way she fidgeted. I wondered if she'd waited for him every night there was a show. If she'd worried, as I'd heard mothers did, every second until he was under the safety of this ramshackle roof. I wondered most of all if she knew he was a murderer. And how he came to have such power.

After some time, she sat on the first step, bathing in the moonlight. Watching stoically. And though I debated it, preferring the solitude, eventually I gave up and joined her, sitting vigilant as we both stared at that tree line. Waiting. Her for comfort and me for answers. It would have been the perfect time to search the house, had she not been there.

"When Orin was a boy, he would race up and down those trees, fighting imaginary villains," she said, likely to fill the growing silence. "He swore to always protect me, and he's never backed down on that promise."

I said nothing, though I didn't think she wanted me to, anyway.

"When he was a teen, barely a man at all, he made a deal with the devil and followed through on his boyish promise. Freeing me from the Maestro and giving his life instead. I'd spent so many years tied to that man. Freedom was the only thing I'd ever wished for my son, and he'd given it away."

My head snapped to her. "He bargained his whole life?"

"Not quite all, but most. Before the show, before the theatrics of it all, Drexel was just a man. He'd have moments that made him a monster, but I think we all do. Things turned dark, and he began collecting people. Turning to crime to get what he wanted. Your father threatened to imprison him, and because that wasn't a war Drexel wanted, he created his gods-damned show instead. Slowly seeping money away from this kingdom and your father's."

"And building his own."

She nodded. "I wouldn't be surprised to see a blue band around the wrist of Icharius Fern. Drexel has never been one for the politics of it all, but he's loved every coin that has ever fallen into his hands. Every person, to a degree. He loves to flaunt his power and the things he collects. Sometimes I think he wants to conquer Requiem. But other times, I realize he just likes the chase. I don't think he's ever cared to be worth his death. He's always wanted the spotlight, instead."

I wanted to ask how she knew so much about him, but the answer was obvious. And likely one she wouldn't openly share. She must have loved him. Any and all information was a tool, a weapon to be collected, though. So, I considered how I might broach the question.

We heard the ruckus before we ever saw them. Althea screamed for Elowen to clear off the table. Two small horses burst from the tree line, dragging a reluctant cart behind them. A parade of people ran for the house.

"Oh, gods," she cried, leaping to her feet and dashing inside.

I moved to the far end of the porch, gripping the railing as the cart came to a halt, and the giant man lifted Orin's limp body, carrying him inside. Paesha was next, then sobbing Althea and the child. I didn't notice the little white dog with long brown ears until a cold nose pressed into my hand. Several more somber faces followed.

"Come on, Boo," the old man said, slapping his thigh until the dog turned, darting into the home.

The second everyone crossed the threshold to the house, I flung myself over the railing and climbed until I stood on the balcony I'd jumped from on our wedding night. The window was still broken, the sheer curtains tumbling in the wind. I took a step before seeing a cello in the corner. Far more worn than the one he'd played so beautifully on that stage.

I crept inside Orin's room, but without being able to turn on a lamp, there was hardly anything more to discern than what my memory held. Sliding a hand between the mattress and the bed frame, I sought Chaos but came out empty-handed. I found a blade beneath the pillow, but it wasn't mine. There was nothing behind the mirror or any of the dusty art on the wall.

The creak of worn steps was my only warning before the knob turned. I dashed under the bed, confident if anyone had been paying close enough attention, they would have seen me. But Althea had come and gone within minutes.

Orin's bedroom held no answers. And Chaos was still missing. With nowhere else to go, I climbed to the roof of the Syndicate home. Three chairs sat gathered in the corner of the flattened portion of the rooftop, surrounded by more black railings. Lying on my back, just above the open balcony, I watched the stars in the sky, wondering how my life had gotten to this point. As the mist grew thicker, the clouds covered the clear night, rain threatening to pour down. Voices trailed up from Orin's bedroom.

"Careful," Althea hissed.

"Back off, buttercup. He's got to lay him down." The sharp edge of Paesha's tone was unmistakable.

"I still don't understand why." Althea's voice was quieter than before.

"Don't be ridiculous, Thea. He married the Death Maiden. He stole the king's bride. Then refused to turn her over. We had a godsdamned plan, and he fucked it all up."

"Paesha." The old man's soft voice was hardly audible. "Whatever your plan, it was reckless. And speaking ill of the Death Maiden as she lurks around this house is dangerous. Even for you, Huntress."

Huntress?

"Well, I don't really care if she hears me, Hollis. Do you hear that, Maiden? Come down from your fucking perch."

I could almost picture those mismatched eyes glaring at me from the window.

But if Paesha was the famed Huntress... if she could use her magic to locate things and people... she could find the Life Maiden. Maybe she already had. Maybe she'd been the one to tell the Maestro about Orin. If I could crack this, convince him to help the people, then I'd finally contribute to this world. Something stirred within me, confirming this was my purpose. I needed to be here. Requiem needed balance.

The distraction of his injuries might have been a good time to slip inside and look around the house, but if I were caught on the first night, I'd never get back in, and, more than anything, I needed to tread carefully around Paesha. There was no way she hadn't used her magic to seek out the Life Maiden. I desperately needed whatever information she had. Surely, if it were my husband, she would know.

"We can do this later." The gruff voice of that large man felt weak compared to Paesha's fierceness.

"Jarek is right," Elowen said, ripping me from my thoughts. "This isn't the time. Orin needs peace."

Minutes of silence passed. Eventually, the door clicked shut. He lived, then. That was a mercy. Though I wasn't sure whose.

Orin began moaning. The guttural sound so wretched, I wondered if the hellhound actually did hold the power of Death's harbingers. Maybe he hadn't escaped fate quite yet. I thrummed my fingers against the rooftop in time with the raindrops, wondering if I was listening to my bonded husband die. The gash in my abdomen had sealed once more, thanks to his attention, but it hadn't healed as much as I would have thought, had he truly been born of life with the power opposite of mine. The ache remained.

I stood, staring up at the small patches of moon peeking out from behind the weeping clouds until I was soaked through. Even then, I waited several moments more before climbing down to the balcony and sneaking back into Orin's room.

His face had only been scratched. Nothing new plagued him beyond the bruising and gash he'd had when he walked onto that stage. Standing here, listening to the moans plague him, the pain audible, my thoughts mimicked his friends. Why had he married me knowing he would piss off his master and equally destroy his own life?

The bandages around his chest might have started white, but the patch of blood was growing. I stared at the hands of a killer, remembering the way they felt on my throat only feet away from where I stood. Orin killed because he could, not because he had to, and that was the difference between him and me. Likely, every life he'd taken had been pinned on me, and I hadn't known about a single one.

The gold band on his wrist, a twin to my own, sat just below the blue one, intersecting a vine tattoo creeping up his bare arm and covering his shoulder. The sharp turn of his jaw and the way he held his eyes tightly shut, even while sleeping, called to me. This was the man who'd stood in my castle bedroom and promised me the world. But this was also that man'd who buried a blade in my gut and locked me in a room.

"I hate you," he mumbled, an eye peeking open. "You're the worst mistake of my life."

I positioned myself over him, our faces inches apart as his blood dripped onto the floor in a perfect rhythm.

"Hate is such a cruel word, Husband."

He shifted. His movement wasn't fast, but I waited, letting him pull the blade from beneath his pillow and press it into my ribs.

I leaned closer, the sharp tip ripping my shirt. "Do it. I dare you."

CHAPTER 19

"He's bleeding again," I told the crowd of concerned faces as they watched me walk to the front door of the Syndicate house. "You wrapped the ribs too tight, and he can't breathe. That's why he's moaning. Your bandage isn't going to do it. You'll have to cauterize the wound."

"Absolutely not." Paesha leaped from her seat in the small sitting room full of mismatched furniture and a patterned rug tamped down to its last days. "That's dangerous."

I rested my hand on the knob, considering my words carefully. "Unless you know for sure the hellhound cannot kill in this world, he's on the brink. I know what death smells like. And even if they can't, if they are somehow bound to the same rules as the rest of Requiem, his skin will remain shredded unless you bind it together. At the very least, he needs to be stitched."

She shifted toward me, a fight in her hands and fury in her eyes. But she said nothing else. Instead, she turned. "Hollis, start a fire." Her voice softened as she faced the little girl and her dog. "Quill, take Boo and go to your room. Practice your singing, okay? Cover your ears."

"No." The child set her glare. "I can help. I'm not afraid."

"It is not your fear that we're protecting, Quilly. It's your innocence. Go on now," the old man said, kneeling before the child.

She turned, patting her leg for the dog to follow. "Come on, Boo. We're gettin' the boot."

"Where are you going?" Althea asked, as I twisted away once more.

"Anywhere but here," I answered, opening the door and walking out.

The rooftop of the Syndicate house was soaking wet. The rain had poured down as thunder boomed and lightning cracked across the sky. It hadn't muted the screams, though. Nor the smell of burning flesh that wafted up from below. I rubbed my palm, all too familiar with that putrid scent.

"Why would you choose to stay up here rather than in the house?" Althea's question hadn't surprised me. I'd heard the rooftop door squeak open.

"I don't understand any of you." I watched the rain fall, darkening her hair to a coppery hue. "There hasn't been a single explanation as to why Orin married me, why he tried to kill me, why I was captured, why I was locked up, why I'm just allowed to be free now, or why you expect me to stay. I don't know why I'm still here. Curiosity, I guess."

"You have nowhere else to go. That's why we're all here. This house is a refuge for those who need it. A meeting hall for others. But Orin does things for his own reasons, and we can't speak for him. If he didn't want you to be here, you wouldn't be. That's enough for me."

I crossed the roof to stand before her, rain dripping from my lashes. "Why did he marry me?"

"Why did you marry him is the better question."

"I married him because he lied. He tricked me. Now, answer at least one of my questions."

"If I do, will you come out of the rain?"

Frustration grew inside me, the swell of defiance growing. I balled my fist and turned away. "You people are insufferable."

"Then go. Because no one is sleeping with you lurking around on the roof anyway. We all know who you are. We feel what you're capable of in our own ways. But Hollis says there's still a soul in your body and we should try. So, we are trying. For Orin."

"Hollis has fond memories of a sister with a terrible history. Whatever he has built in his own mind to make her murders okay, he's wrong."

"He watched his mother die and his sister, Dahlia, turn into a monster. He never said she was a good person." Althea stepped toward me, grabbing my hands, her calluses rough against my own. The human contact jolted through me. "He only said you still have a soul, and I don't think he's wrong, Deyanira."

"Until your name shows on my palm."

A twinkle lit her eyes. "You wouldn't care about that if you were truly a monster."

"I don't," I lied.

"Come inside, Deyanira. Sleep in a warm, dry bed. Find your own place tomorrow if you want, but don't stand out here in the rain, circling your own misery. This world has enough of that."

I let her pull me into the house. Let her guide me through a dimly lit hall and down a set of stairs. Not because I was weak and lonely, as I'd let her believe, but because this was exactly where I needed to be to start searching for answers.

She pointed, her voice barely a whisper. "That's Orin's room, remember."

"I'm smarter than I look."

"Perfect." She gestured to a set of wooden stairs without reacting to my sarcasm. "Down there's Paesha's room, next to mine. You wake her before the sun comes up and she'll eat you alive. And you can have this room. It's nothing special, but it's yours if you want it. At least until Orin comes and kicks you out."

She smiled as she opened the door, and I forced one of my own. Maybe that was her sarcasm peeking through. A faint creak outside the room moments after she'd left was the only sign that Althea had crept away, leaving me to my own thoughts once more. I checked the brass knob twice to make sure she hadn't locked me in. The air was heavy with the masculine scent of musk buried with age, as if the room had been sealed off from the world for far too long.

My fingers brushed against the cool, weathered wood of the bed frame. The texture was rough, yet there was a certain elegance to its design, hinting at its former grandeur. I imagined the man who once occupied this room had a taste for finer things. But they'd said this house was a place for people to come and go as they needed, so maybe it was the composition of many and not one man in particular.

I woke to shouting in the hall. To Paesha and Althea screaming at one another. But when I swung my door open and found Orin standing in the frame of his own, pants hung loose on his hips, a fresh bandage wrapped around his chest, tucked all the way to his armpits, everything in the world went silent.

"Ah," he said as he grunted. "Now it makes sense. You might want to find a different room if you don't want to wake up with a knife in your chest."

"Since when do you care if I'm a pin cushion?" I asked, crossing my arms. "And how are you standing right now? You should be fighting for your life."

His eyes scanned me, lingering on the bottom of my shirt

before I remembered I wasn't wearing pants. "I don't care. And let's call it residual adrenaline from being burned, which I'm told was your idea. Did you stay just to watch?"

"Yes," I snapped, walking back into the borrowed bedroom. "Your screams sang me to sleep, asshole."

He somehow managed a dark chuckle over the sound of the door slamming.

CHAPTER 20

I stared into the gold mirror hanging in the Syndicate house, wondering about Ro. Wondering if all mirrors would call to her or only special ones. I hadn't thought to ask, had never needed to know. Lifting a hand to test the magic, I was nearly there before I hesitated and drew my fingers away from the ornate filigree adorning the sides. I'd never gotten it right. How to have relationships with people. How to judge the sincerity of someone's words. I understood the feelings, though. The way Ro's attention had eased a broken part of my soul and how turning me away had wrecked other parts. Our friendship had always been on her terms. Only hers. Whether she would see me or speak to me depended on her mood. Maybe that's how it was supposed to be, but maybe it wasn't. Maybe it was supposed to be something more like Althea and Paesha, who'd screamed at each other this morning for over an hour, but now sat together on the front porch of this patchwork house, laughing, and talking like true friends while Quill chased that white dog through the open field before the tree line.

There'd been a meeting of some type behind closed doors just after breakfast. A few people came, and, though I'd tried to eavesdrop, Elowen had kept me in the kitchen, as was likely her only job. Something was happening around here, and the secrets were only stacking.

I walked away from that mirror, disappointed. I'd seen my father's eyes stare back at me in the reflection, and I could nearly hear his voice telling me to run. That these people, no matter how curious I was, would never really want me here, and I couldn't trust them. I knew in my bones I couldn't. I'd only be staying long enough to figure out why Orin had been able to kill a man. And if Paesha knew where the Life Maiden was, that was bonus information.

My reflection had been scary. Hair tangled, my face gaunt, I looked as if I'd aged twenty precious years in the last week. I stared at the dirt beneath my nails and wished for a bath more than anything. I was a mess. But I wasn't sure I could bring myself to use a public bathhouse. Not because I was shy, but because I couldn't be properly armed.

I crept down the stairs and into the kitchen, sneaking fruit from the counter. Elowen followed, her watchful eyes full of questions.

"I'm not taking your knife."

"An apple isn't going to sustain you for the day. I'll have dinner on the table at sundown. Don't be late."

"Oh, I'm not..." I didn't know what I was doing, actually. "Okay."

"Okay," she echoed.

"Do you know..." I looked down at my shirt. "It's just..."

"For heaven's sake, child, spit it out."

"These are my clothes, but I didn't bring them here. Do you know if I have others? Or where they came from?"

"No, but I bet Hollis will have something. He's in the garden out back."

I walked to the door, resting a hand on the knob. "Why aren't you afraid of me?"

She wiped her fingers on her apron with a laugh. "People have come and gone from this house for years, Maiden. Some stick around longer than others, some are dangerous, some are shy. Some are broken, some are healing. But all are human, and we have our own burdens and stories. The way I see it, you probably haven't been shown a lot of kindness in your life. I'm sure you don't quite know what to do with any of us. But we're only people, like you, trying to make the most of our situations. I am not afraid of you, only worried for my son and that power inside of you. But I think you have a story to tell, as well. And just maybe, you'll find a space here to share it."

I opened my mouth to respond, and nothing came out. I hated that I was feared, but there was comfort in the boundaries. Solace in the solitude. Her words were unnerving.

"The back door is down the other hall on the right."

Hollis, wrist-deep in dirt, was still impeccably dressed, wearing a leather wide-brim hat, though the clouds had lingered. When he saw me coming, he stood, wiping dirty hands on a cloth before pulling out his golden pocket watch to check the time. "Hello, Little Dove."

I wanted so desperately to ask about his sister. She was younger, but already gone. Had been gone for at least twenty-six years. Which meant she'd succumbed to the madness, and it devoured her. She'd killed too many, too fast, and had paid the ultimate price.

"This might seem strange, but Elowen thought you would have a change of clothes for me."

He stroked a thumb over his chin, gesturing for me to turn. I twisted slowly, feeling every bit the fool I must have seemed.

"I'm a tailor. Clothing is precisely the right thing to ask about. I have a simple outfit. Not your usual leather, I'm afraid, but I can make you something soon. Wait here."

As he made his way inside, his gait a bit slower than most, I knelt and continued pulling the weeds he'd been working on in the slightly overgrown garden. I didn't have a clue what I was doing, though, and when a particularly stubborn weed plopped out with a tiny carrot on the end, I jerked upright, glanced at the door to make sure no one was watching, and shoved it into my pocket. Taking three giant steps away, I tucked my hands behind my back and waited, content to leave the gardening to the old man.

He strode from the house with a gentle whistle, carrying a pile of neatly folded clothes. I didn't really care what they were, as long as they were clean and fit well enough.

"Just some pants and a buttoned shirt for you. I hoped you could manage the buttons with your wound."

"Oh, umm. It's not bothering me much today."

"Good. There's a river that runs along the east there, just over that small hill. It's private, and the water's usually still warm for a few more weeks before the frost sets in." He dug into his pocket and laid a bar of soap on top of the pile. "It isn't the nicest smelling, but it'll do. Most that come to stay for a bit use it, and I haven't had a complaint yet."

I didn't remember to thank him until I was already out of earshot.

The path leading to the riverbank was lined with lush vegetation, their leaves rustling in the gentle breeze. The scent of wildflowers and damp earth filled the air, rejuvenating my senses. Beyond the hill, just as he'd promised, in a small clearing, the river flowed serenely, shimmering like liquid silver under the scattered rays of sun battling the clouds.

The water's surface danced over rocks, with ripples enticing me to immerse myself in its cool embrace. I removed my clothes, feeling the weight of the world gradually lifted with each layer discarded. The air was slightly chilly, but I knew the river's touch would be revitalizing.

The riverbed beneath my feet was a symphony of smooth stones and soft silt, its texture grounding me to the earth. I waded until the water reached my waist, and then, with a graceful dive, I fully submerged myself in the refreshing stream, feeling only a small ache where I'd been stabbed.

The initial shock of the water's chill claimed a breath, but as I resurfaced, revitalized, I let out a contented sigh, my muscles relaxing. I ran my fingers through the water. The gentle current caressed my skin, carrying away the sweat and grime that'd plagued me.

I could have stayed in that river forever. Might have tried, had bickering voices not interrupted my stolen peace. I strained to listen, my heart quickening as I recognized the familiar timbre of Orin's voice. I whipped around just in time to see him and Paesha moving down the hill.

I covered my breasts with my hands as if they could see me from there. If I swam to the bank and managed to get out of the water fast enough, I still wouldn't be able to dress before they arrived. There was no escape here. I pressed myself against the partially submerged trunk of a fallen tree, its branches providing some concealment.

But when I'd emerged, keeping only my eyes and nose above the water, I watched as Orin gently shoved her backward, clearly agitated by her attempted help, until he'd barked something rude, and she'd flipped him off before storming away.

He watched her leave, waiting for her to fall beyond the cover of the hill, then moved to the edge of the riverbed and gripped the loose bottom of his shirt. A gentle breeze whispered through the leaves, as if the forest itself held its breath, anticipating what was to come. I should have looked away. But gods help me, the second that shirt came off, I couldn't move.

He dropped his pants just as quickly, and my thundering heart should have given me away. Utter perfection stood on the bank of that river, as if he'd been crafted as my personal punishment for every one of my sins. Orin Faber was an indulgence I'd never let myself experience.

The bandage had already been removed, and had I not been holding my breath, I might have gasped at the condition of the wounds on his side, still fiery red and swollen. Though you could see each individual slash from that hellhound across his stomach, he was far more healed than he should have been. Interesting. He couldn't be hiding the Life Maiden and simply visited her. He hadn't left that room. Not a single person had wandered in either. He was clearly still injured. Still slow to move. But something was off.

Orin's healing was not the only mysterious thing about him. In fact, it might have been the least concerning feature when he faced my direction, revealing a heart so black it showed through his skin. Even the surrounding veins had turned black, growing from his heart like vines. For a moment, I thought it might be the most beautiful, intricate tattoo I'd ever seen, until it throbbed.

As he dipped his foot into the cool river, ripples cascaded outward. He winced slightly, the water's temperature seemingly colder than he had anticipated, yet he continued. Once submerged, he let out a satisfying sigh, and my mouth turned dry, the air heavy.

He smoothed a hand down his chest, holding his palm over his heart, tilting his head back. The sun filtered through the canopy, painting a mosaic of golden hues on the rocky riverbed, the golden light kissing his beautiful face, though I could see the anguish there. What was he? Who was he?

The silt below my feet gave just a bit, causing me to sink. The rippling water, though subtle, might've given me away, had he been looking, but rather than being aware of his surroundings and using caution as most of Requiem did, he remained unmoving, lost in his simple peace, his head staring up to the heavens as if in prayer while running his hands down his pained face. He did not fear this world.

After several moments, he turned back to the bank and grabbed a bar of soap. With slow, deliberate movements, he washed himself, the suds creating a lather that clung to his skin. His long, nimble fingers traced patterns across his chest, and I found myself captivated by the way he cared for his body, every motion exuding a sense of tenderness. My own body responded, forcing me to remember what it was like to have those hands on me. I wanted desperately to turn away, but I could not tear my eyes from him. Each drip of water cascading down his broad chest called to me, and I hated it. He should have been ugly. Monsters always were. Though Death was just as beautiful, and he was the greatest monster of all.

Orin swam closer to the center of the river, lying back carefully until he floated, moving those fingers through the water in a rhythm that told me one of his songs must have been playing through his mind. As if the music he crafted came from a place like this. Tranquil and quiet.

The second his eyes closed again, I shifted my feet, fighting the way the deep mud in the river pulled me down. The rippling water nearly reached him, and I prepared to dive and hold my breath for an eternity, but before I could, he stood, whipping around to face me. "You can come out now, Wife. The show's over."

I jerked, absolute mortification seeping over me as a tingling sensation raced up my back and across my neck, no doubt turning every trace of skin as red as possible. But I couldn't let him have this moment of victory. Each sparring match with him, verbal or otherwise, was a battle, and I would not lose.

Embarrassed as I was, I swam forward just as close to the bank as he was, keeping my breasts below the surface as I boldly stared him in the eyes. "I wondered when you were going to stop fondling yourself so I could leave in peace."

He crossed his arms over his chest, spreading his legs a little further, as if daring me to look. "You know it shrinks in the water, right?"

"Feeling paranoid?"

The corner of his mouth twitched. "Just warning you, in case that pretty color on your neck means what I think it does."

"There is absolutely no way in the heavens or hell that I'm ever going to need that warning." I pushed out of the water unabashedly, walking with every ounce of confidence I could draw from this world. Stepping past him, completely naked and dripping wet, I gathered my hidden things while his jaw hung open. I walked back, ankle-deep in the water once more, closing his mouth with my finger as I growled. "You'd have to get on your fucking knees and beg for it. And even then, I'd rather see you devoured by a hellhound."

He struck hard and fast, gripping my throat as darkness filled his eyes. "There she is." His fingers tightened until I could hardly swallow. "I wondered when you'd come out to play, Nightmare."

I forced a smile. "I'll happily come back to remind you who I am when you can stand up straight."

"It's just a scratch."

I grabbed his wrist and twisted. He gave in too easily, breaking contact because he didn't have the strength to fight beyond the pain of his injuries.

"Funny. Your scratch is bleeding again."

He looked down, and I took the opportunity to storm off, his growl of annoyance following me back over that hill, though he did not.

After dressing outside, I hustled to Orin's bedroom. I had three, maybe four minutes before I was sure he would come waltzing in, but he had Chaos hiding somewhere, hopefully in this house, and I aimed to find her. She wouldn't sit properly above the door frame, but I dragged my fingers over the ledge anyway. I rummaged through his clothes several times, noting how he kept his performance attire hanging and the rest of his clothing neatly folded. He lived two lives, separate, but the same.

It only occurred to me when I heard the stairs creak that I hadn't checked for loose floorboards beneath the bed. But he was coming, so I'd have to save it for later.

Sneaking out, I zipped across the hall, keeping the door to my borrowed bedroom open just enough to watch that infuriating man saunter into his room, whistling in perfect pitch as if he were a fucking songbird. I cursed the golden band on my arm and sat heavily on the edge of my bed.

A crash downstairs turned the house into an uproar of Quill screaming at her dog while Orin's mother yelled about catching whatever he'd just stolen from the kitchen, and Hollis laughing a great, big, belly laugh. Within seconds, my door flew open, and Boo dashed into the room, a whole cooked chicken in his mouth. He tried darting under the bed but didn't fit, so half of him hung out, that white long-hair tail thumping against the floor in victory.

"Boo!" Quill shouted, rounding the corner, only to stop dead in her tracks the moment her eyes landed on me. "Oh, Boo! Please. He doesn't mean to be naughty. He's a really good boy. I promise."

Her big, blue eyes welled with tears as she glanced between me and the dog, bringing her delicate fingers to her mouth. Gods. She thought I was going to kill him. I needed to stop flinging empty threats around so much.

"Please don't be afraid. I promise I won't hurt him. Or you."

She took a tiny step forward, but I suspected that was all she could commit to.

I pushed off the bed and inched backward. Quill looked at Orin's door, no doubt for a place to run if I made any sudden movements. Smart girl.

Falling to my hands and knees, I knelt beside the dog, snatching his collar and dragging him out. He still had half a chicken in his mouth, but when I tried to take it out, he snarled.

Quill gasped.

"That is quite enough," I said, pointing a firm finger at the little beast. He whimpered and dropped the meat to the floor, tongue hanging. I buried my hands into his soft fur, scratching behind his dark copper ears until his leg began twitching. "Yes. You are a good boy, aren't you? A good, naughty boy."

He pressed his nose to my face and licked, chicken breath ruining the bath I'd had, but it was worth every second.

"I've always wanted a dog," I said.

Maybe an animal would have loved me loyally. However, my

father never agreed, and it wasn't a battle I was willing to have as a child. Somewhere along the years of becoming Death's Maiden, I'd let the dream go.

"I think he likes you," Quill whispered, daring to step into the room.

"They say dogs are excellent judges of character." Hollis stepped out from behind the door, as if he'd been there to protect her, just in case.

"What does that say about Orin and what happened last night?" she asked, peeking at his room again.

"I don't think hellhounds count, Quilly," he answered, patting her on the head. "Best take the chicken back to Miss Elowen and see if there's anything to be salvaged."

She groaned, shoulders slumping as she grabbed Boo's collar, swiped the chicken from the floor, and pulled her dog to the hall. "I'm going to be on dish duty for a week, thanks to you."

I waited until she'd gotten all the way down the stairs before I asked, "Is she Paesha's daughter?"

Hollis laughed. "No. But I can see why you think that. She and Paesha have a special bond. There's a lot in abandonment that only those who have been through it can understand. But she's really all of ours now. Lady Visha gifted her to the Maestro, but he didn't know what to do with her. The Syndicate takes care of her, but she's her own person. She's got an old soul, that girl."

"So, she's just alone?"

He tucked his hands behind his back, dipping a chin. "I think we're all a little bit alone. Don't you?"

I hated the way his piercing gaze felt so personal. As if he truly did know something about me.

"Some of us chose to be alone, Old Man."

"Yes. And some of us are plagued by it."

ORIN HADN'T LEFT the house. I'd been hoping to follow him again, but, though I paced in my room, waiting for him to make a move, it seemed he knew it and sat idle out of spite.

The second I opened the door, he did the same, leaning on the frame with one arm while tenderly holding his stomach with the other as he lifted a brow. "Going somewhere, Maiden?"

The way his dark glare pinned me to the spot irritated me. I couldn't see the murderer in those eyes. Perhaps because I loathed seeing it in mine.

"Am I not allowed?"

"Thank you for asking permission," he answered with a smile curling his lips. "I think you better stay here today."

"It was rhetorical," I shouted after he shut his door. "I'll leave if I damn well please."

"But where would you go?" Quill's shy voice from the other end of the hall surprised me.

Her muted footsteps were not nearly as loud as the limp that tormented Hollis most days. But the surprise came from her choice to speak. She hadn't spoken to me again after the chicken debacle with Boo. Likely because Paesha kept her at arm's reach. The Huntress couldn't control the dog, though, and he'd plowed into my borrowed bedroom every single morning, burying his wet nose into my cheek until I crawled out of bed and snuck him a handful of whatever food I'd managed to sneak away. Mostly for his loyalty, but also because there was something so soothing about being enjoyed. As if the world surrendered to me just a teeny bit.

Quill didn't live solely in the Syndicate house. She had a strange attachment to the Maestro, and, though I wanted to figure that out, as well, I couldn't solve the mystery of my new husband, find the true Life Maiden if it wasn't him, and start poking around Drexel Vanhoff without inviting more trouble than it was worth. I'd have to pick my battles.

"That's the beauty of adulthood, kid. You can go wherever you want, whenever you want." I raised my voice. "Take notes, Husband."

She'd vanished back down the stairs with no more questions, and I hadn't pushed.

Through the following week, I'd made small talk with Hollis and had been as gentle with Quill as I could be, but she was still completely terrified. The mind of a child was innocent. But their mouths were loose and their secrets easy to coax free. She was my target.

Lying in the garden, when the back door slammed open and her sweet little voice called for her pup, I pressed my lips together to hide the smile from a well-laid plan.

"Boo!" she shouted, hands cupped around her mouth as she faced the river.

I sat up slowly, making sure she knew I was there. I didn't want to scare her, just... help.

"Ha-have you seen my dog?" she asked, hiking her dress to get down the stairs.

I shook my head. "No."

"I'm not allowed to chase him over the hill."

A fact I knew.

"I could go with you, if you want."

She dropped the bottom of her dress, tapping her lips with a finger as she contemplated. "Will you leave Elowen's knife here?"

"Cross my heart," I promised.

"Okay, but we can't tell Paesha. She says you're dangerous."

"Paesha is smart, and she's right. I am dangerous. But not to you."

Shoving the toe of her boot into the dirt, she managed a small smile. "Well, Boo listens to you, and sometimes he growls at Paesha, so maybe you're not so, so bad. Maybe just medium bad."

"I'll settle for medium bad," I said, holding my hand out toward the child.

She swiped her curls from her face, showcasing her hesitation. But as I dropped my hand, she reached forward and took it anyway.

"Medium bad," she whispered to herself.

"How old are you, Quill?" I asked, as we followed the trail I'd taken earlier with the dog, leading him away from the house.

"Eight and a half. How old are you?"

I couldn't help the genuine smile. "I'm twenty-six, twenty-seven next month."

"Oh! We can have a party. Orin can play, and Paesha can dance, and Thea will make you something so neat. Probably not a knife, though, because... you know. But maybe a necklace like she made me for my birthday, see?"

She pulled a tiny locket from beneath the lace collar of her little dress. "It's got a picture of the Maestro in there. But it's kind of hard to make out."

"The Maestro? Why him?"

"He's my friend. And he keeps me safe. And he gives me candy, and I get to sit in a special seat on show nights."

"I see."

"Paesha says he's dangerous, too. But he's only small bad. If he's mad, he's mean sometimes, but only to bad guys. Not to me."

"Did you think he was mean to Orin? Is he a bad guy?" I waited, genuinely curious to see if she seemed to know anything at all about him.

"Orin is my best friend. I might marry him one day, too. Like you did."

I bit my bottom lip to keep from laughing. "Oh, yeah? He'd probably be a much nicer husband to you."

"Probably if you were only small bad and not medium bad, he'd be nicer to you, too."

"Probably," I agreed, marveling at how right she was. But I needed to redirect the conversation before we got to Boo. Stepping on my bootlace without her noticing, I drew up short, kneeling to retie it as I let go of her hand. "You never answered my question. Do you think the Maestro is mean to Orin?"

She bit her bottom lip and looked away, contemplating her answer. "Yes. I do. But I don't think he meant to be. The Maestro said it was a little bit of an accident because he thought the hound was going to play with Orin like how Boo does sometimes, but the dog was naughty, and Orin got hurt. And then the Maestro saved him. Because he's our friend."

"Makes sense." I switched feet, untying my bootlace without her noticing so I could delay her. "You know what I think? Oh, maybe I shouldn't say. It's probably just for grownups to talk about."

"I did say eight and a half."

"Right, right. Well, if you're sure you're almost there."

She studied her fingers for a moment. "I'm almost two whole hands. That's pretty close."

"It's just... don't you think it would have been better for Orin if the Life Maiden could have helped him?"

"Everyone knows she can't."

Heart quickening, I finally felt like I was on to something. "Right. But if she could, I mean. If Boo got hurt, let's say, shouldn't we take him to see her?"

She stopped, her eyes doubling in size. "But how could we when everyone knows she's dead?"

The hair on my arms rose at her very blunt response. She was dead. 'Everyone' to a child was such a small group of people. Only those close to her. A secret well-kept, and if she had somehow found this out, it explained why Drexel held her close. Why the Syndicate kept her closer. Why she'd been treated with such favor. Had Orin killed the Life Maiden for Drexel and wasn't really harboring Life Maiden power?

"You're right," I answered numbly, wondering what the off-kiltered balance of power with only one of us meant for the world. "Everyone knows."

"Except Paesha and Thea. But Paesha can't find her, and Thea is a... oppymis."

"Oppymis?"

"Yeah, you know. She always sees things brighter."

We crested the hill, the child's confession confusing me more than ever as we peered down at the riverbank.

"An optimist?"

"Boo!" she shouted, tearing away from me to tackle her very muddy dog, who'd lay on the bank, chewing on a bone I'd left for him, his red collar miraculously stuck on a random piece of fishing twine that'd been haphazardly discarded.

"Well, what are the odds?" I tugged on my slipknot, setting the dog free, but he didn't budge, unwilling to give up the bone.

"Come on, you big oaf." Quill threw her entire body weight into the pup. He didn't give an inch.

I swiped the bone, and he was off the ground in a second, diligently at my side.

"Good boy," I muttered under my breath as he shoved his nose into my pocket, smelling the bits of roast I'd saved for him.

We walked toward the house together in mostly silence, save the giggles as Boo smothered Quill in muddy kisses when she'd taken the bone. From the top of the hill, she darted for the door, stopped in her tracks, and ran back to hug me.

"Maybe you're only small bad, Death Maiden."

"Maybe." I smiled down at her. "You can call me Dey, if you want to."

She lifted a shoulder. "I'll think about it." And then she was gone, running for the house at full speed, yelling at Boo about having to go to the bathhouse now.

I let the information swirl through my mind, turning the scenarios over and over again. If Paesha didn't think the Life Maiden was dead, then there couldn't be a great secret Quill was hoarding. Or maybe there was, but that wasn't the secret. I was starting to doubt whether any of them knew Orin was a murderer. She never claimed Orin thought the Life Maiden was alive, though. And that was very interesting to me.

I wasn't alone. Elowen was always home, and there was usually someone coming and going, it seemed. Today was quiet, though. Only her. I'd been torn between starting my search for the Life Maiden in the city, or here in the Syndicate house, but after several days of everyone being around, they were finally gone, so I decided to take the opportunity presented and start searching.

"Tea?" I asked, holding the smile that felt foreign on my face as I offered a sleeping tonic to Orin's mother, sitting next to her on the front steps again.

"Thank you, Dey. It never gets easier. Every night they leave, I feel like I can't breathe until they come home safely."

"I've been wondering, how does the Maestro's power work? I thought for every deed, a debt was paid. That's how Lady Visha's binding magic is."

"That would be how it appears, but we cannot claim to know the intricacies of magic or the heart of the wielder, can we, Maiden? The same can be said for Drexel. He values time rather than deeds."

She sipped her tea as I did mine, the soft breeze coiling through her golden-brown hair. I didn't bother answering, just waited until she stifled a yawn with the back of her hand. "Have you ever wondered where the Life Maiden is?"

She choked on her next drink, sitting up a little straighter. "Why do you ask?"

Usually, when someone answered a question with a question, they knew more than they were willing to say. I forced a sigh, moving a finger over the rim of my teacup. "No reason."

"If you're hunting her, don't bother. Paesha's been trying for years."

Interesting, though I'd deduced as much from the child.

"The Life Maiden means nothing to me. It just seems strange that every generation we've had one and now suddenly we don't. The world looks different from a castle. The edges of reality are smoother, and the smiles are less genuine. You never know what's real."

She yawned again. "Yes, I can see how that would be true, but no one knows where the Life Maiden is. The people of this world are close. No one truly has secrets. If one person knew, we'd all know."

"Good point." I wondered if she could lie well while so tired or if she really meant what she'd said, and my entire theory about Orin was wrong.

"Goodness, what time is it? I can barely keep my eyes open."

I nudged her with my shoulder. "If you want to sleep, I can wait for them and wake you if something happens."

"Oh, no." She rubbed her eyes. "I've never missed a homecoming. And the Maestro is furious with Orin for..." Her voice trailed off.

"Marrying me. You can say it. Though I'm not sure why it matters to him."

Leaning on the railing, she let her eyes fall shut. "I'm sure there are two reasons. First, because... because he likes to be in control, and the second..."

"The second?" I asked, startling her awake.

"The second what, dear?"

"You said there were two reasons the Maestro would be mad at Orin for marrying me."

"Ah, yes. Because you are a prize to..."

This time when she fell asleep, I didn't wake her. Of course, I was a prize for a man who could control anyone with a magically binding contract. Without my father in the way, he'd probably be hunting me soon. And by my choice, I was living in a house full of people bound to him.

Paesha's and Althea's rooms were on the second level of the home. Hollis, Quill, and Elowen had the first floor, and Orin and I shared the top. I wasn't sure which room belonged to Paesha, but still, I flinched when the stairs creaked at my ascent. I'd been purposefully avoiding this floor. I wanted them to think I respected their space and so far, aside from the clear avoidance on Paesha's part, there hadn't been an outright tantrum in my presence. After she got over which room I was staying in.

I pressed open the first door, waiting to see if Elowen made a noise from the front door before I stepped inside. It felt strange to lurk without my mask and hood, but also familiar. There was something comforting about relying on only myself, especially in a house full of people who were constantly together. They worked together, ate together, they even practiced together. Paesha was a dancer, a beautiful one. She danced in the garden yesterday as Orin played his cello, her twirls and stretches far more graceful than what I'd seen on the Maestro's stage.

Althea's blacksmith apron lay over the back of a chair. I wasn't sure if she used magic or not, but her room was full of metal parts and drawings of designs. She had cogs and wheels and blueprints all over the place. But somehow, the pink bed coverings and gentle lace still felt like her. I couldn't imagine where to begin rummaging. And for now, I wouldn't. Though there was one particular area I felt drawn to. I'd be back to search that spot soon.

Paesha was my target. I quietly closed the door, standing in the hall with my breath held for just a moment. The house remained quiet. Slipping into her room next, I glanced at the window facing the tree line, watching for a hint of movement. Nothing.

Things were thrown everywhere, with no rhyme or reason. Books were stacked from floor to ceiling, and performance costumes were tossed in the corner. She hadn't made her bed, nor cleared her nightstand in probably forever. I smirked at the red panties hanging from the lamp before carefully winding my way through. Paesha didn't need to keep her space clean because she was magically gifted with the ability to find anything she needed. But she might also know if things were moved, and, based on the way she watched me enter and exit a room, I'd bet my last coin she'd set a trap in here for me. Because it's exactly what I would have done if I had something to hide.

I started with the books. She must have meant to read every book in existence before her one-hundredth year. And she'd made a pretty good dent. Unless she was just a collector. But something in the way she kept to herself but always had a strong opinion, the way she studied every little detail and held eyes on Quill, told me she was studious. Observant.

Breaking down Paesha the way I had Death's victims made my skin crackle with anticipation. I loved the hunt. Not the outcome. I loathed the outcome. But there was something so satisfying about using my brain and wits to solve the mystery that surrounded every person. Most of her books were of the battles drawn out between ancient Silbath and Perth. Of the lineage of the kings and the histories of gods. She had a few fairytales scattered about, which surprised me. She didn't seem like the whimsical kind of woman I figured those would attract. But then, what did I truly know about people?

Paesha was a collector. Stacked along her walls were shelves of things. Metal containers with buttons and spools of dusty strings, albums of pictures, and jars of dried flowers. Shoes for dancing hung from her floor-length mirror, and... I paused.

The mirror.

It was nearly a twin to the one Ro had gifted me in the castle. I carefully stepped closer, smoothing a hand over the golden filigree. Could that be a coincidence? Hers was cleaner, newer. There were no signs of wear along the edges, no handprints from wishing for entry into a hidden world. There was no buzz of magic, no silvery ripple. It was just a mirror.

I turned, staring at the bed. If I were storing information about the Life Maiden, I'm not sure where I would have hidden it in this mess. Honestly, I might have left it in plain sight. Or not in my bedroom at all.

I thought about what Elowen had said about the Maestro considering me a prize. But he'd never needed to hunt me. The hand of Death was a beacon in a world full of immortals. He always knew where I was. The Life Maiden, though... There's no way he wasn't hunting for her. Each day that passed without her only made her more valuable. And Drexel Vanhoff was a collector.

Bound to him, as Paesha was, if she had information, *he* had information. Unless she knew how to hide it from him. But I didn't think his magic came with loopholes. Without rooting around the room and moving things to dig, I wasn't sure if I was going to find anything in this mess.

I moved back to the window, thanking the old gods for a

full, bright moon, then checked the tree line one more time before falling to my knees beside the bed and swiping my hand below the iron bed frame. Nothing. I'd drugged Orin's mom to sleep with poppy milk tea that was likely far too potent for her petite figure. I'd waited patiently for days for everyone to leave this godsdamned house. I needed this moment.

If I didn't find the Life Maiden, I had no true purpose beyond Death's calling. I'd never bring a single thing to this world. Each foul and despicable thought and word anyone ever had against me would be my only truth. And I refused to be the enemy. I was not like them, those that came before me. And I'd search every inch of this world until I proved it.

My skin practically crawled with the desire to pick up the clothes covering the floor and toss them to the side. Frustrated, I wanted to destroy this place just as much as I wanted to preserve it. But since I couldn't, and there was not a single clue to be found that wasn't buried within the millions of pages of books she had or lost beneath a sloppy mountain, I tiptoed back to the open door, cursing Paesha Vox and her gloriously disastrous bedroom.

I almost walked out. Almost let her win. But when the screaming from outside began, a repeat of the last time they'd come home, I threw the door back open, racing for the window. The doorknob crashed into the wall, causing a frame to fall, but also marking the wall. A hoard of silhouettes broke through the tree line.

If I blew my cover, if they knew I was simply staying in order to find answers, they'd force me to leave. And sorting through all my husband's lies would be so much harder from the outside. I snatched the cracked picture from the floor and propped it back up over the nail head peeking from the wall.

The front door slammed open. My ears began to ring. I glanced at the weathered frame for one more second, hoping I'd gotten the angle right, as if she wouldn't notice the giant crack in the glass. But the smiles in the painting halted me. Even as Hollis called my name.

There were five people. First, Paesha, her beautiful sun-kissed skin a near match to the familiar face beside her. Orin. Impeccably dressed in a suit, as he usually was, he held her hand in his, smiling brightly. A genuine grin that must have been created by an absolute artist able to imagine such a thing because I'd never seen him look that way. His eyes twinkled. Paesha was just as happy, staring at the side profile of another man standing just a bit taller than Orin, slightly hidden by the collar of his coat. His arms were slung over the shoulder of a third man. Althea stood on the opposite side, her face flushed, leaning on a sword she no doubt crafted herself with a smudge of ash on her chin. These must have been important members of their little Syndicate.

"Deyanira?" Hollis called from the base of the stairs. "Come quick."

"Coming!" I shouted, muffling my voice with my arm so he couldn't discern where I was.

I closed the door as quietly as I could, sneaking up one flight of stairs before loudly crashing back down them to make it seem like I'd been in my bedroom. I tossed my hair and pinched my cheeks for color as I jogged down to the entrance of the Syndicate house.

Althea's eyes were red-rimmed as she dragged a sleepy Elowen through the front door. Hollis held Orin up with the last bit of strength the old man could likely muster.

I rushed forward, taking Orin's other side. "Was it another hellhound?"

"A sword fight," Hollis answered, pulling his hand away from Orin's ribs to reveal the gaping wound. "One he had no chance of winning."

"Just a scratch," Orin moaned, his head falling backward, revealing the gash in his throat.

"Where are Quill and Paesha?" I asked carefully, head snapping to Althea.

She covered her mouth with the back of her hand before bursting into tears. "Quill is missing."

CHAPTER 23

The wretched groans of Orin Faber as his mother tended to his wounds from his bed were nothing compared to the somber faces standing at the front door, waiting for Paesha and Quill to arrive safely.

I thought of the little girl who'd been so innocent when we'd spoken, and I'd felt guilty for tricking her, though nothing much had come from it. She'd been kind, even when she was scared, and that was far more than I could say for half the world's population. But what did it mean if Drexel's charge was missing? Had he hidden her away somewhere? Or had she been taken right under his nose? I couldn't help the worry as I glared at the damned tree line.

Lit by the full moon, the trees in the distance were easy enough to see, but the shadows remained dark, and each rustle of an oak branch was paired with a tiny gasp before disappointment.

"How long does it usually take Paesha to find someone?" I asked.

"It varies. Sometimes days, sometimes minutes... There."

Althea jerked a finger toward a figure emerging from the darkness before she darted out the door.

Hollis was quick to follow, but not quick in general. I walked behind, unsure of where I fit into this particular situation. Paesha would not want me involved. But Quill was a child, and I could help. I wanted so desperately for the world to see me that way. It wasn't long before my steps quickened, and I'd passed Hollis and nearly beat Althea to Paesha.

"This doesn't concern you, Maiden. Go back to the roof, or wherever you like to lurk."

"Where is she?" Thea asked, ignoring Paesha's cruelty.

"I'm not saying anything until she goes away."

I crossed my arms over my chest. "I can help. I know you think I'm a snake, but if that were true, I'd have already struck. I know this world, and just like you, I've hunted in it. Let me help you."

"Orin's out of commission until further notice," Hollis said from behind, finally catching up, his presence deflating some of the animosity. "I won't have this bickering when one of ours is missing. Where is she?"

Paesha's scowl would have shredded me to pieces if looks could kill. "I've got a read on her, but it's not great. She's in Icharius's castle."

Her admission dropped into my gut like an anchor in shallow water. The king's angry fists slid across my mind as I remembered his reaction when he realized he'd been swindled out of a wife. I hadn't thought about that moment for a while.

"Where's the dog?" I asked, starting back toward the house.

"Boo's with a friend of ours. Someone we trust. He'll be fine for now," Thea said. "Where are you going?"

"I'm going to need more weapons," I answered. "And you're going to give them to me."

"I'm not waiting for you, Maiden," Paesha shouted, headed to the trees.

"You can go on your own if you want, but I know exactly how to get into that castle. I know my way around, and I know what's going to be there when you get into the castle. So, unless you want your own capture tonight, fall in line, Huntress. Because I'm only doing this once."

Thea ran after me, passing me up the stairs and darting into her room. I followed, and she looked over her shoulder, considering for only a second before she sighed. "This is probably a really bad idea."

"I can confirm it is. But there's no time for debating. Slide your little wall there and let's go."

"My... you knew?"

"One of these days, we'll break into the Perth castle, and I'll show you mine."

A smile lit her pretty face. "I've seen it. It's okay."

"Okay?" I asked, drawing back.

She winked and slid the faux wall to the side, revealing a second room. "We snuck into your castle to get your clothes after, well... when Orin crashed your wedding. I got curious. But I prefer my collection more."

I was frozen to the spot, nearly reaching out to steady myself on the post of Thea's bed. "It's... gods, Thea. It's incredible."

"I tinker," she said, lifting a shoulder. "Take your pick. But if you break it and I can't fix it, we're fighting, Maiden."

I shuffled forward, stroking my hand down the twisted pommel of a sword, before studying the ornate collection of throwing knives, each narrow handle perfectly shaped and carefully carved. Chain whips and daggers and crossbows and contraptions I'd never seen filled the hidden room. But it was more than that.

"You do have power," I said in awe. "These are far too beautiful to be anything but."

"I don't advertise it, Dey. Promise you'll never take one of these without my permission. I can't... I don't want to..."

I lifted the chain from the hook, swiped two daggers, and let my hand rest over the sword before deciding to pass.

"I get it."

She bit her lip, sliding the wall back into place. "They're art."

"Not weapons for Death. It's okay. I understand more than you think."

I missed Chaos. And I would have loved to storm into Orin's room and demand her return, but if they hadn't told him Quill was missing, there was likely a solid reason. He was too damaged to be helpful, and breaking into the Silbath castle with a man that could barely keep himself upright sounded like a good way to fail.

Paesha was waiting on the front steps when we walked out. "Armed to the teeth, Maiden?"

"Just the way I like it, Huntress. Now, we're going to have to steal a carriage, unless you have one hiding around here?"

"I know where we can get one." Hollis stepped in.

Paesha's mismatched eyes scanned Hollis, softening. "Are you sure it's not too much, Hol? You can stay."

"I won't slow you down. But I can drive the carriage."

"Great," I piped in, hustling for the trees before I called over my shoulder. "Here's the plan. Hollis and Thea stay in the carriage; we won't be able to take it through the gates at the castle. You're going to have to circle. Stay close enough for us to find you, but not enough to raise suspicion. He's a new king, and I'd bet my own death he's doubled down on guards."

"He's taken the Perth guard," Hollis confirmed, falling behind. "Moved everyone off the border. Perth has completely fallen."

Five years ago, ten even, if someone had been brave enough to tell me that would ever happen, I'd have laughed in their face. My father was cunning and guarded and everything a king should have been, aside from compassionate. But maybe kings weren't meant to be kind. Maybe they were forged from iron and ruthlessness. History had surely proven that to be true. All the more reason to worry for that wide-eyed little girl likely surrounded by strangers. Enemies even.

By the time we'd gotten to the carriage and within two blocks of the castle, I could taste the citrus tang of Paesha's magic in the air. Thea gripped the edge of her wooden seat. She could feel it, too. Paesha concentrated, her power seeming more peaceful than mine, but I'd rarely witnessed anyone use magic. Ro's was different. A granted entry, but not a continuous stream.

The beautiful Huntress sat back, her long lashes falling onto her dark face as she closed her eyes and got lost in her power. The air in the enclosed space filled with my envy. I'd never feel an ounce of my magic and not loathe it. Not cower. Not hate myself a bit more.

"She's still there," she said, the smoky tone of her voice calm. "I can't tell exactly where, but I know she hasn't moved since I checked last.

"How does the magic work?" I asked, scooting forward.

Those mysterious eyes fluttered open. She began to speak and then stopped, staring out the window.

"I'm not trying to pry if it's personal. I'm just wondering if you're able to see anything when you find her or if it's a feeling you get. If you have any visions, I can probably figure out where she is and save us some time."

"We're on the same team here, P." Althea nudged her friend with a knee.

"It's different every time. This time, I can see small bits of light on a far wall. I can tell she's in an empty room, sitting in a corner. I saw the hallway earlier. There were several guards."

"Do you remember any paintings? Sculptures? Windows with a view? Something that could give us a point of reference?"

"As if you have the whole castle memorized," she said under her breath, slumping backward.

"I do."

Both heads snapped to me.

"You have your powers, and I have mine."

"There's a painting on one of the walls of the former king. He's holding a scepter and riding a stallion."

I searched my memory. We couldn't afford to make a mistake, or we'd all be in deep shit. And as the Huntress, Paesha was likely just as valuable to Icharius as I was. "Black or brown?"

"What?"

"The horse. Was it black or brown? There are two paintings, and the halls are on opposite sides of the castle."

"Gods, you really do have the whole place memorized."

"It's not that impressive," I assured her, lifting a brow to Paesha for an answer.

"I'm not sure. Maybe brown."

"Thea, does your magic allow you to bend metal, or does it lend more to the design and ingenuity?"

"I can build anything, given the proper tools and time."

I shifted to face her. "How well can you destroy something?"

"Thea's a badass, Maiden. What do you have in mind?"

"We're going to need a distraction. Let's go."

After instructing Hollis and telling Althea the plan, we left them behind so we could get as close to the moat as possible. We waited, crawling on our bellies through the grass in the dark until we could go no further without being spotted by the cluster of guards walking the parapet.

There was not a break in guards, not a single angle the king's men didn't have covered. The last time I'd come, Bram Ellis's guards were scattered. These men, dressed in full armor, stood nearly shoulder to shoulder, staring down at the world.

"Why are they prepared for battle?" I asked, mostly to myself.

"Half of them probably hate the other half, for starters. And if a usurper didn't live in a constant state of paranoia for an uprising, he'd be mad."

"No one wants a war. No one is going to come knocking down his doors. The people are going to follow the strongest player for protection, and there are no other pieces on the board. Icharius won. In a single week."

Paesha swiped at the grass in front of her. "The Maestro is far more powerful than the new king, Maiden. Should he desire that throne for even a second, it would be his. And some would argue that your playing piece is still very much on the table."

I scoffed, ducking to keep myself hidden. "I don't want a throne. I don't even want a husband. I just want to be left alone."

"I'm sure your victims felt the same way."

I studied her eyes, searching for hatred but finding mostly pain. "I'm sure they did."

The air was thick with tension, and the weight of our daring plan pressed upon us. We had to enter the castle without alerting the guards, and the diversion unfolding before our eyes was our ticket in.

Right on cue, the portcullis launched halfway down the stone bridge over the rancid moat as if it'd been kicked by a giant. At the same time, the bell in the tower on the far side of the castle came crashing down, its thunderous tolling echoing through the courtyard. The cacophony was a jarring symphony of chaos, a stark contrast to the usual stillness of the castle grounds. Amidst the clamor, a few of the guards started to panic, their armor clinking as it shrank.

"Remind me never to get on her bad side," I said, darting for the murky water.

"Told you she was a badass." Paesha grinned at me, and, for the first time, I saw a crack in her wall.

Several moments later, dripping in disgusting water, the smile was gone, replaced by absolute detest. "If you ever have a brilliant plan again, remind me to run in the other direction."

"At least we didn't have to take the sewers. The ones by Beggar's Alley in Perth are bad enough to make you question every choice made in this life and your past lives."

She shook her head before scrunching the water from her hair. "Oh, I know. You should see the ones around Misery's End. The mold down there grows on the backs of the rodents."

"Thanks for that visual."

"Consider it payment for the slop we swam through. We made it in. Now what?"

"We're going to have to go back out that way, so don't bother cursing me just yet." I pulled a throwing knife for each hand from my jacket, feeling bare without my mask. "The last time I was in this castle, I ran into a child. I don't know the court Icharius keeps, but we'll have to stay vigilant. We go up the stairs and down the left corridor. Most of the walls lining the outside and through the middle of the castle have passageways behind them. You can get through undetected if the king isn't using them for his guards or his lovers."

She pulled the sword from her back, and I turned and led her out. We barely got the door cracked before metal on metal screeched down the hallway.

"The godsdamned thing just fell," a guard shouted.

"It's the Maestro. He's coming to get the kid."

"Shit," Paesha breathed into my ear.

"Our distraction might have been a little too big," I whispered, grabbing her hand to yank her down the corridor as soon as it was clear.

We ran. I didn't look back, didn't question whether she could keep up or if she had any doubts. My heartbeat matched my steps, and judging by her silent breaths, hers did, too. Though neither of us had acknowledged it, if we were caught, there was no way we were getting out of here. But maybe that was the plan. Maybe Quill was bait.

"Use your power," I hissed, yanking her into the secret hallway. "Has she been moved yet? They're going to make it impossible to get to her."

The sweet taste of citrus filled the space. "Same place. Keep going."

"I sure hope it was the brown horse."

Avoiding the dusty walls, we soared through the passageway until we couldn't go any further. In the heart of Icharius Fern's castle, I could hardly take a full breath. If not for the danger, then for the proximity of the scorned man.

"Definitely this way, Maiden. I can feel her now," she whispered, peeking over my shoulder as I cracked the door open. "Let me lead."

"It's not safe. Let me go first."

"I think I can take care of myself," she hissed, pushing past me.

I chased after her with a growl. "There's bound to be—"

A giant hand reached out from around a corner, grabbing her by the throat and lifting until she was dangling. She wrenched the helmet off the guard, digging her fingers into his eyes until he dropped her as I caught up.

The guard started wailing, alerting the entire kingdom of Silbath where we were.

"Go!" I shouted.

She ran, taking a turn I wouldn't have, but she knew where she was going, and I had to trust that as the sound of stomping and shouting guards grew louder behind us.

"Guards!" she yelled back at me, seconds before she was captured by another.

I whipped a dagger into the small space between his armor, and he fell to his knees but still held Paesha by the hair.

"Go get our girl, Deyanira," she said. "I'll be right behind you."

"Let me—"

"Enough fighting, just save Quill!" she yelled as another guard ran for us.

I couldn't take the time to argue, nor could I save them both. And she knew it. She made her choice. But Quill never got one. Running past the painting of the prior king, eyes flicking to the brown horse, I slammed my entire body into the door, every bit of my skin crawling with adrenaline as I prepared for whatever I'd find.

It swung open on impact, revealing tiny Quill clutching her legs to her chest, face stained with tears, and three armed guards, swords out, standing vigil.

"Quilly, I know you're scared," I said, allowing a dangerous calm to settle over me. "Close your eyes and cover your ears. Sing Orin's favorite song as loud as you can."

CHAPTER 24

Quill's sweet, shaking voice filled the room as time stopped. I wasn't here for Death. I would not kill these guards. But the way all three took a collective step toward me raised the hair on my body. I wasn't sure I would have a choice by the end of this fight.

I gripped the perfectly shaped handle of Thea's whip, letting the metal teeth glimmer in the lamplight as I snapped it once, inviting anyone who wanted to try me to step forward.

They moved at once, and I launched into action, serenaded by the voice of an innocent as I ripped into Icharius Fern's guards. Strategically, I aimed for weak spots in the armor, loosening the buckles and unfastening the straps, shifting left and right as they lunged and missed, none of them properly trained. One grabbed me around the waist and hauled me sideways. I used the momentum to bring a leg out and kick the helmet from another before planting a knife into the armpit of the man holding me.

He yelped, and I fell to the floor in a crouch. Whipping the chain across another's armor, sparks flew in a warning.

"You get to decide for yourself today. You live or die by your next moves. That little girl and I are leaving this room. Are you?"

Each guard paused, the static in the air thickening. The one with a gash in his pit darted for the door. Two remained. They surged as one, both blades flying for me. I leaped from the ground, soaring over the one with no helmet and coiling the whip around his neck as I came down. The blood spatter was silent, even as I loosened the whip with a flick of my wrist just in time to keep his head on his shoulders. He fell to his knees regardless, grasping at his wound as he crawled on the door.

The final guard was a beast. His sword nicked my arm, and he'd plowed a shoulder into my stomach, and had I not dodged, in the next drive, he'd have been on top of me. But Paesha's desperate scream from the hallway and the way Quill's back went rigid was enough to make the decision I'd been trying to avoid. We needed to get out of the castle, or we were never going back.

"Forgive me," I whispered to the guard, causing him to still.

He knew. And I knew.

And it was over in the next move. Three throwing knives. Three beautifully crafted weapons of art had found their home with less effort than it took to keep him alive. Quill's final note of her beautiful song ended the second I snatched her from the corner and ran like hell.

I couldn't save Paesha while carrying Quill. It was far too dangerous. Every second that passed, the worse it would become for the Huntress at the end of the hall. An overwhelming sense of dread flooded me as I contemplated my own escape. My own free will.

"Keep your eyes closed, do you hear me? Cover your ears and don't look," I told Quill, setting her down behind a pillar. "I promise I will come back for you."

"Okay," she whispered, her face full of terror.

Paesha was putting up a valiant fight, but there was only a slim chance we were walking out of this castle. I cracked the whip, drawing attention to distract the two guards, giving her a window to back away and join my side.

"I know you hate me, but if we don't do this together, we won't do it at all."

She slid a hand over a brow. "Agreed."

The men rushed forward. She held her blade steady, bending slightly in the knees.

"I don't want to kill them."

She scoffed.

I whipped the chain forward. It coiled around their feet before I ripped it backward. "I'm serious, Huntress. I won't kill them if I don't have to. I'll take them down; you take them out."

"And when that stops working?" she asked with a grunt, as another guard rounded the corner.

"Don't speak as if you're already defeated."

A man surged forward, reaching for her. I slung a dagger across his hand. When he drew back, Paesha struck, sinking the tip of her sword into his stomach. Had it been my blade, he would have died. But since it was her, he'd survive it, and I envied her for it.

Another two guards appeared, and I whispered so only she could hear me. "Don't let them pass. Stay on my left. The second there's a break, we run." I turned to stare viciously into those cold, mismatched eyes. "There's a painting around the corner. It's a woman holding a red vase. If this goes to shit, grab Quill and take the passage behind it. The hinges are on the right side, and they squeak when you open it."

Her breath caught as she realized what I was saying. I would be the one to stay behind.

"That's not an option, Maiden."

I lowered my chin as the guard she'd been fighting closed in.

"No one gives a shit if I'm captured. Quill needs you to get her out of here. She's just a kid."

"Together, then."

Paesha was a whirlwind of steel, her sword silently slicing through the air with beautiful precision. She'd trained, and it showed. I couldn't help but notice some of her movements reminded me of Orin's. We fought, battling in sync, stacking, letting the bodies of her victims fall into a pile. But the guards kept coming, and we were tiring.

They charged in waves, and while Paesha moved like a dancer, I moved like a killer, taking them down one by one. She was quick and precise. But she was not trained like I was. Our only advantage was how little experience these men had with true fighters. War had only been a promise for so long now, so most knew nothing of its brutality.

After what felt like an eternity of battling, of taxed muscles and aching shoulders, we managed to thin their ranks, though the bodies had piled up. A very distant part of me could feel the coil of Death's power thrumming in my veins. Urging me to take the immortality of the maimed. As if I'd lusted for the blood of the fallen. And maybe I had, especially when I'd killed that single guard. But the post-power fatigue hadn't come to me and, as far as I knew, neither had Death. Though maybe he lurked, waiting for more to die.

The Huntress drove her sword into the throat of the last guard to come for us. Minimally, he would never speak again. Likely, he'd struggle with every breath for the rest of his hundred years.

"Go!" I shouted, spinning on a heel to grab Quill from where she stood, eyes shut, ears covered, sobs wracking her body.

I led the way, leaping over the thrashing and moaning men, who were too ignorant to have saved themselves. The hallway was stained with so much blood, nearly as much as she and I had been, but we'd almost made it to our escape route.

"Wait," Paesha hissed, jamming an arm out to stop me from leaving the hall. She pointed to her sword before gesturing for us to press our backs against the wall.

I held a firm hand over Quill's mouth to hide the sobs as Paesha's battle cry pierced the air and she lunged, jamming her weapon out just in time to cut the guard down. But she'd missed, the blade bouncing off his silver armor.

With only the top of his face hiding behind a steel mask, the beast of a man looked down at her with a terrible grin before snatching her around the throat and lifting her from the ground. Her legs swung wildly, and despite my hand, Quill released a gut-wrenching scream that filled me with so much fear I could hardly concentrate.

Gods. I'd have to kill two men today.

I didn't have time to process what kind of monster that made me. Setting the child down for the second time, I ran forward, throwing all my weight into a kick at the back of his legs. He fell hard to his knees but hadn't released the Huntress. I went in with my dagger. Paesha scraped at his clutched hand with her fingers. He swung his massive arms, unable to get to a standing position, thank the old gods.

In the heat of the moment, the bloodied hall became a blur. She lunged forward. I threw a dagger, the man stilled, and Paesha froze. Seconds later, he was on the ground, unmoving.

"Come on, we have to go!" Her tense voice forced the world back into motion.

The dark passageway was not empty. We'd tucked against walls and held our breaths, keeping Quill as quiet as possible but allowing her to run on her own. She hadn't balked at the spiderwebs, nor squealed at the mice. She was as determined as we were.

It hadn't occurred to me to ask if she could swim until we'd jumped into the disgusting water.

"Hold your breath, Quilly," Paesha said, treading the murky filth, her voice quiet. "Just like Orin taught you last summer, okay?"

I scanned her eyes for a reason behind the tremble in her words but saw nothing there. It wasn't until we were peeking out of the water on the other side, staring up at the parapet, that I saw her wince. She'd be fine, of course, but she could slow down our escape. And we couldn't afford to draw anyone toward the Syndicate house. Not if we were going to hide Quill. It seemed few knew where she stayed.

Cradling her side as we pulled ourselves out of the moat, Paesha slowed before reaching Hollis and Althea in the carriage.

"Show me," I demanded, the second we were racing through the city streets.

"Mind your business, Maiden," she answered with an eye roll.

Thea hugged Quill. "What happened?"

"She's hurt," I answered, never taking my gaze from the Huntress.

She pulled a trembling hand from her side, revealing a deep gash in her abdomen, dark red blood seeping out. "It's just a scratch."

"Careful, you sound as ridiculous as Orin."

I pulled my blade and ripped a long strip into a blanket I'd found under the bench seat. Though she cursed her the entire time, she let Thea tie the wound.

Hollis steered the cart around the two cities while Paesha sat with her hand pressed into her stomach quietly. We had to make sure we weren't followed, though the minutes ticked by achingly slow. Each foot, each block its own victory and torment.

Several passes of wary soldiers marched through the Silbath streets just off the Silk Road. When Hollis jerked to a stop, I wrapped my hand around the only weapon I had left and said a silent prayer as Althea forced Quill under the bench seat and used her soot-stained apron to cover the child.

"If he looks in here," I whispered, grabbing Thea's hand, "do not try to use magic."

Paesha's faint voice was hardly a sound at all. "They will know, Maiden."

And she was right. Two dead guards had sealed my fate. If Icharius Fern wasn't already furious with me, I'd just slighted him for a second time and left the bodies to prove it.

Hollis's nervous laughter from the front seat, where he likely gripped the reins like his life depended on it, filled the night air with palpable tension. But no guard came. We lurched forward, and the sound of the horses' hooves clacking down the cobblestone streets carried us all the way north with no more delays.

Paesha could barely stand by the time we made it to the front door. Still, Elowen rushed forward, falling to her knees in front of Quill and hugging her before she ever laid eyes on the Huntress. But once she did, she sank further. Defeated. "If the members of this house do not stop getting shredded to pieces, we're going to have to build a hospital next."

If the dark circles below her eyes could be used as measurement, she hadn't slept, and the sleeping tonic I'd given her was likely its own form of torture to her mind at this point. But she was direct, calling orders and forcing Paesha onto the couch.

"What happened?" The gravel of Orin's sleepy voice melted down my spine as he came from behind me.

"We had to get the kid," Paesha said, forcing a smile.

"Get her from whom?" he asked with a grimace, immediately taking Quill's hand.

"The new king," the child said quietly. "But Paesha and the Maiden saved me."

"She's family, right?" Paesha said, weakly.

He pushed past me as if I weren't there at all, kneeling beside the Huntress as he took her hand. "She's family." He kissed her fingers, and the golden band around my wrist throbbed. I couldn't watch him love her while he was married to me, but I also couldn't look away. Had I missed a deeper connection between them?

"Looks like you lost the fight, P," he said, moving his fingers over her fresh stitches.

"Elowen says the blade cut something internally. She's supposed to dance tomorrow night," Thea said, bringing a cup of something warm to Paesha.

Orin swiped Paesha's sweaty brown hair from her forehead. "Did you go on the boss's orders?"

She shook her head.

He sighed. "At least it was only a soldier's blade. Drexel can find a new dancer for a week. You'll be better before you know it."

Her eyes flashed to me and back to him. I could see the way she fought with her words, though it took me a bit to put it all together.

My chest tightened, forcing the gasp. "It wasn't a guard's blade. It was mine."

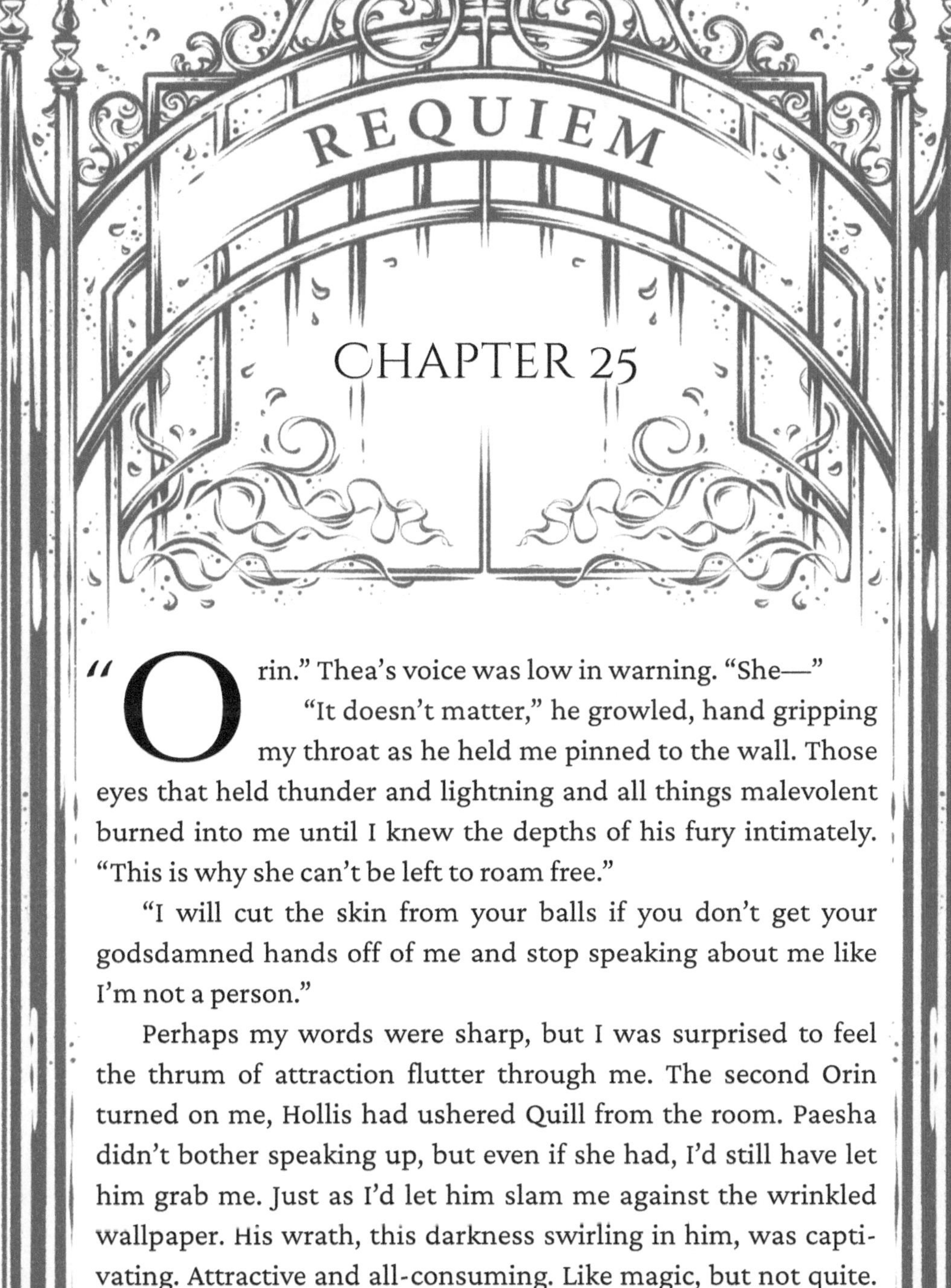

REQUIEM

CHAPTER 25

"Orin." Thea's voice was low in warning. "She—"

"It doesn't matter," he growled, hand gripping my throat as he held me pinned to the wall. Those eyes that held thunder and lightning and all things malevolent burned into me until I knew the depths of his fury intimately. "This is why she can't be left to roam free."

"I will cut the skin from your balls if you don't get your godsdamned hands off of me and stop speaking about me like I'm not a person."

Perhaps my words were sharp, but I was surprised to feel the thrum of attraction flutter through me. The second Orin turned on me, Hollis had ushered Quill from the room. Paesha didn't bother speaking up, but even if she had, I'd still have let him grab me. Just as I'd let him slam me against the wrinkled wallpaper. His wrath, this darkness swirling in him, was captivating. Attractive and all-consuming. Like magic, but not quite. A very big piece of me wanted to push him as far as I could. Force him to come undone and reveal himself. Reveal the beast that was hiding within.

I wouldn't ask about it, though. He didn't need to know what I knew. I wanted no more of his lies, and I was far better off discovering the truths on my own. He pushed his forearm into my throat, and I smiled, much to his dismay, refusing to fight back, though I could tell something in him wanted me to. He wanted my beast just as much as I wanted his.

"If she dies…"

"Do put your fangs away, Husband. She's not going to die."

"Are you a god now, Deyanira? Do you know what the future will bring?"

I jammed a fist into the sword wound on his side, knocking the air from his lungs. Though, to his credit, he didn't step away. "I know what your future holds if you don't stand down."

"Enough," Paesha finally cut in. "Let her go, Orin."

"There will be no more meetings in this house. No one else comes and goes until further notice."

"Orin," she said again, pleading.

"Tell me I'm wrong," he seethed, words strained with pain as he glared at me. "You stay in this house on your own, or I will lock you back in that room. You are danger incarnate, Nightmare."

"And what does that make you, Orin?"

That darkness within him coiled to the surface. His eyes turned black, face red with rage. The question was right there, sitting between us.

I know, I wanted to scream at him. But I didn't. Instead, I jammed another hand into his side until he backed away.

"If you try to lock me away again, I will burn this precious house of yours to the ground. And then I'll bury you in the ashes. I've given you the benefit of the doubt time and time again. And I've tried. Gods, I've tried to show you all that I am not the monster you make me out to be, yet the only person in this fucking house that trusts me is the damn dog."

I was not their enemy. Perhaps I was nosy and seeking answers to questions they would not provide, but I wasn't going to hurt them. If I could help it.

He hesitated, slightly shifting his weight, the tension easing, if only a little. But it vanished in an instant, replaced by the anger, the familiar dance between us that made it easier to keep him at arm's length.

"The only reason the dog trusts you is because you steal food and keep it in your pocket. Don't twist reality."

His words were a weapon he probably didn't know he wielded so well. A gentle slice to my heart. I nodded slowly before shoving past him and walking straight out of the house. He stormed after me, the door slamming against the frame.

"Deyanira," he commanded.

I kept walking, a tidal wave of emotions wreaking havoc. I wasn't surprised by his words because he'd hated me for longer than I'd known he existed. But I was only human, whether he believed it or not.

"Deyanira," he shouted again.

I rounded on him, balling my hands into fists. "Do not speak my name as if you have any power over me."

His shoulders sank, the broad frame of the monster shrinking to human size. "I didn't mean that. What I said about the dog."

I reached my hand into my pocket and pulled out the treats I'd been saving, letting them fall to the ground. "Yes, you did. But since we're dabbling in honesty tonight, tell me why you married me, Orin. You hate me."

He moved forward, crowding my space, filling every inch. Grabbing the back of my neck, he pulled me close, and I let him. If only to feel the contact from another person. To stroke that kernel of madness in me that wanted him. Even now. Even when I fucking hated him, I wanted him. And I'd only just realized it.

The darkness in his eyes seemed to fade beneath the moonlight. "I need to hate you."

"Why?" I didn't mean to sound as weak as I felt.

He pulled me closer, squeezing those fingers along the back of my neck. Time slowed in his grip. The world stopped. "Because as long as I hate you, you cannot destroy me."

"That's where you're mistaken."

"So you see my dilemma?"

His hand flexed at his side, as if standing close to me required so much from him. I pushed away, breaking the trance the moment had over me.

"I see a coward. And a liar. That's all."

"Look harder, Nightmare."

But there was nothing beyond the mask. A shadow maybe, but nothing more.

"You never answered my question. Why did you marry me?"

He blinked several times, his gaze shifting between mine. "Because I had to."

My eyes fell to the blue band on his arm, resting just above the golden one.

"Drexel forced you to marry me and now he's punishing you for it?" I asked.

"The Maestro does whatever he wants on the whims of his own desires. I am bound to those whims."

"And now me."

He held a hand out. "Come inside, Maiden."

"Tell me where my dagger is. Tell me, and I'll come inside, and I'll stay, like the good girl you wish me to be."

The tic in his jaw was his only response.

"That dagger is not the weapon. I am. I just broke into the king's castle, killed two of his guards, and put down a lot more in order to rescue a little girl you claim as family. I got your best friend out, and they captured no one. Without the dagger. But it's the only thing I have in this world."

"Fine."

An infinitesimal gasp from me lit his dark eyes as he spun on a heel and walked back to the Syndicate house.

Moments later, he left me standing in the hall while he escaped into his bedroom. I'd have to be more thorough with my search next time. When he emerged with Chaos wrapped in a cloth, my heart skipped. As if all the broken pieces of me were slightly mended by the presence of an old friend.

"I'm trusting you to keep your word, Deyanira. Stay in this house."

That was only one on a long list of his mistakes.

I'D NAPPED, waiting for the rest of the house to fall asleep. Paesha didn't smell of death, and the magic within me hadn't stirred. She wouldn't die. Despite that, the floors creaked, and movement sounded throughout the house for far too long as her friends checked on her.

Eventually, really only minutes before sunrise, I slipped past the tree line and stepped into Silbath, hustling through the sleeping city to cross the Hallowed River and stand in my father's lost kingdom, with Chaos strapped to my thigh.

Though the morning crept her way into the world, she wept, filling the sky with the dark hues of blue that promised a storm. As if she'd known what I'd planned for this day and delivered darkness as a favor.

Problems ruled the world. Icharius Fern, from his stronghold, but also the Maestro from Misery's End. And every day that passed was a race against time. The people needed something to hope for, a beacon that wasn't a Maiden who promised an early grave.

So, I would hunt and sacrifice and fail over and over until I found my missing counterpart. The balance the world needed. And standing at the base of a cracked stairway, staring up at a temple that screamed for me to turn away, was truly step number one, thanks to the ancient map on Drexel's office wall.

The lightning mirrored the turmoil within me. The concept of life and healing was both intriguing and unsettling, and as I found myself at the threshold of the Goddess of Life's temple, a place that had been abandoned for centuries, the thought of what lay within sent shivers down my spine.

The rain pounded against the ancient walls, nature's way of warning of the dangers that might await me. But duty and curiosity gnawed at my heart, compelling me to keep going despite my apprehensions. The temple might've held remnants of the goddess's once-vibrant power, a power that I, as a harbinger of Death, feared could consume me whole.

Drawing a deep breath, I closed my eyes to steady my racing thoughts. Part of me wanted to turn away, to retreat to the familiarity of the shadows and the rooftops that'd raised me, where Death's embrace was certain and understood.

I peered through the narrow gap between the door and its frame. Darkness cloaked the interior, and my mind conjured images of forgotten guardians and ancient curses, ready to pounce on any intruder who dared disturb their sanctuary. The sound of distant thunder rumbled like the growl of an ancient, snarling beast, as if warning me that the temple's secrets were not mine to discover.

I carried my own power, one that resonated with the ebb and flow of life and death. But this temple held a different energy, a kind I'd never encountered, an energy of creation and growth that had long since been dormant.

Steeling myself, I pushed against the heavy door, the stone grating against the ground with a groan as it slowly gave way. With each creaking inch, the anticipation built, the fear and excitement intertwining like fragile threads of fate.

I shouldn't be here, and I knew it. Of all the places a Death Maiden could roam, the temple of Eiria was not one of them. But the overgrown willow tree in the back of the temple, its gnarled roots breaking the marbled tiles on the floor, beckoned me. Beyond the dust and dirt, beyond the crevices of filth and abandonment, a force of nature had claimed this temple.

Breaths short, with a bit of fear coursing through my veins, I shuffled through, noting the stone archways and sculptures of naked women draped in fabric circling the room like porcelain guardians. Time had worn down the details, but their eyes still followed me as I moved.

"Where is she?" I whispered, as if the room could answer. "Tell me how to find her."

The tree, though growing in a solid stone building with no access to sunlight beyond the small bits that likely poured in through the stained-glass windows, shifted. I whipped around to the door, wondering if a phantom breeze could have swirled through, but I'd shut it behind me.

I stood within inches of the temple's intruder, the delicate branches of timber lending to the cascading leaves kissing the floor. But it'd moved. I knew it in my soul and felt it in my bones. Pushing the branches to the side, I stepped under the lush canopy, feeling a pulse so strong that all sense of fear vanished. A perfectly laid trap as I shuffled forward and placed my palm against the trunk of the mysterious tree.

Bright, searing light blinded me. Burned me. Raced through my body so ferociously, my back arched to a degree it wasn't supposed to. I screamed. From pain and regret. From the life I'd been given. From the image of every face that flashed across my mind, reminding me I was an abomination in this temple. Of Death. In a place so pure. I thought my spine would snap and my veins would burn to ash. My skin would turn to forgotten embers. I'd ignored the warning in my mind when I'd stood at the door of this forbidden temple and still, I'd entered. Still, I'd damned myself.

"She needs me," I croaked. "I must find her."

I crashed to the floor, my legs eagerly giving out.

"Please," I begged the residual power. "Please help me."

But, though the static of lingering magic drifted in the air, and though I'd begged from the depths of my soul, there were no answers. Not from a goddess. Not from a damned tree. Not from a neglected temple in the heart of a decaying city. Nothing.

There would truly only be one way to get the answers I needed. And though I could hear my earlier self fighting with Regulas, refusing to cater to his desire for torture, I'd finally seen the truth.

Pain.

And malice.

The wrath of Death's Maiden would be the only thing that opened the lips of the silent, tortured people living in fear of a mysterious king and a powerful crime lord.

And so, I prowled.

The abandoned halls of the castle I'd once called home shook me. I'd met no resistance at the gates. In fact, there was no one at all. Not a guard, not even a vagrant who'd gotten brave enough to try to climb the wall. The echoes of my footsteps were my only companion as I walked the familiar steps and stood outside my old bedroom. In another life, another reality, I was a princess, too. Royalty. Revered. Now? I wasn't sure what I was.

I'd climbed the clock tower and sold off valuable jewels, convinced my father's castle was full of traitors, yet every treasure so far remained. Each painting untouched.

My room hadn't changed since that veil had fallen over my face. Not a pillow out of line. But someone had been here. Orin had stolen clothes at some point. Or had it been Paesha or Thea? Surely, not Hollis.

As I walked around my room, I considered the old man and the hope he'd placed in me. As if I could make right the wrongs of his sister, Dahlia. Maybe he hadn't trusted me, and that was wise, but he'd been kind and warm. He'd been more than most.

And when he was near, there was a sense of calm unlike anything I'd ever known. Unlike anything I'd ever gotten between these walls.

I changed from the outfit I'd borrowed from Hollis, covered in the blood of the castle guards no matter how hard I'd tried to clean it. I preferred my own leathers. Black as night, perfectly fitted, with tall leather boots, straps for weapons, and my beloved hood and mask.

Sitting on the edge of my bed in every bit of clothing that marked me as Death's Maiden, I considered ripping it off. I considered wandering the castle in search of a woman's gown, with delicate lace and layers of skirts and corsets and giant bustles to distort my figure into something that stroked a man's desire. I wondered for a fraction of a second if Orin would prefer that before cringing and shoving that thought into the trash.

But still, his words lingered in this fateful room.

"Marry me, Princess Deyanira Sariah Hark.... You could have been anyone. Any age, any beauty. And yet, it was as if the heavens conspired, and fate itself intervened to grant me this privilege."

We'd been standing in front of Ro's mirror. He was so handsome, with dark hair and a perfectly pressed suit. The flawless emulation of the part he played. And he'd looked at me without the darkness that I'd known him to harbor. As if that lighthearted man I'd married was actually in there somewhere, hiding behind his hatred and the black veins surrounding his heart.

The deep patterns of the rug were worn thin before Ro's mirror. I moved to dig my boots into the fibers, remembering how many times I'd stood there and been denied access to her. When I was young, I'd never wanted to leave her sanctuary. The home of a woman who showed me kindness and genuine smiles when no one else dared look me in the eye.

Something in my reflection was different, though it took me

several minutes to figure out what it was. Not the pout of my lips, nor the light dusting of freckles along my cheeks. I stepped closer, blinking several times until I realized a few clusters of my lashes had turned white. Drained of color entirely.

The residual power in the temple had left a permanent mark on me. Nothing glaring, but a warning to stay away, all the same. I should have burned it to the sodden ground out of spite.

I slid my hands over the filigree, watching the silver reflection, waiting for Ro to welcome me into that space that'd saved me from so many nightmares. From myself, just as Orin had said. Nothing. I was unwelcome.

I wondered if I could stay. How long would it be before the new king's men came to claim this castle as a second stronghold in this world? On that thought alone, I packed a bag, mostly with my prized weapons, plucking a few to replace the ones of Thea's I'd lost. I snagged a handful of jewelry for security and a couple of changes of clothes before heading to the single room in this castle I'd never been allowed.

My father's. And it'd been plundered. The only space in the castle they'd cared about.

Torn, deep-red curtains hung askew off a broken rod, letting only trace amounts of blue, stormy light in to showcase the ransacked bedroom. I moved my fingers into the fresh gashes ripped down the surface of the large, ornate wooden desk, stepping on the shattered glass from the broken lamp on the floor. Broken quills and spilled ink pots were the lasting sign of my father's devotion to his work. He'd kept a small bed in the corner of the cavernous room, and I wondered what it had looked like when my mother had been alive. Had the bed been massive then? Had it been warm, the fireplace always burning? A sanctuary that was strictly theirs, or had it always been a cluster of rooms that were mostly for work and sleep only when their bodies grew so tired they begged for reprieve?

He'd been hunting for the Life Maiden for so long—since my birth, it'd seemed. Surely, there was something here. But when I approached the stack of papers sitting in the corner, rather than finding pieces of relevant information, I found a list of names. Familiar names. He'd kept a tally of each of my victims, just as I had, though the most recent deaths were not yet etched into my back.

I flipped through the pages. Sometimes his handwriting was carefully scripted and sometimes a blur of names nearly illegible. I felt each of them on my back, each flower, and again thought of Ro. My heart ached. My father had been cruel. But he was my only family, even in his hatred. Still, I was broken because of him. I wanted what the others at the Syndicate house had.

I shuffled the bag on my shoulder and turned away, scanning the vacant room for signs of anything else that might be useful. It hadn't taken long for a spider to weave his web over the bookcase along the wall adjacent to the vandalized desk. Swiping it away, no spider in sight, I pulled the books that weren't already thrown to the floor, studying each title. Though none seemed significant, mostly lists of ancestry and battles long since won, when I slid the final book from the shelf, all the pages fell to the floor. As if they'd been ripped from the binding or hidden within.

Curious, I thought for sure there must be something here, but as I read through the papers, it was only a ledger of births, similar to the ledger of deaths I'd found. I frowned, scanning the names. Most were those of my father's court, here in the castle and some scattered through the city, but not as many. Of course, he hadn't kept track of every child. His courtiers were far more important to him. More than I was.

I shoved the papers back into the book and tossed it into my bag, regretting destroying the spider's new home for nothing.

Everything had been for nothing. And a bit of me sympathized with Regulas in that moment. If my father had charged him with finding the Life Maiden and he'd come up as empty-handed as I had, he'd likely been on the receiving end of Demir Hark's wrath. Mostly he'd deserved it, though. If not for lack of trying, then because he was an asshole.

I didn't spend any more time dwelling. Instead, I stood at the door of my father's castle and wondered if I had the strength to use the threats and force he'd wanted me to. Could I hold a blade to an innocent man's throat and demand information? Yes. Yes, I could. But I really didn't want to have to do that.

Drops of rain fell onto my cheeks in a scattered pattern of defeat and sadness. I could no longer define what my life was, beyond waiting for Death to wrench me into his dark court and deliver a name. I thought I could find her. I was wrong. And I was nothing.

Spiraling through my despair, it wasn't until two giant brown eyes stared down at me, floppy ears covering half of Boo's face before I realized I wasn't alone on the rooftop of the only place I'd thought to come back to. Despite my feelings, I smiled, sitting up to scratch him behind those golden ears as I glanced at Quill, standing in the doorframe, a halo of warm light from the house illuminating her wild, curly hair. She held a worn blanket in her arm, but her eyes were red and full of tears as she stared at me.

I peeled myself from my perch, soaking wet, and carried Boo to the door.

"Are you hurt?"

She shook her head, looking between me and her pup.

"Hungry?"

"No," she whispered, bottom lip beginning to quiver.

Kneeling before the child, I kept a safe distance so I wouldn't scare her. "I can't help you if you don't tell me what's wrong. You have to be brave enough to speak it."

She nodded, her little pink nose sniffling. "You're scary."

"I am," I agreed, though I hated to always be seen as the embodiment of fear. "Does it bother you to be near me? Shall I leave?"

"No," she said quickly. "You're scary to the bad men. But you're my friend. And if you stay with me, then they won't come and take me again."

"Ah. So, I am not your villain."

She forced a smile. "You're theirs."

I stood, reaching a hand down for the child to take it before leading her back to her bedroom.

Only when I'd avoided entering her room did she tug on my hand. "Will you stay with me? Please. If they come and they see you here, they will leave."

"I can't stay forever, Quill."

She pointed her face to the ground, eyes falling. "Will you for just this one night?"

"Okay, kid. Just this one night. But let me change out of these soaking wet clothes."

"Will you wear your fight clothes... just in case?"

"If it makes you feel safer, I can. I'll be right back."

"I'll come with you," she said, practically clinging to my leg. Poor thing.

That night, she lay in her small bed, cream-colored blankets pulled all the way up to her pointed chin. Boo leapt from my arms, circling a spot that was likely his no fewer than fifteen times before finally plopping down. She patted the bed beside her, and I crawled in, lying on top of the blankets, holding my breath as she snuggled next to me. I could have cried at the contact. At the pure soul of a child who seemed to see me more clearly than anyone else, as if her mind wasn't fogged over by the stories of past Maidens.

I swirled my hands through her brown hair, smoothing the tangles as the full moonlight finally broke through the clouds and filled her small room with its silvery light. I thought she was asleep until she drew in a heavy breath.

"One day, when I get to dance on the stage, will you come and watch me and Boo? He's getting pretty good."

I chuckled. "Of course, I will, kid."

"You can bring me flowers," she said quietly, the sleep heavy in her voice.

"I promise I will. But why do you stay with the Maestro? Truly?"

Her eyes fell shut on a giant yawn. "Because he is my friend. And he's supposed to keep me safe. He promised."

"But he didn't?"

"It must have been an accident," she said, so sleepy the words came out as one.

"Take it from me, Quill. It's far better to learn to protect and rely on yourself in this world. You can't trust anyone."

Perhaps it was the fresh wound of standing in his bedroom, but I'd heard my father in those words, and I didn't regret them at all.

"Okay," she said several moments later, likely from within her dream.

I lay for hours in that bed, nodding off several times, but I grew so afraid she'd wake to my face and scream, realizing the bad guy was actually the one she'd invited into her room, I eventually rolled carefully to the side and stood. Boo poked his little white head up, peeking at me with one eye open and a small growl in his throat.

"Good boy," I whispered, patting his head as he yawned and lay back down. "You are a big, ferocious beast."

I turned to walk away when a hint of movement outside Quill's window caught my eye. And though I couldn't see his handsome face, I'd know that silhouette anywhere now. The question was, where was he headed so late at night? And how quickly could I catch up?

I stayed as far away as I could, stalking Orin as he snuck through Silbath, crossed the bridge to Perth, and stood under a streetlamp, the mist of the dreary weather bathing him. As he watched the road, adjusting the leather gloves on his hands and then the brim of the hat on his head, I waited, wondering why he'd dressed so fine.

He paced for a moment before slipping into the shadowed alleyway nearby. The moon had been a blessing thus far, but it made the darkness darker, and he knew that. I'd been born to hunt, though, and the rooftops had never let me down.

He watched over his shoulder enough, and I wondered if he felt me nearby. The beggars in the alleyways paid him no mind, and, aside from the occasional lady of the night he'd kept a wide berth from, no one else seemed to notice him. Eventually, he leaned against a wall near the Badger Hole, checking his watch several times. A rat got too close, and he stomped his foot to scare it away, drawing the attention of birds that hoped he had food.

The wretched cough of a man that sounded as if he'd been sick for most of his life, the kind that weak lungs attacked, could be heard in the far distance. Over the whimpers and pants of those half-naked and frantic a few blocks down, he began to whistle. His perfect pitch carried a tune as haunting as his cello and as dark as his heart.

The sharp jaw of his silhouette was unmistakable. For everything there was to absolutely loathe about the man, Orin was truly beautiful. He kept a clean shave, his hair always combed. He wore suits as if he were a man of stature, and even his gloves were never without their own shine.

And he was mine. Something in that thought caused the band around my wrist to pulse, and when he paused his tune to whip around, as if his marriage bond had also pulsed, I sucked in a sharp breath and ducked low. Just in case. When I peeked back up, I had just caught the coattails of his jacket as he entered the Badger Hole. Two seconds later, I would have missed him.

I leaped over the railing and climbed down the old apartment building I'd been squatting on and casually strolled across the cobblestone street to peer in the window. He'd settled into a booth in the far corner of the old room, his back to the door. Making sure my hood was up, I debated the mask before deciding to forgo it and just walk in.

No one seemed to notice me as I slipped into a high-top table closer to the door. When he ordered two drinks and slid his gloves off, I held my breath, searching the bare skin of his palms. I was sure there would be a name there. But his palms were blank. And I'd been so distracted that I'd nearly missed the woman who swept across the room minutes after the drinks had been delivered.

With chin-length hair and slanted eyes, donning the most beautiful feminine face I'd ever seen, I smothered my gasp with the back of my hand, wondering what the fuck Ro was doing with Orin.

CHAPTER 27

Ro had kept me at arm's length my whole life, and I was only now realizing it. When the title had been stripped away and my world crashed down, she hadn't come until I was on her turf, in the Scarlet District. And even then, she'd ushered me down a hallway and right...

Gods.

She'd delivered me to Orin, who'd been waiting in the alley the night he'd stabbed me. She might as well have had a leash because I'd blindly followed. My skin crawled. And then the fury ignited. Starting in my chest and fanning outward until my fingers shook, my heart raced, and I saw nothing but red. Whatever game I'd been tangled in, however ridiculous I'd looked before, knowing the truth made me that much more foolish.

But the thing that really got me, the single point that crept up my spine and gripped me in a chokehold, was the fact that Ro might've been working with the Maestro. All this time, all these years, had she been in bed with the biggest crime lord in the realm? Anyone worth their death knew to stay away from him. She couldn't possibly be tangled up with the lackey and not the overseer. I'd learned firsthand she preferred the top of the ranks.

At first, I wondered if they could be lovers. I wouldn't put it past Ro, but I didn't know enough about Orin to make that assumption conclusively. They'd never leaned into each other during their lengthy conversation. They'd only shared a friendly smile here and there, as they seemed to discuss something much more serious.

My nerves rattled, as if my body were urging me to stand and walk over. To let them know I'd caught them red-handed. But as always, I kept it to myself, letting the truths fall into place around me until I could work it out on my own. I didn't need any of them, and I'd seen enough. Still, I could feel the challenge boiling.

A drunk man stumbled into my table. I'd hardly noticed until he turned with a sloppy smile, bearing exactly three yellow teeth. Eyes too heavy from alcohol scanned me in a sweep of realization as he stumbled backward, slamming into another table.

"Mai—

"Shh," I cut him off, gripping Chaos on my thigh.

He froze, pissing himself as I stood. Something in that moment, the fury, the edge of my self-control, the magic maybe, wanted me to lash out. To fall victim to the desires of bloodlust that ran deep in my veins. To whip my arm across the innocent man's throat and watch him bleed, just as the harbingers that came before me would have done. Watch the people scream and scatter. See the look in Orin's eyes when he saw me standing in a pool of blood, confirming every thought he had of me.

And I would have fucking smiled. I would have waited for Death to come just to watch the entire place fall into chaos because I was so angry. Odds were the drunk wasn't so innocent. He'd probably done vile things, as we all had. As I had, even in my poisonous thoughts.

I shoved myself away from the table and walked out, heart racing. Breaths staggering. Drowning in the thought that this could be what the others had felt before the madness took over. This could be the breaking point. I willed myself to see reason. Think logically. Be smart. Everything revolved around one single person. Each piece of the puzzle led me back to Drexel Vanhoff, the Maestro, the monster. Including Orin, but I'd rather have poked my eyes out with toothpicks than deal with him when I was so furious.

As if the world was slowly fading to madness, each of its dwellers more desperate for reprieve than ever before, the faint smell of smoke coalescing from the opium den blocks away from Misery's End turned my stomach. I wondered if Drexel was there, with his red mustache twisted into a fresh curl as he sat upon an imaginary throne in his favorite section, watching the lower ranks of Silbath slip into their drug-induced haze. Or was he barking orders to his lackeys, forcing innocent people to pay him what few coins they had, threatening to break them if they didn't comply? Perhaps he was sitting in Icharius Fern's castle, discussing the capture of Quill and the loss of his guards.

Either way, the theater was quiet. I clung to the opposite side of the street from a woman barely dressed, with her long, slender leg hung over the shoulder of a man on his knees. She made eye contact with me, but I couldn't tell if the gasp was for me or him. I adjusted my hood, glad to have the mask across my face, and circled the back of the building. I'd wanted to get back into Drexel's office, but there were fresh bars covering the windows. Thea's handiwork, most likely.

Even when the city slumbered through the night or the day, the theater itself was likely guarded. But the warehouse behind, the one with the tunnel that passed under the street, might not have been. And if it was, then I'd test my luck and see how far it carried me.

The building had no windows, and there were so many decaying marks along the side that one might wonder how this could belong to the same man who took such care with the details and beauty of his grand theater. But that was likely the point.

Much to Drexel's dismay, I was sure the warehouse was easy to break into. A well-placed pin in the lock, a few shakes, and she gave way with ease. But when the door slammed shut behind me the second I stepped inside, a sense of dread began to seep in. The fear I held was not from the possibility of confrontation, but rather the way the door had slammed. The finality of the sound, as if stepping into this world had exposed me to the man that hunted me my entire life. His absolute control over his magically bound men meant, regardless of their fear, they would not stop if he commanded my capture. A soft creak underfoot echoed through the space as I began to explore. The warehouse was a treasure trove of items essential for running the burlesque.

Corsets of various colors and sizes were draped over ornate dressing screens, their intricate lace and silk hinting at the allure of the performers who wore them. Feathered headdresses and sparkling hairpins adorned vanity tables, indicating a place of opulence and glamor. Though the outside of the building was in ruin, the inside was exactly as I'd imagined.

A cluster of delicate handheld fans, some bearing exotic painted scenes and others with intricate patterns, rested on a nearby table alongside a stack of posters that beckoned patrons to witness the spectacular performances. Rows of costumes caught my attention, dresses that shimmered with sequins and beads, tassels swaying sensually with every imagined move-ment, and gloves that extended beyond the elbow. They reminded me of Hollis and the care he'd taken with his needle-work. Bathed in the dim light of the sitting room, a needle pressed between his lips as he took so much care with each stitch.

Mirrors lined one wall, reflecting the ghosts of twirling dancers and passionate rehearsals. Unmoving, I listened to the static in the air for a breath or a step, any sign of a guard or a performer that might have stayed or snuck in for shelter. But none came, and the outside world felt a million miles away from this space.

I placed my fingers on the ivory of the polished piano, holding my breath as I plinked a black key. Again, I listened for the sign of anyone at all. But none came. I took only a moment to admire the contraptions Althea had likely built. Large mirrors and swings and even a giant jewelry box with moving pieces for a dancer to poise upon. She was far too talented to be wasted on the likes of the Maestro when she could have truly done something for this world. I wondered about her debt as I searched the dimly lit space for the access point to the tunnel.

Something in the air changed. A charge, raising the hair on my arms, my spine going ramrod straight. I hadn't heard the warehouse door open, but I knew, deep in my soul, as if there were a tether between us, that Orin had crept inside. And gods, did he fill the massive space. His presence was like a full-grown, otherworldly beast being shoved into a box.

"Deyanira," he hissed, the sound of his voice making me shudder.

I'd been caught. There was no way I could search the theater or get back into Drexel's office with him following me. The only real option was to escape while I was ahead. To cross under the street and take out Drexel's men at the front of the theater on my way out. Or I could turn around, make Orin a target, and leave him on the warehouse floor. At least with him, I knew what I was getting. One man. Easily subdued.

Silently, I scoured the wall, staying hidden as I held my breath and shifted until my fingers moved over a hinge. Perhaps I could spare him. But the door was massive. Tall enough to move all the props and performers back and forth on a show night. There was no way Orin wouldn't hear it open. And if, by some miracle, he didn't, he'd certainly see it.

"Come out, come out wherever you are, Nightmare."

Having no choice, his footsteps creeping closer, I slid the door open and darted into the tunnel. I hoped there would be something to use as a barricade, but the space was nothing more than an upper landing of a wide, dingy stairwell.

A small blue glow from somewhere below beckoned me forward, and I gladly ran for the light. My stomach fluttered, not from the prospect of being caught, but from Orin, my husband, chasing me.

His boots scraped against the threshold as he followed. I felt the curse on his lips moments before he uttered it aloud. Still, I ran, aiming for the other end of the chilly tunnel. I felt him before I saw him closing the distance. As if something within me had spent these last days more aware of him than anything else, even if I'd hardly seen him, and when I had, the words were short and the glares long. He silently gave chase, but I was faster.

I expected a second set of stairs to lead me back up to the theater, but the opposite end of the tunnel showcased a door instead. Keeping within the walls of my hood, I twisted the knob, but it was locked.

There was no keyhole. Panic rose as his footsteps drew nearer.

"Deyanira, stop," he commanded.

But I didn't listen, frantic to open the door and get away

from him. Based on his footsteps echoing, he'd already made it halfway through the tunnel. Heart racing, I felt the shaft of the knob, searching for a switch or anything to trigger the locking mechanism. Nothing. I stepped back. Scanning. Three metal buttons glimmered in the faint light.

I tried to imagine Althea. What kind of contraption would she have created with the buttons? But as he closed the distance, there was no time to mull it over. I slammed a palm over all of them, just as a firm hand landed on my shoulder and yanked me backward, saving me from the stone door that plummeted from the ceiling of the tunnel.

"Tell me, Maiden," he said, moments after the dust settled. "What part of the word stop was difficult to understand?"

Glancing over my shoulder, I finally laid eyes on him. His brutally handsome features twisted into something vicious. Something so beautiful, it would always make me falter. And I hated the vulnerability that came with that. Trained to be nothing more than a killer, the sound of my husband's voice lured dangerous desires to the surface. His very presence was an alarming distraction.

I shoved away from him, my hood falling with the motion. Instead of answering, I dug my fingers under the stone to push the door back up. It didn't budge. Spinning away in frustration, I ran back the way we'd come, only to find another stone wall covering the door.

Orin held a cocky grin on his face, hands in his pockets, the dim blue lamp in the tunnel casting a halo around him. "Life lesson. Never push every button. One is always a trap. And the Maestro loves catching mice in his tunnel."

I glared. "How do we get out?"

"We don't."

"What do you mean, we don't?"

"Althea designed this with mechanisms at the doors. She

doesn't make mistakes. Neither of us will be getting out of here until someone retracts the stone at either end of the tunnel."

"And how long will that take?" I asked, though I wasn't sure I wanted the answer.

"Two days, if we're lucky. Three, if rehearsal is canceled before show night."

Trapped. Gods. The walls began to move, inching inward. This couldn't happen. I'd paint this tunnel red with his blood if Death came. He had no idea of the danger. I swallowed the rising anxiety, keeping the fear from my face.

"Three days? I'm not staying down here with you for three days."

He scanned me slowly, dark hair falling across his brow, the murky light framing his sharpened jaw. "Oh, I wouldn't worry about that. You're far better off asking what's going to happen when we're found."

I stormed forward until I was close enough to see those rare gold flecks in his eyes. "I'm not afraid of your master. Nor his lackeys."

He was so swift, I hardly registered the movement until his fingers were around my throat, pressing me up against the wall, the darkness I'd become so accustomed to baiting me. "Then what are you afraid of?" His touch was like fire against my skin. He squeezed, his grasp threatening.

"Being trapped underground with the vilest human I've ever laid eyes on."

Orin leaned in, pressing his forehead to mine, stealing my breath as my body reacted to him, unraveled for him, until he bared his teeth and practically growled. "Then I guess we have something in common."

I snatched Chaos before he could make another move against me and brought her to his throat. "If I press hard enough to slice your esophagus, you'll drown in your own blood before you have a chance to bleed out." I moved the blade to his ribs. "If I thrust with enough force, I can open the chambers of your heart and cause excruciating pain before you die, writhing on this sodden ground." Down and to the side, I pressed hard enough to snap the beautiful threads of his lovely suit. "But if I really wanted you to suffer, I'd take my time, immobilizing you before removing each organ while it was still warm and attached, sending you into shock long before you passed out and never woke up. I do not fear the Maestro because he is not worthy. Not when I've stared Death in the face and denied him. But do not tempt me, husband."

"Yes, Nightmare," he purred, moving his hand down my throat until it rested on my sternum. "We've established the fact that you can kill. But can you live?"

CHAPTER 28

He was beautiful. Fueled by anger and frustration, he sat against the door, with his head tilted back and eyes closed. I wanted to hate every last thing about him, but that was one thing I couldn't do. Still, I knew there had to be good in there. I'd felt a shred of kindness when we'd stood before that mirror, and he'd stared into my eyes. His words were lies, though. And maybe he truly was nothing more than a performer.

The chill from the evening settled into my bones. The dark tunnel didn't provide an ounce of warmth as I clutched my knees to my chest, avoiding the damp wall. The tall ceiling had been an obvious choice to move their contraptions back and forth, but trapped in the bowels of the cold earth, I loathed them all the same, knowing the heat, what little might reside down here, was likely lingering along the stone ceiling.

I turned my face away from Orin, staring instead down the long prison, wondering when the sun would rise, replaying all the moments that led us to this point. The second I'd laid eyes on that prick, my entire world had spiraled out of control. Now, essentially homeless, as poor as a drifter on Beggar's Row, perhaps eventually he'd push me so far that I'd become the villain he believed I was.

"Here."

It took every bit of self-control not to flinch at his proximity when I hadn't heard him move. I couldn't look at him. His suit jacket plopped down over me, and, out of the corner of my eye, I could see him planting his feet, as if waiting for the battle of wits to recommence.

"It is customary for a gesture of kindness to be followed by a thank-you. No rush, Deyanira. I'll wait for you to discover manners."

The sharp tang of metal filled my mouth as I bit my cheek to save him the tongue lashing. But when that fucking boot began to tap, when that cheerful whistle left those pouty lips, I leapt to my feet and shoved his jacket back at him. "I don't want your pity."

The coat fell unceremoniously to the damp floor.

He didn't move an inch. "I preferred you more when you thought I was groveling at your feet, promising love and an eternity of affection. You should smile more."

Rage—unbridled, cold, feminine rage exploded from me. I planted a palm into his chest, shoving him away. "You are the most selfish, infuriating, hypocritical, misogynistic pig I've ever laid eyes on. And that's saying something, considering I've prowled Requiem, stood in the grime of Beggar's Alley, hunted the Silk Road, and spent too many long nights in an opium den when I was younger. You're worse than the Maestro. I hope you know that. Gods. You're worse than the king."

"Which one? Alive or dead?" he asked with a smirk, as if he'd taken so much pleasure in my anger.

"You'd be worse than all of them if they crawled back from their graves as fucking monsters."

He shifted forward, right back into my comfort zone, resting a hand on the wall beside me, his body so warm against mine, I had to remind myself I hated him as he smirked. "Feeling warmer, Wife?"

I faltered for a second, realizing I'd played right into his hands. Baring my teeth, I snapped. "I hate you."

He leaned forward, his cheek pressed against my temple as the deep timbre of his voice raced down my spine. "I hate you, too."

I pushed him away again. "I don't think you do. I think you enjoy this game of cat and mouse. Every conversation is a battle, and every interaction is infuriating. You could try being nice, for once."

"I just handed you my jacket. I let you stay at my house."

I snorted. "The house you try to force me to stay inside?"

"The house that keeps you away from everyone that would rather see you dismembered than lurking on the streets."

"Because everyone thinks I'm out here murdering people because I want to."

His jaw tightened. "And why is that?"

"You're wrong." My hands shook. From the anger or the cold, I wasn't sure. "I've never killed a single person because I wanted to. I didn't ask for this. And the worst thing you can do is lock me away. If that were the answer, I'd still be rotting in my father's dungeon."

He faltered, but only for a second.

"You don't understand, and you never will. I can't stop it. If the power takes over, I will claw my way out of a prison. I'll tear the skin from my bones without a coherent thought in my mind to get to Death's victim. I will rip off my own arms. I'll fade into madness and kill everyone I can find until the name

I'm given is dead. This magic is a burden. It's devastation. It's cruelty. And if I could stop it, I would. But Death's will trumps everything..." I paused, debating the vulnerability I didn't want to show. But I was weak. "And your hatred of me makes it ten times worse. I know it means nothing to you, but we are bound. And everyone else in my life is dead. It doesn't have to be this way." My voice broke on that final word. "I'm tired, okay? Just leave me alone."

I turned to walk away, but he grabbed my arm, forcing me to look at him. "I didn't know."

Breaking free of his grip, my shoulders fell. "Of course, you didn't. You never asked. You just assumed. Like everyone else. Just because Paesha and Althea had a choice with their magic before Drexel trapped them doesn't mean I do."

"Tell me why you came here. Why did I chase you all the way from Perth?"

I thought maybe a little truth would make him hate me less. Casting my eyes to the ground, I dug a toe into a groove between two carefully placed bricks that made up the tunnel floor. "I'm searching for the Life Maiden."

He barked a laugh, but when my head snapped up and I glared, he covered his mouth. "I'm sorry. It's not funny. Sorry."

Tiny wrinkles around his eyes betrayed his hidden smile. If he carried any guilt about hoarding secrets, about the missing power, they didn't show on his face at all. In fact, the surprise had cast further doubt on my initial assumption about him. The idea was so far-fetched. How could harboring life power make him a killer? How would the Maestro possibly have the sway to change magic? I was wrong. I'd have to start over, which made me bitter.

"What good are you doing for the world, Orin Faber? Tied to a man who collects people as servants and trades away children who trust him? And don't tell me that's not what happened with Quill. There's no way she was taken under everyone's nose without Drexel having something to do with it."

He stopped for a moment; the wrinkles vanished as his hand dropped from his face. Amber eyes searched mine for something I didn't think he'd find.

Eventually, he spoke, softer, more genuine, peeling away a layer of his mask. "I never claimed him to be a hero. If I could be free of him, I would be."

He rolled the sleeves of his collared shirt as if he'd needed a distraction. Those two bands, one that belonged to me and one to Drexel, sat like weights around his wrist. He rubbed them as if it would make them go away. But, of course, it didn't. I searched the muscles of his forearm, wondering if I'd see those black veins again or if it was a tattoo, and my mind had only played tricks on me, but nothing else marked his arms.

"I know you gave your freedom for your mother's. That's the only thing that allows me to close my eyes at night, knowing I sleep near a monster."

Bending down, he picked up the jacket from the floor and swiped a hand down it to clean the mud. "She told you?"

"She did," I said, leaning back against the wall for only a second before I remembered it was freezing cold.

"She's never been good with orders." A genuine smile lit his face, and it was the most handsome thing I'd ever seen. A moment of amenability before his gaze cut to mine, and he turned, brushing away the moment. "You might as well give up searching for the Life Maiden and focus on the missing people instead. If Paesha can't find her, there's no way you will. And the Maestro has commanded it, so it's not like she's giving a half-hearted effort. She has no choice."

"But why wouldn't she be able to find her?"

"Because she's never seen her, she doesn't have a name to hunt. She has no connection to her. You could tell her to find a red bootlace and she'd have it in less than three minutes. But with no point of reference, there's nothing for the magic to cling to."

"Wait. Missing people?"

"You don't know?"

I shook my head. "No clue what you're talking about."

"Perhaps we'll leave that for another time, then."

He held the jacket out toward me once more and lifted a brow. Letting my stubbornness falter, I took it, burying my arms into the sleeves that were far too big. It smelled like him. Of the perfumed oils he'd used to clean my hair and the soap he'd bathed in the river with. Of something masculine laced with something softer.

A moment became a lifetime as we stared at each other. I understood the toxicity with this man. The fighting and the anger. The hatred and the violence. I understood the desire even, living in the tension he'd curated the moment he'd stepped into my palace bedroom. But I didn't understand this moment. And I wasn't sure I could trust myself to work it out, given my jaded history. I knew sword fights. I didn't know people. Or genuine feelings.

"Thank you," I whispered. "For this."

His eyes darkened. "So civilized, Nightmare."

"Must you ruin every moment of peace?"

He stepped back into my space, and this time I didn't move away. "Every one." He curled an index finger under my chin, lifting my gaze, staring at me so closely that the golden flecks in his eyes shimmered. He was obsessed with touching me, it seemed.

"Are you waving your white flag, Husband?" I managed.

"Let's call it gray."

I smiled. "I don't think you understand the terms of war.

People don't walk around with various shades of flags in their pockets, depending on their mood."

"I don't believe you know war either, Maiden," he whispered, long lashes kissing his cheeks as he blinked. "People don't just walk around threatening every single person they come into contact with when they feel uncomfortable."

"Oh, that's not war. That's self-preservation."

A thousand volts of lightning could have struck the ground around us, and I wouldn't have felt more charged than I did standing here before him, without the veils of anger. He was no more than a breath from me, staring down, and, though I didn't realize I'd been moving, my back collided with the wall. But he'd followed effortlessly. As if it were a dance, and I was the lead.

The cool embrace of the stones pressing against my back was not enough to break the trance. Though judging by the lazy gaze, perhaps I was the one beguiling him. But just as soon as that intoxicating moment passed, he pushed off the wall and stepped away.

"You should try to sleep."

I looked anywhere but at him, knowing I'd see the mask again. "It's too cold to sleep down here."

"Floor's dry by the door. It sits on an incline to help angle the props. You could use the jacket as a blanket if you want."

I didn't want to. I wouldn't fall asleep here. If I woke up in Death's court, I couldn't control what would happen when I came back to this reality. But I'd always preferred my own company, so I walked away.

The space was dry but still freezing, and though I'd put the jacket over my head so I could pretend I was alone, I just couldn't let myself trust him, even with Chaos gripped tightly in my hands. I held my breath, listening for him until my teeth chattered. A few times he puffed hot air into his hands, rubbing them to keep warm.

"Do you want your jacket back?" I peeked down the dark blue tunnel, through the small mercy of lights that'd remained on.

He smoothed his hands down his thighs but shook his head. "You keep it."

I lay my head back down, shivering, the cold so gripping I felt as if I'd bathed in an icy river and then rolled in a snowbank. My toes had long since gone numb. He paced and jumped around, and if I were sleeping, I'd probably have been woken and annoyed.

Sitting up again, I locked eyes with him. "We both know the solution here."

"We do," he said, blowing into his fingers again.

"Come on, then."

He stalked up the tunnel, his figure growing until he towered over me. "You sure, Maiden?"

"I'm going to start calling you Icky again if you don't call me Dey. I don't want to be the Maiden, and every time you say it, I want to slice your tongue from your mouth."

"You are so dramatic," he said, plopping down beside me.

"Dey," I followed.

He nudged me with a shoulder. "You are so dramatic, Dey... No... I think I like Nightmare the best. You're so dramatic, Nightmare."

"I hate you." I yawned.

We sat pressed together for hours. Until the cold waned and the conversation ran dry. Until my eyes grew heavy and his stories of performing grew slower.

"You can't let me fall asleep," I said for the third time.

"I'm not." He sighed. "Stay awake."

He wrapped his arm around me, and I listened to his heart-beat until it'd nearly lulled me to sleep.

The second my head nodded, he jammed a finger into my ribs. "Stay awake."

"How many hours do you think it's been?" I asked, forcing my sleepy eyes open.

"Three weeks."

His joke was the last thing I heard before the exhaustion took me.

CHAPTER 29

"**H**onestly, it's just a blade. Thea can fix that with her hands bound."

I glared. "You nicked the tip. Anyone worth their death knows, once it's compromised, a dagger is never going to be the same."

He held Chaos up to the faint light, squinting. "This tiny scratch? It's fine."

Snatching the blade back, I slid her into my holster and smirked when his jaw dropped.

"Don't act like that. We have nothing else to do."

"Using my knife as a pencil is no longer an option. Find a rock or something."

He flashed an arrogant smile before crossing his arms over his broad chest to stare down at me. "You're just mad because you haven't won a single game yet."

I shoved him playfully. "I didn't have the same upbringing as you did. Or did you forget you had to teach me how to play?"

"How could I forget? You keep reminding me every time you lose."

I'd woken with a start, steeped in a pile of dread until I oriented myself, remembering I was trapped in an underground tunnel with a man who had tried to kill me weeks ago. His arm was draped heavily over my body, and his warm breath caressed my ear. He'd snored softly, and I lay there, afraid to wake him. Afraid that when he woke, it would be those dark eyes that stared at me, hated me, and not the amber ones that made him only a man.

Maybe the eyes never truly changed, but the hatred and the glares did, and that was the balancing act I'd learned to expect from him. He woke shortly after I did, but I only knew because of the change in breathing. Because we'd both lay there longer than we should have. Afraid to jostle the other and admit that there were seeds of companionship, if nothing else. And gods. I'd been so alone I couldn't peel myself away from that man's embrace if I'd wanted to.

"We should go over the plan again," he said, squatting on the floor to look for a rock.

"As long as you don't turn my dagger into a blunt object by playing children's games on the walls, I think we'll be fine."

"Got one," he shouted, swiping a pebble from the ground. "Did you have any better ideas to pass the time?"

"Almost anything else."

He held out a hand. "Calm down, Dey. I meant ideas that don't involve being naked."

"So did I," I scowled.

"I saw that look in your eyes this morning," he teased, drawing a giant square on an unmarked section of the stone wall. He stepped back to admire his handiwork before examining the rock again. "It's not perfect, but it'll do."

"Let's take a break."

"Afraid to lose again?"

I pressed my hand to my chest dramatically. "Oh, yes. I'm so worried. Failing at this game is ten times worse than oh, I don't know, Drexel opening one of these doors and finding us down here."

"I've told you he won't," he said, face serious. All hints of play gone. "It'll be one of three people: Hollis—which would be ideal—Ebert Roper, who might not matter if I bribe him well enough, or Cassius. Cassius will be a problem. He doesn't care about anything but the boss's favor. He'd run over his own mother with a team of horses if it won him a single nod. He's not bound to Drexel. His mind is twisted, Deyanira. If he gets a hold of you, he'll... well, he's just not going to."

"If he gets ahold of me, he's standing far too close. You can worry about Paesha and Thea, Hollis and your mother, Quill and even Boo, but you don't have to worry about me. There's not a weak bone in my body."

He moved in, resting his hand on my shoulder. "You're still vulnerable. You married a stranger after thirty minutes of persuasion."

My mouth fell open, but I couldn't argue that.

"I don't say that to be mean, you know? I say it because it's true, and it's a weakness. And he'll use any weakness to get to you, just like the boss will. And Cassius is only the stepping stone. Drexel is the real problem. You have to stay away from him. He can't know where you're weak. He can't speak to you. Ever."

"I've been avoiding him my whole life. I know that."

He brought heavy hands to my shoulders before lifting my chin to gaze into my eyes. "Promise me you'll stay away from him. If he binds you, he'll make you kill anyone that stands in his way. Anyone at any time. He'll take advantage until you have no soul left, Dey."

"I promise. I was weak one time, and I learned my lesson the hard way."

Smoothing his palms down my arms, he grabbed my hands and held them between us. "I know it doesn't feel like it, but you can trust me. And you can trust Paesha."

"You do understand what you're saying, though, right? Since the night we were bound, the Maestro has been punishing you. But he forced you to marry me. If he wants me, you have to deliver. And no one understands the magical compulsion more than I do. That means I can't trust you. I also..." I paused, wondering how far I could take this. But we were at a place and time we may never get back. Where neither of us could run, and we weren't trying to hurt each other.

"Was that a complete thought?"

His smile, so rare behind his dark features, made me weak. I didn't want to break the fragile strand of kindness between us. But I also didn't want the secrets. And he'd been with Ro, whether he wanted to talk about it or not.

"I saw you kill a man in Perth, Orin. I know you're a Death Lord."

He laughed. A genuine, full-belly laugh that had to have been heard on the streets above us. I pulled away, crossing my arms over my chest.

"I don't know what you saw, but I think we both know you're the only person here beholden to Death." He flashed his bare hands in the air. "No names here."

I studied him for a second, searching for signs of a lie. "I know what I saw."

"You're wrong, Nightmare. I'm not a Death Lord. I've never been given a name by him."

"So, you're going to stand here one moment and tell me I can trust you when you know I can't because you are not your own person, but then still lie to me?"

He pulled me toward him. I wanted to fight, to push away and demand answers. But the way his broken expression held me, I just couldn't. "I need you to understand that I cannot speak to you about this."

I searched his pleading eyes for the truth. "Can't or won't?"

"Can't."

Whatever the truth was, the Maestro had forbidden him from speaking of it. And at the very least, I understood magic. He was bound. And that was that.

"Okay," I said, softening. "I won't push."

A creek at the opposite end of the tunnel leading to the warehouse snapped us both apart, shattering the moment as we launched into action.

"Stick to the plan," Orin hissed. "Don't move unless I tell you to."

"I'm not an idiot. Go."

He ran to meet whoever opened the door. And though I was strictly warned I couldn't kill anyone without giving myself away, as if that was my only skill, I still loosened the strap on Chaos, deciding to take my chances. If the guard he was worried about happened to come down, I'd strike first and ask questions later. Murder was not a skill. But dancing around it was.

The grinding of stone on stone filled the tunnel. I was poised, ready to attack, should Orin give any signs of distress, but rather than a fight, a clear, sharp whistle echoed through the space. My shoulders dropped. No danger.

Walking forward, I kept a hand on my blade, unwilling to trust what I didn't see with my own eyes, but it was only Paesha standing at the top of the steps, leaning on the frame in full performance attire, including a white feathered headdress. Likely an excuse to be in the warehouse if she needed it. With a corset and glimmering earrings, the glamor against the softness of her curvy body was stunning. She'd left the snaps at her thighs hanging loose but still worked in the dark stockings and high heels. No wonder the Maestro gave her the stage to command. She deserved it.

"You two playing nice, or do you need a few more hours down here?"

Orin shoved past her. "Took you long enough."

"It's only been a day. Calm down. I knew where you were the whole time." She followed behind him, then turned over her shoulder. "Coming?"

I hustled, though her watchful eyes didn't miss the way I held onto Chaos's hilt. We stepped into the soggy night air, jogging over the streets to leap into the waiting carriage. Hollis snapped the reins up front, and we tore off down the street.

Of all the scenarios Orin had given, he never once mentioned Paesha. And truly, I thought it was because she would never come for me. Maybe for him, but then, if he'd fallen to my blade, she would have been the one to find his body, and maybe that was a trauma she wasn't ready to face.

But as she and Orin bickered with each other in the carriage I'd once been kidnapped in, I couldn't help but look at the floor and think of how far we'd come in just a few short weeks.

"There's something you need to see," Paesha said, nudging Orin with her knee. Her eyes flashed to me. "You too, Maiden."

I held my breath as she reached into her cleavage and pulled out a piece of parchment she'd folded and hidden away.

"Why now?" I asked, snatching the wanted poster from her hands. "Surely he didn't care for those soldiers."

"He cares that you didn't marry him," she said, voice low. "He didn't give a shit about those guards, but he does want you captured."

I rolled my eyes. "No one is going to be foolish enough to—"

"It's a lot of money, Nightmare," Orin cut in, taking the poster. "Money makes desperate people dangerous."

"It also makes them foolish," I said, slumping back in the

bench seat to stare out the window as the final traces of the city faded away.

"Even still, it's best if you stay—"

"I will not be held prisoner. I don't give a damn what he does."

"Why does it feel like it's taking them so much longer tonight?" I asked Hollis, who sat dutifully on the front step, watching the tree line with Elowen.

Hollis pulled at the red thread he was using to sew a button onto the Maestro's jacket. "Because it is. And you're making it worse, Little Dove. Come hold this."

"Careful, Dey. Someone will think you care," Elowen said with a forced smile.

I sighed and pushed away from the door, moving to the stoop to hold the string while Hollis snipped it. Without needing direction, I wrapped it around a spool and hooked it into the notch, just as he'd shown me weeks ago, after Orin and I were trapped in the tunnel for a night.

"There!" Elowen shouted, standing to squint through the darkness.

"It's bad," Althea said when they got close enough, her red hair a beacon as they ran for us. "So bad, Paesha sent Quill home with Jarek."

"She can't stay with strangers," I protested. "If the king comes for her..."

Thea stepped into my view, grabbing my hands with her soot-tipped fingers. "The Maestro decided that Orin will be the closing act for the rest of the season. Every night of the performance, he's to fight until only one man is standing."

I shook my head. "He's a decent fighter."

"Tonight was Cassius, and he was allowed weapons, but Orin wasn't."

I blew out a steady breath and started for the cart he'd been brought home on. "Why is he doing this?" I demanded of Paesha. "If this is about me, why doesn't the Maestro just make him turn me over?"

The two women shared a glance as Elowen and Hollis joined us.

"What?" I asked, unwilling to look down at the broken and battered body I was sure to find.

"Orin made a deal with the Maestro the night after he married you."

My ears began to ring. I didn't want to be a bargaining chip. "What kind of deal?"

Althea took my hand. "He bound himself to the Maestro in exchange for his mother's life debt."

"I had fifty years left," Elowen whispered.

Paesha cleared her throat. "He was seventeen when he made that deal. He would have been freed at sixty-seven. But he made the Maestro agree that we couldn't be forced to turn you over."

"And?"

"And he gave the rest of his hundred years for your safety."

CHAPTER 30

Eiria's Temple was less ominous without the storm raging. Still, I'd waited outside as Paesha inched forward.

She stood at the steps, bathed in moonlight, staring back at me. "You should really be standing somewhere that's not so damn obvious."

Rolling my eyes, I took a step back into the shadow of a nearby building. She blinked several times before squinting. "That's really creepy."

I couldn't help my smile as the fiery woman turned and disappeared into the Goddess of Life's temple. Absolute betrayal had surged through my veins when Orin told Paesha I was searching for the Life Maiden. I'd tried to trust him with my secrets, and he'd immediately gone to her, placing a sliver of that wedge between us once again. But when she cornered me in the gardens the next day, I realized if I let go of the reins and we worked together, maybe that was better than failing on my own. And her eagerness for the hunt officially obliterated any lasting thoughts I had of the missing person secretly being Orin.

I could have counted every damn brick on the building I leaned against by the time the Huntress exited the temple. She sauntered across the street without a care in the world, trying to fix her eyes on me. Clearly, she hadn't been using magic.

When I stepped into the light, she smirked, bumping a shoulder into me. "Tell me that's not magic."

"You're blind for an infamous Huntress."

"Well, you're fucking mouthy, and I don't use magic when I don't need to, so I guess we're even."

We started the journey from Perth back to the outskirts of Silbath, agreeing we wouldn't speak a word of our mission on the streets. Paesha had warned me the Maestro had ears every-where, and I knew Lady Visha was the same.

Breaking the tree line was starting to feel like stepping into a different realm. One that started as a prison but had shifted into a haven for the misfits of this world. Requiem held the grit and gore, the aftermath of an ancient war still present on every surface, but this sanctuary beyond? I could breathe here. Think and feel. Even sleep, though Boo had been finding his way to the foot of my borrowed bed. Each night when I'd taken him back to Quill, she'd begged me to stay with her. I wished I could have relieved her fear, but the settled mind of a child was unbreak-able when it came to trauma.

"Nothing?"

"Just the flowery tree, like you said. Tell me again, why is this so important to you? I know a healer would be a reprieve for us, but why do *you* care?"

"Spend your life being the murderer in a world full of immortals and tell me how it feels to be the villain. Finding the Life Maiden is the only thing that will make me different from... them."

"You're worried about being compared to the other harbingers?"

"I'm not worried about it, Paesha. I *am*. My legacy is only bloodshed and tombstones. My soul is damned. I just wanted one single thing to vindicate it." I took a harrowing, desperate breath. "Did you get any sense of her? Anything your magic could bind to?"

She swiped a stone from the ground and tossed it to me. "You see that rock? Now that I've touched it and I've laid eyes on it, you could hide it anywhere in Silbath and I'd be able to find it in seconds. But if you picked a random stone, I'd try, and the magic would fail."

"A rock is just a rock until you can identify it." I nodded, tossing it to the ground. "That's what Orin said, too."

"The temple was a long shot anyway. It's been abandoned for so long. Whatever happened to you, there was probably just residual power. Of all the people that should have entered—" She stopped short, grabbing my arm. "Shit."

I snapped my eyes to where hers had landed. Black as night and foreboding, the Maestro's carriage sat waiting outside of the Syndicate house.

"He's never come here," she breathed. Turning toward me, she grabbed my arms, her face nearly frantic. "You have to hide, Dey. Go back into the trees. I'll come get you when he's gone."

"And if he asks you where I am?" I started toward the house.

"Orin's going to lose his mind if you walk into that house. The Maestro will bind you. It's not worth the risk."

I paused. "Do you think he won't come back? Do you think he won't punish all of you until he gets to me?"

"Don't kill him, Maiden. If you fail… if you try…"

I let those words fall over me for a second. "If I tried to kill every evil person in this realm, there would be few left standing. Everyone is someone else's villain. I'm not going to kill him. I'm not even going to try. Because if he dies, so must Visha and those that do their bidding, and down and down we go, until there's no line. If I'm going to do anything for this world, it won't be by leaving a trail of bodies. But the next time you wonder why I care about finding the Life Maiden, just remember where your mind jumped when you considered my next move. I'm always only going to be the murderer. Until I'm not."

She stumbled over her words, snapped her mouth shut, and nodded, her beautiful face solemn.

"Orin's already getting the sour end of his deal. If I can't save him, then maybe I can save the rest of you the trouble."

She kept close to my side as we approached the house. The carriage was empty, but the door was wide open. When we entered, Elowen's quivering voice could be heard from the kitchen. I removed the strap holding Chaos in place, locking eyes with Paesha. She shook her head, glancing down at my readied hand.

A great, big laugh, overly dramatic, as if the man stood on a stage, filled the house. Drexel Vanhoff sat at the kitchen table, his red mustache perfectly coiled, Hollis's most recent suit fitting his broad shoulders perfectly. None of his fineries were enough to distract from the scar on his cheek. The fake smile on his ridiculous face wavered when his dark brown eyes fell to my hand. "There's our girl."

The possessive look in his eyes, the way they glistened with desire, shook me to my core. His power, not his magic, but just his ability to fill a room with fear was palpable. Elowen gripped the edge of the counter, forcing a smile, though she couldn't have been cowering any further away.

"There's tea," she managed, a tremble behind the façade. "Can I get you a glass, Deyanira? Paesha?"

"No." I glared, forcing myself to be strong in a moment when years of cultivated fear should have warned me to play nice. "What do you want?"

The smile, disgusting and so over the top, never wavered. "I came to visit my friends."

"The people who live in this house are not your friends. They are your prisoners, Drexel."

He raised a bushy eyebrow. "I see you've taken on your father's eloquent way with words. But you're wrong, Maiden." Challenge filled his eyes before he shouted, "Quill, my darling, please come here."

Ice slid down my side as the child bound into the kitchen, arms full of dog. Her genuine smile next to that of the serpent was sickening. One look at Drexel and Boo began to struggle in Quill's arms until he wrestled free and darted behind me. A low rumble in his throat as the Maestro laid a heavy hand on Quill's shoulder.

"We're friends, aren't we?" he asked the child, voice softening as he nodded, coaxing the answer.

She tucked herself into his side, agreeing. "Of course, we are."

The serpentine look on his face as he looked back at me turned my stomach, hardening the veins in my body as fury coaxed Death's magic from slumber. With a wary gaze shifting between the two of them, I felt more than saw Elowen slowly slip out of the room. But Paesha took her place, moving to my side.

Drexel chuckled. "One day, Huntress, you will look upon me without defiance."

"Perhaps," she answered, crossing her arms, but she softened the second she looked at Quill.

"Be a dear and go retrieve that secret ledger you found four weeks ago. Don't be seen and try to avoid the man at the back door this time. I expect you to be in my office in two hours."

She held her place for only seconds. There was a battle spoken between them as she tried and failed to resist the pungent magic seeping from Drexel. Something in the way he commanded her felt so familiar. And I hated every step that forced her out of the room and out of the house. Though likely a mundane task to send her away, she had no choice. It was only then that I realized she and I were not so different.

"Quill," I said sweetly. "Take Elowen and Boo to the garden and show them that new flower we found growing by the peonies. Tell her the story you made up about how it got there."

"But I—"

"You may go," the Maestro purred, giving her the leave she would not take from me.

When the room was empty, the smile dropped. "Sit, Deyanira. We have much to discuss."

"No."

"Suit yourself."

"What do you want?"

"First, I want you to take that hand off the knife on your thigh. I am not your enemy."

"You are not my *anything*."

The smile returned as he leaned back in the wooden chair, forcing it to creak. He placed a gloved hand onto his cane and heaved himself from the table to come near.

"I am the only person that stands between your friends and your true enemies. I know you were in my tunnel. What is it you were searching for?"

My lips flattened into a thin line. "I don't know what you're talking about."

"Oh, I think you do."

My eyes shifted to the door, as if the glance alone would conjure Orin. Though I knew the safest place for him was as far from the Maestro as possible.

Cold metal graced my cheek as he used his cane to turn my

face back to him, back to dark eyes that shouldn't belong to this world. "Would you like to play a game, Maiden?"

"I'd rather be trampled by a thousand horses."

"Such... charisma." He flourished a hand. "You would do so well on my stage."

I didn't respond, instead tapping my toe as I waited for him to leave, hoping I could get rid of him before Orin returned, and Elowen came back inside. She was clearly afraid.

"I'm not interested. Will that be all?"

"Do come and see me when you realize I'm the reason King Icharius hasn't captured you yet."

I blinked slowly, holding my face as uninterested as I could muster.

"Until next time, then," he said, yellow teeth gleaming as he leaned a little too far on his cane and hobbled out of the house.

The problem wasn't the threat that had always been there, but the spoken words I'd have to think through to make sure he hadn't just bound me into a trap I didn't even see.

"Every single word?"

"As fast as I could write them," Hollis said, standing at the top of the steps, holding a small book with his detailed account of my conversation with his boss in one hand and his pocket watch in the other.

"And?"

"We'll have to show it to Paesha. She's usually around for his contractual bindings."

"I agreed to nothing."

He lifted a bushy white brow, frowning at me, his thick mustache hardly moving. "He asked you to remove the hand on your blade. Did you?"

Fear rippled through my stomach as I tried to replay the strained conversation. "I don't think so, but I've dealt with Lady Visha, Old Man. I know how to guard my words."

He ambled down the steps, giant blue eyes staring into mine. "He is far more cunning than her. I can promise you that, Little Dove. Small concessions lead to bigger traps when battling the Maestro. You must be careful to avoid him."

I sighed, letting my shoulders drop. "Thank you for trying to save me."

"You are worthy," he answered, all the sincerity he could muster coiled around the sentiment.

"Why?" I asked, feeling so vulnerable after throwing up every wall possible in front of Drexel. Something in the old man had continued to bring me a sense of peace. It was as if his soft words and gentle nature gave me balance. But it was more than that. It was his time that meant the most. His instant loyalty and kindness.

"He knows you will not kill, Dey. He wouldn't have come here if he was afraid of that. And while that's a problem for another day, it also should prove to you that you're different." He took my hand, the wrinkles and age marks glaring. "There was a point when I could see that my sister had succumbed to the darkness. Her smiles faded away, and nothing she did felt genuine anymore. The fear from others had fed a dark part of her soul. She would walk into a room and those who didn't cast their eyes away became victims. When I was a child, Dahlia's predecessor gathered a group of people at the portcullis of the Silbath castle and murdered them, one by one, until the king agreed to give her an audience. And when he did, she made heavy demands. None could be denied."

"I've read about her," I said, embarrassment striking me.

"Do you see, Little Dove? You have power you refuse to wield, and that's your choice. That is why you are worthy of my friendship. I may just be an old man with a sad tale, but that has to count for something."

I gripped his fingers. "It counts for everything. But we need to find a way to make Quill see how dangerous he is. He's using her to threaten me, and that's not going to end well."

He shook his head. "She's safe with him. I can promise you that."

"No one is safe with him."

"Don't think about dancing in Misery's End, Quill. Imagine you're on the stage of a ballet, and thousands of people have come to see you dance. Extend your leg... now the arm."

Sitting on the stoop of the Syndicate house, watching Paesha teach Quill while Althea worked tirelessly in her forge, had become some kind of normal. The sun bathed the large grass field in a warm glow, and the tips of the long grass swayed gently in a cool breeze. Thea's hammer struck metal in a hypnotic cadence, giving Paesha and Quill the perfect excuse to escape to the field. The faint trace of wood smoke from the hearth inside the house coalesced with sharp tangs of heated metal. This twisted form of peace, of implied freedom, settled in my bones like an ache. A longing.

We'd collectively agreed to keep the Maestro's visit from Orin. He needed no more distractions while fighting for his life every night. And though Quill had been reluctant, she'd promised Hollis, and that was good enough for me. Paesha had spent a dedicated amount of time looking over the words Hollis had written, confident I hadn't made a single mistake in my words.

Quill threw her skirts to the side, giggling as Paesha demonstrated a graceful spin, got caught in the grass, and lost her balance. The child threw herself onto Paesha, and Hollis's chuckle wrapped around my heart like a hug.

I watched for a while longer, letting the smile settle, hoping it would always be like this. But then I remembered the reason Thea was in the forge. Not because she wanted to be, but because she'd been ordered. And she hadn't slept in days.

I circled the house, shuffling past the garden, letting the

heat from the fire warm my face as I stood in the doorway. The metal she was working on glinted with a fiery intensity, shifting in color from deep reds to bright yellows as it absorbed the heat. Sparks erupted with every impact of the hammer, creating brief moments of brilliance that scattered like miniature stars against the backdrop of the forge.

It was art. And skill. All wrapped into one as she swiped a hand across a sweaty forehead, showcasing her brilliant red hair before letting her hammer slide into its loop on her belt. I might've believed this was peace for her, bringing as much comfort as Paesha's dancing, had the firelight not given way to the tears streaming down her face.

"Can you take a break?" I asked gently.

Her green eyes welled with tears as she shook her head and dropped several lumps of coal into her fire, coating her gloves in black soot. "He's ordered it. The magic won't let me stop."

"For three days, Thea? Can't you use your power?"

Her legs shook from weakness as she buried a rod into the bright flames. "Of all the people in the world, Dey, you should know that all magic comes at a cost. I've used so much it's exhausted me. And the magic doesn't create the art, only moves the metal. He wants a masterpiece."

I was familiar with the bone-deep exhaustion of using Death's power. Of times when I wanted nothing more than to sleep for a week after it quieted. It wasn't as bad if I took longer, giving my target more time, but being tired seemed like a small price to pay to give someone extra life.

Thea, though? She was exhausted. It showed in the circles below her eyes, the weakness of her muscles. The Maestro would work her into the ground, and it wouldn't cost him an ounce of sleep. Yet this woman had always been kind and gentle. She smiled more genuinely than anyone I'd met. Her laugh was like a song in the belly of a temple, rare and treasured.

"Let me help you. Tell me what I can do."

"Honestly, I'm almost done. Just a few more frame pieces, and then everything has to be moved to the theater anyway."

"You sure? Do you want me to bring the wagon?"

She shook her head, wiping another bead of sweat away, leaving a trail of soot across her forehead. "I'm sure."

"I'll bring you some water."

"I've already got it," Hollis said, coming from behind with a glass. "Can you fight it long enough to take a drink this time?" he asked, skirting around the fire to stand nearer to her.

She nodded, drinking deeply. The old man came to stand beside me, bumping his shoulder into mine. "Best leave her to it. The distractions will only take her longer."

"I'm not just going to leave her alone back here to suffer. That's not right."

"Do you prefer an audience or your shadows when you have no control over your kills, Little Dove?"

I found my place on the steps once more, every strike of the hammer like a slice across my patience, coaxing a sleeping, angry beast within me to wake and stew. To pace and plot.

Paesha had changed the game with Quill, no longer teaching her to dance but to fight. I watched for only minutes before approaching.

"Feel free to jump in, Maiden." Paesha stepped back, gesturing to Quill, delivering the distraction my heart needed, though it didn't deserve it while Althea struggled mere paces away.

I circled the child once, rubbing my temple as if in evaluation. She grew three inches taller, jutting her chin out, as Boo jumped at her heels, trying to distract her.

"You have to process the fear before you can defend yourself, kid. Everyone forgets that part. If someone happens to grab you, there's a visceral reaction before logic can take over. Do you know what that means?"

She shook her head, that wild halo of curly hair falling into her pretty face.

I knelt down to her level. "If a bad man sneaks up behind you, grabs you, and runs off, it's normal for you to feel so scared you can't think of what to do. But the quicker you can get past that, the faster you can save yourself. Make sense?"

"I guess."

"The best thing I've learned to do is replace that emotion with another. Anger is powerful. It will urge you to use more strength and feed your adrenaline. Wanna try?"

She lifted a tiny shoulder. "I'm not scared of you."

I snatched Boo from the ground, and she gasped, stumbling backward. Hugging the pup before giving him a good scratch behind the ears, I continued. "That's the reaction part of your brain. You didn't see it coming, and you did nothing to stop me."

"Okay."

She knew I wouldn't hurt the dog, but still, she pulled him from my hands.

"All fine and dandy, Maiden, but maybe move on to the self-defense part," Paesha said, her eyes locked on Orin emerging from the tree line.

"Be loud, Quill. Shout and scream and make sure everyone around you knows what's happening. And then you fight like hell. You kick, you punch, you don't hold back. Aim for the nose like this." I thrust my palm upward. "Then kick them between the legs as hard as you can. Never worry about how much it's going to hurt you. Don't hold back."

"Got it," she said with a firm nod.

"Remember what I told you about trusting people?"

She held the dog closer. "Trust no one more than myself."

Orin cleared his throat behind her. "What are we up to?" The deep bruise around his light eyes was the worst of his injuries from his most recent performance. Whatever the fight had been, he'd clearly won.

"Teaching Quill how to defend herself," I answered, rising from the ground, though I still wasn't at eye level.

He rolled his sleeves to just below his elbows, nodding. "Great. Let's see what you've got, kid."

Quill snorted. "I'm not going to hurt you."

He scrunched his nose with a kindness in his eyes I'd only seen in fleeting moments. "I'm tougher than I look."

"Maybe she should practice on Dey instead." Paesha picked at the hem of her sleeve, stepping backward, the draw in her voice making it clear she thought Orin to be more fragile than I was.

"She's eight," he answered with a scoff.

I held his gaze for just a moment, lifting my brow to question him.

"Honestly, you two. Worse than my mother. Come on, Quill. Show me what you've got."

"Well, we haven't practiced it yet," she answered, throwing her hands on her hips.

"Quill, go stand next to Paesha," I said, grabbing Orin by his black shirt sleeve. "You come this way."

He followed with no hesitation. "I think she's starting to pick up on your attitude."

"Oh, right, it's definitely not Paesha's shining personality coming through."

Orin chuckled. "So, what have we learned so far? Running away?"

I'd planned to warn him, but the cockier he got, the more

interested I became in the show. "Something like that. Just run up and grab her. Let's see what she does."

He rubbed his hands together. "She's just going to laugh."

"I don't think you're giving her enough credit, Icky."

He froze, rising to his full height. "Call me anything else in the world, Wife. That one has to go."

"Okay, Fluffy Bottom. Full speed, right at her."

The edge of his mouth lifted, though he tried to hide the smirk. "There's something wrong with you."

"Yes, well, aren't you the charmer."

"Depends on the day."

"I'm gathering that."

"Will you two stop flirting and get on with it?" Paesha yelled.

"We're perfecting the element of surprise," he answered without missing a beat. "Mind your business."

"Some of us are hungry," Hollis yelled from the front step.

"Fine." He turned to me, pulling his blade from his side. "Hold this. And don't get any ideas."

I flipped the weapon in my hand once and then twice. "Pretty brave to hand the Death Maiden a weapon."

"Last time I checked, you were a weapon without needing the blade."

"Let me guess, your little baby nose still hurts."

"You knocked me out, Deyanira. Out cold. On the damn floor."

"Ah, so it's your ego, then." I flipped the blade one more time. "Noted."

"I hate you," he said with a playful growl before tearing off across the yard, hesitating for a second to make sure Quill was ready, and then lifted her, spinning in circles. His laugh was short-lived as the child began screaming like a banshee, burying tiny fists into his face, and jabbing him in the nose, just as I'd shown her.

He fell to a knee, clearly trying to put the wild thing down without hurting her, but the second he let go, she screamed again and planted her foot right between his legs. He fell to the side in a heap, and she launched herself at him again. Paesha had to tear her away, fighting back her laughter as Quill turned into some kind of rabid beast.

"Good job, kid," I whispered, taking her hand as we headed inside, leaving Orin to wallow in the field.

Thea hadn't joined us for supper, but eventually, the door opened, and she dragged herself inside, came far enough into the kitchen for Elowen to hand her a sandwich, and off she went, likely directly to her bed.

"Do I have to?" Quill whined from the table, shoving a potato around her plate as she kicked her feet back and forth.

"Bath house or river, your choice," Paesha answered, rising.

With a groan and a heavy eye roll, the child slipped from the table, dropping the potato onto the floor for Boo. "Bath house, I guess."

"I'll come, too," Elowen said, following them out of the kitchen. "It'll be a nice treat."

Once everyone had left the kitchen, Orin wandered in, his tender steps eliciting a pointed grin from me. When his playful temperament shined through, I wanted nothing more than to find a way to make those moments last. I wanted him to see me, look at me. There were times when I even wanted him all to myself. Because I craved him. Even in the darkest moments. And I didn't care what that said about me.

"I blame you for turning her into a wild animal," he said, sitting carefully as he reached for the loaf of bread.

I ran a finger over the rim of my glass. "You say that as if it's an insult, but the best people are always the wild ones."

"That explains a lot about you, Nightmare. Pass the butter?"

Sliding the dish across the table, when he reached forward, our hands connected, only slightly, but neither of us pulled away immediately. He'd never been one to deny a chance to touch me, and while others may not have noticed, having so little physical contact in my past, I always would. The bite when he'd called me Nightmare had faded, though, no longer a weapon.

"She likes you, you know?"

I nodded, pulling my hand away. "I'm told I'm only medium bad."

He pinned me with a stare, scraping the butter from his knife to the bread. "Quill is a terrible judge of character."

I smiled. "She's pretty sure she's going to marry you, so I'd have to agree, Fluffy Bottom."

"Call me that one more time."

I stood, circling the table. He spun in his seat as I curled a finger under his chin. "Feeling insecure, Husband?"

He snatched my hand, holding it in place. "I much prefer *Husband.*"

"Could have fooled me."

"Sit back down, Wife."

Shaking my head, I tried to pull away. "I don't take commands from assholes."

He held firm, rising to full height, staring down at me. "Then consider it a request."

"Say please," I whispered, unable to control the way he commanded my racing pulse. I didn't want to be attracted to him, but gods, he was stunning. The angry, possessive exterior was a hard shell around the kindness I knew to be living inside of him. Though buried deep, it called to me more than his darkness.

"Please," he purred.

I backed away, reclaiming my seat as I held eye contact for as long as possible. He leaned forward, clasping his hands before him. "Let's say you're standing at a crossroads. At one end is a child, alone and scared, and on the other an old woman, lost. You can only help one of them. Who do you choose?"

"You made me sit down to ask a theoretical question?"

"I want to know you, Deyanira. I want to understand you better."

"I'd pick the child."

"Why?"

"Because eventually, the old woman is going to run into someone who will care enough to help. She's not scared, and you never said she was alone, but you were sure to add in the anguish of the child, and honestly, a child is a much bigger target for despicable people than a lost old woman who probably doesn't have a pot to piss in. They'll get nothing from her."

"Interesting."

"You'd pick the old woman?"

"No. I'd choose the same as you did, but I'd probably have to think about it longer."

"Not too fast on your feet, huh?"

He scoffed. "Let's say you're—"

"No. I get to ask a question now. That's how this works."

Popping a piece of bread into his mouth, he gestured for me to continue.

"One side, Icharius, the other, Drexel. And you *have* to choose one to save and one to die."

"Too easy. I'd kill the Maestro in a heartbeat. Too much history there."

"Icharius literally took over the world in a matter of weeks, and you still think Drexel is the bigger enemy?"

"No." He wiped his mouth with a napkin, settling deeper into his chair. "I think Drexel and Icky are in something together. I'm not sure what it is. I don't think the boss willingly gave Quill to the king, but I do think that whole thing is suspicious."

"Everything both of them do is suspicious."

"Who would you pick?"

"Is that your question?"

Lifting a shoulder, he nodded. "Sure."

"I'd pick the new king. And not because he's got a bone to pick with me. But the Maestro has been manageable for years. He's a problem and a ruthless crime lord, but he's not shaking up Requiem the way Icharius is. I don't know, the king just feels more dangerous."

"Because of the mystery?"

"I guess." I waited a beat, wondering if I should truly ask the question burning in my mind, partially afraid of the answer. "Life Maiden on one side, me on the other. Who do you save?"

There wasn't a soul alive that would pick me. I knew that. *I* wouldn't even pick me. But I needed him to say it. I needed him to place the distance between us again. Because this was getting too comfortable, and each day I waited for him to come home made me spiral deeper into an illusion that somehow Orin and I could find a path. But rather than answer right away, he stood and moved to the doorway. With his back to me, I felt a small piece of my heart break.

"You could lie," I whispered, letting myself be vulnerable. "You could lie, and I wouldn't be mad."

"I'm not going to lie to you, Deyanira. I'm going to choose you." He turned back to look at me, a swell of emotion in his eyes I'd never seen before. "And I think I need to find a way to process that. I should choose the good of the world. I should be their hero. But I think when it comes down to it, I'd rather be yours, because you have no one."

I don't know how long it took me to move from my seat.

He'd long since gone; the room had grown cold and dark. The others had returned home. And yet I sat there, repeating those words in my mind, wondering if he had actually lied on my command or not.

I'm going to choose you.

CHAPTER 32

"You snore."

Orin's growly voice woke me from an afternoon nap. Leaning against the door to my room in a white, long-sleeve shirt and black pants, arms folded across his chest, he pinned me with a heated look. I'd never seen him dressed so casually.

"Why do you enjoy being such a hateful dick?"

He smirked. "Because I know deep down you enjoy it. Why so tired?"

The back of my eyelids felt like sandpaper. The pure exhaustion from magic still vibrated through my aching bones. I could have slept for days, and that thought scared me. I would have. In this home with these people. The Syndicate house was safe for me, even if I was loath to admit it.

"I was out late. I had something I had to take care of."

"I know what you were doing. You don't have to dance around the truth."

Wiping the sleep from my eyes, I sat up, tossing the blanket from my feet. "You hate me for it, and there's nothing to be done about it, so I'd prefer to avoid the topic."

"Man or woman?"

I didn't want to answer, but I understood why he asked. Why those amber eyes beseeched me. "Woman. Caroleena Befrene. Know her?"

He looked at the floor, likely racing through his memories, but eventually shook his head. "Silbath or Perth?"

"Perth."

He raised a brow. "You okay? Any trouble from the king?"

"Oh, yes. I forgot to mention I was kidnapped and beaten and barely made it out with my virginity intact." I walked to the door.

"Virgin, huh?" He smirked. "Your sarcasm knows no bounds, Maiden."

"Neither do your questions."

I meant to walk past him, but he snatched my arm, spinning me before drawing me so near that I could smell the soap on his skin and see the gold flecks in his eyes again. Something primal raced across his features. I'd tried to discern the look, but it was gone within seconds. Still, my body thrummed, wholly aware of his hands on me.

"Do you have something to tell me?"

I drew back, wondering how he'd heard of Drexel's visit.

"Not that I can think of," I lied.

"There's... What's different about your eyes?"

"My eyes?"

"Some of them are white," he growled.

"Oh, my lashes? I don't know. Must be something that happens with Maidens sometimes. That's my guess, anyway. Nothing dangerous, I promise."

It wasn't that I was unwilling to tell him about the temple.

But nothing had come from it either time I'd gone, and I didn't want questions to lead to the Maestro.

"Come outside with me, Nightmare."

"Ask nicely," I whispered, so faint, if he leaned in to hear, our lips would have touched, and that very thought heated my skin.

A dark chuckle left his lips, and I couldn't help but glance at them. Couldn't fight the pull. "Please?"

I wanted him to touch me. Almost as much as I wanted him to hate me. Because in both ways, there was passion with Orin. His guarded feelings were always a storm.

"Lead the way, Husband," I managed.

He waited several more moments. His eyes glued to mine, the war within mimicked on his face. We were perfect enemies. We fought so beautifully. And in scattered moments, I preferred that anger, the fury he gifted to distract from every other problem in this world. Because I knew what to do with anger. I knew how to coax it, how to stroke it. But I had no idea what to do with the rest of this.

He pushed away from the wall, took my hand, and led me down the steps. There was a heartbeat between those joined fingers. Our bond, throbbing.

Hollis and Althea waited by the front step for us, both sets of eyes gleaming with delight. Paesha followed behind, her ever-present scowl a comfort through the myriad of emotions and confusion.

"I had a genius idea," Althea said, bouncing on her toes, cheeks rosy, having fully recovered from the heavy workload weeks ago. "Orin needs to practice."

He scoffed. "I don't need to practice. Just condition. Train."

"And I'm a dancer, not a fighter," Paesha added, though her words were drawn as if the admittance pained her. I'd seen her fight. She was both.

We moved into the giant opening between the house and the tree line.

"So, you want me to kick your ass until it doesn't hurt anymore? Toughen you up a bit?"

The side of my husband's beautiful mouth lifted. "Think you're pretty tough, Maiden?"

"I seem to recall the last time we fought, I left you knocked out on the floor. There's no thinking involved here. I'm tough, and I know it."

"I've got a coin on Dey," Paesha said, nudging Hollis.

The old man chuckled. "I'm not taking that bet."

"I'll take it," Althea said. "But we have to make it a fair fight. No one can use their hands or weapons."

Orin halted, turning to me with a sly smile, his eyes never leaving mine as he addressed her. "How am I to take down the mighty Death Maiden without my hands?"

"Get creative, husband," I answered.

The citrusy smell of magic, that rich, pure scent of raw power filled the air. I turned to see Althea holding cuffs out toward us.

When Orin groaned, she smiled sweetly. "We can't have anyone cheating when there's money on the table."

"I would never cheat," he said, holding out his wrists.

"Oh, yes, the honorable Orin Faber, who tricked his wife into marrying him," I countered.

His smile faded as he waited for Althea to latch the metal rings around his wrist.

"You don't have to put your hands behind your back," she said, studying my stance.

"The cuffs themselves are weapons. Hands, elbows, forearms, and shoulders can still be used. I'll play fair. But I'm not sure this is the best idea you've had."

"Two coins on Dey," Paesha said.

"Deal." Althea grinned before looking at me apologetically. "Sorry, Dey."

"Don't be. You'll be the one buying drinks tonight."

She laughed, the soft sound filling the space around us as the links clicked in place, and she skipped away to stand next to Hollis. I'd never in my life understand that level of happiness in a world so terrible, even though, somewhere over our time together, I'd begun to feel the gentle roots of friendship digging into my heart. I didn't trust myself enough to truly call any of them that.

"I'll be nice." Orin moved to stand feet shoulder-width apart, his eyes practically burning a trail along my skin.

"I really hope not," I purred. "Because I refuse to make the same promise. You want to learn? I'll teach you. But it's never going to be because I'm nice."

"Go!" Althea shouted, clapping her hands.

Orin raced forward. I easily stepped to the side, and he stumbled, losing his balance. It was nothing to stick a foot out and watch him fall to the ground without using his hands to brace himself.

"Do we help him up?" Althea's sweet whisper made everyone but Orin laugh.

"I can still hear you."

"Right. Sorry."

He rolled to his back, and she grabbed his hands, grunting as she yanked him to his feet.

"Don't lead with your head, Husband. Dead giveaway."

"Pun intended?"

"Always."

He planted his feet again, trying to shake his arms out. "I don't want the advantage."

"Take the advantage. You need it," Hollis shouted from the side.

"Thea," Orin growled, "switch my arms to the back. Make it fair."

She ran forward, gripping the cuffs until they fell free. Once ready to start again, he nodded to me.

"Go!"

He wised up and didn't approach at all this time. I moved in close, light on my feet as I bounced back and forth. Orin watched for several seconds before lunging again. His intention was to plant a shoulder into my gut, but rather than let him, I spun and landed a kick right to the side of his face. To his credit, he didn't fall a second time. But the cheerful redhead behind us gasped, and I didn't miss the way she reached for Paesha's hand.

I could scare them all right now. I didn't want to do that. I'd found a semblance of a home here, and beyond that, I'd never had to wonder from one night to the next if Regulas would be standing at my door, waiting for me.

When he came again, I let the hard sole of his boot land on my stomach. But when he straightened, he scowled before lifting a brow.

"Good job," I said, forcing a breathless tone.

The next time, he tucked a shoulder, and I pretended to move too slowly. He made contact, and I stumbled.

"Change your mind?"

"No," I said, keeping my voice level.

"It's not exciting if you don't have a blade in your hand, Maiden?"

I hated when he called me Maiden, and he damn well knew it.

"Take the handcuffs off, Althea," he said, standing upright.

"But—"

"Take them off," he demanded, and I didn't have to look at

his eyes to know there would be darkness there. A darkness that was so, so familiar to me.

Thea did nothing at all, made no movements, spoke no words, but the cuffs fell with a clink to the ground. I locked my fingers together, refusing to take the bait. He stepped to me and swung; I dodged with ease. He threw a knee; I took it in the gut. Another swing; I stood and let it shake me to my core.

"Stop it," he growled.

"Stop what?"

He pulled a blade from his boot and held it in his hand. "You know what."

When he swung, I blocked but did not strike.

"Paesha's going to be pissed if she loses money because you're scared of a fair fight." His voice was so quiet I almost didn't hear him.

"I'm not scared of a fair fight," I whispered. "There could never be a truly fair fight between us. The first fight we had, I was poisoned. You know this is a bad idea. I don't want to hurt you, and I don't want to scare them. There's a difference."

"You might be good, Deyanira, but you're not that good. You got lucky before. I know what I'm doing. And I trust you."

Those final words were such a shock to my reality. Trusting me was foolish. Because, just like him and the rest of this band of misfits, I was not my own person. Still, something in the way he'd said those words empowered me.

I flashed my eyes to his fingers. "Loosen your grip."

"What?"

"Loosen your grip on the blade."

"No." He jabbed the knife forward, and I twisted, grabbing his wrist, snapping it backward, and stealing the weapon.

"If you hold the blade too tightly, you cannot manipulate the way you thrust. It is meant to be an extension of your arm, but your fingers can bend. Loosen enough that you can rotate your wrist at the last second." I held it out for him. "Try it again."

He stubbornly gripped it the same way he had before. A challenge. When he moved, assuming I would do the same thing, I trapped his thrust-out hand, snatched the knife, and flipped him onto his back, planting the blade just above his Adam's apple.

Paesha slowly clapped her hands, but I couldn't look at Althea and see the fear that would surely be there. Instead, I watched the face of the man who never feared me, even when he hated me.

"Good girl," he said smoothly, pushing away the blade. "Do it again."

The next time he came for me, I tried something different, meaning to strike him in the kidney on his initial step, but he'd been ready and blocked, his face nothing but concentration. Spinning to move with the momentum of his forceful counter, I dropped and swept a leg out, once again knocking him down.

"This is honestly sad," Paesha said, clearly bored. "No wonder you're getting your ass handed to you every night, Orin."

"I'd like to see you try," he said, peeling himself from the ground.

"Okay."

My breath caught in my throat as they traded spots, but I held my composure, masking the surprise by finally looking at the others. Hollis dipped his chin to me, and Thea hadn't lost her smile. Maybe they weren't afraid.

"This is a really bad idea," I said when the Huntress took her mark across from me.

"Thea," she answered with a grin, tossing one of the discarded cuffs to her friend. "I need a sword."

Within moments, I faced off with the Huntress. She'd taken

a traditional stance, elbow near her ear, point facing right at me. But her posture was immaculate, her sun-kissed skin gleaming beneath the rays that poured out from the clouds as if they were eager to watch such a beauty perform.

She'd overextended her muscles, though, far more focused on her initial pose than what she might actually do from that point. Had she been on stage, it would have been a marvel to see, but in a real fight, in the bloody hallways of a king's castle, she'd be so easy to tip over, I might have laughed, if not for the severity on her face.

"You sure?" I asked.

"Ask me if I'm scared, Maiden."

I rolled my eyes. "You should be."

"Two coins on Dey," Hollis shouted, shoving his hand into his pocket, though I could only see him out of the corner of my eye.

No one took the bet, though.

"Go," Orin barked.

I held my hands behind my back again, holding my feet planted as she lunged. "If I had a blade, I'd strike from the right and throw you sideways." Stepping away from the tip of her sword, I spun to face her. "You can think like a dancer in sword fighting, except for one thing. You have to bend, Huntress. If you keep the legs straight..." She lunged again, but I was way ahead of her. "Your lead-off is too big, and I can predict what you're doing from a mile away."

She smiled, something wicked and stunning and maybe even terrifying. "Noted."

"Are you paying attention, Orin?" Thea asked.

I could feel his eyes on me, but when I turned and heat raced down my body at his assessing gaze, I couldn't hide the blush. Nor the pause in focus. Paesha came at me again, and while I was distracted, she nicked my arm, slicing into the loose sleeve of my shirt.

Thea gasped. But it wasn't nearly enough to stall me as I jumped right back into motion, letting the thought of that beautiful man's attention fuel every muscle in my body as I waited for her to turn and strike. When the blade came down, slicing through the air in a perfect arc, I simply stepped back, letting it bury into the dirt before kicking Paesha's wrist. She yelped and released the handle, I snatched it away before the hilt hit the ground, and in one smooth, terrifying motion, brought the blade through the air and stopped an inch before her head, eliciting a beautiful smirk from her and a gasp from Orin.

"Ready," Quill yelled from the front door, breaking the spell over all of us.

Althea sighed. "Oh, thank the gods. That's enough for today."

I dropped the sword to the ground, and it shriveled back into the cuffs it'd been formed from.

"I'm not sure if this was the greatest distraction I've ever witnessed or the worst," Hollis said, leading the way to the house.

"Distraction for what?" I asked, following him.

But Orin grabbed my hand, stopping me as the others walked away. "You really are a brutal little thing, Nightmare, but next time you hold back, I will find a way to coax that lethal demon from you and force her to come play with me."

"I can promise you that's one side of me you never want to see."

He pulled me to his chest, and I let him, relishing in the way our bodies felt when so close together. An ache building within my heart, my head wishing it wouldn't.

"I'm beginning to think there are no sides of you that

wouldn't absolutely destroy me." He brushed a strand of hair from my face, letting his fingers linger on my flushed cheeks. "Even the rare smile is enough to weaken a man."

"I've learned to never trust your flattery," I said breathlessly.

"Deyanira—"

"Come on," Quill yelled from the door, though I hardly heard her over the racing of my heart.

"We better go inside, Deyanira Sariah Faber, Death's Maiden, wife of a lying flatterer."

CHAPTER 33

"Surprise!"

The gathered family, with Orin at my back and Hollis, Thea, Quill, Paesha, and Elowen before me, had been scheming. And when they yelled, my first instinct was to reach for a weapon. I hated that twisted side of my mind.

"Happy birthday," Orin rumbled into my ear, his palm burning an invisible mark onto the small of my back.

A birthday was a pressing reminder of our eventual mortality and release from this world. Some celebrated with gifts and pleasantries as they could, but most said nothing, did nothing, preferring to closely guard every second of their one hundred years. Knowing that you would die on your one-hundredth year felt like sand in an hourglass, slowly ticking by, to people who had true happiness in this world. But to the rest of us, we'd begun the countdown for a different reason. Anticipation and not fear.

It wouldn't be hard to figure out my birthday. As a princess, my birth was supposed to be a day of celebration in Perth, but the banners had been covered in black, the flags withdrawn, and the note pinned to the gate of my father's castle announced my mother's tragic death. My birthday had never been one of jubilation. Only mourning. Only bitterness in a cold castle when every servant and every court member had been sent home. Hallowed halls and fasting. That was how my birthday was spent.

I shook my head, trying to make sense of it all until I remembered a conversation with Quill right after I'd come. "You betrayed me, kid."

"It was a good plan, huh, Paesha?"

The Huntress mussed the little girl's hair. "Sure, it was."

"I made you this." Quill stepped forward, handing me a rolled piece of paper. "And Elowen got me the paper and the paints, so it's from both of us."

Unrolling the parchment, I couldn't help the warmth that spread through me, the heart-wrenching sweetness at her depiction of the group, me included. Orin and I stood together in her painting, and she'd been so meticulous about including the small dagger on my thigh. Everyone was there. Hollis, with either a sword or a massive needle, it was hard to tell, though the needle made more sense. Althea, with a big heart drawn onto her chest and a smile on her pretty face, Paesha, drawn in feathers as if she were dancing, and she'd drawn herself holding Boo's paw while Elowen held a birthday cake.

"It's incredible. Thank you." I swallowed the lump in my throat, wishing I could dart up the stairs as I spiraled into a place that knew I didn't really deserve this kind of love. But equally, I wanted to take this moment and freeze it, holding it tenderly for as long as I could. Because, though Requiem was so, so broken, in our own way, we were not. And maybe I truly did belong here.

"Don't cry, or I'm going to cry," Althea said, stepping away from the stairs as she held out something rolled in brown paper.

"Really, you don't need to go through the trouble."

"This is an honor, Dey."

Opening the package as everyone stood in a circle watching me, I worried that whatever may be inside, I wouldn't have the reaction they expected, and they'd be disappointed. But when I peeled back the final layer and stared down at the dagger in my hand, I nearly stumbled.

"Thea..." I forced a breath into my lungs to steady my racing heart. "Gods, Thea."

She bounced on her toes again. "It's a twin to Chaos. But I like to think of her as a counterpart. The curves in the handles are opposite, so one for right, and one for left. I matched the design as closely as I could, and Elowen picked the ruby. I was hoping you would call her Serenity. Because they are day and night. Darkness and light. Chaos and Serenity."

Elowen had been standing at the door with hands clasped to her chest and small tears in her eyes. "I hope you like it."

I didn't have words at all. There wasn't a word in our language that would convey the gratitude. And it wasn't about the blade, though it was a masterpiece. It was the gesture. The knot in my throat grew larger, my nose tingling as I struggled for breath, hoping to hide the tears that made me weak.

Drawing in a steady breath, I thanked Elowen and Althea, but when they moved in to hug me, I turned rigid. Awkward and unable to convey anything that I was feeling. They were warm, and I was cold, and that's the way all of these weeks between us had been. But neither had faltered in their kindness. Not when I was sneaking around the house because I didn't think they would give me answers, nor when I was angry and defiant. They were kind. And I was not worthy.

"My turn," the frail voice of the old man in the back said, bringing a large package out from behind his back.

I moved to stand before him, knowing that at any moment I

was going to fall apart, and I'd have to run. But measured movements and his steady, calming gaze held me in the moment as I tugged the laces on his gift and let the paper fall away.

"It will fit you perfectly," he promised as I pulled the black clothing from his hands, holding the leather to my chest. "I've reinforced your pockets for blade tips and made the fabric more breathable. It's darker than your other outfits, as well. I've been experimenting with a dye that will keep you hidden."

I didn't understand how they could all give me things that would help me be the monster they'd once hated me for. The tears were genuine and the pounding in my chest, deafening. "Thank you," I managed.

"I tried to tell him the dye was unnecessary, but he didn't listen," Paesha said. "You've got that shadow thing down."

Orin cleared his throat.

"I didn't say it wasn't a nice gift," she said, tossing me another parcel. "Mine's just better."

"Technically, I had a hand in that one also," Hollis said, a lightness to his voice I wished I could bottle and keep forever.

"Fair," she countered. "But maybe don't open that one in front of the kid."

Drawing back, I pinned her with a questioning gaze. She lifted a shoulder and moved toward the kitchen. "You'll see."

"I wish I could find the words to thank you all. They just don't exist."

"We know," Quill answered, setting Boo on the floor. "Can we have cake now?"

"Dinner first," Elowen ordered, pushing her to follow Paesha.

"Come with me," Orin whispered over my shoulder as the others shuffled into the kitchen, his smoky voice walking down my spine, stealing my breath.

He took the pile of gifts and set them on the couch before

holding out a hand. I let my eyes trail down the gap where his shirt wasn't fully buttoned, the blush heating my skin as I searched for those dark veins and found nothing but his knowing stare.

"When you're done gawking..."

I rolled my eyes. "I wasn't gawking. Just wondering why you haven't had that missing button replaced on your shirt."

He shifted close, pinning me against the wall. "Do you always blush when you lie, Nightmare?"

"Wouldn't that be so convenient for you?"

He smiled and snatched my hand, spinning away. As he led me up the flights of stairs in the patchwork house, I fought the lingering sadness in my heart. It must have been sadness, because why else would I want to break down and cry? But I understood none of it. They'd been so kind. So genuine.

And in that moment, I wished I could have spoken to Ro. I wish I'd had the courage to step into a mirror and hug her and apologize for being so angry with her for only giving part of herself to me. I understood it now. Because as much as I cared for the people in this house, they would never have all of me either. I was still a warrior. Still a harbinger, and I wanted to always shield them from the darkest parts of me. And maybe that's what Ro had been doing, as well.

When Orin pushed open the door to the rooftop, I nearly fell over. The rare, evening sun bathed the rooftop in a warm hue, and the elegant silhouette of a cello stood proudly against the chimney, its polished wood and graceful curves adding an air of sophistication to the picnic set directly in the middle of the space.

"Will you take your evening meal with me, Wife?"

I pushed beyond the emotions, relying on sarcasm to see me through these foreign, tender moments. "So formal, Husband."

His broad smile as he bowed at the waist made my heart skip a beat. "I aim to please."

"I think you aim to flatter. We've discussed this."

He moved to stand before me, resting his hands on my arms. "How am I doing on that front?"

"Marginal."

His laugh was contagious, though the demon within me still told me he was not to be trusted. Trust no one. Rely on no one. I was the only person I could ever truly count on. And his nefarious boss was still very much a problem. All of this could be a ruse. A game to trap me, as Drexel had tried to do my entire life.

"Are you ready for your gift, Nightmare?"

Forcing the smile to smother the negative thoughts, I nodded. "You really didn't have to go through the trouble."

Again, he laughed, pressing his forehead to mine. "Paesha threatened to chop my balls off if I didn't play nicely today. And with her, those are never empty threats. So, I wrote this song for you."

He spun me around. I glanced over the rooftop as he counted the balusters before pulling me sideways, into his perfect position. "Stand here."

Sitting behind his gleaming cello, he rolled his sleeves with careful precision, baring the twin bands on his arm before he began. He drew the bow across the strings, and the air was suddenly filled with a haunting melody that seemed to caress every corner of my soul. The first notes resonated through the open space, carrying an ache and longing that reached deep, punctuating the feelings the day had already wrought. It was as if the cello was an extension of Orin's very being, an instrument he used, a tool to pour out his heart.

Thick lashes fell to his cheeks as he closed those beautifully darkening eyes and let himself fall into a cocoon of sound that transcended the physical realm. Each note was like a brushstroke on an invisible canvas, painting a vivid picture of emotions that I had buried within. Memories, dreams, and unspoken desires surged to life, given form by the gentle touch of his fingers on the strings.

As the melody unfolded, I felt myself swaying to its rhythm, my heart dancing in time with its cadence. Tears welled in my eyes, a bittersweet mixture of joy and sorrow spilling over. The cello's lament spoke to every hidden thought, every buried feeling I had ever harbored. To the nightmare. He had unlocked the door to my heart, allowing the floodgates of emotion to burst open, and that was Orin Faber's true power. The ability to pour so much into something he loved, there could be no question of his raw talent.

Unable to bear the weight of the moment, I sank to my knees. The rooftop seemed to vanish, and I was suspended in a world where only the music, the man, and I existed. The notes cascaded over me like a waterfall of sound, washing away my inhibitions and leaving me raw, vulnerable, and utterly alive, but walking the very fine line of heartache.

I knew the danger here. What it meant to allow anyone close to me. But I equally wanted that so much, my very soul cried out for it. I wept, tears streaming down my cheeks unchecked, as the cello's melody continued to unravel the tapestry of my existence. It was a catharsis, a release of all that I had held tightly within me for so long. The beautiful man on the rooftop, his fingers moving with a grace that seemed to defy gravity, was a conduit for the symphony of my heart.

I was in so, so much trouble.

When the song ended on a long, mournful note, I kept my face buried in my hands. But Orin sat beside me, taking a long, deep breath before pulling me to his chest, wrapping me in his arms until the rest of the world was merely a memory and remained silent. Until the tears dried, my mind quieted, and only he and I remained.

"Why did you cry, Deyanira?"

"Should you ever play that song, and it falls on hardened ears, just know that your audience has no soul, Husband."

He rubbed my back. "That could never happen. The song belongs to you now."

CHAPTER 34

"What was it like? As a child?"

I sat across from Orin on the picnic blanket, watching the setting sun with a full belly, tender heart, and so many questions about the reality of my life.

"Being a princess was all I knew. My father wasn't kind. I didn't know a thing about my mother. He refused to speak of her. He took down every painting of the two of them and had them destroyed so I could never lay eyes on her. She was his and never mine. He loved her, and when I killed her, I killed a piece of him, too. The part of him that was still human and soft."

"You didn't kill your mother, Dey."

I cut a glance at him, watching the lingering, warm sunlight caress his sharp jawline. "That's how it works. Her death was my first kill."

"No." He shook his head. "You were a baby. You had no control."

"I have no control now, Orin. Even when I fight it, even when I've tried everything else, madness takes over until I'm no longer in control of myself."

"I hate the madness for you. If I could will it away, I would."

"It's not like your life is ideal, if we're discussing the pitfalls. Being bound to Drexel is a dangerous entanglement, and we both know it."

He took a final swig of his liquor before swinging the ice around in his glass. "I'm sure you know he wants you, too. You've been a target for a long, long time. But you have to stay away from him. If he has control of you... he will force you to use that magic. He'll make you perform your murders on a stage in front of hundreds, night after night, turning you into a spectacle."

"It's worse than that," I agreed. "There's something... something I want to tell you. Something no one knows of harbinger magic."

I couldn't believe the words had left my mouth, and the second they had, I regretted it. But how could I go back after teasing such a secret? "You mustn't repeat this. At all costs necessary, you have to find loopholes to make sure no one, not even Drexel, ever knows."

Setting the glass down, he twisted to face me fully. "If it risks your safety, Deyanira, do not speak the words to me. I can't vow them into silence."

"You've given me a home, Orin. You put these amazing people in my life, and I fought you every step of the way. I know you were forced into marrying me, and I know it's not what either of us wanted. It was the worst of circumstances months ago, but there's peace here now. Because you've pushed for it and done things to protect me, even if you felt in your soul I didn't deserve it. I trust you, and this is something I can share to prove that to you. The only gift I can give is the truth."

He nodded. "Okay, Wife. Tell me about the Maiden's secret."

"Our power is not infinite. There's a reason the Maidens of

the past didn't decimate the world, regardless of the bloodlust. Because all magic comes with a cost, and the cost is chipping away at the fabric of who we are. It's likely why there were Maidens that died before their hundred years. Never because Death called them to his court early, but because they'd depleted themselves. The reason Death does not call me into his court every night is because the power is too strong, and when wielded too often, I could die."

He considered my confession for several moments, running a finger over the smooth rim of his glass. "Every time a Maiden kills, they use the power? Even if they choose the kill themselves and not Death?"

"Fractionally, yes. When we were in the castle to save Quill, I could feel the beast within me wake. Even though the choice to end the guards had been solely mine, I know Death will come for their souls, eventually. I know without question that I will see every single soul I've reaped again when I enter Death's court for the final time. Even my parents.

"The Maestro is dangerous on many levels. But he doesn't know the boundaries. If he captures me by contract, he will slaughter so many for a show, a thrill. He's been hunting me since I was a child, and the strongest reason to stay the hell away from him, if not for the lives of the innocent, is because he'll put me into a grave."

"I'd never let him do that."

"My father, King of Perth, couldn't control him. Neither can you."

Orin ran a hand through his hair, staring off into nothing. "It's no secret that he wants you…"

I studied the hard planes of his face, the way his steady breaths lifted his broad shoulders, the way the orange glow of light illuminated the amber flecks in his eyes. I could see the guilt on his face, in the turn of his brow. The discomfort was thick in the air, reminding us that our beginning was sparked by Orin's easy lies.

"He can't have me..." I whispered.

"He's a patient man, Nightmare."

"When I was twelve, maybe thirteen, I'd been standing at the door, wondering when the staff would return. My father always sent them away on the anniversary of my mother's death because that's all this day was to him. Anyway, a tall man with bushy black hair and a red jacket and the most elaborate top hat I'd ever seen walked up the circle drive and stood at the base of the steps, carrying a large white box with long black ribbons. I remember he pulled the hat from his head, flourished his hand, and gave me the box. I didn't understand birthdays at the time. I'd never heard of them. But he'd wished me a happy birthday from his boss and walked off. The second my fingers gripped that ribbon, my father shouted my name. He took the gift and made me watch as he tossed it into the fireplace in the grand hall. Maybe Drexel is patient, but I learned how to play this game from a ruthless man a long time ago."

Orin rubbed his eyes with his palms. "I thought having only one parent was something we had in common, but you never had a parent at all, and I'm sorry for it."

"Don't be." I stretched my arms above my head, staring at the final rays of sunlight. "For all his flaws, I know something in him had cared for me. Even if it was only the sliver of my mother that showed through, whether he wanted it or not. He taught me to be strong in a world where the weak never truly survive the hunters." Pausing, I chose my next words carefully. "When I met you, you said I'd killed your brother, your father, and your neighbor. I'm sorry. For what it's worth."

He faded into silence, seeming to slip a million miles away.

So, I continued, if only to fill the awkward silence. "It seems odd to me that Death would choose so many people close to you. Your father and your brother?"

He was silent for a few minutes before answering. "Ezra wasn't my real brother. But he was my best friend. I might have lied about my father. I really don't know who he was. You're welcome to prod my mother for information, but she's never given in to my questions, so don't hold your breath. Whomever he was, I have to believe he's dead now. Because how could he just walk away from her?"

I stewed on that for several moments before saying something I immediately regretted. "Do you think the Maestro could be your secret father? And maybe he never really left?"

His head snapped to face me, his perfectly combed hair falling into his face. "No."

"It's just that… your mother spoke so kindly of him from long ago, like he used to be a sweet memory, and now everything has changed."

"Drexel Vanhoff is not my father. He's my uncle."

I couldn't hide the gasp. "Your uncle is having you tortured every night?"

"When he came into his power, darkness slowly rotted away all semblance of kindness. My mother never danced on his stage. She worked tirelessly for him, cooking and cleaning, and even helped to spread the word about his show. She was beholden to him out of the love of a sibling, long before she was bound."

I thought of Elowen working as tirelessly as I'd seen the others. I thought of the Maestro's men stalking the alleyways at all hours of the night. I thought of the way their eyes had lingered when they'd tried to hunt me, and the fear hidden behind obligation. What horrors and heartache Orin's mother must have witnessed for the love of a brother. "Maybe we shouldn't talk about such terrible things."

He stood, holding out a hand. I took it, letting him pull me to my feet before walking to the edge of the rooftop. His fingers gripped the railing as we stood side by side, watching the final traces of color in the sky melt into night.

"Tell me something happy from your childhood."

I smiled. "I had a friend. Or what I believed a friend to be when I knew no better. Now I'm not so sure."

My ears burned red, anticipation growing in my gut as I considered telling him that I knew about his friendship with Ro. But why was that my business, and why would I risk shattering the very fragile strands of friendliness budding between us? I was not his keeper, and he was not duty-bound to me.

"How'd you meet her?"

"She was older. She'd been so kind when no one else had. She'd protected me in a way and taught me about life in others."

"Deyanira." His eyes were so full of sadness that I wondered if we really could forge a friendship after all. We'd covered the hard topics. The ones that caused such heartache between us, but really, we'd danced around them, as a performer always would.

I waited for him to tell me it was just too much. That I couldn't stay, and though there was something in both of us that may have wanted that, it could never be, but before any revelations could be made, the door opened, and Paesha and Thea joined us.

"Did we miss it?" Thea asked. "Shit."

"Every time," Paesha said, staring at the spot where the sun had just set.

"Are we, uh... interrupting anything up here?" Thea's smile was far too eager, even with a face smudged with ash and her apron covered in soot.

We moved away from each other before speaking in unison. "No."

"Great." Paesha sauntered over to the checkered blanket and lifted our glasses one by one, refilling them with Orin's favorite amber liquor, then handed them to each of us. "Because I need to dance."

I'd heard them up here several times in the past, sometimes with music and sometimes without. But they'd always gathered. It usually started with laughter and fell into silence, slipping back into the house only hours before the day began.

"Happy Birthday, Maiden." The Huntress clinked her glass with mine. "May you see your one-hundredth year with peace."

"Cheers." Thea joined, removing the apron and tossing it to the floor.

"Happy Birthday, Nightmare."

Orin's voice rumbled through me, an edge of sadness laced within. Just when I thought we were burying the hatchet between us, I began to feel as if possibly we'd resurrected it instead, both aware of how hard it would be, of the history that began between us long before we'd ever met. I'd taken the lives of people close to him, and he'd wrecked mine. Or so I thought... months ago.

"Good day or bad day?" Orin asked, turning to Paesha as he slammed his drink back and set it down.

"Bad day," she answered, eyes falling.

He took her hand and pulled her to the center of the rooftop. They swept the blanket away and began to dance, spinning and moving as if they could both hear the pulse of an ethereal song that no one else was privy to.

She spoke loud enough for everyone to hear. "He's never coming back, and I'm not strong enough to get over it."

I wasn't sure what kind of man would ever walk away from someone so beautiful, with so much passion and fierceness, but whoever had hurt her didn't deserve the redemption she clearly would have given. She was heartbroken, which really explained so much about what I'd seen from her. Dangerously loyal and incredibly protective, anyone would be lucky to stand by her side.

After whatever song they'd both heard ended, Orin slipped from her arms and moved to his cello. My heart leapt with anticipation. If anything, I'd learned I would never hear a note of music again without picturing the face he made the second those eyes fell shut as he escaped into his own melodious world.

"It's not a bad day because of your birthday, if that's what you're thinking," Thea said.

"I wasn't," I whispered, because Paesha's ornery smile had been so genuine earlier.

The Huntress extended her body, twisting and turning. Each movement was a carefully orchestrated symphony of sensuality, a tantalizing ballet of curves and contours that seemed to stir the night air. But the second the music had started, that haunting first note that Orin always delivered with absolute perfection, her tears began to fall.

There was no question that every step she made had been performed hundreds and hundreds of times, each twist a conjuring of emotion as she moved, not as a performer in a burlesque show, but more. Divine.

"Dancing with our ghosts again?" Hollis asked, joining Thea and me along the iron railing as he clicked his pocket watch shut and slipped it into his coat.

"I guess so." She shrugged, handing him what was left of her drink.

As the old man tipped the glass back, I couldn't help my burning question. "What kind of a man would leave her and never come back?"

Hollis choked on his drink as Thea's jaw slacked, her usual cheerful tone turning grave. "She traded a life of servitude to the Maestro to save him, but it didn't matter because once the Death Maiden has your name, there's nothing to be done. His name was Ezra Prophet, and he didn't leave. You killed him."

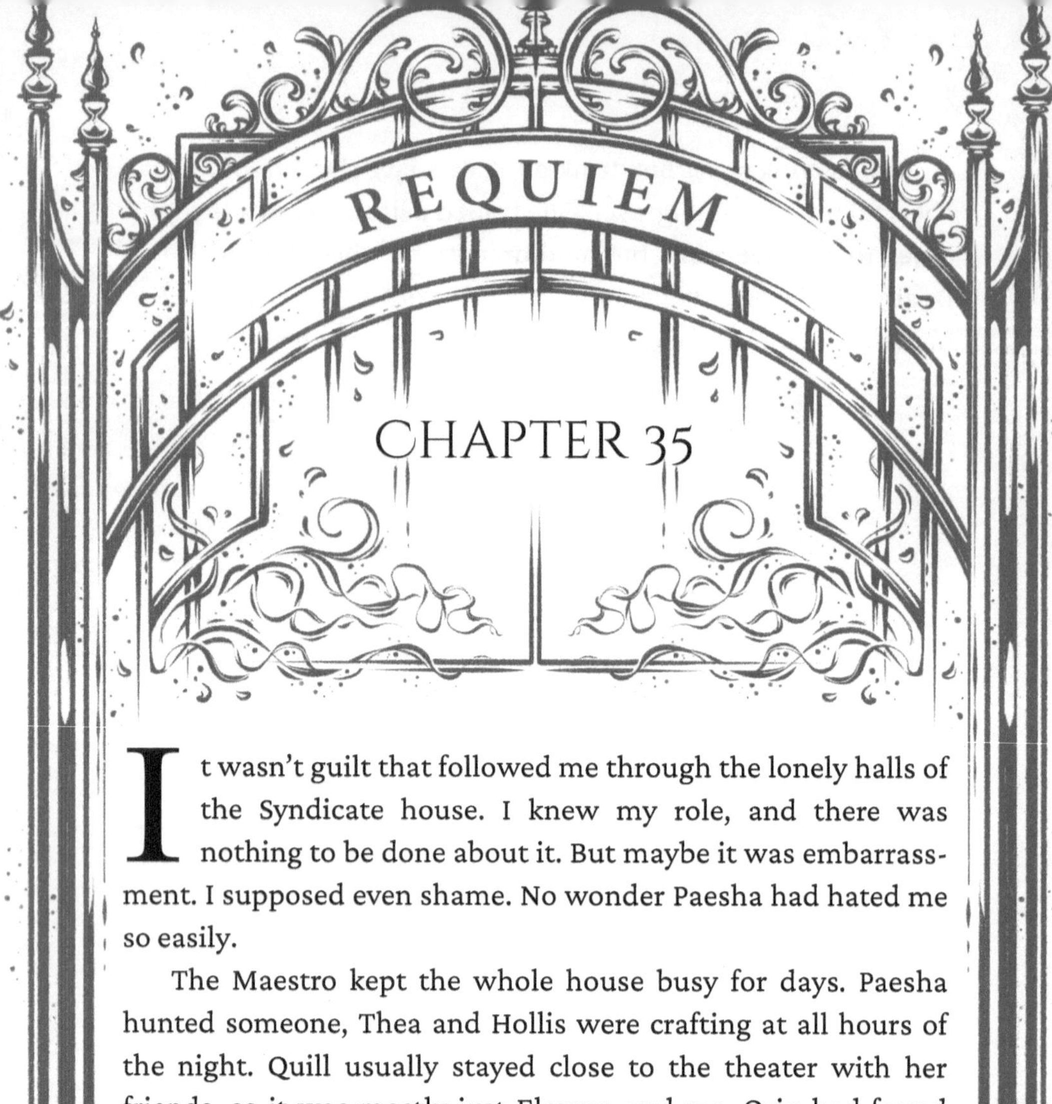

It wasn't guilt that followed me through the lonely halls of the Syndicate house. I knew my role, and there was nothing to be done about it. But maybe it was embarrassment. I supposed even shame. No wonder Paesha had hated me so easily.

The Maestro kept the whole house busy for days. Paesha hunted someone, Thea and Hollis were crafting at all hours of the night. Quill usually stayed close to the theater with her friends, so it was mostly just Elowen and me. Orin had found every possible excuse to stay away, solidifying the wedge. Elowen went to shop for groceries, and the rest were called to practice for the show. Even the dog had somewhere to be when I did not.

There was only one person I could think of to keep me company. Someone who might have answers to several of my burning questions. But she'd been so distant. Even preferring the company of Orin over me. Still, I snuck into Paesha's room and stood before the familiar mirror, holding my breath. Letting the anticipation buzz below my skin. Hardening myself in case she didn't welcome me.

I'd convinced myself whatever friendship I'd had with Ro was long over. As soon as I wielded no power as a royal, I was of no use to her anymore. But when the silvery reflection rippled, her invitation clear, I hesitated, wondering if I should really face her after all my hateful thoughts these past months.

But something within me needed closure from that part of my life. So, I stepped through the threshold, into the hall of mirrors, and descended the familiar steps to find her standing, arms crossed, waiting for me.

"Took you long enough," she huffed in greeting.

"I've tried to come so many times. You've denied me. You don't get to turn my absence on me when you're in control."

"There's a new king, and he's bad news. I've been spying and busy."

"So that's where you've been? Just lurking in mirrors?"

She scowled. "I don't lurk. I just happen to hear things from my hall. I cannot be held accountable for people with loose tongues."

Narrowing my eyes, I fell over the edge of my fury, letting it show, regardless of the consequences. "I've been married off, assaulted, imprisoned, nearly murdered, homeless, and denounced. I've seen you for five seconds when you ran into me at Lady Visha's, and then you vanished. I understand you're busy, but are you my friend or not, Ro? Just be honest."

Her deep eyes filled with hurt. "Of course I'm your friend. But that doesn't mean I can be available to you all the time. I'm sorry if that's hurtful, but friendship doesn't mean codependency, Dey. I have to keep an eye on this world if I want to survive in it. It's the only way I can protect my friends."

"Friends as in plural."

"Just because I'm *your* only friend doesn't mean you're mine."

My spine straightened. Maybe I'd relied too much on Ro and this distance was to teach me one of her many lessons. I'd wanted her to confess about Orin, though, and she hadn't. "I have other friends. Good ones. But there's so much pain and history there, I don't know how to navigate it."

"I'll always be here when you need me most, but it's important that you learn to live out there, too. I cannot be your crutch... Come on," she said with a heavy sigh, her cropped brown hair pushing into her face. "Let's sit as we used to and catch up."

I followed her through her quaint little home, swiping the long vines from the ceiling to pass by until we entered her parlor. Of course, everything had been completely changed since the last time I'd visited. "I'm afraid we'd be here for days if we had to go over it all."

She lifted a shoulder. "I've got nowhere to be today. You?"

"I've got nowhere to be, forever, unless Death comes. Because I'm wanted by Icharius Fern." I sat heavily on her plush green couch, letting the full cushions nearly swallow me.

"No one is brave enough to hunt you." She poured tea into two dainty teacups and set a beautiful tray on the table between us. "But the king is trouble. And I'm afraid he's been working with the Maestro, which is an even bigger problem."

"A problem we've already seen. And I'd like to believe that no one is brave enough, but let's be honest. I can be overpowered. My lovely new husband was proof of that." I waited, a subtle nod to the elephant in the room. But she never acknowledged the mention of Orin, so I continued. "I won't kill if I don't have to, and as soon as these idiots start figuring that out, I'm going to be in trouble."

"If they come for you, Deyanira, you *will* have to. And that's what makes you dangerous. Or have you forgotten those two guards so quickly?"

My skin bristled, cheeks heating as I realized she'd been watching me. "You know I haven't."

"But you saved that child. A child with a lot of power for such a little thing." Ro pinned me with a stare. "Don't you agree?"

"I don't ... Are you confirming Quill has magic?"

"You are not the foolish princess you used to be, Deyanira. Why else would the king want her?"

"That wasn't for power. Drexel forced my husband to marry me because he wanted to slight the new king. Icharius took Quill as punishment."

"Interesting theory. But why is Orin being punished by his keeper for following his commands?" She drew the last sentence from me as if she already knew the answer and wanted to lead me down the path of understanding. But I hated the proverbial leash and the upper hand she wielded so casually.

"Because he's a fool and made a deal for my safety, and Drexel is trying to break him, make him ask for something else instead of protecting me."

She swirled a finger along the edge of her teacup, considering the facts. "I think you need to pay closer attention to those you keep company with."

I regarded her with a hint of skepticism, my gaze lingering longer than usual. "What do you know?"

"When it comes to Icharius Fern and Drexel Vanhoff, they keep their secrets locked very tight. I have few facts and many suspicions."

A wash of cool calmness settled over me as I leaned forward, placing the teacup on the table, prepared to slip back into the predator I'd always been. Because, after everything that'd happened, I couldn't trust her any more than I could trust Orin Faber, even if I desperately wanted to.

"And when it comes to my bonded husband and his housemates?"

She thrummed her fingers together, a smile creeping across her face as she matched my energy, scooting in, entering the battle of wits I wasn't sure I was prepared for.

"Why did you agree to stay in their house?"

Wondering if this was a time to stop sharing information with Ro, I chose my words carefully. "Where else would I go?"

"Do not answer a question with a question and expect to get information from me."

"That was a genuine response. My father's castle is abandoned but probably still being watched by Drexel and King Icharius."

"Yet you visited the clock tower to collect trinkets to sell to Visha. You could have slept there."

"And then you delivered me to my husband so he could stab me in an alley and capture me. Which one of us is the asshole here?"

She stood. "He stabbed you because you're a godsdamned fool who wouldn't stay put. You cannot go to Visha and ask for a single thing. She's trouble, and she'll bind you to her, and then where will you be? Naked on the streets? Bent over her filthy couches for whatever scum she welcomes in her doors? A thug? A lackey? Turning Visha into a crime lord with power that will overtake Drexel. That's what you will become. He collects magical people, but you're the ultimate prize here, and somehow you forget that."

"I haven't forgotten a single thing!" I rose to stare into her eyes, irritated that she was so much taller than I was. "You could have let me come here, but you didn't fucking answer. I had nowhere else to go, and I was trying to protect myself. You think I don't know what these assholes want from me? You have no idea what I've been through."

She softened, if only a little. "I know what you've been through. But sometimes we have to take the journey alone. Even if I wanted to be there for you, had I stepped in, would you be where you are now?"

I considered that, deflating. "No. But you make it seem like I shouldn't be there anyway."

"Oh, you definitely need to be there, Dey. You just need to keep your eyes and ears open. Be smart."

"Then tell me what you know and what you suspect, and let me be the judge of where I should and shouldn't be."

"Quill is powerful. But you must keep in mind that they are all bound to Drexel. If he demands it, they must listen. Even if it means lying to you."

"Then how do I free them?"

She faltered, a gasp catching in her throat. "You don't. You stay far, far away from that man."

It didn't really matter if I kept my distance because he was always going to be a problem until I solved it. And I was done with hiding in a house and watching the only people around me suffer because of him. I needed to steer the conversation away from that, though. Ro wasn't going to solve that issue.

Sitting back down, I reached for my tea, casting my eyes to the floor. If she needed to think she'd won this, then fine. Because I had other problems.

"Are we done?"

"I didn't come here to fight with you."

"Then why did you come?"

"I've been trying to find the Life Maiden, and I think that's a lost cause. I've never asked because it would have only been for my father before, but now, I don't know. I just need to find her."

"As she is your counterpart, I think something in you probably urges you to seek that balance of power. But there are no traces that I have seen. Just like the missing people."

I'd almost forgotten about the missing people with everything else going on. Orin had brought them up, as well. And then I remembered that it'd taken me longer to search for a target the time before last. Normally, the magic led me by compulsion because it was nearly sentient and all-knowing. Something within it was also a hunter. But something was wrong. As if the soul had been able to hide.

"The Huntress hasn't been able to locate them either. And one of them she knows. No one can find them, but someone's hiding it."

"Is that why you were with Orin in the Badger Hole?"

A familiar smile of an old friend reached her eyes. "Took you long enough to ask about it."

"Why wouldn't you two just tell me you knew each other?"

"Your new husband is a very private person. And I've only seen you once since then. There was no time for catching up."

I sat back on the couch, examining my nails rather than looking her in the eyes. "How do you know him?"

"Requiem is a small realm. We have similar circles, and our concerns are aligned. No one knows where the missing people are going, but I have a suspicion the new king has something to do with it."

"Do you think the missing people could have something to do with the missing Life Maiden?"

Ro's slanted eyes narrowed carefully as she studied my blank features. I wondered if she'd realized I had steered this conversation with precision. I no longer cared that she'd been with Orin, but if she thought that was the most important thing, perhaps she wouldn't be so guarded with other information.

"Here's what I know. You think everyone is going to find out you don't kill for sport and won't be afraid of you. But everyone thinks these missing people are your victims. I'll admit that even I thought so. Until someone from Misery's End vanished on a night you were accounted for."

"So, they've been watching what I do, and that's why they want me to stay there."

"I think that was maybe the plan at the beginning. But things have changed, and now your husband will not share a single word about you with me."

"And that's why you finally let me in."

"I let you in because we are friends, even if you like to argue and be ridiculous." She reached into her pocket and pulled out the familiar box with my mother's jewel on the top. "How many flowers do you need, Deyanira?"

I sighed. Conversation over. "I need four."

THIS WAS A TERRIBLE IDEA. The most dangerous of all ideas I'd ever had. But, as the warehouse filled with some of the most beautiful people this world had to offer, I fell in line with them, shuffling into the space as if I belonged there.

Everyone prepping for tonight's show moved with a purpose, completely unaware of the murderer among them. Women dressed in little more than lace robes sat in a line before the mirrors, applying heavy shades of makeup and gossiping about their boss's newest recruit. A fierce woman holding a clipboard and barking orders directed everyone with a shrill voice. I knew who it was without needing an introduction. They called her Genevieve. And there wasn't a person in the house that cared for her. Not even Quill, who'd befriended a monster— several, in fact.

I kept my back to the woman, moving toward the tunnel to

gain entrance to the theater without announcing my presence to Drexel if I could help it. I'd borrowed a green velvet gown from Althea's stash, stole a matching hat from the old man, and had spent the better part of an hour trying to dress appropriately. With my hair tucked and movements no faster than the fifty or so people scrambling about, I blended in well enough.

"That is how it's meant to be worn. This may not be a brothel, but we have a show to put on." Hollis's voice comforted me, even if I didn't want him to know I was there. He'd been tucked in a corner, tightening a corset on a red-haired woman while arguing with another about his latest masterpiece.

If something didn't change, that man would live out his final years tied to the Maestro. And though I knew he loved what he did, there was a better life for him. His level of kindness didn't deserve the entrapment.

Pressed against a back wall, I watched a world I'd never seen before. Quill and Paesha were nowhere to be seen, but I'd kept my eyes glued to Orin as I waited for someone to go down the tunnel. He faced a wall, scribbling frantically onto music sheets, with disheveled hair but dressed in a finely pressed blue suit and boots so shiny I could likely see my reflection. Hollis would allow nothing less.

The aged posters adorning the wall promised shows of grandeur and seduction. Suggestive silhouettes of curvy women in sensual poses had been a common theme amongst them. They drew my attention along the dimly lit space until I found Althea, sitting on a worn-out chaise, studying a giant blueprint of her next contraption, brows knit in concentration, even a pair of goggles on her head.

This was a different world for them. Here, they were different people. The bands on their arms made them servants. But it seemed that they had each found a way to embrace it regardless. The silver lining. Or the perfectly laid trap the

Maestro had planned when he'd wrapped them all into contracts.

"Twenty minutes, you scoundrels. We'll start with 'Satin Sheets Serenade'. Then 'Ballad of Temptation' will follow."

I didn't miss the way Orin's back straightened, cutting a glance to Althea. She'd made almost the same move. I sank back a little further, shuffling behind a rack of feather boas and sequined gowns.

"'Masquerade Minuet' is still slow after the bridge, ladies. Get your asses moving. I want no excuses about the shoes this time. It's three and four and then back to your mark."

The woman with curly blonde hair pulled the glasses from her nose, letting them fall until the pearl chain around her neck holding them went taut. "Where's Paesha?"

Thea jumped from her seat and scrambled forward, nearly tripping over the giant metal ring she'd been working on. "She's coming. The boss sent her to work on something else."

The woman rolled her eyes, moving a giant feathered quill across her parchment in earnest.

"No. Please, Genevieve. She'll be here. She promised it wouldn't take that long."

"How I run the boss's show is none of your concern, Althea Washburn. Go... build something."

She waved her off with a hand, and some of the other women snickered. Thea's face turned red, and she tucked her head and hustled back to her work. By the time I left the room, I wanted to punch no less than eighty percent of the people within, starting with Genevieve, who'd spoken down to Hollis twice for the way the women picked at their costumes and then went after Thea again when Paesha sauntered in three minutes late.

The Huntress's eyes found mine before she'd made it three steps into the room. She looked at me and then at the door to the tunnel. Then back to me again with a slight shake of her head. After my conversation with Ro, I believed I'd made a connection I'd missed before, but I would need someone to confirm before I did something I'd ultimately regret.

I beckoned her with a finger and slipped into the tunnel as she approached Genevieve. Minutes later, she stood at the top of the stairs, staring down at me.

"Whatever you're doing here, don't."

"I need you to tell me something."

She snorted, moving down the stairs quickly. "If it's that important, I probably can't."

"Look, I'm sorry, okay? I know why you hate me, and I haven't had a chance to apologize. If I could take it back and give him back to you, I would. But I can't, and there's only one way to make this right. For everyone."

"Famous last words, Dey."

"Does Quill have power?"

My blunt question was met with a sharp breath. I wasn't sure if she couldn't or wouldn't answer, but I didn't need her to. Not when I could see the answer written on her face nearly as clear as the truth Ro had given. Those in the Syndicate house were my friends, and I was mostly safe with them, but they were keeping secrets. Because they had to or wanted to, I wasn't sure. But none of that mattered.

"I'll see you at the house, Paesha."

"Deyanira," she said, voice low in warning.

I didn't look back.

"Maiden," she hissed.

But her warnings would get neither of us where we needed to be. At least someone knew where I was, in case this night went very, very badly.

CHAPTER 36

The view from the balcony of Misery's End was like a different world. Though the heavy black curtains rose with a gust of anticipation, and the eager crowd moved to the edge of their seats, the Maestro strode out with his infamous cane clacking in perfect rhythm. That repulsive smile plastered across his face, lifting his curled red mustache, infuriated me.

"Ladies and gentlemen, wanderers of peculiarity, seekers of sultry, and brave souls who dare to tread where shadows dance and dreams unravel—welcome, oh, welcome, to the beautiful Misery's End, where no two shows are the same, and our deepest desire is to teach you what lust truly is, to make you feel as if your feet stand upon this beautiful stage. As if your body is moving to the pulse of..." He paused, pointing his cane at the orchestra nestled in the sunken pit in the heart of the audience. They responded right on cue, their barrage of instruments thundering through the theater. The Maestro whipped his cane back, and silence fell. Back and forth, he conducted from the stage, leaving the audience to follow the ebb and flow until they moved when he did. They leaned when he leaned. Frowned when he did. Until he conducted his audience as thoroughly as his musicians. "Just a little warm-up," he roared, sweeping his arm to the side. "But first, we must introduce our future's diamond."

All eyes followed his gesture as Quill, dressed in delicate layers of crimson lace, pearls, and makeup, rose from the ground in that massive gold birdcage, her swing rocking back and forth as she smiled and waved proudly to the crowd. If looks alone could kill, Drexel would be dead upon his stage. The manipulation of an adult by anyone was disgusting, but the orchestration of such tactics upon a tender child was nothing short of abhorrent.

The Maestro's cackle swirled around the room like hands, gripping every single person as he spoke with so much flare my stomach twisted into knots. It seemed only I could see beyond the mask.

"Lean closer, my delectable darlings, and bear witness to a world beyond the mundane. Yes. I know why you've come." He chuckled, the nuance of the sound practiced and particular. "I extend an invitation that promises an indulgence like no other. Behold a coven of the sensuous and the forbidden, where every tantalizing movement is a serenade to the senses, an invitation to embrace your innermost cravings. Within these doors, a woman's body is an art form, and a man's is a display of strength and grit."

He crossed the stage, the echo of his cane a taunt as a cymbal rattled in the pit, and slowly, very slowly, the music began in a crescendo. The Maestro flourished a gloved hand, holding it extended to the audience. That swine-like smile melted into something far more sinister as his finger curled. "Take my hand and surrender to temptation. Allow yourselves to be ensnared in the intoxicating dance of Misery's End."

In a heartbeat, the entire theater went dark and silent; the only palpable presence was the magic coating the air. Quill's magic. The reason the Maestro had kept her so close. The reason the king had tried to take her.

The audience gasped, holding their breaths for a beat and then another before the stage fired back to life. Drexel was gone, and four women stood in suggestive poses, with arched backs and poised hands above them. A single minor key of the piano played. The women shifted to strike new poses. Again. And then again. I leaned forward on the balcony, letting myself get lost in the way they moved. Each stance, a choreographed dance meant to weaken one's resolve. Barely dressed, poised behind perfectly placed feathers, the women turned at once, grabbing their black top hats. Four men stormed across the stage as the steady beat of a drum led each step.

Upon reaching the women, the men stopped, holding out a hand for their partner to lie back on before he stroked his fingers between her breasts, stopping just below her navel. The drum beat once more, the women stood, and a piercing note filled the theater as the dance changed. The women fell to their knees before the men. Reaching for them. Pulling back. An easy flow, perfectly timed, each tantalizing move making me feel as if I should look away. As if I were an intruder on a moment far more intimate than a moan and thrust in a dark alleyway. I couldn't help but think of golden eyes and thick forearms holding me. Of the sounds Orin might make and how that thought heated something inside of me. The burlesque show was indeed a lesson on lust.

I might have believed the first performance was a dance of yearning for what we could not have, but that was never the story the Maestro would sell. *"You can have everything this world has to offer,"* the posters had said. *"Step inside Misery's End to learn how."*

Flashing a glance at Quill in a gilded cage, fury stirred within me. I'd hoped to come here and feel differently. To find that, in their own way, they were happy with the lives they led. And maybe some small part of them were. But Quill. She was not a tool. She was a child. And the way her giant eyes stared at that stage in wonder rattled me to my core. This was not okay. And I had the power to stop it. *Only* I had the power.

My thoughts were a downward spiral as the show continued. The only constant upon the stage was the heavy theme of seduction and the blue bands around every wrist. Each person bound to the Maestro. Each smile forced. Each twist and turn, every inch of bare skin, his. Every note played, and every light that fell was plucked from his delusional mind.

There were so many things that man had done that most wouldn't hear of. Though it could never be proven, it was whispered among the streets that he kept the opium dens full, and when my father had sent guards to the border, he'd been the one to fund the response in Bram Ellis's name. He'd sent Paesha to find the innocent. But it wasn't enough to know where they were, as she had told me one night. There was far more value in her ability to find his target's weaknesses.

The very same man that stood on that stage and welcomed the world in, hunted them. Plucking them from their seats with a skewer, learning what they needed most in the world, and offering it on a silver platter with a single fine line, entrapping them. A meticulous spiderweb that never missed a fly.

I watched that little girl twirl in her swing, listening to the music. Tapping her tiny foot. He was a predator lurking in shadows, and she was his prey. Eventually, he would pounce. It was enough. It had been enough for years. And tonight, Drexel Vanhoff would finally learn his lesson.

Two beautiful knives provided a balanced weight on my thighs. Their perfect curves, a seduction of their own as I peeled away from my seat, fighting Quill's compulsion, and began to hunt the Maestro. He hadn't been in his box. Nor had he come back to the stage. Which meant he was likely in his office.

I snuck through the upper portion of the theater quietly. Incapacitating the guards, who were probably not perfect citizens but likely wouldn't have done half the shit Drexel forced upon them, had they the choice. I tried to keep that in mind as I laid them out in the hallway one by one, not dead, but also not a threat to me.

The glowing light from beneath the door was all I needed to see before I stroked Chaos and Serenity and kicked the damn door in, staring into the bewildered eyes of a red-haired villain.

But shock melted into elation as he drank me in. Death incarnate, come to reap his soul. He must have been mad to sit before me, poised behind his desk, and grin. I drew the blades.

"So, they were wrong about you, Maiden."

Stepping into the office, I chanced a glance behind the door to make sure no one was there before slamming it shut.

There was no fear.

Why?

I didn't answer. I'd spent years holding my tongue with Death. Instead, I gripped Serenity's handle tighter, the embellishments digging into my skin, grounding me behind pulsing fury. The beautiful tone of Orin's cello crept up the stairs and beneath the door. The Maestro's requiem.

"We can both win here. I can protect you from the king that hunts you. Your palm does not bear my name, and we both know that to be true. Your beloved master is sworn to me. That blade will never strike home."

My ears rang as something beneath my skin buzzed with horror. "You could never force Death into submission."

His smile grew as he stood, weight heavily shifting onto the cane. "Perhaps the devil is in the details, Deyanira. May I call you Deyanira?"

"No."

"No matter. The name is not important." He thumped that cane three times on the wood floor and waited for my reaction.

I slid Serenity into her sheath, pulled a throwing knife, and watched as it slammed into his shoulder. Drexel's body jerked on impact, and finally, the wretched smile faded as if his own mortality, the blood that began to seep down his arm, reminded him that he truly was at Death's mercy, no matter the deal he'd made.

"Death is a master of deal-making, Deyanira," he said behind clenched teeth. "I know my place in this world, but do you know yours? Rumor has it you refuse to kill for him. Yet, here you are. Willing to kill for yourself. You think I'm the monster, but what does that make you?"

"I've never claimed to be anything *but* a monster." I flung another throwing knife. It landed exactly opposite of its counterpart.

The door slammed open behind me, and Paesha rushed in, holding Quill in her grip. I looked between them, unsure of what I expected.

"You have to take Quill away. Get out of here."

Her eyes sang a thousand apologies as she pushed the little girl toward the bleeding sadist. "You know I can't do that."

"Drexel?" Quill whispered, eyes glued to the wounds in his shoulders as she circled the desk to stand beside him. "What happened?"

"The Maiden and I are having a slight misunderstanding, nothing to worry about."

Rage powered through my entire body until I shook. "Get away from him, kid."

"But he's my friend. He keeps the bad guys away, just like you do."

"No. No, he doesn't."

"If you think I had anything to do with her kidnapping, you are mistaken, Maiden. She is far, far too precious." A forced laugh filled the room as the Maestro's giant hand landed on the girl's shoulder, and he turned his words to her. "Just a game, little one. Just a game." But when his eyes cut to me, I could see the venom behind the glare. The warning. The promise of pain.

"I want to make a deal," I blurted, caught between her safety and my rage.

Another laugh. "Of course, you do, pet. Everyone wants to make a deal. But what could you possibly offer me?"

A game, then. One of careful ledges and dangerous slopes.

"I wish to speak to Paesha alone before I tell you. Those are my terms."

"Of course, my dear. Shall I cover my ears? I'm afraid my arms aren't working. Quill, my darling, would you mind removing these blades?"

"No!" Paesha yelled, darting across the dimly lit office. "I'll do it."

She'd meant to save the child from the horror, and I was grateful for it, but equally sickened by the lengths Drexel would go.

The squelch of the blades' removal twisted Quill's face, though she wouldn't look at me. I'd hurt her, even when I'd been trying to save her. But if being her villain kept her away from the claws of the Maestro, I'd take that role to my grave.

I shifted forward. "It has to be a true deal, or I walk."

The sharp tang of magic filled the air as he spoke his next words. "I will allow you two minutes of privacy and no more. You may not leave my theater, nor speak to another soul. If you do, you're mine forever, Deyanira Hark. Do you agree to those terms?"

"No," I answered. "You must also agree that you cannot and will not ever ask Paesha about the conversation."

"I agree that I will not ask or seek to discover what is to be said. Are those the final terms?"

"No."

His eyes narrowed. "I'm listening."

"During our time, she must be allowed to speak to me without any of your agreements preventing her. It's only fair that I walk into this deal as knowledgeable as you are. And if you fail to uphold your end of the bargain, you are bound to me, just as I am bound to you if I fail. An even trade."

Clenching his teeth, he gripped the edge of the desk. "I agree to your terms. Do you agree with mine?"

Heart hammering in my chest, sucking in a sharp breath full of a lifetime of warnings and fear, I lifted my chin. "Yes."

A searing pain leeched around my wrist, binding our magical deal. Paesha ran into the hall, snatching me on the way out.

"You are a godsdamn idiot," she hissed.

My voice was hardly audible and full of panic. "There's no time; we have two minutes. I'm going to do something far more ridiculous anyway. Confirm for me, Quill can affect emotions. That's her power?"

"Yes." Her brows rose, shocked at her ability to answer.

"And the Maestro cannot bind her to him yet, true?"

"True. Her age is limiting his power."

"And if I make a deal with him, will Quill help me, or will she be too upset that I've attacked him?"

She lowered her chin, realization falling over her. "I'll talk to her. She will help you." With a pause, she rose to her full height. "And I will help you, Maiden."

"Do you know where the Life Maiden is?"

"No." Her shoulders shrank. "And he has demanded I find her. I have to search every day, but I don't know what I'm looking for. Or who. I'm sorry."

I took her hand. "And I'm sorry for Ezra. If this all goes to shit, just know that I never wanted any of this."

Leaning her head to mine, she closed her eyes. "You're forgiven. Just don't fuck this up, or we're all in trouble. What's the plan?"

Stepping away from her, I shook my head. "He's already looking for a loophole."

We walked back into the room to find Quill waiting beside him.

Paesha reached out a hand. "Come on, Quilly, let's go back downstairs."

"Is this your wish?" the Maestro asked me, an eyebrow lifted.

I said nothing. He'd meant to trap me within the two-minute window. If I spoke to anyone but Paesha, I was his. Forever. So, I waited. And waited. Counting up in my mind until no less than five minutes had passed.

"They are not needed for you and me to bargain, are they?"

He glanced at his watch. "Clever girl."

"Check your other wrist." I smiled sweetly.

When he drew back the opposite sleeve, revealing the deep blue band, he nearly fell out of his chair. "What is this? What have you done? Your minutes are over."

"Well, Drexy-poo, can I call you that? I feel like I can. You see, making deals is a tricky business. I was bound to your terms for two minutes, but you, sir, are bound to mine for life. Shall we revisit the conversation?"

His eyes doubled as he sank back, suit jacket still covered in blood. "No. I remember."

"Should you ever ask about our conversation in the hallway, even trying to find a loophole verbally, which I'm sure is already spinning through that messy head of yours, you fail your part of the bargain, and you become bound to me for the rest of your life."

"You don't have the power to bind me."

"No, Drexy. But you do. That's your own magic turned against you. Pity."

"Get out of my office."

I lifted Chaos, picking the dirt from beneath my nails, feeling more myself than I had in ages. I'd forgotten who I was when my world had been swept away, but no more.

"Perhaps you didn't hear me," he said, standing, gripping the edges of his desk for balance. "Get. Out."

"Don't you want to know how to get rid of that band? I mean, if you want to keep it forever, that's fine, but I'm willing to make a much more lucrative bargain with you."

I knew he couldn't resist the urge. An offer from Death's Maiden sitting on the table. But I'd outsmarted him once, and he wouldn't allow that a second time. I'd need to be very, very careful.

"Speak the terms and I will decide."

"I will perform on your stage, in front of a normal audience one time. If I can earn a standing ovation, then you will let my friends, specifically, Paesha, Thea, Quill, Hollis, and Orin, free from their debt to you. And if I cannot do it, then I will fall in line and become your weapon. There's not a person on the planet you cannot ask me to kill. And you cannot turn me over to Icharius Fern or his men. You can do nothing to prevent me from performing."

His eyes glistened with mirth as his power began to fill the room, igniting with the spoken terms. "Five shows. I decide the performance, and you have ten minutes on stage each time.

Should you fail, you are mine for life. There will be no loopholes, Maiden. And once this deal is struck, the other bargain is void."

"No. I agree to these terms only. The prior bargain cannot be terminated until this one is. I will perform in three shows, and within ten minutes of the performance start, I must have a standing ovation. You cannot do anything to keep the people from coming or standing or clapping, and it must be a single act on the stage. You cannot ask me to do anything more than the rest of your performers do, nor can you ask me to kill anyone. I also will not fight Death's hounds, so don't even think about it."

"Watch your words, Maiden. I won't agree to bind my mind's thoughts."

I rolled my eyes. Magical deals were so nit-picky. "Fine. You can think about it, but you cannot ask it. I won't fight them. And you can never speak of the details to Paesha, Quill, Orin, Thea, or Hollis."

"No. Never is eternal, or have you forgotten the lesson you've just taught? I will not ask them a single question about this bargain until after the final grain of sand falls on your third day. And then I am free."

"Fine." I shrugged.

"And should you fail, you are mine forever." He lifted an auburn brow. "You seem to have conveniently left that tidbit out."

Holding myself as still as possible so he could not determine which of us was the real predator here, I nodded. "For the rest of my lifetime. Not forever."

"Final terms?" he asked with a dangerous smile.

I circled the plan over and over again, making sure there was nothing that I couldn't manage. It felt secure. And though warning bells were firing in my mind, I could see the nerves on his face. He carried the same thoughts I did. This was incredibly dangerous. But the freedom of that house, of Thea's kindness and Hollis's love, of Quill's carefree spirit, and Paesha's fierce loyalty, and my husband's future all came down to this one moment.

"The shows must be the next three consecutive; you cannot drag them out. Whatever your normal schedule is, that is when I will perform."

His cocky grin faltered, ire staring back at me in human form as he spoke through clenched teeth. "Final terms?"

"Final terms."

Again, the magic seared my wrist, sealing the deal with a power I had no business messing with. Because from this day forward, until I could free them all, I was bound to Drexel Vanhoff.

PART TWO

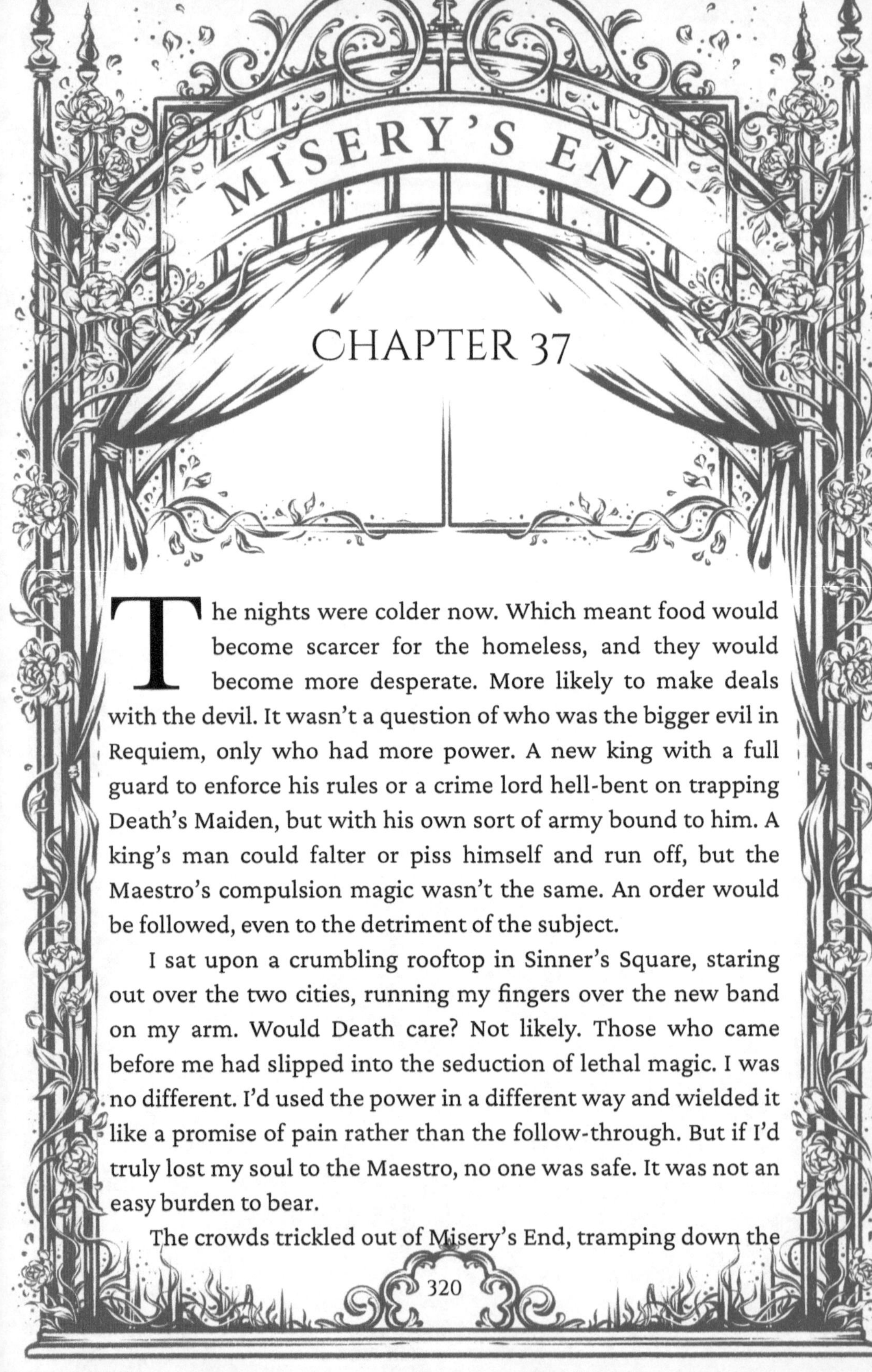

MISERY'S END

CHAPTER 37

The nights were colder now. Which meant food would become scarcer for the homeless, and they would become more desperate. More likely to make deals with the devil. It wasn't a question of who was the bigger evil in Requiem, only who had more power. A new king with a full guard to enforce his rules or a crime lord hell-bent on trapping Death's Maiden, but with his own sort of army bound to him. A king's man could falter or piss himself and run off, but the Maestro's compulsion magic wasn't the same. An order would be followed, even to the detriment of the subject.

I sat upon a crumbling rooftop in Sinner's Square, staring out over the two cities, running my fingers over the new band on my arm. Would Death care? Not likely. Those who came before me had slipped into the seduction of lethal magic. I was no different. I'd used the power in a different way and wielded it like a promise of pain rather than the follow-through. But if I'd truly lost my soul to the Maestro, no one was safe. It was not an easy burden to bear.

The crowds trickled out of Misery's End, tramping down the

streets with their threadbare coats pulled tight to battle the icy breeze while slipping back into Requiem's dire reality. I waited, giving those headed to the Syndicate house long enough to get home and settled before I snuck in. But when I opened my bedroom door and found Paesha pacing inside, she brought a finger to her lips before I could question her. Less than three seconds later, Orin slammed the door open, eyes nearly black and a hint of those eerie veins peeking from beneath his collar as if they'd crept up his neck. His broad shoulders heaved as Orin's wild eyes met mine, sweeping down my body, searching for gods knew what. Still, that gaze burned a path so strong it was as if I could feel phantom hands wrapping around me, pulling me toward him.

I opened my mouth to explain. To promise him I would be careful with the dangerous deal I'd made, but the Huntress grabbed my arm and squeezed. A warning.

"Where have you been?" he demanded. "Why weren't you home when we got here?"

He didn't know yet. *Good.*

I didn't want to lie, but his fury drew my own, and starting another fight with him was not on my to-do list after the evening I'd had. Confident the blue band on my arm was hidden, I drew a long, exasperated breath. "I went for a walk. I'm tired of being cooped up in this house."

"How rough it must be for you," he growled.

Paesha moved in front of me. "Calm down, Orin. She's not your prisoner. Or have you forgotten?"

"Since when are you on her side?" he asked, glare shifting between us.

"Since she kicked your ass in the front yard, and I won that bet. Look around. Everyone's fine." She stepped forward, resting a hand on his shoulder. "Just because you think it's your job to protect us all doesn't mean it truly is."

"It *is* my job," he argued.

"Last time I checked, I was grown."

"We have only us, and if we aren't careful, this world will end us."

She shook her head, a golden-brown curl falling loose. "Whatever fate the old gods have damned us to, it's not that. But we're a team. Remember the first night you found me on the streets and forced me to come stay here? And Ezra stayed up all night because he was confident you'd made a huge mistake bringing in the infamous Huntress? And you told him he worried too much... You didn't have to take his place when he died."

"P..." Orin's voice trailed off as he softened.

"We know you lose sleep and pull strings we don't know exist to make this little haven safe. But life's short, and you're allowed your own joy, too. Take a breath. I'm starting to worry about you."

He smoothed a hand down his face, shoulders falling. "Give us a second?"

She nodded, twisting toward the door. "Come find me when you're done, Dey."

"Okay," I managed, the first word I'd spoken.

"Be nice," Paesha said, throwing an elbow into Orin before disappearing down the hallway.

We stood in silence, staring for several quiet moments.

"I see you're in one piece tonight?"

He crossed his arms over his chest. "The boss was busy. The show wrapped early. I guess he's planning something big for tomorrow."

"Well, I'm glad there's no cauterizing wounds or bandaging gashes tonight. I think we're running low on supplies."

He scratched the back of his head, though he seemed... nervous?

"What?"

"Walk with me?"

I didn't hesitate to take his outstretched hand, but the moment the connection was made, I suddenly fell right back into that place that made me feel so lost. I wasn't the confident woman trapping an asshole into his own power. I was just a woman, standing with my new husband, so, so aware of every single one of my shortcomings.

He led us out of the house quietly, never letting go of my hand. We were several paces away from the house before he spoke. "I thought... I'm sorry I yelled. It's just... When you weren't home tonight when we got here, I had this terrible feeling something bad happened. In the past, I told myself you were out hunting and murdering and slaughtering, and I'd sit and stew with that until I couldn't. But this was different. I knew you weren't. I know you wouldn't unless Death gives you a name. But this sense of dread just came over me, and I couldn't shake it. And then you weren't home, and no one had seen you. I thought maybe the king..."

He was beautiful in the moonlight, confessing without saying the words that he cared. That he'd worried about me. I lifted my free hand to his cold cheek, and he closed his eyes, turning into my touch.

"I'm sorry everything is broken, Deyanira. But I want to fix it. I don't think I'm supposed to want that. Hell, I don't think I'm supposed to want you, but here we are, and I can't help the way my heart fucking aches for you."

He moved a hand into my hair, pulling me until we stood chest to chest. I had to tilt my head back just to peek into those eyes that wrecked me. And there, for just a moment, I wondered if I would ever look at him without hoping he would touch me.

"It does?"

"There are days when I wish you would draw that pretty

blade from your side and slide it right into my heart because I think it would hurt less than wanting you and telling myself I can't have you."

I pulled away, shivers creeping down my arms at the loss of his warmth. "Why can't you have me? Am I not enough?"

"*I* am not enough. You are the stars and the storm, Wife. Somehow, you're both peace and destruction. Nightmare and a daydream. You're hell and home. Fear and solace. Slumber and panic. Kindness and rage. Light is easy to love, but I've seen your darkness, and I want that, too. I crave it. I want to fucking drown it in. But how does any man live up to that? Deserve that?"

I smiled. "I've heard it starts with stabbing, so I think we're halfway there."

He yanked me to him again, stroking his thumb over my cheeks, brushing the tips of my white lashes as my heart pounded against his, melting something inside of me. "The problem is there's darkness inside me, too, and no one can ever know about it."

I swallowed a gasp as I realized what he was saying. A silent confession if ever I'd witnessed one. He really had killed that man. And if the Maestro ever learned of it, he wouldn't need me when he could exploit his nephew so much easier. "Then don't tell a soul. Never speak of it aloud."

Dark lashes fell to his cheeks as he drew a steady breath. "Never a soul," he repeated.

The chilly breeze wrapped around us as we stood inches apart, lost in each other and the moment.

"It's cold," he whispered. "Let's go back inside."

"One more minute?" I could hear the shameless plea in my voice, and I didn't care. The second he learned about my deal with the devil, marking me as reckless as he feared, everything would be broken anyway. So, we stayed like that, lost beneath a sea of stars, standing in secrets so fragile, the world was sure to break soon, and our tender moments would become simple casualties of the truth.

The front door clicked shut, and he hung his head. "Paesha's probably in her room. I'll see you in the morning."

Conversation over. He had held back, and I could do nothing but stand there like a fool, wondering how he could pour his heart out to me with such confessions and still walk away. But then I considered the way he fought. The war mounting inside of him. I was his problem. I'd been his enemy. And those truths didn't just vanish with a few moments of vulnerability.

Each step to Paesha's room was a heavy one, coiled in confusion and sadness. Maybe I should have told him the truth out there, but it would have only complicated things more than they were. As long as Drexel had a grip on him, he would never let himself get closer. There was too much danger in weaknesses.

My knuckles grazed the Huntress's door so quietly, I didn't know if she'd hear me, but when it swung open, revealing the disastrous room, she grabbed my forearm, yanked me inside, and shut the door.

She crossed her arms over her chest with her mismatched eyes pinned to me. "It would do him some good to have a little fun, Maiden. Honestly, you, too. The tension in this house is too much. Why haven't you kissed him yet?"

"Is that why you dragged me in here?"

"No, but gods, if I have to sit at one more dinner with the two of you eye fucking, I'm moving out. What's the deal?"

"First of all, there's no eye fucking. I don't even know what that is. And there's too much bad history. Too much fighting."

"Fighting is just passion. Get over it. Trust me when I tell you, life is too short for sitting around, wondering what might have been. I'd give anything to fight with Ezra again."

Smiling sadly, I moved away from the window. "I bet you were a force to be reckoned with, Huntress."

The moment the memories threatened to haunt her, she shook her head and began clearing a path to the chair, also covered with clothes. Gathering them in her arms, she tossed them onto the floor and sat, swinging her legs over the arm. "What's the plan?"

"I've bargained that he cannot ask you anything about this, but it's best to keep it between you and me, and we're going to have to bring in Quill."

Repeating the entire conversation with the Maestro, she went over and over all the words spoken with me until we both determined it was a solid plan. Risky, but there was hope.

"So, you'll teach me how to dance?"

She snorted. "There's no way you're going to truly learn by tomorrow night's show. But I have some pointers I can give you. As long as you're half-naked and aware of the beat, you'll be fine. If you can fight, you can dance. Just... touch yourself a little more. And yeah, we're going to have to bring in Hollis, too."

"Stop making that face," Paesha growled, trying to put makeup on my lashes. "It's going to smear, and no one's gonna clap for smeared mascara."

"I will," Quill argued, sitting on the kitchen table beside us, legs swinging back and forth as she fed Boo from her dinner scraps.

"Thanks, kid." I shared a smile with her, and for the first time since she'd walked into that office, she smiled back.

"We're sure he's not coming home, right?"

"Thea promised to keep him busy until showtime. She's

going to be pissed when she finds out we didn't tell her. But she'll get over it."

"It's just our secret," Quill said again, a truth she'd been repeating all day, as if being in on the plan made her feel important. "And soon, everyone is going to be free, and then maybe we can open up our own theater. You can still dance, P."

"Imagine," Paesha said, dusting pink blush across the little girl's nose until she giggled. "And you can perform, Quilly. No waiting for a grumpy old man to let you. No more bird cages."

She adjusted the dog on her lap. "And Boo can come, and I'll teach him to jump through rings and stuff."

"That sounds lovely. Why don't you run upstairs and get ready. We have to leave in ten minutes."

With a squeal of excitement, she leapt from the table and dashed toward her room.

"She's fine with leaving her *friend* behind."

"It's not her fault she isn't scared of him. I've been in her shoes." She gathered the makeup from the table and set it into a large bag as she continued. "When I was a kid, the Maestro hunted me, too. Before he had Misery's End, my father was bound to him. Back when he was still a mystery to most and I felt like I was in on something important. I don't know how he figured it out, probably ordered every secret from my father's mouth, but as soon as he knew I'd shown Huntress power, he began challenging me. It was a game. *Find me a red shoelace and I'll give you a treat. See if you can find a man with a perfect circle birthmark. There's a book in the library in Perth. Bring it to me.* And every time I did, he made such a big deal about how important I was. IIe was learning my boundaries and how my power worked quicker than I was. He knew I'd never find the man because I'd had no contact with him, but I could find the book because I'd seen it on his desk. He's clever and cunning. Dangerous, but oftentimes fair. If he really wanted to swing his hammer, he would cleave the world, but mostly, he's a greedy collector."

"That's why you stick so close to Quill. You're protecting her the only way you know how."

She nodded. "I can't save her from him. He's forbidden my interference. There are... things we are not permitted to speak aloud."

"Like how awful he is?"

She stared at me as if in confirmation. "But I can bring her home and make sure she's safe. She's smart, and eventually, my hope is that she will see the monster behind the mask. He's not a pervert, thank the gods. He just thrives on curating fear and controlling others. Every person is a quest to be conquered and collected."

"But why hasn't Elowen told her?"

"Because the Maestro knows what he has in Orin. The heart of a mother will never compromise the safety of her son. She treads lightly, or the boss takes her missteps out on him."

"So how did you end up bound to him? Or is that too personal?"

She set her bag on the kitchen table, picking at the loose strings along the frayed handle as she considered her answer, and then became wholly consumed by it. "I was always a smart kid. I figured him out a long time ago. I'd stick around for shelter and food when my father started spending more time at the opium den than at home with me. I refused him for a really long time, Dey. I knew the cost." She paused, voice filling with an ache. "But then I saw you. That first night in an alley in Sinner's Square. And I just knew you were hunting Ezra.

"The next night was the same, but I was hunting you, too. When you showed up twice, his fate was sealed. I couldn't think straight. Couldn't breathe for hours. He'd held me in his arms and promised me it wasn't him. I'd still gone to Drexel. And in my distraught mind, I'd forgotten to measure each of his words. He'd agreed to help me if I would bind myself to him for the rest of my hundred years. He said he would try to find a way to stop the Death Maiden." She forced a laugh past sad eyes, never really looking at me, but each word had taken her further and further into a memory that would have her dancing with his ghost, as the others had called it.

"Paesha," I whispered, trying to bring her back to this moment.

But she was too far gone. Too fragile. "His attempt was half-assed, and it didn't matter. I had three more days with Ezra before you snuck into his place and killed him in his sleep."

Every breath into my lungs hurt. Every inch of my skin, red with embarrassment and shame. It wasn't enough that he'd died. Not enough that I'd been his murderer. I'd even had a hand in her imprisonment to the monster. "If I could—"

"I know, Maiden. You don't have to apologize again."

I stood, grabbing her arm firmly. "If ever I was going to question my sanity in this bargain, I take it back right now. I owe you this. I won't let us down."

"Ready?" Quill stood in the door to the kitchen, her perfect soft blue dress trimmed in white lace, painting her into a picture of innocence.

"Don't let *her* down," Paesha answered. "She's the future, and she's important."

"I don't think I'm wearing it right," I said from behind the curtain as Hollis's stomping boots gave away his pacing back and forth in a quiet corner of the theater's warehouse, opening and closing his pocket watch as if by habit alone.

"You're not meant to fight in it, Little Dove. You're to seduce. Consider your end goal."

And though his presence was typically calming, there was nothing comforting in this tragedy of a contraption. "If my end goal was to embed rubies into my asshole, I think we've made it."

"May I see?"

"My jeweled asshole? If you must. But I can't walk."

He whipped the curtain away and glared at me. "I would never design something that would incapacitate you. Oh! Good gods, you've put it on sideways. Do you not see the clasps? Who taught you to dress?"

I returned the scowl. "Well, it sure as hell wasn't Lady Visha."

"No doubt about that." He chuckled, pulling his brimmed hat from his head, revealing the waves of silver locks. "At least you got the heels on right. Might I help you?"

"I think you're going to have to."

Several minutes later, he stepped away, wrinkled hands clasped to his chest. "It's the most stunning piece I've ever created. Turn."

I spun as instructed, lifting my hands so he could examine the rubies covering my skin in clusters, only in the most important parts, strung together by invisible pieces of mesh and dainty lace that made it look like the jewels were skin, woven together with intricate metal clasps, camouflaged behind the red jewels. He held out a black lace robe, as if that would somehow make me feel less exposed.

Hollis lifted my chin with a gentle touch. "Don't lose your fire, Little Dove. Sex sells, and you've got to sell your soul to the crowd if you want to wipe away their fear enough to make them stand. The greatest hurdle of your life is before you, and not because of our freedom, but your own."

"Maiden?" a trembling voice said from somewhere behind me. Genevieve stood holding a rolled parchment tied in a black ribbon, exactly the kind used in my mysterious birthday packages. She'd clipped her wild blonde curls from her face and painted her lips red. "The boss asked me to give you this."

I scowled, daring her to step toward me. She'd been mean to Thea, the kindest person on the planet, and maybe today was the day she learned a lesson. Rather than pulling the parchment from her outstretched hand, I turned to the old man. "Hollis, my friend, I need my blades."

He looked between the woman and me before nodding and shuffling back into the dressing area.

"You must—"

I shot a hand up, stopping her. She stumbled backward as if I'd already struck her.

"I don't speak to hateful people without weapons. Now be a good girl and wait right there."

Her eyes bounced around the room, looking for anyone that might help her, but most of the performers were already backstage. There were times when I loathed the fear. But then there were others that empowered me, though I would never admit that to a soul.

"Arms up," Hollis said, stepping close.

I kept my eyes glued to the woman as he fastened the jeweled straps around my hips. We'd agreed that featuring who I was without pulling the blades would make the audience feel something, and where I took it from there would depend on my performance. But I was confident. Even if I had to stand there and threaten each of their lives to force the ovation, I would. Because that was not against the Maestro's rules.

"Do you see how close he stands?"

She nodded slowly, feet frozen in place.

"Do you think there's a reason he doesn't fear me?"

Again, she nodded.

"Speak it."

Her mouth opened and immediately snapped shut.

"Speak."

"Because you are friends."

Lifting Chaos from my belt, I twirled the curved handle. "And what do you think happens when people are mean to my friends?"

"Deyanira." Hollis meant to protect the woman, but only because of his own fear. No doubt, Drexel had given her too much leash, and she needed to be reined in.

"Speak," I demanded again.

"They... You..."

I stepped forward, sliding my dagger back into its sheath. "Do you know who else is my friend?"

She shook her head, glancing to Hollis for an answer, though he said nothing.

"No. You don't. So, watch what you say and how you say it to every single person, Genevieve, because I know where you sleep, and I'm *very* good with weapons."

She nodded frantically, sweat clinging to the blonde curls framing her face.

"You're dismissed," I purred, plucking the parchment from her hands.

The clack of her heels faded away, and the old man stepped in front of me, taking my hand and whispering, "If ever you question your strength, remember the kindness inside of you has its own power. Your morals and restraint are your true power, Little Dove."

"Too bad it's not dancing," I said, reading the carefully scripted lines of the message.

Maiden,
Darkest soul, your mountain to climb
In shadows cast, can brilliance shine?
No battles fought, no weapons held,
Dance alone, silent laments spelled.
No need for blades, nor show of might,
Onstage you'll shimmer in the night.
With weapon poised, but ne'er to employ,
Seduce the crowd, your presence a joy.
Ever yours,
DV

"Right." He flashed a kind smile, pulling the paper from my hand. "You can't pull your weapons, but you can take them onstage." As he so often did, he lifted the long golden chain from his pocket and clicked open his beautiful watch. "Time to charm the masses."

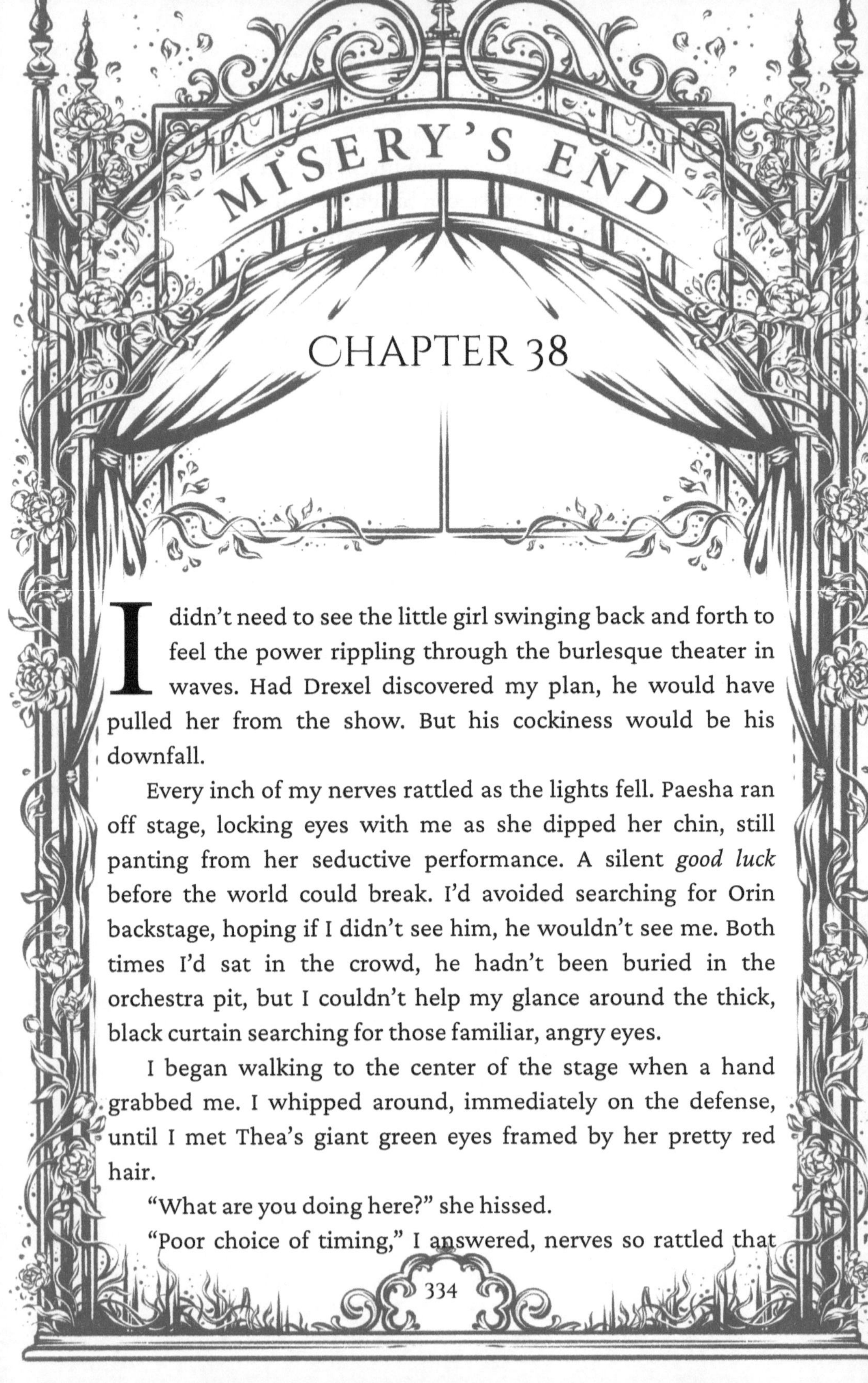

MISERY'S END

CHAPTER 38

I didn't need to see the little girl swinging back and forth to feel the power rippling through the burlesque theater in waves. Had Drexel discovered my plan, he would have pulled her from the show. But his cockiness would be his downfall.

Every inch of my nerves rattled as the lights fell. Paesha ran off stage, locking eyes with me as she dipped her chin, still panting from her seductive performance. A silent *good luck* before the world could break. I'd avoided searching for Orin backstage, hoping if I didn't see him, he wouldn't see me. Both times I'd sat in the crowd, he hadn't been buried in the orchestra pit, but I couldn't help my glance around the thick, black curtain searching for those familiar, angry eyes.

I began walking to the center of the stage when a hand grabbed me. I whipped around, immediately on the defense, until I met Thea's giant green eyes framed by her pretty red hair.

"What are you doing here?" she hissed.

"Poor choice of timing," I answered, nerves so rattled that

every heartbeat was a thunderous echo in my chest, each breath a chore.

"They have to clear the stage before the next act."

"I *am* the next act, Thea."

She stumbled backward, head snapping to some point across the space. "You can't be serious. What did you do?"

"Later," I said, ripping myself away from her strong hands to move to the center of the dark stage.

The soft murmurs of the crowd did not cease. A gasp did not come. I waited and waited until movement at my side caught my attention. Though nearly pitch black, a single light at the very back of the cavernous room had been left on, and I could just make out the shape of a giant hourglass being wheeled out. Thea's handiwork, no doubt. A man turned, showing only the white of his eyes as he grabbed a handle on the side of the contraption and spun, effectively starting my ten-minute timer before sneaking behind the curtain just as the final bit of light vanished. That's what Thea was worried about.

I sucked in a heavy breath, ready for the music to begin as the soft sound of sand falling accompanied my racing heart. But the spotlight never came, and the stage was too dark for the crowd to see me.

In shadows cast, can brilliance shine?

The fucking loophole. Of course, he didn't care if Quill was here. It wouldn't matter if they couldn't see me. Each grain of sand became a crackle of panic.

I wasn't a singer or a poet. I wasn't a dancer. Nor an actress with a grand soliloquy. I was just a desperate woman with no plan and a lonely heart. I ran to the side of the stage, halting at the very last second. Was I allowed to leave the stage? I couldn't remember. But it didn't matter because everyone behind the curtains was gone. Not a soul remained. I whipped around, facing the audience, who'd grown louder and impatient in the dark theater. Trying desperately, I could not make out a single face.

Minutes had passed, and the chokehold of the Maestro's grip on my destiny tightened until I could hardly breathe. I fell to my knees in a contraption of rubies made by an old man who'd shown me nothing but kindness. I squeezed my eyes closed, covering my ears, shutting out the groans of the crowd as I pictured the stage in my memory. Each step, each wrinkle in the black fabric curtains, each lamp, the golden birdcage showcasing the eventual capture of an innocent child.

Gods. The stage was encircled by a border of oil lamps. Oil. I crawled forward, hands outstretched, searching almost blindly for the edge. If I fell off, my fate was sealed. Several more minutes had already passed, though. Precious minutes. Gathering the lanterns as fast as I could, spilling the oil in an arc that ended at the base of the hourglass, I hustled. Ripping a small piece of the lace, I created a wick. Gathering my courage as adrenaline coursed through my body, I rested a hand on Chaos's pommel. The instructions were clear. I couldn't draw a weapon. The heels, though glorious and lethal in their own way, would do nothing for me. I had no flint. No metal at all. Only a slickened floor and absolute panic.

But that wasn't true. I did have metal.

Sending a prayer to whatever god would hear my plea, I wrapped a hand around a cluster of rubies trailing down my side, and screamed as I ripped the clasp free in one smooth motion, striking it upon the iron base of the hourglass. No spark. But the crowd fell silent.

Again, I struck. Again, I failed.

And though I felt alone, and like I was falling from a cliff, a single, glorious cello note pierced the stale air. I knew without looking it was him. As if I could feel him through our marriage bond, a heart as desperate as mine when he'd realized the stage was not empty.

The next spark was a perfect arch into damp fabric, igniting the entire stage in one fell swoop. I couldn't see beyond the burst of flames. Could hear nothing but the soft beginning of a single cello's lament. Because, though the orchestra had been ordered not to play, somewhere behind me, my husband had no such order.

A hush fell over the crowd as they drank me in, as they saw the desperate eyes of Death's Maiden standing upon a burning stage in woven rubies. Quill's magic pulsed like a heartbeat. One shared amongst friends. And so, I danced. Stretching my arms and trailing my hands over my body as I'd seen the women that commanded the stage do. The fire was my partner, an unpredictable and passionate companion. I had started it for light, but now it was a living entity, mirroring my every move, casting eerie shadows as the heat licked my legs, and I swung my hips, hoping I looked half as sensual as Paesha.

Floor crackling, fire spreading, I smoothed a hand across my collar bone, pretending the touch belonged to Orin. I spun, touching my breasts, keeping my chin down as if I were not afraid. As if the world were truly mine and I was in control. As if I coaxed the fear from the audience and molded it into sinful lust, daring them to want to touch me. To hear the sounds I would make, should they be brave enough to try.

I couldn't see the red-haired man in that special seat atop his theater. I couldn't hear the growl that had surely come from him. But I hoped he watched. I hoped he watched and every godsdamned vein in his body filled with ire as his precious stage burned because he'd tried to outsmart me.

That desperate act sat upon my soul as a giant fuck you. Turning the stage to ash pushed me onward as Orin's song grew in volume and tempo. I sauntered closer to the fire, feeling its warmth against my skin, a fierce contrast to the cool air that now seemed like a distant memory. The audience's faces were a blur, their sounds muted by the crackling inferno that stood between us. I reveled in the solitude of the flames, the sensation of being both isolated and connected.

My fingers brushed against the hourglass as I circled it, my touch gentle yet deliberate. I could feel the sand slipping away, each grain a fleeting moment in time. I danced. I danced for the people that had become my friends, but also for myself. Breaking free of the chains of a princess and the angry words of a mourning father. Of the glares from a fallen kingdom and the fear in that child's eyes on my wedding day. My body responded to the haunting music. My hips swayed in rhythm, a slow undulation. I spun and spun as gracefully as a sword fighter and threw my hands in my hair until the grains of sand had nearly vanished and the fire had grown from my ankles to my shoulders, concealing me. The music ended on a crescendo. I collapsed to the floor, breathless and spent.

And then they stood. From Quill's magic or a frenzied attempt to see over the flames and get another glimpse at Death's Maiden, I wasn't sure, but they stood. The applause erupted like a tidal wave, washing over me in a rush of sound. I had danced amidst the flames, a phoenix rising from the ashes of my own creation. It was a battle hard fought and barely won, but victory, nonetheless. I crawled from that stage, avoiding the eyes of the performers that ran to extinguish the fire.

"I think it's fair to say there won't be a show tomorrow night," Paesha said. She handed me a robe with far more coverage than the one I'd been given from Hollis as I climbed the steps from the tunnel into the warehouse, holding my broken outfit in place as best I could.

"Probably a good thing," Thea said, pointing behind me.

I didn't have to look to know who she'd seen, but I was a

glutton for punishment, spinning to stare directly into the angry face of Orin Faber, storming forward with a permanent scowl and a glare that might've set the stage to flame without the production I'd needed.

"What the fuck have you done?"

Closing my arms over my chest, I leveled a stare. "Too many things to recall. Keep up, Husband."

He moved so close I could feel his rapid heartbeat as if it were my own. His eyes dipped low, mouth falling open, and I reveled in the way he stared, knowing he wanted to hate it, but he couldn't.

"Eyes up here."

He ripped his jacket off and wrapped it around my shoulders, gripping the lapel to yank me close. "You forget, Nightmare, you belong to me."

"I'm no one's property," I managed, though the words were a struggle beyond the way I'd needed him to touch me, to ease this ache within my body that truly did belong to him.

"We will discuss this at home."

"Looking forward to it."

QUILL HAD FALLEN asleep on the couch, snuggled up with Boo as she'd waited for Orin, like the rest of us.

"I still can't believe you guys didn't tell me," Thea said, closing the book she'd been trying to read for an hour. "I could've helped."

"For the thousandth time, you did help," Paesha said, scooping her arms under the sleeping child. "Come on, mutt."

Thea gasped. "Don't call him that. He's a good boy."

"Consider it a term of endearment," she threw over her

shoulder as the sleepy dog slunk off the couch and followed her up the stairs.

"Soon," Hollis said, following my eyes to the clock. "He's got to work his anger out before he gets home. Just be patient."

I should have followed him. I knew what was coming. I'd hardened myself the entire trip back, as Paesha explained the bargain in detail to Althea. She'd tried to remain optimistic, but they'd never witnessed anyone escape the clutches of the Maestro, so the worry on all their faces was warranted. I hadn't seen his trick tonight coming, and now I'd have to be more prepared for the next show. Whenever that might be.

The Huntress no more than sat back down on the couch before the front door slammed open. The squelch of boots stomping through the entryway toward the sitting room matched the looks we each passed as we waited for Orin to join us.

"Son," Elowen said, standing immediately.

"Everyone out," he answered.

"Orin." Paesha stood.

He shook his head. "No. Don't start with me. You were in on this. What the fuck were you thinking?"

She moved to stand toe to toe with the furious man. "The only person I loved enough to sell my soul to the devil for was Ezra. And that took years. I never tried to save my father. Your mother. Not even you. So don't you dare stand there and berate her for loving us all enough to sacrifice everything. We don't deserve her. We captured her and hated her and would've taken turns with a shovel in the graveyard. But don't you forget that you chose to marry her, even with all that history. Don't forget that you brought her here, locked her in this house, and have made life hell for her ever since." She placed her hands on his chest and shoved, a break in her voice as she continued. "I don't know what's happening to you. I see the anger taking over more and more. There's darkness creeping through your veins, and you're mean. Deyanira is not dangerous, Orin. You are."

She pushed away from him and stormed up the stairs. Ever the warrior. I stood in my corner, though her words had left me in a state of shock. Somewhere along the lines, a friendship had bloomed between us. Maybe her mourning soul recognized my lonely one. And maybe she'd actually just been really good at her job as a Huntress, and she'd captured me, just as the Maestro wanted. But she hadn't wavered since the moment we'd rescued Quill all that time ago. And Orin had done nothing but brood.

Thea quickly hustled out of the room, followed by Hollis, and though Elowen stopped to rest her hand on her son's trembling arm, she averted her eyes and scurried down the hall.

"You have to get out of it." His voice was low and threatening, every bit the tone I'd expected.

"I think we both know that's not a possibility."

"Why do you absolutely insist on doing everything I explicitly ask you not to do? You were supposed to stay away from him. He's fucking dangerous."

I rose. "So am I. Do you think I wanted to do this? I went into that office to kill him, and he dangled Quill in front of me. He used her to keep me from murdering him, and I had to do something. Paesha thinks I'm trying to save you for love, but she's wrong. I'm doing it because it's the right thing to do. Because despite the way you hate me, I still think you're worth saving. You gave the rest of your life for me, but I don't fucking want it."

I shifted just in time to see him pull the blade. He shouted in anger, eyes never leaving mine as he whipped the dagger through the air, slicing right past my head as it stuck into the wall.

"You are such a tantrum-throwing child."

Ripping his blade free, I mimicked his motion, letting the

blade fly as it shot directly between his legs and clattered to the floor of the hall behind him.

His eyes lit in defiance as I stepped around the coffee table and brushed past him. He snatched my wrist, whipping me around until I was close enough to see the tips of the black veins creeping up his neckline. A breath caught in my throat, a momentary distraction as he moved like a predator, grip firm until my back collided with the wall.

There was so much fire and passion in everything he did. Orin's hand loosened, fingers trailing down my arms in an inferno that left me yearning for him to touch me somewhere else. Anywhere else. I don't know if it was the fact that we'd both silently decided this would never be a real marriage, or because of how hot the hatred burned when we let it, but there was something keeping us right here, stuck in a moment that we weren't strong enough to walk away from.

He gripped the side of my face, eyes searching mine for permission or hesitation. I wasn't sure. I grabbed his wrists, boldly slipping into a place I couldn't escape from. His dark lashes fell to his cheeks as he seemed to breathe me in, broad shoulders lifting and falling as my knees weakened. I wasn't sure if I should kiss him or stab him.

Instead, I warned him. "I will never be a compliant wife."

He leaned close enough I had to tilt my head back to look at his brutally handsome face. "I would expect nothing less."

"Don't tell lies, Orin. It's not an attractive trait."

He smoothed a thumb over my bottom lip. "Maybe I don't want you to be attracted to me. Maybe I'm the monster in disguise, and my anger is to protect you... from me."

"I don't need to be protected from someone I am not afraid of."

His hand slid down until the heartbeat in my neck throbbed

against his palm. His fingers tightened. "Are you flirting or fighting with me right now, Deyanira?"

"Neither. I'm simply standing here, willing to face your demons rather than back away and leave you alone with them. I know them as intimately as you do. There's madness within the darkness you're hiding, isn't there?"

"Yes," he said quietly. Fiercely. "And I think it's you, the way you consume me. You are the darkness."

I shook my head, smiling. "No, Husband. I am the abyss that calls to your shadows, the tempest that matches your storm. We are not mere darkness, we are the symphony of our scars."

He leaned his forehead to mine, holding my gaze steady within his own. "Two sides of the same coin."

I could not answer. Could hardly swallow over his tight grip on my throat. Minutes passed by. Years even, locked in that moment with him. His lips were inches from mine. His solid body pressed into me, as if he could not get close enough. My skin hummed with desire. Each second building an ache low in my belly until the tension between us swelled to an immeasurable degree.

Do it, I begged him silently. *Kiss me, you damn fool. End the agony.*

But instead, he pushed away, the war between madness and sanity returning. "End your deal with the Maestro. Find something else to offer him. Give him the fucking world, Deyanira. But do not give him yourself. You had no right to make that bargain. You already belong to me."

And with that, he stalked out of the room, snatching the dagger from the floor as he went.

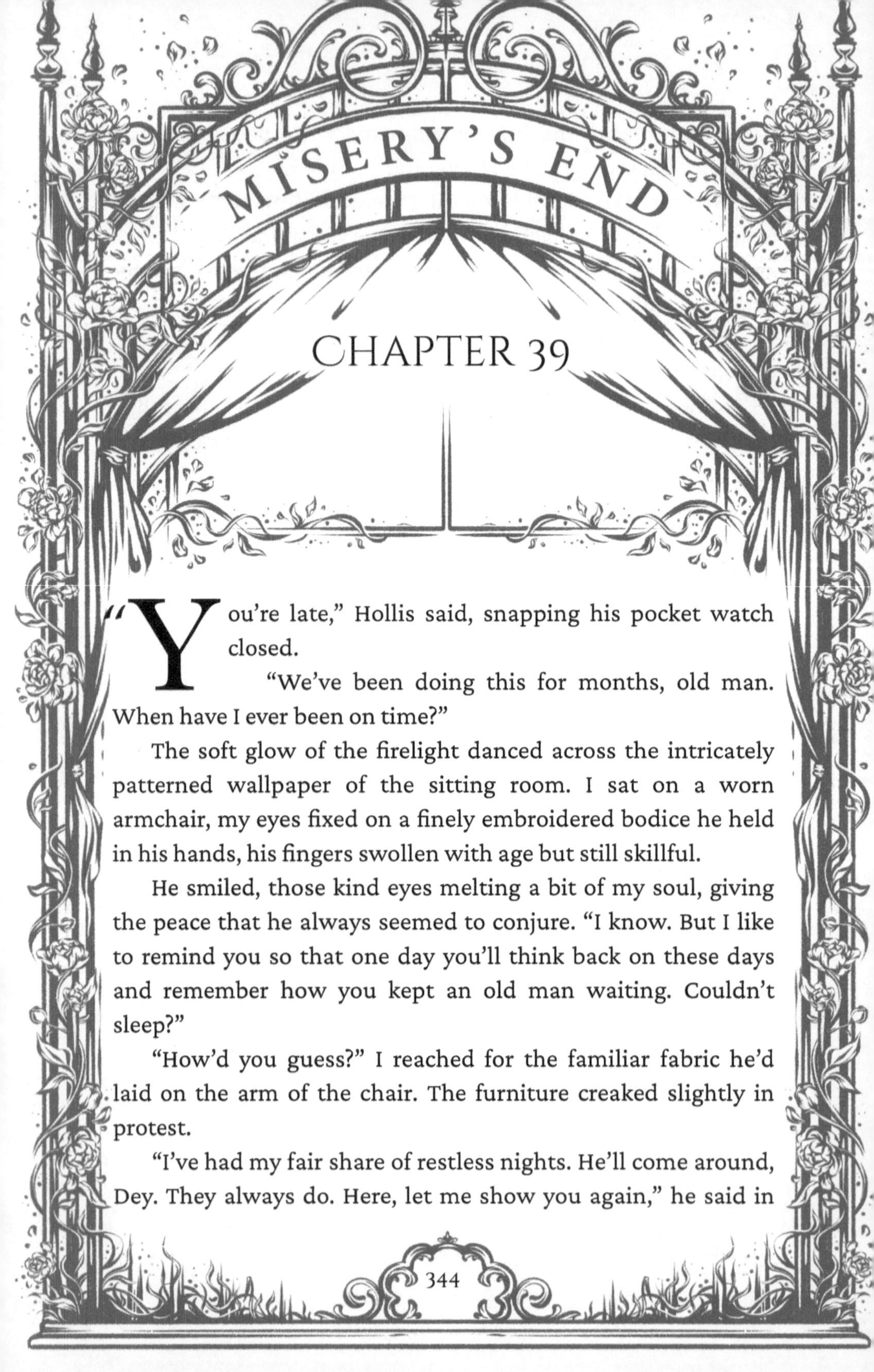

MISERY'S END

CHAPTER 39

"Y ou're late," Hollis said, snapping his pocket watch closed.

"We've been doing this for months, old man. When have I ever been on time?"

The soft glow of the firelight danced across the intricately patterned wallpaper of the sitting room. I sat on a worn armchair, my eyes fixed on a finely embroidered bodice he held in his hands, his fingers swollen with age but still skillful.

He smiled, those kind eyes melting a bit of my soul, giving the peace that he always seemed to conjure. "I know. But I like to remind you so that one day you'll think back on these days and remember how you kept an old man waiting. Couldn't sleep?"

"How'd you guess?" I reached for the familiar fabric he'd laid on the arm of the chair. The furniture creaked slightly in protest.

"I've had my fair share of restless nights. He'll come around, Dey. They always do. Here, let me show you again," he said in his gentle, raspy voice, beckoning me to move the bodice onto my lap.

"You can show me a thousand times, and I'm always going to tangle the string on the knot. You know this."

"Such a pessimist, Little Dove."

I handed the project back to him. "Someone has to balance out Thea's optimism."

"Speaking of balance… any leads on your pursuit?"

I shook my head, releasing a heavy sigh of defeat. "I think it's a lost cause. I hate to stop hunting for the Life Maiden, but the only things I have are the pages from my father's study. And you know we've poured over them. There's nothing that really matters in there. I need to focus on my bargain with Drexel now."

He snipped a long golden thread from his spool. "Do I need to lecture you on how foolish that bargain was?"

"Do I need to lecture *you* on lecturing *me*?"

He laughed. "You know what I think you need?"

I wiggled my eyebrows. "Hard liquor and a good fist fight?"

"Fun, Deyanira. I was going to say fun."

"Same thing, Old Man."

He rolled those watery blue eyes. "I see so much of my sister in you. It's uncanny."

"Will you tell me about her?" I asked, giving up on watching the way he stitched so I could swing my legs over the arm of the chair and listen. I always gave up. He'd insisted on my learning a new skill to distract my mind ages ago, but it never went beyond the first few minutes until I started asking him to tell me stories. Sometimes the others would join us, filling the room just to hear his tales, which never included his sister. He'd always skimmed over parts of his stories that involved her. Hollis had raised Dahlia, he'd told us one day. His father worked every hour he could, and the old man, just a child then, was left behind to tend to the motherless infant.

I hoped Dahlia had known how lucky she was to have him, though I doubted it in her later years. Still, my heart ached as I witnessed his sadness. As I looked at a man who had accepted me with no boundaries and did his best every day to make me feel like I was someone worthy of him. But I wasn't. These moments weren't about learning to sew or his past. They were about time. And though his was fleeting as he neared his one hundred years, he'd given me every second he could because he knew no one else had. And that foreign act of love burrowed itself so deep into my heart, there were days when I looked at him and hated the world more. What had he done to deserve a life of servitude? And what had I done to deserve a man who had delivered tranquility to my erratic soul?

Hollis faded into himself, as he so often did, and I worried I'd asked the wrong question.

"You don't have to. I could go back to destroying that shirt if you want."

He cleared his throat. "No, no. It's okay. I've wondered when you'd ask. Only it seems none of our stories have the same light they did when I was young."

I moved to sit next to him on the couch, taking his hand. "I can tell you from experience, the light may dim, but it never goes out. Whatever you thought your memories to be with her, if you can still hear her laugh and picture her smile, those moments were real, however tainted they may feel. She had no choice, Hollis. The madness is debilitating, and she was merely a victim."

He squeezed my fingers, eyes glossing over. "I used to call her Little Dove, too. When Dahlia was little, before she trained and shut herself away from everyone, she would sit at the picture window of our apartment and watch the birds fight the rats on the street. One day, she'd begged me to take her to the library, but my father had forbidden us from leaving. The next morning, she was gone. I was terrified something had happened. Maybe someone had broken in and taken her, or worse. She was born with a target on her back, as you know. I searched for hours and hours, worried sick. But then I remembered her request, and there I found her, sitting on the floor of the library, tucked between two giant bookshelves.

"She wanted to know about the birds. She'd shoved a book into my face and told me about doves. How they'd been a symbol of peace forever. She wouldn't sleep that night until I promised her I'd find one." He sat back on the couch, lifting the bodice once more. Tugging on his shimmering string as he whispered. "I never did fulfill that promise."

"Because there is no peace; not really."

He looked at me and smiled sadly. "You're my peace. You have the light she lost, and every day, I think it grows a little brighter."

"I'm fairly certain that's not the case."

"When was the last time you threatened to kill someone?"

"I told Thea an hour ago I was going to chop her arm off if she didn't stop whistling."

"The very same Thea that you're trying to save from the boss?"

I smirked. "Threatening the loss of a body part is a term of endearment."

THE DANCING GHOST was a wretched hive of debauchery and depravity, a place where shadows clung to every corner, and the stench of spilled liquor and cheap cigarettes hung thick in the air. As I entered, the low hum of drunken laughter and clinking glasses fell silent, like the closing of a heavy iron door.

Clad in dark leathers, hood, and my notorious blade on my thigh, I was a ghostly figure amidst the riffraff, with my reputation preceding me. My heart dropped into my stomach when I laid eyes on the bald man at the end of the bar. I thought I'd never see him again, had hoped for it at one point, but Paesha had come through once again. There he sat, hunched over, a dirty mug in his trembling hand, his eyes bloodshot from hours of intoxication, beard grown and more haggard than I'd ever known him to be. That's what the streets would do to a person. Especially one that had so far to fall.

"Careful, Little Dove. Drexel's men are everywhere."

"I'm more worried about the King's Guard. Maybe you should have waited outside," I said from behind my mask. "Stay beside me. Don't make eye contact with anyone."

"This wasn't supposed to be violent," Hollis said calmly as we stalked to the back of the room.

"I never promised that. You don't know him like I do."

The man at the bar turned, blinking several times before falling backward from his stool and scrambling away.

"Hey, Reg, how ya been?"

"How... how'd you find me?" He backed himself against the wall, though I hadn't moved an inch.

"Even you aren't daft enough to forget the Huntress's power. Did you think you were safe?"

"Stay away from me."

I tsked, reaching for my blade. Old habits died hard. I'd half-expected a word from Hollis at my back, but he remained quiet, steady, calm.

"We need to have a little chat, and since I'm feeling generous today, I'll let you decide if we do that here, or we take a walk outside."

His bloodshot eyes tracked my hand as he stumbled side-ways. "I'm not fucking following you anywhere. Do I look like some kind of godsdamned fool?"

"I'm going to assume that's a rhetorical question."

I stepped closer, placing the flat of the blade beneath his scruffy beard. The tavern took a singular breath, and I didn't need to look to know all eyes remained on us as I pinned myself as the villain they'd all known me to be.

Regulas, my father's hand and the enemy of my childhood, gritted his teeth, turning red as he glanced over the room, looking for a single person with enough balls to stop me. He paused in the far-right corner, where Drexel's henchmen had gathered around a table, their leather gloves and nice coats a dead giveaway the second we'd entered.

"You're going to tell me everything you know of the Life Maiden, Regulas."

He scoffed, eyes snapping back to me. "What makes you think I know anything at all?"

I stepped in closer, keeping my voice down. "My father was a wise man. He was hunting for her my entire life, and you were so, so desperate for answers. Do you mean to tell me, with every resource available to you and years of hunting, you didn't find a single clue? Yet my father kept your sniveling ass around, and for what? Entertainment?"

"I'd rather take my secrets to an early grave than help you, King Slayer."

Hollis cleared his throat, peeling the hood of his cloak down to reveal his aged face. Regulas gasped, glancing between us.

I hitched a brow, confused at his recognition of my companion.

"Don't you see? She isn't trying to help herself. She's trying to help everyone else. Why would Death's Maiden care about her counterpart, if not for the good of the realm? You took an oath, Regulas Carstark. I stood in that audience and watched you do it."

Of course. Hollis had been born in Perth. I'd nearly forgotten. I'd come with force, but he'd come with logic. As always.

"You can take my oath and shove it up your ass, Hollis Bennet, you fucking maggot."

Twenty-seven years of pent-up rage exploded from me. I dropped the blade, more interested in the blood of the man than his soul. I snatched him by the neck in a single strike and slammed his head against the wall. Not once, not twice, but three times, until his eyes rolled back, and his fat hands no longer clawed at mine. Chaos erupted. People began screaming that Death would come soon. Most scrambled for the door.

I saw nothing but red as I dropped Regulas to the floor and placed a boot over his thick neck, feeling Death's magic stir within me as I imagined the crunch of his windpipe. He blinked up at me, likely grasping to stay conscious.

"You can say all the disgusting things you want about me. You can tell the world how you tortured me when I was a child. How mean you were and just how far your head fit up my father's ass, but don't you speak a word against that man again."

"Kill me now, Maiden," he rasped over the blade. "End this misery."

I smiled, shaking my head with a glare. "I don't think so, Reg. I'd rather watch you stew in it."

"If I tell you—" His words were interrupted by a cough. "If I tell you what I know?"

"Deyanira," Hollis warned, pressing his back to mine, the pummel of his ornamental sword driving into my spine.

I ignored him. "You have three seconds, Regulas."

Another cough.

I lifted my boot a fraction of an inch. "One."

"Dey," Hollis warned.

"Two."

"The Life Maiden is in Perth."

"Where?" I growled.

"We don't know. We just know there are more births and faster healing on that side of the realm. There have been no other signs. Your father... he imprisoned people for years to get them to talk. No one knows a thing."

"That's not enough, Regulas. Enjoy the rest of your miserable years."

I spun on his scream, just in time to see Drexel's henchmen closing in, surrounding us.

"Oh, godsdamn it. Does he breed stupidity over there, or is this just a special occasion?" I pulled several tiny blades from the leather bandolier strapped across my chest.

Hollis yanked his sword free, his old body moving gracefully into a fighter's position. I thought he'd only brought it to intimidate, but I was wrong. Clearly, the old man had more stories to tell.

Still, this was not a battle I wanted or needed. Three days had passed since I lit the Maestro's stage on fire, and I regretted nothing. There was a difference between surviving and living, and the more time I spent at the Syndicate house, the more those two things felt very separate. Requiem wasn't a world built for people to live, only survive by whatever means necessary. We had grit and were selfish on our best days, but I would not condemn Hollis to Drexel's punishments if I could help it.

One of the men closest to the door lit a cigarette, the bright cherry casting his face in orange. "Going somewhere, Maiden?"

"You see? That's the problem. You know who I am and yet your little balls tell you to stand there unafraid."

"You can't touch us," another said, shifting in toward Regulas behind us. "The boss says you're in debt to him now."

"Hate to break it to you, boys, but your boss is a liar. Now... I've always been generous. Ask my friend, Regulas over here if you don't believe me. So, I'm going to give you two options. One, sit back down at your seat, and I'll have the barkeep send a round over on me. Or two, you're all going to be lying on this floor in a pile of blood and piss within three minutes. Your choice."

They exchanged glances amongst themselves until the one at the door spoke again. "Well now, I think you've misunderstood our meaning is all. Me and the boys were just coming to make sure you didn't need our help. Isn't that right, boys?"

They mumbled their agreements, and Hollis's shoulders sank in relief. Within minutes, we were outside and headed back to the carriage we'd stolen from Drexel's hoard.

"Okay, Hollis?"

"Got my blood pumping." He patted my leg before snapping the reins. "You did the right thing, Little Dove."

"With the Maestro's men?"

He chuckled. "Well, that, too. But I meant Regulas. He's always been a snake."

"How do you know him?"

"I don't, really. *Of* him is more like it. Awful, awful man."

"You knew that's who I was hunting. Why'd you come if you hated him?"

He shared a sly smile. "I wondered if he'd changed. And if not... I was hoping you'd make him bleed."

"I had no idea you were so vengeful."

"Anyone who talks to my girl that way... he deserves what he gets."

I laid my head on his shoulder as we carried on. "Thanks for always having my back, Old Man."

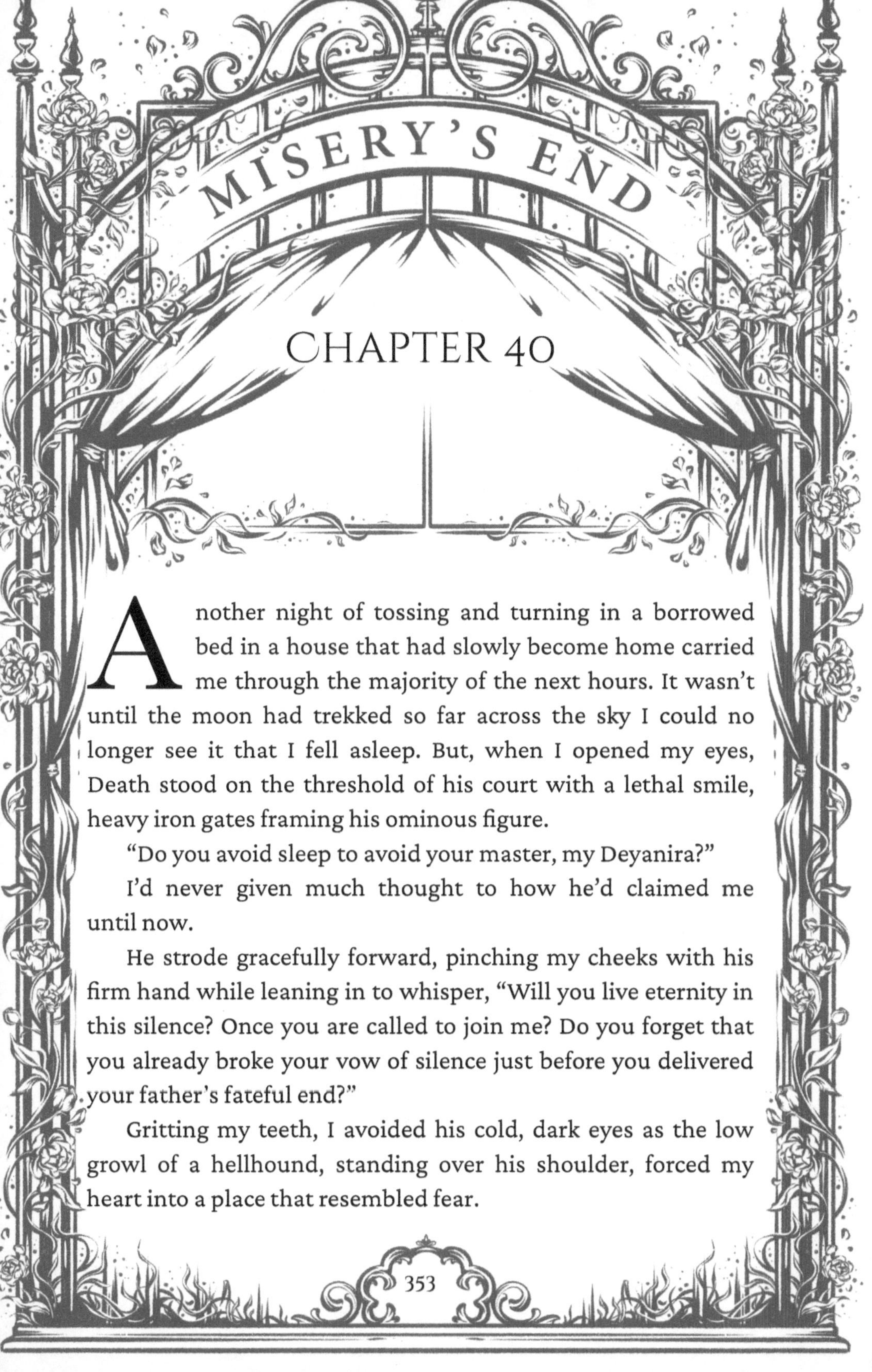

CHAPTER 40

Another night of tossing and turning in a borrowed bed in a house that had slowly become home carried me through the majority of the next hours. It wasn't until the moon had trekked so far across the sky I could no longer see it that I fell asleep. But, when I opened my eyes, Death stood on the threshold of his court with a lethal smile, heavy iron gates framing his ominous figure.

"Do you avoid sleep to avoid your master, my Deyanira?"

I'd never given much thought to how he'd claimed me until now.

He strode gracefully forward, pinching my cheeks with his firm hand while leaning in to whisper, "Will you live eternity in this silence? Once you are called to join me? Do you forget that you already broke your vow of silence just before you delivered your father's fateful end?"

Gritting my teeth, I avoided his cold, dark eyes as the low growl of a hellhound, standing over his shoulder, forced my heart into a place that resembled fear.

Death's low cackle rattled my bones. "Your stubborn will shall get you nowhere in the afterlife, my darling."

He'd never pushed beyond forcing my eyes to his. A concession I would always grant him: the upper hand in his realm of darkness. There was familiarity in those evil spheres. Of the madness that consumed me should I fight the magic. Of the days lost in opium dens and clawing my way through a prison wall until my nails were filed away and fingertips bloodied and raw. Of twenty-three souls taken in one fateful night. Of the flowers tattooed on my back in remembrance. It took everything I had to hold that glare as his fingers trailed down my arm and gripped my wrist.

"I have a good feeling about this one," he purred.

The pain was quick and all-consuming, burning the flesh as he dragged his nail through tender skin. His wretched smile as he waited for me to scream held me upright. It hurt. Beyond the pain of a dagger in the gut or a lonely heart. He'd made it worse for his own sick pleasure.

When the name was given, he pressed his cold lips to my cheek and whispered, "I will break your stubborn spirit," before fading away.

I jerked upright in bed, closing my hand in a fist. Was that a warning? A threat linked to the name he'd given. All of a sudden, I had names that I needed to protect. Names that I could not bear to see.

When I knocked on Paesha's door moments later, tears streaming down my face, she pulled me into her bedroom without hesitation. Thea was already there, sitting on her floor, folding laundry.

"Gods, Deyanira. What is it? You look like you've seen a ghost."

But the Huntress was far more observant. She moved in front of me, voice soft. "Who?"

"I don't know," I managed. "I'm too afraid to look and see one of your names."

Thea stood, taking Paesha's side. "What if you don't? You can't hunt someone without the name, can you?"

The magic within me pulsed as if in defiance of her statement.

Look.

With tight fists, I banged my hands into my head. "Don't talk to me."

Look.

Oh, gods. Oh, gods. He'd threatened me, hadn't he? Fear unlike anything I'd ever known grabbed me by the throat, stealing every full breath. Every steady heartbeat.

Look.

I buried a hand into my hair, pulling, if only to remind myself that I was only a human. Just a woman with a god's dangerous power coursing through her.

"Hey, stop," Althea said, rushing to grab my unmarked hand.

"You have to lock me away. You have to find a way to stop him."

Paesha grabbed the wrist of the other hand. "You know we can't do that. If Drexel announces a show and you aren't there, he will own you. And those names will be a lot closer to home and a lot more frequent."

I nodded, swallowing the lump burning my throat. "It'll be his name. It'll be Orin's."

Look.

Squeezing my eyes shut, I forced that voice into the abyss of my own mind. Fighting a losing battle.

"Show us," Paesha whispered. "We will help you."

I shook my head, trying to break away, but they did not relent. In fact, the Huntress grabbed my shoulder and jerked me back to sanity. "You are not alone. Let us help you. We'll do it together, no matter the name."

My eyes fell to the floor, catching the moment they locked hands. Paesha's tan skin a beautiful contrast to Thea's.

"Let us help shoulder your burden," the blacksmith insisted.

"It will be his name."

"Breathe," Paesha commanded, even as the magic thrummed. "Turn your head and let us look first."

I nodded, following the instructions, though my heart could barely stand the seconds that passed after Paesha pried my hand open. They'd been silent. Too silent.

Look.

"No."

"Dey?"

Look.

"No!" I shouted.

My heart leapt into my throat, suffocating me until my ears rang, hearing only that madness inside of me.

Look.

"Stop it!" I cried, yanking myself free of the women to crumble to the floor, gripping my head as I rocked back and forth.

"Deyanira Faber, stop this immediately."

It wasn't the firm voice of the Huntress, nor the soft tones of the blacksmith. It was Hollis. He stood in the doorway in a sharp-fitting red suit, face full of pity as he looked me over.

"You have to warn Orin. You have to tell him to run. Please."

"It isn't his name, Deyanira."

My head whipped to Paesha. "I... What?"

"It's not Orin." She locked eyes with Hollis. "It's Tolen Santus."

Thea gasped, words shaking. "Are you sure?"

The old man cut a glance at me before looking over his

shoulder and pulling the door shut behind him. "Well, that's going to be a problem."

I finally dared a peek at my palm, confirming the stranger's name. "Every death is a problem."

I swiped away my tears as I let the calmness wash over me. No matter the name, it was a burden I loathed, but how could I go my whole life with the repetitive fear of their deaths? Being alone, though it came with its own tribulations, made this part so much easier to bear. Maybe Orin was lying, and he was actually protecting himself.

"Because I've been hunting him for a while, and I cannot find him."

I blinked slowly. "You've been hunting the Life Maiden longer, have you not?"

"This is different," Thea interjected. "Tolen used to be part of the Syndicate. He's our friend. *My* friend. Paesha knows him well."

"The missing people? He's one of them now?" I asked.

Thea helped me to my feet, eyes glued to my hand as she said, "What happens if you can't—"

Her words were halted by a gasp as indescribable pain raced over my palm, nearly taking me back to the floor. I clenched my teeth, ripping myself free of her grasp as white clouded the edges of my vision.

"What the—" Paesha snatched my hand back, looking down at it and then back to me. "Did you do something?"

I blinked past the tears. "No."

"Holy gods," Thea whispered. "The name changed."

"What?" Jerking myself away again, I studied the burning edges of freshly seared skin.

"Gresidia Fischer," I mouthed, shaking my head. "That's never happened."

"Do you think..." Hope grew in Thea's eyes. "Do you think he's safe, then?"

"I don't know, but we need to call a meeting." Hollis rushed out the door as the rest of us stood in shock. Within minutes, he'd returned. "I'm sorry to say it, Little Dove, but you're going to have to hustle with that death."

"Why?"

He pulled a roll of parchment from behind his back, the black ribbons long enough to touch the floor. "Looks like the boss got the stage fixed. We have to report by nightfall."

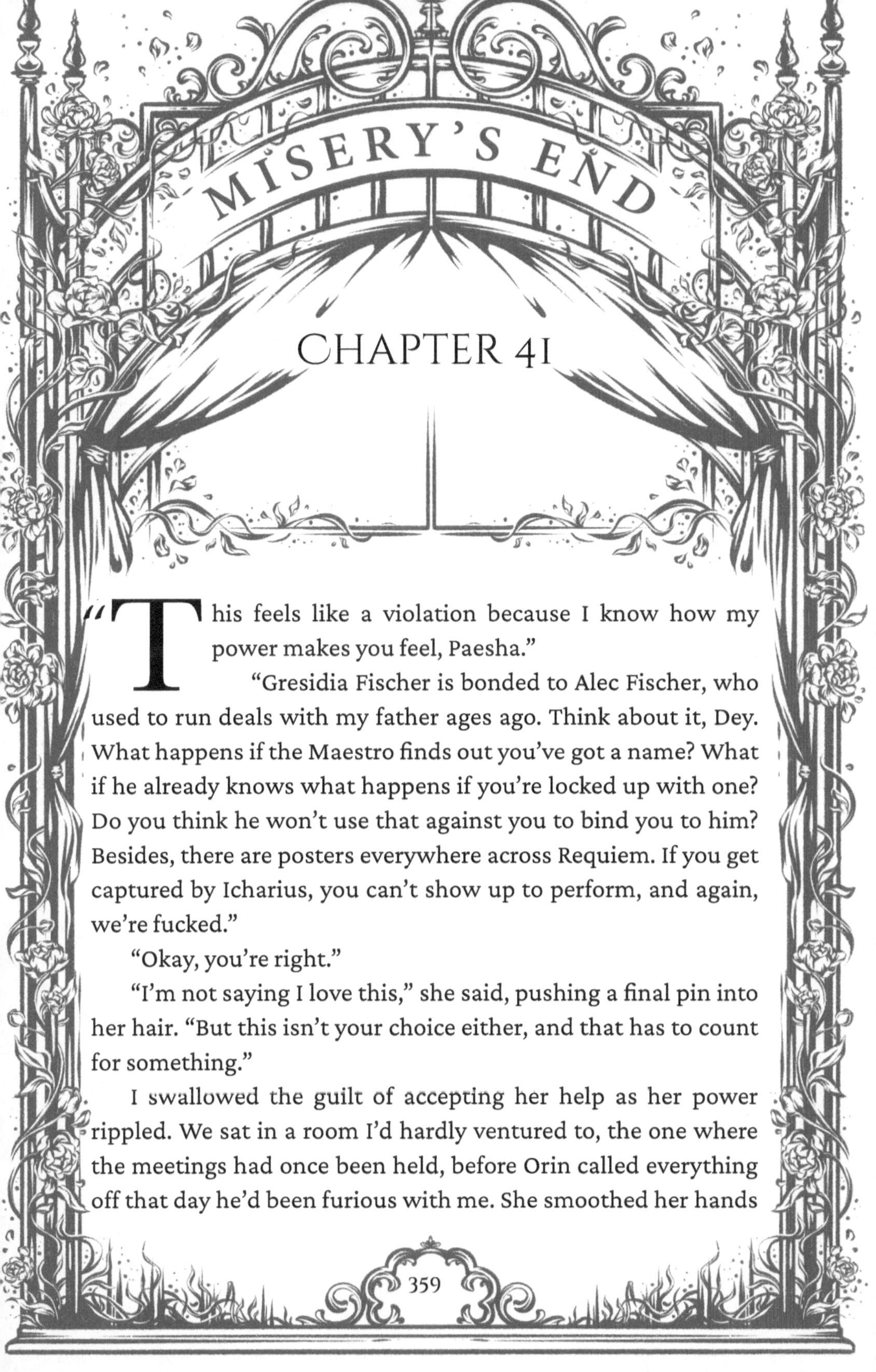

CHAPTER 41

"This feels like a violation because I know how my power makes you feel, Paesha."

"Gresidia Fischer is bonded to Alec Fischer, who used to run deals with my father ages ago. Think about it, Dey. What happens if the Maestro finds out you've got a name? What if he already knows what happens if you're locked up with one? Do you think he won't use that against you to bind you to him? Besides, there are posters everywhere across Requiem. If you get captured by Icharius, you can't show up to perform, and again, we're fucked."

"Okay, you're right."

"I'm not saying I love this," she said, pushing a final pin into her hair. "But this isn't your choice either, and that has to count for something."

I swallowed the guilt of accepting her help as her power rippled. We sat in a room I'd hardly ventured to, the one where the meetings had once been held, before Orin called everything off that day he'd been furious with me. She smoothed her hands over the intricate map of Requiem, far more updated than the tapestry hanging in Drexel's office.

I held my breath, listening to her fingernails slide over the grooves of the fabric, while I waited.

Within minutes, she'd tapped the icon for the Gambler's Quarter in Silbath. "At least it's not too far from Misery's End. If it takes a while, you can go directly to the theater. There's an opium den right around here, and I'd bet my death she's headed that way."

I didn't want to admit that I knew exactly the one she'd spoken of. That I'd been in that hell hole once or twice.

"I hate rushing this."

She ignored my hesitation and jutted her chin toward the parchment in my hand. "Problem number two, now. Let's hear it."

I let the paper unroll across the map as Hollis and Althea stepped in to get a better look.

Maiden,
Whispers of fate, a deadly embrace,
Destiny bound in a dangerous chase.
He stands by your side, a phantom so near,
Near a god, a shadow to revere.
With weapons in hand, a dance they partake,
A tango of souls, eternity and pain at stake.
The stage is their battlefield, passion their cry,
Entangled in a waltz where truths and lies vie.
Ever yours,
DV

"Do you think he's found a way to make you kill someone?" Thea asked, pointing to the word *deadly*.

"The deal was clear," I said, beginning to pace. "He cannot

ask me to do anything more than the rest of his performers do, nor can he ask me to kill anyone."

"Maybe he's done something wild and invited Death to the stage," Paesha said, pointing to the third and fourth line.

"That could be. Near a god might indicate Death, and he is revered." Hollis pulled a chair from the table and sat down heavily. "Imagine."

I shook my head. "He can't do anything to keep people from coming or clapping or standing. And the last line doesn't really make sense. But if Death shows up, no one will be brave enough to move."

"Technically, he's not stopping them, though," Thea whispered. "They could stand; they just won't."

"Then that's his loophole. But what's the solution?" Paesha took the opposite side of the table to pace, biting at a nail. "There's no true way for you to fight Death; the weapons would be pointless."

"That's it," Hollis said, banging a hand on the table as he stood. "You don't have to fight him. You have to make him leave before the timer is up. The crowd would cheer for that alone."

"Easy enough. I'll just ask him to kindly fuck off."

Thea snorted. "Great plan, team."

"No, seriously," Paesha said, freezing. "Can you ask him to leave?"

"I can ask him, but I don't think he'll listen."

"What could you offer him in exchange?"

Sucking in a sharp breath, I realized. "Words. I've never spoken to him in the Death Court, and he hates it."

"Never?" Thea drew backward, surprised.

I lifted a shoulder. "I bellowed in pain once, and he loved it so much I vowed to never make another sound in his court."

"I think it's time to break that vow, Maiden."

SHE HADN'T SCREAMED. Hadn't even acknowledged my presence as I stood before Gresidia Fischer, with Chaos in one hand and Serenity in the other. I'd felt sorry for her as she'd crumpled to the stained floor of the vacant opium den. But then I always did, to some degree.

Death had come and gone with little more than a sinister grin. Perhaps a promise to see me later. I wondered if I should have made the deal with him then, twisting the Maestro's plans. But I was not a fool. Not entirely. If I gave away that I knew anything at all, it would give him far more time to consider a bargain with me upon that stage. And the one thing the message *had* been clear about was the fact that we were meant to dance with weapons. I'd need every upper hand I could muster.

"AND THE WEAPONS?" I asked, standing before a mirror in the warehouse with Althea and Hollis behind me.

Thea shifted her apron to the side, sliding a hammer into a loop on her belt. The dress was stunning, only revealing in the short length of the skirt and the plunge between my breasts. When I twisted, each golden tassel on the shimmering costume glistened and swayed, drawing my eyes to the motion and shape of my hips. Still, I was tired. Death's power always left its trace on the weight of my bones.

"I made this for you," Thea said, holding out a thin belt made of chain mail. "You can't cut the metal links, so you're less likely to lose your weapons if someone tries to slice it off, but you can still move in this without it being restrictive."

"It's beautiful."

"Thanks." She beamed. "Took a little bit to make the gold strong enough, but I think I've worked out the kinks."

"Maiden?" Genevieve's voice crept over my shoulder. "The Maestro has asked to see you in his office."

"Why?" Hollis, Thea, and I asked in unison.

She shrugged, taking a tentative step backward. "Only the messenger, I'm afraid."

"You'll be okay," Thea said, gripping my hand as she always did.

After all these months, the connection no longer jarred me.

"Of course, I will. Any word on Paesha?"

"She's in three numbers tonight, but she's meeting with some others," she said, glancing around, "to tell them of the name change. Just in case anyone has any ideas. She said, 'Respectfully, don't forget to move your hips.'"

"Somehow, I'm doubting the *respectfully* bit. Does Orin know yet?"

"He and I got into a fight earlier when I was trying to tell him, and he stormed out. Something's..." Her eyes began to water.

Squeezing those fingers back, I leaned in. "He's got a lot on his plate right now. The Maestro isn't making his life easy, and I'm afraid I'm not either. Try not to take it too personally."

She forced a smile, a tear falling anyway. "We better go, Hollis."

I decided not to run through the tunnel in case the plan was to try to delay everything by indirectly imprisoning me. It only took me a few minutes to jog across the street, wind my way through the crowd, and force the guards at the back door to let me in.

Approaching the office, I lifted a fist to knock, but before I could connect, it swung open to reveal Orin, red-faced and furious, dressed in the most perfectly tailored black suit I'd ever seen him wear. I stumbled back, searching his eyes for whatever might've happened, but he brushed past me without so much as a second glance. And I would be lying if I didn't acknowledge the sting. To hate me when it was only him and I was one thing, but to do it so publicly was another.

"Maiden, please come in." The purr of Drexel's theatrical voice raked down my spine, causing my flesh to rise, begging me to shake away the disgusting sound. "Close the door behind you."

I did no such thing, choosing to stand in the doorway with my arms crossed. "What do you want, Drexel?"

He clicked his tongue behind his teeth, shaking his head. "It will always be a battle of wits with you, I see."

"No. It would take two competent parties to form a battle, and from where I'm standing, your side of the room is lacking the requirements. What do you want?"

His smile was nauseating. "Only to wish you good luck this evening. Your first night was a surprise for both of us, I believe."

"No. No. I'm quite sure watching your stage burn was a shock to you, but your little act of darkness was no surprise to me at all."

"Not one teensy bit?"

"If that's all, I really have to get back. I was busy being busy."

He thrummed thick fingers over his desk. "Sounds awful."

Rolling my eyes, I pushed off the door and walked away, calling over my shoulder. "I can assure you there are worse things."

"Break a leg, Maiden. Or two, if you feel so inclined."

I couldn't help my smile. There was no doubt in my mind he'd genuinely meant that. I'd won that little battle.

"STAY CLOSE?" I asked Paesha as she panted from the side of the stage.

She'd just performed the most erotic dance I'd ever seen, removing layers of clothing only to reveal smaller layers beneath. She'd hung from the ceiling by a strap on her wrist and spun until the stage seemed to swallow her whole. She was a dream, and there was just no way I could follow such a talent.

"Promise," she managed. "Quill's all set. I've asked her not to watch, though."

"Good plan. Death is beautiful but terrifying, and she's easily manipulated."

"Tell me about it," Thea said, joining Paesha's side.

"Don't forget your goal here. It'll be a tango. Flip that dress around, twirls, touching, keep your feet moving until the music is still. You have to pull a blade. The audience is most likely to respond to you if you're giving deadly lust. Don't hold back, Dey."

Watching every prop dragged from the pitch-black floor forced my pulse to quicken. Nothing smelled of smoke from the fire; no signs of damage plagued the dark burlesque. Quill's golden cage had even been polished. She swung from her perch with a giant rainbow sucker, watching the audience with an innocent smile.

The lights finally fell, indicating Misery's End was ready for her final act, though I was confident the onlookers were not. Steeped in lush magic, holding them to their seats, keeping their hearts surging, the end would surely leave them aching for more.

My heart pounded in rhythm with the bass drum that echoed through the theater, beckoning me from the side of the stage. I gazed out into the darkness opposite of me, the shadows concealing the identity of my partner, though the hourglass had been turned. I didn't want to bargain with Death any more than I had with the Maestro, but I'd have to accept it and trade one brand of evil for another.

A surge of shock raced through me like lightning as the spotlight sliced through the darkness, revealing an unexpected figure. It wasn't Death shrouded in the fearful depths of shadows he relished, but Orin, his anger radiating from him like an aura, his eyes darker than I had ever witnessed. Despite his presence, the audience's focus barely shifted. Their attention remained steadfast on center stage, their gazes captivated by Death's Maiden. By me.

The low bellow of a masculine voice ripped across the theater in a growl as another light ignited, rimming the singer standing in the center of the orchestra pit in a vibrant red hue.

Orin stalked forward. I matched the cadence of his steps as the music built, closing the distance between us, swaying, each step firm and deliberate, with Chaos and Serenity beaming in the spotlights. Black eyes stared into my soul as he reached for my waist, forcing me against him. He would lead this dance of seduction.

"Arm up," he ordered so only I could hear him.

I raised my hand, and he snatched it, his massive fingers engulfing mine.

"Move with me, Deyanira." Orin's commanding voice was a purr and growl, and I melted a touch in his embrace.

But there was no time for swooning over a dangerous man when the angry music roared to life, and he whipped me around, tassels flying, and locked my arm behind his neck, my back colliding with his broad chest. The way his calloused fingers, rough from playing his cello, slid down the bare skin on my arm, sent a rush of heat directly through me. Orin's warm breath trickled along the sensitive curve of my neck.

The passion laced with anger was unending when he spoke. "This is the price we both pay for your careless bargain."

"Is it so painful to be seen in public with me?"

"Painful? No."

His hand creeping across my stomach, splayed wide to hold me firm to his chest, he stomped and swayed, and before I could catch a breath, he spun me again.

"Foolish. Yes."

Quill's magic felt different, pounding through the room in a thick coating of lust. More than intrigue, more than awe. It was suffocating.

We glided across the floor in a rhythm that was charged with tension, gazes locked on each other. Every moment between us to this point, every fiery argument, and every lingering touch raced through my mind.

He dipped me, holding me by the small of my back while trailing a single finger down the exposed skin between my breasts so very slowly. I gasped, nearly slipping, praying he would go lower, crowd be damned.

"Focus," he demanded.

Jerking me upward, Orin stopped mid-turn, yanking me in, staring directly into my soul as he lifted my thigh, until those thick fingers pressed firmly into flesh, stretching every muscle, testing just how limber I could be.

"Does it feel good? To show them you're my weakness, Wife?"

His confession shocked me, but he must have known it would. The mischievous grin that inched across his beautiful face gave him away and heated me thoroughly. He danced with perfect grace and posture, and though each powerful grip was met with stone-cold eyes at the beginning of the song, somewhere in the middle, the thin line of his pouty lips had faded. He'd softened. Whipping me around, yanking us together over and over. Immersed in the power that held us both writhing with desire.

I wanted him to touch me. To slide his fingers over a body that thrummed for him alone until he could feel just how much I needed him. But when I circled him, fingers splayed across his broad chest, I could see the same in his eyes. I could feel the reaction to my touch in the way he pulsed, leaned toward me, and responded to only me. And gods, did I love the command of him. The weakness we'd shared as his gaze burned into mine. All eyes were glued to us, watching as that handsome creature seduced me on a stage of lies, just as the poem had said.

Instead of removing Quill, as had been my fear, the Maestro had likely asked to use her magic more powerfully at this moment because he had planned to use it against me to create a distraction. Probably she'd agreed because, to an innocent child, that might've been helpful, if not for the fiery passion that already held the space between us charged with tension. This was a place Orin and I were intimately familiar with.

Drexel's plan might have worked, had Orin not been so perfectly clever and wholly aware of the games his boss played. He had never let me falter. Never once loosened his grip. Perhaps his confession of weakness was a lie, but I could see the desperation on his face. Could feel the small gasp and smaller exhale every time I touched him.

The music slowed, still a genuine spice to the sharp notes, but a challenge, nonetheless, forcing our bodies together as our feet stilled. That grip of his was unwavering. He reached between my legs. I had no clue what he was doing, what our next move would be, but at that moment, I didn't care. When he lifted, spinning me as I stretched, the only thing I could think of was how close he was to parts of me that could've been his.

I landed soundlessly, and again, the music took off, carrying us across the stage, locked in each other's arms.

"Your blades, Nightmare," he rumbled into my ear as soon as he'd pressed me up against the icy exterior of the giant, golden hourglass. "Focus."

I'd nearly forgotten, so swept up in him and the way he'd consumed me flawlessly. Removing the latch that held Chaos in place, I waited until we were nose-to-nose again. The next dramatic note, I whirled away, pausing at the final graze of our fingertips before slicing the knife through the air with another spin, fully in control as the crowd gasped the second my dagger landed upon his throat without so much as nicking him.

He hadn't flinched. He'd trusted me so fully, so uncomfortably, I nearly stumbled on the heel of my gold stilettos. Completely unphased, in one sudden motion, he struck, stepping forward, weapon be damned, and grabbed my throat.

The music grew into a glorious escalation, drums, strings, even the singer dragged my anxious nerves to an absolute peak as I managed a glance at the fading grains of sand seeping through the funnel of the hourglass, swallowing around his grip.

"Forgive me," he whispered seconds before I dropped the blade, and his lips captured mine with an intensity that ignited an inferno within me. It was a kiss born of passion and aggression; a collision of conflicting emotions that melded into something all-consuming. His mouth was demanding yet tender, his grip on me unyielding yet gentle. Our lips moved with a desperation that spoke of months of tension, of battles waged and unexplored desires.

The world fell away as the kiss deepened, becoming a whirlwind of sensations that left me dizzy and yearning for more. In that stolen breath of time, the winds had changed, our hostility transformed into a fusion of need, a realization that the lines between lust and conflict were blurred beyond recognition. When we finally pulled away, our foreheads touching, I knew that this kiss had rewritten the rules of our dance, setting us on an unknown path.

The theater was quiet. Absolutely, deathly still. And then, as if a dam had burst, the crowd erupted into a frenzy of applause and cheers that reverberated through the theater. The sound was deafening, a tidal wave of approval crashing over us. It wasn't just our dance they celebrated; it was the raw intensity, the palpable connection that had ignited between us and blazed to life in that unforgettable kiss. And my husband had absolutely conducted that.

He bowed quickly once before walking off the stage as if nothing had happened. I watched him go, feeling every gaping inch he placed between us as fast as he could. But when I turned back, the crowd who'd stood so boldly faded into darkness as the back of the theater burst to life, every guard, every man at Icharius Fern's disposal pouring in, weapons drawn, all eyes on me.

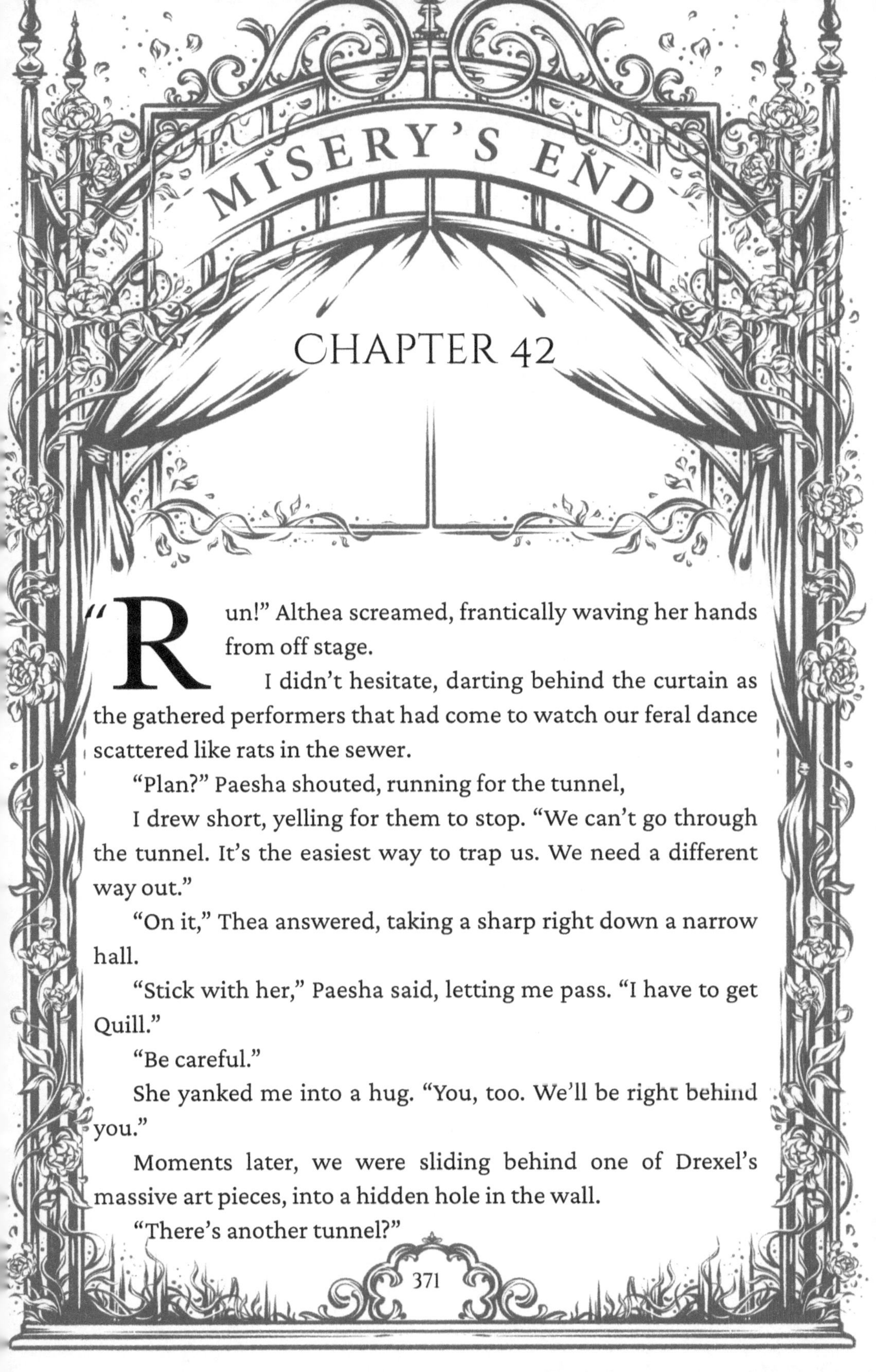

MISERY'S END

CHAPTER 42

"R un!" Althea screamed, frantically waving her hands from off stage.

I didn't hesitate, darting behind the curtain as the gathered performers that had come to watch our feral dance scattered like rats in the sewer.

"Plan?" Paesha shouted, running for the tunnel,

I drew short, yelling for them to stop. "We can't go through the tunnel. It's the easiest way to trap us. We need a different way out."

"On it," Thea answered, taking a sharp right down a narrow hall.

"Stick with her," Paesha said, letting me pass. "I have to get Quill."

"Be careful."

She yanked me into a hug. "You, too. We'll be right behind you."

Moments later, we were sliding behind one of Drexel's massive art pieces, into a hidden hole in the wall.

"There's another tunnel?"

The handle of Thea's hammer, hanging loosely on her belt, slid against the wall of the metal tube as she reached for my hand. "Syndicate use only. No one else knows it's here, not even the Maestro."

"Gods. You put this down here with your power?"

"For special occasions like these." She beamed. "Come on."

We ran for what felt like forever, twisting and turning through the narrow tunnel buried beneath the city. A masterpiece. A labyrinth depositing us into a small room beneath an old apartment building within the heart of Silbath.

"Keep going. Up these stairs."

Letting her guide the way, I gripped the iron railing in the hall, taking the steps two at a time, just as she had. "This is Ezra's old place. We've been using it as a backup meeting spot since Orin kicked everyone out of our house."

"How big is his apartment?"

"Not just the one, silly. He owned the whole building. Four little homes." Thea took a deep breath, resting her hand on the knob of the furthest door from the stairs we'd climbed. "The others... they can be a little rough around the edges."

I leveled a serious stare. "So can I."

"Good point." She pushed the door open, stepping aside so I could take in the room littered with strangers. In the middle of a long, droopy couch, Elowen sat sandwiched between two men, likely older than Orin. One, the large man that'd helped him the night he'd stabbed me, stood, moving his body as a shield between us.

Elowen shooed him away. "I've told you a hundred times, Jarek, she's perfectly safe. Stop this." She rose, coming to rest her hands on my arms. "I'm sure you have questions. I'll start from the beginning. Shall we sit?"

The dusty paintings and tapestries hung along the walls had lost their luster, matching the worrisome faces of the gathered people as they watched the door. The entry room had clearly been transformed into a meeting space, filled with as much seating as they could fit. The lamps were dim, as if to hide the secrets of the Syndicate, and, though it was tidy, dust had begun to collect on the chair rail circling the space.

I followed her to an empty couch crammed in a corner. She lifted a blanket and spread it across her lap, tucking her dark hair behind an ear. "When Orin was a boy, he would bring home every stray child he could find. We'd feed them and clothe them as best we could, offering shelter for as long as we could. We'd asked both kings to help fund the house, to help with food and coin, but we were denied. We try not to get involved with the politics of it all. We just help those who need it and keep our heads down."

"We're not here to fix the world," Thea added. "We're just trying to make life easier for those who need it most. But some of the people we'd been helping started disappearing. Tolen Santus, for example. And, at first, we thought it was because of you. But even when you were at the house, and we knew you hadn't left, it was still happening."

So, they hadn't been a great crime ring or their own version of the law. They weren't even warriors. Just a group of people trying to do right by the world.

"That's why Orin wanted me to stay there?"

Thea stepped forward. "We never meant to make you feel like a prisoner. But we wanted to know what was happening. And we couldn't risk the Maestro finding out about any of it. We knew he wouldn't demand answers if he didn't know anything, so we've been working together to keep everything from him, even searching for the Life Maiden."

I drew back, shaking my head. "Gods, you could have just asked. I would have given you my victims' names."

"And trusted you to speak the truth?" Jarek rested an arm on the back of the couch.

"Who are you to question me? You don't even know me."

His accusatory eyes narrowed just as the door slammed open, and Paesha, Hollis, and Quill rushed inside.

"Orin?" Elowen asked.

Paesha shook her head, eyes cast to the floor. "He said he had some stuff to sort, and he'd be here as soon as he could."

"How many would you say there were, Dey?" Hollis asked, stepping beyond the door to take a seat in one of the old wooden chairs lined up against the wall.

"At least fifty, not including any that might've been in the halls."

"Just tell us what happened," Elowen interrupted. "Nyx saw the soldiers leaving the castle and came to get me, but we've heard nothing else."

"They're hunting me. I should have known it would happen. They found out I was in the last show, I'm sure."

"Well, you killed two of his guards, and we incapacitated a lot more. The new king might've been scorned when you left him at the altar, but now he's pissed," Paesha said. "The only thing we can do right now is wait it out."

"I have to perform in the next show, no matter what. If I don't..." My voice trailed off, unwilling to reveal the stakes to strangers.

Elowen leaned into me. "You better make a plan then, because my brother isn't going to miss the opportunity to see you captured before you can walk out on that stage."

ORIN NEVER CAME. And though I knew it was foolish, I found myself on the rooftop of the apartment building, still dressed in the golden gown, with a heavy blanket wrapped around my shoulders. I stared out over the city, listening to the gritty ambiance of Requiem. Far off in the distance, the clock tower in Perth orientated me. Beyond that, my father's castle could hardly be seen, bathed in shadow, a reminder that even the strongest could be slain. No one took their title into eternity. In Death's court, people were nothing more than wandering souls.

Every movement in the city below snatched my attention as I watched for armor, but more than that, I sought a broad figure with a heart of stone and enough stubbornness to break me.

"You'll catch a cold," Hollis said, startling me. I whipped around just in time to see his smile curl. He walked to the edge, wrapping age-marked hands around the rusted railing. "Care to share your thoughts with an old man?"

"Trust me, whatever's twirling around in this brain isn't worth the time it takes to speak it."

"Oh, Little Dove. We all see the way you look at him."

"I'm not supposed to care," I whispered. "Caring makes me vulnerable and weak. And all we do is fight. He hates me."

"No. He doesn't. You just make him feel things he'd rather believe are not possible. In all my years, I've learned that when it comes to matters of the heart, there's nothing rational about it. And just when you think you've got it all figured out, you find out you know nothing at all. If he didn't care, he wouldn't have traded the only freedom he would ever know for your safety."

We watched the crows peck along the cracks in the ground, bathed in the blue cast of the streetlamps. A hunched figure, wrapped in layers of worn clothing, stepped a little too close, and the birds scattered, cawing their disapproval as my mind spun with confessions best left unspoken.

But I was weak. And more than anything in the world, I needed a friend. This friend.

"It's just... There are these moments I have with him that

feel so raw and real. Where the man behind the anger that consumes him comes out, and that version of him is so kind. The night he married me... I know he lied, Hollis. I know he was doing it because he had to. But there was a sincerity there, in his hopes for the world, in the way he'd looked at me. And I've spent every day since longing for the way he'd made me feel."

I swallowed the thick lump in my throat, leaning my head on the old man's shoulder when he wrapped an arm around me. My nose stung, giving away the tears that pooled in my eyes. I tried to force the heavy emotions away, but there was safety here with Hollis. A space he'd created where I was never judged. "You've always made me feel like more than what I am. Thank you."

He chuckled, leaning his head to mine. "You are more than you believe yourself to be, my girl. He'll see the light one day, I'm certain."

"But what if I truly am only darkness?"

"You aren't. But if you were, then he would see the cataclysmic depths of you and wonder how you find the will to light up a room, all the same."

I swiped away the tears freezing my cheek. "How did you get so wise, Old Man?"

He sighed, watching his breath plume in the chilly air before drawing back his sleeve to reveal an aged golden band on his forearm. "I loved a woman once. Promised her the world, and I intended to keep that promise. I didn't have much more than the clothes on my back and a spool of thread in my pocket, though. So, I stitched her a bracelet and promised to replace it one day with a gold band. I wanted everything with her. The home, the children, the world."

I was almost afraid to ask. "What happened?"

He lifted his chin to the silver moonlight, eyes falling shut as a single tear fell, wrenching my heart into pieces. "My sister killed her."

Old men weren't supposed to cry.

JAREK SLAMMED a handful of posters onto the table the next morning at breakfast, his massive brown hand wrinkling the whole stack as he slumped so heavily into the metal chair beside Quill, I thought it might break. "We've got a problem."

Sliding my glass of water to the side, I lifted the paper, eyes gliding down the beautifully crafted message.

Step into a realm of wonder and awe,
Misery's End awaits you.
Unlike anything you've ever witnessed before
A final act that will leave you eager for more when Death's
Maiden takes the stage.

Tonight only – Admission will be free.

I NEARLY CHOKED on my own gasp. "What the hell is he planning?"

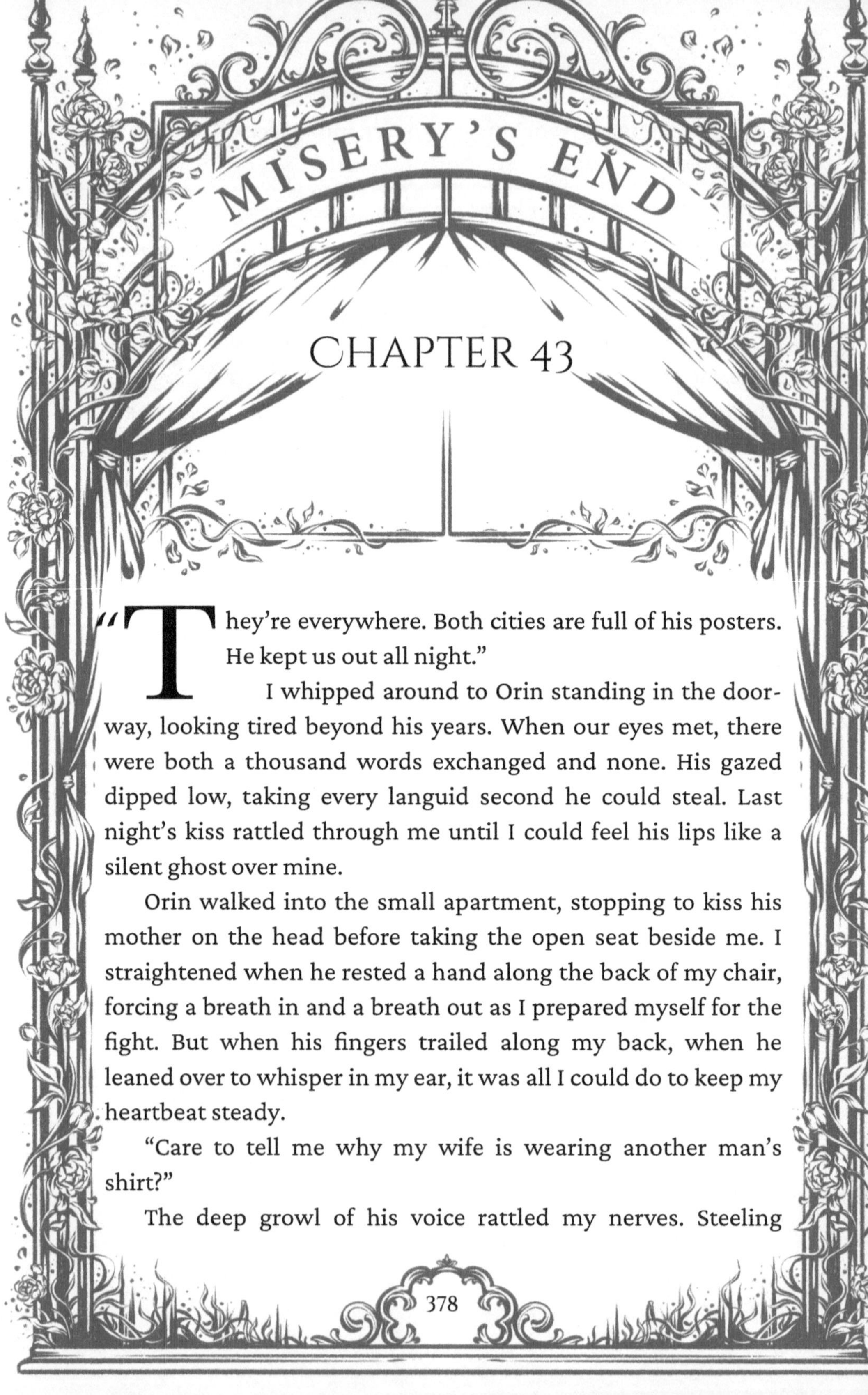

CHAPTER 43

"They're everywhere. Both cities are full of his posters. He kept us out all night."

I whipped around to Orin standing in the doorway, looking tired beyond his years. When our eyes met, there were both a thousand words exchanged and none. His gazed dipped low, taking every languid second he could steal. Last night's kiss rattled through me until I could feel his lips like a silent ghost over mine.

Orin walked into the small apartment, stopping to kiss his mother on the head before taking the open seat beside me. I straightened when he rested a hand along the back of my chair, forcing a breath in and a breath out as I prepared myself for the fight. But when his fingers trailed along my back, when he leaned over to whisper in my ear, it was all I could do to keep my heartbeat steady.

"Care to tell me why my wife is wearing another man's shirt?"

The deep growl of his voice rattled my nerves. Steeling

myself, I pushed away from the table, ignoring the way his arm dropped, sliding down my back as I stood.

"No."

The plink of my glass on the counter was as loud as the pulse thundering in my ears. This infuriating man was so good at breaking me, so damn good at making me aware of every move he made. I didn't even have to look to know he watched me disappear down the hall and escape into a tiny bedroom.

Door slamming open, he stalked forward. "Gods, Deyanira. When are you going to stop fighting me?"

I scoffed. "Two seconds after you stop fighting me."

"I wasn't, and you still ran away."

"I guess I'm too used to the way you hate me."

He took three steps toward me, and Serenity was drawn before the fourth. Orin's golden eyes flicked to the blade, unbothered as he closed the distance between us, gripping my hand on my own dagger, shoving it away so he could grab the collar of the oversized shirt Paesha had brought me. "When you speak, I can hear the battle. When you glare, I can feel your repulsion. And I can't breathe when you are near. I can't think or see beyond my own rage. Whatever power you hold over me is a vicious form of torture. And I am weak for you. Only you."

"This isn't repulsion, nor weakness, Husband. This is fucking obsession. Every day. Every second. And maybe I'm a masochist because I don't want to be without it."

"You don't know what you're asking for, Nightmare."

My eyes dropped to his lips, the tension as thick as castle walls. "Yes. I. Do."

The world shifted abruptly, as if time had bent to his will. One moment he'd been seething, and the next, his mouth crashed onto mine with a searing urgency that left no room for restraint. The press of his lips was an oath to our shared longing, a craving that consumed us both. I found myself trapped between the solidity of the wall and the hard contours of his body, a willing captive in a dance of fervent need. The thought that I should resist was a fleeting echo, easily drowned out by the primal desire coursing through me.

I came alive with the need of him, my body responding as it always had with his touch. Breasts growing heavy, legs weakening, warmth pooling as we finally, finally let the walls between us fall. And I wanted him. Every inch. I wanted to writhe beneath him and pant his name. I wanted to hear his breath catch the second before release. I wanted the peak of my desire to last an eternity at his fingertips until he drove into me so hard I could not bear it. I wanted him to take it all. And keep it.

His hand slipped into my hair, possessively deepening our kiss. My lips parted, an invitation he accepted eagerly, his tongue brushing mine with a practiced tease. Clutching his shirt, I pulled him closer. The wave of longing spiraled. The taste of him was my complete undoing. With every movement of our lips, the world faded into insignificance, leaving only the intoxicating pull.

Eventually, our need for air forced us to part. The lingering touch, a bittersweet reminder of what I'd longed for. Our eyes remained locked in a silent exchange. A wordless confession of how much we needed each other. Breathless, we stared, the electricity of our kiss still crackling in the air, binding us in a spell we were reluctant to break.

"You deserved so much more than the stolen kiss on the stage." His eyes searched mine as if seeking answers to questions we both feared to voice. "I'm so tired of fighting you. Of fighting myself. I know what I want. I've known for a long time, but I've been so angry, trying to convince myself that you were the problem. But it's always been me. That first night in your bedroom, there was a light in your eyes, unlike anything I'd ever seen. So much grit and defiance. But at the wedding, when you'd pieced together what I'd done, I watched that damn light fade, and it ripped everything I thought I knew about myself to shreds. Every day, I check to see if it's returned, if you've rediscovered the happiness you had before I stole it from you, and it never has. I'm sorry I broke you so thoroughly. I don't hate you. I hate me."

"Orin..."

"Give me everything. I want your sadness. Your guilt. I want your happiness, too. And every moment that makes those lips curl into a smile." He leaned down, breath hot against my neck. "I want to hear the little growls you make when we fight. And I want to hear you purr my name when we are not fighting. When I am buried between your beautiful legs, I want every breath and every pant."

He kissed me again, desperately, as if he hadn't wished on a falling star, but instead upon my lips. His touch was a brand, his fingers lingering on my skin as he spoke, leaving an imprint that matched his words. "I'm not asking you to love me, Dey. I'm not even asking you to like me. I just need you to forgive me."

I forced myself away from him, shoving space and time and the ability to think between us. He was all-consuming, but I needed truth. I needed to trust him. "If you want my forgiveness, then tell me honestly. Did you kill that man in the alley?"

Amber eyes fell to my swollen lips. "Yes."

A jolt of shock betrayed me as I stumbled further away. "You lied?"

"Yes."

"Why?"

He moved in, brows dropping. "There's nothing I can say that will justify it."

"Try," I demanded, placing a palm on his chest to hold the distance.

"To protect you and keep you from hunting answers you won't find."

"Are you a Death Lord?"

He raised a shoulder. "I don't know what I am. I've never seen Death. I've never been forced to kill a specific person."

"You hated me for who I was when you were exactly the same."

He nodded, eyes on me once more. "No one knows. Not Paesha, Hollis, not even my mother."

"Then why would you tell me?"

"Because someday, Death will come to reap my soul and punish me for breaking his promise to the people. And when he does, somebody needs to know why."

The ache in his voice, the way he'd laid himself bare, revealing a sacred part of himself, held me in place.

"Can you forgive me?"

"Don't be greedy, Husband."

"He's in his castle. Nowhere near the theater."

"And Drexel?" Orin asked, shoulder pinned to mine as I stroked the dog curled in my lap while we sat on the dusty couch pressed against a wall of the Syndicate's apartment.

"He's... At Lady Visha's."

Boo raised his head as Quill bounded into the room. Plopping down beside me, she gave the pup a hug, giggling when he licked her little face.

"Now's the time to move, then. We have to get into that theater as soon as possible."

He was up and moving without a second thought. Hustling around the apartment, pulling a few weapons from a slew of nooks and crannies, and plopping them onto the table.

"Throwing knives, Thea. As many as you can."

She shoved away from the table, running for the kitchen. "How attached are you to the silverware, P?"

"What?" Paesha ran after her, hollering, and then Thea started yelling, and before anyone could discern what was really happening, Elowen came back into the living room and dumped a drawer full of utensils onto the table.

The two women followed right behind her. I stood. Orin grabbed hold of Paesha, tugging her away as he cradled her into his chest. Quill stepped in, taking her hand.

"It's faster if I can start with metal," Thea said, so quietly I almost hadn't heard it.

Something in my heart broke when Paesha nodded, and Thea drew her hammer. I bit the inside of my cheek at the Huntress's uninhibited sob. They were his. This apartment was Ezra's home away from the Syndicate house. And little by little, it'd been pieced away, given to those in need. Those who suffered until all that remained beyond the dusty memories were the things Paesha must have held on to.

"Paesha?" I whispered.

She turned; a rare moment of weakness settled onto her beautiful face.

"We don't need them. Keep your silverware."

She shook her head, leaving Orin's arms to stand before me, her back to the table as she gripped my hands, resting her forehead on mine. "I have to let him go, Maiden."

Swallowing the lump in my throat, I threw my arms around her and held on tight as the hammer struck as true as the magic that filled the room. When Thea drew it away, a tiny throwing knife had taken its place. On and on she went, each strike causing Paesha to jerk in my arms.

"I'm sorry," I said, so only she could hear me. "I'm so fucking sorry."

She sniffled. "What is a simple fork compared to the freedom of a friend?"

ARMED TO THE TEETH, every member of the Syndicate that was able to join us wound their way through the tunnel, back to Misery's End, in silent determination. I wasn't foolish enough to believe they'd all come for me, but the man on my right, eyes cold and dark as he led the charge, had, and he wasn't shy about that declaration. Nor were Paesha and Quill, who'd packed in behind us, swords strapped to their backs and worry in their eyes.

Even Elowen had come. And though her son had argued, when she'd put her foot down, he silently retreated. This was not my moment, not really. It was theirs. Because if I somehow made it to that stage, it was their freedom on the line just as much as my own.

We'd argued over Quill coming. Most of us wanted her to stay away from the place. I'd sworn I could perform whatever he wanted without her, but we also trusted no one else to keep her safe, and we had no choice but to believe the Maestro coveted the power she promised more than appeasing a king that did not scare him. When Paesha mentioned he would ask where she was and they would be forced to answer, giving away their second hideout *and* the girl, the argument was over, and she and her pup had come along, though no one was happy about it.

"I think I don't want to be friends with Drexel anymore," Quill confessed halfway through the underground labyrinth.

The others halted, but most were bound by magic to not interfere. I had no such bindings. Maybe Elowen was afraid of the Maestro's anger, but I wasn't.

"I think that would be a very wise and mature decision," I said, kneeling before the child.

"Do you think so, too?" she asked, giant blue eyes staring into Paesha's.

I knew she couldn't answer. I knew the panic in her eyes was that of the Huntress trying to fight the magic that bound her words.

"Of course, she does, Quilly." I reached for Boo, pulling him close as a distraction. "And so does this little rascal. If you don't want to go tonight, you don't have to. I will take you somewhere safe. And no one else will know, so he won't be able to force them."

She shook her head, letting her power swell in the hallway. "Do you feel that?"

I nodded, the magic pulsing through me.

Hollis leaned against the wall, closing his eyes. "That's love. As pure as it gets."

I watched as each member sank into that feeling, shoulders dropping, faces softening.

"You can choose the emotion?"

She smiled, nodding. "And this one's for you."

She flung herself at me, arms wrapping around my neck. "I have to save you tonight, like you saved me because I love you."

I fell backward, letting the words that had only been spoken to me once in my whole life repeat over and over in my mind. Until the world turned blurry behind my tears and the innocent soul of a child healed something damaged within me.

"You don't have to save me, kid. I can save myself."

She pulled away, placing her palms on both sides of my face. "Do you think the Maestro will hurt me?"

I shook my head. I didn't want her to be afraid, but I also truly believed he wouldn't.

"Then if you love me back, you will let me come. We're a family. We have to stick together."

She squeezed my cheeks until my lips puckered. Boo barked, and she giggled. "You're not even medium scary anymore. You're just Dey."

"Just Dey," I repeated. "But we have to go now, okay?"

She moved back to Paesha, the woman who'd been more like a mother to her than anyone else, then turned and grabbed Hollis's hand. "Family, right?"

"The best one," he answered as we began the rest of our trek down the hall.

"Stay here," Orin ordered, placing his hands on the hidden door to the theater a while later.

Moving to stand beside him, I drew my blades, letting the feel of their solid handles kick-start my adrenaline. "You couldn't pay me enough coins to sit in this tunnel while you go offer yourself as bait."

His lips parted to argue, but as his eyes fell on his mother and shifted to Quill, he stopped, likely realizing what was at stake. He nodded, swinging the door open. When it was only him and I in the silent, dark theater, he reached for me, for my hand, steadying both of us as we moved like wraiths.

But the theater was completely empty. Not a soul. Not a heartbeat. Absolutely no one had come yet. Early though it was, we'd been so confident there was a battle to be had. Winding through the halls, we searched the rooms; even Drexel's office was dark and empty.

"It's in the terms, he can't hand me over to the king," I said, pausing in a hallway.

"That doesn't mean he can't step out of the way."

"Think about it, though. His posters are promising the greatest show ever and free admission. He's not going to do something like that without cutting off Icharius. Drexel's been playing this game a lot longer than Icky. He's smart. Too smart. He's been running these cities for a long time."

Orin stroked a thumb across his bottom lip, eyes flickering down the dark hall. "True. But you're saying we have to place bets on which beast has the biggest bite right now."

"That's never going to be a question. Drexel's always going to win that war. There's no way Icharius isn't where he is because your boss had a hand in it. I just can't figure out the puzzle. Have you... have you ever tried to..." I slid my thumb across my throat rather than speak the words aloud, just in case. "I know he's your uncle, but..."

He leaned closer to breathe his answer into my ear. "Yes. Twice. But he never knew it was me, and he never died."

"Maybe his claims of bargaining with Death were real."

I took a step to continue our journey back to the hiding Syndicate members, but he stopped me. "In hours, this theater is going to fill with people. Probably more than ever before. If he's truly making deals with Death, promise me you'll be careful. Stay hidden until showtime, even if we're all called away. Make no more bargains, okay? In and out."

I nodded as he pressed his lips to mine. "This marriage is only getting started, Wife. I won't see it end before I have a chance with you."

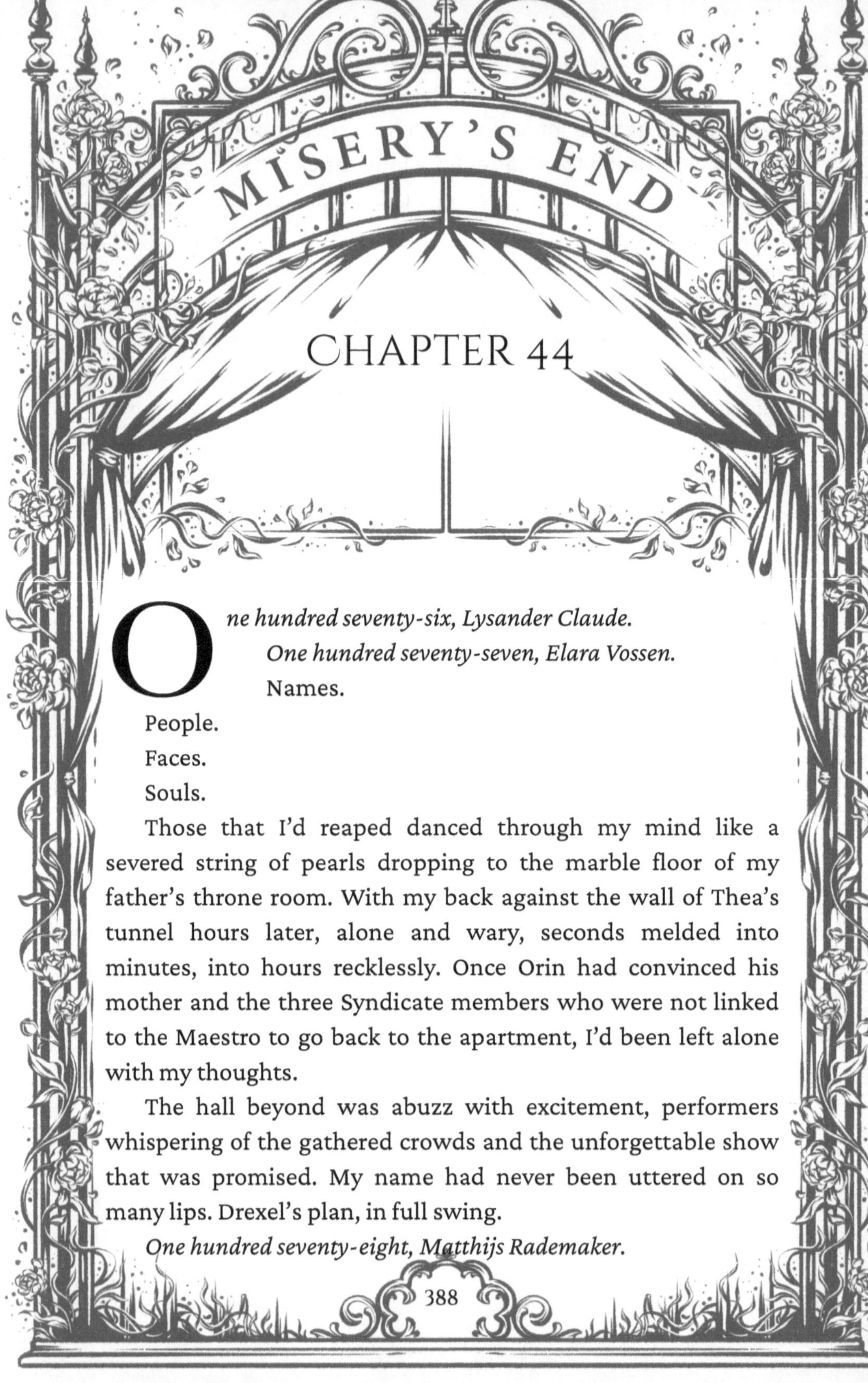

MISERY'S END

CHAPTER 44

One hundred seventy-six, Lysander Claude.
One hundred seventy-seven, Elara Vossen.
Names.

People.

Faces.

Souls.

Those that I'd reaped danced through my mind like a severed string of pearls dropping to the marble floor of my father's throne room. With my back against the wall of Thea's tunnel hours later, alone and wary, seconds melded into minutes, into hours recklessly. Once Orin had convinced his mother and the three Syndicate members who were not linked to the Maestro to go back to the apartment, I'd been left alone with my thoughts.

The hall beyond was abuzz with excitement, performers whispering of the gathered crowds and the unforgettable show that was promised. My name had never been uttered on so many lips. Drexel's plan, in full swing.

One hundred seventy-eight, Matthijs Rademaker.

One hundred seventy-nine, Seraphina Klaase.

The others had gone hours ago, slipping into the line of performers one by one to prepare for whatever tonight's show would bring without friction. And while I imagined they'd dressed in their finest, keeping Hollis on his toes, I also pictured Orin, sitting before his polished cello on a dark stage, a single spotlight on him as he poured every worry, every truth, and every lie into those notes he'd so carefully crafted.

His kiss lingered on my lips even now, alone and hidden in a hallway, letting the nerves the Maestro had conducted so flawlessly build to a crescendo, reminding me that the anticipated fear was far more potent than unexpected fear. A well-crafted plan.

"Deyanira?" Thea's whispered voice surged through me. She pressed the door open to peek around the corner, eyes sinking as she took me in. "It's clear, but we have to hurry. The show's about to start."

I jerked back in surprise. "It is? Is it late already?"

"Orin wanted to wait so you couldn't be locked in anywhere else. Genevieve has your performance orders, and Hollis is ready to dress you backstage."

We slipped out of the secret space, and I hurried through the mass of performers, most dressed in little more than lace and strategically placed feathers. Tentative eyes landed on me as we rushed. Each one of them held their breath as if I'd pluck them from their spot in line and kill them without a thought.

I turned my face to stone, cool calm pouring over me. I used to think the shadows protected me from other's fear of my presence, but the reality was, they only kept me from seeing it. There would be no hiding today, not as I was put on display, ready to perform whatever dance or fight or song the Maestro demanded. He couldn't ask me to do anything more than the other performers, and in this moment, when all eyes would be on me, I was grateful for the forethought of that contingency.

"Quickly now," Hollis said, pulling the black leather outfit he'd given me for my birthday from a rack of sequined gowns and elaborate masks and jewels.

"How did this get here?" I asked, heart thundering as all the pieces fell into place.

His eyes were as sad as my own as I slipped into the outfit I'd loved so thoroughly.

"He doesn't want me hiding who I am. He wants to parade me before everyone like a puppeteer."

"I've been his puppet for many years, Little Dove. I promise you'll still open your eyes tomorrow, and sometimes that's the only silver lining of a day conducted by Drexel Vanhoff."

I took a steadying breath, gripping his hand as Quill's magic filled the arena, and the music from the orchestra pit sprung to life. Hollis handed me each of my blades, and after I'd strapped them on, he held a small leather box with a golden skull embedded into the top toward me.

"What's this?"

"Open it."

I flipped open the lid and gasped. Lifting the necklace from within, I studied the intricate little flower, embedded with a ruby stone that matched the ones in Chaos and Serenity's hilts.

"The flower was Orin's idea. The stone was Paesha's. The chain was from Thea, and I stitched the box. Whatever happens tonight, Deyanira, we are with you. Bargaining for our freedom in place of your own will probably be the greatest feat of your life. But regardless of the crowd's final moment, you are ours now as much as we are yours." The old man cleared the lump in his throat, his voice turning hoarse. "I never had a daughter, but if I did, I can't imagine anyone I'd rather have her be more like."

My eyes shifted between the cerulean blue of his, taking in

every wrinkle, every age mark, every sign of kindness on his weathered face. I could hardly manage a breath. "I'm scared."

He took the necklace from my hands and circled me to clasp it before spinning me around. "You are brave, and you are strong. There's a light in you. Being scared only makes you human, Deyanira. Not flawed."

"Maiden?" Genevieve held the final scroll out to me.

The crowd roared to life, filling the air backstage with so much applause and screaming, I nearly dropped the rolled parchment.

"They're in a mood tonight," she warned tentatively before hustling away.

"Of course they are. He's promised them the show of a lifetime." Orin's voice was like a balm. An anchor in a tumultuous sea of trepidation.

"I didn't think I'd see you," I admitted, taking a second to admire the pressed coattails and top hat as he shifted firmly to my side.

Each time I'd encountered Orin, up until this moment, kindness was a chore. A battle to wage before there was light. But, as if something had twisted, as if our kiss had changed the game, he'd come without a storm. Without fury and madness. Only him. A semblance of the man I'd married on that rooftop with dreams of a peaceful world and a wife that'd chosen him, even when he hadn't truly had the same choice.

"He would have had to cut my arms and legs off to keep me away," he purred into my ear. "What's the performance?"

Hollis moved to my other side as I gripped the silk ribbon bow and tugged. The theater fell silent beyond the rush of my thudding heartbeat.

Maiden,

Good Luck.

DV

"What is that supposed to mean?" Orin asked, ripping the scroll away to read over the words before flipping the page back and forth. "Didn't the other ones have more information?"

"Yes," I said numbly as the lights flickered on and off.

He squeezed my hand before placing it into Hollis's. "I'm up. You'll figure it out. Okay? Just be careful. There are guards in the crowd, and I think the king is in the box with the boss."

"He's here?"

The lights flickered again.

He nodded, taking two steps away before coming back to kiss me soundly. "Be so careful," he whispered.

The reflection of worry on his face and the crease in his brow conjured the same feelings in me. I'd never been able to figure out the Maestro ahead of time before, but I wasn't sure I could worry about that. Not with the king present, his men close by, and Quill on full display.

"Deyanira," Hollis said as I tugged him through the performers packing the sides of the stage when the music began. "Perhaps we should stay away from the stage until it's time for you to go out."

"Why would we—"

My words were clipped short by the reflection of a sequin bouncing across his face. I whipped around, expecting the stage to hold Orin and his cello, only to find him dancing with four completely naked women, save the glittering high heels. He slung a hand out to the side, taking the waist of one woman while he spun another, and the crowd was eating it up. His movements were slow. As slow as they had been with me. Jealousy raged through me like a storm before I was even prepared for the emotion.

His eyes. They would betray his conviction, I was sure of it. For whatever he might've been forced by his uncle to do, I'd know and feel the truth there. I'd only needed him to spin my way. But he held his back to me, falling to his knees before one of the women, grabbing her thigh as she flung a bare leg onto his shoulder. He could have tasted her. Right there in front of the entire crowd. My stomach turned. My whole body became numb.

"Little Dove," Hollis said.

But I couldn't respond. I couldn't move at all when I watched the woman dance away, and he crawled across the floor on his knees for her.

Look at me, I pleaded. *Look at me, godsdamnit.*

I needed to see it in his eyes. The repulsion. The anger.

Another woman danced forward, using a giant handheld fan of feathers to block her naked body as she twirled around him, chin low, eyes seductive as fingers trailed across his heaving chest. His head fell, and the performer flashed a wicked smile, lifting his chin and shaking a finger at him.

The crowd turned feral, laughing and clapping with the rapid tempo of the music.

I knew it wasn't his fault. I knew this show was meant to rattle me, break me, but still, I couldn't help the envy that seeped through my mind like wildfire. Orin was not mine. As much as the bands on our wrists linked us, and though he'd kissed me until the world became obsolete, neither of us had earned the right to lay claim over the other.

A hand slipped into mine, though I barely registered the way it felt, and I wasn't sure who it was. Then another hand. Soft and gentle. Thea and Paesha. My friends. Truly the greatest women I'd ever known.

Family.

The crowd knew, of course. Who he was. Who we were together. They'd come to see the Death Maiden, and now they watched her bonded husband fawn over other women because I was not and would never be truly worthy of a man's loyalty. That was what they would say. The story the Maestro spun to eviscerate me before I'd ever take the stage.

"It's not real," Thea said into my ear before her hand fell free of mine and she slipped away.

I nodded. I was far more than this envy. More than arbitrary control in a battle of wits. I didn't need to see his face to know this wasn't what Orin wanted. I needed to learn to trust. To let go of my father's voice in my ear reminding me that I was and would always be alone.

They'd removed his jacket as he danced, and I wondered how far they would go. Would they take him down to his bare skin? Would I be able to stand on the side of the stage and watch it happen? Just as my nerves vibrated, locking down my muscles, coiling deeper and deeper within me, until I didn't think I could bear to watch a single second more, his gaze finally lifted to mine.

A broken man stared into my soul, so distant from the acts performed on stage, my feet shuffled forward. The woman at my side anchored me.

"If you step on stage, you might start your timer. Or break the deal," Paesha hissed, still as stone beside me.

She was right, of course. Still, that glorious golden band, inches below the blue, throbbed on my wrist.

I am with you.

He couldn't hear me or read my mind. But the unspoken words lingered, just as he grabbed one of the women, twisted her away, and kissed her, half a second before the lights fell.

With the roar of the crowd, the stage was cleared, and each

of the performers, including my husband, was ushered off the opposite side. I didn't have time to process anything that'd happened before a drum roll sounded and the hourglass was wheeled onto the stage. Every light in the theater burst to life, just as the final stagehand made fearful eye contact with me and turned the hourglass.

The crowd fell deathly silent. My breaths, short. I'd forgotten everything about my performance, so caught in my own damn jealousy. A small push from Paesha and I was thrust onto an empty stage in the middle of a silent theater, with no instruction and now less than ten minutes to win the freedom of almost everyone in the world who mattered to me.

I looked back once, but she was already gone. Everyone was. Not a single friendly face greeted me, and you could have heard a pin drop in that theater. Something prickled beneath my skin. Something screaming at me to focus, to think, to do something other than stand here like a fool.

Under the glaring lights that left no shadow for comfort, I stood alone, facing a sea of impassive faces, the lack of amusement a palpable force. There was no grand display, no one to share the stage with. Just me, the audience, and the ticking of time.

My only saving grace was Quill.

Quill.

Pivoting to that golden birdcage, I nearly fell to my knees when I realized the swing was empty. Her power, gone...

Orin's dance was a godsdamned distraction.

I spun, running off the edge of the stage, but inches before I got there, I froze. If I fled, he'd own me. All of us. I moved back to the center of the space. With no choice left and time slipping away, I drew my blades.

The hourglass continued its unrelenting countdown, each grain a blaring reminder of our fate. Doubt began to creep in, but I pushed it aside as I stretched my muscles outward and moved, slicing silent daggers through the air in a dance of my own design.

The audience remained unmoved, a collective wall of detachment. A lone voice in the center of the crowd booed. And then another and another. Heart cracking, I glanced up to see the gleeful faces of Icharius Fern and Drexel Vanhoff on a sickening display. Blood rushed to my ears as the Maestro gestured behind me.

Hollis stepped onto the stage, his age and frailty hidden beneath the finest suit he'd worn, each golden button, each feather tucked into his hat pristine. The audience erupted. They'd come for one reason only. The greatest show they'd ever witness, just as they'd been promised. Because they might have feared me in an alley, but here, I was nothing more than a spectacle.

"What are... why are you out here? You can't be."

So much love poured from his kind eyes as he looked only at me. I couldn't stand the agony.

"Deyanira," he began.

I shook my head, stumbling away. "No. No. He cannot force me. That was the agreement. We made a deal. I won't do it."

He followed, reaching for me, but again I moved, each of my limbs growing heavy as I turned cold with fear. "Stay back, Hollis."

"The posters," he whispered. "They promised Death's Maiden."

"I *am* Death's Maiden," I roared, not at him, not for the audience, not for the honor or recognition. As a punishment to myself. For the monster I was. "They've already got me."

"Kill him! Kill him!"

The growing chant from the audience was like standing in a cell and watching the prison door slide shut, damning my eternity. I truly thought the people of Requiem were better than this. But in the end, they only wanted bloodshed. They wanted the show. And Drexel had known that. I tried to swallow my panic. To force a breath as the clock counted down.

How could I have been so damn foolish?

"Kill him! Kill him!"

Every word from the audience deepened the hue of red over my vision.

"He cannot force me, Hollis. That was the deal."

The old man stepped closer, plucking Serenity from my hand as if it were the easiest thing he'd ever done. "He found the loophole, Little Dove. He hasn't asked you."

Each step away was an effort. A chore. The world around me seemed distant, blurred, the bright lights and the sea of faces reduced to mere background noise. My hands trembled slightly, and I clutched the remaining dagger, seeking an anchor in the midst of the storm.

Trying desperately to swallow the lump in my throat, I thought of the first time I'd seen Hollis's smile. I thought of his kindness and belief in me, even when I didn't believe in myself. The Maestro might as well have sealed my fate because there was no way in this life or the next that I could or would perform the task implied but never requested.

I turned my back to the old man, clenching my teeth as I squeezed my eyes shut against the pain thrashing through my heart. A drum in the orchestra pit began a steady rhythm in time with the audience's demand for murder. This was agony. This was the greatest form of torture I would ever know.

"You must," he said, standing before me, though I hadn't heard him move. "Do you know what happens to a harbinger if they kill too many? If the bloodlust consumes them?"

I nodded, swallowing again. "I'll die for you, Hollis. I don't care. Send me to Death's court if that's the cost of your freedom."

He shook his head, his own tears glistening in the lights. "What is one life in exchange for the masses? He'll make you kill more than your soul can handle. More than an simple old man, if he gets the chance."

I could hardly see past the tears to take in every wrinkle. To admire the sharp green suit he wore. The crowd's chanting became its only entity, a life form taking shape as they demanded, not just blood, but a soul reaped by Death.

"That one soul is the purest love I've ever known," I whispered, tears falling freely.

His eyes lingered on the hourglass. "Me, too, Little Dove." He brought his shaking hands to my cheeks, forcing the theater to disappear. "Don't let this world break the goodness buried within you. Hold on to it."

"Stop it, Hollis. Don't." I began to pace. "Let me think."

I had to get away. I needed space. Time. I needed a plan. But no matter where I went, he followed. Standing too close, insisting I do the unthinkable. The stage was too small. The crowd, too loud. Every sound became an echo, a thunderstorm in my addled mind. Every move I made caused my stomach to roll until I was sure I'd be sick.

The sand.

The time.

The sadness... the devastation.

"Kill him! Kill him!"

I couldn't swallow. I couldn't breathe.

"You must give them what they demand, or it could be anyone up here tomorrow, and you will have no choice at all."

"This is not a choice."

He turned the hilt of Serenity toward me, lifted my shaking hand and forcing her into my trembling palm.

"Kill him!"

"Let me save you," he said, stepping forward until the tip pierced that beautiful suit. "I've lived the better part of my one hundred years. It's time for you to live yours."

I tried to back away again but was met with the cool wall of the hourglass.

"Kill him!"

"Deyanira," he said again as my ears rang.

"No. Send someone else out. I don't care who. Go find someone else."

"It will be me. Don't ask me to condemn another."

My chest tightened at his plea. He'd been everything a father should have been to me, and I hadn't had long enough with him. Words caught in my throat as I tried to speak, a knot of grief gripping my voice.

"I love you," he mouthed. "Do it now."

Each breath I took felt constricted, as if my chest had been clenched in a vise. His hand rested on my hand holding the blade as I stared into his unwavering eyes. And though his fingers trembled, the smile on his face was steady. Calm. Just as he had been.

The choice was no choice at all. Take twenty years from Hollis or an immeasurable amount of lives later. It could be Paesha standing here next time, and then Thea and Elowen. Even Orin. Faces of a thousand strangers floated through my vision as I pictured the mass of people Drexel would have me kill.

"I'm ready, Little Dove."

"Forgive me."

Somehow, I managed to pull back and send that blade home. Right into the heart of the best man I'd ever have the pleasure of knowing.

The crowd stilled as everything halted. When Hollis gasped,

my world became ensnared in that fleeting exhalation, accompanied by the macabre dance of blood that stained my hand when he gracefully crumbled upon the stage.

Locking eyes with the Maestro over the top of the roaring audience bursting to their feet, I made him a silent promise of death, just as the curtains fell.

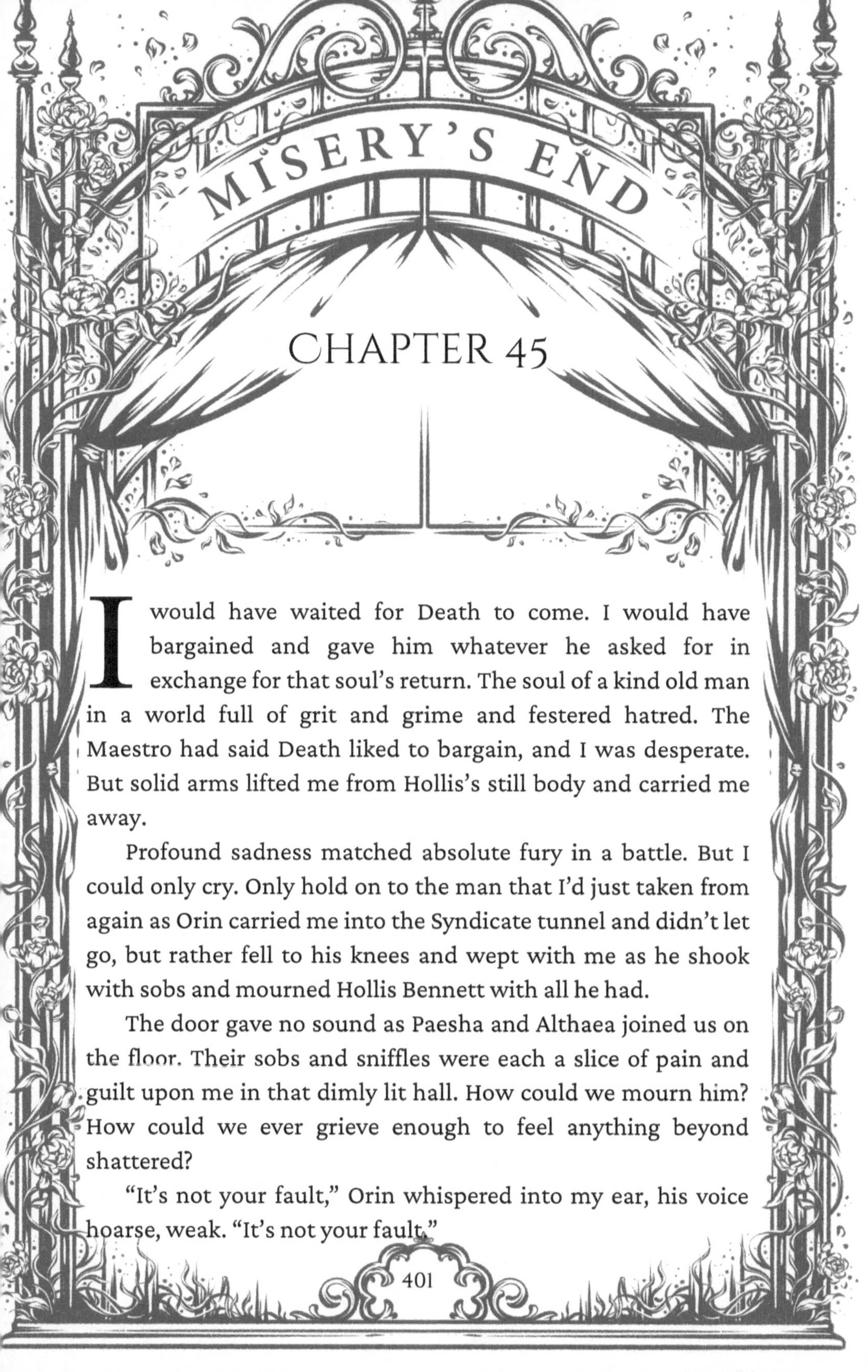

CHAPTER 45

I would have waited for Death to come. I would have bargained and gave him whatever he asked for in exchange for that soul's return. The soul of a kind old man in a world full of grit and grime and festered hatred. The Maestro had said Death liked to bargain, and I was desperate. But solid arms lifted me from Hollis's still body and carried me away.

Profound sadness matched absolute fury in a battle. But I could only cry. Only hold on to the man that I'd just taken from again as Orin carried me into the Syndicate tunnel and didn't let go, but rather fell to his knees and wept with me as he shook with sobs and mourned Hollis Bennett with all he had.

The door gave no sound as Paesha and Althaea joined us on the floor. Their sobs and sniffles were each a slice of pain and guilt upon me in that dimly lit hall. How could we mourn him? How could we ever grieve enough to feel anything beyond shattered?

"It's not your fault," Orin whispered into my ear, his voice hoarse, weak. "It's not your fault."

"Of course, it is," I cried, trying to push away from him. "I made that fucking deal. I did this."

"No, Dey. Hollis made a choice."

I shifted in Orin's arms to look into the somber face of the Huntress. "What?"

She swiped at her tears. "Drexel called us all to his office and told us what would happen. He made us choose who would be the one."

"It should have been me," Orin growled.

Thea laid her head on his shoulder, her red hair nearly glowing in the lamp light, voice raw as she whispered. "Hollis volunteered before any of us could answer, but we all tried to take his place."

I pushed out of Orin's arms, standing. "And Quill? She's fine?"

Paesha drew back, "Didn't you see her?"

"Quill wasn't in the cage when I went out."

They exchanged wary glances before everyone was on their feet.

"Quill was never mentioned in the boss's orders," Thea said.

Paesha burrowed into her power without prompting. The sweet taste of her magic filled the space, as her lashes fell to damp cheeks.

Orin paced, broad shoulders stealing the width of the hall while so many emotions must have been flooding through him. "She was there when I performed. She kept her eyes covered the whole time."

"Something happened when the lights went out, before my... before..." I couldn't say his name. It sat like embers on my tongue, as if I had no right.

"We've gotta get out of this tunnel," Paesha snarled. "It's too hard to see above ground."

"Should I go find Boo? Meet you guys back at the apartment?" Thea asked.

"Just be careful. Stay the hell away from Drexel. If he touches you, cut his fucking arm off, got it? Exchange no words. Not one. Swear it."

"I swear."

The darkness I'd been so used to rushed to the surface as Orin burrowed into his own anger. I would not begrudge him those feelings, though, nor would I step into his path as he shoved past us and took off running toward Ezra's apartment building.

"Keep trying," he roared at Paesha as we ran.

"What the hell do you think I'm doing?" she snapped back.

We soared through the tunnel. Paesha, still in a corset and lace skirts, didn't miss a step or slow at all. The moment we were out of the tunnel and racing up the stairs, the door to the apartment flew open to Elowen standing there, apron on, twisting a rag in her hand with worry. Her eyes flashed to Orin's wrist before she could likely comprehend our panic.

"What happened?" she asked, stepping to the side so we could slip in.

"Paesha?" Orin's low-timbral voice was laced with an unhinged danger even Elowen didn't balk at. Paesha coiled into her power once more.

"Please," Orin's mother whispered after several moments. "Just tell me what happened."

Several of the other Syndicate members gathered around her, and I shifted until I was all the way to the back of the room. But Orin could not answer beyond his own panic, and Paesha was concentrating on searching for Quill. That left only me to speak the words that would slice her heart. Only me.

"We won and lost in the same moment," I managed. "He made me..."

I couldn't do it.

"Orin?" Elowen whispered, staring into her son's dark eyes.

He moved to stand before his mother, softening, if only just a fraction, as he took her hands and brought them to his mouth. "You should sit down."

She shook her head, trembling as she searched his eyes. "Hollis?"

He nodded, catching her before she hit the floor. Her wail broke the last string of composure I'd held on to. I'd done this. Not just to them, but to every person I'd killed. I didn't think I could hate a single person more than I hated Death, but I was wrong. I hated myself so much more.

Stumbling down the hallway, I tried so hard to keep the tears I didn't deserve from burning my eyes. I crashed into a picture but caught it before it hit the floor. These were Paesha's precious memories. The last she had of a lover I'd taken, as well. Gritting my teeth, I rehung the frame, just to catch a glimpse of myself in the mirror hanging beside it. I looked like hell. I felt like hell. I wanted to plant a fist into the godsdamned glass as punishment to myself.

When the reflection rippled, I swallowed past the lump in my throat, shaking my head. "Not now, Ro."

But again, the glass rippled.

"If you get to pick the times, so do I."

I walked the rest of the way down the narrow hall, careful to avoid the paintings as I stepped into the room I'd had the night before. I needed to be alone. Not just in this moment, but forever. I needed to get away from everyone. They were free now. I'd done what I could.

But Quill was missing, and I couldn't slip away until I knew she had been found.

The room, once a stranger's sanctuary, had become a prison for my guilt and grief. The candlelight cast dancing shadows on the walls, eerie figures that seemed to mirror the torment within my soul. I'd been so lost in my own misery, when the bed sank beside me, I jumped. Orin's large hand closed over mine, but I pulled it away.

"If I could spare you the burden of our bonded marriage, I would, but I can't stay here." A shuddered breath rattled through me. "I'm never going to look at you and not see his face. I'm never going to be able to sleep in that house and not hear his laughter. He was the first person that didn't judge me, even when he had the most reason to. I can't imagine what it will be like for you. To even sit beside me must..."

"Ask me what I want before you run, Deyanira."

I managed a glance at his pained face before I couldn't hold the stare.

"I'm sorry about Hollis. I'm sorry about who I am."

"I know it hurts, but our hearts will heal. And what we choose to do from this day forward will always be because of those moments on the stage. I'm sorry, too. I'm sorry your life is full of suffering. But it doesn't have to be."

We sat in silence for so long I thought we might never speak again. My throbbing heart had slowed. My anger numbed as I considered what my future would really look like. How things had changed in an instant. Not just for me, but for everyone I cared about.

"I thought you had a choice, Dey," Orin said, finally. "I thought Death delivered the name, and the deed was done by will alone. And I was so angry. I blamed you for Ezra. And for the others. I thought if we could keep you in, then none of us would live in fear of your power. I was trying to save the world from you when really, I should have been saving you from me."

"Thea's here." Elowen's soft tone was full of sorrow as her gentle knock on the door broke the desperate spell over us.

Orin helped me stand, holding my hand and never letting it

go as he pulled me toward the hall. I glanced up at the mirror as we passed, and it shimmered again. Faltering for a second was all the hesitation he needed to jerk around, just to make sure I wasn't doubting the promises he'd just made.

"I have an idea," I said. "But I'll have to do it alone."

"No."

"Orin…"

"No is a complete sentence, and that's my answer."

I tugged him back toward me, pushing him against the wall. "You do not get to say such lovely things one moment and command me the next."

His fingers trailed up my skin, grazing my jawline before he leaned in, whispering, "Remember you said that."

I gripped the collar of his shirt. "It's Ro. I'm sure of it."

His eyes turned dark as he considered my words. "Ro wouldn't have taken Quill, Deyanira. She's not on their side."

"No. I don't think she is. But I think that's why Paesha can't find her. Ro's hiding her."

A line formed between his brows. "How's Ro going to hide Quill in Perth?"

He clearly didn't know about her mirrors. And I wasn't sure what to do with that. I didn't want to lie, but her truth was not mine to tell.

"How many hidden tunnels are there under these cities?" I asked.

"None that she would know about." He eyed me carefully, and I wondered how far he'd possibly let me get without following. Based on the grip he hadn't loosened, I'd bet my death it wasn't far at all.

"Dead end, I guess," I said, lifting an easy shoulder. "Maybe Thea found something."

His careful gaze lingered for only a second before walking

the rest of the way down the hall. The gentle flick of Boo's tail upon the worn couch cushion was a stark contrast to the restlessness that seemed to permeate the room. Paesha, with her intense glare, paced back and forth. Her usually composed demeanor, anxious. Elowen was nowhere to be seen, having likely vanished into the kitchen. Several other members of the clandestine Syndicate lingered around, their hushed conversations creating an undertone of tension in the air.

"Anything?" Orin asked Paesha.

"This is not happening. It can't be," she answered, with a shake of her head.

"Take a break," he ordered, pulling a chair out for her. "You're only going to exhaust yourself."

Paesha relented, though the worry never left her beautiful face. As she sank into the seat, I inched closer to her, making eye contact until she felt my stare. While Thea kept Orin's attention, I glanced toward the hall and back to the Huntress several times before she took the hint and stood once more.

"I need a drink," she said, grabbing my arm and hauling me toward the hallway. "Help me find enough glasses."

Out of view of the others, I wasted no time. "I think I know where she might be, but I'm going to have to go alone. Orin isn't going to let me, so you need to keep him distracted while I get out of here."

"You're lucky I trust you, Maiden."

"Can you keep him distracted or not?"

"Well, yeah. For about five seconds, before he's going to ask me to find you using my magic."

"But you're so, so tired," I reminded her. "You need a break."

She glared. "I can buy you five minutes."

I was halfway down the hall, headed toward the bedroom when I whispered, "Better make it six."

She never saw me snag the mirror from the wall. Still, I closed my eyes and said a silent prayer to the old gods before I set it on the floor, waited for another rippling in the silver surface, and jumped, effectively falling sideways into Ro's eerie hall of mirrors.

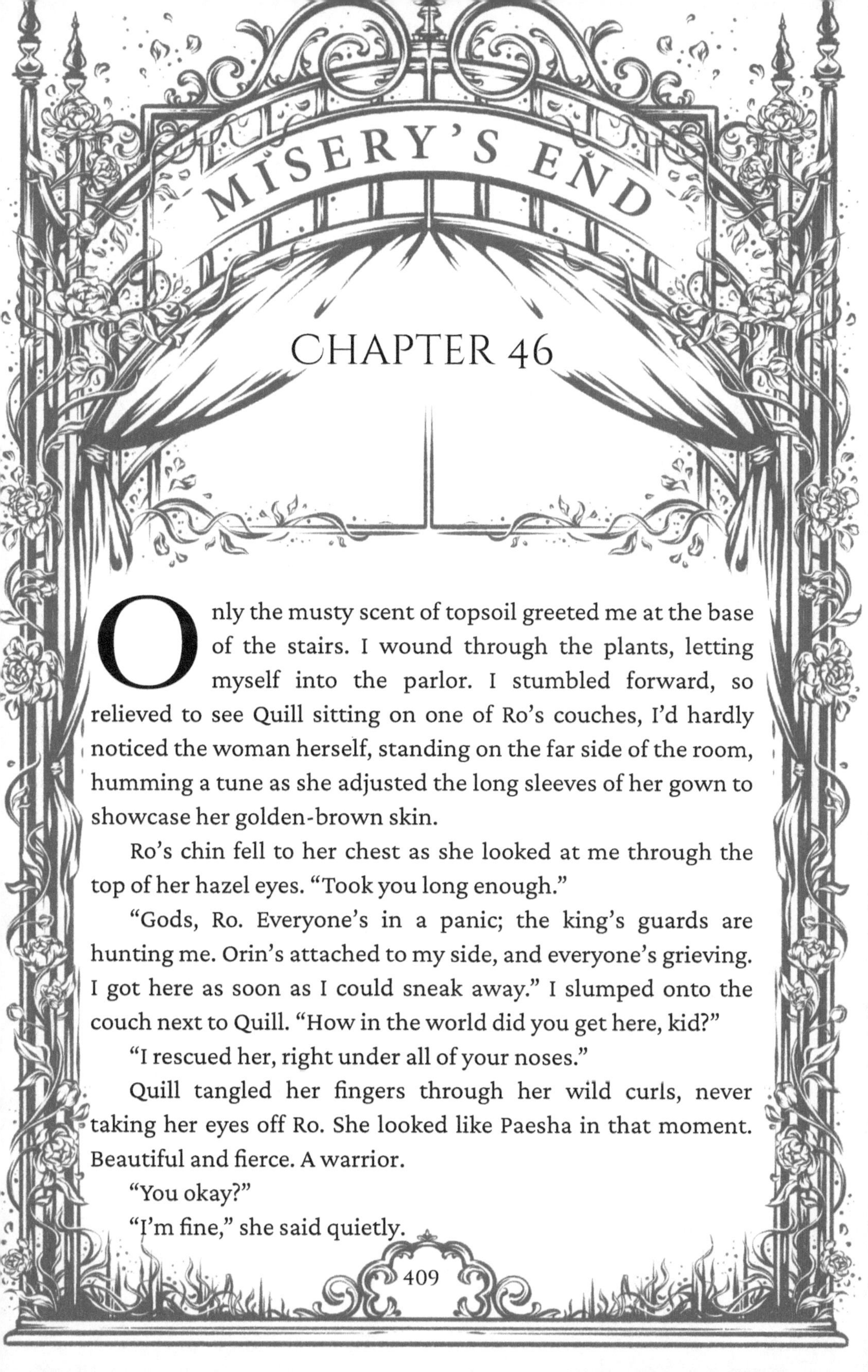

MISERY'S END

CHAPTER 46

Only the musty scent of topsoil greeted me at the base of the stairs. I wound through the plants, letting myself into the parlor. I stumbled forward, so relieved to see Quill sitting on one of Ro's couches, I'd hardly noticed the woman herself, standing on the far side of the room, humming a tune as she adjusted the long sleeves of her gown to showcase her golden-brown skin.

Ro's chin fell to her chest as she looked at me through the top of her hazel eyes. "Took you long enough."

"Gods, Ro. Everyone's in a panic; the king's guards are hunting me. Orin's attached to my side, and everyone's grieving. I got here as soon as I could sneak away." I slumped onto the couch next to Quill. "How in the world did you get here, kid?"

"I rescued her, right under all of your noses."

Quill tangled her fingers through her wild curls, never taking her eyes off Ro. She looked like Paesha in that moment. Beautiful and fierce. A warrior.

"You okay?"

"I'm fine," she said quietly.

"Wanna tell me what happened?" Sitting on the couch, I pulled her little fingers from her hair and held tightly.

She took a steady breath. "Orin was dancing, and the lights went out. Someone pulled me off my swing and covered my mouth."

I shifted closer, wrapping an arm around her, though I cut an angry glare to Ro. "I'm so sorry, Quilly."

Ro raised her palms, taking a step backward. "Careful, Maiden. That part wasn't me."

"It was the guy dressed like the other guys that took me last time. You know, the one with that mark on his face?"

I had no idea who she was talking about. "One of the new king's men?"

"Yeah. I could see over his big, old, fat fingers, so when we got to the hallway, I bit his hand and kicked him between the legs like you showed me."

A flash of pride soared through me as I pictured the small child catching the man off guard.

"I don't think it really hurt him, but he let go for a second, and I ran away. But then this lady jumped right out of a mirror in the hallway and captured me again."

Ro pointed to her arm. "For the record, she bit me, too."

"Everything's a weapon," Quill said with as much sass as she could muster.

I hugged her tighter. "Everything can be. But Ro is friends with Orin and me. She would never hurt you. She helped take care of me when I needed her, too."

The child rolled her big blue eyes. "That's what she said, too, but you said we could never trust anyone but ourselves, so I tried to get away. Now, that lady says I'm stuck here forever and ever, and I'm never going to see my dog again."

"Ro!"

"She bit me!"

Quill jumped from her seat. "You stole me. And now my friend is going to kill you, huh, Dey? 'Cause we're family."

I couldn't help my smile. So much fire in such a wild little thing. "No, kid. I'm not going to kill her. I'll yell at her really good, though, okay?"

She jerked her arms over her chest with a pout and sank back onto the couch, her pink lace dress billowing around her. Eventually, she was going to learn about Hollis, and I was sure her fire would be put out. So, I let her live in her anger a little longer because at least that meant she could still feel something.

"I jumped into a mirror to get here, and we can't leave the same way if you don't want your power exposed."

"You understand what happened here, don't you?" Ro asked, sitting across from us on a high-back chair that might've been a throne in a larger size.

"You saved her from being captured by Icharius Fern."

"Do you think Drexel would have just casually let someone take his prize?"

Quill's hands tightened in mine.

"There's something between them. I'm just not sure what it is. He said he would protect her."

"Yes. An easy lie for a notorious performer. Be careful, Deyanira. You've just given him all the reason in the world to come after you."

I stood, pulling Quill to my side. "I hope he comes. It'll save me the trouble."

She glanced at the child and back at me. "Just don't forget what you have to lose now."

"The next time Drexel Vanhoff is before me, he will be on his knees and weeping. If not for bartering away the kid, then for every other offense in his life. I'm not worried about what I have to lose, because this isn't a game. It's earned retaliation, and I will end it."

She stood, her movements as smooth as a viper rising, eyes vicious and glistening. "There's my girl."

We followed Ro through her house and back up the stairs, though I had to pull Quill through the mirror, leaving Ro behind. The girl's distrust for anything at this point was warranted, so I didn't fuss too much as we darted out of a little shack in the heart of Silbath and toward the apartment building hiding the Syndicate members.

If looks could kill when the door flew open and Orin found us standing there, they would have been digging my early grave. But Thea flew around him, grabbing Quill and swinging her, breaking the tension.

"How did you get out?" he asked as I stepped into the apartment.

"There are these fun things called windows. They're used for fresh air, sunlight, and prison escapes."

He reached around me to close the door, coming so close, his warm breath fell on my cheek as he whispered. "Sometimes I think you mouth off just to see if I'll punish you."

I grabbed his collar, lowering my voice as I countered, "You may want to reevaluate the difference between punishment and pleasure."

His snarl would have garnered a laugh, had reality not felt so heavy. But I knew these next moments would be hard. Especially as Thea sat Quill on the couch and the rest of the group moved around her. Sandwiched between Elowen and Paesha, Quill stilled as they both grabbed the child's tiny fingers.

Orin left me standing at the door to move a chair out of the way in order to squat right in front of Quill. Her curious features became somber as Thea set Boo on her lap. She looked carefully around the room, taking in each face until the pieces fell into place.

"Where's Hollis?" she asked, her tiny voice slicing every heart in the room to pieces.

Orin patted her knee. "Do you remember on your birthday last year when Hollis made you that beautiful green gown and told you it was because the color reminded him of his wife's favorite color?"

She nodded slowly, swallowing.

"And how he missed his wife so much sometimes it made him really sad?"

Another small nod.

Orin's breath was shaky; his eyes never left hers though, even when a tear slipped silently down Paesha's cheek. "Hollis is with his wife now, Quilly."

You could have heard a pin drop anywhere in the city as every person in the room stared into the face of that little girl. I held my breath, guilt crashing over me in waves when tear-filled eyes flashed to me.

"No." Her tiny word was so quiet at first, I'd questioned whether she'd spoken at all. Until she repeated herself. "No!" She pushed Boo from her lap, jumping from the couch to stand in front of me. She knew, of course. As far as she was concerned, only I had the power to do it.

"Say he's lying," she demanded.

"I wish I could."

Tiny hands struck me as she shoved and shoved. I hardly moved, but she screamed, the sadness so raw, I let myself fall to the floor, if only to be on her level.

"He was our family," she yelled. "He was mine, and you took him."

"I promise I didn't mean to."

She crashed into me, trying to push me away. I sat there on

the floor, letting her. Willing myself to feel and take her pain, though I knew it would never be enough. An ache grew so heavy in my chest that when my nose stung and my tears came, I didn't bother trying to hide any of it, not even in a room full of people that hadn't moved.

"I'm so sorry, Quilly."

"I hate you. You're not my family, Deyanira."

"Quill," Orin whispered.

The little girl spun, took one look at him, and began to wail. My throat turned to sandpaper, refusing to let me swallow. I'd never forgive myself for taking him from her. No matter what pain it'd saved the world, it wrecked hers, and that was a permanent scar on my heart. This was an agony I couldn't save any of us from.

Elowen carried Quill to a room in the back of the apartment, Boo following close behind. I stood, aiming for the door, but Orin caught my hand.

I jerked away, broken and angry all over again. "Don't touch me."

"Deyanira," Paesha said, as if she had some kind of say over me.

I shook my head, unable to see any of them beyond the tears flooding my eyes. "What kind of a monster does that to a child?"

I walked out of the apartment completely destroyed.

I STARED out over the city of Silbath, watching her come alive as the moon trekked across the sky, coaxing the seedy underbelly from its chambers, pulling the sprawling masses of sinners to their perches. Night workers took their corners, bathed in glowing streetlamps, stomping their high heels until the rats scattered and birds cawed in defiance.

Drinkers fell into step, headed toward the taverns and opium dens as if in a hypnotic state; some limped, and some were missing limbs. The signs of Requiem's deterioration shown on their bodies like sequins in a spotlight. This was my world. This was where I belonged.

"I know you're there," I said, balancing Chaos on my finger, flipping it back and forth and letting myself get lost in the muscle memory.

"Why do you always run to the rooftops?" Orin asked, stepping from the shadows to swipe Chaos from my grip.

"Solitude."

"You can't just escape this, Wife."

"I'm my own person. I can do as I please. Haven't you had enough? Aren't you tired of this yet?"

"No. Never. I want a thousand lifetimes. If you go, you're only pausing a clock on something inevitable. Because I will find you. And I will bring you back to me over and over again until you learn that I will never give up on this. You became mine the day you stood on that temple and bound yourself to me, and just because I'm free of my uncle, doesn't mean I wasn't willing to give away the rest of my freedom for you. That hasn't changed just because this world is cruel."

I forced a smile as I buried my fingers in his soft hair. "Did you just threaten to stalk me for the rest of our lives?"

He grabbed my hands, kissing my fingers. "Don't act so surprised, Wife. When have I ever let you get too far from me? I can't promise you're not going to want to bury that blade into my gut a time or two before this is all over. But I can promise I will still chase you. There will never be a part of me that doesn't crave you. Even in madness, you're my only desire. In rage and fury. In weakness and wonder. You may question whether I am sane, but I am wholly yours. For a thousand lifetimes. Eternity is not going to be long enough."

"And Quill?" I asked, skimming over his beautiful words.

"She's just a kid, Dey. She'll be okay. You'll be friends again tomorrow."

"If you think I left because of Quill, you're wrong." I stole the blade from him, sliding her into place on my thigh. "I just want to give you all space to grieve without the murderer sleeping under the same roof."

"Hollis's murderer sleeps in a four-poster bed made of iron and old money, under no roof of mine."

"Yes, and if he knows what's good for him, he's going to sleep with one eye open."

He shifted in front of me, curling a finger below my chin to force my eyes to his. "If we're going for revenge, Nightmare, we're going to need three shovels. One for my uncle and one for each of us because in the end, it will consume you, and then saving you will consume me. It's a never-ending cycle of pain and suffering, and it rarely leads to true satisfaction. He wants you to come back to him. He's likely already got a plan in place. Staying away from him is the worst thing you could do when he wants you so badly."

"The worst thing I could do to him is force him into eternal damnation with me so every moment of his afterlife is ruined by all the ways I can find to torture him."

I didn't miss the way his eyes narrowed. The way they shone, even with darkness seeping from me in waves. Leaning closer, he brushed his lips over mine, his shoulders full of tension easing as if he couldn't help himself. As if the mere contact brought him solace.

"Then I will find the shovels, and we will dig the graves."

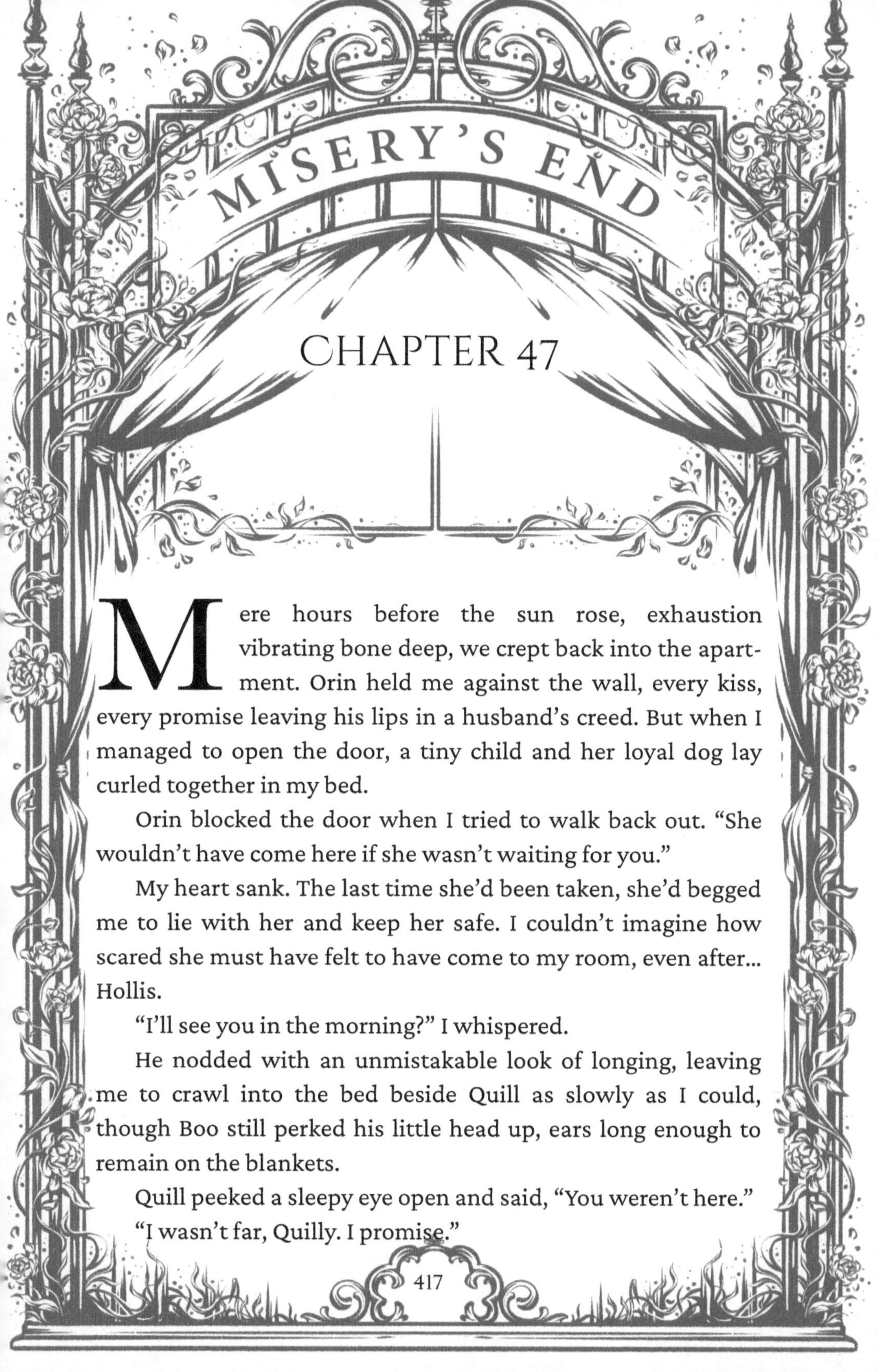

CHAPTER 47

ere hours before the sun rose, exhaustion vibrating bone deep, we crept back into the apartment. Orin held me against the wall, every kiss, every promise leaving his lips in a husband's creed. But when I managed to open the door, a tiny child and her loyal dog lay curled together in my bed.

Orin blocked the door when I tried to walk back out. "She wouldn't have come here if she wasn't waiting for you."

My heart sank. The last time she'd been taken, she'd begged me to lie with her and keep her safe. I couldn't imagine how scared she must have felt to have come to my room, even after... Hollis.

"I'll see you in the morning?" I whispered.

He nodded with an unmistakable look of longing, leaving me to crawl into the bed beside Quill as slowly as I could, though Boo still perked his little head up, ears long enough to remain on the blankets.

Quill peeked a sleepy eye open and said, "You weren't here."

"I wasn't far, Quilly. I promise."

"I'm sorry I got mad at you. I'm still sad, though."

Tucking a wild brown curl behind her ear, I whispered, "I'm sad, too."

"You had to do it?"

I lay for several minutes, tracing lazy circles into Boo's patch of white fur as I considered an age-appropriate response. I didn't think it would do Quill any favors to shelter her from this twisted world, but equally, she needed to be able to close her eyes at night.

"There was a choice. Either what happened, or I would have to do everything the Maestro says for the rest of my life. Anyone he got mad at or if he wanted to put on a show, I would have to kill them, just because he said so. He would have been able to give me any name tomorrow and I wouldn't have been able to stop it. And then your family would have remained under contract with him. And now they're free."

She cupped her little hand over my cheek, eyes falling heavy as she whispered, "*Our* family."

We stood at the foot of the fresh grave, the damp earth beneath my boots sending a shiver up my spine. Orin remained at my side, one hand tightly gripping mine, the other holding Quill's, a silent pillar of strength in the midst of shared sorrow. Elowen held a bouquet of dark lilies, her eyes glistening with unshed tears.

The chilly morning had cast a shroud of fog over the graveyard, and the city lay in slumber, as if mourning alongside us. With Althea and Paesha planted directly across from us, something here felt like peace, even if it was truly torture to speak our final goodbyes.

I'd perched on a rooftop near Tolliver's Pointe and watched

the funerals of my victims more times than I could count. But I'd never truly understood the raw pain and heartbreak until this morning, when we'd walked away with absolutely nothing beyond the finality of Hollis's life and the simple pocket watch Orin had tucked into his own coat.

I'd thought maybe something in our private funeral would be soothing, a balm, but there was nothing there beyond the visceral pain etched into the faces of those crowded around.

Collectively, we'd decided to move back to the Syndicate house, come what may with Drexel Vanhoff. We needed to let our lives move forward. And maybe he'd owned the world, but they were free of him now, and the only way they would ever truly feel that was if they stopped hiding.

When we approached, I'd expected the door to be hanging off the hinges, the whole place to be ransacked by Drexel's henchmen, out to deepen the wound, but no one had come. Nothing lay in shambles, and the weapons in Thea's forge hadn't even been touched. But that had been its own statement. He'd come eventually. It would be on his time. Which was fine, because Chaos and Serenity would be waiting.

"It's weird," Paesha said as she pushed the door open. "Even before the Maestro, I'd lived on a schedule he'd crafted. When Ezra would have to report to shows, when I'd danced at Misery's End by choice, but now, I don't know what to do with myself."

Thea nodded. "The magic is gone, and the only thing I want to do is go to the forge and work. For myself. For us."

"A new routine will come," Elowen said, pushing the door open. "We just need some inspiration."

"And a hot bath," Paesha added, climbing her way up the stairs. "I'm going to sleep. No one wake me for at least a week."

"I'm going to bed, too," Quill said, pulling Boo behind her.

Orin waited until her door shut to say anything. "We need

to do something for her, or I'm worried Hollis's death is going to be so damaging she will never fully recover."

"No one fully recovers from death, son. We just learn to breathe with it in the room."

"When do we get to breathe again?" Thea asked, leading us out of the entry hall and into the sitting room. "Because right now it feels like never."

Elowen patted her leg as she sat beside her. "It will come, Althea, I promise."

"What about the Life Maiden?" I asked from the door. "Why don't we all shift focus to finding her? Give Quill a new purpose."

"I was thinking more like a horse or something," Orin said.

"I think you might have to accept that the Life Maiden is truly not here, Deyanira. Maybe there was too much corruption in the world for her to be born."

I shook my head. "It just doesn't make sense. I am her counterpart. We are the cost for each other. How can I exist and not her?"

Orin wrapped an arm around me. "I know how much this means to you, Dey. Maybe we take a few days to make sure Drexel isn't sitting around waiting, and then we head to the library in Perth. See if we can find some answers. Probably not where the Life Maiden is, but we could try to follow history back to the end of the wars and see what we can learn about the first one."

"That's something, I guess."

We sat in silence for several moments before Thea jumped up and ran out of the room, calling over her shoulder. "I know what we need."

"Was that a complete thought?" I called after her.

She came back, holding one of Elowen's pans.

"Thea," the older woman warned, tucking her dark hair behind her ear. "Thea, don't you dare."

She smiled excitedly, her freckles distorting as she scrunched her nose. "I'll turn it back, I promise."

"Last time you said that, I ended up with three knives instead of the four you started with."

Thea looked at me, but I threw my hands up defensively. "I haven't stolen a knife in forever."

"You're supposed to back me up here, Dey. This is important."

"Fine. I stole the knife for overnight snacking in my room."

"Real convincing." Orin smirked. "Great team player, this one."

"Can we please get back to the brilliant idea?" I asked, jutting my chin toward the pan in Althea's hand.

"Yes," she said as she rubbed a palm over the flat side of the skillet, then spun it until it changed into a building before our eyes.

"It'll take me a little while to work out the logistics, but we could let Quill help with the artwork, and we'd need to figure out the water, but..."

"A bathhouse," I breathed, peeking through the large arched windows to the sunken craters in her imagined floor. "Could you really manage it?"

"That's a big project, Althea."

But Orin plucked the metal box from her hands, spinning it to take in the details. "We could pump water from the river if we dig a trench at an angle, and if we used the forge and the right piping, the fire could double as a heating element for the water."

"I can handle design and all the pipework. We'd just need glass for windows and stone for the floor. Everything else can be metal." Thea bounced on her toes, so excited it was contagious.

"Imagine," Elowen said. "Our own bathhouse."

"We could even run a pipe to the kitchen for hot water," Orin added. "You'd have to pump a lever to get it here, though, but I bet Thea could figure it out."

Orin's mother sighed. "Keep the pan, Thea. It'll be a worthy loss."

ALTHEA WAS A GENIUS. At breakfast the next day, she'd introduced the idea to Quill and convinced her she was going to need a lot of help with the design. The kid took it very seriously, stealing all the paper she could find in the house to jot down her ideas until they'd settled on a plan together. Paesha joined the plan-making, and by the time Orin and I slipped away a few days later, they were already thoroughly distracted from the loss of Hollis. Quill had cried a few times before bed, but I'd diligently climbed in with her and Boo, staying well beyond the rhythmic snoring. Lying beneath the silver moon shining into Quill's bedroom, for the first time in a long time, I felt like we were all going to be okay. And somehow, life was going to become simpler, though the lingering threat of Drexel still sat upon our minds.

"LOOK AT THIS ONE." Orin slid a book across the long wooden desk at the library, leaving a streak in the dust. "It talks about the final battle."

Upon entering the library for the first time, he'd stumbled backward, out the door, and all the way to the street to stare up at the old building again, just to make sure it was in fact the library and not an abandoned temple. We figured it had been at least a decade since anyone had been here. And while it smelled of old wax and leather binding, the decay had started creeping in, eating at the wooden floors, vines breaking through the windows to creep up the walls. Thea decided once they finished the bathhouse, this would be her next adventure. And there was a promise in that. A way to help the world we could all be a part of, even if we never found the Life Maiden. But still, we tried to make sense of it all.

I thumbed through the ancient pages, relying on the dim light of several candles as I turned each page tenderly, reading of bloodshed and loss while Orin stared at me intently. His heated gaze was more distracting than he'd likely planned for it to be.

"It's weird because the way this is written, it seems like the gods were still involved in these battles. And the world, so much larger than just Perth and Silbath."

"I thought so, too," Orin said, shoving another book at me. "But look at this."

"I've seen this before." I ran my fingers over the map. "It's the same one from Drexel's office."

"Right. Two cities."

"But the temples are all named here. As if the gods were still around." Closing the book, I set it in the pile of things we'd found useful. "My father always told me when we were at war, the gods had abandoned us, and Death came and gifted everyone a hundred years of immortality in order to save us from each other."

"According to these books, the gods hadn't abandoned us at the end of the war. That happened later."

"But why?"

Orin sighed, stretching, leaning so far back in the chair that the hem of his shirt lifted, showing a glimpse of his muscled body and dark veins. "I guess that's a question for another day. Let's go see how the others are doing. I'm exhausted."

Rubbing my eyes, I nodded. "Me, too. And honestly, I'm starting to wonder if this is a lost cause."

"Of course, it is. If she could have been found, I think Paesha would have done it by now."

"You don't have to come, Orin. I don't mind doing this by myself."

He circled the table, closing the distance to rub my shoulders. "It's important to you that we exhaust all our options. So that's what we'll do. If you told me you wanted to find a way to reach the moon, I'd be here for that, as well. Your desires are mine because you are mine, Wife. And then, when all else fails, we'll find something else to occupy our time."

Standing, I spun to wrap my arms around him. "What did you have in mind?"

Something dark crossed his face as his dangerous gaze raked over my body. "Nothing decent. I can promise you that."

"Thank the gods. I hate decency."

He stroked a finger over my bottom lip, heating me thoroughly. "I was hoping you'd say that." Brushing a gentle kiss on my lips, he grabbed my thighs and lifted me onto the desk, deepening the kiss until every part of my body answered to his touch.

When he gripped my throat, before sliding his hands back, holding the dark waves of my hair to bring me closer, I moaned against his mouth. We'd been alone here before. We'd taken these moments for stolen kisses, but he always stopped. Always pulled away.

This time, when he broke the connection, I snagged his shirt and brought him forward again. Maybe he wasn't ready to cross that line with me. Maybe he was still trying to work through it all, but I was so ready for him. Desperate for him, even. Each night, I ached for him. Dreamed of him opening the door to my room and crawling into my bed. But he never did.

With Orin's body pressed to mine, I could tell he was hard for me. I knew he wanted more than passionate kisses in an old library. The way he clenched his fist at his side, the way he held his breath. He was holding back.

"What's wrong?"

"You'll never understand it." His strained whisper intertwined with his breath hot on my collarbone as he kissed my neck. "I've spent a lifetime reining myself in, controlling everything around me. Every move I've made. But this is a new kind of torture."

Drawing back, I took in the pain on his face. "Why?"

"Both of the villains in this world want you. And it's made me believe that maybe there are three."

"Icharius and Drexel... who is the third?"

"Me. Because should any harm come to you, Deyanira, I will become the thing of nightmares. I will bring this world to wreckage. It's the only thing I can give you. My only promise."

I reached for his face, stroking the smooth, hard edges, staring into the depth of his amber eyes. "I can protect myself. I don't need anything more than this, Orin. Only you. All of you."

He grabbed the back of my neck and jerked me forward, controlling everything as he kissed me once more, full of possession and steeped in desire. "You don't know what you're asking for."

I locked my hands behind his neck. "I know exactly what I'm asking for. What are you so afraid of?"

He smirked, a glint in his eyes as he leaned his head against mine. "Whatever this is, it's not fear. It's fucking obsession. It's the chase. The capture. The godsdamned overturn of everything I thought I knew about what a man and woman should be. I want to savor every moment for eternity. I won't rush, because the craving, the anticipation, is intoxicating. I will drag these moments out for as long as I can because once we cross that bridge, Wife, we burn it to the ground and never look back. Nothing else will matter to me."

A smile played on my lips. "That sure of yourself?"

He growled, biting my earlobe until a shiver crept down my spine. "I'm not just sure; I'm absolutely, irrevocably, and undeniably certain that when I take you, we will be lost to each other for the rest of time."

And though I wanted nothing more than to believe every promise he delivered so perfectly, he'd all but admitted he was holding himself back. This marriage was born of beautiful lies, yet even flowers couldn't escape the taint of poison in a seed. There was more to Orin's story than what he'd allowed himself to share.

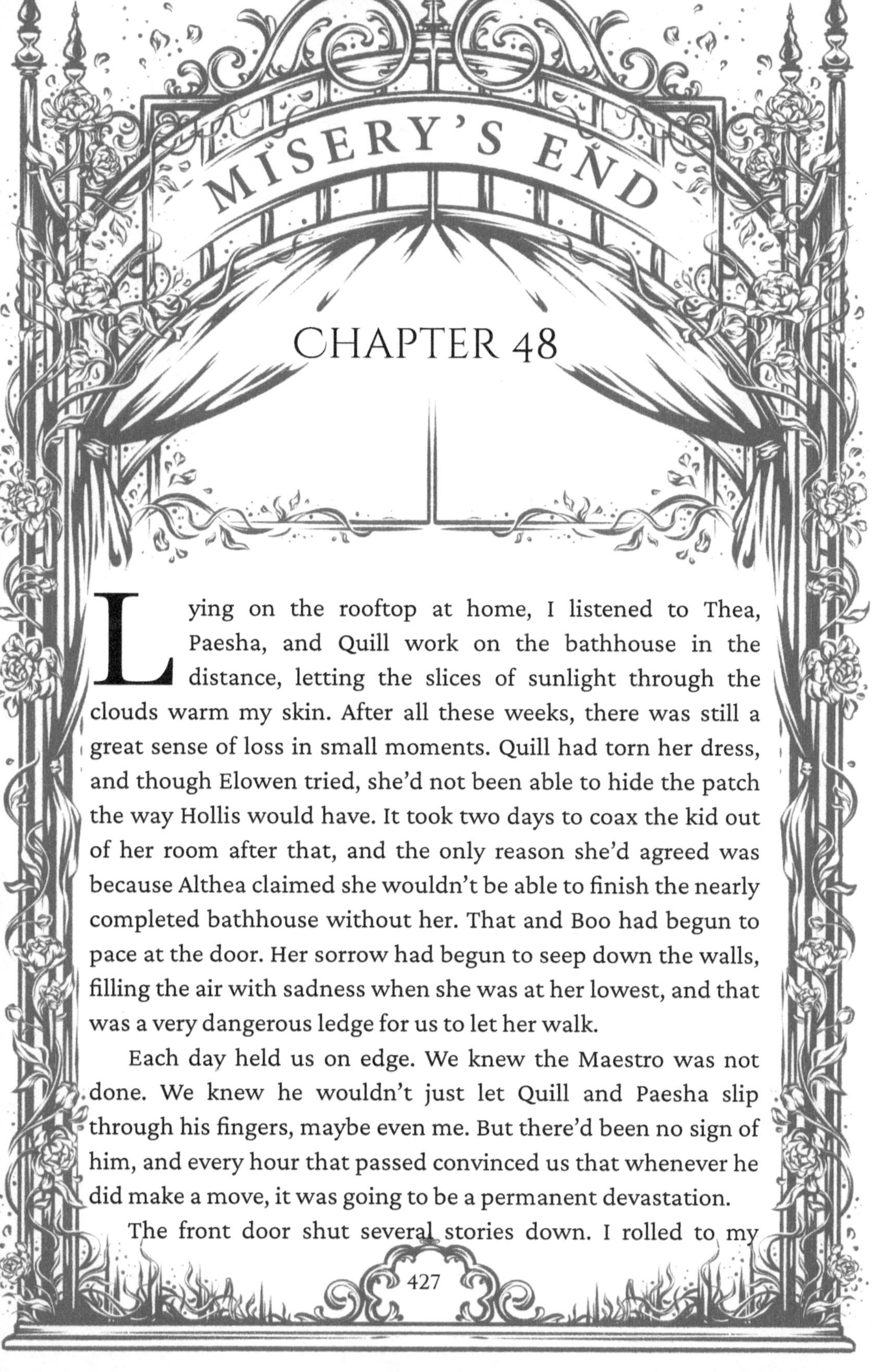

CHAPTER 48

Lying on the rooftop at home, I listened to Thea, Paesha, and Quill work on the bathhouse in the distance, letting the slices of sunlight through the clouds warm my skin. After all these weeks, there was still a great sense of loss in small moments. Quill had torn her dress, and though Elowen tried, she'd not been able to hide the patch the way Hollis would have. It took two days to coax the kid out of her room after that, and the only reason she'd agreed was because Althea claimed she wouldn't be able to finish the nearly completed bathhouse without her. That and Boo had begun to pace at the door. Her sorrow had begun to seep down the walls, filling the air with sadness when she was at her lowest, and that was a very dangerous ledge for us to let her walk.

Each day held us on edge. We knew the Maestro was not done. We knew he wouldn't just let Quill and Paesha slip through his fingers, maybe even me. But there'd been no sign of him, and every hour that passed convinced us that whenever he did make a move, it was going to be a permanent devastation.

The front door shut several stories down. I rolled to my

stomach, watching Orin cross the yard more quickly than normal. When he looked over his shoulder toward the roof, I ducked, convinced he was trying to make sure I didn't see him. For all the distance we'd come, he still had secrets. And maybe I should have let him have that space, but there were promises of a future between us, and I held nothing back.

Curiosity got the best of me, and I was chasing after him before I realized what I was doing. We'd never discussed his ability to kill after that first conversation, but there were still unanswered questions, and the last time he'd snuck out like this, there'd been a singular purpose.

That was night, and this was day, though, so maybe I'd had it all wrong. Still, I followed him through Silbath, taking the long way around Misery's End, crossing the stone bridge into Perth, past the clock tower, turning south through the grave-yard, and heading directly into the Scarlet District.

Paranoia crept over me as I kept an eye on my back now more than ever. I'd seen the extra patrols of guards, had caught the way Orin avoided certain streets bogged down by Drexel's henchmen wearing long coats and twisted mustaches, as if they wanted to be the Maestro. He'd avoided going anywhere near the temples, his hatred for the gods shining through, even in the paths he chose to take.

Orin moved with a direct purpose into a narrow alleyway between two towering apartment buildings. I kept my distance, watching him from above, but as if he could feel me watching, he turned, studying the broken cobblestone streets around him. I ducked, holding my breath as I counted to ten, giving just enough time for him to pour over his surroundings. When I peeked my head up, he'd turned away, leaning against a building once more.

Drawing Hollis's pocket watch, he studied the time, danger rolling off him as a door swung open and a man emerged, holding tightly to the elbow of another man. Neither of which I recognized.

Still, Orin was quick. A strike to the throat and the man being detained was free to run. And that's exactly what he did. Though limping, he never once looked back to his savior as he bolted away. The other man, though? He'd fallen to his knees, hands held before him as if in prayer, begging my husband to show him mercy. I didn't need to hear the words spill from his trembling lips to know the darkness in Orin's eyes at this moment.

The ground seemed to rumble for a flash of a second, and the man collapsed to the ground, no longer moving. Orin's shoulders sank. He didn't bother checking for a pulse. As if time were not on his side, he raced down another alley, his coat billowing behind him.

I crouched, frozen in shock. I'd seen it happen before, but I'd somehow convinced myself it wasn't real. That it couldn't be. Even with the confession. I waited moments more, anticipating Death this time, confident he'd come, take the fallen's soul, and return to his home. But again, it wasn't Death. Only a creeping shadow, there and gone before anyone would know what happened.

I wasn't sure if I could catch Orin. I thought maybe I'd be better off heading home. But sheer curiosity forced me to hop across an adjacent alley, letting the sun set as I chased a man that always knew exactly the right words to say to hold my heart in his hands. Even when I knew I should have been more careful with it.

With each footstep, I remembered his words in my mind. His promises to choose me when I thought he hated me. The way he kissed me. The way his eyes burned for me. Whatever his secret, whatever he thought he was protecting me from, I could still feel myself falling deeply, maddeningly in love with him. Poor bastard.

On the backside of an opium den, closer to my father's castle than I was comfortable, he stopped again, this time for less than two minutes before a stunning woman emerged from the back door, her breathtaking beauty betraying her identity as she hugged my husband and pulled him down the street, to which he diligently followed.

When Ro and Orin slipped into an old building, I followed right behind them, jealousy expanding like a wildfire in my heart. I wanted so desperately to trust both of them, but this felt wrong. This felt like a secret betrayal before I'd even gotten an answer. I'd learned over these past months that I truly knew nothing of people. Of friendship or family or love or loss. So how could I claim to know anything about jealousy?

The hallways of the apartment building were narrow and smelled of old piss. Stained carpet and dented doors filled the space as I held my breath and followed the echo of Ro's heels all the way to the back end of the building, around a corner, up a single flight of stairs, and further down another hallway. When I'd nearly caught up to them, turning the final corner, I drew up short. Could my heart really handle what I might find in this moment? Did I really want to see them embrace as lovers or see his lips on another woman? Though my heart ached at the mere thought, I was not a coward. And I would never be able to look at myself in the mirror if I walked away.

The door to the apartment they sank into was left ajar. And I'd never felt like a bigger fool than I did, peeking inside to find Orin's eyes locked with mine, arms crossed over his chest, tapping his fingers as if he'd been there for hours, waiting for me to arrive.

"Took you long enough," he said with an eyebrow raised.

I peeked around him to see Ro sitting on a golden couch that looked oddly similar to one I'd seen in her home.

"Where are we?"

He flashed a curious glance at Ro and then back at me. "You've never been here?"

"Of course, she has; she's just confused." She pinned me with a stare, but I shook my head, unwilling to play her game.

"No. I've never been here. And just as I won't let you lie to me, Orin, I'm not going to lie to you."

Ro rubbed her face, the eye roll almost audible. "Fine. Come sit down. Both of you. Where to start..." She tapped a finger to her chin, scooting to the edge of her ornate couch. "Dey first, I think.

"She's never been here because I have another home I usually invite her to. That covers that."

And it did, I supposed.

"Orin, on the other hand, is harder. Perhaps we should have some tea. Maybe something stronger?"

I had barely sat down before pulling away from Orin's grip on my hand and standing. "Just get to the point. I've been patient long enough."

"Your husband has the ability to kill, yet he is not a Death Lord."

I tucked my chin to my chest, pinning her with a stare. "I've gathered that much already."

Orin cleared his throat, reaching for me, but I took a step back. "Start talking."

"It's not like your power. Death doesn't come. I don't get names. I just... how do I explain this?" He turned to Ro, but she only lifted a shoulder.

"Try the beginning," I said, throwing my hands on my hips.

Ro cut in. "Deyanira, sit down."

"I'm fine standing. None of this explains why you two are sneaking around Perth."

"Remember that time when you locked yourself in your father's dungeons, and the madness set in so deep you clawed your way free, and…" Ro's voice trailed off, but it didn't stop the embarrassment and shame from crawling across my skin. "You spent a good amount of time lost in the opium dens, and I basically had to drag you out, kicking and screaming?"

Without directly telling him, I'd said as much to Orin in the past. Still, I hated the way that memory haunted me. I sank into the couch, ignoring the pity on his face. My voice was little more than a whisper. "How could I ever forget the way they ran? The screams. The bloodshed. There were twenty-three deaths that day. Twenty-three people that happened to be standing in my path. I can never let that happen again. The madness that has never left or the nightmares from what I became. I tried to lock myself away, and it saturated me in bloodlust. So badly, the only thing I could see beyond the red were the faces of my victims as they fell. I killed until I found a way to stop. But I'll never forget it."

"The madness?" Orin asked gently.

"I'm not a terrible person."

He narrowed his eyes. "Of course, you aren't. Why would you need to defend that point to *me*, of all people? You've seen the darkness I harbor, Dey. You know most of this truth, though the words haven't been spoken."

Managing a breath, I nodded. "Tell me what's happening."

"I go to a place that's consumed by hatred. Slowly, over days, sometimes weeks, I become dark. Hateful. Hard. It's my own kind of madness, all-consuming until I kill someone."

I swallowed my pride, reaching for his hand. "Anyone?"

"Anyone. But Ro… she helps me. She finds the criminals, and they are who I hunt. Because I have to. Not because it was ordered by Drexel. He doesn't know. It's my choice. Otherwise…"

I knew that fear so intimately it hurt. "If you… I don't understand. The abhorrence you had for who I was, was real. Why would you hate me so much if you knew why I had to do it, too? If you'd experienced what I did?"

"I told you. I thought you had a choice, just like I do. And with the people that are missing, it just made sense that you were killing them. But I never meant to hate you, Deyanira. Not one day. When the darkness sinks in, it makes me hate everything. Even my own mother. And unless I'm with you, every day is a chore."

I shook my head, pulling away. "What do you mean, *unless you're with me?*"

He shifted closer, taking my hand, stroking a thumb over my knuckles as he cast his eyes to the floor. "That night in your room… I wasn't there to marry you. I was there to kill you."

A single sharp breath hissed between my teeth. "But I thought your uncle forced you to marry me."

Ro cleared her throat. "Be careful what truths you seek. Some are harder than the lies you find so comfortable."

"Stay out of this," I ordered, eyes like daggers as I threw a glare at her, pulling away from Orin again.

"Deyanira."

"No. You don't get to do anything but tell the truth. If one more lie slips from those lips… so help me gods…"

"My uncle had nothing to do with me marrying you. That's why he punished me during every show. Icharius was pissed, but the boss was furious. He's always called the shots and pulled the strings on the streets, and I slighted him."

"Tell me why, Orin. Why did you marry me?"

He looked at Ro, so much anguish on his face it physically broke me. But rather than respond, she simply stood and left the room. Likely seeking the drink she'd hoped for at the beginning of this.

My heart wasn't ready. My mind wasn't. Not for him to stand, take a knee before me, and drop his head. "I'll never be able to redo that day. And in many ways, I'm not sorry for it. You've been my match and my balm. The only thing I have ever truly needed in this world."

"Enough with your pretty words." I slipped Chaos from my thigh on instinct, bringing the blade below his chin to force his eyes to mine. "Tell me why you married me."

He swallowed, never moving away from my dagger, letting it nick his neck rather than allow a sliver of more space between us. Holding eye contact, he shrugged out of his coat, rolling the sleeve of his shirt to show me the black veins creeping down his muscled forearm. Slowly, he used his other hand, sliding it over my wrist. The darkness faded, accompanying my gasp.

"When I kill, it stays the magic. But when I touch you, it recedes. I accidentally grabbed you that night, and it changed everything. I didn't know what else to do. It was death or marriage once you woke, and... I'm sorry."

The betrayal was more lethal than the knife in my hands. Inch by inch, I felt the crack and then the shatter of my heart. Everything had been a lie, and he carried that willingly. The threat of tears burned like acid, their scalding trails etching the painful truth deeper into my wounded soul.

"You could have told me so long ago." I ground my teeth together, letting anger cover the sadness. "You let me be the fool in front of everyone. Did they all know?"

He nodded, a tear slipping down his cheek, landing on the cold, unforgiving steel of the knife pressed against his throat. "Not about the murders, but they knew about the madness."

"That's why they let me stay," I whispered, the blade dropping to the floor. "It's all been a façade. Even Quill? And Hollis? Gods, tell me Ro didn't send you to kill me."

He opened his mouth to speak and quickly closed it. And that was all the confirmation I needed. She wasn't perfect, but she was all I had then. And even she had wanted me dead.

I ran until I couldn't hear him calling my name anymore. Until the shadows were no longer a comfort to me, and the rain had soaked through every layer of clothing I'd worn. Until the crows scattered at my presence and the rats hid among the alleyways. And in that moment, pausing at the end of a street I hardly recognized, I realized I was truly alone, with nothing but my slain trust and the bitter taste of a life I once thought I knew.

How could I go back? How could I look any of them in the face knowing what they'd all been hiding? I'd freed them. I was willing to be imprisoned by a man I thought to be the greatest villain of this world... and for what?

I wasn't sure when my tears ran out and only rain fell upon my skin. Soaked to the bone and weary, I wandered aimlessly, so lost in my own misery, I let my guard down. So much that I hadn't noticed the looming silhouette of a broad man standing beneath the glow of the streetlamp, nor the cane planted into the ground to steady him.

"Is our precious Death Maiden in distress?" The squeaking of Drexel's leather gloves gripping his cane tighter felt like its own kind of warning.

I said nothing, unable to conjure the anger swelling within me any more than the numb sadness. He stepped closer, the clack of his walking stick muted by the sodden cobblestones.

"I know you think I'm a scoundrel, Deyanira, but I am a giving man. Tell me what you want in this world, and I will see it done. There are no limits to my power."

Ice filled my veins. "I want nothing from you. I can't be bought."

He chuckled, the deep red curl of his mustache bouncing with the sound, mimicking the scar on his face. "Everyone has a price."

For a second, I wondered if I did. If there was anything this man could do to take away the betrayal wreaking havoc within me. But I knew better. I knew he would only see that pain tripled in size. He was everything I thought he was, including Orin's scapegoat. And I hated him with such a visceral passion, I couldn't see past the red lining the edges of my vision. Serenity was a cool comfort in my hand as I charged for him, stopping only a single step away. "Tell me the price for your life, Maestro."

He lifted his cane, attempting to swipe my blade away, but I grabbed the end and jerked him forward until he sat at the edge of Serenity. Again, he smiled, his jagged scar setting me on edge. I'd never looked at the man as anything more than a villain, but in this moment, as he faced his own death, he was attractive in his own right. Rough, confident, everything a man should and shouldn't be in one single package. I could see a hint of Orin behind those eyes. Even a dash of Elowen on his face. He'd been only a person once, until this world twisted him into something far more vile.

"You don't have the nerve, Maiden."

My flesh rippled at his spitting use of my title. As if disdain was not a strong enough emotion to convey the jealousy over my power.

"You have no idea what I'm capable of right now, Drexel."

"You're right. Let's play a game, shall we? Take that beautiful blade and plunge it into my heart." He gestured to the ground. "Watch me take my final breaths right here in this puddle."

I inched forward. I wanted to. Gods, I did. If not for the years and years of suffering he'd brought to this world, then for my own aching heart. But even now, at the pinnacle of my own sorrow, I knew his death would offer no solace. Still, I could free the world from at least one of its problems.

"Do it," he purred. "Bury the blade, Deyanira. Or are the rumors true? Have you not the conviction without the command from Death?"

I hesitated for only a moment. I could and would do this. A hardness settled over me with my decision as I drew Serenity backward, watching for the second those eyes turned from calculated to cold fear.

But Drexel Vanhoff was only the distraction, one Icharius Fern probably didn't need, as an army of men stepped from the shadows, surrounding me with faces hard and weapons drawn. I didn't bother fighting them. I simply slackened my shoulders, letting Serenity clatter to the saturated ground, no longer feeling an ounce of attachment to it as a hundred burly hands grabbed me.

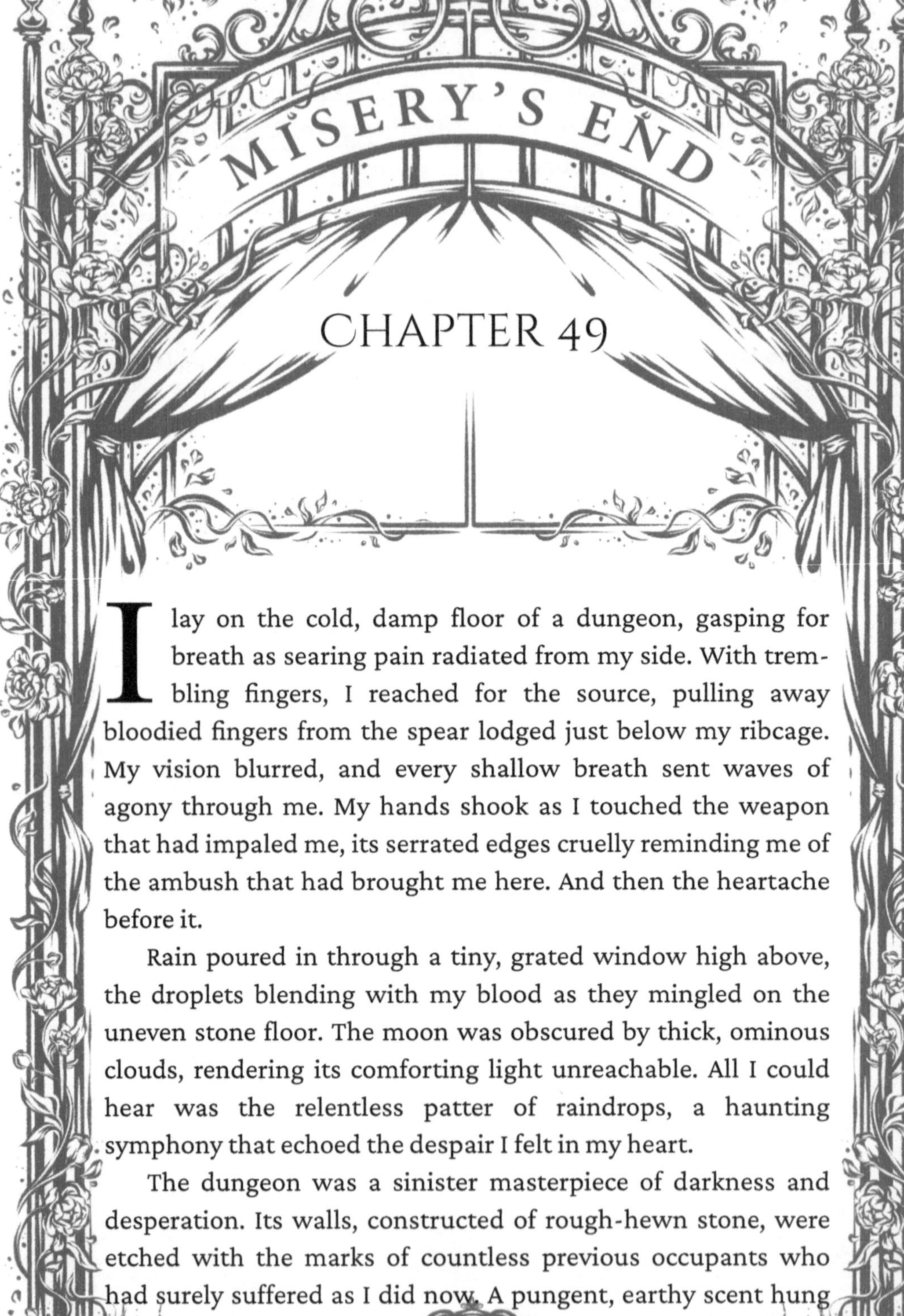

CHAPTER 49

I lay on the cold, damp floor of a dungeon, gasping for breath as searing pain radiated from my side. With trembling fingers, I reached for the source, pulling away bloodied fingers from the spear lodged just below my ribcage. My vision blurred, and every shallow breath sent waves of agony through me. My hands shook as I touched the weapon that had impaled me, its serrated edges cruelly reminding me of the ambush that had brought me here. And then the heartache before it.

Rain poured in through a tiny, grated window high above, the droplets blending with my blood as they mingled on the uneven stone floor. The moon was obscured by thick, ominous clouds, rendering its comforting light unreachable. All I could hear was the relentless patter of raindrops, a haunting symphony that echoed the despair I felt in my heart.

The dungeon was a sinister masterpiece of darkness and desperation. Its walls, constructed of rough-hewn stone, were etched with the marks of countless previous occupants who had surely suffered as I did now. A pungent, earthy scent hung in the air, a combination of mildew and the lingering stench of misery.

The cell was barely large enough for me to stretch out my aching body. Chains dangled from the walls, their rusty links clinking with every gust of wind. The flickering torchlight in the corridor outside only deepened the shadows within, casting eerie, dancing shapes that seemed to mock my predicament.

In the far corner, a rat scuttled by, its beady eyes gleaming with malevolent intelligence as it disappeared into a crack in the wall. The rat, it seemed, was the only other living creature in this forsaken place, and its presence only served to remind me of how utterly alone and vulnerable I was.

I closed my eyes, trying to shut out the pain, the misery, and the relentless sound of the rain. But even in the blackness behind my eyelids, I could see the faces of Drexel and Icharius, the men who had orchestrated my abduction, and beyond that, Orin sat there, too. Far more handsome, much more dangerous, and everything I thought I needed in this world.

But the biggest fear I held in these moments wasn't the rats nor the weapon I'd eventually have to remove; it wasn't the rain or the chill that set into the air or the king that would eventually descend those steps. It was falling asleep. It was standing in Death's court and being given the name of a person I wouldn't be able to hunt. It was the madness. Always the madness. And with that truth came an ounce of compassion for Orin and the decision he'd made to trap me into a bonded marriage. Though I could never forgive him for the lie, I'd forgive him for the choice.

The pain in my side was unbearable. My fingers fumbled along the length of the spear, slick with my own blood, until they found the grip at the end. Gathering every ounce of strength left in my battered body, I took a deep, shuddering breath, and with a clenched jaw, I seized the spear's shaft.

The agony intensified as I pulled and twisted, the sensation of the weapon being torn from my flesh sending waves of nausea through me. My vision blurred, and I bit down hard on my lower lip to stifle a scream, refusing to give anyone listening the satisfaction of hearing my pain.

Just as I felt the spear leave my body, the door at the top of the stairs swung open with a creak. Panic rose, mingling with the searing agony. I had to hide the weapon, to buy myself a few precious moments.

With a desperate heave, I shoved the spear toward a filthy straw pallet in the corner of the cell, gritting my teeth against the blinding rip that threatened to consume me. The spear disappeared into the darkness just as the first footsteps echoed down the stone stairwell.

I sank back against the cold, damp floor, my breath coming in ragged gasps, my blood-slicked hands trembling. The figure in the doorway came into view, a silhouette framed by the flickering torchlight from the corridor.

"I see you're awake and trying to be resourceful." Icharius turned to a guard, gesturing for them to open my prison door.

"B-but, Your Grace," the guard protested.

Icharius was fast, striking like a serpent, his movements so quick before my blurred vision, I might not have registered it at all, had the man not crumbled to the floor the second after his neck was snapped.

"I do so hate it when they disobey a direct order. We're still in training, you see. They haven't quite learned to fear me as much as they fear you, Maiden."

He stepped to the side, his boots sliding across the pool of my blood so I could see the darkness rise from the ground and smother the man, just as it had with Orin's victim.

I swallowed my gasp. "Who are you?"

Plucking the key from the fallen guard's belt, he turned it in the lock and strode forward fearlessly, kneeling as he brushed a finger over my bruised face. "I was born a Death Lord, your male counterpart, long before you came to this world, Maiden. I think the real question is, who are you?"

"That's not possible," I grunted, willing myself to sit up, holding my hand over the wound at my side. I had no idea who'd given me this particular injury. If it were him, I would die. "I am Death's Maiden. I've seen his realm hundreds of times."

"Yes, those hellhounds before the gates really are something, are they not?"

He'd been there, then. I glanced down at his hand, searching for a name, but he wore leather gloves, likely to keep his secret. He'd conquered the whole world with his lie. No wonder the Maestro hadn't shut him down, nor challenged him when he came for Quill. He knew. And he was afraid.

"Andros!" he shouted, sending a jolt of pain through me when I flinched.

The next guard came warily down the steps, each careful move measured. "Yes, Your Grace?"

"You will come and sit in the cell with our precious Maiden. I'm told her will is strong, and I am to break it."

Nothing made sense to me. I squeezed my eyes shut, willing my vision to focus as weakness in every limb of my body pulled me toward the ground.

"Oh, no. You must stay awake, Maiden. I have so many delicious plans for us." He gripped me by my hair, tilting my head back until I winced, the pain reverberating through my entire body. "I'd heard you went gallivanting in the temple of Eiria." He twisted my face, looking into my eyes, but not fully. Instead, at the white lashes, no doubt. "If you kill this man, I will let you sleep and heal."

"Go fuck yourself," I mumbled.

The king's blond hair fell across his brow as he laughed.

"Maybe later, sweetheart." Grabbing my arm, he yanked the black leather sleeve up, dark eyes pinned to the gold band that became his ultimate embarrassment. "I've dreamed of this moment."

As he drew the ax from his side, I screamed, scrambling away, no matter the pain it caused, adrenaline forcing me to unsteady feet. I snatched the spear from where I'd hid it, holding it toward the king, though I knew I wouldn't be strong enough to impale him. I was hardly able to stand.

The moonlight crept across the cell, the clouds giving way just enough to showcase his sinister smile as he nodded. "The ferocity is inspiring, dear. Come, Andros. I believe she needs a night to sleep on it."

A foul stench filled my prison as the guard stepped away, walking as if he'd just ridden a horse for three days. He'd shit his pants watching me go for that weapon, and I couldn't help but feel bad for him as he passed over his fallen comrade and followed the king up the stairs.

I stood there for over an hour, muscles trembling for relief, while I stared at the body on the floor, using the weapon that'd broken me as leverage to hold my body up. I needed a plan, and I needed it yesterday. What did forcing me to kill give him? Why would that be important to him? He knew who I was, but what was happening that seemed to be breaking the rules of the world? Orin could kill. Icharius could kill... but he'd specifically called himself a Death Lord when Orin had insisted he wasn't.

"Deyanira?" Paesha's voice broke something within me. I couldn't help the weakening of my stance.

"Here," I said, the word escaping somewhere between a whisper and a plea.

"Godsdamnit, Thea. Hold the fucking boat still."

"I'm trying," Althea answered.

I could almost picture them following Paesha's magic to the

window of my cell, forcing them into a boat because they couldn't get to me from within the castle. But they'd come. For me. Even when I'd doubted everything I was to them the second I got a chance, they'd still come. Maybe not with Orin, but in spite of him.

"How do we get you out?"

"I'm hurt pretty badly." I shifted to the window to keep my voice down. "Spear to the side." I wondered for a second if I should warn them about the king's hidden power. Their betrayal and lies had cut me so deep. Everything my father had always told me about trusting others became the truest wisdom I'd ever been given. And those wounds cut deep, nearly severing my heart. I'd risked everything for them. And they'd lied. But I could never look myself in the mirror if I didn't take the higher road. "Listen to me. Icharius can kill. He's a Death Lord. I don't know how. But you can't come into this castle. He won't hesitate."

Althea's voice shrank. So small, I could barely hear her through the small window. "He's what? I don't understand. How?"

"I wish I knew," I answered quietly. "But I think that's where all the missing people have gone."

I heard a clunk, as if she'd fallen into the boat.

"Gods, Thea," Paesha snapped. "You'll tip us into the piss water. Be careful."

"P," she said, voice almost numb. There was a pause between them. A breath and a realization. "Tolen's name... the change."

Their friend wasn't missing. He'd died at the king's hand.

"I'm sorry, Thea. I know how close you were." A sniffle and another splash of water before Paesha's voice grew quieter. "Is anyone with you, Dey?"

"No."

"Can you reach the bars? I can take them out, Dey. Can you crawl up the wall?" Thea said, a renewed sense of urgency seeping through the night.

I reached as far as I could before the pain in my side raced up my body, stealing my breath before taking me to the floor. "Can't. It's too hard."

"I'm not leaving you in there, Deyanira," Paesha swore. "You either figure out your own escape, or I'm coming in for you, king or no king."

"Give me a day. Let me see what information I can gather and let my side heal. Come back tomorrow at this time if you can get around the guards. I'll try to find a way to reach the window."

Paesha's words crept through the small window with frightening severity. "Once Orin finds out where you are... all bets are off."

I placed my hand on the cold stone wall, wishing I could just take it down. Not for him. But for the women who had come regardless of the danger. "Then don't tell him. Stay in the apartment if you have to. If he gets reckless and mistakes are made, someone's going to die."

"Just don't let it be you, Maiden."

I swallowed, my sadness letting the moment hang between us. "Paesha? Thea?"

"Still here," Paesha whispered. "For as long as we can be."

I nodded, though I knew she couldn't see me lying in the fetal position in a puddle of my own blood, feet away from a dead body. "Thank you for coming." I managed another haggard breath. "If I don't—"

"Don't do that," she hissed. "Don't lose your fight. No goodbyes. Not one."

"I think I need to sleep now."

"Just be careful," Thea said, full of worry. The metal from

their boat scraped against the stone exterior for several silent minutes, even as my eyes drifted shut.

I woke hours later to a guard sleeping on the stairs. If they came back, he'd be a problem. Still sore, though not as bad, I closed my eyes and replayed every moment I had with the family that was never truly mine. I think I'd learned what love was in those stolen days. Somewhere in the laughter of an old man and the kindness of a worried mother. The reach of a child and the embrace of two fearless women. And though I hated to admit it, I learned more about love with Orin than anywhere else. I'd let myself be vulnerable with him. Full of anger one moment and heaps of passion the next. I'd learned that love, no matter the depth, would always leave a mark on your soul. Even if you walked away from it, that wound would never heal. Love was finding yourself lost in the world and realizing that, in the arms of your family, you had discovered the most profound and enduring sanctuary, where your heart could always find its way back home.

Maybe it was formed on a lie, and maybe they'd been the ones to keep it, but they were still my family, and until they cast me away, that was home. There would need to be a conversation. Apologies from both sides because I'd gone there at the very beginning under false pretenses, too. I wasn't perfect. But I needed them. With or without Orin. The second I'd stood before Drexel Vanhoff, I'd wanted to run in the other direction. Straight back to Orin. I wanted to take away the pain in his words for both of us. He'd lied, and I didn't know if I'd ever get over that, but that mark he'd left on my heart remained.

The door creaked open again, jarring the so-called guard to wake. I imagined morning had come, though I wasn't sure of the time, and the window betrayed nothing when the sun remained hidden. A bevy of people descended into the dungeon. Staring into unknown faces, I rose on slightly steadier feet, preparing myself for the final man who clomped down the steps like a horse, his layers of clothing making him look two sizes bigger than he likely was. With furs over his shoulders and a sword strapped to his side, he took up more room than anyone else by half as they lined up outside my cell.

"Good morning, King Slayer. Did you sleep well?" Icharius drew his sword and dragged it along the bars as if he were playing an instrument.

"Quite well," I sneered. "So kind of you to ask."

"I thought we could start this day with a game. Do you see these wretches?"

I studied my nails rather than give away the rapid beat of my heart. "No. I've gone blind overnight."

He laughed, though it was so disingenuous it caused my skin to prickle. "Look at the faces. Study them." Gripping the face of the youngest woman until her gaunt cheeks disappeared behind his gloves, he pulled her forward. "Do you think she deserves to die?"

"No," I answered, frankly.

He shoved her away. "You don't know her. How can you be so sure?"

"I have no interest in your games. What do you want from me?"

"I told you. I'm going to break you, just like you broke my poor little heart." He dipped those words in enough sarcasm that one of his guards flashed a smile.

I said nothing, turning away to sit on my cot.

"Andros!" he screamed, calling the guard from yesterday to step forward. "Open the cell."

I didn't look as several of the small crowd gasped, indicating they believed I was a bigger threat than he was. They had no idea. That was a world he'd built. But there was something else here. Something I believed Icharius might have been putting together far quicker than I had.

The moment the cell was open, he shoved Andros inside and quickly locked it. "You will kill him, Maiden, or every hour on the hour, someone from this group will fall prey to... my skills. Take one life to save ten lives; that's the choice you're faced with. Shall I bring in a giant hourglass for you, or can you count?"

I ran for the bars, shaking the iron in my hands as I threatened him. "The only death you will see from my hands will be your own, King. Only yours."

He laughed all the way back up the stairs as the group followed behind him. I'd played this damn game before. He knew I would choose the greater good. But why did he care? Why did he *need* to push me?

"He's trying to anger you, Princess," Andros said with a look of grim resignation. "You need not fight him. Just kill me and be done with it."

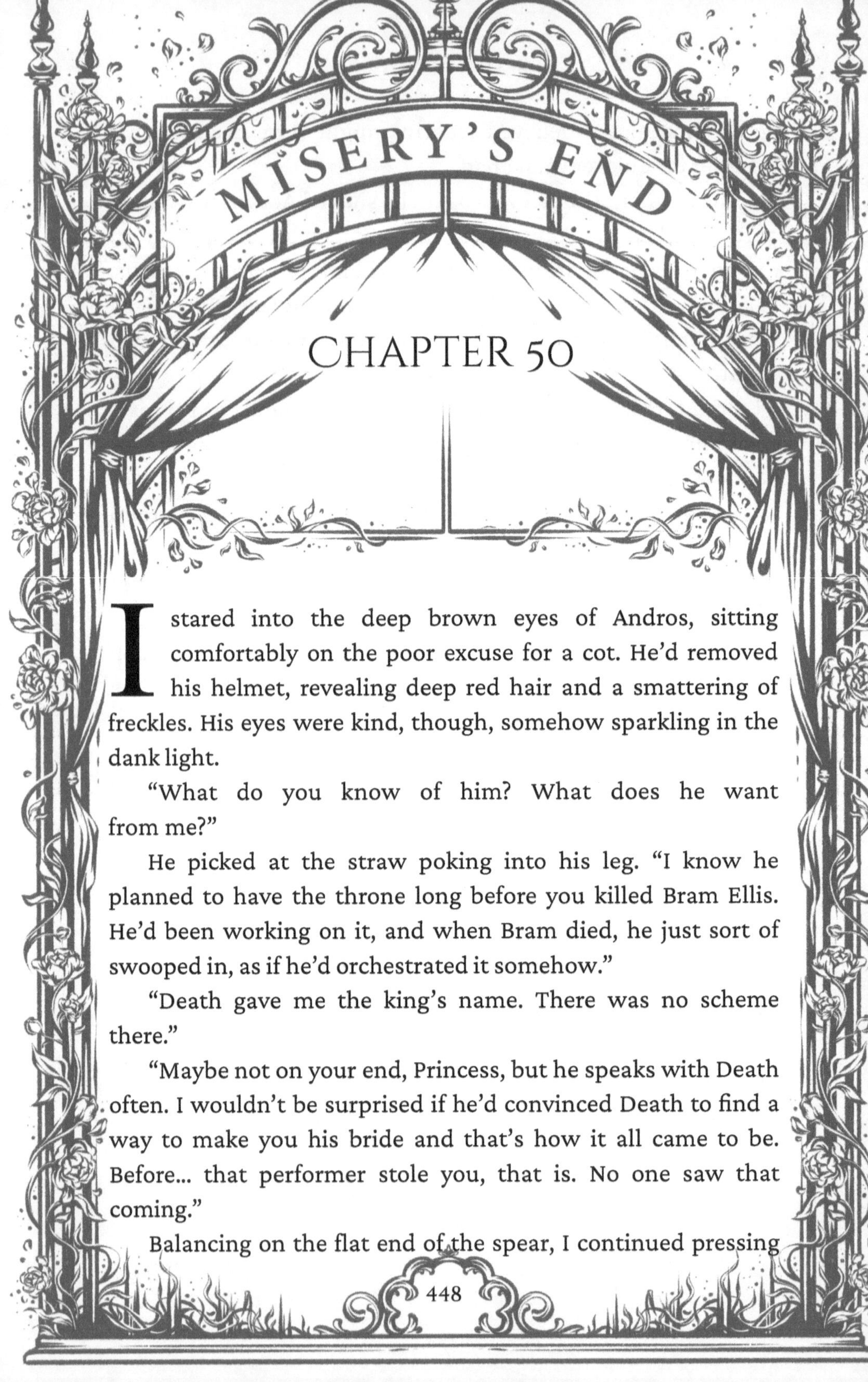

MISERY'S END

CHAPTER 50

I stared into the deep brown eyes of Andros, sitting comfortably on the poor excuse for a cot. He'd removed his helmet, revealing deep red hair and a smattering of freckles. His eyes were kind, though, somehow sparkling in the dank light.

"What do you know of him? What does he want from me?"

He picked at the straw poking into his leg. "I know he planned to have the throne long before you killed Bram Ellis. He'd been working on it, and when Bram died, he just sort of swooped in, as if he'd orchestrated it somehow."

"Death gave me the king's name. There was no scheme there."

"Maybe not on your end, Princess, but he speaks with Death often. I wouldn't be surprised if he'd convinced Death to find a way to make you his bride and that's how it all came to be. Before... that performer stole you, that is. No one saw that coming."

Balancing on the flat end of the spear, I continued pressing for information, using kindness as a weapon against the poor fool. "What does he want with Quill?"

Andros lifted his shoulder. "Is that the kid? No idea. We don't have many kids around here, ya know. Not like Perth."

I rolled my eyes. "There aren't many in Perth either. This might shock you, but the Life Maiden is missing from *both* cities. All of Requiem."

"Right. Right."

I thought back to my father's birth ledger, remembering how most of the babies were documented with addresses closer to the castle. And then Regulas's supposed confession of the Life Maiden's whereabouts, though after countless hours in the library, I'd decided he was lying. But Andros's words sank in, and I felt a knot forming in the pit of my stomach. Something buzzing, just on the edge of realization. It was as if a long-forgotten puzzle was coming together, piece by piece, revealing a picture that I had never expected to see. I had always known I was different, but the realization was both perplexing and frightening.

My eyes wandered to the spear I had been using as a makeshift crutch, and I couldn't help but notice that the dull ache in my side had faded away completely. I recalled the numerous times when Orin's injuries had healed remarkably fast. And I'd directly affected his madness. My presence was a balm to his tormented soul. Not because we were bonded.

Because *I* was the missing Life Maiden.

I stumbled backward, my mind running in circles as I searched my memories for any signs saying this couldn't be true. I'd stood in Death's court. His power was the only one I felt in my veins. If this was true, how could Death have power over Life? How could madness consume me, yet I was the answer to Orin's darkness? Maybe I was wrong.

It didn't matter. Not as the door from above crashed open

and Icharius Fern came stomping down the steps, whistling a jovial tune. Though I didn't think I needed to, since he'd been too sure of himself to take the spear, I still tossed it toward his guard sitting on the cot, with his eyes cast to the floor. There was a time to play games and a time to get serious, and at this moment, he'd expected to find Andros lying on the floor.

But when he came close enough, his cold eyes pinned to the kind man sitting on the cot, the final low note of his song faded away. "You had one godsdamned job."

"I've never been a good worker," I said. "Ask the Maestro; he can confirm."

"We could have ruled this world with Death's blessing. Two weapons on a black throne. But you had to go and fuck that up."

Face turning as red as the lights outside of Lady Visha's brothel, he stormed up the stairs, dragging one of the older women who'd been in the group down the stairs by her hair.

Andros jolted to his feet, gripping the iron bars. "Please, Your Grace. She's done nothing wrong."

"You will not speak," he said, the red fading to purple as fury consumed him. "Which life will you take, Deyanira? Andros's or hers?"

"Mine. Choose mine," the woman said, her eyes locked on the man in my cell.

It took only a glimpse of the two to see the similarities. The pointed nose, the kind eyes, even the red hair. The only distinction apart from the size and sex was her age. His mother, no doubt.

My stomach turned. A perfectly orchestrated plan by a disgusting man. When I said nothing, Icharius slammed the woman's head into the bars, splitting the flesh on her forehead as she cried out in pain.

"Princess," Andros pleaded. "Take your spear and end this."

"Princess?" The king's anger shifted into humor as he glanced between us. "Were you a son of Perth, Andros?"

I looked at Andros once more, never considering he may very well have been one of my father's subjects.

"I am a son of Perth, Your Grace. Until my last breath."

The king clicked his tongue. "Pity you shit yourself in front of your banished princess. Maybe you could have had a chance. Now make your choice, Deyanira. Which of your people will you kill?"

I balled my hands into fists, gritting my teeth. "I will not choose."

The sharp tip of the spear pressed into my spine with enough force that, on instinct alone, I jerked around, gripping the handle, and smashing it into Andros's gut.

"I'm... I'm sorry, Princess. But you must make a choice. You must choose her. Kill me. Please. Save my mother."

"This isn't my choice. It's his. I don't want any of this."

The king smashed the woman into the bars again, letting her crumple to the floor in tears. "Please," she begged. "Don't let him die for me."

Andros fell to his knees, crawling across the floor to reach his mother. But when his arms passed through the bars, the king pulled his ax. I screamed, lunging for the guard, intending to pull him away, but then it happened—a swift, merciless swing of the king's blade, and Andros's arm fell to the ground with a sickening thud. Time seemed to freeze as the prison filled with the echoes of his agonized screams. Shock washed over me like a tidal wave, freezing me in place as I stared at the gruesome scene before me. Andros's blood covering his poor mother.

A burning, seething anger rose within me. This was the ruin of our world. This man who had taken Requiem for his own would never be stopped if I didn't do it myself. I wasn't going to choose Andros or his weeping mother. I knew now, beyond a shadow of a doubt, he would be my next death.

"You win," I said meekly, leaning on the spear as if I were still severely injured. "I will kill Andros at your request. But I insist you let him die in his mother's arms. Those are my terms."

The king smiled. The symphony of wails filling the chamber didn't stop him from reaching for the key on his belt and unlocking the prison door. So used to being the strongest person in the room, he'd forgotten the monster he'd just set free.

I tucked my arm beneath the guard's good one, helping him scoot on his stomach beyond the threshold and to his mother. They were a sad, pitiful sight, but Icharius was nothing more than triumphant smiles as I stepped outside and pressed the spear to the back of the guard's trembling neck.

"No, please," his mother cried, but the only return she got for her unwavering love was a kick to the stomach from the ruthless king.

I struck hard and fast, lifting the spear to crack it across his smug face. He was strong, though. Too strong. He'd taken the blow like a statue, grabbing the end of the weapon and shoving it toward me to throw me off balance. It worked. I stumbled backward. He leaped over Andros, coming at me with all his might. I waited. Closer and closer he came. A moth to the flame. But the flame would always burn the most. In a practiced move, as he lunged for me, I spun to the side, swiping his blade from its scabbard and jamming it into the back of his right leg.

He fell to one knee, ripping his ax free once more and throwing it at me with such force, it didn't spin end over end. It simply flew straight for me. I shifted right, but not fast enough to avoid the blade altogether as it sliced across my shoulder.

"Not very smart, throwing your weapons, King."

"Enou—"

The king's command was cut off by shouting up the stairs.

Starting with a few voices, in just minutes, the entire castle began to quake, followed by the familiar, bellowing tone of my furious husband.

He'd come for me.

Icharius's shock was short-lived as I hauled back and lunged, nearly driving the king's own sword into his chest. Instead, he twisted, grabbing the hilt of the blade right on top of my hand, forcing my back to his stomach, twisting and straining until the blade was pressed to my neck. His breath was hot against my ear. I was strong, but he was stronger. And though I didn't have it in me to stop fighting, I knew I'd lost. I knew that blade to the throat would spur my final descension to Death's court. A beautiful twist of fate between me and all my victims. I wondered if I'd gasp.

But instead of death, a jolt of power unlike anything I'd ever felt rippled across the realm. Icharius went stiff at my back before falling heavily to the stone floor. I spun around, intending to help Andros and his mother escape. But Orin's power had already killed them.

Because not only had he come, he'd shattered the world to get to me.

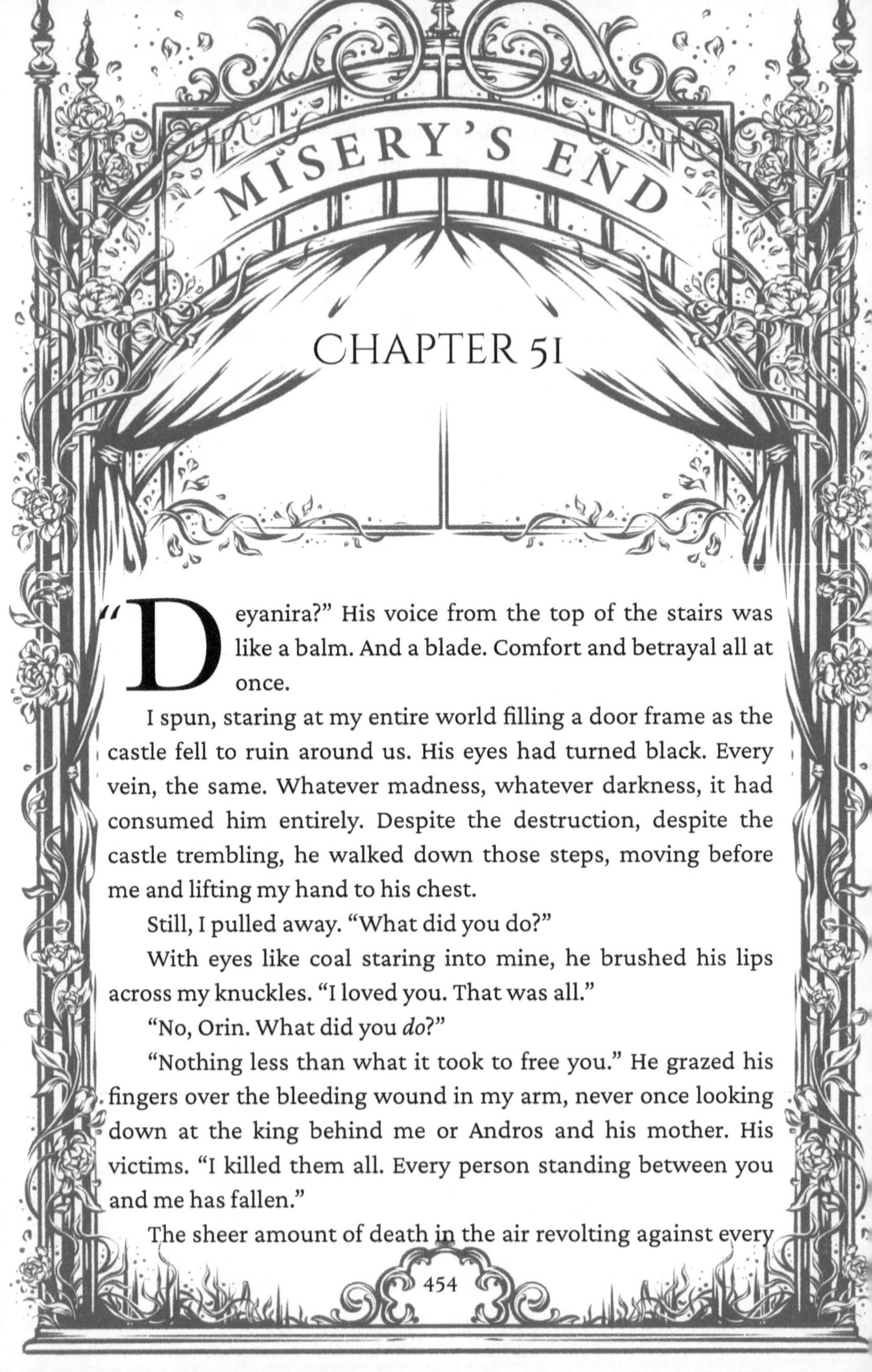

CHAPTER 51

"Deyanira?" His voice from the top of the stairs was like a balm. And a blade. Comfort and betrayal all at once.

I spun, staring at my entire world filling a door frame as the castle fell to ruin around us. His eyes had turned black. Every vein, the same. Whatever madness, whatever darkness, it had consumed him entirely. Despite the destruction, despite the castle trembling, he walked down those steps, moving before me and lifting my hand to his chest.

Still, I pulled away. "What did you do?"

With eyes like coal staring into mine, he brushed his lips across my knuckles. "I loved you. That was all."

"No, Orin. What did you *do*?"

"Nothing less than what it took to free you." He grazed his fingers over the bleeding wound in my arm, never once looking down at the king behind me or Andros and his mother. His victims. "I killed them all. Every person standing between you and me has fallen."

The sheer amount of death in the air revolting against every moral code I've ever known caused churning in my stomach. It was as if I could feel each petal withering away on my back. As if those deaths were somehow less than because of Orin's massacre for my freedom.

I needed to decide quickly. To leave with the man I was bonded to or run away from him. In the midst of my anger and heartbreak, I couldn't deny the truth that gnawed at me. Some part of me loved him, too, despite his deceit. It was a maddening contradiction, a fierce and passionate thing that had grown in the darkest corners of my heart. I knew I shouldn't feel this way, that I should turn away from him and never look back.

"I will do whatever it takes, Dey. Whatever apology you need, I will deliver it. Whatever my punishment need be, whatever the lesson, I will learn it. I'm sorry for deceiving you."

I wanted to berate him, to unleash the anger that had been burning inside me, but there was no time, and he seemed so… fragile. But I couldn't process any of that as the castle walls continued to fall.

"We don't have time for this. We have to get out of here, and then we'll talk." I took a hesitant step toward him, losing my footing as another rumble shook the remains of the castle.

And then we ran.

Stones rained down from the ceiling, and the walls shuddered. The sound of crashing masonry echoed, and we had to duck and dodge to avoid being struck by the debris.

The stairs were treacherous, slick with moisture, and crumbling underfoot. I stumbled but refused to fall. I couldn't let the castle become our tomb. We burst into the torch-lit hallways, gasping for breath as I surveyed the shocking death and destruction around me. The castle seemed to weep, the tapestries smoldered in the flickering light, and the paintings of the past monarchs trembled on their hooks, falling one by one to the ground.

Dashing through the building as fast as we could, the distance between us grew. I was faster and more agile, and I hadn't thought to look back. To check on him.

He screamed my name from the back end of a hallway, and I turned just in time for a wall beside me to groan. I backed away, unsure of where to go. But it was too late. Another tremble and the whole thing collapsed right on top of me, turning the outside world dark.

Orin's voice was muted shouts in the distance. I could hear his agony above my own for only moments before everything turned silent, and the whole world slipped away.

I wasn't sure how much time had passed. I peeled my eyes open, seeing only wreckage as strong arms carried me without pause through Silbath. He hadn't just taken down the castle. Orin's unchecked power had cleaved the world, destroying over half the city. Eventually, I closed my eyes, unable to see any more of the damage, the shattered brick streets, the crumbled buildings, the smoke and horror of it all. He'd promised to break the world to get to me, and he'd kept it.

I'd been placed in my bed, my boots had been removed, and when the blanket was pulled to my chin, I finally let go and allowed myself to fall asleep. I braced myself for Death's court. But instead, I dreamed of nothing at all. Only a deep pit of darkness swirling with the light that must have been buried inside of me. Because though it wasn't confirmed, somehow, I'd been born of life and death.

I woke to a tiny cool hand on my cheek and big blue eyes staring into my soul.

"Are you really awake this time or pretend awake like last time?"

I managed a smile, though my head throbbed. "I'm awake."

"Oh, good. Elowen said Boo can't come in here until you're really awake because he was making circles on your bed. Can I let him in?"

"Sure," I whispered, feeling like I'd swallowed a thousand needles.

The little girl hopped down, handing me a glass of water from the nightstand before cracking the door open. The small dog had been there, curled up and snoozing just outside.

"She's awake!" she screamed, with nothing held back whatsoever before nudging her dog. "Come on, you big lug." Quill tugged once on Boo's collar, and after peeking his head up, he leaped from his spot and dashed into the room, though he did not immediately get on the bed. Instead, he placed his paws at the edge and sniffed my face, as if making sure I was okay before jumping.

"Told you," she said, the second the dog found a comfortable place to make his circles before plopping down. "We're the same now, right? You were stolen, and I was stolen?"

"Yeah, kid. We're the same."

She crawled back into the bed and placed her hand on my cheek again. "Paesha says you're really mad, and you might leave, and if you do, then we can be sad, but we can't ask you to stay. Promise you won't tell her I said that?"

"Promise."

"But are you going to go away?"

I cleared my throat, buying time. I really wasn't sure what was going to happen. I knew this had become home, but how could I stay if I couldn't trust any of them? What kind of a fool would that make me? Still, I couldn't tell Quill that. She'd never understand it. So instead, I sighed, reaching down to bury my fingers into Boo's soft coat. "I need to think about it. Is that okay?"

She twisted her lips, clearly considering my answer. "That's not a no?"

"No. It's not."

"But it's also not a yes, so I guess that's okay."

Three soft knocks sounded on the door before it swung open, revealing Paesha in a beautiful golden gown, the long side of her warm chestnut hair curled back flawlessly, showcasing her tanned skin. "The most I've ever gotten from a lover is flowers. And here you've got mass destruction."

I couldn't even force the smile.

She pinned Quill with a look. "Time to get changed, Quilly."

The child giggled and slid from the bed. Boo followed his kid, loyal as ever as she bound down the stairs.

Paesha stepped inside the room, and I forced myself to sit up, noting I was mostly stiff, but otherwise, not in too rough of shape. Thea followed close behind, her red hair pinned up in a beautiful golden broach that matched Paesha's dress, though Thea wore a loose white gown. I stared beyond them both, into the eyes of Orin's mother, the concern on her face more prevalent than anything.

"Okay?" she asked, inching inside to stand at the foot of the bed.

I nodded, though a lump grew in my throat. I really wanted to throw the blankets over my head and cry, from shame and embarrassment and maybe even from anger. But I knew why they'd come. And I knew I needed to be the first to speak here.

"When I was young, the first lesson my father taught me was never to trust a soul. He said the world would sooner chew me up and spit me out than show me kindness. And he was right for my whole life. Every twist and turn that led me, guided me, were those words."

"Dey," Thea whispered, but I held up a hand.

"I thought—" I swallowed the lump in my throat. "I

thought I could come here and learn your secrets and figure out Orin's secret. I'd seen him kill, and that's the only reason I came back that day Thea freed me. I'm assuming you've gathered by this point that he has power?"

They nodded.

"I'd thought I was so smart, and you all were so naïve. I started this friendship on a lie. I tied Boo up down at the river and convinced Quill we could save him, just so I could ask her questions about you."

"This isn't necessary," Elowen said.

"And you?" I laughed, though a tear betrayed my feelings. "I slipped you a sleeping tonic so I could search the house. That's how I knew about Thea's armory. I'm apologizing for those things because honesty is the only way forward. So, I'm sorry. For being the worst of us. And I know you knew him longer. You'd loved him harder. Your loyalty to him trumped the friendships we'd grown. I get it. I wish I'd known, though. I wish one of you would have told me I was only here because of my touch."

"No one told you that because it isn't true." Paesha stepped closer, lifting her skirt to sit on the edge of the bed. "We didn't tell you because we wanted to keep you here with us. We knew you'd be pissed, and we knew you'd run."

Another tear fell. "I would have. I did."

Thea smoothed a hand over a wrinkle in the blanket at the foot of the bed. "He'd gotten so dark and so mean. And by the time we were all on the same page about telling you, he'd become so attached, we knew neither of you would forgive us. So, we had to sit back and wait and hope that when it was time, we could find a way to salvage this family."

"We are a family, Deyanira, the six of us. As a mother, I needed you to help my son. I won't deny that. But I also needed you here. We all did. We still do." Elowen shuffled closer. "You can consider this tough love, but I'm not going to allow you to run off without the apology you deserve. You can take it or leave it, but just know that after all this time, none of us were pretending to want you here. We love you."

I traced the stitching pattern on the quilt folded over me, the tears still falling, though now it was a release more than anything. Letting go of twenty-seven years of emotions I'd never been allowed to feel without being weak.

"You're safe here," Elowen said. "And we'd like you to stay. Not because of Orin. Because your place here is deserved."

A simple throat clearing from the doorway sent a ripple of anticipation through me. The women filed out of the room, revealing the most stunning man I'd ever seen standing in the hall, wearing a black suit, tie, tails, pocket square, and all. He looked just as I'd remembered him. The darkness gone, the light honey of his eyes returned.

"Is it safe for me to enter?" he asked, a playful lift to his brow, an attempt to ease the tension, no doubt.

"Define safe."

"If you have to ask, I'm safer in the hall."

I cast away all attempts at lightheartedness, lowering my chin to glare at him. "People died, Orin. A lot of them. And for what? Me? I wasn't worth a single one of their lives. And if I were bold enough to sit here and say I was, it still doesn't change the fact that you've lied to a degree I can't and won't get over. The night I met you, you played the part of a man, smitten at first glance, willing to sweep away the Death Maiden for the good of the kingdom. And I hated you the next day. I wanted you gone in those moments more than anything. I'd cast you lower than every other person in this realm. But every day that's passed since then, you climbed step after step, redeeming yourself, becoming the man I'd hoped you were all those months ago. I was such a godsdamned fool to have believed you. Again."

"No." His skin paled, confident shoulders sunken in. His breath rattled as he managed to draw it. "I hated myself, too. In so many ways, I thought we were the same. Most know Death delivers the names of his preferred victims, but the details get lost in gossip. So many before you have killed far beyond those demands; no one knew the truth anymore. Not even Hollis, who watched his sister succumb to the madness. But I thought I did. I thought somehow there'd been a mistake, and two were born with Death's power. I could make choices and so could you. But you chose a woman that helped my mother raise me. And then Ezra. My brother. My best friend. And the grief from those losses was all-consuming."

"So, I deserved to be lied to because you made assumptions that were wrong? And even when you learned that, it wasn't enough to speak the truth?"

He closed the distance between us, falling to his knees on the floor beside me to take my hands. "No. I never lied to you. I didn't tell you the whole truth, and I'm sorry for that, but you came to your own conclusion about the Maestro forcing our marriage, and I just couldn't tell you otherwise because I knew you'd run. I needed you far more than you've ever needed me, and I thought if the woman who tried to kill me several times knew that, it would just be another weapon for you to yield against me. But I fell in love with my enemy, and as the truth unraveled, I couldn't bear to lose you for so many other reasons. For the smile you give when you think no one is looking, the way you feed that damn dog so much he doesn't eat his supper anymore, for the way you love my family so fully, for Hollis. Because he loved you more than all of us, I think.

"I was selfish. I just kept holding on to the moments I had with you because I knew the end was near. Every single night, I've prayed to gods I don't know the names of to help me find a way to keep you. You always deserved the truth. I don't care how complicated this gets. I still want you."

He looked so hard into my eyes I could feel every second between my heartbeats, could feel each lingering moment like the ticking of a dying clock.

"I'm sorry, Deyanira. You deserve so much better than this bond between us. I know you never chose it. And I wish I could say this just isn't meant to be, but I can't speak those words. That truly would be a lie. We are meant to be. You're my counterpart. You are the balm to my broken soul, and though you hate it, you know I am the only man you want. When I kiss you, your knees weaken. When we're alone, your eyes linger." He stood, closing the distance between us, leaning over the bed. "Whatever it is you need to forgive me and stay, speak it, and it is yours. There's not a single mountain I won't climb."

"Omitting the truth is exactly the same as lying." I needed to speak the words aloud to convince my heart of the same, because I was weak for him. And I loved him, even in this vat of pain.

"I know it is, love. Please. Let me earn you back."

I placed a trembling hand to his cheek, closing my eyes. "I wouldn't even know where to start forgiving you."

He tucked a finger under my chin, lifting. "At the beginning. This time, you have all the truths and all the choices."

"What do you mean?"

"Marry me again, Deyanira. Choose me. And us."

CHAPTER 52

He'd left me lying in bed with a choice to make. He hadn't pushed, hadn't forced me to decide, had only gone for a second to bring a package to my room from his and close the door behind him. I stared at the brown paper-covered box for a long time, eyed the letter scripted with elegant writing—his, most likely—and lived in the torment of my heart. Eventually, curiosity won out, and I caved, snatching the letter.

Deyanira Sariah Faber, Death's Maiden,
Princess to the fallen kingdom of Perth, the sharpest
of blades and greatest of hearts,
The choice is yours. I will wait for you in the
garden until midnight. If you don't come, we will
not chase you. We will let you live the life you
choose in peace.
Orin Faber,
the most sorrowful of husbands

My eyes lingered on my title from Death far longer than it should have. Death's Maiden but also Life's, or the God of Life, whoever that was. The second that thought had come to me, a thrum of peace rippled through my body, as if my soul embraced a foreign power I'd never realized laid nearly dormant within me. I hadn't told him. And I wasn't sure if I should until I had no doubts.

Still, I slid the box across the bed, pulling it onto my lap. Tearing the packaging away, I tossed it and the lid, gasping as my fingers grazed the black silk fabric within, lying beneath Chaos. The writing on the note inside was not from Orin's hand. The letters were smaller, clean, but with a different edge to them.

Deyanira,
As I write this letter behind the stage where
you and I will share our final words, I want you
to know that I am grateful for this escape. I
choose this end. I choose to be with my beloved once
more.

I fear for you, my darling. Hidden truths will fester, and while we all played a part in this deception, just know that I've witnessed his hardest days made easier by your simple touch, and I was not strong enough to deny him the escape. I am sorry. There will come a day when truths unfold. I've asked for this letter to be delivered at that time because my final lesson, and possibly the most important I will ever leave you with, is to love your family through the masks they wear and the hardships you will all endure.

When Dahlia smiled, even when the madness had consumed her, I couldn't stop loving her. My sister was part of my first family, but you, my dear girl, are my second. The one I chose.

Do this old man a favor and choose them back, though none of us deserve you.

I will see you in eternity with open arms, no matter your choice.

Hollis

Such heartache should not have been meant for humans. Losing that old man was an agony I wasn't prepared for, but mourning him was so much worse. Fine one moment and all-consuming the next, I couldn't think beyond the sadness and the pain of missing him. I blinked away tears I wished I could have controlled. I forced a breath to fill reluctant lungs. With the heaviest of hearts, I lifted the black silk gown from the box and moved my fingers over the lace edging on the open back and then the threading that was nearly invisible in the flawless masterpiece. He'd touched these pieces, and no doubt, had worried over each stitch, as I'd seen him do a hundred times. Hollis was the only man in my life to ever truly treat me as a princess *and* a person. Never as Death's Maiden, simply a kindred spirit.

I wasn't sure which way I'd go: if I'd walk out of the front door or the back. But I slipped from that bed and put the dress on all the same, letting the cool fabric hug my skin until I could almost feel those fragile arms around me. I hoped I truly would see him in Death's court when my time came. But I couldn't pretend to know the true workings of eternity. I had no idea what lay beyond the gates of hell. Past the hellhounds, and into a realm likely steeped in fear. Or if I would truly go there. If I was Death and Life's Maiden, who would lay claim over my soul?

With a strong, steady breath, I opened the door and descended the stairs, stepping into the sitting room to take in the moment. A vase of Elowen's flowers sat in the center of the coffee table, dying, drooping, mirroring the deflation of my heart. I reached for the peonies, their once-bulbous shape now limp. Desperately searching for a power that wasn't solely Death's, I burrowed deep, looking beyond the blackness that sat within me, searching for something light. A pinprick of luminescence, nearly drowned in a vat of dark, drew me nearer. I reached for that bit with all my grit, wishing for it to be enough. More than its counterpart. A vibrant wave of color wicked up the peony as I wrapped my whole self around that light. Its gentle petals grew with life in my palm, confirming the power buried within me. Heart pounding, I watched as it bloomed anew, rejuvenated. But only for a second before the opposing power took over like a snarling beast and turned the flower to ash.

For every day, so would be a night. For every life, a death. For every win, a loss. All things came with a balance. I thought of Orin, knowing he stood in the garden as time ticked away. He was my perfect counterpart. And I was his.

The night air was cool and filled with the gentle scent of jasmine as I stood at the edge of the garden, hidden in the embrace of the shadows. The moon hung low in the sky, its cool light casting a soft, ethereal glow over the scene before me. Hollis's fabric cascaded like liquid midnight.

As I took that first step, the grass was cool and slightly damp, with dew that had settled on the garden in the quiet hours of the night. The soft rustling of leaves in the nearby trees whispered secrets of the centuries, as if the very world were holding its breath, awaiting the union that was about to take place.

Orin stood there beneath an intricate golden archway. His eyes widened in surprise, and then a slow, incredulous smile spread across his face. It was a moment of pure understanding, a moment when he saw into my heart and knew that I had chosen him over all else. Each footfall on the cool earth resonated with a reassuring solidity, the sound echoing through the stillness like a heartbeat. The gentle melody of a distant nightingale filled the air, its song a haunting, sweet serenade that seemed to accompany me on my journey toward him.

The rest had come. Had waited for my final decision, just as he had. My heart, once heavy with hurt and darkness, beat in harmony with the rhythm of my steps. I released the pain, the doubts, and the shadows that had clung to me, and I felt as if I were walking on air. The weight of forgiveness and love lifted me higher with each step, propelling me toward the man I had chosen to marry, the man I had chosen to love despite it all.

"You came," he said simply, reaching his hand toward me.

It might have been a simple gesture, had I not known the

reality behind it. My touch was life and light. An escape for his darkness. And taking that hand would be accepting that as truth. As my fingers slipped into his, I couldn't help the warm smile.

He pulled me near, smoothing his thumbs over my cheeks as he spoke. "I promise to do whatever it takes to coax this beautiful smile every day for the rest of my hundred years."

"Is that your vow?" I asked, wrapping my arms around him.

Touching his forehead to mine, he whispered, "I didn't think you'd come."

"Me either."

Paesha cleared her throat, reminding us both that we had a full audience and a yawning child doing her best to stay awake, though her eyes had glossed over, and the dog at her feet snored louder than the bird singing in the distance.

Orin gripped my wrist, rubbing a finger over the golden band before placing his own directly on top of it. His eyes, deep and unwavering, met mine with a profound sincerity beyond ordinary boundaries of mortal love. "My promise, Wife, goes far beyond a life of happiness. I offer you a vow that reaches into eternity itself. I will stand by your side through all the storms that may come our way. In a world where uncertainty reigns, I vow to be your anchor, your steadfast companion, and your refuge in times of sorrow. I pledge to honor you not only in the light but also in the darkest of hours. At the end of this mortal life, when Death walks beside us, our love shall defy the limits of eternity. It will be a testament to the enduring power of the human heart. I vow that our love will be our legacy left behind, not our power. With Death's blessing and the gods watching over us, I bind myself to you from this day till death."

Orin's vow ignited the magical bond we shared; the bands at our wrists illuminated the night as our friends gasped. I couldn't pull my eyes from his, though. Couldn't stop repeating his solemn vows in my mind as the words washed over me. When we'd married, he'd laughed when I accidentally bound him to Death's court, and here he'd promised to come with me on his own accord. Forever.

"I don't have any promises to make beyond one. I vow to always be a safe space for you. When the darkness consumes you, I will be your light, your beacon. I will never let you fall. With Death's blessing and the gods watching over us, I bind myself to you from this day till death."

Our soft and gentle kiss was accompanied by the applause of those who loved us most. Before I could take a full breath after such an emotional moment, we were encased in hugs.

"We have a wedding gift for you," Quill said through a yawn. "Oh, and thanks for staying."

"The bathhouse is ready," Thea continued, bouncing on her toes.

Paesha added, "I snuck in earlier. It's divine."

Orin grabbed my hand, leading me away from the others. "Good night," he called over his shoulder.

And in unison, all four of them called in sing-song voices, "Good night."

The building was just as it was last I'd seen it. A long building that was more a work of art than anything else, made from opaque glass and intricate metal designs. The filigree of Thea's handiwork crept up the building in such fine detail, I worried if word got out, our small reprieve from the world would become a beacon to those curious enough to wander through the tree line.

But the outside was nothing compared to what lay within. Orin's hand faltered when we stepped through the doorway, taking in details fit for a king. No. A god. A golden arch, twin to the one we'd just stood under, welcomed us inside. Beyond that, pools of steaming water dipped into the marble floor separated by white pillars, smothered in vines of delicate golden leaves. Had this bathhouse been built in the realm of gods, it still would have been noteworthy. Thea had outdone herself, and there would never be another building in this world to compare.

The air was heavy with the intoxicating scent of fragrant oils and burning wood in the fireplace along the farthest wall, and I could feel the warmth wrap around us nearly as heated as the amber eyes that watched only me. The full baths steamed, sending tendrils of mist curling through the air. It was as if we'd entered a hidden realm, far removed from the wreckage of the world.

Orin's knuckles traced the black silk along my side, his voice low and husky. "Choose your bath, Wife."

I led him towards the largest sunken basin, its water shimmering like liquid gold in the firelight. We stood there for a moment, our eyes locked, the promise of pleasure building between us. After circling, searing me with his gaze, Orin began to untie the ribbon at the back of my neck, the only fabric holding the dress up.

He massaged the tattoo that covered my back, his burning contact causing a wave of desire as each inch of vine held his attention. "So lovely," he whispered into my ear as the silk gown pooled to the floor. Brushing his lips across the base of my neck, it took every ounce of control not to completely come apart for him right there. I'd needed this moment so desperately for so long; had craved his touch. Even in anger, I planned to savor every bit.

Turning so my breasts pressed against him, I tugged on the bottom of his shirt until it was free of his pants. Button by button, as I held his fiery gaze, I undressed him. Each movement elicited a pulse of need until he stood gloriously bare. His body like that of a fallen god.

I rose to the tips of my toes, locking my fingers behind his neck as I dropped his shirt to the floor, joining my gown. Smoothing my hands over his tight, muscled chest, over each black vein creeping from his heart, my knees felt weak when he slid a thumb over his bottom lip and closed his eyes, dragging in a measured breath.

He kissed me once, viciously, with hard determination, every jagged edge of his madness peeking through to form the entirety of the man he was and not the masks he wore. Not all good and not all bad. He lingered somewhere in between, just as I did. But we would always call to the darkness within each other, even unintentionally.

Deep golden eyes stared down into mine as he pulled back, his lips swollen as he stroked his fingers down my arms, dragging a moan from me. Heat pooled between my legs from the way he stared at my bare body, frozen as if he could not trust himself to keep from ruining me.

"Tell me you are mine," he growled, wrapping my hair around his fist, tilting my head back. "Tell me this is forever."

I dug my nails into his arms and dragged them down until he hissed, delight showing on his stunning face. "I am yours and you are mine."

I sauntered away, swishing my hips, until the fiction made my clit throb with need. Moving to the edge of the steaming bath, the fire heated my back as I dipped a toe in. Orin's face lit with menace, cocking an eyebrow as he dared me to continue. Dropping my chin, I stepped in, the hot water lapping over the edge and onto the floor. Still, he stood. Still, he stared, locked in time, as he watched every inch of my body disappear. My breath left me, though I wasn't sure if it was from the strain on his face or the temperature of the bath.

I dipped below the surface, letting my hair soak completely through. By the time I came up for air, he'd already moved, the spell broken, or perhaps only amplified as he approached the bath. I turned, leaning against the opposite edge to watch him descend the steps, holding my gaze.

"Stand up, Deyanira. Let me look at you."

"You didn't marry a demure, obedient woman, Orin," I reminded him, sinking lower. "If you want me, come and get me."

I needed him. His fingers on my skin, his lips on mine. The few feet between us felt like miles as those eyes burned into me, devoured me, tracing up and down my body until my swollen slit ached with a desire only he could release.

"You are a stunning little nightmare," he growled before plunging into the water, emerging inches away, grabbing my hand and spinning me until my back pressed against him fully. He curled around my body, reaching low, kissing the curve of my neck, water dripping from him as calloused fingers crept down my stomach. He stopped just above my core. When I lifted to my toes, his dark chuckle as he moved away amplified that vivid ache for him.

He reached into a basket sitting near the ledge. Dipping a cloth into the water, he held my gaze as he lathered, each corded muscle of his body tight, his skin so golden, flickering in the light of the flames, I needed nothing more than to run my fingers down the grooves of his body. Instead, he gestured for me to turn around. He surged forward until the water lapped at my waist.

Pulling my back flush to his chest again, he began. Inch by inch, he circled the cloth over my sensitive skin until it came alive beneath his touch. Warm breath caressed my ear, trailing down my neck. Orin was relentless. Bringing my body to life as if it were an instrument for him to learn. Fingers grazed the lower swell of my breast, forcing a small gasp as I filled with anticipation of his touch.

"Take a breath, Wife. I have no plans to rush this."

"It's cute that you think you're in charge."

His grip tightened, a hand sliding up to my throat. "You can have every other moment, but I own this one. I will lead, and you will follow. You will let me show you how much your body already belongs to me. Do you understand?"

I had no fight as he bit my earlobe, before sliding his hand back down, becoming slow. Painfully, blissfully slow as he washed my body, sliding that cloth up my thighs and between my legs.

"Answer," he growled.

"Yes."

"Good girl."

Gathering oil from the basket to drip over eager skin, apt fingers dug into my shoulders in a back massage that melted the world. I crossed my arms over the ledge, laying my head down and closing my eyes, giving him full access to massage every flower down each vine of my tattoo. His searing touch, the one that drew my power so effortlessly, left a burning path of need straight to my breasts before pooling in my lower belly. There was no rush, as he was sure to let me know, and he took his time, rubbing circles in perfect rhythm.

"I plan to turn those little mewls into screams, Nightmare, but I certainly appreciate the warmup."

"You talk too much," I moaned.

He grabbed the ends of my hair and yanked, balling it into a fist as he pulled me flush to him once more. "Be nice or you'll be punished. Those are the rules."

"If I had a blade, I'd pull it right now, just to see if you kept your word."

He laughed, that lung-crushing, heart-stopping laugh that was always so rare from him. "It wouldn't have been a proper wedding night without a threat of violence."

I turned to face him, pressing my naked body against his as I snaked my arms around his neck. "Wedding nights without daggers are never proper."

He traced a finger down my side before leaning down to kiss me. "Tell me what you want, Nightmare, and it is yours. It's been yours since the day we met."

"Only you, Orin. I just want us." I rested my hands on his chest, over the darkness taking root there. "And eternity."

He prowled forward. I closed my eyes, droplets of water falling down my cheeks, my heart pounding, my nerves standing on end with the promise that salacious look on his face delivered. I couldn't handle the way I needed him. Couldn't process the tremble between my legs begging for his touch. In one motion, he grabbed my waist and lifted, helping me to sit on the edge of the bath so I could stare down at him as he drank me. His jaw slacked, and a tongue flashed across his bottom lip.

Hands still slick with oil, he slowly spread my legs apart as he inched toward my core. Orin's fingers drifted close, so fucking close to where I needed him most, tracing fiery circles against my sensitive skin, heat pouring off him.

"Do you like it when I touch you here, Wife?"

I nodded.

He shifted a tiny bit closer, until the anticipation of his next move, the absolute need to feel him inside of me, thrummed.

"How about here?" His deep voice was strained and controlled, but only just.

"Don't play with your dinner, Orin. Or do, but please do it soon."

"Is that a plea, Wife?"

"It's whatever the hell you need it to be," I breathed.

"Yes, it is." With a wide grin, he stroked his fingers over me once, circling my clit, satisfying one small need by stoking another as he pulled his hands away and tasted me on them. "So fucking sweet. Just as I imagined. Gods, Deyanira."

I practically panted when those eyes met mine, watching me as he slid his thumb over me again. I buried my hands in his dripping dark hair. Aching for more. For him. The threads of our bond pulsed with need, just as I did.

He dug his fingers into my thighs, pulling me closer to the ledge, burying his face between my legs to claim the soft flesh waiting for him. Tongue flicking over me in a perfect rhythm, pushing his fingers inside, a pure, feral growl left him, the sound vibrating my thighs. He spiraled, eyes turning dark and dangerous as he tasted me in a way that carried me to the deepest pit of desire and the very height of sensitivity. Tilting my head back, fingers pulling on his hair, every second, every stroke, was torment and ecstasy. I needed to fall, to burst as he grazed his teeth over me, but I also never wanted him to stop, never wanted that plunge.

But still, I shattered. Still, I cried out his name, limbs trembling, begging him to stop, to relent for just one moment. Every muscle failed me as I lay back, the cool stone floor kissing my skin as I dragged air into my lungs, knowing I needed more of him. All of him.

He leaped from the water, splashing, dripping all over me as he lifted me from the floor and carried me to the rug before the fire, the flame's heat licking my skin dry as Orin perched above me, watching. Resting my hands on the sides of his face, I studied this version of him. He was so many things. Dark and unbreakable in dire moments, and tender in others. But whatever he was from one moment to another, it was usually fleeting, a battle he constantly waged. My equal. My everything.

As if he could read my thoughts, he pressed his lips to my ear. "Don't look at me like that, Nightmare, or we will never leave this bathhouse, and your eternity will be spent naked and writhing below me."

"I wouldn't complain."

A soft kiss to white lashes grew to feral nipping at my lips and breasts. He took himself in his hand and slid his tip right down my slit. I arched. He groaned. And then he surged forward, filling me completely before he withdrew and thrust again with a groan of contentment. Until our shared breaths became one, until the chaos of the moment turned calm, reliable. A steady rhythm. Until I knew each ridge of his cock, and he knew the walls that welcomed him. Until there was no light or darkness. Only him and I and a lingering promise of forever that took root, winding its sharpened talons around the core of this world, anchoring us both.

As he changed his pace, I raised my hips to meet him, and Orin took that as a sign that I needed him deeper. He lifted my leg, resting it on his shoulder, stretching those muscles. I couldn't have held back if I'd wanted to. I no longer had control over my body. I was his entirely as he stroked me, stretched me, and filled me to the brink, overwhelming my senses until I screamed his name. Addled thoughts coursed through my mind as I tried to remember anything beyond the unbridled pleasure of Orin pulsing inside of me.

He collapsed beside me, breaths ragged.

Though an ache settled between my legs, I twisted to face him, letting the fire warm my back. "You never washed."

"I know. I was saving it for round two."

THE SUN HAD RISEN before we'd snuck off to the house, crossing the grass, still damp with dew, creeping in and up the stairs until we fell into Orin's bed, getting lost in each other once more. It'd started with a kiss to my shoulder, and before I knew it, I was naked again, never feeling like I'd get enough of him and us and the eternity that waited.

When the exhaustion was finally too much, when our bodies were slick with sweat and our breaths ragged, I let my eyes fall shut. He curled up behind me, his warm body wrapping perfectly around mine.

Three breaths into the oblivion of sleep, I felt myself falling as I was yanked into Death's court, and that stunning face I'd seen so many times was deep red and full of fury.

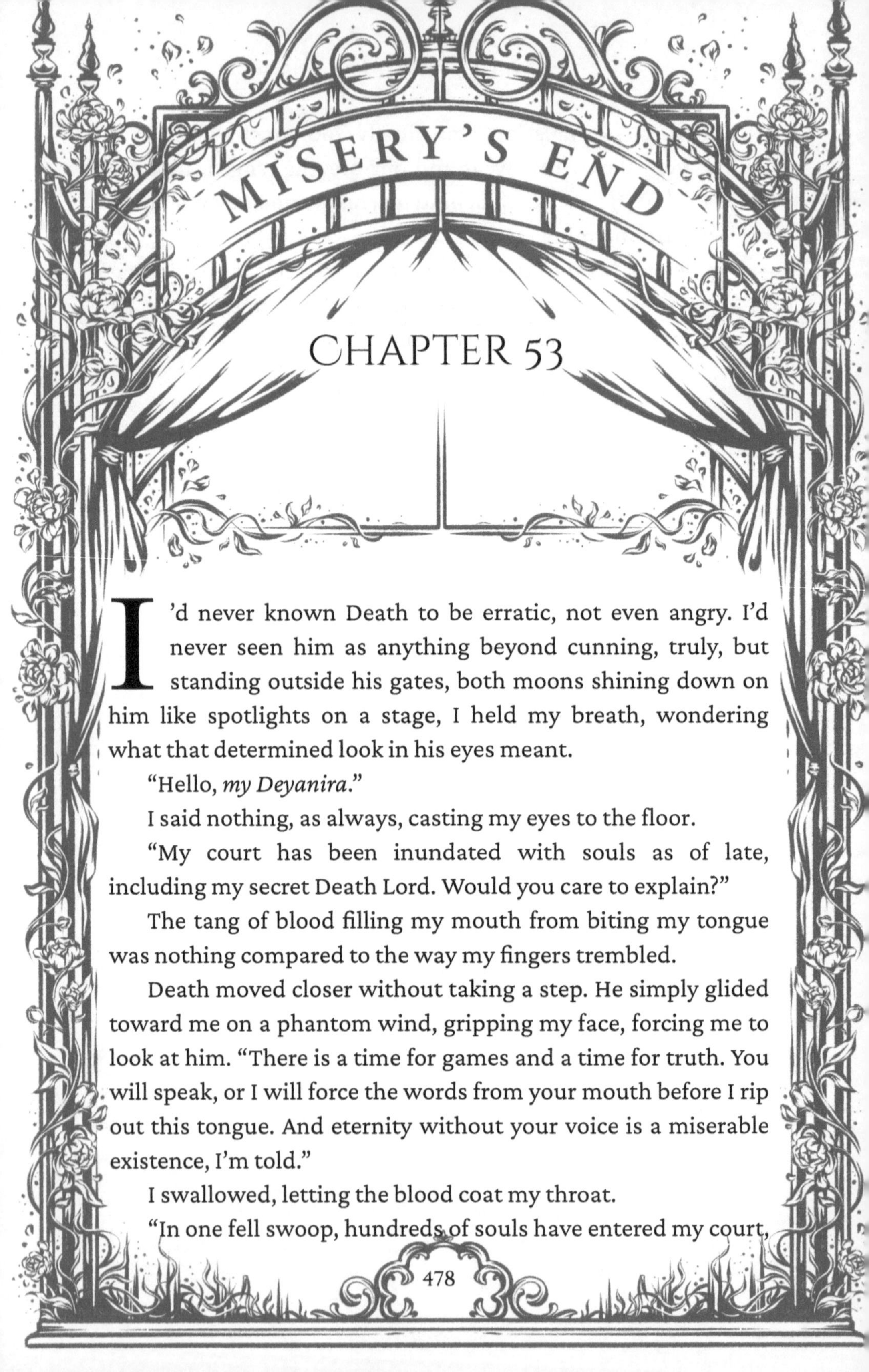

MISERY'S END

CHAPTER 53

I'd never known Death to be erratic, not even angry. I'd never seen him as anything beyond cunning, truly, but standing outside his gates, both moons shining down on him like spotlights on a stage, I held my breath, wondering what that determined look in his eyes meant.

"Hello, *my Deyanira*."

I said nothing, as always, casting my eyes to the floor.

"My court has been inundated with souls as of late, including my secret Death Lord. Would you care to explain?"

The tang of blood filling my mouth from biting my tongue was nothing compared to the way my fingers trembled.

Death moved closer without taking a step. He simply glided toward me on a phantom wind, gripping my face, forcing me to look at him. "There is a time for games and a time for truth. You will speak, or I will force the words from your mouth before I rip out this tongue. And eternity without your voice is a miserable existence, I'm told."

I swallowed, letting the blood coat my throat.

"In one fell swoop, hundreds of souls have entered my court, though none can name their murderer. Not a blade to the throat, as is your signature, but death by magic. *My* magic. And Icharius Fern has assured me you have a name. Tell me who holds power that should only belong to my chosen."

I squeezed my eyes shut, panic rising within me as I realized what he was saying. Somehow Orin truly did have magic gifted from Death himself, but that wasn't the surprise. It was the fact that he hadn't known about it. And I had seconds to defy the only god I'd ever known in order to protect a man that held my heart.

"Give me the name, Deyanira. I will not ask again."

I stood firm, my lip curling in disgust as I held my ground. He could condemn me to his court right now and I still wouldn't speak Orin's name. I would spend an eternity suffering before I let Death have him.

He dragged a sharp finger down my cheek, leaning so close there was no doubt he could see me tremble. Though not with fear, but anger because of all the gods, we were left with one that would rain misery on a suffering world for his own pleasure. But what difference did it make who held such power when Death could take whatever he wanted from our world? He had gifted each person of Requiem a hundred years of immortality, but his magic remained. I remained. The Death Maiden had been his promise that should the world fall to pieces, he would bring it down. Why would he need Orin? Why search for one with that power unless... he couldn't? Perhaps his magic was not infinite.

I will see you in a few days, my beauty. I have a good feeling about this one.

Death is hunting someone.

The realization melted over me as I stepped backward. He was hunting Orin's power.

"I see something in your eyes, Deyanira. Tell me what it is."

Another step backward.

He snatched my hand before I could move again, yanking me toward him as he purred with delight in my ear. "The first and last time you disappoint me lives in this moment. Shall we start close to home, then?"

"No!" I roared, trying to pull away. But there was no escaping Death's absolute hold as his power raced down my arm.

"She speaks." He chuckled.

Again, I tried to fight him, pulling away, though I had no idea how I would escape beyond his grasp. I didn't matter, though, not as white-hot pain raced across my palm, burning my flesh to embers as a name was given. A name I couldn't bear to see.

"Look, Deyanira."

I couldn't. Squeezing my eyes shut so he would not see the tears, I willed myself to wake, but the hold did not waver, and the heat of Death's court didn't retreat.

"I will hold you here until I see your face. Do not test me, my darling. I'm far better at this game than you are."

He could've gripped my throat and ripped all the air from my lungs. He could've shoved his hand into my heart and squeezed until I felt as though he'd ripped it from my weakening chest. But he hadn't. All those sensations were my own as I crumbled to the ground and held those burning letters to my chest, so afraid to see which of my family he'd selected.

"Look," he demanded again. And, as though the power of his words ripped my will in two, my eyes fell to the name burned into my palm, just as every piece of my heart shattered.

Orin Faber.

The love of my life.

My husband.

The single death I would never recover from. The man that

had carried me would now die at my hands. When I glanced up at Death's beautiful face, it twisted into something far more grotesque. He delighted in the visceral pain throbbing within my soul.

"Thank you for sharing this moment, my Deyanira. I will see you soon." He pulled me from the rocky ground with a firm grip on my bicep. "I have a *really* good feeling about this one."

And then he was gone. His court fell to darkness as my dream faded.

The cool sheets of our bed grounded me, though the tears were silent. I could feel him lying there, the arm wrapped heavily around my waist, the soothing breaths on my ear.

Orin.

The magic pulsed; a hairline tinge of madness curled around his name in my mind, and I thought I'd be sick with the panic of it.

As slowly as my racing heart would allow, I slipped from the bed and darted down the hall, tears running freely. Ripping Thea's door open, I ran to her, shaking her awake with all the fear and hysteria present on my face, I was sure.

"You have to wake up," I cried. "You have to save him. I can't stop it. You have to help me. Thea. Please."

She was up in seconds, ripping the blankets away with a fury as my panic became her panic.

"Slow down, Deyanira." Her words were measured and calm, an attempt to bring me a semblance of peace, but there would be none for me. Not now. Not ever.

"Look," I answered, shoving my palm into her face. "You have to lock me up, Thea. You have to make chains with magic. Something I can never escape from. You have to save him. Please."

"Oh, gods," she whispered, pulling my hand toward the small light in her room to take in the name.

She shook her head, her own tears welling as she stood from her bed and threw her arms around me. "Please don't do it, Deyanira. Please."

Her words, the plea in them, sliced into my heart. After all this time, she knew I didn't have a choice, but still, to hear those words on her lips only made the wound dig deeper.

"You have to lock me up," I cried again. "Somewhere he cannot find me."

"I can't. I could never. We'll find another way."

"No," I hissed, pushing her away far more forcefully than I'd wanted. "Unless you want to see him die, Thea, you've got to."

"If your intention is to wake the whole house, you're nearly there," Paesha yawned from the door. "What's going on?"

But the second she took in my face, her eyes fell to Thea cradling my palm in hers. And then she knew. As if the words had been spoken aloud, she knew.

"There's only one way to save him, Paesha."

She nodded. "We have to get you out of here. Where do you want to go?"

"No," Thea's voice broke. "You can't be serious. I'm not doing this. You've seen her madness, P."

She grabbed Thea's boots and threw them to her feet. "I've also lost the man I love, and if I could have taken his place, I would have. Get dressed, Thea. We're leaving."

The blacksmith complied, sniffling the entire time she slipped her feet into her boots and chased us out the door.

"We have to go somewhere he'll never think to look because he will come for you."

"A temple," I whispered. "He hates them. Pick any, I don't care."

"The Temple of Eiria. The one with the tree. He knows what happened the last time you were there. He'll never expect you to go back."

We had minutes, I was sure of it. If Orin woke and I was not beside him, he'd come for me. He needed me beyond the healing he drew from our connection. He loved me, and as I looked over my shoulder at that house one final time, letting my fate seal with every hurried step, the crack in my heart reminded me that I needed him, too.

The magic would not be stayed, though. Not as a dagger to his throat flashed across my mind. I blinked several times as we ran past the tree line, beyond Misery's End, through the devastating wreckage of Silbath. This is what he'd done to get to me last time. A show of his desperation through the lower half of this crumbling city. What would become of the world when I vanished?

Thea had stopped to get a small chain from her forge, claiming it would be easier to have something to start with, but before we'd even reached the stone bridge to Perth, she'd had to hand it off to Paesha to take a turn carrying it. As we ran, she'd been winding her magic over the links, using power to turn each one unbreakable.

The door to the temple was still cracked open, likely from the last time Paesha had gone in to search for signs of the Life Maiden. Standing on the steps outside, I took one final look at the world beyond before following the others, Thea's growing chain now dragging on the ground.

When Paesha had come, she swore the willow tree in the middle of the temple was dead, but looking at it now, at the unique little flowers sweeping down the branches, I would have never believed her. With gnarled roots climbing the stone walls and the canopy nearly filling the ceiling of the abandoned temple, something had come to life here. A protest against the presence of death in the Temple of Eiria.

As if the magic within me knew what I'd planned, it hissed in my mind, nearly burning through my thoughts until the only thing I could think of was Orin standing before me. I'd been lost in those phantom amber eyes when Paesha yanked on my arm, pulling me back to reality.

"You're sure you want to do this?" she asked for the third time.

Run.

My eyes traveled on their own accord, following the path we'd walked into the building, settling on the early morning fog beyond the temple door. It took every ounce of strength I had to fight Death's compulsion.

"I have to," I said, a knot building in my throat. "And you need to do it now, Thea."

She knelt, placing her palm on the first link of the chain and then the floor. Pulling her hammer, sparks flew as she got to work. The second the iron linked around my wrists, suffocation and sheer panic rose like a tidal wave. How far would I go? What would my future become? It didn't matter, though, not when I thought of his.

The women came to stand before me, Thea bringing her palm to my cheek. Her touch was filled with a tenderness that spoke of a love that had grown between us. "They will not break. The more you struggle, the tighter they will become, so you won't be able to leverage yourself free, nor harm yourself trying." Her breath shuddered through her, a tear slipping down her cheek. "Eventually, they will hold you bound to the floor."

The green in her eyes shone like a thousand emeralds behind those tears. She opened her mouth to say more, but nothing came out.

I sighed, the weight of the world resting on my shoulders as I stood bound to that temple floor. "I'm sorry you had to be the one to do this. If I could have spared you..."

"No." Paesha stepped forward, placing her forehead to mine.

"You don't have to be the one to apologize, Dey. Your power is a curse, but we'll find a way to free you both. I swear it."

"Just don't tell him where I am. I need you to promise it."

"We promise," Paesha whispered.

Fight them. Escape.

Already I was finding it hard to remember these were not my thoughts. Perhaps stirred by the finality of their stares.

"Tell Quill... I love her."

"We will," Thea managed, though she sobbed.

"And when he threatens you, you lie. Do whatever you have to do, but never forget that Orin is dangerous. And desperate, dangerous people make ruthless decisions. He can't think I'm suffering, or he will bring down the rest of this world."

"I'll handle it," Paesha promised. "And we will see you again, Deyanira. I swear it."

I saw the irony of asking them to lie for me to him, just as he'd asked them to do, and though I felt like a monster for it, I saw no other way. The only thing standing between Orin and an early grave was three women who loved him desperately and chains that I could only pray would hold me despite the guaranteed madness.

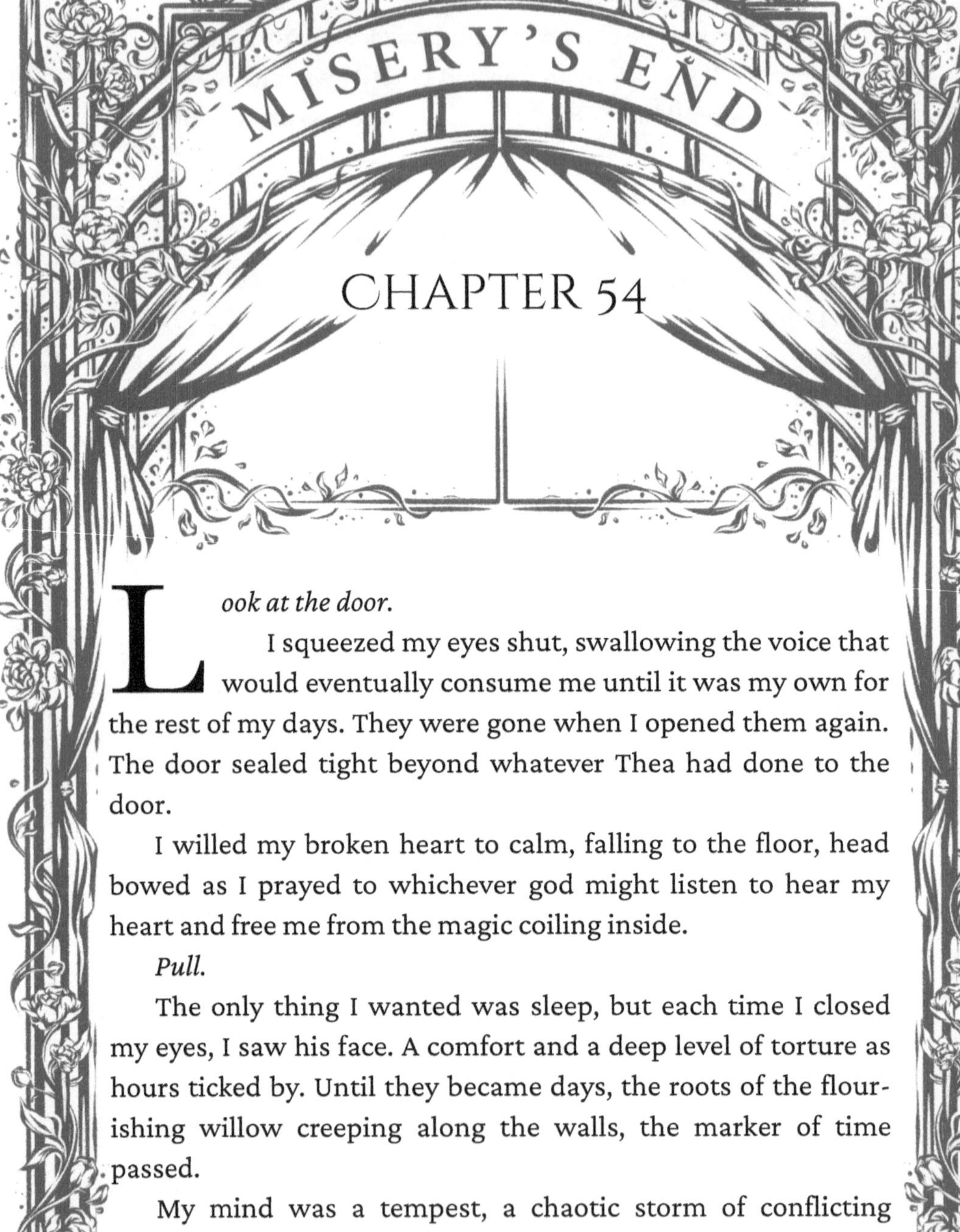

CHAPTER 54

ook at the door.

I squeezed my eyes shut, swallowing the voice that would eventually consume me until it was my own for the rest of my days. They were gone when I opened them again. The door sealed tight beyond whatever Thea had done to the door.

I willed my broken heart to calm, falling to the floor, head bowed as I prayed to whichever god might listen to hear my heart and free me from the magic coiling inside.

Pull.

The only thing I wanted was sleep, but each time I closed my eyes, I saw his face. A comfort and a deep level of torture as hours ticked by. Until they became days, the roots of the flourishing willow creeping along the walls, the marker of time passed.

My mind was a tempest, a chaotic storm of conflicting thoughts and emotions, of my strong will versus Death's power. The magic within writhed like a serpent, taunting me with whispers of murder. It promised release from my chains, from the torment of my own mind, if only I would let it in.

"One, Anika Sariah Hark."

My raspy words were sandpaper in my throat.

Orin Faber.

"Two. Garrit Faden."

Orin Faber.

"Three. Marian Achlen."

There is nothing more beautiful than a blade piercing smooth skin.

"Four," I cried, trying to cover an ear with my shoulder as the chain weighed me down. "Leander Galen."

Drip. Drip. See his blood fall upon this floor. Red. Beautiful. Scarlet.

"Five... Ave... Ave..."

Orin Faber.

"Orin Faber."

Breathe.

Take a breath. His.

Focus. Spiral. Pull. The floor.

The cool stone floor. Slack waning. Lie down.

Stand up.

"Five. Aveline Elara."

Orin Faber.

Strong jaw, hair as dark as night. Nightmare. Golden eyes, pouty lips.

"Pouty lips."

Yes.

"Sleep."

No.

"Sleep."

The chains bit into my flesh, my struggles in vain as they held. My nails clawed at the cold stone, leaving trails of desperation behind. I could feel the magic's tendrils probing, seeking the chinks in my weakening resolve. Tears streamed down my cheeks as I wrestled with the darkness within.

"I won't let you," I hissed through gritted teeth, my eyes wide and wild, reflecting the torment of my fractured soul. "I won't break." The words were a promise to myself more than anything. To him. The man I believed was struggling just as much as I was, however far away he might be.

The temple seemed to respond to my internal turmoil, its timeworn walls creaking and groaning as if they, too, felt the weight of my inner battle. Shadows danced in grotesque patterns around me, mocking my helplessness. And I needed them. Every one. My only company as time dragged on.

There were moments when I wondered if Death would come and break Thea's chains. If he would capture Orin and deliver him just to watch the severing blow. But I continued to fight against every second. Until I wished away his face in my mind, until I refused to look at the name on my palm. Until I forgot what it felt like when he'd caressed my skin and tasted me.

"Deyanira."

Orin's voice ripped through the temple like an axe. Reality from my heart's greatest desire was becoming so hard to discern. But the deep growl in that voice woke the dormant magic, stirring it to life with vigor.

He comes.

"No. He can't."

The visions began again. Orin stood before me, so much pain and anguish on his face. Hands free from chains and trembling, I ripped the blade across his throat, feeling only satisfaction as he fell to the ground.

My heart stumbled over itself as I forced measured breaths.

"No."

Yes.

I couldn't squeeze my eyes shut and not see his face. I couldn't look upon reality and see nothing but eternity without him. The walls moved in. Everything shifted. Turning threatening as my nails began to dig into flesh on my palms. Until my blood dripped to the floor and Thea's magic pulsed. A warning in the chains. Should I continue, they would hold me to the ground rather than let me stand.

But I needed to stand. I needed to fight.

Yes.

"No. Stop."

Each breath became labored as his phantom voice snapped through the room again. "Deyanira Sariah Faber."

It was beautifully timbral and held so much emotion. I couldn't escape the way it crept over my skin like a balm, taking me to a place that was only ours. In darkness and in madness. In all the safe havens we'd built together, the way his voice carried me to peace was a power not of this world. Not of Death or abandoned gods. Of love. And desperation.

The madness conquered my own horrors, though. As the great door swung open and Orin stood within the frame, eyes pinned to me, I lurched for him, desperate for my blades.

You don't need them. You need only his blood. His pain. His body. His life.

The snap of my bones as I dislocated both shoulders fighting the chains did nothing to stop the way I lunged for him. Iron digging into skin, drawing my blood did not deter me. Thea's magic failed as I ripped the chains from the floor and ran for him. For a moment, there was relief on his beautiful face. Until he realized I had become the thing of nightmares. I was his enemy.

No matter the way I fought the power, still, I ran. Still, I watched those chains as they swung through the air, ensnaring him. Still, I watched them rip him to pieces until everything in my world shattered as what was left of Orin Faber turned to shadow.

Trembling, I pushed away the magic, searching beyond the darkness inside of me until I could see past it. Until the door was shut once more, and Orin was nowhere to be seen. Until my heart ached for him as much as it found relief that those images were not real. Only the madness rotting my mind.

But again, I heard my name.

"Deyanira."

"No," I cried.

That word didn't dance on phantom power. It was real. And so was he, banging on the door of the temple. He repeatedly beat on the door. I'd always known he would find me, just as he had the day he broke the world. And though I loved him more for his devotion, I hated how cruel fate could be to a man who could love so passionately.

He screamed my name until his voice grew hoarse. Each syllable paired with a tear on my cheek. Because I wanted him just as fiercely as he wanted me. And somehow, as if the temple bent to the will of Death, the giant willow shuddered, and the door came down in a thud.

He didn't stand there by magic or illusion. He was real.

"Why?" he demanded, storming into the room, nearly swallowed by his own darkness. The veins on his body had crept up his neck, kissing his jawline. His eyes were wholly black, and each breath was a tidal wave of fury. "You left me. You just fucking left me lying in our bed."

"I'm sorry," I whispered before another vision of his death flashed before my eyes. Just a throat slice this time, silencing him.

You. Not Death. Not madness. You want him. You need him. You fight.

The poisonous thoughts were mine. My thoughts. Mine.

Every choice. Every gasp. Every death. Every drop of blood. I wanted this. I craved this. I needed death. His end. Him. The satisfaction. The pleasure. The pride. The weapon. The blood. The blood.

The blood.

"Stay away."

At my words, he dashed forward. "Fight it, Deyanira."

"I can't," I whispered, feeling the tic in my neck as I yanked on the chains. "You have to leave."

Kill.

"Now, Orin."

"I need you. Every second of my life, I need you. Not because of the power. Because I love you. My world doesn't exist without you in it."

The blood.

"Stop it," I commanded the voices, trying to cradle my own head, though I couldn't reach beyond the chains. "It's too loud."

"Dey." He took a step toward me. "I won't let this happen." Another step. "I know what this feels like." Again, a step.

"Orin, please. Don't make me your murderer."

"I am not afraid to wait for you in eternity, love."

"Stay away from me."

"If there's a single part of your heart that convinces you that I'd sit back and let you suffer for the rest of your life just to spare me the passing of mine, you don't know the depth of my love for you." He moved before me, so close I could feel him and every bit of the tiny inch that remained between us.

"I need you to be an illusion. Please don't do this."

He reached for the chains attached to my feet first. That deep bevy of power rumbled through the temple, until the tree shriveled, the pulse of whatever remained within it cowering at Orin's magic.

My heart did not beat. Seconds did not pass. Everything

stood still as that beautiful man fell to his knees before me and lifted Chaos like an offering, his head bowed. "My life was yours the second I met you, Deyanira. Take it and free yourself."

A terror like none I'd ever known overcame me. I could feel the madness within me, the malevolent power, clawing at the edges of my consciousness, trying to take control. My body convulsed, the edges of my vision turning an ominous shade of black.

I gasped for breath, feeling the struggle within me intensify. *The blade. The blood. The gasp. Ours. Mine. His.*

I reached for that fucking blade, having no control over my movements. Not an ounce. I didn't want to feel the cool metal. I didn't want to remember the way the grooves dug into my hands.

"Please run," I whispered, limbs shaking as I fell to the floor before him, knees touching.

But he met my eyes fearlessly, every bit of fight I'd known him to harbor gone. "I will not. You fight it, Deyanira. Fight it or let it take me because I refuse to be the reason you suffer."

"How can you not see putting your death in my hands is no different?" I tried to swallow, but the lump in my throat had grown sharp, the few breaths I could manage, a chore.

I bowed my head, the only movement that was my own as my arm crossed my body. A single slice. One strike and he'd be gone from me for the rest of this lifetime. I fought to summon the dormant Life Maiden magic, praying it would not be a repeat of that poor peony. My desperate need to save Orin circumvented any doubt that might have settled in my mind. But the darkness clawed back, relentless.

The agony of my mental battle was overwhelming, and I could hear Orin's voice, a distant, smoky sound that resonated through my entire body. Seeking the power was not enough. I let it grow, let it rip that pinprick source open until it became a wildfire within me, sending Death's power to the furthest recesses of my consciousness. Darkness could only thrive where light failed to cast its radiant touch, but in my soul, I forged a blazing sun, banishing the shadows into oblivion with every breath of my unwavering spirit.

The sharp edge of madness faded away until the inside of that temple held no trace of torment. Chaos slipped from my hand. With a wail, I reached for him, throwing my arms around his neck, kissing him until my lips had gone numb. Living in a place of freedom I didn't know could exist.

"How?" he asked as we stood from the ground.

"I found the Life Maiden, Orin."

His gaze shifted between my eyes, waiting for me to say the words I wasn't sure how to voice. Without a doubt, the feeling that resonated within me, thrumming just below my skin in the most radiant, rejuvenating wave of euphoria was not only the relief of my escape from Death's thrall, but power that started right here within this godless temple.

He brushed the tip of his thumb over the outside corners of my lashes. "I think I found her, too. Only you could harbor life and death and somehow still be undeniably your own person. More than a vessel, more than a conduit. So human, yet so much more than any person walking this realm."

"Isn't she spectacular?"

Death's voice ricocheted through the chasm of every fear I'd ever harbored. His footsteps were silent as he paused to pluck a familiar flower from the magical willow tree that turned to ash at his touch. "The backdrop of your betrayal is uncanny, my beauty."

He practically floated toward us, and though I'd wanted to step between him and Orin, my husband took my hand and shifted in front of me instead.

Orin's low growl was nearly feral in his chest as he managed to stare down at Death, though they stood eye to eye. Something in that moment stole my breath. Fear of the one I'd believed to be the true villain of the world, or fear for the man that was my world, I wasn't sure. But it was more than that. A realization before the words were spoken. An absolute truth that stole the very breath from my lungs.

Death stared at Orin, his eyes widening for a fraction before a stunning smile crept along his full lips. Lips that now brought about a shock jolting through me. I'd seen his devastating beauty before and knew that none could match him ... except, the man facing him. Orin, whose lips were so similar to Death's, though marred in a frown.

"I should have known," Death said, placing a hand on Orin's shoulder. "Only my blood would be powerful enough to defy the gods. Let's go home, son."

Son.

The world turned to icy dread and confusion.

Orin's grip slackened. I grasped for him, yanking on his hand for him to spin. To face me. But there was only darkness in his eyes. Death. His father.

"Orin?"

He didn't answer. All of his features, each one I'd cherished, hardened. He was lost in an instant as hatred filled the eyes that stared down at me. Before I could reach for that Life Maiden power, before I could save him, they both vanished into a pool of shadows, leaving me feeling like the ground had crumbled beneath my feet, my heart heavy with the weight of a truth I had never expected and an absolute severance of my soul.

"I will come for you," I whispered into the abyss, hoping he'd heard me before the shadows dissipated.

What lies had Elowen told? And what truths had Ro kept, having known how to appease his power?

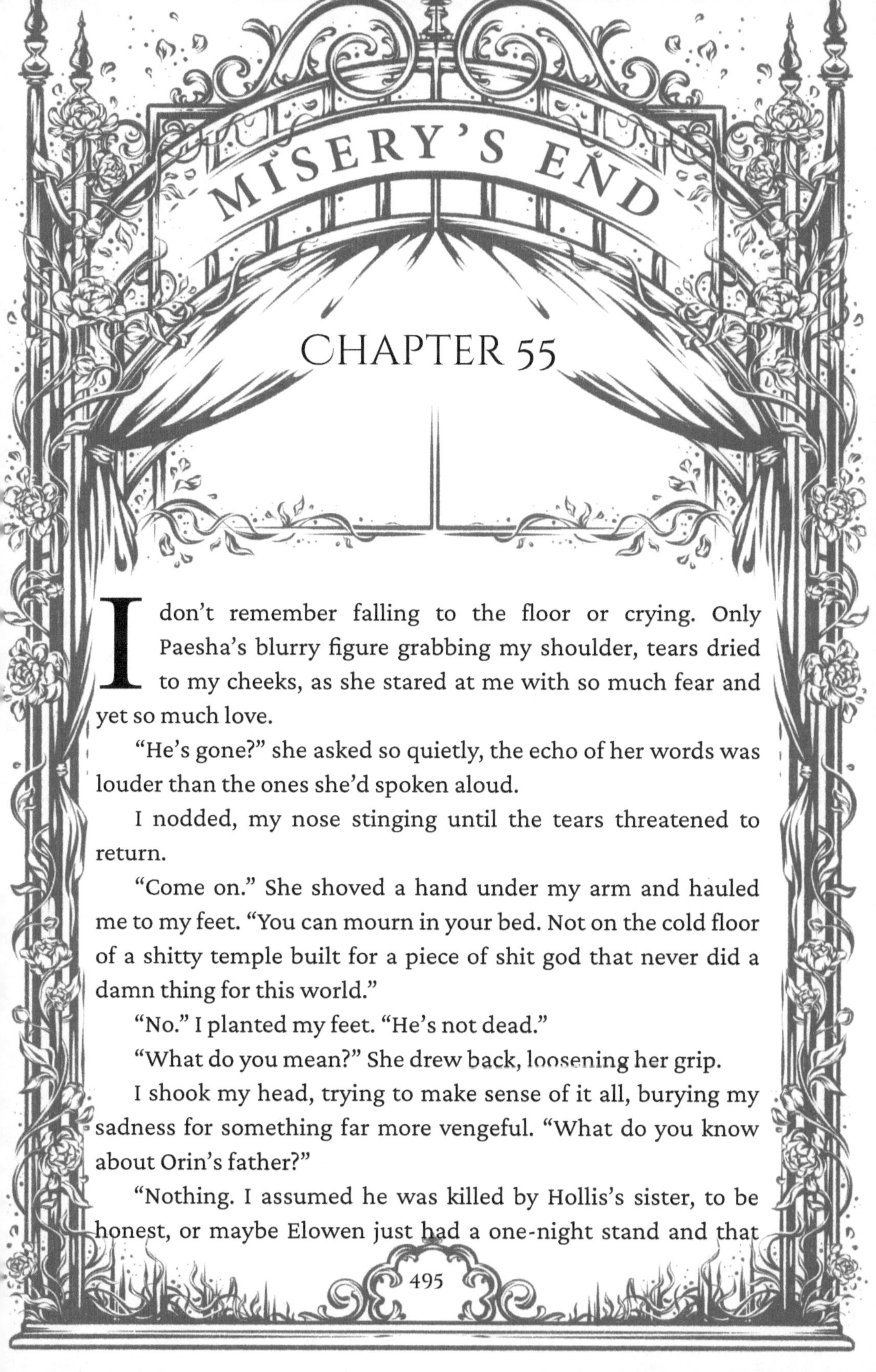

MISERY'S END

CHAPTER 55

I don't remember falling to the floor or crying. Only Paesha's blurry figure grabbing my shoulder, tears dried to my cheeks, as she stared at me with so much fear and yet so much love.

"He's gone?" she asked so quietly, the echo of her words was louder than the ones she'd spoken aloud.

I nodded, my nose stinging until the tears threatened to return.

"Come on." She shoved a hand under my arm and hauled me to my feet. "You can mourn in your bed. Not on the cold floor of a shitty temple built for a piece of shit god that never did a damn thing for this world."

"No." I planted my feet. "He's not dead."

"What do you mean?" She drew back, loosening her grip.

I shook my head, trying to make sense of it all, burying my sadness for something far more vengeful. "What do you know about Orin's father?"

"Nothing. I assumed he was killed by Hollis's sister, to be honest, or maybe Elowen just had a one-night stand and that was all there was to it. He's never brought it up, and I've never asked."

"Well, I think it's time we start asking Elowen questions because Death called him his son and then they vanished. Together. And Orin didn't even fight it. The second Death touched him, he was... lost." If a heart was made of a thousand pieces of emotion, all of mine shattered with those words. "I was supposed to save him. And I did. And it didn't matter."

"I'm coming with you." Paesha's cold stare was final. "If you need help searching, I'm going. Whatever you're after, Maiden, whatever you need."

Her eyes searched mine for a fight, but I simply plucked a flower from the ground and pulled her out of the temple, hoping I'd never have to step foot in that place again.

"Not dead?" Elowen asked, skin turning pale as she fell into a chair at the kitchen table.

"I don't know if it's permanent. If there's a way... If I can get to him. He didn't die, Elowen."

"But you're the Life Maiden?" Thea asked, gripping Elowen's shoulders to give her comfort. "And your other power is what? Gone? How could you get to Death's court without..."

"Dying?" I lowered my voice so Quill wouldn't hear me. "I don't know. Orin told me his world didn't exist without me, but mine doesn't exist without him, either. We are bonded. I have to find a path to him. And I think it starts at the beginning." We faced Orin's mother in solidarity.

"He was so handsome," Elowen said, her eyes glossed over as she lived through a memory. "My brother introduced us. He'd given me the night off from the show and let me go with this... stranger. I'd always wanted to fall in love, and I thought I had, in one night. He'd spoken of a future together. He'd promised to help me find a way out of Drexel's new magic. He was so dark but so light, and we drank and danced, and he laughed. Gods, the way that man laughed. I can still hear it, even after all these years. And the next morning, I woke up naked. And alone. And I didn't even care. Not when I'd got that one night of happiness. My belly swelled, and I knew Orin was a blessing from a god. A baby I might have never had, otherwise."

I swallowed my shock. "I'm so sorry you were left alone."

"I'm not," she said, forcing a smile. "Because I was never truly alone."

I paced the floor, Elowen's story lingering in the stagnant air.

"What's your plan?" Althea asked, eventually.

"I think I have to start with Ro. She was helping him. She knew about his power."

"Or you start with Drexel. He seems to have Death's ear," Thea said.

Paesha shook her head. "I think the Maestro died when Orin cast his magic to save you. No one has seen him."

"Pity." I stared down into Elowen's blank face. "I would have loved to see him fall."

I'd seen a small bit of the destruction on the journey to and from the temple, but we'd stuck close to the Hallowed River both times we'd gone. Still, the Maestro's death, if that's truly what happened, felt like a robbery in the grand scheme of things, with all the heartache he'd caused. Not just to me, of course, but the pained look on Elowen's face had nothing to do with a fallen brother. She'd lost her son. And Drexel, her own flesh and blood, had played a part in that.

I knelt before Quill, rubbing my hands through Boo's soft hair one final time before pulling the child into a hug. "You are brave, and you are strong. Never stop fighting for what you believe in, Quilly. Do you hear me? Dreams are worth chasing, and family is worth trusting."

She nodded, a sob escaping as she buried her face in the crook of my neck. "You'll try to come back though, won't you?"

I pulled away, looking deep into those stunning blue eyes. "I will do everything I can to come back to you, but I can't promise it."

"Orin won't be alone, and he needs family, too," she said, swiping a tear. "But I'll miss you."

"I'll miss you, too, kid."

I closed my eyes the second she wailed and flew into Paesha's waiting arms.

"Hey, Quilly," Paesha said gently. "Don't worry. Things have a way of working out, right?"

Quill nodded, still staring at Paesha as if she'd never see her again. I thought Paesha would argue the point, reassure her she'd be back by nightfall, whether I was there or not, but she didn't. Whatever goodbye the two of them shared, it wouldn't come with promises from Paesha. Maybe she worried about what was to come and didn't want to leave Quill feeling abandoned if neither of us made it back.

Paesha had taken Quill in when she'd been taken from her mother's incapable hands and placed into Drexel's. And though she'd still have Thea and Elowen, the child had already experienced more loss than she ever should have. It was hard to say goodbye to her, but for me, it would have been harder to stay here if there was any chance I could get to Orin. To save him from whatever Death had planned. I only hoped my path forward brought Paesha back to that child's arms.

Death was hunting something, and if he'd taken Orin the

second he learned of his power, who knew whether this realm would survive or if it would fall if someone didn't stand in the way. I knew leaving was the right choice for me. And I knew Quill would have the others to watch over her as I chased my husband's captor.

"I'll see the library fixed. And maybe we can move through the cities and rebuild," Thea said, her voice shaky as she held Elowen's hand, who'd lost all sense of the world the second she'd remembered her night with Death. As if a spell had fallen over her and she couldn't wake from it.

"Just take care of yourself and the others." I chanced a glance at Elowen so Thea understood. "No spotlights. Stay under the radar. The clock tower, should you need it, has some jewels. There's more in my father's castle. I'd make that my first stop in case the others get the same idea, now that there is no king and no law. Call in the rest of the Syndicate members and build a stronghold here, Thea. When Paesha gets back, recruit where you can. Don't worry about the outside world until you have yours well in hand."

She nodded. "I've got this. I promise. I'm stronger than I look."

Paesha moved to my side. "You're looking pretty fucking strong from where I'm standing, sister."

With a final hug, Paesha and I disappeared into her room and stood before the mirror I knew Ro was watching. There was just no way she didn't have eyes on this house and ears on Orin and his deadly power.

When the mirror did not ripple, I ran a hand over the glistening filigree to the side. Still nothing.

"What if she doesn't let us in?"

I slammed my hand against the glass, watching it crack into a spiderweb. "She's more than meets the eye, and she's got secrets. If she doesn't want to share... then I'll break every mirror in this godsdamned realm, and we'll see how she fares from there."

"Guess we better bring more weapons."

"On it," Thea called from the hallway.

STRAPPED DOWN with Thea's armory, Paesha and I stood on the front step of the Syndicate house for only a moment, each finding our own resolve to walk away without looking back. But the second that pup barked, we both looked over our shoulder to see all three of them standing in the door, waving, each motion full of sadness and finality.

"Are you sure about Visha?" Paesha asked, using her power to hunt down the brothel owner.

"The last time Ro showed up unexpectedly, it was in the Scarlet District. I've caught her there twice, once with Orin and once at Lady Visha's. I'm sure."

"There's a huge risk even stepping foot into that building."

"Then I guess it's a good thing I have nothing to lose. You don't have to come if you don't want to. You shouldn't go where I'm going anyway."

"I'll go as far as I can before I have to get back to the others. This is a fight I can handle, and Orin would never want you to do this alone."

The destruction was vast. Far more than I'd known. It seemed as if a quarter of Silbath had fallen to rubble in the aftermath of Orin's wrath. And each step I'd taken over the rubble was laden with guilt. The stones slipped beneath our feet as we wove between the buildings, finding reprieve once we reached the bridge to Perth, the city that remained untouched. And likely where the majority of survivors had run.

"I bet Beggar's Alley is full of people right now," Paesha said, adjusting the sword on her back as we crossed over the Hallowed River. "All those people…"

"We can't think about them. If we do, we'll never leave."

She pinned me with a stare. "Are you sure the Life Maiden *should* leave the world like this?"

"There's no part of me that wants to be without him, Paesha. I can't imagine a pining, sad Life Maiden is worth a thing to this world. I know what it's like to be with him; I can't possibly accept life without him. He broke the world for my freedom, and I'll burn down Death's court for his." I stepped off the bridge, turning toward the Scarlet District. "The night I met Orin, he said we could choose each other before the world forced us. I chose him then, when I shouldn't have, and I choose him now because there is no other way for me."

"They say Visha is more cunning than the Maestro. Her *petals* are more devoted to her. Makes her more dangerous."

I pulled Chaos from my thigh, missing the weight of Serenity on the other, accepting that the blade had been lost to the vagrants the second I'd dropped it. "She is dangerous, Paesha, but so are we."

The massive black man standing at the back door of Visha's brothel didn't so much as flinch when we approached. Nor did he bother to look at us at all. He simply pushed the door open, releasing a growl as we stepped inside the dimly lit space.

A soft murmur of conversation and laughter floated through the air. I knew the layout by heart, each room discreetly tucked away from prying eyes. As we made our way deeper into the establishment, our steps fell into a rhythm that felt almost automatic. The lush red velvet curtains framed each doorway like a promise of escape, a brief respite from the world outside. But that's exactly what Lady Visha's brothel always had been. She'd constructed a private world within these walls. Her own kingdom nestled into the heart of another.

The sound of a piano drifted towards us, the haunting melody tugging at memories I wasn't sure I was ready for. Of Orin playing on stage and the audience melting like liquid in his hands. He'd always been a spectacle. A haunted mystery.

Paesha followed behind me, her fingers trailing over the curtains and eyes lingering on the suggestive artwork down the hall until we entered the open room of velvet couches. Cordelia made eye contact with a gasp and hustled away.

A burly man sat opposite the room, gazing over the top of a newspaper. His eyes snapped away from me the moment recognition lit his face, but they landed easily on Paesha, drinking her in.

"I've got a nice place for you to sit over here, pet," he said, patting the cushion beside him.

She scowled. "I'd rather sit on the business end of my own sword."

"I'd love to watch," he breathed.

"Honestly, where do men get the audacity?"

I nudged her with my shoulder. "I'm pretty sure it's somewhere in that wrinkly ball sac skin."

She grinned. "That explains so much."

The man, clearly offended, tossed his paper to the side with a snarl, attempting to stand.

I whipped a tiny blade from my bandolier, and it landed right between his legs. "I fucking dare you."

He cleared his throat and plopped right back down, spreading his legs for the blade embedded into the couch. Paesha sauntered forward, gripped the knife, and pulled it free, just as the man gulped. "Waste not, want not," she said with a smirk.

"You've got a lot of nerve coming into my sanctuary, Huntress." Visha's words were sharp and full of venom.

Paesha brushed golden brown hair over her shoulder. "I do,

in fact, have a lot of nerve. Thanks for noticing, Lady V. Always a pleasure."

Impressed as I was with her snark, Paesha's smart mouth was surely going to get us in trouble if we weren't careful. We didn't have time to fall into Lady Visha's debt.

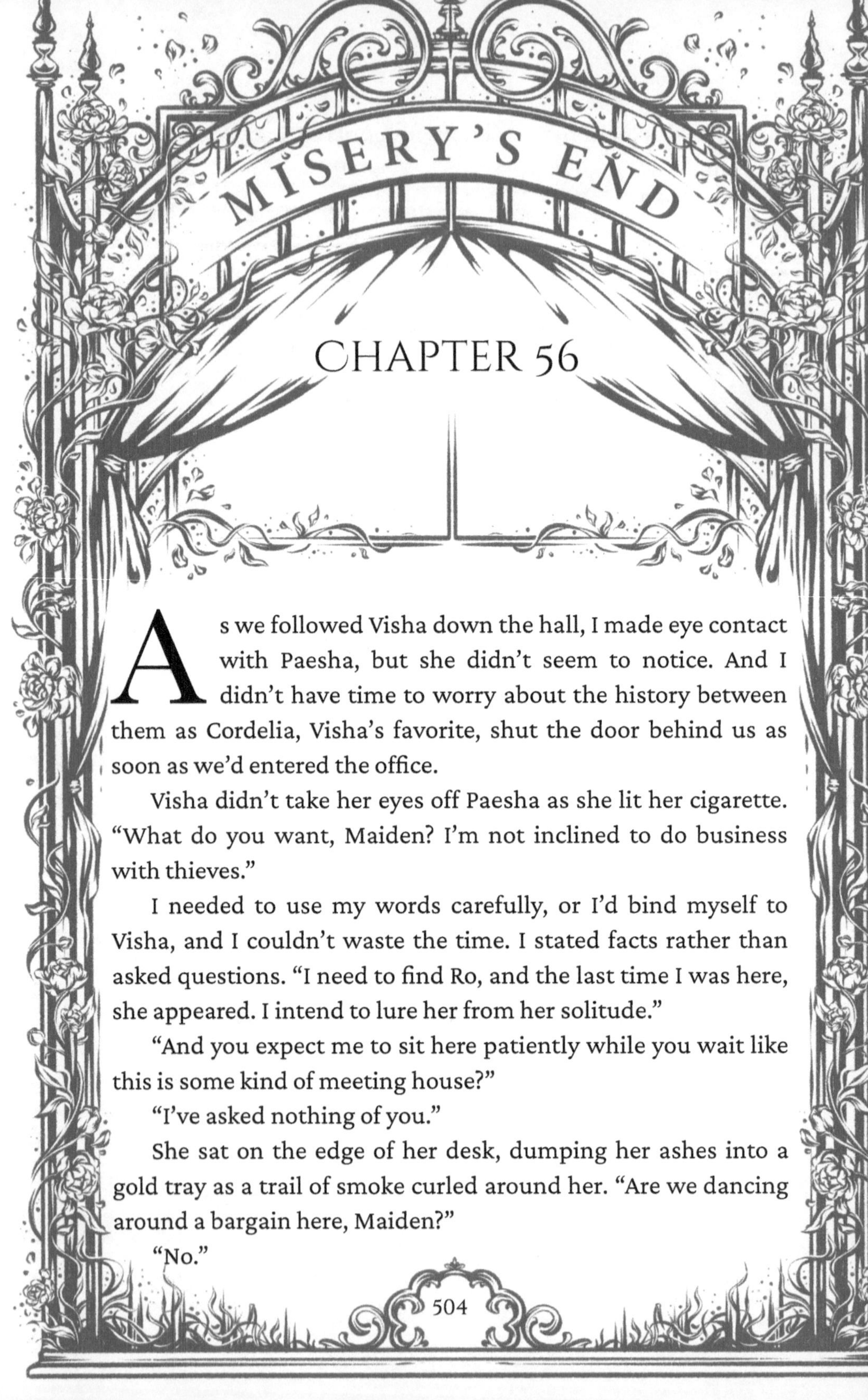

CHAPTER 56

As we followed Visha down the hall, I made eye contact with Paesha, but she didn't seem to notice. And I didn't have time to worry about the history between them as Cordelia, Visha's favorite, shut the door behind us as soon as we'd entered the office.

Visha didn't take her eyes off Paesha as she lit her cigarette. "What do you want, Maiden? I'm not inclined to do business with thieves."

I needed to use my words carefully, or I'd bind myself to Visha, and I couldn't waste the time. I stated facts rather than asked questions. "I need to find Ro, and the last time I was here, she appeared. I intend to lure her from her solitude."

"And you expect me to sit here patiently while you wait like this is some kind of meeting house?"

"I've asked nothing of you."

She sat on the edge of her desk, dumping her ashes into a gold tray as a trail of smoke curled around her. "Are we dancing around a bargain here, Maiden?"

"No."

"Yes."

Paesha and I'd answered at the same time, though I swallowed my gasp at her willingness to be bound to the woman.

"No," I said again, crossing my arms.

She narrowed those cunning eyes, taking a slow drag on that cigarette, the tip illuminating her beautiful face. "Then sit down, Maiden. If you're not here to bargain, you're wasting your time."

Anger coiled within me as I teetered on the edge of my own control. This wasn't a game to me. Orin's life, his freedom, wasn't something I wanted to gamble with. But the players in this realm, those who could make any difference , would always set the rules, and those in need would play along or be left to slaughter. It had always been that way, and I didn't know why I expected this to be any different. Fortunately, Paesha had spent a lifetime in this world. She knew exactly which mask she needed and when to slip it on.

"For starters, don't speak to Death's Maiden that way, or you're going to lose more than your little book, understood?"

"What do you want, Huntress?"

"We want you to tell us how to lure Ro from hiding. And before you start trapping us with fancy words, in exchange, I'm going to get the book I stole from you for the Maestro. I know where he keeps it locked up and exactly how to get into the safe. There will be no other terms."

"Deyanira stays here while you go," she said, far more amiable than I'd anticipated. No dealing, no debating, clean and easy.

"Deal, but if I'm not back by midnight, she goes free," Paesha said, turning toward me. "I'll be back as soon as I can." Pulling me into a hug, she whispered, "Don't let her fool you; she cannot trap you into a bargain without her book."

"You might have mentioned that before we got here," I hissed.

"I forgot," she said simply, stepping away. "Have fun, ladies."

She hadn't forgotten the book. She'd forgotten she was free of Drexel's bindings. He'd probably forbidden her to ever tell, so she didn't, keeping all his secrets that were now hers to share as she wished.

"Please see Miss Vox back to the main door, Cordelia. I'd hate for her hands to get sticky before she's left the building."

"You really are so uptight, Lady V. Loosen the corset."

Visha lifted her middle finger as Paesha blew her a kiss, walking out of the room in front of Cordelia with her chin held high.

"The friends you keep are dangerous," the brothel owner said, moments later.

"That's how I like them."

"Me, too." She smiled, staring at the door. "Just don't tell her I said that. It ruins the fun. Tell me what you want from Ro."

"It's none of your business."

Realizing Lady Visha couldn't actually force me into a contract, nor had she truly bound Paesha, made the words come easier, but still, my truths were my own, and I wouldn't say any more about Orin than I needed to.

"She's always protected you, Deyanira. Don't you ever wonder why?"

"Ro was my only friend growing up. She was all I had. I'd like to think it was because someone actually gave a fuck."

"Then where is she now?"

I plucked Chaos from my thigh and began to clean beneath my nails. "Obviously, I don't know where she is, Visha. Otherwise, I wouldn't be here."

Shoving the end of her cigarette into her golden ashtray, she snorted. "Some friend."

"Why do you care?"

"I don't," she said with such finality I let the conversation end.

We sat in silence for hours, Cordelia coming and going from the room like a wraith, silently serving her master without speaking. I'd begun to worry about Paesha, wondering if she'd run into Drexel and he was alive after all, until she walked in unannounced, slamming a giant leather-bound book on the desk before Lady Visha. The brothel owner's shoulders visibly sank as she moved her fingers over the etchings in the leather.

"Try standing before a mirror and calling her by her real name: Cythronia Eiria, Goddess of Life, Truth, and Reflection," she said simply, lifting the book to her chest as she walked out of the room.

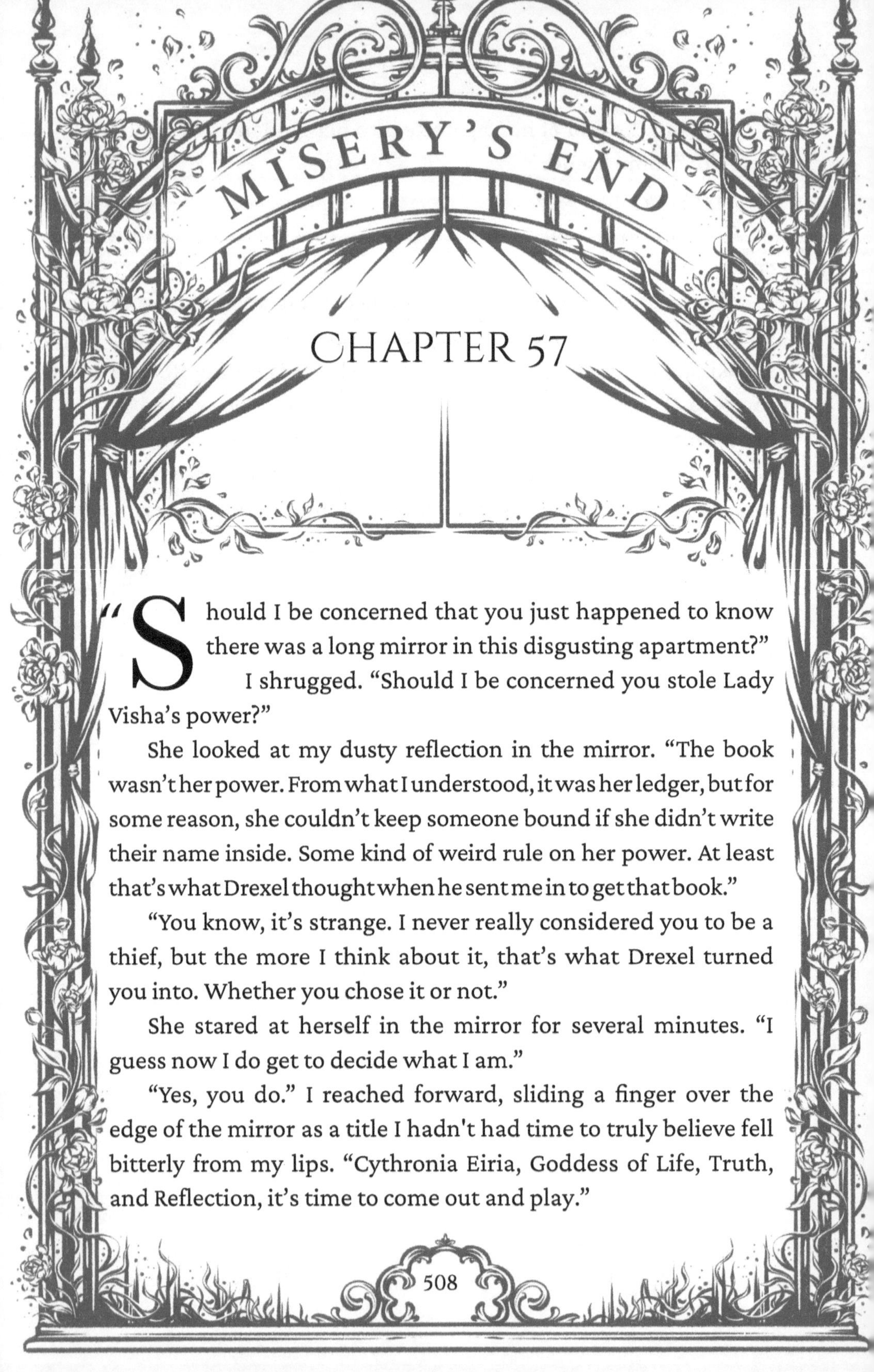

CHAPTER 57

"Should I be concerned that you just happened to know there was a long mirror in this disgusting apartment?"

I shrugged. "Should I be concerned you stole Lady Visha's power?"

She looked at my dusty reflection in the mirror. "The book wasn't her power. From what I understood, it was her ledger, but for some reason, she couldn't keep someone bound if she didn't write their name inside. Some kind of weird rule on her power. At least that's what Drexel thought when he sent me in to get that book."

"You know, it's strange. I never really considered you to be a thief, but the more I think about it, that's what Drexel turned you into. Whether you chose it or not."

She stared at herself in the mirror for several minutes. "I guess now I do get to decide what I am."

"Yes, you do." I reached forward, sliding a finger over the edge of the mirror as a title I hadn't had time to truly believe fell bitterly from my lips. "Cythronia Eiria, Goddess of Life, Truth, and Reflection, it's time to come out and play."

For a moment, the mirror didn't respond. And I thought for sure I was going to have to keep my vow and start hunting down all the mirrors and breaking them, just to lure her from her hole, but eventually, the glass rippled, and we were able to step beyond the threshold and into an open clearing I'd seen one other time.

"I don't like to be summoned," Ro said, standing with her feet shoulder-width apart, arms crossed and glaring at the two of us.

"A goddess, Ro? Really?"

She rolled her eyes, and I couldn't help but think of how ungodlike that gesture was. "The writing was on the wall, Deyanira. But that's not why you're here."

I pulled the tiny flower from my pocket, withered as it was, and held it out toward her. "Why did you choose this design for the tattoos on my back?"

She plucked a small white petal and studied it for several moments before softening. "Because I knew when it was time, you would figure it out."

"Why didn't you just tell me? Of all people, Lady Visha had to. How did she know?"

"Because she's a nosy cunt." She dropped the petal to the ground, walked directly past us, and through the mirror. We shared a glance before following, both hesitant to trust a goddess in a godless world. But when we stepped through, we entered the hall of mirrors I'd originally expected.

Traipsing down the stairs, I pushed the door open to her sitting room as Paesha took my side, still silent.

"Thirsty?" Ro asked, pouring herself a drink.

"Seriously, why didn't you tell me, Ro?"

"Humans are fickle, and you are the ficklest of them all. So consumed by the guilt of the dark magic, you couldn't see the light. Telling you wouldn't have made a difference until you were ready to use it. I dropped hints, but you were obtuse."

"But Orin…"

She froze, staring between us both. "Yes. Orin. What happened? I haven't been able to see anything in the majority of Silbath in days, and it's not safe for me to leave."

"Not safe?"

Her voice became otherworldly, as if it carried two tones of absolute command, seeking the truth, as was her godly charge. "We'll get there. Tell me what happened with Orin. Now."

"Long story," Paesha said. "I'll condense. You and Orin were keeping secrets, even though we'd told you not to."

"That's not keeping it short, Huntress."

"Right." She glowered. "But it was worth saying. Anyway, Dey ran off, Drexel caught her, and turned her over to the new king. The new king wasn't being very nice, and it pissed Orin off, so he… you know, just killed a bunch of people, and broke the world to free her, and then Death—"

She held up her hand. "I can pretty much guess what happened from there. Thank you."

I narrowed my eyes at her. "So, you knew he was Orin's father?"

"Yes. Of course."

"And you instructed him to kill me?"

"I put you both in the same place at the same time and hoped for the best."

"That's awfully… meddling of you, Goddess."

She shrugged. "I have my own reasons. You were properly trained. Now's not the time for pity parties, Maiden."

"So we never were friends? I was just a pawn?"

"Why must we always come back to this? Your constant need for validation is exhausting. Of course, we are friends. I wouldn't have bothered if we weren't. Did you not fall in love with him, Dey? Did your life not start over because of him? The road was messy, but the destination was the right one."

"Why are we talking in circles?" Paesha asked. "Can we please get to the point? What the fuck is going on, and how are we going to get him back? Those are the questions we need answers to. The rest of this doesn't matter."

"We'll start from the beginning. Or *a* beginning, I should say. Have a seat, ladies."

Paesha sat so close our thighs touched. Ro poured amber liquid into three glasses, and though Paesha snatched the one offered to her, I passed, waiting for answers.

"Most of the history of Requiem as you know it is false, though each piece is laced with truth." She sat in the chair across from us, her long legs slipping from her red silk gown as she crossed them. "Requiem is a world ruled by the gods from their home in Etherium. When war broke out here, Reverius, the Keeper of the Realms and Highest Sovereign, banned every god from returning to Requiem. Some still found a way, pining for those who worshiped them. Some took humans to their beds and left babies in the bellies of women. That's where traces of power can be found." She took a sip of her drink. "Like you, Huntress, the blood of Alastor, God of Lost and Broken things runs through your veins."

"Oh, I bet you loved him," Paesha said.

"I love my brother enough," Ro answered defensively.

"I'm sure there's a point to all of this," I said, interrupting.

"But this story doesn't begin with Requiem; rather, it ends here. For now. Because one particular goddess, who held the Keeper in the highest esteem, never left the comfort of Etherium. She'd worked from the heavens to cast her power below. Some would say this seclusion made her naïve. Especially when Death snuck into the realm of gods, fully convinced he could kill the Keeper and take his place as sovereign. But

Death got distracted and fell in love with that naïve goddess. Every day, he returned to our realm, showering her with promises of eternal glory. Until he was discovered.

"As punishment, Reverius threw Death and the goddess he'd obsessed over, from his sacred realm, damning *her* to live eternity in Requiem. To safeguard her eternal damnation and shunning, the punishment she took for allowing such a being into his realm, the Keeper took away Requiem's ability to die, creating another immortal world where Death's power was not welcome and would not work. Reverius knew that Death would otherwise hunt the soul of his lover and draw her into his court for eternity.

"But Death was cunning and desperate to find his lover. Willing to pay whatever cost the magic demanded, he used a dark curse to bring forth a harbinger: a person able to traverse the immortal realm and kill in his place, sending the soul of the fallen directly to his infamous court. The price, however, was a counterpart, a Life Maiden, able to bring fertility and healing to a world suffering from battle scars that spanned lifetimes. Death never saved Requiem from war. The Keeper did.

"Centuries later, Death was still hunting for the soul of his beloved. A single harbinger in a realm of two giant cities was not enough. Time was his enemy, as he had to lie in wait a full year before he could deliver a new name to his Maiden or Lord. But his power was not absolute. It was not without flaws. And so, he found another way to outsmart the gods. Another power, another cost.

"Siphoning the Keeper's power from the human's immortality, he was able to draw his Maiden into his realm while she slept, delivering names far more often. But one day, his greed grew too plentiful, his harbingers too lethal, and the fragile magic broke. Immortality was ripped away from the humans, and they were left with one hundred years of life.

"Death was all too happy to wait, believing all the world would fall at once; every soul, upon reaching one hundred years old, would cross their final threshold and enter his eternal court. But when the first to fall did not come, and the soul was reincarnated back into this eternal realm, Death became irrational and desperate. And so, a new plan was concocted. A new magic, born. A new price, paid."

My jaw ached from the way it dropped, eyes wide as I listened to Ro tell Death's tale. "Wait... wait. You're saying... all of this is just because Death fell in love? Some asshole god got pissed off about it and decided to punish him by locking her into a realm and kicking Death out of it with magic? And since Death can't kill her and take her to his court, the harbingers are just... hunters? Arrows he's blindly shooting through a keyhole of a locked door? That's all we're doing... But he *has* been here. He comes to collect the souls."

"Only to you, Deyanira. With Orin and Icharius, his shadows have collected; the rules don't restrict his ability to reap a soul. Only to take a life. And since he's never truly appeared to Orin's kills, likely he had no reason to believe it was anyone but Icharius. I think he feels your kills differently. Acutely. Because your magic is not only dark; it's also light. Now, you have a choice to make. Will you let Orin fall victim to the darkness, or will you save him?"

The way she looked at me with such challenge in her eyes made me question every bit of her story until one truth became glaring. Each piece of Ro's carefully laid plan came together so nicely, had I blindly trusted her, I might not have seen the small part she'd left out.

I have my own reasons, she had said.

Rubbing my hands together, I let the tension build in my shoulders, laying my own trap. She'd meddled, pushed, and twisted, all in convenient times for this single moment, and it gave me the final advantage I needed to protect the ones I was leaving behind.

"I don't think I can do it," I said with so much finality, I hoped Paesha followed along. "There's no true way to get to Death's court, and if I somehow managed, how would I save him? What advantage could we possibly have over Death?"

Paesha studied the look on my face but said nothing, trusting me fully, just as I'd hoped she would.

"You're the Life Maiden. You can use that magic to defeat him."

"You must have confused me with someone else. If I can figure out how to get there, I'm getting Orin and getting the hell out of there."

"No!" she shouted, jumping to her feet. "His power will continue to haunt you if you do not see this through to the end."

"Why do you seem so desperate?" Paesha asked, rising at the same time I did.

"Because," I answered, "we're staring at Death's missing lover."

"I never loved him." Ro seemed to shrink into herself. "He was so dark and obsessive, so dangerous. Maybe there was a part of me that was intrigued, but there was no love or love lost. He was delusional."

I leaned in, narrowing my gaze as if it were a weapon. "For someone who holds the value of truth to the highest level, you're such a talented liar."

"I can imagine it's very easy to stand there and point the finger at me, but I need you both to consider taking a step back and looking at the bigger picture. Not at me or the fact that my future has been destroyed, my eternity stolen, but at everything. The root of evil here is Death. The man who forced the madness onto a child, Deyanira. He pulls the strings of this world so flawlessly. Who do you think gave the Maestro power? He wasn't born to that; he bargained with Death for it. Every lashing your husband took was because Death made that deal. Every bit of suffering Elowen experienced was because of the lies Death spun. Who do you think elevated Icharius to king? Death. And who thought to put his Death Lord and Maiden on the throne of a world he's damned? Death. Those flowers on your back and every hateful glance you've ever received are because of him. Not me. I tried to bring peace to you when you had none. I knew the Life Maiden magic hidden within you would never be strong enough if you didn't have light in your world. Death manipulated your history to make himself a god, and you are only a pawn. Consider your evils and sit in the truth."

"So that's why you've been hiding in mirrors. You've been so involved in my life because you knew I was the only one with the power to enter his court and use my opposing magic against him. You've played every single piece perfectly. Including Orin's and my *chance* meeting. Because you knew I needed a reason to go. A reason to want Death gone."

"You're fucking twisted," Paesha said, grabbing my hand to keep me grounded. "Did you convince him to break the world, too, so his father would finally figure it out and come for him when it was most convenient?"

She popped her mouth open, then shut it again as she fought for words to argue.

"You did," Paesha gasped. "You did this."

I tugged on the Huntress's arm, holding her to my side.

"If I can't get him back, Goddess, I swear to every holy temple, on the grave of every fallen god, and the dais of the rest that I will find a way to make you pay, whether you choose to take responsibility or not. If I have to reach into the heavens and pull Reverius from his fucking throne to save Orin, I will."

"Shh," she hissed. "You mustn't speak like that if you have a will to live."

"Then I think it's lucky for all of us that I don't. But here's what you're going to do for me. Althea, Quill, Elowen, and Paesha are being left behind in a broken world with no rules and no ruler. Requiem is bound to fall into ruin. And you're going to protect them by whatever means necessary. If that means you bring them into this world of yours, you're going to do it."

"Humans don't make demands of gods, Deyanira."

"Then I'll take my ass home and do nothing to save you, and the next time Death comes to my dreams, I will tell him exactly where you're hiding."

"You wouldn't," she gasped.

I glared, staring at the woman who was always too beautiful for this world. "Fucking try me."

She sat for several moments, picking at her fingernails before thrumming them along the arm of her chair, contemplating.

"I will protect Quill, Thea, and Elowen as best I can, Deyanira, but Paesha... she has to go with you."

"I'm not bargaining her life," I argued.

She shook her head, turning to Paesha. "It's not a bargain. You're the only one with the power to find the path."

"You've got my magic confused. I've never been to Death's court, and I can't find something I have no familiarity with."

"I can offer the doorway, but you must follow your magic to Ezra."

All color leached from her face as she tried to swallow and failed. I handed her my drink, and she threw it back, nearly choking on the burn. Eventually, she took my hands, that set of stunning eyes shifting between mine.

She didn't have to say the words. I knew her answer long before the question was ever given. Still, she spoke, severing all hope. "I'm sorry, Deyanira. But I can't leave Quill behind. I've accepted that I will spend eternity with Ezra when my time eventually comes. I know I'm needed here just a little while longer. And I didn't say goodbye. I just left her. If I don't come back..." She shook her head, stepping away from me. "She'll never recover from it, and I think that might be dangerous for Requiem. She's powerful."

"I know," I whispered, feeling so utterly lost. He'd been right there, attainable. And now there was no path forward.

"Please," Ro said. "Please reconsider. I've promised to look after the child. She can come here. I helped raise Deyanira from her own sorrow as a child. I can do the same for Quill. I'll protect her."

Paesha was quiet for a long time, staring at the floor. She didn't want to be the reason Orin suffered, and I knew it. But Quill was like her own. And still so young. I couldn't let her guilt eat at her for another second. And I couldn't let myself become defeated.

I slipped my hand into hers, squeezing. "I'll find the path on my own, Paesha."

As if she hadn't heard me, she lifted her head, staring at Ro. "If I go, can I come back?"

Ro sighed. "If there is a way, you will be the one to find it."

"Are you sure you don't want to say goodbye to Quill, just in case?"

Paesha shook her head. "I'm coming back for her. If I say goodbye beyond what I already did, she's only going to worry. Her mother abandoned her. Her father abandoned her. She wanted a friend in Drexel so bad, and he cast her to the side. I'm her constant. More than anyone else. It has to be this way, or she will panic."

"Okay," I answered. "I promise when the time comes, I'll help you find the way home."

We stood in a room of mirrors I'd never seen before, the air thick with an eerie, hushed tension. The chamber seemed suspended in a timeless void, its boundaries obscured by countless reflections of ourselves. The walls, the ceiling, the floor—all surfaces, every inch of them—were adorned with mirrors, each one casting our likenesses back at us, multiplying our anxious faces into infinity.

"Ready?" Paesha reached for my hand with a faint tremble. "Don't let go, okay? Whatever happens?"

At the center of the room loomed the ominous mirror that beckoned us toward an irreversible journey into eternity. So unlike the others, with a dark frame of ornate wood that seemed to absorb the very light around it. Its surface was not pristine; instead, it carried an ebb and flow of shadow.

"In case I forget to tell you, Huntress, thanks for coming. See you on the other side," I said, taking one final deep breath and leaping into the mirror.

PART THREE

WHISPERING GROVE
AURELIAN GATE
DEATH'S CASTLE
LAKE OF LOST SOULS
GRIMWOOD THICKET

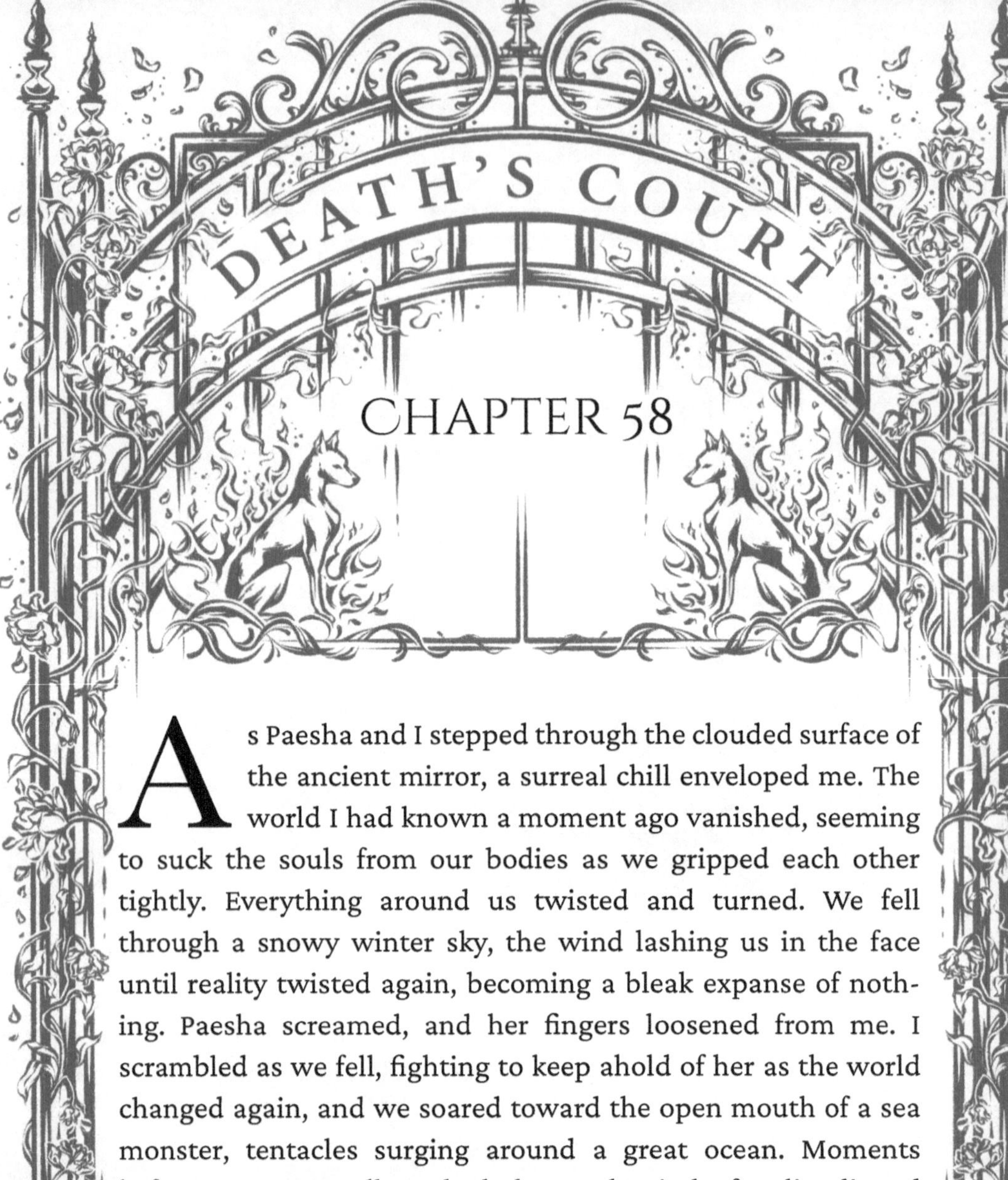

CHAPTER 58

As Paesha and I stepped through the clouded surface of the ancient mirror, a surreal chill enveloped me. The world I had known a moment ago vanished, seeming to suck the souls from our bodies as we gripped each other tightly. Everything around us twisted and turned. We fell through a snowy winter sky, the wind lashing us in the face until reality twisted again, becoming a bleak expanse of nothing. Paesha screamed, and her fingers loosened from me. I scrambled as we fell, fighting to keep ahold of her as the world changed again, and we soared toward the open mouth of a sea monster, tentacles surging around a great ocean. Moments before we were swallowed whole, another jerk of reality dipped us into a world of two great moons.

"Stop!" I yelled. "Here. We're here."

She threw her other hand around me, chestnut hair whipping in my face as we fell to the black stone ground, into a familiar realm that seemed to defy the very laws of reality. Climbing to our feet, catching our breath, we exchanged a determined glance, a silent vow to protect each other at all costs.

Massive wrought-iron gates, ancient and foreboding, stretched into the obsidian sky, which hosted two moons. Their intricate designs seemed to writhe with a life of their own, like serpents coiled and waiting to strike. The gates, framed by the swirling mists of the underworld, stretched into infinity, their spires disappearing into a dark abyss. The ironwork was as cold as death itself, and I couldn't help but shiver as a gust of other-worldly wind brushed against my skin, carrying with it the faint scent of withered roses and distant, echoing whispers.

The ground rumbled beneath our feet, and from the depths of the shadows emerged Death's hellhounds. With eyes that gleamed like fiery embers and snarling jaws that dripped with anticipation of our demise, they were monstrous creatures.

The sharp slice of Paesha's blade being drawn from its sheath drew their attention. I thought back to her battle in the castle and how she'd nearly fallen. I'd meant to save Orin, but maybe letting Paesha come was a terrible idea.

"Stop it," she hissed. "I can see the look in your eye, Maiden. We live together, or we die together, right here and now. If you start doubting me, this fight is over. Knock it off."

The dogs began to circle us as I pulled several small throwing knives.

"You're right. I'm sorry!" I yelled just as the beast closest to me lunged.

The hiss of steel and gnashing teeth filled the air. I'd never trained to fight something so massive, and even if I had, he was so strong. His one leg stood higher than I was tall. The only thing I could think to do was slice and slice and slice, crippling him as I kept moving, dodging teeth and claws. I wanted to look back, to make sure Paesha could handle the other beast, but if I looked away, I'd die, and she was right. I needed to trust her, even when I heard the grunts and the low growls. Even when every nerve ending I had stood on end and adrenaline raced through my body. A tuck, a roll, a dodge, a swing. Over and over. The battle became a dance. A cadence that waited in anticipation for one of us to falter. A single misstep and we'd be crushed beneath a paw, or worse, eaten.

The beasts did not grow weary. Not a pant, no sheen of sweat along their slick black fur, which glowed blue in its brightest places in the moonlight. Only the deep ruby red of their eyes held me in panic. Every other piece of my body wanted to stop for a second and rest.

Paesha's back collided into mine as we were gathered together by the hounds. She reached for my hand, gasping for breaths. I took it, though I knew what it meant. We falter, we fall.

"Can we run?" she asked, desperately.

I struggled for a breath. "I don't know where we'd go. This is as far as I've ever been allowed in this court."

"Look," she gasped, pointing to the legs of the closest hound.

I had to squint my eyes to see beyond the deep shadows of fur, so dark it trapped light. But the soft pink flesh exposed by her sword had closed. My stomach turned.

"Oh, fuck me. We can't kill them. Everything here is already dead."

She looked over her shoulder to where the mirror we'd come through had stood, but it was gone. There would be no escape. Round and round the beasts stepped, watching us, giving us a moment to catch our breaths before they devoured us.

"Can you try your Life Maiden magic on Fluffy over there? If you can get close enough to touch him?"

"Fluffy? Yeah, right before it fucking eats my head off. I'll just reach out and grab a tooth as an experiment, okay? Because

Fluffy's looking awfully damn hungry. And that one's drooling." I tried the only thing I could think of, stretching a trembling hand forward, still gripping the scabbard in my other. "Hey, Fluffy. Remember me? I pet you once. Or... one of you. Might have been your brother... Ruffles. I'm nice. Not dangerous at all."

"Really convincing," Paesha hissed.

I swiped my hand across my forehead, wiping away the sweat threatening to drip into my eyes. Fluffy growled, burning eyes locked on my blade.

"How much do you trust me?" I asked, sliding Chaos into its sheath.

She barked a laugh. "Of all the times in the world to ask that question, Deyanira..."

"Put your sword away. Don't let them see it."

"No. No way. Not going to happen. If that fucker decides to have me for dinner, I'm taking out his esophagus on the way down."

"I support that decision. But Death once told me they wouldn't attack if I drew no weapons, and he didn't demand it."

"And you just *now* thought to mention that?" she asked, still holding her sword between her and the prowling dogs.

"This might come as a shock, but I don't trust him as far as Quill could throw him, and, if I didn't want people barging into my house, I'd probably lie to them about how to get past my death doggies, too."

"I see your point," she said, tucking her blade into the sheath.

The hellhounds froze, still eyeing us warily, but they stopped circling.

"Is it working?"

"Only one way to find out." I jutted my chin toward the gates of Death's court. "Shall we?"

"Quick question before we go," she whispered. "Can we die if we're already stuck in Death's court?"

"I don't know the rules. Let's go with no."

"So, if they eat us, we're stuck in their stomachs?"

My lip curled in disgust. "Gods, I hope not."

"Okay, well, if you get eaten, I'll cut you out."

"So kind," I said, sharing a smile before she yanked on my hand, and we bolted through the gap the dogs had left, slipping between the spindles of the gate rather than trying the handle.

"Let's hope that was the hard part," Paesha said, staring behind us at the hellhounds that moved back to their guarded positions as if they'd never seen us at all.

"I'm guessing it wasn't." I stared at the labyrinth of dead trees that lay between Death's forbidding castle and the dimly lit path we now stood upon.

CHAPTER 59

The overgrown garden within Death's court loomed before us, a twisted mass of gnarled trees and tangled vines. The air was heavy with an unsettling aura, as if the very essence of despair and decay clung to each leaf and petal.

"We're going to have to go through that," Paesha said, resting a hand on her sword's hilt, though she didn't draw it.

There was no way around the overgrown barrier. It stretched as far as the moonlight fell, and farther, into the depths of the shadows beyond, somehow growing in the eternal nighttime, thriving as the foreground to the towering black castle beyond.

"Looks like it," I answered, beginning my path forward.

"What's the plan once we get to people? I mean, are they people? Are they ghosts?"

"I've seen Death in all forms, but mostly corporeal."

"Just keep your wits about you. If the hellhounds were the welcoming committee, you can bet this isn't going to be a walk in the park," she said.

"No shit. What was the first clue?"

She pointed to the largest spider web I'd ever seen, glimmering in the moonlight. "That."

As we made our way through the maze of vegetation, whispers floated on the breeze. Ghostly voices beckoned from all directions, their words both haunting and enticing. They spoke of long-lost desires, regrets, and the echoes of souls trapped in eternal torment. The garden had become a distorted canvas for the voices of the departed, and we were the only ones there to bear witness.

Paesha's multi-colored eyes darted around, her expression growing distant and transfixed. Enthralled by the spectral echoes, her gaze fixated on a figure that materialized among the overgrown foliage.

"Ezra?"

I'd never heard her sound so weak, so sad.

I reached out to Paesha, desperate to break the spell of illusion that gripped her. "He's not real," I pleaded, my voice filled with concern. "It's a trick. Stay with me."

She covered her ears, squeezing her eyes shut. "I hate this place. Why won't they stop?"

I wasn't sure how to comfort her. I tried moving closer, placing a hand on her shoulder. But the large figure in the distance took a step toward us, and her resolve faltered, her longing overriding reason. My heart broke at the hope in her eyes, the vulnerability in trembling fingers that dropped to her side.

"I have to see, Dey. I need to know."

Reluctantly, I followed her careful steps, my heart full of worry as the madness stirred by Death's dark forest seeped into my mind and glimpses of faces I'd recognized flashed by. The voices of madness whispered to me in fragmented, disjointed phrases that sent shivers down my spine. They were like riddles from the abyss, their meanings elusive and maddening.

"Lost echoes... shadows dance..."

The words seemed to shift and swirl like mist, making it impossible to grasp their true intent. They were fragments of memories, half-formed thoughts, and cryptic prophecies chasing us as we moved toward Paesha's mirage.

"Blood-stained hands—eternity beckons."

I stumbled over gnarled roots, my mind struggling to make sense of the whispers, but for some reason, I still tried, as if it were a puzzle I needed to put together in order to leave the forest. The maze around me pulsed with a malevolent energy.

"A sacrifice."

"Puppet strings."

"Madness calls... embrace the void..."

The darkness deepened, and I struggled to maintain my grip on reality as the forest itself seemed to warp and twist, gripping my mind and the pressing need to solve an undefined riddle. Paesha's figure ahead of me became a distant specter, and I felt as though I were descending further into the abyss. Though my heart thundered and every warning bell my brain could muster rang, I still couldn't help the way I chased the mystery rather than my friend.

She was almost out of sight, nearly lost to the deep shadows formed by two full moons when her voice rang through the chaos threatening to trap me.

"Ezra!" she screamed, her silhouette charging forward as she threw herself into the very solid arms of the form she'd been chasing. I'd expected her to fall, the specter to vanish, but instead, his hands wrapped around her, lifting her and swinging until her feet left the ground, and she kissed him. The laughter mixed with sobs spurred my feet to run to them both.

"I told you he was real," she cried, holding the sides of his striking face.

And though most of his features were hidden in the darkness, with his smile and the way his dark eyes held her so tenderly, I didn't bother questioning it. Somehow, he'd come.

"You shouldn't be here, kitten. You were never supposed to come. Unless..." He paused, the wheels of his mind turning until finally, his head jerked to me, studying each of my features, measuring me up until he sneered, pushing her behind him.

"I may not be able to kill you, Maiden, but I know exactly how to make your eternity a nightmare."

"Ezra," Paesha whispered, pulling him back. "I came here willingly. We didn't—"

He clapped a soft hand over her mouth. "Be careful, my love. Everything here has ears. And they come. I just happened to beat them out the door."

"Who comes?" I demanded, reaching for Chaos, though I wasn't sure what good our weapons would do here, considering everyone was already dead.

"We do," a sickly sweet feminine voice called from behind Paesha's lover. "And our master has summoned you, Deyanira."

I stepped around Ezra's large figure to take in a massive line of women and men, all thrumming with a power that was so familiar. Death's magic seemed to agitate beneath my skin, renewed and vigorous as it was drawn forward. Every one of Death's harbingers, a group of warriors he'd reaped, stared at me, oozing bloodlust and madness. For the first time in a long time, I felt real, genuine fear undulate over my bones.

DEATH'S COURT

CHAPTER 60

"We need to find Orin," Paesha whispered to Ezra as we followed the collection of Death's harbingers through the gnarled gardens. Icharius Fern held a position in the middle, but he'd kept his face down and his mouth shut. I'd almost forgotten he was there at all, as it seemed he wished everyone to. What level of madness had he waged war with through his own life? Hiding his power so flawlessly had to come with a price.

Ezra pressed his lips together, shaking his head, still staring into the shadows. Whatever he was afraid of, it held him invisibly by the throat, as if he'd learned a hard lesson we hadn't yet.

The harbingers were insufferably slow, taking their time, likely to let our fear build as we climbed the steps. The grand, marbled corridors of Death's castle were exactly as I'd imagined they would be from beyond the court's gates. The opulence of the surroundings clashed with the underlying darkness that permeated every stone and every inch of the fortress. A twisted sort of beauty, but then so was Death.

The walls rose high, adorned with intricate carvings depicting scenes of suffering and despair. Flickering torches cast eerie shadows, dancing along the cold, polished floors. The air was heavy with a suffocating stillness, broken only by the echoing footsteps of our group, shuffling forward.

When Ezra reached for Paesha's hand, her shoulders relaxed, and though a ping of jealousy rattled through me, unsure of the state I'd find Orin in, I was so happy for her. She'd loved as desperately as I had; she'd danced with his memories on the rooftop countless times until she'd cried herself to sleep. She'd never let go of him for a day. Had come to hell, following her love of him, her soul be damned, and she'd made it through. Come what may, she deserved the smile that tugged at her lips, even as fear held us both firmly on the ground.

Little by little, they inched away from us, Ezra holding her further and further back, until it was clear that whatever my summons would hold, he would protect her, keeping her far away from Death, and for that, I was grateful.

The former harbingers and I walked the center aisle, our steps measured and resolute. I refused to look ahead, to see those hard eyes watching me. The seats lining the aisle drew my attention instead, and as my gaze swept over them, a chill gripped my heart. Each seat was occupied by a familiar face, those whom I had condemned to Death's court. An audience of my victims. How fucking poetic.

Their eyes, filled with both resentment and resignation, bore into my soul. They were corporeal ghosts of lives extinguished, a haunting reminder of the choices I never truly had. But guilt still gnawed at me.

A tugging on my conscience pulled my eyes from my victims to the dais. To Orin, standing strong behind the throne of golden skulls his father sat so comfortably in. My knees weakened and steps faltered. His once-vibrant eyes were hollow, consumed by unfathomable darkness. Veins of black snaked beneath his collar, a visible manifestation of the madness that gripped his very being.

My heart shattered as I realized that his father's power had swallowed him whole, erasing the man I loved. I couldn't stand to see him like that, yet I couldn't bear to tear my eyes away either, even though he didn't seem to notice me. He hadn't come to my side the way Ezra had come for Paesha. He hadn't moved an inch. Orin was lost. Just as I'd feared. Though standing here now, in the heart of Death's court, I finally realized there was likely no way of ever being able to save him, not under his father's watchful eye, as Ezra had warned us, and even if I could, where would we go? How could we return?

Building up the courage, I looked into the hard face of Death next, his beautiful features so similar to Orin. I wondered how I hadn't seen it before. Perhaps it was the angles the moon's light cast through the vaulted windows above or the identical robes they both wore. Maybe it was the obsidian eyes or impassive faces, but seeing them side by side was eerie.

Each time I'd let myself look into Death's face, a serpentine smile had formed, and he'd stroked my cheek just as Orin had, always keeping hands on me. Now that I knew the truth of my power, I realized why. Not for healing, as my husband needed, but to keep the darkness, his potent magic, stronger than the other, mostly dormant within me.

When he looked away, the smile finally forming, I followed his gaze to a woman standing at the bottom of the steps between us. Her eyes were fixed ahead, as if trapped within an unyielding trance. Vaguely familiar features mirrored my own, causing a surge of recognition that sent tremors through me. My mother, the woman whose death had carried me into this world, marking me *his* before I could ever belong to anyone else. An innocent child, Life's Maiden, robbed of a happy beginning.

She stood maybe fifty steps from me, stirring a whirlwind of emotions—a longing for a mother's love and the profound ache of loss. But perhaps more intense than that was a festered anger that had coiled for so, so long, I thought I'd burst soon, staring back at Death, the monster that'd taken everything from me. My past and my future. And he'd done it with that smile on his face, calculating and cunning. *Bastard.*

Curiosity got the best of me. I whipped my head around, staring in the direction my mother was until I found two familiar, hateful green eyes peering directly into mine. My father. Scorned by his own death. Based on the way my mother watched him in disbelief, I could only imagine that Death had held them apart, saving their happy reunion until this moment, though neither looked jovial.

"My lovely Deyanira," Death purred, rising from his gilded throne to melt down the steps and stand before me. "Welcome home."

"I'd say thank you, but I'm not feeling very grateful at the moment."

"She speaks again." Pure delight lit every one of his features. "Such a lovely voice. Though I prefer the time you screamed. Shall we revisit that moment?"

I glared. "Don't fucking touch me."

"Why do you look at me as though I'm the villain? Look at the room. Look at the faces. You damned them, not me."

I barely heard him over the roar in my ears. "You made me your monster! I never meant for any of them to die."

The group of harbingers behind me all began to laugh, the cacophonous sound snaking through the room until it ignited a fire in my veins. I wasn't like them, and I never would be.

"Such a temper." Death clicked his tongue, so cool and collected while I felt like I was falling apart.

You never, ever lose your fight. You never let someone defeat you. You never falter. You stand. You step. You rise.

Ro's voice rattled in my mind as I thought about the way he'd pursued her. What it must have been like to be the object of his obsession after all these years. An obsession that spanned lifetimes and twisted worlds. The very pit of who he'd become was nothing more than a desperate man, a being, chasing a woman who didn't want him. I made him weak in my mind. As small as I possibly could, until I stared down into those black eyes with pity. There was only one way forward. I would become his villain. And I would do it silently. Because even gods could fall.

"Feel like a little reunion with mommy dearest?"

He snapped his fingers, and from the shadow of a giant pillar stepped Drexel Vanhoff, pallid skin full of sweat, red hair a mess, and smelling like the piss stain on his pants. He shuffled forward, lifting a key from his neck and holding it out to Death with trembling hands. The man who'd been such a villain had fallen to meek compliance.

"What's the matter, *Maestro?*" Death purred, rolling the word. "Cat got your tongue?"

Drexel said nothing, casting his eyes to the floor. I chanced a glance at Orin, to see if he cared about the fall of his uncle, but he hadn't moved an inch, gripped by the darkness that claimed him. My heart hammered, and my skin crawled. I'd never felt so trapped within my own body, wanting to go to him, to save him, and also biding my time. Still, the invisible bond between us hummed, but only on my end, it seemed.

Without a word, Drexel slunk back to his shadows, and Death held the skeleton key toward me, letting it swing back and forth between us, that fucking smile never leaving his face, begging me to slam a fist into it.

The knife on my belt grew heavy, an urging to pluck it free and bury it into Death's heart. But he could not die. None here could. The power that made me his in Requiem turned to ash in eternity.

"Take the key, Deyanira. Free your mother."

I fell into mock compliance, gripping the key and snatching it away before walking to the base of the steps, staring a familiar stranger in the face, and freeing her of the chains around her wrists.

"Be careful," she mouthed.

No 'hello'. No 'nice to meet you', no hint of emotion. Simply a warning before she glanced over my shoulder, locking eyes with my father once more. How she must have wished she could get to him, just as I pined for Orin, steps away, locked in darkness.

I whipped around, walking back to Death as if I didn't care for the woman at all, and tossed him the key.

"Say thank you."

The challenge in his eyes lit me on fire. I couldn't. Wouldn't. No matter how much I'd sworn to bring him down. I'd never bend for him, and he knew it. Likely counted on it. So, I stood, chin high, mouth pressed shut as the audience grew restless, uncomfortable. Because who was I to challenge Death?

"Say thank you, Deyanira."

One steady breath in, one breath out.

He leaned in, so close I could smell decay on him, the truth behind his beauty. "Do not make me look like a fool before our special audience," he growled into my ear.

A blink. And another.

His breath was fiery hot along my skin, causing my flesh to rise, as the familiar pulse of power radiated from him. But when he reached for my face, to grip my cheeks as he'd always done, his fingers hissed against my skin. Yanking his hand back, he tried to hide what had happened. Tried to keep his composure, though he looked at me in utter shock. It wasn't his power I'd felt at his proximity. It was mine.

"Orin," he said, his self-control wavering. "Take our new guests to the pit. Both of them."

DEATH'S COURT

CHAPTER 61

I didn't buckle when Orin descended the steps like a minion and stopped before me. I didn't waver. I held my chin high and my body rigid, though internally I struggled.

Look at me, I begged him, stroking the end of our bond.

But he did no such thing. I inched away, convinced he would reach for me, that my power would break the trance on contact. But he didn't move.

"Ezra," Death called, "bring the lovely Huntress forward."

A chill ran down my spine, echoing the gasp of the room when his deep voice responded, "No."

"Perhaps you didn't hear," Death answered. His voice hardened as he curled a finger toward the man until he fell to a knee, veins protruding to fight the pain. "I said, bring your guest to me."

The only response was a grunt as Ezra struggled to stay upright.

"Stop this," Paesha cried, trying and failing to lift her lover from his knees.

"No," Ezra said again. Love was the only thing that gave him power over Death, foolish as it might have been.

"Please do take care of this, son," Death crooned, stepping back and stroking a finger over his forehead as if dealing with unruly children.

"Orin, don't," Paesha cried, leaving Ezra behind to dart up the aisle. "That's your family. Your real family. Ezra is your best friend, your brother. You *know* him."

But when he shoved past her toward Ezra, I did the only thing I could think of and darted for him, whipping Chaos from my thigh and hurling it, end over end, until it grazed his arm, tearing his loose black shirt and falling to the ground between the two men.

He spun, obsidian eyes full of hatred as he snarled.

"Come and get me, you bastard," I taunted, shifting from one foot to another, sliding right back into a place that was so familiar to us both. I saw the recognition flash across his hardened face.

Death commanded him to stop as he stormed my way, but he didn't listen. Not as he crowded my space, not as he sneered, not even as he reached for me, gripping my throat with such anger, had the contact not instantly pierced the darkness, he might have ripped my damn head off.

"There you are, Husband," I rasped, gulping over his grip, luring out the man buried within.

He bared his teeth, still fighting the power. "Maiden."

Not wife. Maiden. He'd forgotten me.

"I think you mean *Nightmare*." I painted a sly smile, fighting to keep the relief from my face when the Orin I'd known peeked through. When he faltered, though, I doubted anyone had seen. He was there, so far away, but still there. And he was mine because I'd never feared his darkness. "Please continue to fight, my darling. I love a good challenge."

Words he'd once spoken to me left my tongue like a promise. A vow to save him, even if he couldn't hear the meaning. Fingers tightened as the room held unnecessary breaths. I imagined they all wanted to see my eventual demise, but I only focused on my love for him. Willing him to feel it as potent as the power within me.

Death's hand crept over his son's shoulder. "There, there, son. We all know she is a monstrous little thing, but do try to control yourself. Take all three to the pit and meet me for dinner." He spun on a heel and walked out, robes billowing in a phantom wind behind him.

Orin's grip on my throat fell away, but still, he grabbed my arm, hauling me down the aisle. I reached for Paesha, snagging her hand and pulling her behind us. Ezra followed without command. He would not leave her. And I think, though I didn't know him at all, I loved him instantly for the way he loved her.

The second we were out of the hall, I called forth the Life Maiden power, pushing and shoving on it, willing it to free him. He faltered. His footsteps halted. His shoulders fell, and those amber eyes flew to mine. His grasp on my arm tightened as he shoved me into an alcove without a single word, pressing his body to mine, kissing me with more fervor than I'd known him to ever hold as he buried his hands into my hair, eliciting a moan. Letting the power pulse, I slipped my hands behind his neck, my cool fingers caressing his sweltering skin as I let him devour me. Until my belly pooled with desire, and I wanted nothing more than to let the world fade away and demand he kiss every inch, taste every part of me, defeating any hint of Death's power over him as I pushed more and more magic between us. I could do this. I could save him. I just needed enough time.

But Paesha cleared her throat, ripping us from the heated

moment. The second he stepped away, all signs of him were gone once more.

"Dey," she said, her voice low in warning.

"I know," I stammered, still reaching for him, though he'd faded back to darkness.

"We need—"

"I know," I snapped, a piece of my heart breaking.

Orin snatched my wrist and continued our winding journey through Death's dark castle.

"At least it's not the Lake of Lost Souls," Ezra said as Orin slammed shut the door to the room we'd been shoved into, his footsteps immediately fading away on the other side of the door.

The pit was a chamber carved from the very bowels of Death's castle. Its walls were hewn from gray stone that absorbed whatever feeble light struggled to penetrate the abyss. I choked on the air, thick and stifling, carrying with it a noxious scent that made every breath a laborious effort.

The meager illumination from scattered dim torches revealed the horrors of our confinement. Chains, thick as tree trunks, hung from the towering ceiling, their ends disappearing into the inky darkness above. Each chain bore cruel-looking manacles that swayed ominously, awaiting their next victims.

"Don't look up," Ezra said, swinging an arm over Paesha as he held out a hand to me. "I'm Ezra Prophet. Thank you for making it painless."

I took his hand, though I couldn't pull my eyes from the door. "It seemed like the least I could do."

"Come on." Paesha wrapped me in a hug before leading me to a bench along the far wall of the room. "We'll figure it out."

"Whatever happens," Ezra said, his words turning shaky, more fearful than when he'd denied Death, "it's not real, okay? Just keep telling yourselves that."

"What's not—"

Paesha's words were cut off by the high-pitched scream of some kind of monstrous beast stepping from the shadows just as all but one torch went out. Long, haggard hair and needle-like claws scraped the stone floor as venom dripped from tapered, razor-sharp canines. Within minutes of the beast's appearance, though it hadn't come closer than the very edges of the light cast onto the jagged floor, it became a symphony of screaming and crying. Tortuous sounds clawed its way from the beast's throat until it was maddening.

I covered my ears, just as the other two had done, but the screaming echoed off the walls until, like a blade to a throat, it stopped. Suddenly and without warning.

"Cover your eyes!" Ezra shouted, as if he'd had his fair share of time in this version of hell, and he knew exactly what to expect.

I'd spent too many seconds considering that, not listening to his command. When the torches flared to life, illuminating the entire cavern, the gaunt faces of a thousand ghosts stared back at me, their eyes as ruby red as the hellhounds, all smiling, each one making my skin crawl.

"Look harder," one whispered, floating back and forth, back and forth as black, oiled hair covered most of her face.

I couldn't tear my gaze away, couldn't stop the rise of my own panic when she rushed forward, her terrifying face only inches from mine before she disappeared, and another came for me. Ignoring the two with their eyes well covered, the spectral whispered the same maddening thoughts I'd heard in the forest outside of the castle.

"Death's Maiden... blood's mistress... soul's keeper."

Twisting my head away, I glanced down at movement on my arm, jumping when a spider the size of my palm appeared, crawling up my arm. I couldn't escape, couldn't force my eyes closed.

"Riddle whispers... chaos echoes...thief..."

I slammed my hands over my ears, trying to block the echo of sounds that drove me deeper and deeper into a place I was far too familiar with.

Hello, Maiden.

"No!" I shouted, pushing against Death's madness.

The reprieve is in her blood.

A visceral desire to see the crimson drops of Paesha's blood spilling onto the cracked stone floor crept into my mind. To see life leave her eyes. To watch Ezra fall over her body, taking even more from him than I already had.

I rocked back and forth, humming to block the sound. The need. The blood. The blood.

The blood.

"Stop," I pleaded, losing my sense of self in seconds as I stared into the eyes of the ghosts, watching tears of blood dripping down their faces. I wished I could run my fingers through it. Paint the walls with it. Bathe in it.

I drew a breath, fighting for myself. For her. For him. For every ounce of resolve I'd ever have, as my trembling hand gripped one of the daggers strapped to my chest.

"It's not real," I told myself.

"It's not real," Ezra echoed.

She cannot die. She's already in Death's court. I cannot kill her. I repeated the mantra in my mind until the voice of madness laughed back at me.

She has not yet died. Take it. Take her life.

"No," I managed to whisper.

Yours.

Mine.

Ours.

No.

The blood.

The blood.

The body. The soul.

"Stop," I pleaded, feeling myself weaken, the small handle of the throwing knife vibrating against my palm. Paesha lay in Ezra's lap, slender hands over her ears, face twisted in pain.

I had no pain.

She had pain.

Sweet, beautiful pain. Like the slice of a blade across flawless skin. Like the final breath of a dancer at the end of a performance.

A gasp.

A gasp.

I gripped the edge of the bench with my free hand, watching the pulse of her heart in her throat, the artery luring me.

"It's not real!" Paesha screamed, momentarily breaking the trance.

I drew a heavy breath into my lungs, remembering that I was no longer Death's. The darkness was not the whole of my being. I belonged to Life, too. To happiness. To birth and healing. To laughter and a family who loved me. To her.

Drawing forth the light that'd almost vanished within me, I fought against the darkness until the voices were silenced. Until saving her was not enough. Until every bit of light begged for escape, and then I let it. Releasing the power, allowing it to surge through Death's pit. Filling every crevice, each shadowed corner with pure, blinding radiance.

"Dey?" Paesha squinted at me. "You're kind of glowing."

A tear slipped down my cheek. "I'm so glad."

She had no idea the battle I'd just fought, and I hoped she never would.

"Impeccable timing," Ezra said, drawing both of our attention to the open door.

Every part of my body froze. I couldn't move. Or breathe. Nor think beyond the old man standing there, his kind eyes and simple smile a balm to a racing heart.

"Hello, Little Dove."

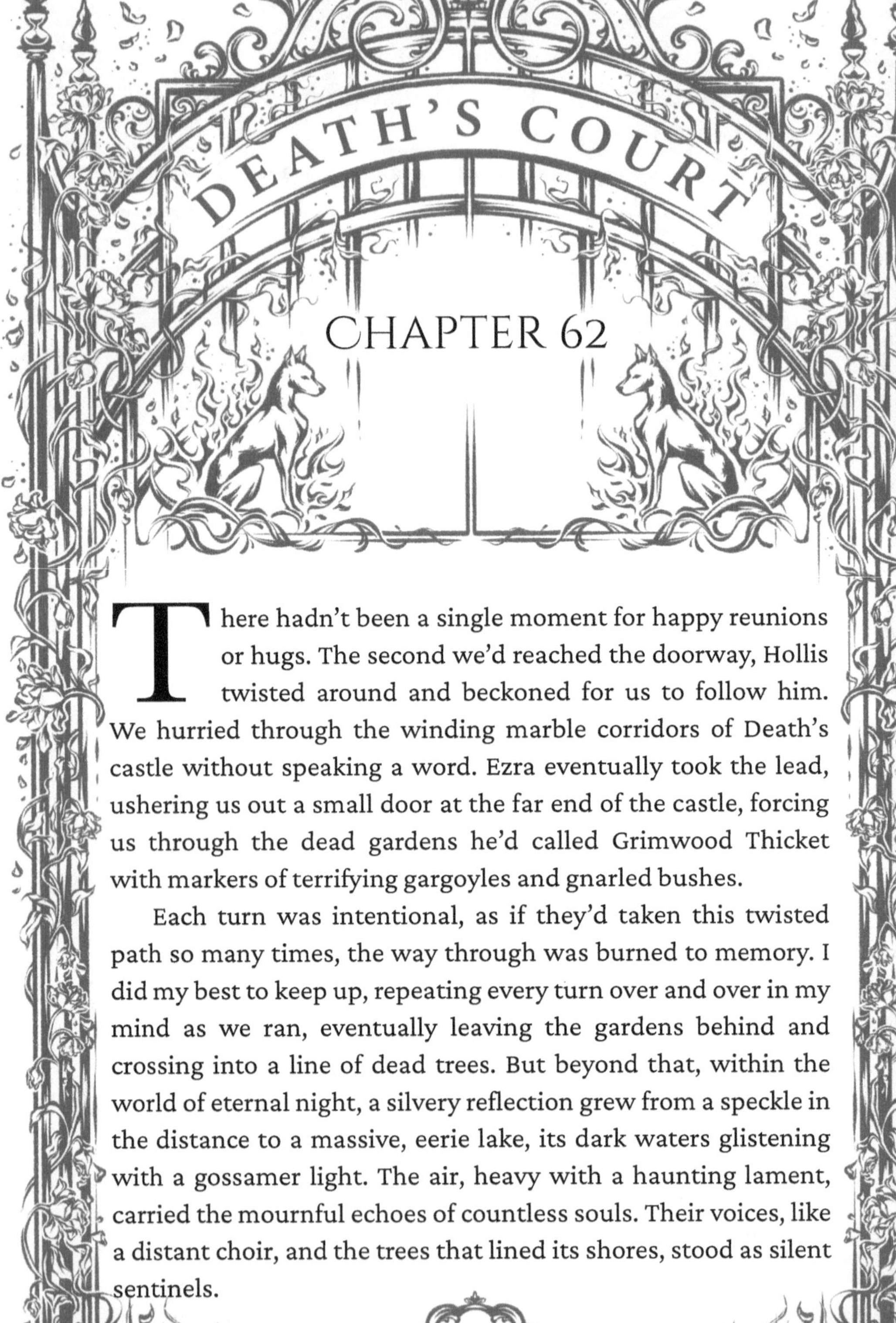

CHAPTER 62

There hadn't been a single moment for happy reunions or hugs. The second we'd reached the doorway, Hollis twisted around and beckoned for us to follow him. We hurried through the winding marble corridors of Death's castle without speaking a word. Ezra eventually took the lead, ushering us out a small door at the far end of the castle, forcing us through the dead gardens he'd called Grimwood Thicket with markers of terrifying gargoyles and gnarled bushes.

Each turn was intentional, as if they'd taken this twisted path so many times, the way through was burned to memory. I did my best to keep up, repeating every turn over and over in my mind as we ran, eventually leaving the gardens behind and crossing into a line of dead trees. But beyond that, within the world of eternal night, a silvery reflection grew from a speckle in the distance to a massive, eerie lake, its dark waters glistening with a gossamer light. The air, heavy with a haunting lament, carried the mournful echoes of countless souls. Their voices, like a distant choir, and the trees that lined its shores, stood as silent sentinels.

The second we stopped, I darted for Hollis, wrapping my arms around him as he chuckled, that familiar sound coating something that felt so raw and so bruised within me. "I missed you, Old Man."

"Careful, Little Dove," he whispered into my ear. "You don't want anyone here knowing you have a heart, or they'll find a way to use it against you."

I pulled away from him, studying his deep blue eyes. "Your bonded wife? Is she here?"

He nodded, but his smile faltered. "I see her when I can. Death tends to keep us apart." When Paesha hugged him, he buried his face into her chestnut hair, but I could see the worry there, just below the surface.

"What's going on, Hollis? Tell me what he's done."

"The only currency in this realm is fear. You live with it, or you cultivate it. Those are the two roles. The reaper or the sower and I expect he'll come for you again soon. If you let him see that Orin is your weakness, he's going to find a way to break you both. You have to stay away from Orin. He's not safe."

I lifted a shoulder. "He's never been safe, and that hasn't kept me away yet."

"I mean it, Deyanira," Hollis snapped, his words more forceful than they'd ever been. "This is your eternity. Don't let yourself be fooled into thinking you can hide from Death in his own court. He loves the cat-and-mouse game, but you're always going to be the mouse."

"What is this place?" Paesha asked, kneeling to stare at her reflection in the water.

Ezra grabbed her and yanked her back, just as a translucent hand broke the surface, reaching for her. She looked at me then, fear coating her stunning eyes, though her golden skin had been leached of color by the greedy light of the silver moons.

Ezra pointed. "This is the Lake of Lost Souls. The final

punishment Death deals to those who don't bend to his will. See the souls? They're condemned to circle the bottom of the lake, forever seeking a final breath they will never be granted. Once you breach the water's surface, not even Death can save you."

"A graveyard," Hollis added. "He doesn't come here often. It's not exactly safe, but there isn't an inch of this realm that is."

"Deyanira?"

I spun at Paesha's gasp, not recognizing the voice until I saw the face standing in the tree line. "Mother?"

Instead of walking away, the Huntress moved in, taking my shoulder as my father stepped from the shadows behind her, his hand not lovingly in hers, but gripping her shoulder as he pushed her forward. I saw it then. That look in her eyes I'd seen so many times before, though I hadn't known it for what it was with Ro. The fear. The control from a man that was once a lover. My father was a reaper.

His fingers tightened on her, knuckles turning white as she hissed, shrinking until he stopped.

"I needed to see you," she said softly. "One more time, if only for selfish reasons. You really are so beautiful and so grown. I can hardly believe it."

She reached until her fingers were a hairsbreadth from my face, but my father yanked her back. Paesha grabbed my hand, holding me in place, vigilant at my side. Ezra grunted, taking the opposite so I was sandwiched between them.

"How long do you think I'm going to let you jerk her around before I kick your ass, Father?"

"Do not speak to me that way, Deyanira. You were raised better."

"No. I really wasn't. The last time you and I had a private conversation, you hit me in the face and threatened me. Do you think I give a shit what you have to say? Get your hands off my mother."

"Stop this," the woman who looked so much like me snapped, interrupting what I'm sure would have been a fun battle of wits between us. "I've come with the only advice I can offer. You must seek out Death, child. Find him and take whatever consequences he deems fit for your intrusion. To take him as an enemy is not the eternity you want."

"Are you telling me this because you want to or because you have to?" I asked, tilting my head.

I didn't miss the way she turned to him, cowering as he glared. "It's true."

I pulled away from the others until I was within striking distance of my father. "I would like to take a walk with my mother. And you're going to stay here with my friends. Got it?"

He scoffed. "You have no power here."

In one motion, I snatched my mother free of his grip and punched him in the face. "I'm a pretty quick learner. I can't kill you, but I *can* torture the hell out of you, and pain is pain in any realm."

Ezra stepped forward, gripping my father's shoulder exactly like he'd held my mother. "Perhaps a lesson in kindness as we wait."

I threw him a grateful glance, and he bowed slightly, his hazel eyes catching in the moonlight, though even when he'd bent, he was still so much taller than I was.

Once out of earshot, my mother cracked. "Listen to me. You have to stay away from Orin. Do you understand? I saw the way you looked at him, but whatever you remember him to be, he's gone. He belongs to Death now. His will is not his own."

"I don't—"

She threw a hand up. "There are things you don't know. Things I don't know if I have time to explain."

We stayed well away from the edge of the lake, but she hardly peeled her eyes away, even as she scrambled for words.

"You don't have to save me, Mother. I'm grown, and I can make my own choices."

"Orin only exists because of you," she rushed out.

"Orin is older than I am, so that's not true at all. Please, Mother."

"Deyanira Sariah Hark, you listen to me and listen well. You'll have one single chance to hear this story, I'm sure of it."

I paused, crossing my arms, trying to swallow my pride. "It's Faber. I'm listening."

"Do you want to know why Death came, had a son, and then abandoned him? All magic comes with a cost, and when Death's power was restricted by the gods when they made Requiem immortal, he leeched the immortal power in order to create his harbingers because he's hunting a soul in Requiem."

"Interesting." I knew this, but Ezra had said everything had ears, and there were few I trusted enough to share anything with, so I let her continue as I remained silent.

"It wasn't enough for him to have a single weapon. He's greedy. So, he took a human woman to his bed, his seed bearing him a son. He believed he stole the power and the very breath of his heir to gain the ability to overtake the magic of the next born Life Maiden. Orin was meant to die after that, and Death was sure the last strand of your Life magic had sent his son to the ether rather than this court."

My heart plummeted into my stomach. "How could you possibly know this, and why would you tell me?"

"I've been here for a long time, Deyanira, and the only thing I've sought for years is this answer. I could feel you in my belly. The pure joy and healing and love that radiated from you before you were born was immense. I always thought you would be the new Life Maiden after Sorenia, your predecessor, was killed. But then everything turned dark, and I came here. I knew it was wrong. Broken somehow. If I give you nothing else, daughter, take this knowledge. He will surely cast me into the Lake when he learns of my betrayal anyway."

"Mother," I whispered, taking her hand. "What in the gods' names could you have done to get this information? Surely, he's not keeping a diary."

She smiled, so sad it was haunting. "He keeps consorts." She brushed a dark lock of hair behind an ear, letting the moment and her confession hang between us until the silence grew unbearable.

"I don't know what to say."

"You don't need to say anything. Just listen. Death wants no heirs, no one vying for his position. The bond that you share goes beyond your marriage, but don't fool yourself. Orin's darkness is strong enough to swallow you whole, as it was always intended to. His existence was a price paid and nothing more. Believe me, his father sees that power for what it is now. He intends to send him to Requiem as soon as he has control and bring it down. Every person will fall. Every soul will be reaped. And the price for that kind of magic will be Orin himself. And likely anyone tied to him. Run far and fast, Deyanira. Or this lake will look like a sanctuary when Death truly gets ahold of you. He'll play with his food first, but he never leaves the table hungry."

I turned to her then, staring into foreign eyes, into the face of a woman who was taken from me before I could even know the love of a mother. Yet she'd still made her own sacrifices. She'd found a way to love me beyond death. "I didn't grow up gentle. I'm not a reticent person. I don't like gravy, and sometimes flowers make me sneeze. I prefer the cold side of a pillow, and I'm not a morning person. I taught myself to walk, and when Father hired a tutor to teach me to read and write, I taught myself instead because she was mean. I prefer rooftops over grassy fields, and I'm not scared of heights. I can't play an instrument or sing, and I accidentally married the wrong man. But he was the right man. The only one for me. He loves me just as much as you do, and whatever part of me that's bound to him is where my future lies. Be it darkness or light, an eternity at the bottom of this lake or upon a throne of skulls, I will not leave him to suffer his father's madness. And while I'm grateful for your words, there's truly nothing you could have said that would have changed my mind. I've never been a runner, Mother, only a Maiden."

"Dey—"

"You're suffering. I can see it in your eyes. Let me try to bring you a bit of peace. A little of those final moments of happiness in Requiem." Reaching for her hand, I pulled her into a hug, holding my breath as I called for the power I was always meant to have. She gasped as light formed between us. Not the blue or silver light of nighttime, but something warm and inviting. Calm and healing.

But one moment I was holding my mother, wishing her peace, and the next, the light of her soul was ripped away from her body as skin and bones turned to embers, and she was released. Free. The tiny orb of light circled me once and then twice, and though I wasn't sure if my mind conjured it or if it really happened, I could've sworn I heard her whisper, "Thank you," before she vanished altogether.

"What the hell?" I said, mostly to myself, as no one was nearby.

But a sinister voice answered. "You've released her soul to reincarnate, and now you'll do the same for me."

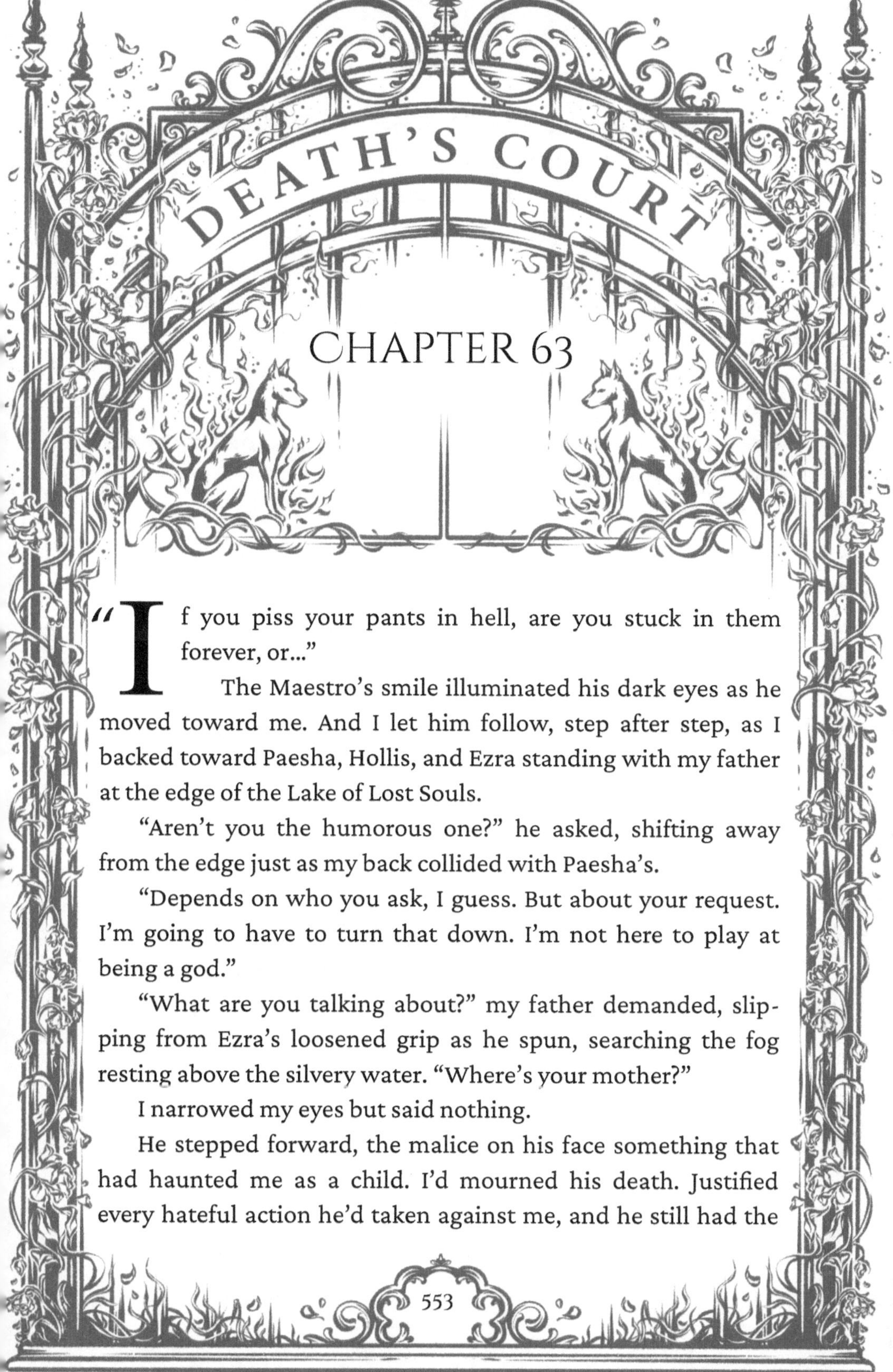

CHAPTER 63

"If you piss your pants in hell, are you stuck in them forever, or..."

The Maestro's smile illuminated his dark eyes as he moved toward me. And I let him follow, step after step, as I backed toward Paesha, Hollis, and Ezra standing with my father at the edge of the Lake of Lost Souls.

"Aren't you the humorous one?" he asked, shifting away from the edge just as my back collided with Paesha's.

"Depends on who you ask, I guess. But about your request. I'm going to have to turn that down. I'm not here to play at being a god."

"What are you talking about?" my father demanded, slipping from Ezra's loosened grip as he spun, searching the fog resting above the silvery water. "Where's your mother?"

I narrowed my eyes but said nothing.

He stepped forward, the malice on his face something that had haunted me as a child. I'd mourned his death. Justified every hateful action he'd taken against me, and he still had the gall to look at me like that. I'd chosen peace with him relentlessly, but even I had my limits.

"Where is my wife?" he demanded again.

"Free."

Without warning, Drexel lunged, grabbing Hollis from my side, slipping his arm around his neck, and dragging him backward toward the edge of the lake.

"No," I screamed, but Ezra held me back, snatching Paesha, as well.

"Don't get close to the water," he growled, staring at Drexel, who'd taken my father's side.

Hollis squirmed, and I couldn't manage a single breath as my heart began to pound in my chest. I couldn't lose him twice.

Drexel's face twisted into something unhinged, desperate. Menacing eyes growing wide, he ran his fingers through his hair until it stood on end. "You think *I* like bargains, Deyanira? Death loves them more. He made me what I was, gave me power that wasn't owed to me for a night with my sister. I did his bidding and look where that got me. I'm done. I want to be freed from this purgatory, and I won't go back to that castle. I won't be locked in the pit again. You will free me, or you know what's coming."

I inched forward, yanking myself from Ezra's hold as I swiped two throwing knives from my chest. Drexel's laugh and his fucking smile as Hollis feared for his eternity ignited a torrent of fury within me.

"If you think the pit is bad, wait until you see what I have planned for you."

"You would never," he sang, the voice of a performer coming out. "You're too pure."

"Put the weapons down, Deyanira. They do you no good here," my father ordered before turning to Drexel. "I can promise you she's always been the thorn, never the rose. Don't hold her to standards. She'll only disappoint you."

I studied our surroundings for an answer. Help of any kind. But only the shadowed branches of dead, gnarled trees loomed above us. My shoulders fell as I looked to see Paesha struggling against Ezra while he hauled her backward.

"Let him go!" she screamed. "Take me this time, Maestro. Take me."

"Beautiful Huntress," he purred. "Happy reunions. How was our little Quill last you saw her?"

She froze, slowly standing upright. "Why?"

Drexel's grin became maniacal. "One doesn't make enemies of Death's Maiden without certain... safeguards in place."

"What did you do?" Ezra asked, the growl in his voice terrifying.

He lifted a shoulder. "It doesn't matter now, does it? We're here, and she isn't. Though I do hope to see her again in my next life. See how she fares with her new troubles. Don't you, Hollis?"

"Let him go," I warned, wondering what I truly would do if he didn't comply.

"Go ahead, Dey. Give him another chance at life so I can find a way to kill him slower next time," Paesha said through gritted teeth.

His doubt of my conviction to damn a life was twisted. The war within me had already ended. I was just like everyone else. Not all good, not all bad. Existence wasn't black and white. It was gray. I was gray because some deaths were warranted. Still, I took a step backward, and he followed, moving slightly away from the edge of the water. Another step, and again, he followed. Predictable.

"Throw your little knife, Maiden. It makes no difference to me. I'm already dead."

"Oh, this isn't for you." I lunged, snatching the front of

Hollis's perfect white shirt, ripping him from Drexel grasp as I twisted and blasted the throwing knives into the branch of the dead tree now hanging above us. We tumbled to the ground the second the crack echoed through the night and the limb fell, crashing into the Maestro's stomach, where Hollis had been. He stumbled backward, sheer panic on his face as he reached the slippery edge of the Lake of Lost Souls.

He yelled, throwing his arms out to catch his balance. Only then did I notice how close he'd been to my father. The Maestro reached for him, scrambling, snatching his sleeve. I tried to get up. Tried to get to them. Even when neither deserved it, I still tried. But it was too late. In a breath, they both crashed into the murky water, though it didn't splash. Didn't ripple or wave. Simply... devoured them.

I held my breath, guarding my heart as I prepared for the guilt to break me. Nothing came. Only a calm numbing. Only a pulsing sense of justice.

Still, Hollis laid his hand on mine as we sat on the decayed ground. "I'm so sorry, Little Dove."

I shook my head. "Don't apologize for them. They made their own choices."

Ezra and Paesha came to help us up, but the color had completely washed from her face as she stared into the murky water.

"P?" I whispered.

"I'm fine."

"Hey." Ezra spun her until her back was to the water, holding the sides of her face tenderly as he forced her gaze to his. "It'll never be you, Kitten. I'd drain the fucking lake before I let that happen."

She smiled, nodding, though her fingers trembled along his. He pressed a quick kiss to her forehead before leading us away from the water.

"Do we sleep in hell?" Paesha asked, stepping around a fallen branch.

"We do whatever we want until he calls," her lover answered. "And he will."

"Apart from the lake and the pit, what else do we need to be aware of?" I asked.

"Death has had an eternity to twist this realm into a place of pure pleasure and unmatched torture. If I began to list them, we'd be here for hours. Just stay close until we can figure out a way to get you home."

I stopped, wondering if I should run. If I could trust Ezra as much as the others. Paesha tugged on his arm until all three paused.

"You don't know me, so I'm going to give you the benefit of the doubt here. I'm not going back unless it's with Orin."

"Orin is gone," he shouted, throwing his hands up. "And each second you spend trying to free him, you're putting everyone around you in danger. Respectfully, you should have had a better plan before you got here, Maiden. Because the only thing you can do now is survive."

"He's still in there. You saw him in the hall."

Ezra rushed toward me, gripping the collar of my shirt, hauling me closer. "He's nothing more than Death's lackey, and you're fooling yourself if you think otherwise. His actions are demands of his father, and that's it. My brother is *gone.* That *thing* that looks out from his eyes ate away his soul. Orin would have never laid a hand on me."

"You have three seconds to get your fucking hands off of me or I'm going to make you wish you had the lake to escape to."

He growled, baring his teeth. "Your threats mean nothing here, Maiden."

I gripped his wrist, anger building.

"Dey," Paesha whispered.

"One."

He tugged me closer, hazel eyes nearly gleaming in the moonlight. "Two."

"Stop this," Hollis pleaded from Paesha's side as she ran forward, shoving herself between us until Ezra's grip faltered, and he let me go.

She kept her back to him, a plea in her eyes as she held her hands up. "He's only trying to keep me safe."

"I know," I roared. "What do you think I'm trying to do for Orin? He needs someone. He needs me to remind him who he is."

"Okay," she said softly, as if she were speaking to a wild animal. "We'll find him. We'll do it together."

"*We* won't," Ezra said with so much finality the twist in Paesha's heart showed on her face.

"I will," Hollis said, moving to my side. "I will stand beside you, come what may."

The Huntress turned, facing the love of her life. "I will, too," she breathed. "Because if it were me, Orin would come. He would crawl his way through any battleground for me." She stepped forward, placing a hand on Ezra's chest until heaving breaths turned steady. "And if it were you, I would be the one to start the battle."

"You don't know this place like I do," he said, shaking his head.

"No, my love. I don't. I know you, and I know your fear is warranted. But Deyanira is my family, too, and she needs us as much as he does."

His eyes shifted between hers, and I felt like an intruder on a pivotal, private moment. He practically shrank, leaning his forehead to hers. "Then I will follow you into the depths of hell and grow wings for your escape."

Ezra threw a halfhearted apology my way as we continued

following whatever path he'd chosen. I didn't condemn him for putting her safety above everyone else. He'd lost her and was likely to do irrational things to keep her now that they were reunited. But that kind of love was dangerous to me. He was dangerous.

"If not the lake, then perhaps the grove?" Hollis asked, with a note of reservation in his tone.

"You of all people know why that's a bad idea, Hol," Ezra answered. "But I can't argue that it's probably the best option for a single night."

"I'm fine with anywhere but the lake," Paesha said.

I leaned down, swiping a dead leaf from the ground to keep my hands busy. "What's the threat there?"

"It's best you see it for yourself," Hollis answered, a tiny skip to his step as he hustled forward, nearly overtaking Ezra's long strides.

Beyond the patch of trees bordering the Lake of Lost Souls, a glowing blue light shone in the distance. As we neared, though Ezra's steps had grown slower, the lights grew, until we were close enough to see them for what they truly were.

"What is this?" I asked, staring up at the silvery bark emitting that soft blue glow. I swiped my hand through the gentle mist that made the area feel almost dreamlike, immediately feeling a pull to step into the heart of the grove, as if I could feel the safety within, the promise of peace.

"The Whispering Grove," Hollis answered, leaving us all behind in a trance.

"It's a sanctuary amidst the horrors of Death's court for the spirits known as the Whispers," Ezra said, standing pointedly outside of the glow cast to the soft, mossy ground. "The Whispers are a collection of souls that found themselves so entranced by the grove's allure they became trapped within."

I tossed the remnants of the crumbled leaf I'd been picking

at to the ground and stepped into the cool light, immediately feeling the pull, the cool brush of a calm promise. "So, they get to spend eternity in peace? Sounds terrible," I said with an eye roll, turning to follow Hollis.

Ezra's step within came with a gasp from Paesha. I whipped around to see him, half the form of a human and half luminescent spectral, his eyes growing sad as he moved backward. "I've spent my fair share of time in the grove, Maiden. Most of us have. There's a mask of peace, but this is Death's court, and the Whispers are trapped here. When he comes to play, it's absolute torture. He's peeled the skin from my body. Broken every bone. Made me watch as he murdered everyone I'd ever known in visions of torment. Death's single currency is fear, and he comes here to collect it."

Paesha joined him just outside of the barrier. "We'll, umm. We'll just be out here," she said.

"You're safe," he assured her, stepping back into the light. "I won't be taken overnight. And Death has been... extra vicious lately. Orin's massacre has given him a crop of new souls to torment. He only comes here when he has to. I think because something in the magic tortures him, too."

"But Hollis?" I pointed to where the old man was fading down a hill. "Why did he seem so eager?"

Ezra sighed, his hazel eyes darkening. "Because his wife is a Whisper, and if he spends much more time here with her, he will become one, too."

"Does he know?"

The giant man nodded. "He's made his choice. This will eventually become his eternity."

THE EDGE of the Whispering Grove was hard to step out of. Having spent hours there, waiting for them to fall asleep, each moment coaxing me to wait just a little longer and a little longer until the Whispers came. Like haunted ghosts, they circled, smiling, each face kind as they promised I could stay forever.

We will protect you, they'd said. *Don't listen to the things you've heard, Maiden. The grove is safe. The grove is happiness and love. The grove is...*

I'd had to cover my ears to block them out, and the moment I did, they vanished, content to let me feel the euphoria of the grove without the badgering.

Paesha fell asleep in Ezra's strong arms, his snoring never seeming to bother her. Together, they looked so peaceful and happy it made my heart ache, but it also solidified my decision. She'd come for Orin and for me. But if we dug deeper, I knew it was for Ezra, too. Even though it meant leaving Quill behind. Ezra was her eternity. And he was right. Every decision I made put her in more danger than she deserved.

She needed to get back to Quill, and I'd promised her a way. I couldn't let anything happen to her before it. So, I left her, wrapped in his strength, knowing that no one would protect her or love her as hard as he did. And that was the best thing I could ever wish for her. She needed these moments before they were gone. She'd earned them.

The trees beyond the Whispering Grove felt colder, darker than they had before. There were more people within the forest now, more souls really, though they were corporeal, like those in Death's throne room. Most faces seemed gaunt, most people keeping a distance, but not all were alone. They didn't speak, though. Not a single hushed tone crept along the cool breeze. They were scared. All of them. As I should have been.

Still, I followed the silhouette of the looming castle in the distance. Each moment that passed felt heavy, as if it would be the one that captured Orin fully, the moment he could no longer fight. There wasn't a part of me that could sleep in a mossy grove, knowing intimately the darkness that held my husband by the throat. I hadn't come here for safety. I'd come for him. He was mine. Fierce and merciless and unmoving. But mine.

I thought I'd have to search the entire castle to find him. I'd resolved to accept any form of torment along the way, but when he stepped out from behind a tree, cloaked in his father's black robes, shrouded in darkness, and eyes full of hatred, I found that perhaps I wasn't truly ready for torture.

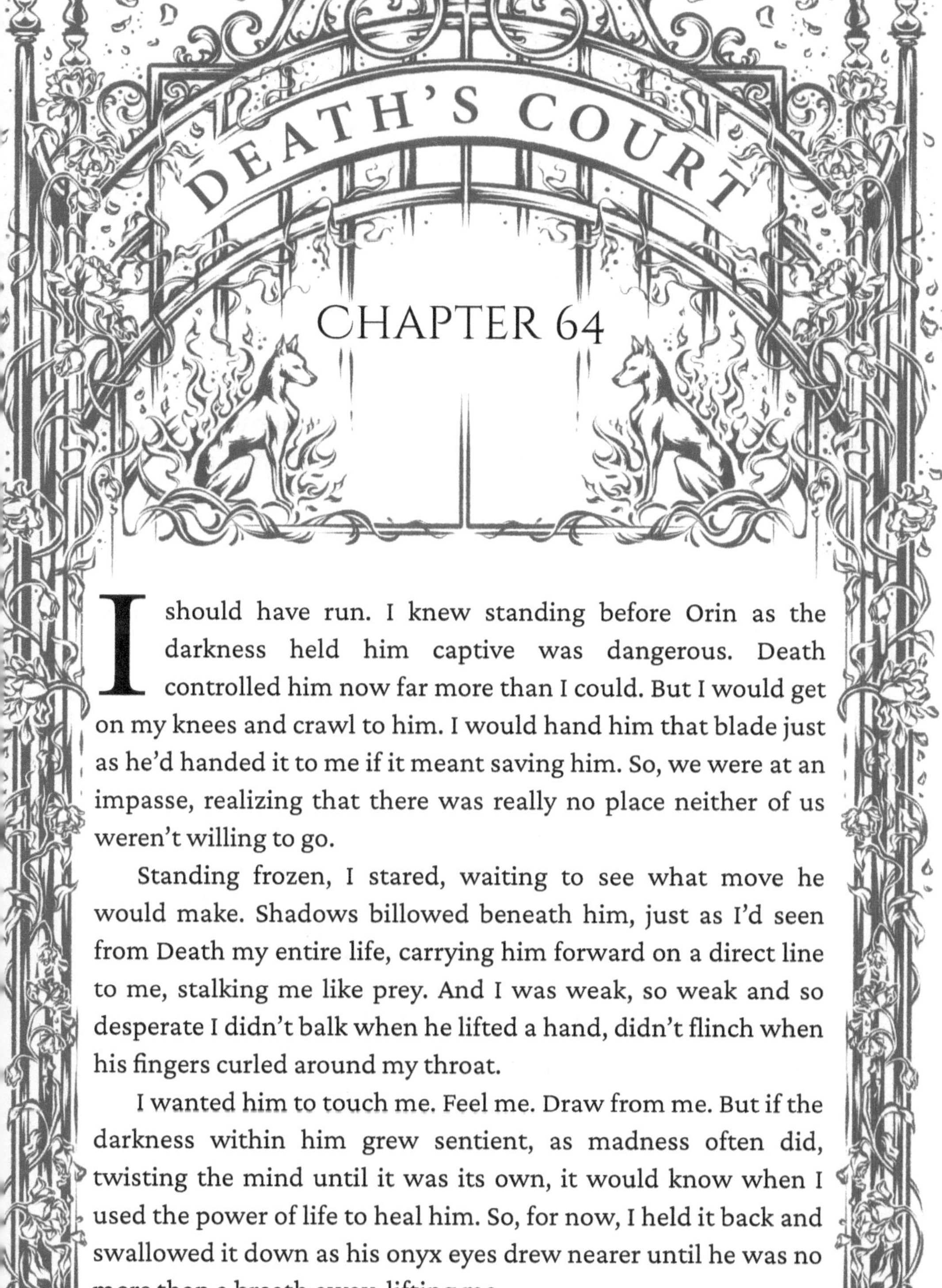

CHAPTER 64

I should have run. I knew standing before Orin as the darkness held him captive was dangerous. Death controlled him now far more than I could. But I would get on my knees and crawl to him. I would hand him that blade just as he'd handed it to me if it meant saving him. So, we were at an impasse, realizing that there was really no place neither of us weren't willing to go.

Standing frozen, I stared, waiting to see what move he would make. Shadows billowed beneath him, just as I'd seen from Death my entire life, carrying him forward on a direct line to me, stalking me like prey. And I was weak, so weak and so desperate I didn't balk when he lifted a hand, didn't flinch when his fingers curled around my throat.

I wanted him to touch me. Feel me. Draw from me. But if the darkness within him grew sentient, as madness often did, twisting the mind until it was its own, it would know when I used the power of life to heal him. So, for now, I held it back and swallowed it down as his onyx eyes drew nearer until he was no more than a breath away, lifting me.

"You...Why am I drawn to you?" he asked, his voice so strained it broke my heart.

"Do you not remember?" I rasped, reaching for his fingers, releasing the smallest tendril of power. A flash of color lit his eyes on contact, followed by a gasp. "See me, Orin. Feel me. Know that I am here, and I love you."

His grip on my throat loosened before he jerked away, smoothing his hands down his face, so much agony shining through as he tilted his head back and groaned. Seconds turned into minutes until he settled enough to come back to me, gentle fingers on my face as he swiped his thumbs across my cheeks.

"Nightmare..." He sighed. "What were you thinking coming here?"

"Would you have come for me?"

"Of course, I would have, but you don't know what he's like. You don't know what I'm becoming."

Placing my hands on his chest, I began to argue, but the screaming in the distance halted me.

He closed his eyes, placing his forehead to mine. "It will be over in a minute, love."

But then another scream followed, and one more, until a flash of darkness stole him. He tried to pull away, but I latched onto his neck, forcing the contact, forcing a little bit of magic through in a desperate moment. Hoping like hell he wouldn't be released the way my mother had. But he had never died. This wasn't his soul touching me. It was him. All of him. His shoulders relaxed, and a full breath filled his lungs.

"Can't you see I'm not safe? You have to run while you still can. Go home, Deyanira. Live. I am only his son now. Only his."

"You are *not* his," I growled. "You are mine. And I will stand between you and Death until he forgets you exist. Until the gods return. Until they all fall. Until this realm becomes a pinprick of a memory in a universe that transcends time. He can do whatever he wants to me, and I will not bend. I will not break. I will not leave you."

"I am dangerous!" he yelled, stepping away, eyes flashing black, teeth clenching.

I got right back in his face, shoving him, pushing him to fight with me, to be with me in whatever capacity he could. "Not to me."

"To everyone."

Another scream, another pained look on his face as he tried and failed to fight the pull to it. He turned away, taking several steps toward the sound. I grabbed him, yanking his wrist until he spun back. "Stay with me."

He took a shuddering breath, facing the castle, then back to me, waging war. "Whatever your plan is, all of your eternity is mine. Should it be torture or rivalry, I will help you conquer it. Should you wish the souls of Death's court to their knees, I will build a mountain of bones for you to stand on. I will forge a crown and place it on your head, and I will be the first to bow. And I will eviscerate anyone who does not follow suit."

The gleam in his eyes shifted through a thousand emotions until he landed on hunger. He was on me in a second, hands on my face once more, lips to mine in desperation. Tongue and teeth as I opened for him, letting him taste me, have me in whatever way he wanted. Shadows enveloped us, creeping from the ground and smothering us in darkness as I gasped, but he gripped my waist, holding me steady until they fell away, revealing a dark room lit only with candles. So many candles lined the floor in clusters, and the ivory wax dripped carelessly, circling a bed in the center of the room.

"Are you afraid?" His words were a brush against my lips and also laced with their own level of fear, as if I would deny him.

Tension coiled low in my belly, remembering what it felt like to have him inside of me. Worshiping me. "I don't fear the dark, Orin. I need it. And you need my light. We are bound because of it. Touch me. Use me. Take whatever you want from me because I am yours."

I let the magic free until my skin began to glow. He traced a finger over my palm. Then slid a hand to the buckle holding the last of my throwing knives to my chest. He let them fall to the floor before gripping the ends of my shirt and pulling it over my head, the fabric brushing my overly sensitive skin, desperate for him to taste every inch. Shadows surrounded both of us, stealing the remnants of our clothing in less than a breath.

With a flash of darkness, he moved backward, head tilting as I lost him in that moment. I watched as he became consumed, instantly changing into something feral, someone far more dangerous. I lowered my chin, a dare in my eyes as I stalked forward.

"You want me. You know you do."

"I want to watch you suffer," he said.

"Then come and get me, Husband."

He wasn't tender as he laid a palm against my chest and shoved me against the wall. Still, that contact was enough to push the power back, spinning his hatred into lust.

He pressed his hot mouth to a nipple, sucking as he dragged me toward the bed, his hold never faltering, drawing the light to counter the dark. He moved a hand down my thigh, resting it where Chaos should have been as he nipped my neck. I moaned. With a flick of his wrist and a tendril of shadow, my blade appeared in his hand. "You really should keep better care of your weapons."

"I'll try harder," I managed, as he dropped the blade to the floor.

I reached for the button on his pants, but he pulled away,

clicking his tongue with a salacious grin. "Naughty Nightmare. There's no rush."

But again, as he held a distance, the darkness took over.

I spread my legs on the bed, drawing a finger down my slick center, stopping to circle my clit as I held eye contact. His jaw ticked when I gasped at my touch, arching on the bed, inviting him closer, inviting him to claim me as he once had.

"Don't you want to taste it, Husband?" I moved my fingers to my mouth, and he faltered, stumbling forward. "Come closer and I'll let you. I promise."

He glared.

I smiled, sliding my palm down my body again, plunging two fingers into my own core, toying with his anger.

He reached for me with greedy hands, flipping me over on the bed as he fell on my back and hissed into my ear. "You deserve to be punished for that."

I lifted from the bed, pressing into his hard cock and wiggling. "Then do it, Husband. And make sure it fucking hurts."

With one hand gripping my waist, holding me up from the bed, he slammed a palm across my ass. The quick, sharp sting raced over me, eliciting a moan before he smoothed his fingers over the spot.

"Again," I begged him, forcing as much contact as possible.

His eager compliance was a dream. Orin reached around, circling my clit as he growled from behind me. "This won't be gentle."

I could hardly think around the sensation of his perfect strokes, but still, I trembled with eager anticipation when he wrapped my hair around his fist and yanked me backward at the same time he slammed into me with absolutely no warning. He groaned, pausing for only a second before pulling out and thrusting once more.

I clenched around him as he violently pounded into me over and over again, unaware of the magic pulsing through every place his body touched mine. Without warning, he withdrew and flipped me onto my back, kissing me with a desperate hunger, teeth digging into my bottom lip, as golden eyes met mine.

"Hello, Husband," I purred.

Panting, he dropped his forehead to mine. "Hello, Wife."

Gripping my hips, he pulled me closer, driving himself forward once more as he gazed down into my eyes. I reached up, running my fingers through his thick, dark hair. He found a steady rhythm, driving himself forward almost brutally, setting me on fire.

"Don't stop," I moaned, arching into him, muscles seized as euphoria built between us. "Don't you dare stop."

He paused, bending to whisper into my ear. "Keep making those fucking sounds, and I won't have a choice, Nightmare."

He thrust again with a newfound fervor, driving me up and up until I clenched the sheets in my hands, racing for my climax, and cried out his name, vision gone as sheer pleasure coiled around us, exploding as one.

I COULDN'T SLEEP, not even within the comfort of Orin's arms wrapped around me, not as he traced circles into my skin, our legs tangled together beneath silk sheets. If I closed my eyes and fell asleep, everything could change; he could fade back, and I wasn't ready to let him go.

"What do we do?" I breathed, breaking the silence between us.

"Death is stronger because of the fear gripping the souls

locked in his court. It's not just that he enjoys the fear. It fuels his power. Intensifies it."

I considered that for a while, lying in bed, matching my breathing to Orin's while remembering all of my time with his father. I'd always held my tongue, though he'd tried to break me. Always denied him, though he'd pushed me. It was more than that, though. It was the challenge. That cat-and-mouse game. Maybe that's why he'd chased Ro so relentlessly. Perhaps in his own twisted mind he did love her, but it was more likely that he was obsessed with her and the chase. The centuries-long game between gods, where humans of the world became the wreckage of the pursuit.

"He never came to you after you killed someone, did he?" I asked, mind wandering.

"No."

"It was the same for Icharius Fern. He sent shadows to collect the souls, but he appeared every single time for me."

"Of course he did," Orin answered, following my thoughts. "He needed to make sure he wasn't losing you to Life."

"He's been stroking his power within me since that first kill when I was a teen. Every month, sometimes several times a month, he called me. Not because he had to, but because he wanted to make sure the Life Maiden power remained dormant."

"Exactly." He slid his fingers into my hair as I twisted to look up at him. "But you've never been easy for him, and he likes your fight."

"Has he told you that?"

"No. But I know what it feels like when you fight back. I've been on the receiving end of that glare, and maybe he and I are alike because, when I see it, I want nothing more than to challenge you. I can't help it."

"It's true," Death's eerie, smooth voice said as he appeared, standing at the foot of the bed. "I do enjoy our little games."

I gasped as Orin's shadows covered me in fabric. Jerking upright, Orin began to shout in pain. I turned my bare back to Death, reaching for Orin, ready to reveal the full capacity of my power to save whatever agony Death had planned when the entire room fell to shadow and the bed beneath us vanished. The man beside me disappeared, though I could still hear him writhing in pain.

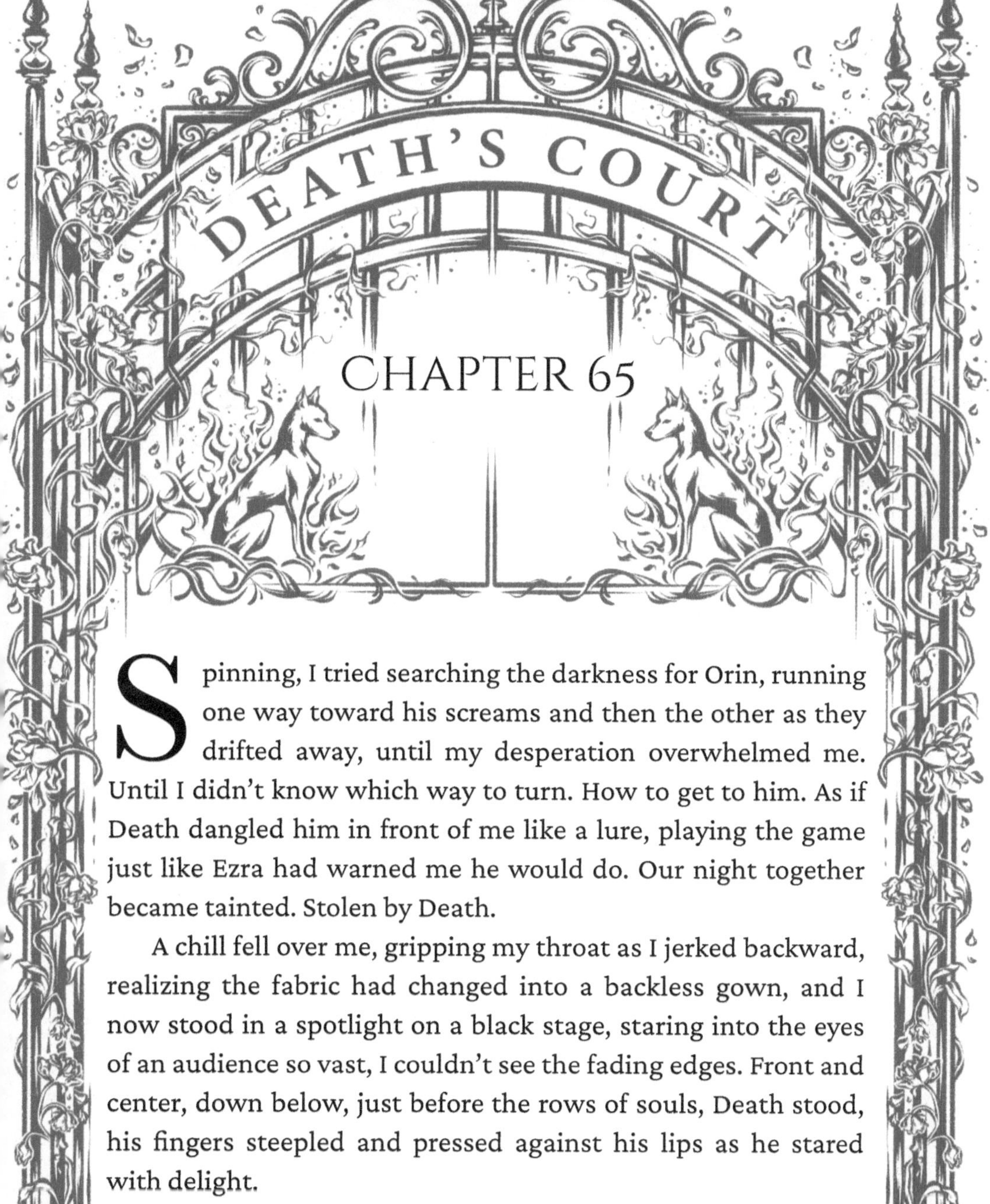

DEATH'S COURT

CHAPTER 65

Spinning, I tried searching the darkness for Orin, running one way toward his screams and then the other as they drifted away, until my desperation overwhelmed me. Until I didn't know which way to turn. How to get to him. As if Death dangled him in front of me like a lure, playing the game just like Ezra had warned me he would do. Our night together became tainted. Stolen by Death.

A chill fell over me, gripping my throat as I jerked backward, realizing the fabric had changed into a backless gown, and I now stood in a spotlight on a black stage, staring into the eyes of an audience so vast, I couldn't see the fading edges. Front and center, down below, just before the rows of souls, Death stood, his fingers steepled and pressed against his lips as he stared with delight.

Then the screaming started again.

Orin.

To my right, locked in a familiar golden birdcage, lying on the ground and writhing in pain lay Orin. I tried to move, to get to him. Touch him. But I couldn't. My feet were stuck to the stage.

Death's laugh silenced the restless crowd, the fear palpable among the thousands and thousands of souls. Those dark features were narrowed on me, the challenge sitting between us as he lowered his chin. "Dance, Deyanira."

I didn't let the surprise of his command show, though I felt it in my stuttering heart. "Respectfully, go fuck yourself."

His response was almost giddy. "Sometimes you can be so predictable."

He pointed a long finger toward Orin, who stopped screaming for merely a second, warm eyes flashing to me.

"Please," he trembled, reaching a hand toward me. "Send her home."

His screams began again. He gripped his head, squeezing his eyes shut. Death's cackle reverberated off walls so dark, I could not see them at all. "Why would I do that when we could have so much fun together? We can break that stubborn will, *together*. I have been waiting so long for this day. Dance, Deyanira, and I will make it stop."

I flinched. Giving in was too easy. It's not what he truly wanted. And if I caved, even though every single thing in my body wanted to free my husband from his torture, I knew Death wouldn't stop there. So again, I refused. Shaking my head, though a tear fell, and my breaths ceased.

"Not even one teeny, tiny sway for your husband's sanity? I think you've been lied to, son. I don't think she loves you at all."

Orin roared, fighting whatever monster consumed him as he pulled himself to his feet, staring at his father, though every black vein showed and every muscle grew taut. "You know nothing of love."

His father jerked at those words, the surprise of Orin's conviction to stand and fight evident within his wide eyes. But the shock was there and gone in a flash. Mirth melted into fury at the challenge from his son before a group of people that were meant to hold only fear. Never hope. And in that moment, Orin was hope. He was everything his father could never be. And that was a huge problem.

A set of stairs appeared, and Death took them, one by one, eyes never leaving his son as he prowled forward. The cage flew to pieces, golden shards of metal flying everywhere. They stood toe to toe for only a moment before Death reached out and placed his thumb to Orin's forehead, taking him to his knees.

"Good boy," he said. "But I'm afraid we have a problem. You see, we must remind everyone who you are. What you are. And why you can never be anything more than that."

He spun, his dark cloak flaring behind him as he took several steps away. Orin pinned his eyes on me. I could see the fight at first, the struggle to defeat his father's darkness. But it lasted only a second before he shifted to pure anger, then absolute rage as he ran across the stage, snatched me by my throat, and lifted me from the ground, his beautiful, brutal face void of any recognition.

I tried to grab his hand to send him my power, but he was quick, and I wasn't prepared for him move, to slam me into the ground so fucking hard the air was stolen from my lungs and the wooden planks of the stage shattered below me.

A stabbing pain seared my side, and I couldn't gasp over his grip. There was not an ounce of mercy in his eyes. He was gone. I squeezed the hand holding me, scrambling to loosen the fingers that crushed my neck.

"Son," Death said, so calm it felt like a violation to this rancid world.

Orin released me, staring down as I turned to the side that hadn't been impaled by a massive splinter of wood and coughed, the sound becoming a choke as whatever damage he'd done to my esophagus refused the air to pass. I closed my eyes, the tears on my cheeks my only companions as I fought for a breath.

The rattled sound was a small but mighty win against Death.

Orin grabbed my arm, lifting me from the ground as his fingers closed around the board that stuck out from my side. There was a single flash of empathy before he yanked, freeing me of the wood but sending me back to my knees, blinding white pain claiming me.

For several moments, there was nothing beyond the agony of the splinters left in my body and the torn flesh at my side.

But that sickening peace found in pain was ripped away with Death's next words. "Tell me why you chose to have those flowers placed on your back. Who put them there?"

I gulped down air, the world reforming around me. On my hands and knees before Death's entire court, I vomited.

Before I could think of a passable lie, Death had taken Orin's place above me. He crouched, waiting as the shadows he commanded settled along the stage like fog on a lake, taking away the bile, the blood, the splinters and repairing the wood. He leaned forward, careful not to touch me as he whispered in my ear. "Tell me about the flowers," he hissed. "Where did you get the markings?"

I didn't even consider responding.

Shadows snatched my hair and yanked my head back so hard I saw stars. "Tell me or I will make you wish you were never born."

"Too late," I spat.

"Son," he crooned. "What do you know of these marks on your lovely wife's back?"

Orin's answer was numb, forced. "One for each life she's taken."

"And their origin?"

He lifted a stiff shoulder.

"A game, then," Death announced to the crowd. "A parade, if you will."

He paced along the edge of the stage, hands clasped behind his back. A few waves of his power and Orin was back in a new birdcage, this one adorned with golden skulls along the top. Death's shadows grew from the floor, winding around my ankles like shackles before snaking up my body, a violation that churned my stomach. The shadows slipped up my arms, forcing them to spread wide. He twirled a finger, and they twisted, tightening, pinching the skin until I hissed. He'd made sure I stared directly at Orin, not to the audience held in captivated awe by their jailer's show.

"Dey," Orin whispered, darkness gone but full of fear, brows knit together. "I'm here. I'm with you."

Should he reach his hand through the cage, he might've been able to touch me, but I couldn't move. The more I struggled against the magical bonds, the tighter they became.

Death stepped into my line of sight, squeezing my chin. I wiggled, trying to pull from his grasp, but there would be no escape.

"Speak their names."

My mouth formed a thin line.

"So beautifully stubborn."

In a flicker of motion, a long, corded leather whip appeared in his hands. "You either say the names or tell me where you got that tattoo."

"I will not break," I spat.

His breath curled hot around my ear as he whispered into it. "Yes, Deyanira Sariah Faber, you will. And you will do it so beautifully our crowd will weep."

He shoved my head to the side, forcing me to look out to the people. I nearly vomited again when I saw one green eye and one blue staring back and me, full of tears, as Paesha held the hand of her lover, a massive hellhound standing guard behind them both.

"You will speak, or maybe she will take your lashings for you."

He didn't wait for me to respond, circling like a vulture. The backless dress had been planned. He knew what he was going to do with me the second he saw the tattoo when I was lying in that bed... the familiar flowers that belonged to Ro piqued his curiosity, his desperation to win the game with her.

Ro. A goddess. But also, a victim. The one who'd saved me when I didn't know I needed saving. The one who'd never *truly* asked me for anything but to keep her secret. The one who'd promised, should her name show up on my palm, she would hold the blade, she would take the guilt. And she'd saved Orin, too. She'd found a way to keep his darkness at bay; she brought us together. And she was a victim. I could and would be strong for her because I couldn't die here. Only suffer. Just as she had been doing silently for centuries.

The anticipation of pain caused every muscle to shake. The whip cracked through the air, its sharp sound reverberating before the angry strike, biting into my flesh like a thousand venomous serpents. I gritted my teeth, swallowing the cry that caught in my throat. Death circled as his hollow eyes bore into mine, waiting for my decision. I knew what he demanded, and the weight of the choice pressed down upon me like a mountain.

Orin screamed. He'd never recover from watching me suffer. There was a bit of darkness that would never leave him now, and I accepted that as warm blood trailed down my back.

"Garrit Faden," I managed behind locked jaws, purposefully skipping my mother.

Death smiled, turning to the crowd. He pointed to the man who'd been the first to truly haunt my dreams, and Garrit surged forward on an invisible string of magic, his lifeless eyes and sunken face every bit as dark as I'd remembered.

The second lashing was faster, snapping through the air on a wave of promised pain, ripping into the flesh of my back as I arched.

"Marian Achlen," I managed.

She was plucked from the audience, but this time, I couldn't look her in the eyes. Instead, I held mine locked with Orin. He growled, and Death responded with another wave of pain in his direction, taking him back to his knees, though this time, he was silent, too. An unspoken oath between us. You could bend us, but we would never break. And so he rose once more.

The third crack of the whip, accompanied by another name, ripped so much skin from my back, I felt it hang, dangling. The fourth shredded me, taking away my breath as I stared at Orin, his fist in his mouth to keep from crying out. Maybe not for himself, but the sight, I was sure, was its own nightmare come to life.

With the fifth and sixth lashes, each crossing each other, I faltered, my head hanging, my bones rattling, my heart fading. I managed a glance to the side, managed to see the group of my victims standing there, watching. Some were horrified, while some felt vindicated.

"I mourned you," I whispered, though I wasn't sure they could hear me. "I honored each of you. I remembered your names, and I've carried you with me all this time."

They probably didn't care, but I did. I needed to remind myself that I was human. I was partially light, not only darkness that everyone in Requiem believed me to be.

Death became maniacal, hardly giving me time to say the next name before ripping through another row of flowers, delighting in his twisted show as the crowd on stage grew. The crowd down below stayed silent, and Orin, my loyal, sacrificing husband, slowly sank back to the floor of that cage.

My skin peeled in ribbons, and I stood in a pool of my own blood. I thought I couldn't die—I was confident, in fact. But slowly, the edge of my vision faded, the world spun, and whatever contents had remained in my stomach had long since been discharged.

The only thing I could hear were the sobs from Paesha, the crack of the whip like a metronome, and the names I'd delivered from memory. The ones I'd spoken so many times before, I didn't have to dig through my mind to find them. They sat, waiting on the threshold.

With the next lash, the arch of my back, the white-hot searing pain, I gasped. Finally showing Death the suffering he so loved.

"Stop this!" Orin yelled, unable to stand it any longer. The way his voice broke, the way he remained on his knees, the way he looked at me through tear-filled eyes, I knew we had to be near the end. "Let it be me. Gods, let it be me instead. She can speak the names and I will stand for her."

"No," a deep voice boomed from below. "I will take the lashings."

Ezra. The strong and loyal man who would bend for only one. Would break for her, too.

"No!" Paesha yelled. "I'll do it. You threatened her with me. Let it be me."

I had suffered too much blood loss, suspended in the air by shadows. I could no longer feel my hands or my legs. Even my back had grown numb between whippings. I could still feel my heart, though. The way it beat for all of them. The icy spirit within me that still would not give him what he truly wanted.

But when Death circled me again, the scarlet blood dripping

from his weapon of choice up his dark stage, I raced through every crevice of my mind, searching for a way out of this. If not for me, then for them.

He knelt outside of Orin's cage, reaching through the bars to take his chin, letting the darkness radiate until all emotion swept from Orin's face, the final tears that fell, meaningless. "I can see we just haven't given her enough motivation, son. And I grow bored. Go back to your realm, find the little girl, find the blacksmith. Find your mother and send their souls to me."

"No!" I screamed, the very pitch of desperation racing through the night. "I want to make a bargain."

His head snapped sideways. "Will you tell me how you came to have that tattoo?"

"I'll do more than that. If you agree to my terms, I will tell you where to find your missing goddess."

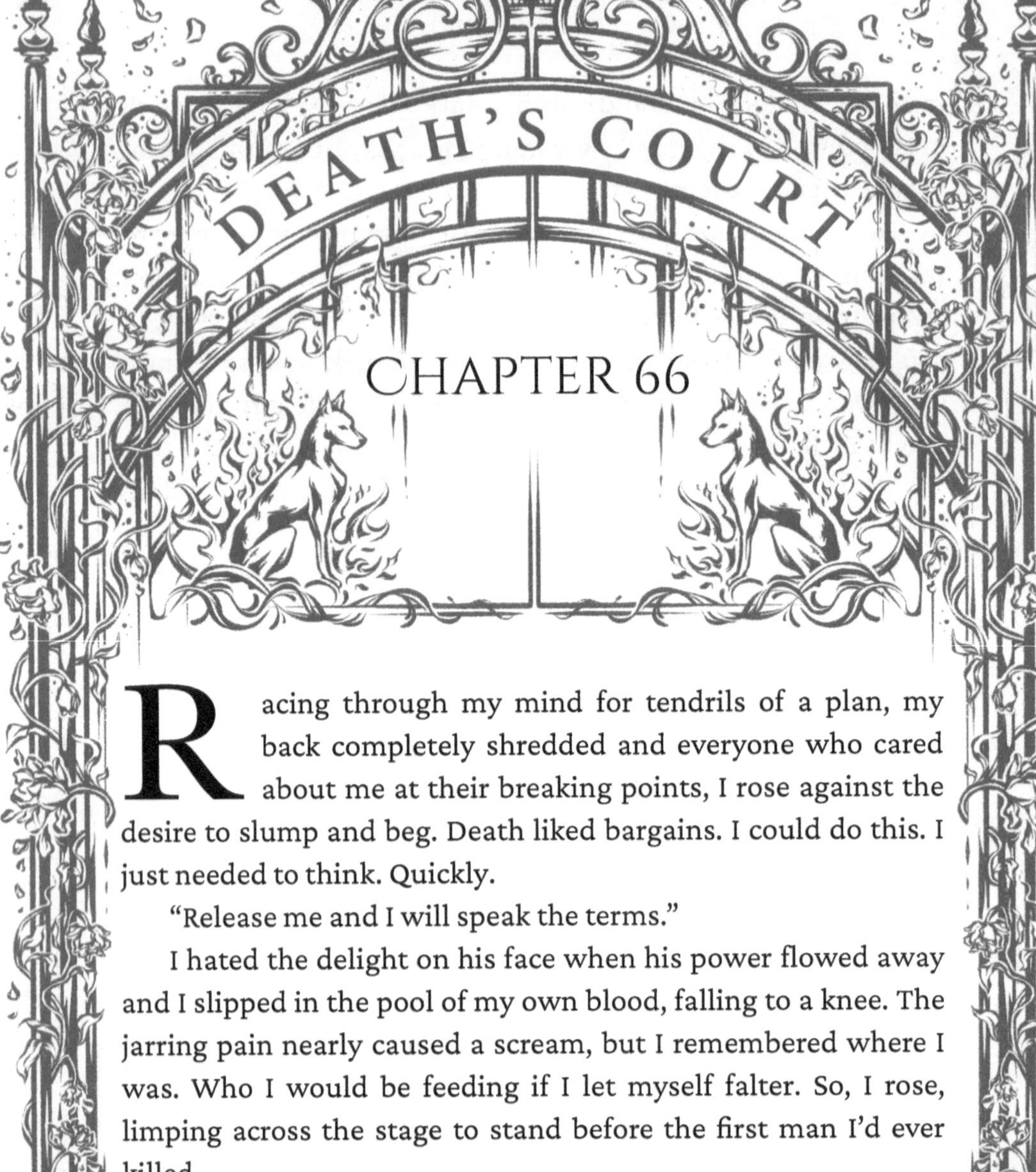

CHAPTER 66

Racing through my mind for tendrils of a plan, my back completely shredded and everyone who cared about me at their breaking points, I rose against the desire to slump and beg. Death liked bargains. I could do this. I just needed to think. Quickly.

"Release me and I will speak the terms."

I hated the delight on his face when his power flowed away and I slipped in the pool of my own blood, falling to a knee. The jarring pain nearly caused a scream, but I remembered where I was. Who I would be feeding if I let myself falter. So, I rose, limping across the stage to stand before the first man I'd ever killed.

"I am sorry. If you can trust me for even a moment, and you have a desire to leave this place, I will prove it to you."

The man narrowed his eyes as the crowd that had become restless and uncomfortable with Death's gruesome show stilled. He took my hand, and I walked him to the front of the stage. He said nothing when I held too tight, using him to keep my balance as the world swayed below me.

Cold steel wrapped through my veins as I turned to Death.

"Your bargain?" he asked, so intrigued he'd let his magic recede, the cage around Orin flickering as if it were only an illusion.

"The only thing stronger than fear is hope," I yelled, loud enough the crowd could hear every bit of diction in my words as I planted a palm into Garrit Faden's chest and let my power ripple. Just as my mother had, his body turned to ash, and his soul was released.

I couldn't hear the crowd's collective gasp over Death's absolute roar.

Still, I shouted. "You replace your fear with hope and take away his power. Find me and I will release you," I shouted, just as the world was enveloped in inky black shadows.

The banks of the Lake of Lost souls had crumbled, expanding the body of water as if Death's anger had rattled the world. But I was too foolish to be scared, too reckless to be careful. Too desperate to listen to the warnings that had been Ezra's mantra since the moment we met.

That man had stood for me, had offered to take my suffering, and I'd thought he didn't care for me at all. When in reality, as I peered over the lake and watched Orin dangling above it, gripping Death's shadows wrapped around his neck, I realized Ezra cared beyond rage. Beyond reason. He cared enough to try to keep us all safe, no matter the cost to him. Because they were his family. His weakness, just as Orin was mine.

And Death knew it. My heart plummeted. All resolve melted away as sheer panic rose until my fingers went numb. Until my breaths were shallow and all I could do was look out over those dangerous waters and pray to any of the gods to help us. Because I was only a single soul drowning in an eternity of Death's wrath.

Still, I dared to stare him in the eyes. To appear more than what I was. Because the only other option was to fall to my knees and beg. Death's eyes, once cold and calculating, now wild and frenzied, like an unhinged predator on the brink of madness. He began to pace, steps uneven and disjointed. The shadows billowing beneath him flickered, and he jerked.

"If you want to know where Cythronia is, you will release him."

"Are those the terms?" he asked wildly. "You have no power here. Not really. Do you think your little parlor trick was enough to change the minds of thousands? You're already mine, and you damn well know it. You're desperate now. I can see it. I can feel your fear like a vibration. I can fucking taste it."

Each step I took was poised and deliberate, a mirror to the quiet assurance that settled over me like a cloak. "You're wrong. I'm not dead, and you have no power over me. I'll never be yours because I already belong to him."

I didn't need to point for Death to know who I meant, and he flinched as if I'd struck him. The very existence of his son was a threat to him, just as my mother had warned while standing in this very spot.

"You would've never gotten past my hounds if you weren't dead, Deyanira. Don't tell lies."

I smiled, matching one I'd seen him share for over a decade. "You're the one who told them I wasn't a threat, don't you remember?"

He swept a hand toward Orin, and the shadows mimicked his gesture, until they became an extension of him, their tendrils matching his shape, no longer ribbons of murky shadows but fingers wrapped around his son's throat. He lowered his arm, watching only me. Waiting for me to cry out.

But instead, I played the final card I had in the game. The one I'd saved. The wild card that might've gotten me nowhere. "If you do this, Reverius, the Supreme Sovereign and Keeper of

All Realms will ban you from every world, not only Requiem and that of the gods. Everywhere, across all time and all realms. You will become obsolete." It was a lie, one pulled from desperation and yearning. Ro had given me the name of the highest god. She planted the weapon and trusted me to wield it wisely.

"You dare speak that name to me? He has no power here."

Daring another step, I pushed. "Yes, he does, and I think deep down you know it. That's your fear. That's why the Whispering Grove bothers you. Your *own* fear threatens you there. But I'm still standing here, willing to make a bargain with you. A simple one. Release him, and I will tell you where she is."

The severity on his face flickered to worry. He was weakening, and he knew it. The hope I'd planted on that stage was growing, as he did not return to them immediately to reignite the fear.

"Only Orin can send Cythronia Eiria's soul to this realm now that you have no harbinger in Requiem, and only I can tell you where she is. For now. Unless she runs again."

"She loves me," he yelled. "She doesn't run. She is lost and waiting for me to find her."

"Oh. Is that what that is? I must've misunderstood her."

Death's eyes narrowed once more, but this time, when his power flickered, Orin dropped, his legs falling into the water as he screamed in agony. The Lake of Lost souls had captured him, and though half of him remained above the water, his very soul was being ripped from his body, inch by inch, ethereal hands clawing at him.

I broke. Screaming. All the strength and resolve I'd ever built against Death slipped away as everything turned ice cold. Watching Orin be taken from me, knowing the finality of that pit of water was like staring but not seeing. Speaking with no sound. As if Death's bloodied whips had wrapped around my heart. I screamed again. For every lashing, every time he'd seared a name into my palm. Every time I'd taken a life, each second of his madness that poisoned my soul. Down and down, Orin fell. I didn't want to see it, but I couldn't look away when those golden eyes flashed to me. When a calmness fell over him as he accepted his fate.

"Live, Deyanira," he managed. "Love another."

"No!" I crawled, fucking crawled, on my hands and knees to the water's edge, ready to plunge. My eternity would already be filled with longing without him anyway.

Death's thick fingers gripped the back of my hair, ripping me away from the bank as he pulled his son from the water and dropped him unceremoniously to the ground, smothering him in so much darkness, I couldn't see a limb, his face, or a slice of his clothing.

Orin's father kneeled, sliding a finger across my neck, stopping where my heart pounded furiously. "Your scream was more perfect than I remembered. Thank you for your fear. He will be such a good tool to control you."

Pure rage rattled beneath my skin. "The funny thing about me is, I've never done well with controlling assholes. Ask your son."

With no hesitation, I launched myself at him, driving my fingers around his neck as he fell backward, skin searing beneath my palms just as he'd burned me over and over again. He laughed at first, until the first pulse of my power surged through him. And then it was there. Death's own horror. Sweet, delicious fear. Pushing and digging deeper and deeper into the pit of my magic, a place I'd never bothered to explore, I dove, letting the power heal me as it took from him. I heaved everything I had at Death as he thrashed beneath me, fighting and swinging and shoving his shadows, trying and failing to knock me away. I felt them surge urgently into my body, searching for his darkness. But they were denied. Only light shone through. My light. Ro's ultimate revenge.

He stared back at me, so much less of a being than he had been. He was still in there, though, not defeated. Not gone. Weakened. Just as I was. Bone-tired and drained of all power, I continued to reach for more. I needed more. But there was nothing.

I'd lost.

A hand slid over my shoulder. "You cannot remove Death, my love."

Fingers still tight at his father's throat, I peered up at Orin beyond my tears and anguish to see his eyes still so dark, his veins still black, though he spoke with his softest voice.

"Fight back, Orin. Fight *back.*"

"I am darkness," he answered, falling to his knees beside me as his father gripped my wrists, shoving away the final remnants of light.

A slew of fresh tears fell as I tried to hold on, to pour from an empty well. "No. You are perfection, and you're mine, not his. Fight back."

Orin's voice became so soft, so vulnerable, it eviscerated my heart. "Will you stay with me, my love? In the shadows?"

"And in the light and every shade between," I whispered.

Death's shadows pulsed, sending me flying backward, knocking the breath from me. "It's over," Orin said, calmly twisting his hand to reveal the slender curves of Chaos before plunging my blade into his father's heart. "I accept my role as Death."

CHAPTER 67

We stood hand in hand, staring down at the burned edges of the ground where his father had turned to ash. There was no fiery moment of passion between us, no celebration of victory. Only the daunting insecurity of what our future would look like now that Orin had become Death.

"I don't blame him," he said, "even if he was demented. If he loved her or thought he loved her half as much as I love you, I can't. I would have hunted you to the end of the universe. I would search the worlds for you. And I would have burned it all down until you stood before me."

"The difference is, this is real, and I will never run."

He chuckled. The first hint of healing I could have hoped for. "But you did run."

I leaned against him, yawning. "In my defense, you stabbed me."

"True," he said, tugging me away. "How's your back?"

"Healed, I think. Using that much power, though... I'll probably need to sleep for a week."

He squeezed my hand gently as we walked back toward the castle. "You can have your week, Nightmare. We have an eternity now."

But then I thought of Paesha. Of her vow to return to Quill, and I wondered if she still wanted that, and if she did, how she was going to say goodbye to Ezra, and how we'd find a way back. My heart ached for her. For the dancer that mourned on the rooftop.

The look of relief on both of their moonlit faces as we made it back to the castle might've been welcoming, had there not been a crowd of souls standing behind them, all eyes locked on Orin and me, each one eager for answers and comfort. One moment, I was staring at Paesha and Ezra, the next, they were swallowed by the crowd that rushed for us.

Before we were crushed by people eager to have my promise to them fulfilled, Orin pulled me flush to his side and enveloped us in shadows that were fully his now. We appeared in the same bedroom as before, though the candles had long since melted onto the floor, nothing more than piles of wax.

"Someday, we will explore this castle together, but for now, rest."

"They won't wait and they shouldn't have to," I warned, stifling another yawn as the exhaustion from magic threatened to end me. "And do we know the ramifications of holding Death's court, your court, I guess, with no one here?"

He held the sides of my face tenderly, closing his dark eyes as another rush of shadows swirled around us both. They sent a wave of heat over my skin as his lips brushed mine. "We have forever, Deyanira. There's no rush."

With the retreat of his power, I'd been fully cleaned, the tattered dress replaced with loose pants and an oversized shirt that smelled an awful lot like him.

"I've been in this court for exactly a day longer than you

have. I know almost nothing. Sleep, my love. We can figure it out tomorrow. I'll go talk to them."

"And Ezra and Paesha. And Hollis. And oh, his wife…"

My eyelids grew heavy as he led me to the bed.

"I will find them."

THE BED DIPPED, and Orin wrapped his arm around me sometime hours and hours later. I could have stayed there for a long time, but with each passing moment, even in sleep, I could see their faces. A fraction of the crowd that'd haunted my dreams for so long had done so again, their heavy voices begging me to set them free from the prison I'd damned them to.

And so, I woke, not to sunlight pouring in, but to the steady, silvery moonlight brushing against Orin's sharp jaw, the pout of his lips, and the rise and fall of his chest. He survived. And he was mine, and that was enough to soothe my tender soul.

"This is eternity," he whispered, the heavy notes of sleep rattling his words. "We could just stay in this bed forever."

"Only if we bar the doors and don't mind a riot."

He groaned, wiping a heavy hand down his face. "I'm just a cellist. A performer. I'm not meant to rule a realm or punish people. I can feel the darkness, though. It's like a weight. A burden, but not."

"A duty?"

He nodded, staring into the shadows of the room.

I brushed the dark strands of his hair from his eyes and kissed him. "I am with you, even in the darkness."

"Are you with me in annoyance, too? Because we're about to be interrupted by Ezra."

"The shadows tell you that?"

"Apparently."

Three solid knocks sounded on the door.

"Go away," he roared, pulling me on top of him.

"The next time we climb into this bed, I'll do unspeakable things to you, Husband. But for now, we have to get up."

"Unspeakable?" He lifted a brow. "What could my wife possibly find so scandalous she wouldn't speak it aloud?"

"Hmm. That's a good point. Likely nothing. But maybe I'll ask around for some pointers."

"If you start with Paesha, I'm moving out."

Two more knocks.

"I don't think you can move out of your own castle, Orin."

A shadow passed over his face. "Maybe we'll build a new home and leave this one behind."

I wiggled, pressing up against him until he groaned, grabbing my hips to hold me there.

"You're giving mixed signals. You touch my cock with any part of your body and no one's leaving this bed for at least an hour."

I thrust my hips forward. "Like this?"

"Seriously, Orin. I can hear you talking."

I stifled a laugh as he buried his face in a pillow and moaned.

"Welcome to godlyhood."

He sat up, tossing me to the side in a playful way. "You don't get to make up words just to tease me."

"Oh, I'm about ninety-eight percent sure that's the single perk of being someone's bonded spouse."

He gripped the edges of the pillow beside him as Ezra pounded on the door again. With a playful glint in his eye, he tried to swing it at me, but I was faster and ripped it from his hands, hauling it back to smash it right into his face. "Better luck next time, Fluffy Bottom."

"World's greatest wife," he said, rubbing his cheek.

I hauled myself out of the bed. "I'm kind of pissed we spent so much time fighting with knives when we could have been fighting with pillows."

He laughed. "No, you're not."

"No," I agreed with a smirk. "Not even a little bit."

"We still need to work on that nickname, though. Pretty sure you can't just walk around calling Death *Fluffy Bottom*."

"Pretty sure I can."

"Are there workers?" Paesha asked as all four of us sat together in a long, narrow dining hall with nothing more than a table and no less than forty chairs on each side.

Ezra lifted a tray, the rising steam making my stomach groan in response. "No. The castle caters to gluttony. Before, if you were in Death's favor," he flourished a hand, "you just asked, and it would appear."

"And if you weren't?" Orin kept his eyes locked on the shadows pooling along the floor.

"There are many, many rooms here curated for all kinds of nightmares. I'm sure you'll be fine, Faber, but ladies, don't wander."

Paesha rubbed her hands together, whispering, "Please be sausage, please be sausage." When she lifted the tray to find fresh greens, she slumped into her seat. "No fair."

"Ooo. Looks like you're not in Orin's favor, P. Better work on that."

Ezra leaned over to growl in her ear until a blush colored her cheeks.

I lifted the silver tray closest to me, devouring the bright fruit with my eyes before sliding my fork into the fattest strawberry. "You can have my sausage later, too, Paesha."

Orin's genuine smile didn't cover his surprise. "You could hear him?"

I snorted. "No. But it doesn't take a genius to see the innuendo there. Keep up, Husband."

Ezra laughed. His whole giant body shook, and the deep sound echoed around the hollow room so beautifully that I froze, staring at him with my eyes wide.

"What?" he asked, shoveling in a mouthful of eggs.

"I had no idea you could laugh. You seem so..." I turned to Paesha, cocking a brow. "What's the word I'm looking for?"

"Dangerous."

"No. That's not it." I scrunched my nose before snapping. "Oh. Dickish."

"We're in the business of making up words this morning," Orin said, stealing something off Ezra's plate and popping it into his mouth. "She's got a real talent for it."

"Wait." I held up a finger to stop Ezra as he leaned to whisper in Paesha's ear again. "You can have three of these yellow things, Huntress, if you can guess what he's about to say."

Her mouth twisted into a grin as she stared at her lover, deepening her voice to try to mimic his. "I've got a real talent for something else."

I snorted, almost choking on the berry as Ezra disagreed. "Those yellow things are called pineapple, and actually, Maiden, I was going to say, *Can you please pass the salt?*"

Orin clapped him on the back. "I love you, brother, but you're a fucking terrible liar."

Ezra wiggled his eyebrows at Paesha. "Well, I *am* very talented."

"True," she said, tapping her finger on his nose. "And predictable."

The light humor we'd all desperately needed was stolen

from the room in a flash. The towering oak doors at the end of the hall sounded like they were being shredded to pieces. We leapt from our seats in unison, and Orin didn't hesitate to call forth his formidable shadows. The center of the doors bowed again, following another slash.

"What the fuck?" my husband whispered, whipping his hands to blow the doors open.

Two giant beasts poked their heads in, filling the door frame. The hellhounds.

"Who could have sent them?" Ezra growled, shoving Paesha behind him.

"Relax." Orin moved his chair, sitting back down. "Apparently, they answer to me now."

"Oh, yay! We get puppies."

My loving husband pinned me with a glare. "And apparently, we've named them Ruffles and... *Fluffy?*"

"Come on in, boys!" I shouted before flashing a smile at him. "To be fair, your friend over there named Fluffy."

"True," Paesha agreed. "I think it fits."

The massive hounds pawed their way into the dining hall. The closer they got, the higher we had to crane our necks to see their glowing ruby eyes. Though my heart still skipped a beat, and I had to force a steady breath, I rose and pointed to the floor as if talking to Boo. "Sit."

They obeyed immediately, giant pink tongues rolling out of their mouths as I launched a pancake at each of them.

"Oh, for god's sake," Orin groaned, rubbing his hands through his hair. "We have the universe's biggest puppies."

I scowled. "They can hear you."

Paesha giggled as Orin changed the pitch of his voice to mock celebration, pretending to clap. "We have the universe's biggest puppies."

"Attaboy." I grinned, tossing another couple of pancakes.

Eventually, Paesha sat back in her seat, shoving the plate away. "This was nice. Family breakfast. I still wish Hollis had come."

Orin rose from his chair, waving a hand to clear the dishes.

"That's handy," I said, before turning to the Huntress. "Do we know if he's seen Dahlia yet?"

"Most of the former harbingers stay together. Not that anyone here has been incredibly friendly, but the more friends you make, the more targets around you, and since that group is single-handedly responsible for the majority of the court's deaths, they keep to themselves."

"They're not, though," I argued. "They couldn't help the role they were born into."

Ezra's eyes flashed around the table for backup, but no one spoke. He didn't know about the madness. Just as Paesha and Orin had to learn, so would he.

"I didn't kill you because I chose it. I did it because I physically had to, or I would have been forced to kill a slew of other people while trying to fight it. There wasn't a choice there. Not for me, and not for them either. But I'm still sorry."

He lowered his chin, the depth of his voice all-consuming and serious. "I don't need your apology. You've given it once, and that's enough. But you do have to try to understand the minds of the people here, or you'll never be able to rule them."

"We won't be ruling anyone," Orin said with complete finality. "Every person who wishes to leave can and will. From what I've gathered, I can't do anything about the Lake of Lost Souls, but everyone else can be freed. They can reincarnate, should they choose to, and go back to live another life cycle."

"Even the Whispers?" Paesha breathed.

"Even the Whispers," he answered.

And so we began. With no clocks and no true sense of time, no passing sunlight, nor shift in moon, the day grew long. The discomfort of the castle's sordid memories loomed over everyone, so we agreed to work in the yard just outside. With the help of Fluffy and Ruffles, and the shadows most still feared, Orin and Ezra kept the crowd in line, while Paesha ushered soul after tortured soul to meet with me. One by one, we released them into the ether, setting them on whatever course was necessary for reincarnation.

Even the harbingers had come, including Icharius. They'd kept their heads down and their place in the shifting line, and though I tried to concentrate on each soul that came, I couldn't help but watch as they moved closer and closer.

Hours into the job, the people began to look at me in awe, jaws slacked and eyes wide as I wished them peace and sliced a little more away from my power. Until I was drained and sagging and every bone in my body weighed a hundred pounds. But still, the harbingers crept forward. I wanted to get to them so badly. I pushed myself beyond limits I knew possible. Until they came, shifting in and taking my hands with greater anticipation than most of the others. Because this was not an escape from Death's realm for them. It was an escape from reality. From the memories that haunted them, just as they'd haunted me, and they had all seen so much more bloodshed. They hadn't had a kernel of light in them, keeping the madness at bay.

But they were free now, each one of them fading to embers on a soft breeze as they were released back into the ether.

I pushed myself until I couldn't feel my fingers and every muscle ached, until the back of my eyelids felt like they'd been dragged across a thousand sandy beaches. Until Orin stepped in, pulling me away when I could no longer stand. And each day was a repeated cycle of this one. With hints from Paesha that we needed to find a doorway back, there was pressure to complete this process, even if she hadn't meant for there to be. She wasn't eager to leave Ezra, and I knew it, but still, she worried about

Quill every day, even walking through each potential threat Drexel might've left for her. For her peace of mind, we'd worked together to convince her that Drexel had only said what he'd said to bother her, but none of us could truly know that, and each day she grew more and more wary.

The eager crowd dwindled until we were left with only the Whispering Grove and about three hundred souls who'd chosen to stay and rest in Orin's promised peace rather than return to the unknown of Requiem's future.

I hadn't seen Hollis since Death's demise. I'd watched for him among the faces, of course, and Paesha had gone to check on him and make sure he was still with us, but he hadn't come. Hadn't been able to tear himself away from the happiness he'd found with the spirit of his young wife.

So, when we approached the very edge of the Whispering Grove to find him standing there, staring at a pocket watch with the soft blue light of the trees casting his perfect silhouette our way, we stopped. All of us, hand in hand, staring at the kind old man who would likely leave us all on this day. We drank in the moment, the absolute gift it was to be able to look upon him one final time.

"I'm not ready," Paesha whispered.

I squeezed her hand, swallowing the lump in my throat. "No. But he is."

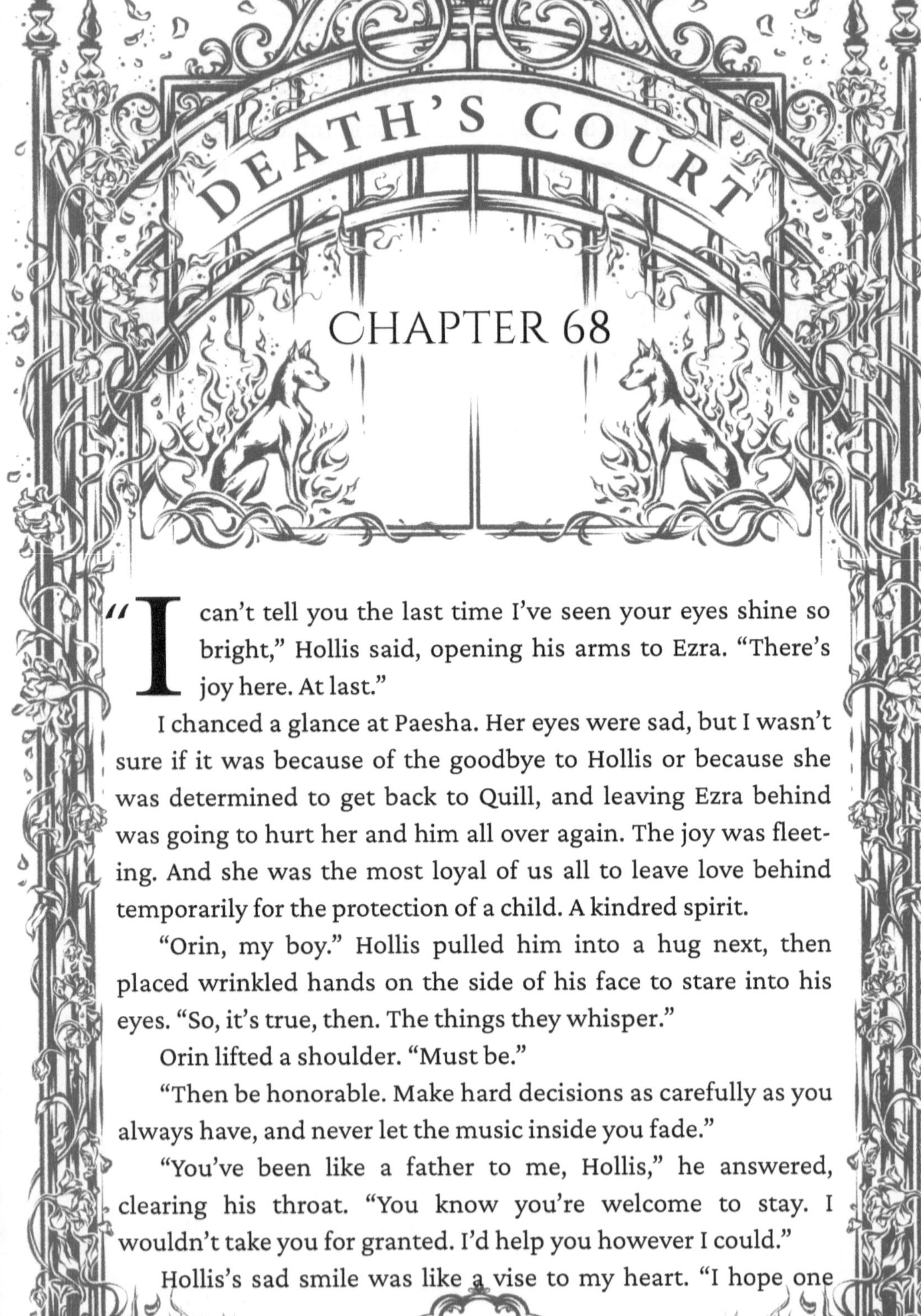

CHAPTER 68

"I can't tell you the last time I've seen your eyes shine so bright," Hollis said, opening his arms to Ezra. "There's joy here. At last."

I chanced a glance at Paesha. Her eyes were sad, but I wasn't sure if it was because of the goodbye to Hollis or because she was determined to get back to Quill, and leaving Ezra behind was going to hurt her and him all over again. The joy was fleeting. And she was the most loyal of us all to leave love behind temporarily for the protection of a child. A kindred spirit.

"Orin, my boy." Hollis pulled him into a hug next, then placed wrinkled hands on the side of his face to stare into his eyes. "So, it's true, then. The things they whisper."

Orin lifted a shoulder. "Must be."

"Then be honorable. Make hard decisions as carefully as you always have, and never let the music inside you fade."

"You've been like a father to me, Hollis," he answered, clearing his throat. "You know you're welcome to stay. I wouldn't take you for granted. I'd help you however I could."

Hollis's sad smile was like a vise to my heart. "I hope one

day you'll forgive me for going, Orin. There's nothing in this realm that you need an old man for. I promise. Except the clothes, but even then, there's bound to be a tailor coming along." He reached up to his chest pocket and unclipped the watch hanging by a chain before placing it into Orin's trembling fingers. "Dahlia gave me this the day I arrived. She remembered how much I loved mine, even in her madness, and she'd been saving it for me."

"I can't accept this, Hol," Orin said, shaking his head.

But the old man simply closed Orin's fingers over the pocket watch and smiled once more. "It's of no use to me now."

"Maybe I'll find you in your next life and return it," he said.

"That would be fine, son. Just fine."

He came to me next, his outline blurry through tears I didn't shed. "No goodbyes, Old Man."

"No goodbyes," he promised, taking my hand. "Would you like to meet my wife?"

I pulled him close to my side. "I'd be absolutely offended if you refused me."

He chuckled. "That sounds like you. Shall we?"

Orin took my other side, but Paesha and Ezra opted to stay behind. The moment we passed the threshold of the blue light cast onto the grove, Hollis transformed, no longer the corporeal form of a man, but rather a spectral, save his old, withered hands. The euphoria I remembered from the last time I'd come kissed my skin, settling into my bones and leaving me with a kernel of longing, not unlike Quill's power. I kept an eye on Orin, though, worried his own nightmares would come back to haunt him, and if he lost control in a place like this, where Death had come to torture the poor Whispers, I wasn't sure he'd be able to fight the darkness. Or what that might do to those of us inside the grove.

The Whispers stayed away, leaving a wide berth. Climbing

the small hill in the center of the grove, a beautiful spectral appeared beside us. Her long hair waving in a phantom wind, doe-eyed and smiling as she swirled around Hollis. She was young, only slightly older than me, and that truth became the very likely reason the old man had chosen this. He could have stayed here with her, living happily in this grove for eternity. But she hadn't gotten to live, not really, and there were likely miles of hard lessons learned between them.

"So, you see?" she asked, circling me.

"I think I do," I breathed, closing my eyes as she spun around me.

"Deyanira Sariah Faber, Princess of Perth, Death's Maiden, bonded wife of Death, and Queen of this court, it is my honor to introduce you to Yvette Louise Bennet, daughter of your great uncle, Atticus Hark."

I gasped, spinning to stare at Hollis. "My great uncle?"

He nodded. "We've truly always been family, Deyanira."

"Why didn't you say anything?"

"I wanted you to know I cared and accepted you without a familial bond. I loved you because of your moral compass and not your ties to my wife. But I did see her in your eyes sometimes."

"I got them from my father," I whispered, staring back at the woman once more, my... cousin. "If you so choose it, I have come to release your soul, Yvette. You will reincarnate back to Requiem, and your new life will be yours alone."

She swirled around Hollis, and they said together, "We choose it."

The curiosity of our conversation or the network of whispering gossip drew the others near, despite Orin's proximity. Still, he boomed, "Stay back if you wish to remain a Whisper in the grove. If you wish to reincarnate, come near."

We'd discussed the best approach since I couldn't make

contact with their translucent forms. Landing on the wave of power I'd used in the pit, I let it ripple across the space like a drop in a bucket and waited, feeling the tiny slice in my heart as Hollis turned to ash, his soul circling Orin and me for the blink of a second before he and the others vanished.

Our steps were heavy. It was easier knowing he'd had the final choice, but still, the ache of missing him again was raw. Lost in our sadness once more, we were not prepared to walk out of the grove and be assaulted by Paesha's blood-curdling scream as she stared up at Ezra, hanging limp in the air, a massive glowing entity holding him suspended by his neck.

"Who the fuck is that?" I whispered.

Icy fingers walked down my spine as Ro stepped out from behind the blinding figure, her chin high, the cast of warm light warming her beautiful brown skin as she gripped the edges of her golden gown, bowed all the way to the ground in a graceful dip and said calmly, "Kneel before your highest god, the Supreme Sovereign, the Unerring Arbiter of Beginnings and Endings, and the Keeper of All Realms."

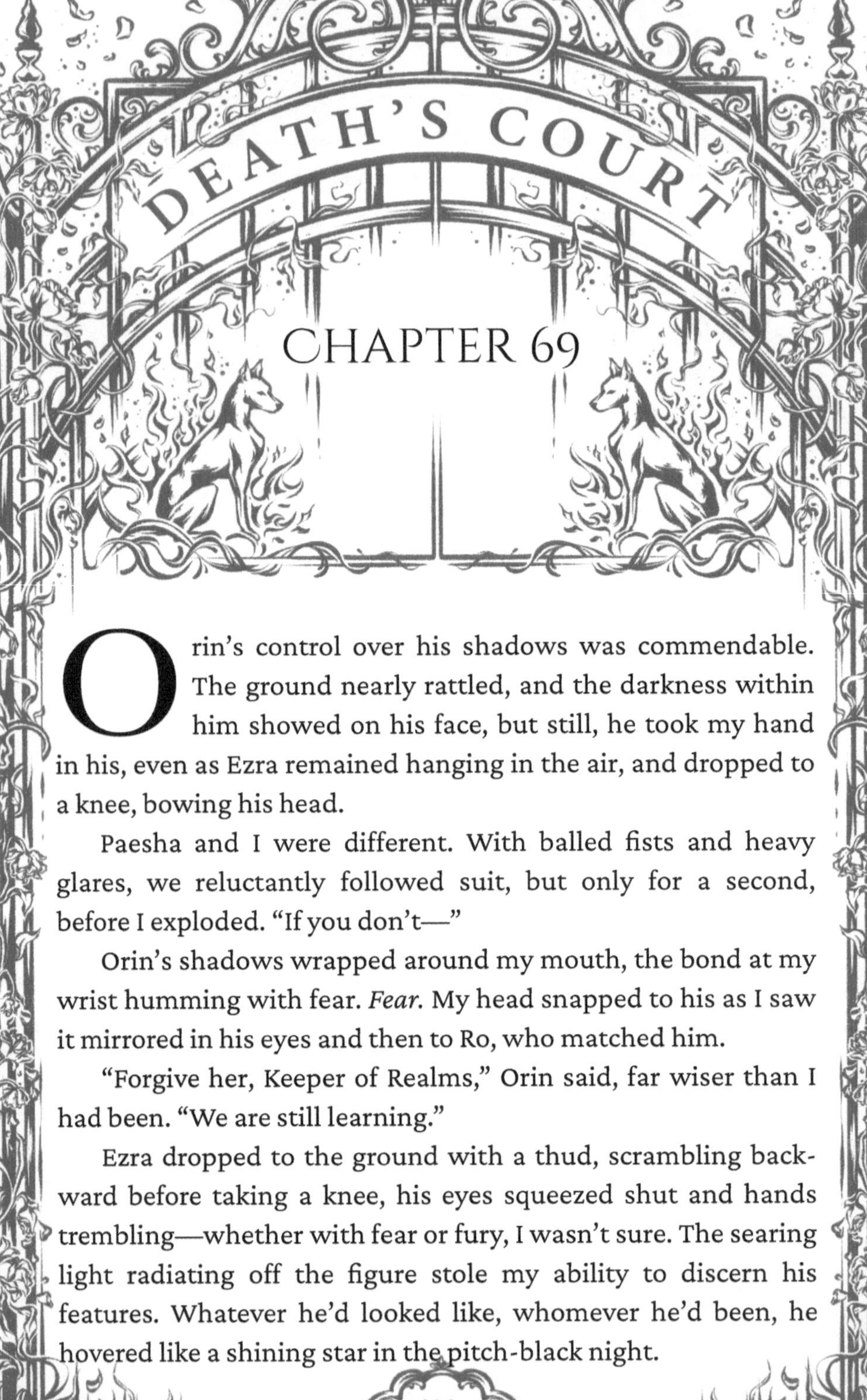

CHAPTER 69

Orin's control over his shadows was commendable. The ground nearly rattled, and the darkness within him showed on his face, but still, he took my hand in his, even as Ezra remained hanging in the air, and dropped to a knee, bowing his head.

Paesha and I were different. With balled fists and heavy glares, we reluctantly followed suit, but only for a second, before I exploded. "If you don't—"

Orin's shadows wrapped around my mouth, the bond at my wrist humming with fear. *Fear.* My head snapped to his as I saw it mirrored in his eyes and then to Ro, who matched him.

"Forgive her, Keeper of Realms," Orin said, far wiser than I had been. "We are still learning."

Ezra dropped to the ground with a thud, scrambling backward before taking a knee, his eyes squeezed shut and hands trembling—whether with fear or fury, I wasn't sure. The searing light radiating off the figure stole my ability to discern his features. Whatever he'd looked like, whomever he'd been, he hovered like a shining star in the pitch-black night.

The great voice of the sovereign lingered with an echo as he spoke. "Rise, Orin Aurelius Faber. In this name, I grant you not merely a designation but a profound responsibility. 'Aurelius' signifies the golden path of wisdom, the radiant thread of divine duty, and the sacred trust of maintaining order.

"With this name, I mark a new beginning of your eternity, entrusting you to wield your power wisely and to keep yourself in perfect order. You are a guardian of the delicate balance between life and death, a sentinel of transitions and endings, and a steward of the realms.

"Consider your role in this world as paramount. You stand at the crossroads of existence. Guard well the boundaries of your duties. You are now tasked with upholding the eternal balance, ensuring that all things flow according to the grand design.

"May the name 'Aurelius' serve as a constant reminder of the luminous path you are entrusted to tread, and may you embrace this divine duty with unwavering resolve. Through your actions and judgments, may you illuminate the way for all souls, guiding them on their journey with wisdom and compassion."

Ro clasped her hands together, a bright smile beaming. "With this gift, Reverius, Keeper of Realms, imparts not just a name but a sacred charge, a reminder of your pivotal role in the cosmic order, and the immense trust placed upon your shoulders."

"The final gift is a portal without the restrictions of your father's. This gift shall be marked in Etherium, the Realm of Gods, as the Aurelian Gate."

The Keeper, still glowing so bright I couldn't make out the edges of his form, swiped a giant arm through the air, and a large door appeared in the forest, so big, Ezra, Paesha, Orin, and I could have walked through it shoulder to shoulder. The void between the frame of the intricate iron weavings rippled, revealing a glimpse into Requiem. "This is the world from which you come." With another wave, the vision rippled, and a different world appeared. One steeped in night and lit by stars, though only a great body of water covered the ground. "This is another of your charges. The Astral Seal is a world with great order and balance far vaster than your Requiem." Again, the picture changed, one of mountains and forests and winding rivers and lakes so still, they looked like mirrors. "Starforge is a dangerous realm. Take care when you carry the spirits from this world, Orin Aurelius Faber. They do not leave with ease."

I grew tired, shifting from foot to foot as Orin took in his role and our future. Realm by realm flashed by until the reflection turned dark and then faded completely. Paesha, though? She watched those worlds pass by in fervor. She seemed to take in every detail and every name. Every picture burning into her memory, each sound of crashing waves and singing birds, of dry desert wind, and the fury of a blizzard captured her.

Paesha cleared her throat. "Reverius, Keeper of Realms and Sovereign of Sovereignty things, can we please see Requiem again?"

"Unerring Arbiter of Beginnings and Endings, Supreme Sovereign," Ro corrected her.

"That's what I said."

"These other worlds are not for you, Huntress," the gleaming god answered. "But this one is, and I can see your heart's desire."

The Syndicate house appeared before us, more specifically, the backs of Elowen and Althea as they held hands, staring into Quill's tidy bedroom. The little girl lay in her bed, with Boo snuggled in a tiny circle beside her as she shook with tears.

"Oh, gods," Paesha breathed, stepping forward to reach a hand toward Quill.

"Your realm has fallen," Reverius said quietly. "With no present ruler and your Fera in distress, there can be no peace."

"Fera?" I asked, stepping forward to stand beside Paesha.

Ro answered. "Quill is rare. Special. She is known as a Fera, which means the bearer. At a baser level, her unique power allows her to bear the emotions of others, sometimes carry them when they grow too heavy, and ultimately manipulate them, should she choose it. Her power has been lost for a millennium. And with eternal mourning, she will bring down that world, and the rest will follow. Because sadness is only a root to which anger grows."

"No," I answered, because Paesha fell quiet. "You said you were going to help her. That was our bargain."

"I've been called back to Etherium." Ro tucked her hair behind her ear. "I'll still help as I can, but my role is vast and demanding."

"You're such a liar. I did *all of this* for you, and you're just... leaving?"

"Such is the way of gods," Reverius said, deflating my anger with a pulse of his choking power.

"Tell me how to go back. Can't I just walk through this?" Paesha turned to Ezra. "I'm sorry, but I will come back to you. Wait for me here and I will come back. She needs me."

"Seventy years is nothing compared to an eternity together," Ezra answered, pulling her into his arms. "I would wait a thousand lifetimes."

"I've allowed the gods to return to Requiem. There is no immortality among humans anymore. No need for Maidens. Humans will live and die by fate alone, as it should be. There is no path back for you, Huntress."

Her spine straightened as she slowly faced the glowing entity. "What?"

"You stand in a realm of the dead, living. The Aurelian Gate is only for those touched by Death. Deyanira was marked by him at birth, but you cannot return to Requiem. Should you try to pass through, you will simply die and return here."

"That…" She glared. "You're supposed to be the supreme god of the fucking realms, and you're telling me that little girl is going to burn it all down, and there's nothing you can do because … why, exactly? You're the master of beginnings or whatever. You can create worlds, but you can't just send me back to save everyone? What the fuck?"

"Tongue," Ro snapped, to which Paesha extended a middle finger.

"There is a way," Reverius said, his authoritative tone consuming the air around him. "But all magic comes at a cost."

"Then pay it," she snapped.

"Why should I? Perhaps the Ether calls to me, Huntress."

"Bargain with me, then," she said, stepping toward him. "Let me try to save the worlds you damn so easily."

"Speak your terms, Huntress," the god said, the edges of his form darkening, if only slightly.

"Send me back and I will pay the cost. Whatever it is, I will pay it."

"Paesha," Ezra and Orin said in unison.

Ezra continued, "Absolutely not."

I moved carefully to her side. "You can't mean that, Paesha. It's too dangerous."

She spun with a glare. "Everyone dies, Maiden. Everyone. Not just dies; they cease to exist. You, me, Orin, Ezra, our family. The Syndicate, every soul across the realms if what he says is true. Tell me you wouldn't make the same deal, pay whatever the cost to save them."

She was right, of course.

Reverius's form waved, and Paesha's mismatched eyes glossed over until they glowed a golden hue.

"What the hell?" I waved my hand in front of Paesha's face, but she didn't move.

Ro stepped forward, her silk gown cascading along the decaying ground. "They're having a private conversation."

"No," Ezra breathed. "Don't let her agree to this, Goddess. Whatever the terms, let me go instead."

An eerie, unearthly smile played across Ro's lips as she shook her head. "That isn't our choice to make."

The Huntress gasped, stumbling back as the light faded from her eyes. She looked only at Ezra as she said, "I agree to your terms, Keeper."

"What terms?" Orin demanded, surging forward to grab Paesha's arms. "What did you do?"

But before he could get to her, before she could be stopped, she spun and took a single step backward, mouthed, "I'm sorry," and crossed through the Aurelian Gate, fading away.

"Tell me the terms," Ezra roared, fists at his side. "What the hell did she just do?"

But the Keeper didn't answer. Instead, his ethereal form flashed, and he vanished. Ro swept a hand through the pooling shadows on the ground before nodding once and disappearing, just as her beloved god had.

We stood stricken, each breath a chore as we stared at Requiem through the gate, wondering what had just happened and what Paesha had agreed to. And then, from one breath to the next, Ezra was running, crying out for his beloved as he, too, aimed for the threshold of the Aurelian Gate.

Orin lurched forward to stop him, calling out his name, but Ezra didn't fade away as Paesha had. He didn't spiral into an abyss or turn to embers on contact. He transformed, glowing brighter and brighter as he grew. Until he stood in a halo of golden light, just like Reverius had. I stumbled backward, eyes wide and skin turning ice cold.

"I... I remember," he said, studying his massive hands before lowering his chin to scowl. "I remember everything."

And then he vanished.

My mouth dropped open, staring in silence at Orin as realization hit me. Ezra was not just any soul. He was a god.

THREE MONTHS LATER

We'd heard nothing, nor seen anything through the gate of Paesha's return home. Whatever the terms she'd agreed to, whatever path she'd chosen, Requiem had not fallen. I'd spent so much time worrying about her. Consumed with searching to see where she'd landed. Eventually, I had to walk away. I had to choose to trust her, just as she'd once demanded. But still, her mysterious deal held my curiosity.

"What do you think it was? The bargain she made?"

Orin slid a hand down my back before shoving me against the wall. "The same thing I thought it was yesterday and the day before that."

I bit his lip before grabbing him by the collar and tugging him down the hall toward the dining room. "'*I have no idea*' is not a guess. Try harder and stop getting distracted. They're waiting for us."

He halted. "Did you decide to wear that dress, Nightmare?"

"Yes."

"And did you think there would be any possible way I could keep my hands off you when you made that decision?"

I grinned. "I was undecided."

"A bit of a hint, Nightmare. The second lace, in any color, touches this beautiful skin of yours, I'm going to grow envious and then plot for its immediate removal. But when it is black? There will be no planning. No masterminding. It'll be on the floor within an hour."

Sauntering toward him, I lifted the long chain of his pocket watch, smoothing a finger over the dove etched into the cover, and clicked it open. "Oh, dear. It looks like we only have fifteen minutes for dinner, then."

He slid a finger below the lace at my shoulder and tugged until it ripped. "Or we could start with dessert."

"Like... cake?"

"No." He smiled, placing his hand on the wall behind me, eyes full of mirth. "Something sweeter."

He commanded his shadows flawlessly now. The wall, now cool against my back, rippled before the handle of a door appeared. With a hint of malevolence, he grinned and twisted. I fell backward into a new room, landing on a bed. With a single wave, the dress vanished, and I lay, splayed before him, naked.

"That might be a new record."

"I do love a good challenge," he purred.

Wasting no time, he fell to his knees, swiping a finger down my slit as he stared into my eyes. "Shall I taste you here, Wife?"

"If you wish."

"Use your words, Deyanira. Tell me where you want me."

"That's not really fair when I want you everywhere."

His dark laugh rattled down my body, heating me all the way to my core as his shadows wrapped around me while he watched. I writhed, arching off the bed as he moved them between my legs, letting them vibrate until they fell open.

He dropped to his knees, dragging his lips up the inside of my thigh, each one a touch of heat as those ribbons of shadow undulated across my breasts, tugging at my hair, bringing every inch of me to life until every brush of his lips and his fingers dug into my thighs lit me on fire. Still, he waited, avoiding that single spot I wanted him most, playing with his shadows, playing with me, until I couldn't breathe. I couldn't think. I couldn't exist beyond the feel of that man.

"Orin..."

"You will say it, or I won't break. I'm a patient man."

He pressed his thumbs closer, spreading me but refusing to touch where I needed him most.

"Taste it, Orin. Tell me how much you like it."

"Such a good girl." He closed his mouth over me, and the moment his tongue swept back and forth, I was done for. My head fell back against the bed. He feathered his tongue over my clit before sucking it in hard enough I gasped. Orin moved closer, lifting my leg over his shoulder and sliding two fingers into me as he tasted and tasted. And then shadows swept in, vibrating around his mouth. I gripped the sheets so hard in my fists, I knew they'd be shredded by the time I fell. Still, I climbed. Each second a mountain. He knew my body so perfectly. Had taken the time to learn every single thing that would break me in minutes.

"Let me hear you come, Wife, and then I'll fuck you properly."

"No," I panted. "Stop."

He pulled away, and I sat up, grabbing him by the shirt and yanking him to me until his lips were on mine. Until I could taste myself. He buried his hands in my hair, pulling my head back as I looked up to the ceiling.

Kiss after kiss, he moved down my jawline before he practically growled, "Why did you stop me?"

"I want you inside me. Not your tongue, not your damn fingers. You."

His clothes were gone in seconds, his tip resting at my core. I lifted my hips, and his eyes darkened as a wicked smile curled across his face. In a single motion, he drove all the way in. I felt every vein, every ridge, every fucking inch as he moved. Not slow and steady, not calm and careful. Orin was feral. And so was I. Still, I couldn't help the scream. The euphoric surprise of glorious pleasure rippled through me as he thrust over and over, until there was nothing but uninhibited need between us.

Rocking my hips, I took as much of him as I could. But it was not enough. It would never be enough. He yanked free, grabbing my thighs and flipping me over. Twisting my hair into a fist, he yanked as he slammed into me from behind, filling me. He was relentless, the musician with perfect rhythm building the perfect crescendo, carrying me all the way up, kneading my hips as he held firm.

Whatever he shouted the second we exploded was lost to me as I spiraled, the burst near blinding as I climaxed, every muscle taut, every sound a whimper.

Until he released the fist of hair and traced a small trail of kisses down my sweaty spine before slapping my ass. "Get back into that lovely gown, Wife. There are people waiting."

Satiated and in a hurry, we rushed down the hall. Orin threw the doors open and prowled in like a king, unbothered that we were late and so many had waited for us.

"Third time this week, sir," one of the souls yelled from the end of the table.

"Yeah. Yeah," Orin said, clapping him on the back. "You've got nowhere else to be, Cadoc."

His shadows poured over the table in a ripple of power.

Trays of food appeared, wine filled the pitchers, and at once, the room sprang to life as everyone dug into dinner. It'd been the same routine for weeks now. Orin drew all the souls to the castle and invited them to live in harmony with us. He'd searched the place high and low for any lost souls or anyone in captivity or being tortured by his father. They'd been given the same options as the others, and slowly, he'd sealed away the darkness left behind. And then they came. A few to dinner at first, but slowly, the room became longer and larger to accommodate as many people that wished to come as possible. He'd hung tapestries of peaceful scenery along the walls when the echoes became too loud. The laughter was deafening. And he'd played. Gods, he'd played the cello for everyone. And some had joined in. Orin created a symphony in Death's court. His court.

"I see you wore the lace again," Ava said, sipping on a glass of wine as she winked at me.

"He really is so predictable. And until you ladies take a cellist to your beds and learn what he can really do with those fast fingers, I don't want to hear a peep from either of you. Any movement on Alexander?"

Nymeria, another of the ladies I'd become friends with, popped a grape into her mouth as she leaned in. "Oh, I believe there was plenty of movement last night. And moaning. That shit's loud, by the way. I'm going to need Orin to move my room away from hers."

Hours later, I lay tangled in bed with my husband, staring up at the ceiling of stars he'd created for us to sleep beneath.

"Are you happy here?"

I twisted to make sure he could see the shock on my face. "Of course, I am. Why would you ask me that?"

"Because this is our eternity, and your happiness is important to me. I know you worry about the ones we left behind."

"I just wish we could be sure she's safe, that's all. But I

understand our limits. We can only go to Requiem when someone dies and their soul needs guidance. There's not a lot we can do for her from here."

"Imagine if Ezra is trying to find her. Would you take that risk? Leave eternity to find me at some unknown cost?"

He smiled, his eyes falling a bit darker when he leaned over and growled into my ear. "I've seen our past lives, Nightmare. Our souls have always been bound. Since before the gods ever appeared in Requiem. But I would not simply find you. I would hunt you, as I have always done. That's not something we will ever have to worry about again. These are our days and our nights. This is forever."

I brushed a lock of hair from his eyes. "Tell me what you did today."

"I went to a new world," he said with a smile.

I gasped. "You've been holding out on me? Dammit, Fluffy Bottom. We've talked about this. I knew I should have gone. Tell me!"

"It'll cost you."

"You're so greedy," I teased, paying the cost of a kiss. "Now, spill it."

"I've never seen anything quite like it. Two worlds within a world, divided by a barrier. In the southern world, there was a land made of floating isles over the sea."

"Are they staying at court, or...?"

"Nope. He was a witch."

"Shoot." I laid my head on his chest. "They never want to come."

"I imagine being severed from their power is tough."

A giant warm breeze moved across the bed, and Orin groaned, glaring at our dogs. "They could sleep in the hall, you know. Or at the gates, like they're supposed to."

"These are my babies. You start talking shit about Fluffy and Ruffles, *you* can sleep in the hall."

"Fine. But I'm getting a cat just to spite you, Nightmare."

"Oooh! A kitty. Can we name her Duck?"

"I think you need to go back to weapons training for your own sanity. You're losing your edge, Wife."

"Honestly, you're probably right."

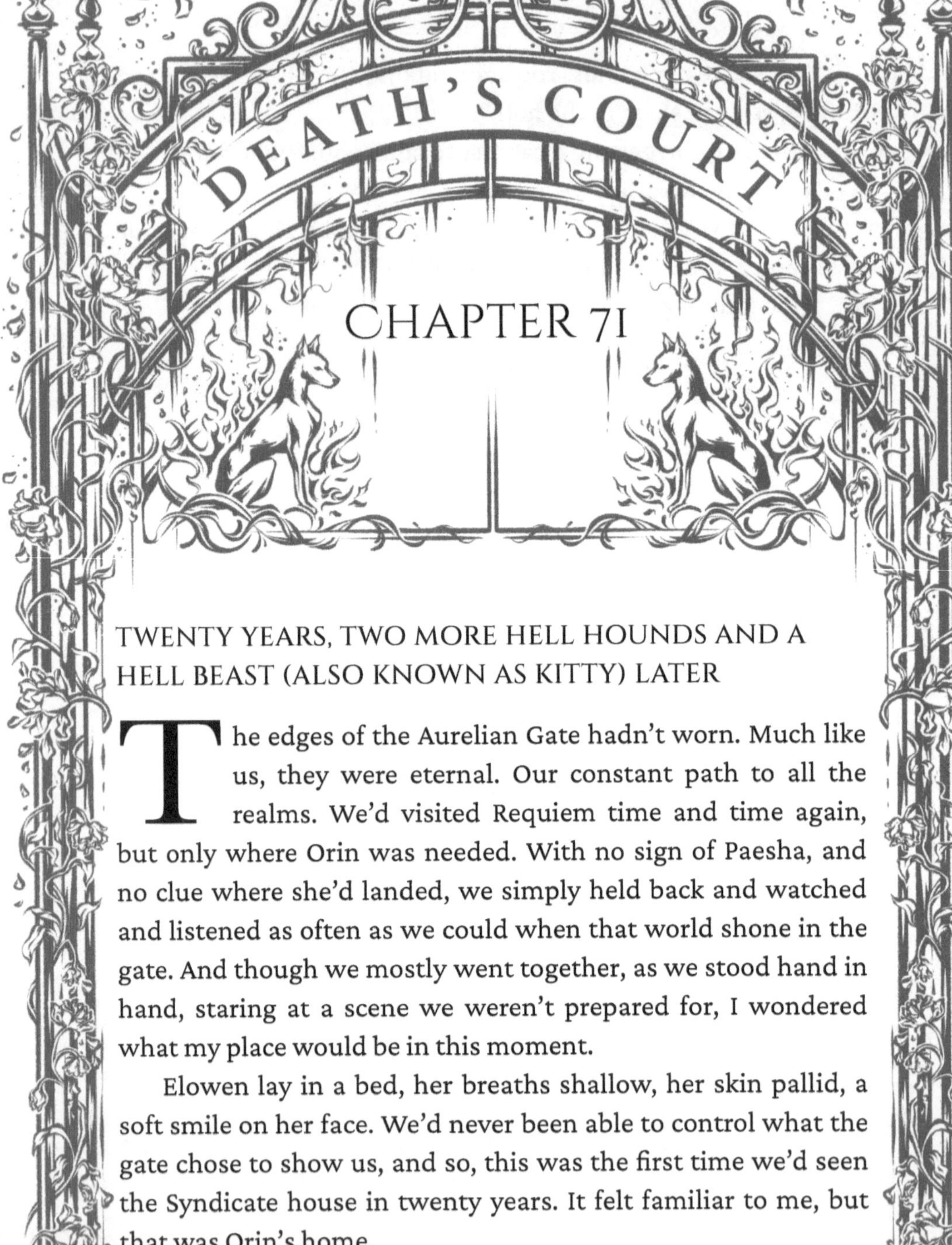

DEATH'S COURT

CHAPTER 71

TWENTY YEARS, TWO MORE HELL HOUNDS AND A HELL BEAST (ALSO KNOWN AS KITTY) LATER

The edges of the Aurelian Gate hadn't worn. Much like us, they were eternal. Our constant path to all the realms. We'd visited Requiem time and time again, but only where Orin was needed. With no sign of Paesha, and no clue where she'd landed, we simply held back and watched and listened as often as we could when that world shone in the gate. And though we mostly went together, as we stood hand in hand, staring at a scene we weren't prepared for, I wondered what my place would be in this moment.

Elowen lay in a bed, her breaths shallow, her skin pallid, a soft smile on her face. We'd never been able to control what the gate chose to show us, and so, this was the first time we'd seen the Syndicate house in twenty years. It felt familiar to me, but that was Orin's home.

"I can stay here," I whispered.

"No. You're coming. Let's just... wait a minute."

Every face circling the bed was sad. I searched the features of the strangers, digging through my memories for anything that might be familiar. Thea's red hair was simple to find, and though she'd aged beautifully, it was clear the world had not been kind to her. Scars marked the hands that held Elowen's, and a permanent flush graced her cheeks. Beside her, though, stood a stunning woman with tears so large, they might've drowned the room had they been able. She seemed older than she should have been. Perhaps also poisoned by the world that never had a heart for a child. It wasn't the tears that drew me to her, though, nor the curly hair that seemed far tamer than my memories, but it was those stunning blue eyes next to her olive skin.

"Quilly," Orin said, with a smile.

There were others, of course. People Orin might've recognized and some neither of us had known. But their sadness was palpable, even across realms. To them, a matriarch would fall today, and they would never see her again. But the concept of death had changed so much for him and me over these years. No longer a deep, soul-shattering severance of reality, but more of an awakening, just a piece of a soul's journey, onward or renewed, and that was all. Death was merely a slot in an endless cycle of life until one decided to step off the ride and live an eternity in the ether or here in this court.

One of the strangers, whose back was to us, took the hand of another. She swayed, inspiring the next person to do the same, and down the line, as a low, soft sound blossomed into a song. She was singing. The most beautiful sound as she inspired peace in a room full of mourning people. She dropped the hand of the closest stranger, circling the others to pull Quill, who sobbed and sobbed, into her arms. Still, she sang and moved, though we were frozen in place. Not because of her song, nor the way Quill remained still in her grasp, but because when she turned and finished her song, the finale of her requiem carrying into our own hearts, one blue and one green eye had shone through her tears. Paesha.

My heart immediately ached with pride. "She did it. She made it back," I whispered.

Orin released a long and steady breath. "Let's just hope she truly finds a version of happiness down there because I don't see Ezra, and that means he abandoned her, despite his power."

"We run on hope, Husband. Are you ready to go get your mother?"

"I hate to take her from them, but I'm ready."

Stepping past the threshold, the familiar chill brought me comfort. The promise of family.

It was nighttime when we appeared in Elowen's room. Only Thea remained at her side. And when we nudged her, hand in hand, she gasped, throwing herself into Orin's waiting arms and then into mine. That bit of cheer was short-lived, though, as she realized what it meant.

"You're Death now? Truly?"

Orin nodded.

"I guess it's wrong of me to be sad when I'm just returning your mother to you," she cried. "But she's been a mother to me, too."

"Of course, she has." Orin wiped away her tears. "She'll be there waiting when it's your time. We all will."

"And we'll throw the biggest party you've ever seen. But live your life, Thea. Find happiness here that's just for you. Be a little selfish, okay?"

"Selfish. Got it." She swiped another tear away, looking down at Elowen. "You've always been the glue. I can put things together, but you've always known how to bring people together, and I never took a second to tell you thank you for building a family around me. So, thank you."

But Elowen didn't answer. Her spirit had already left her body. Thea couldn't see her soul standing behind her; she couldn't feel Elowen's hand rest on her shoulder, nor hear her words. "Goodbye, my beautiful girl."

With that, she stepped away, and into Orin's waiting arms. We walked back through the gate before he spoke. "Hello, Mother."

She pulled him close, studying his face, smoothing her hands over his strong jawline, and running her fingers through his hair as if trying to remember every detail of him. "You haven't changed a bit."

"Immortality is eternal."

"I suppose it is."

"You birthed a god, Elowen. Just don't remind him of that too often. He gets a big head, and it takes days to shrink small enough to fit into the castle."

"Hello, dear," she said, finally turning to hug me. "I hoped I would see you again."

"I promised I would save him, didn't I?"

She patted the top of my hand. "You sure did."

"Mother," Orin said quietly. "You don't have to stay here. You can reincarnate or vanish into the ether and simply... end. You have a choice. All souls do."

"Of course, I'm staying," she said, as if it were the easiest choice in the world. "I've waited twenty years to be with you, son. I'm not leaving now."

The tension fell from his shoulders as he gestured to the castle. "Then let's go home."

Sometime later, I woke from a deep sleep to find the space beside me empty and the mountain of black fur that'd been the reason our room kept expanding, gone. Slipping from the bed, the marble floor cold on the bottom of my feet, I tied a robe around my waist and opened the bedroom door to peek out. And though I couldn't see a thing, a single haunted note echoed down the hallway like a string tied to my heart, tugging me toward Orin. Toward the throne room.

He didn't stop playing when I walked in, hadn't heard the door open. I watched him for a long time with awe and so much respect for the burden he carried with far more dignity than I would have. The moonlight seeping through the window high above lent a godly aura to his presence, highlighting the strong features of his face and the graceful curves of the cello in his hands. The instrument was an extension of his very soul, a steadfast companion during these nocturnal hours. This was where he came when his mind got busy, when eternity felt a little too long to serve.

His music, though hauntingly beautiful, carried an unmistakable undercurrent of peace and fullness. The mournful notes, like whispers from the past, filled the room, mingling with the hushed stillness of the castle. I'd never felt so much peace as I had in that moment. We'd come full circle, him and I. And there would be an eternity of euphoria because of a single moment on top of the roof when I'd accidentally married the wrong man.

"Do you know what the tonic of a song is?"

I'd never heard the piece end, spiraling so far into the beauty of it and our memories. I hadn't seen him look at me either. I shook my head and walked around the massive hounds snoring peacefully on the floor in order to sit on the arm of his chair. He still couldn't bring himself to sit upon his father's throne of gilded skulls.

"It's the most important note in a piece of music. It's the destination, the end. Every other note's single purpose is to lead you back to the tonic."

"That sounds lovely, like poetry."

He set his cello to the side and pulled me into his lap, sliding a lock of hair behind my ear. "I thought I loved you, but I was wrong. We both ran from madness for so long, love was impossible. There's only obsession. Only compulsion. You are not a desire, Wife. You're a godsdamn addiction. Love makes you a weakness. But you're my strength. My future. Mine. All of you belongs to me. Every heartbeat, every breath. Every second of your eternal life is mine and mine alone. In malevolence, in anger, in hysteria and darkness, you are unwavering. You're the crescendo, my love. The pinnacle of every song, the climb, and the purpose. And I will love you beyond the final note."

"I think you need to go back to weapons training for your own sanity. You're losing your edge, Husband."

"I hate you," he chuckled.

THE END

Thank you so much for reading *Till Death*! If you'd like to take a peek into Orin's mind and find out what really happened the day he destroyed the world, you can find the BONUS CHAPTER here.

https://BookHip.com/LKDKQCZ

Keep turning for a peek at Paesha's book title!

SHE MADE THE DEAL
AND NOW SHE MUST PAY
THE PRICE...

Nevermore

COMING NEXT
FROM

MIRANDA LYN

Acknowledgments

Dear Reader,

I wrote this book for you. You carried me through every chapter and every line. As an indie author, it's so easy to feel like you're going to be lost in the noise of others. The noise was loud, the pressure to follow such a successful duology mounted with each syllable until I had to take a step back and remember why I was writing. It was you. It's always been you. Thank you a million times over for seeing this book through the end. Please consider leaving a review, dropping a comment on my socials, and sharing your thoughts with friends. Those little tasks truly make our worlds go round and I have more stories to tell.

To my husband, my ride or die, my love: these may not be our stories but the way you love me sure does inspire them. Though you've never read a page, I want you to know that you're as loving as Fenlas, as loyal as Kai, as resilient as Bastian, and as passionate as Orin. How lucky am I to be married to the main character?

To my girls, this year hasn't been an easy one, but you've all inspired me through your own journeys, and I'm so grateful to be your mom. And, though K hates our group chat notifications, I'd be devastated if they were ever silent. Keep running, girls. You make us so proud.

To Darby and Claire, my dream team. Holy shit... This year came for us so hard. Thanks for every ounce of love along the way. I couldn't do this without you. Not for a second.

To Amanda, for walks on the beach and borrowed names. This story was born on a trip to your house and grew within those walls. You saw me struggle and never judged the wild workings of my mind. Thank you. Can't wait to sit in our rocking chairs on the compound one day like a couple of blue hairs we know.

To Miss Alison VonSchnauzzen and crew, there are not words. Literally none. Your support and ears and unwavering laughter lift me on my hardest days. Thank you a million times over for all of it, because this book would be twice the size if I had to make a list.

To Courtenay, well, Flimsy Kris was a failure, but in our hearts we'll always have that name. Definitely keeping it on the books for future options. Thanks for reading this beast when she was raw and loving her anyway. You know they say – if you can't love her at her worst, you don't deserve her at her best. You deserve this book.

To Kay, Merrit, Jess and Tiff... once upon a time we sat at a table in the restaurant of a wonderland themed hotel, and I told you the *very* rough makings of this story. It was your enthusiasm that saw through the end and I'm so grateful you were all able to be there for that moment and every one since. Your words of encouragement do not go unnoticed. Somedays, they are all that pulls me through. Thank you.

To Jes and Britt, my influencer dream team, thank you for taking a chance on me. Thank you for continuing to support me. Thank you for the friendships we've forged along the way and being such champions of my work.

And finally, **to Jiminy**, you little manwhore. You sang your sweet little song in commemoration of this book for far too long. But you were vigilant. Staying until the very end. Until the last Excedrin and the final acknowledgment. I hope you found your mate, annoying cricket.

PLEASE CONSIDERING LEAVING YOUR REVIEW
THANKS FOR READING!

About the Author

Miranda Lyn is the best selling author of the trending, witchy duology, Unmarked, her debut series, Fae Rising and now she ups the anti with Till Death. Miranda has spent the past two decades reading romantic fantasy novels, and the last handful of years crafting similar worlds steeped in heartache, adventure, love, and loss. Her past work has taken her readers into the heart of a witch, alongside the journey of a high fae, through the oceans with a siren and now prowling the rooftops with Death's Maiden.

She owes it all to that one science teacher that made her write a paper on dirt and loved it so much he read it to the class. And then lectured her for missing class that day. But if not for him, because he probably doesn't deserve the credit since she missed the next day of class as well, then to that little, ol'

English teacher that swept her into a world of creative writing. The only class she never missed.

Check out our website for extras, character art, and exclusive content. www.authormirandalyn.com

To sign up for the mailing list and get access to more exclusive content and giveaways, please visit

https://www.authormirandalyn.com/subscribe

ALSO BY MIRANDA LYN

FAE RISING SERIES (COMPLETE)
BLOOD AND PROMISE
CHAOS AND DESTINY
FATE AND FLAME

TIDES AND RUIN (A FAE RISING SPIN OFF)

UNMARKED DUOLOGY (COMPLETE)
THE UNMARKED WITCH
THE UNBOUND WITCH
THE UNBLESSED WITCH (AN UNMARKED NOVELLA)